Praise for *The Last Jew*:

"Whether it is due to the originality of his broken sty..., ... his characters, or his implacable lucidity, Kaniuk must be considered one of the great writers of our time." —*Le Monde*

"A rich, demanding, life-affirming masterpiece . . . The cyclical nature of history and the repetitive sufferings of the Jews are analyzed with . . . revelatory complexity. . . . Kaniuk employs a virtually Faulknerian dreamlike logic in constructing this intricate fiction . . . [in which] sons seek their fathers, shattered families seek reunion, and embodiments of the legendary Wandering Jew repeatedly reenact the old, sorrowing myth of exodus and hardship and return. . . . Not to be missed." —*Kirkus Reviews* (starred review)

"A true work of art . . . First published more than twenty years ago and newly translated into English, the novel's preoccupations are only more timely today. the exploitation of catastrophe and the deceptiveness of art." —Dara Horn, *The Washington Post Book World*

"A literary masterpiece, mandatory reading for anyone who wants to understand the makings of Israeli society . . . Kaniuk knows the distress of his people. I have not in recent years come across an Israeli novel of such quality and historical insight." —*The Jerusalem Post*

"A fascinating page-turner, epic in nature, [*The Last Jew*] explores Jewish identity in kaleidoscopic form. . . . A brilliant tour de force." —*Library Journal*

"An essential acquisition . . . *The Last Jew* makes heavy demands on its readers, compelling them—as does Faulkner's *As I Lay Dying* or Joyce's *Ulysses*—to find a context and meaning for the fractured perceptions and convoluted lives of the characters that confront them." —*Booklist* (starred review)

"A layered, sweeping panorama of twentieth century Jewish life and identity." —*Publishers Weekly*

"[Kaniuk is] perhaps the greatest writer to fable himself out of Israel and onto the international scene since the tragic early death of the genius Yaakov Shabtai. . . . *The Last Jew* is a masterpiece." —*Jewish Book World*

The
LAST JEW

Yoram Kaniuk

Being the Tale of Teacher Henkin and the Vulture,
the Chronicles of the Last Jew, the Awful Tale of Joseph and
His Offspring, the Story of Secret Charity, the Annals of the
Moshava, All Those Wars, and the End of the Annals of the Jews

Translated from the Hebrew by Barbara Harshav

GROVE PRESS
NEW YORK

Published simultaneously in Canada
Printed in the United States of America

FIRST PAPERBACK EDITION

Library of Congress Cataloging-in-Publication Data

Kaniuk, Yoram.
[Yehudi ha-aharon. English]
The last Jew / Yoram Kaniuk ; translated from the Hebrew
by Barbara Harshav.— 1st ed.
p. cm.
ISBN 10: 0-8021-4295-8
ISBN 13: 978-0-8021-4295-5
I. Harshav, Barbara, 1940– II. Title.
PJ5054.K326Y4413 2006
892.4'36—dc22
2005051396

Grove Press
an imprint of Grove/Atlantic, Inc.
841 Broadway
New York, NY 10003

07 08 09 10   10 9 8 7 6 5 4 3 2 1

The
LAST JEW

The young man got off the bus full of soldiers and hoisted his kitbag onto his shoulder. The bus took off, ants returned from a reconnaissance mission bearing pieces of leaves and stubs of wood, he looked here and there and saw a house, went in and on the table were fresh vegetables, cigarettes, and sweet juices. A woman whose hair had changed from shiny black to gray sat him down at the vegetables and wanted to see him eat. He swallowed the fresh vegetables and smoked a few cigarettes and then he put a few packs into the kitbag and drank some sweet-and-sour juice. She asked him if he was hungry and he said no, no. Then a few girls appeared at the window on the way to a tent. He glanced at them and wanted to ask one of them a question but he didn't find the question and went on sitting. He tried to locate tangible memories in himself but everything was mixed up. Somebody he thought was a commander and wore a ribbon on his shoulder tab asked him a few personal questions and out of his kitbag the young man took papers he himself avoided looking at, and the man studied them, took out a payment chit, and gave it to him. And he said: You'll surely go home, but the young man didn't remember anymore if he had really thought of going home and suddenly he really didn't know where that home was, he only nodded, picked up the kitbag, got into the jeep parked in the yard, and waited. A driver came and asked him what he was doing in the jeep. The young man said he wanted to go, never mind where. The driver looked at him with shrewd amazement and said: All of you came back fucked up, then he bent over the steering wheel and whispered: My brother went, I'm going to Gan Yavneh. The young man said: Take me to Marar. The driver started the jeep and didn't tell the young man that there was no more Marar. When they came the mountain was empty. The young man stood in the road, put down the kitbag, looked at what was a village, and thought, I live not far from here, but the distance between him and his home was now almost imaginary, he started retreating like somebody who truly dreaded knowing who he was.

Late in the evening he came to Tel Aviv and slept near the sanitation workers in the central bus station. A girl coming back from work stepped on him and he didn't say a word. In the morning he ate a bagel and drank lukewarm tea, went to the boulevard, and walked all along it. When he came to a bench that suited him he put the kitbag down again and sat down. He sat without moving from nine in the morning until five thirty in the evening. Most of the time he looked at the house opposite. The balconies were empty.

Children paraded by, carrying a blue and white flag, singing. He felt hungry but he didn't get up. Opposite a window opened and a woman looked at the sky and then closed the window. The cars passed with a frequency that made him try to understand its rules, but he couldn't. He touched the money in his pocket and thought maybe it was time to get up and go. But he didn't get up and he didn't go. A few downcast people walked along the boulevard. They held their hands clasped almost boldly behind their backs and their faces were down. They looked pale but maybe also full of imaginary gaiety; they imagined they were happy. They stopped not far from him; one of them spoke of some great hour that had not been missed and he was glad about the words that sounded familiar to him. Then sights passed before his eyes that he wanted to forget and blood flowed from him and he planned the destruction of the house opposite. He'd place the TNT on the doorsill behind the security wall. Then he'd connect the detonator and then the red wire and the white wire and would retreat to the bench, hide behind the bench, and activate it. The house wouldn't cave in immediately, but would be opened and then, slowly slowly would sink. When he thought about the anonymous people who would die in the house he felt a distant affection for them, almost a yearning, and in the back of his mind the house was gaping and caving in, gaping and caving in, and he took a pack of cigarettes out of the kitbag and chain-smoked a few. Then, thirsty, he found the hose used to water the boulevard, turned on the faucet, and drank. A sanitation worker tried to stop him, but the young man looked at him with controlled rage and the worker thought: Another one who came back, why do I need troubles. The celebration was in other places.

He thought maybe he should have stayed in camp and eaten fresh vegetables another few days. The gloomy woman with silvery hair could probably have suckled him. Then he could have sung to her how they die in
Bab-el-Wad. But he sits here on the bench on the boulevard and the day
is nearing its end and he's not yet aware of anything profound, very important, bothering him. Somebody is sitting here on the bench, he thought,
but who is really sitting here? The thick trees intertwined in the sky created a kind of gigantic purple bridal veil above his head. Their trunks were
oval. The blossoms were also a bit blue. The kitbag was laid on the mown
but almost dead lawn that smelled of mold and dying grass. He felt the
wetness penetrate the back of the bench, which was eaten by old wetness
that hadn't dried. The tree facing him was all gnarled, leaves dropped
slowly like a gentle rain of dead children. When he opened his eyes after
a strained doze, he saw the foliage and the purple blue and could make out
the distant sunset hidden by the buildings, and then he could also sense
the redness and even see tatters of it. The sky growing dim, that whisper
through the purple and blue nimbus. Once again he made out the wall of
the house opposite. The wall was yellowish and tending to rust. On the
balcony a woman now stood and hung up her little girl to dry. The little girl
dropped and then jumped up with a cheer on what might have been a lawn
hidden behind a low concrete wall. And the little girl laughed. What should
have been terror was a loud rejoicing squashed to depression by a black
Ford and the young man on the bench felt a certain regret, something repressed in the back of his mind wanted to see a woman drying a little girl.
The woman vanished from the balcony, a door slammed, another car
passed, and from Habima Theater appeared a young woman in a golden
dress ignited by the twilight with a certain delicate charm, somehow connected with the joy of the little girl on the lawn. She stopped, looked at
him, bent over, his legs heavy, his face tilted a little to the side, and said:
Boaz, Boaz Schneerson, what are you doing here, and he didn't grasp that
she was talking to him. He got up, picked up the kitbag, and from his angle
of vision, when he stood up, a green pin now appeared clasping the young
woman's hair, her lips looked spread in an amazement she was afraid to
express properly, the lips were now clamped hard, maybe as an attempt to
defend herself, the theater on the right seemed shrouded in concave light,
so maybe he burst out laughing. The young woman said: You certainly

don't even remember my name, and he nodded. Then he said: Not your name and not my name, even though you called me Boaz. She said: Boaz, you fell on your head, and he answered: Yes, I fell on my head. Suddenly I'm on the boulevard, what's on at Habima? She averted her face, looked at the thick-trunked sycamores, the sandy square, the building enveloped in gloom, and tried to recall. Her shoulder holding a purse moved, the purse slipped to the ground, her hand clenched uneasily, she tried to bend down to pick up the purse and yet as if she wanted to stay erect, the little girl opposite started throwing a ball against the wall. The spots above the foliage became dark, on her finger a gold ring was seen shining in the light of the prancing sunbeam, and he approached her, looked at the ring, put the kitbag down on the ground, and started pulling the ring off the finger. She said in pain, Stop, you're hurting me, but he said, I have to take off the ring. The ring was small and stuck to the finger and the young woman who was supposed to run stood still; a tiny spot of blood appeared flickering on her knuckle. She reached out her other hand, grabbed hold of him, pulled him to her in an attempt to get away from him; her eyes were bloodshot, the sky now grew dark fast and her hair clasped in a green pin dropped onto her face like a wild screen, for a moment she couldn't even see, in that second he managed to tear the ring off and her finger bled and when she slipped, he grabbed the finger, licked it, and cleaned off the blood. She slapped his face and shouted: You're really crazy, Boaz Schneerson, you're a bad animal, but after he licked the blood from his lips, he said: You shouldn't get married with phony rings, that's what's killing me. She pushed aside her hair, pulled it back, picked up the purse, looked at her hand, felt dizzy, something seemed shaky even in her crotch, and she said: I'm not married to anybody, I wasn't wearing a wedding ring, once when I met you, you went to Hepzibah and bought me a cheap ring. It's funny you don't re-member. You came from the settlement, maybe that was the same ring.

Things cleared up now and that could be seen on his rounded forehead, his hardened body; he thrust the ring in his pocket and picked up the kitbag. You're Minna, maybe we really did know each other, who knows. She leaned on a tree and didn't notice that a dripping resin stuck to her dress and she could see purplish leaves falling into her hair. She said, You said you'd write to me, where were you in the war? And he shook his head and said more to himself than to her, Where the rings were I was too, I've got a collection of gold teeth of dead Arabs. And an ear that my friend, who died, would chew like gum. She tried to smile, the dark grew thicker, the change from evening to night was too swift. So my name's Boaz Schneerson, he said, here, take the ring from me and wait for me, I don't need phony rings. He held out the ring he took out of his pocket and started going away from her, he didn't turn around but walked backward, his face stuck to the sight of her, she stood leaning on the tree, her hair covered by a gloom drenched with leaves, and the little girl opposite yelled: Mama mama I've got to make peepee, a car sprayed water that may have been left there from the sloppy watering. In the thickening darkness the thick, gnarled, ancient sycamores looked like giant memorials, and she looked amazed at his back illuminated in the light in front of the theater that suddenly came on. The light didn't touch the kitbag or his hand and it looked like his hand were lopped off. She thought about a hand chewed like gum. The kitbag was the shadow of a dog that wasn't there. Close to the sand dunes the houses were scattered up to the row of cypresses whose outlines were now erased in the light crushed on their backs; for a moment, a stub of moon was seen above the house under construction and Boaz lit a cigarette, the smoke curled into the street that led nowhere. Maybe he once knew some girl who lived here, maybe it was on another boulevard. Minna's house with the red roof tiles. Everything was too blurred to be caught in a clear picture. She looked abandoned near the tree, far away, and he thought, maybe the little girl doesn't have gold teeth anymore. He stood still in the middle of the street and waited. Then the dull feeling of regret that had started filling him earlier was finished, his mouth was still full of the dampness of blood and then he smiled too. But the gloom covered his smile. When he saw the two headlights of the car heading for him, he thought it was the same car he saw before, even though maybe it wasn't. The lights moved toward him like the limbs of an enemy. And that's what he also said to Solomon on the way to Tel Aviv: Got to search for the enemy even after the war, to search for a proper defeat, and Solomon said: I'm not searching for any enemy, going to screw until the middle of next year, nonstop, stop only to eat fresh vegetables and halvah. The car came close and the driver, who had already seen Boaz, started honking his horn. The honking was mashed, from one of those broken horns, so Boaz felt generous toward the honking, but couldn't budge. The car approached and squealed to a stop; in the light of

the streetlamp, it looked like a big ladybug. Another person was there who
burst out of the kiosk hidden under an awning loaded with a heavy dropping of leaves. The kiosk light was dimmed by the black paint that hadn't
been removed when the war ended; the person who came out of the kiosk
held a pencil and a notebook and was writing something. On his lips was
a smile he had brought with him from the kiosk and had nothing to do with
what was going on outside. Boaz looked from the car to the person and
back, wanted to smash the car, but the notebook in that man's hand excited him to some extent, as if all he wanted to do ever since he had come
down from Jerusalem and knew that the battles were over was to see a person with a notebook and pencil. The driver got out of the car and started
yelling. His voice was low, thick, and the words came out of his mouth a bit
drawled, as if he could think even during anger. The person with the notebook and pencil immediately turned into a witness. You were standing here
in the middle of the street, sir, and blocking traffic, he stated with angry
politeness. And nobody asked him. Boaz, who was sparing with words and
afraid to waste them, let the two men discuss it between themselves. He
put down the kitbag and waited. The person with the notebook and pencil said: People like that should be run over, then they wouldn't stand in
the middle of the street and stop traffic, and the driver said: If I hadn't
stopped, he'd be dead, and he looked at Boaz, who didn't move from where
he was standing in front of the car. The word *dead* inflamed the driver, who
said it with a vague fear, and the person with the notebook and pencil now
seemed dressed with rather exaggerated elegance, on his nose a scratch
was clearly seen that could have come from an illegal chase of municipal
tow trucks, thought Boaz and didn't know if he really had anything to do
with those people, if he really spoke their language, if he understood what
they were saying, and why the shoes of the person with the notebook and
pencil had no laces. They spoke energetically to one another. The notebook in the man's hand shook and the driver wanted to go and then Boaz
approached, with his strong hands that looked so delicate, he grasped the
two heads, held them a moment as they were amazed, coupled them,
moved one head away from the other, and then knocked the heads together. At the moment the smashing of the two skulls was heard, a car was
seen trying to maneuver its way left. From there a wagon with a stooped
carter was seen, and the wagon, unlike the car, passed by very slowly, the

mare was old and weary and the carter was humming a song in Yiddish: There was a queen whose crown was sparkling, sparkling, there was a queen whose tomb was sparkling, sparkling. The two heads now moved away from one another, the car whose lights were still on blocked the picture of the cart and the other car, and after a silent pause, the cart and the car disappeared, the notebook dropped onto the ground and Boaz, illuminated by the lights, quickly tossed the kitbag into the car and when the driver yelled: What are you doing, sir? in his slow defensive voice, Boaz saw on his face the crushed expression of somebody who managed to stun with illogic but certainly with a certain methodicalness. I'm taking your auto, said Boaz, what I wanted was to lie on the street to ask forgiveness from your shoes. But his hands started hitting in rage, the little girl dropped from the balcony, that tranquility.

Minna wants him to remember her, the rage stunned him, a rage that brought a ring down on Minna, I'm sorry, he said, and when he jumped into the car, he yelled: My name is Boaz, but he should have said: I'm Boaz, he started the car and began driving. The stunned driver stood there next to the person with the notebook and pencil, his face crushed from the blow, and the man with the notebook searched for the pencil that might have fallen and clenched his arm that had been hit and Boaz drove fast down the slope of Dizengoff toward the huts on Nordau. He saw people huddled at the coffee shop where a news announcer's voice was coming, and he went on, he stopped at a breached bridge with a few bushes still burgeoning between its tatters and an iron skeleton was seen peeping out of what had apparently once been a complete structure. He parked the car, turned off the lights, took the kitbag, and went. He walked along the street and could smell the blood of the sea. The smell was calming and the crash of the waves was pleasant and demonstrated devotion and obstinacy.

When he lay on a cot in a tent on the seashore, in the small camp for soldiers who returned and didn't know where, or why they stayed there, he thought he didn't remember who Minna was and in fact he did remember, but it wasn't important to him. And then he realized that he was protecting somebody.

In the morning, he passed by a small hotel with a sign on its wall saying: "For Soldiers, Discount and Free Wash." He didn't know what was free and what was discounted and he went in. The clerk was snoozing and upstairs in the rooms, people were groaning. Maybe the clerk recorded their made-up names in his notebook. Boaz asked for what was free and found himself in a bathroom whose walls were filthy and whose mirrors were broken. He asked the man for toothpaste; the clerk was too tired to refuse. Boaz spread toothpaste on a fountain pen he took out of the kitbag and brushed his teeth. Then he wet his face and hair and combed his hair back with his fingers, and the broken mirror didn't give him any idea of how he looked. When he came out, the clerk said something about the war and hope and Boaz asked him if he was interested in buying gold teeth of Arabs. The clerk felt the toothpaste that Boaz returned to him and said: Enough already, everybody's got those jokes. Boaz didn't correct him, but went out, pounded his fist, and saw damp crumbling plaster, his hand was white from the blow and he walked along Hayarkon Street where the sea was seen flickering between the houses. A woman was hanging laundry out to dry and he wanted the sun to burn her men's clothes. When he came to the office, he saw a sign: "Office to Direct Soldiers Who Were Cut Off from Their Units." He climbed the stinking stairs and saw soldiers standing in a line. One of them said, There's a Romanian girl on Third Street, twenty cents a fuck. Boaz waited quietly and chewed imaginary gum. The soldiers wanted gum and he showed them a mouth with no gum. In the office sat a well-groomed officer wearing a handsome uniform, and his eyes were veiled in a panic that became beautiful in a properly functioning smile. Boaz appreciated that national authority. He answered the officer's questions calmly, pulled out the papers, and showed them to the officer. The officer said to him: Oh, you were there too, you deserve more, where's the weapon, they spoke a few minutes and a female soldier came in looking furious and wrote something on a small thin pink paper form. After he signed, he wanted to understand how far the female soldier's gigantic breasts reached, but she turned her back to him and said: Everybody, everybody, and he understood her, maybe in his heart he pitied her, with breasts like those to meet those dark schemes. When he went outside, he remembered dully that he had to go to the settlement, to Grandmother, but he knew the time hadn't yet come, he'd been moving around for a month now, he'd wait another few days. And he didn't know where he had been moving around for a month before he came here, the battles had ended before, he didn't remember what was the last battle, but he did remember saying to somebody, it's good that it's over but he didn't know if he really meant that. Different ants walked in a row toward a hole they had dug and in a nub sat a tree in a big pot. Somebody was watering the tree with a long hose and standing under the awning of a stationery store. From there you could see a big yard behind a house that might once have been a fashionable café. In the yard were pieces of chairs and posts with broken lanterns hanging on them. Boaz loaded the kitbag on his back, spread out his hands, bent down to balance the weight, as if he were walking on a tightrope, and walked toward the courtyard, where cats striped like tame tigers were yowling. He sat down in a broken chair in the courtyard and tried again to think. The ants and the beetles were a sign that his friends really did die and that he really did come back but if he could, he would have asked the officer more questions now, but since it was a waste of effort to go back up, he didn't. He fingered the money they had given him and didn't recognize the money. The money was written with Hebrew letters. That money already has a state, he said aloud and the cat jumped with trained wildness toward a broken lantern and planted its claws in it. So he went to the café not far from there and ordered coffee, cake, and a glass of soda. When he wanted to pay, he gave the waiter all the money and the waiter looked at him in shock, counted the necessary coins, and said, returning most of the money to him, You're funny today sir; but he said finny.

Boaz thought that as a funny, or finny, person, he had to see the car he had taken the day before but he knew that was only an excuse to return to some place, for no good reason, and the car surely wasn't there. He wanted to know where he should go. When he came, he saw the car parked where he had left it. The man from the grocery store who came outside to bring in the margarine thrown on the sidewalk by the driver of the worn-out and squeaky pickup truck said, You looking for an apartment here? There's one upstairs, rent control. Boaz said, That car is stolen! The man pondered a bit and bent over to pick up the margarine. Boaz picked up the case of margarine for him and dragged it inside. The man gave Boaz an Eskimo Pie and he nibbled at it. Boaz said, Cars should live in their own houses. The shopkeeper muttered something and said there were people here at night, but they left. And Boaz said they come and go all the time. Over the counter hung an announcement about food rationing and food coupons and Boaz read it carefully; the shopkeeper said, It'll be hot today. When he came out of the shop, he saw the driver in the distance, he leaped into the yard and climbed the tree. He looked and saw them checking the car and a person who looked like a plainclothes cop searched for fingerprints on the handle. That made him laugh, in the tree, and he slowly came down and started walking. They didn't even see him. He came to the tents, put down the kitbag, put on a clean but wrinkled shirt, and went out. After he sat for hours and looked at the sea, he went to Café Pilz. The music burst out and the waves of the sea looked silvery. He drank two spitfires and Menashke played songs on the accordion. Then they played a rumba and everybody danced. A girl Boaz later discovered in his arms tried to defend herself against the shock on his face. But she accepted Boaz's kiss with empty lips cut off from himself. She was offended and tried to look into his eyes but in the middle of the second kiss, with two spitfires in his belly and his head spinning, he left her slack-jawed and went toward London Square. She yelled something that was drowned in the noise of the sea. He expected her to be the daughter of the driver of the car and would sue him. So he groped in the empty pocket where he used to keep the gold teeth. Then he sat on a rock and looked at a bench not far from him. The bench was surely more comfortable to sit on because in the morning, when he went to the office, he saw that it was repainted. The sea spread out before him. The girl was still yelling, or the yelling was before and only the echo was heard now, the sea was locked because of the dark. The moon shed a little light but it was thin and curved and a car that might have broken down, parked with its lights on and illuminated the wrong section of the sea. Boaz leaned over the rock and behind it were white houses gleaming in the curved light, with eyes wide open he saw nonexistent eagles darting, swooping and a bright path, and a man yelling, they died, got to save the black. Boaz sat there terrified, shrouded in dread from some unknown source, thought about the baby that could have been born if the woman who got an indifferent kiss near Café Pilz was yelling something. Maybe Boaz was a bastard who fell on his head, he thought; maybe that's Minna, did I know her once, or not, Minna, and what does he have to do with all those Minnas, he told the baby kicking inside him: Wait a while, I'll give birth to you, pretty one, with two mothers, three fathers, and two grandfathers. Then he went down to the boardwalk and bumped into wires not reached by the car's headlights. Maybe they were laid here recently when the war was close to Tel Aviv, which always expected wars on her border.

Two young men stood at the door of a café that looked locked. They knocked on the door, but nobody opened it. He could imagine the café owner leaving, escaping in a boat, and not yet back. A girl in a short dress was standing in a shaded niche next to the door. For a moment, she rolled up her dress a little and the two young men laughed and approached her as in a slow dance, she raised the dress as if her hands were the hands of a doctor, but the touch was hesitant, wounded, and the lights of a passing car showed some profound contempt flickering deep in her eyes. The lights of the car that might have broken down were extinguished now and the sea was still silvered, calm, sealed in moon shadows. A cop passed by on a bike now and shone a flashlight on the bench Boaz had almost sat on before. Clouds of suspicions in the place were plastered but tangible. An ancient smell of damp and phony chill came from the park. For a moment he felt a secret bliss that he could feel a common fate with those two young men and share the girl's contempt for their springy steps, but the girl looked scared of the cop, turned around and lowered her dress with perhaps unexpected coarseness, they stood still again in front of the locked door and one of them started weeping. Now Boaz could make out how big they were, like wild bulls he used to see between Marar and the settlement. They were surely searching for a *fille de joie* with braids and a pinafore, their childhood love, he thought. But there was a war, and if two fools like them didn't die, they were superfluous like me. The two strode toward Hayarkon Street and from there to the Red House. In the Red House, somebody was playing the "Internationale" on a mandolin. An unseen woman was singing in a whisper the words that moved toward the sea and were mixed in it. Near the house was a barbed wire fence and two women soldiers with Sten guns were guarding it. The fence was rusty and behind it were only limestone hills and sea. The cannon that may really have stood here once was moved. Inside the Red House a forehead was seen and near it two crests of male hair. The overgrown young men stood facing the women soldiers and spoke coarsely. The women soldiers enveloped themselves in a secret mantle that had long ago been forced on them and tried not to get angry, and, even more, the second one (the first one was fatter) tried not to smile. The girl Boaz had earlier invented with the pinafore and flaxen hair, twelve years old, naïve, now passed by the women soldiers, on her way to a belated piano lesson. The balconies in the house opposite, surely her parents' house, were wreathed in plants and flowers and a pleasant smell rose from the recently watered flowers. The little girl's beauty stunned the two young men walking behind her. They wept aloud again and the two female soldiers tried not to pity them. The little girl saved the moment for him and Boaz saw her laugh with the sudden joy of breasts that may have started sprouting. One of the two women soldiers said: Soldiers come and weep all the time, go know. Right, said the second woman soldier, a lot of weepers returned, what was there, and Boaz said: A lake of tears was there and anybody who returned brought the tears with him, but you guarded the secret ship here and you didn't know. The woman soldier said, The cannon, and Boaz said: But there is no cannon, and she said So what, just because there's no cannon, there's no need to guard? He tried to understand her logic, but the crescent moon now cast its full light and they saw how much his look was shrouded in disgust and they were afraid to get mixed up in some emotional adventure that wasn't yet wanted and they turned their stiff backs on him. The plump one looked better from behind.

At night he slept in his clothes and sweated even though it wasn't especially hot. In the morning he opened his eyes wide to the voice of a person standing over him and looking from his angle of vision as if he were tearing the tent with his kinky hair. The man read Boaz a new order of the day and Boaz, who was already awake and feeling the wetness of his clothes, said: I'm discharged, dummy. The man tried to be friendly. His yellowed teeth seemed to be searching for a more suitable mouth. The man said: That's your shock, Boaz, you don't remember me? Boaz looked at him and didn't remember. He said, fine, let's go, and since he didn't need to get dressed he went outside, took some sand, and rubbed it on his neck and his face. Then they walked among people who seemed for some reason to be rushing like actors in a silent movie. They went into a little café and Boaz was afraid he had lost his hearing. He said to the man: Yell something, and the man yelled, and Boaz said, I heard you, over and out. And then he put a finger in his ear and rummaged around a little while and said, I hear. The man said, He hears, that'll be fine. The woman who owned the place looked at Boaz. She saw how wrinkled he was and because of that she seemed to know his pain personally and she said: Take off your clothes and I'll clean them for you. But Boaz said: There's no point, take some money and bring me new clothes, pick them out yourself. He took off his clothes and remained in a black undershirt and shorts, he also enjoyed her obedience, sat in his shorts and undershirt with a man he surely didn't know, or else he wouldn't have sat with him in a café, and people who peeped inside saw a man in an undershirt and shorts and asked what happened and Boaz yelled: The enemy killed my clothes, that man raped my mother, pretends he's my father. The man laughed and Boaz didn't. He drank coffee and ate a roll and on it he slowly spread margarine and he didn't know if it was what he had dragged in from the sidewalk to the shop earlier or a week ago, and suddenly he wanted to know who Minna was. Maybe she really was the daughter of Gilboa the contractor? Boaz licked the jam from the jar and drank more coffee. At first he tried to count the cups of coffee, then he stopped. The woman came back with a bundle of new clothes and took pins out of the shirt, when the sleeves dropped down, he felt some excitement, as if a baby were born, he tried on the new clothes, took the bundle of old clothes outside and put it next to the bundle of clothes forgotten downstairs by new immigrants peeping from their rented room upstairs, or maybe they were waiting for the right time to bring them upstairs. Nor did they know what to do with the new flowerpots that were given them. The man sitting with him said, You have to forget, Boaz, come back home, they've started searching for you, they said you've been wandering around for a month now, I don't know why they're so worried about you, you've got a grandmother with citrus groves and vineyards and you've got money. What, you need help?

Not me, said Boaz and licked the jar of jam some more.

It says here, said the man, that the battles were hard. Boaz asked where it said and the man showed him a sheet of paper. The paper said Boaz Schneerson, fourth brigade, Har-El. Boaz said: What else does it say? And the man said: It says that you were mobilized in 'forty-seven. That you were trained in boats in Caesarea and then fought in Jerusalem. It says you took part in—and he listed one battle after another until Boaz got bored and stopped listening. The man added, you wound up in an ambush, so what? It says you played dead. That you lay and they shot at the dead, every moment you knew you'd die and you didn't, there were crows and vultures there, maybe hawks? Maybe falcons? Maybe eagles? I can imagine that it was awful, it says here that afterward you got up and there were another two who got up at the same time and you all ran.

I don't remember, said Boaz.

The man smiled and said, they didn't go down to the valley with the dead because the Jews had an atom bomb. And the bomb there was a Davidka shell, which explodes once every seven shots. Fifty percent of the giant shells don't explode. The shells really were gigantic, said Boaz, and they were shaped like an atom bomb.

The Jews got atom bombs from the Elders of Zion, said the Arabs. You drew clocks and you wrote mysterious numbers on the shells so that if they didn't explode, at least they'd frighten. The explosion worked by smell, said the Arabs, if an Arab soldier got close to it it exploded from the smell. The Jews were vaccinated against it, said the man, for example, in Hiroshima not one Jew was killed. The logic was perfect, Boaz said to him. So you were saved, said the man, I don't remember, said Boaz, but added: Grandmother recited Psalms throughout the war and saved me, even the battle I don't remember.

It bothers you to be rehabilitated, said the man.

But I wasn't there, said Boaz, it's a mistake, and the man said, go home and you'll remember, it'll help you. Boaz said, I still need to know who really came out of those battles, not sure it's me. The man listed names of the dead but Boaz stood up and wanted to pay. He said, I don't remember them, the man said, I'll pay, and Boaz saw the hair stuck to his scalp and thought maybe antitoxin for hair, a future invention, and with a razor blade he always kept in his pocket in a wrinkled old cigarette pack he wanted to cut his circumcision, but also the hair of that man, and the bitter rage evoked in him by that superfluous memory.

In the evening, he went down to the seashore. A man sat there sculpting. Boaz watched him. A couple lay between the darkness and the limestone hill, tossing and turning. The sculptor said: So what, I sculpt eternal statues in water. I sculpt Joshua, Moses, Nimrod the hero, Ben-Gurion. Up above they've already started building the last villas of Saints of the Holocaust Street. A party was going on in one of the houses and music burst out of an open window. A boy was dragging sardines and beer to the party.

Near the ledge of the boardwalk were two crows that vanished into the sunset. Invisible walls collapsed on him and Boaz said to the sculptor: That sunset is sweet as fire, and the sculptor said to him, Got to know how to capture yells, and Boaz envied the sand under the lovers. He strode along the ledge of the boardwalk until it stopped. The sea cast a pale light of a city erased of houses, a streetlamp illuminated the sea magic, the iron of the ledge was rusty, and at the ledge stood a young woman and looked at the sea. Boaz stood not far from her and looked at the sea too. He didn't even know that she was standing, at any rate, he surely didn't think of it, he was thinking of Minna, why had he plucked the ring off her. When he discovered the woman he looked at her. She didn't move, as if she were waiting for somebody who hadn't come for some time now. A wild silence was strewn on her face, which she extinguished. She had a pug nose and her cheeks weren't symmetrical. Her eyes turned to him didn't see him. The question conveyed to him in her unseeing look was: How can a young man have eyes that are three thousand years old? Thus they approached one another and then he kissed her with a delicacy he felt she deserved and didn't know was in him. Embracing but each one alone, they ascended the path to the small hotel with the discount for soldiers and a free wash. They got the discount and like everybody else they wrote made-up names. Then she tried to weep and not say anything she'd regret afterward. Too bad I didn't ask her name, he thought several days later, but there was a crib there and they said, That will be our baby, she spoke broken Hebrew and said: There it was bad, and showed him marks on her arms and he tried to tell something and didn't know what, and they laughed because she was the almost imaginary lover of a person whose cruelty Boaz couldn't imagine but warmth flowed from her, that flame that melted her, and at three in the morning she said: I was beautiful and they saw only my back. And he wanted to tell her how beautiful she was now in bed, naked, but he didn't have women he dreamed about years ago and so he was silent. He wanted to understand how they penetrated her, how they didn't ask questions, and his distress became unbearable, he who wanted to be independent in love began pitying her and himself and almost spoke, and then she whispered to him don't say I love, don't you dare, and he got angry that she began teaching him and after they quarreled he brought her water and she drank from his hands, lapped it like a dog, and he got down on all fours and said: Don't love, don't love, and she said see, Hebrew, I don't know but they put into my body that thing to honor Jewish girls and in his mind's eye he saw her standing there alone waiting for somebody else on the beach of Tel Aviv and started wondering whether he had also been there, and the pressure in his chest grew and then he had to hit her, insult her, and before she managed to tell him her name, she got dressed in a hurry and said: I'm going, and he said fine and only afterward, after he lay for an hour and tried to shut his eyes, did he understand what he was losing, but by then it was too late. He thought about the little girl with flaxen hair next to the flowerpots and wanted to understand what was happening to all of them and said I'm Boaz Schneerson and he went down to the pay phone and called his grandmother in the settlement and talked with her for a long time and could sense her wicked laugh.

After he saw the cement in Mugrabi he ate a hot dog in a roll on the square. Behind him flew a distorted picture of Laurence Olivier, and the hot dog vendor tried to prove to him again that Goethe was greater than Shakespeare, less violent, more sophisticated. The clock showed the wrong time and Boaz recalled that in the war they said that after it was all over, they'd hold a brigade reunion in the telephone booth near Mugrabi. He started searching desperately for the young woman he had spent the night with but she wasn't anywhere. Among the things details began to be clear. A man limped toward the movie box office and a woman passed by him, bumped into him, hiccuped, and Boaz laughed. She had cruel small teeth, she dropped a hat, and when she picked it up she opened her purse, took out powder, and smeared it on her cheeks and then in the light of the streetlamp she smeared lipstick on her lips. Since he was stuck to the corner, he could see her gaping mouth, her squinting eyes, her teeth with a little bit of lipstick stuck to them, and then she blotted the lipstick with a handkerchief. Boaz tried to remember the dead, recalled that Menahem Henkin lay next to him, but was dead and his blood stuck to him, so Boaz wanted to break a clothes hanger because Menahem Henkin used to break hangers in his childhood, Menahem Henken told Boaz.

Then he went to see the second show of a film whose name he forgot, and felt as if he had come to the end of the road and where would he escape now, and then the strange event happened to him that I'm telling about in these tapes. Boaz stood at the kiosk and tried to read the headline of the evening paper and very close to the counter, next to a hurricane lamp, stood a young man Boaz was sure came out of the battle the man in the café had told him about. His head was wreathed with a halo of light and his face looked like the face of Boaz that the man had told him about. The kiosk owner said to the young man: So from the ship you were sent straight to the war? And the young man said, No, first I was in the port of Haifa. And the young man was so familiar, when Boaz looked at his arm in the light of the hurricane lamp and saw that it moved from his own shoulder. The young man finished drinking and now hid the newspaper headline from Boaz and over his head hung an ad for Nesher beer. Boaz thought, The betrayals will end for a while, so he also understood that no envy would save him but he knew that signals were sent to him from the depths of the war he had fought in, or that that young man had fought in for him. Headlights flashed and there were still many painted streetlamps from the war and the lights seemed to be caressing the gloom. Thoughts that didn't come from a certain place stuck in his mind and a bird built itself a nest on the roof of the kiosk. The man said: That's a honeysucker, so small, every year he comes and makes his nest on the roof. And the young man asked if that tiny sucker could be the same bird and Boaz who knew the answer from childhood, couldn't have spoken, stood on the side, darkened, terrified, the back of the young man's neck filled him with longings for Minna's finger dripping blood and he tried to remember when he had bought her the ring in Hepzibah where Grandmother thought he was stealing pens and erasers, but he couldn't recall. When the young man moved a shadow seemed to shift or a curtain to be pulled. The kiosk was gaping like a wound. A caprice of chiaroscuro made the young man look as if he were going away into a halo of light, but it was only outlines of non-body.

A man chewing sesame and drinking soda held a fragrant wormwood leaf between his fingers and the smell was tormenting and sweet. The desert wildness in the city street was sudden and assuaged some pain that gnawed in him. The man paid and the young man started walking and Boaz found himself hopping behind him, he was hopping because now he had a pain in his foot, wanted to stop, settle things, but he followed the young man like a blind man. And then he said: That young man took off Minna's ring, loves blood, is disguised as a crow. They eat sesame seeds in Tel Aviv with desert wormwood. I'm walking behind a yell that came from inside me, he said to himself, but what's happening to me, what am I, a car thief, a war-monger, that silence will drive me out of my mind: the young man turned into a dark street and went off toward a house with a thick tree sprouting from it. The tree was dead but the house around the tree wasn't destroyed. The crest of the tree wasn't seen in the dark. He searched for a house number on the wall and didn't find one. The name of the street wasn't written there either. The fence was low and beyond the house tombstones were seen, the dark obliterated the tops of the tombstones, but one tombstone was seen clearly and even the writing etched on it was seen prominently, maybe because of the light falling from a window where a broken shutter didn't block it. Then it became clear that aside from the tombstone lying here waiting to be moved to the cemetery, this was a cemetery for dead cars, maybe even the spoils of war. A person was walking in the yards, he had stones in his pocket and was searching for cats to throw the stones at. The cats looked like flashes in the headlights of the passing cars, slithering around tree trunks that looked as if they didn't have crests. The young man looked as if he were hesitating. I wanted to go back, he'll say years later, as an end of a story about people searching for themselves, I wanted to go back like a melody played long ago. In the yard the young man entered you could feel rusty nails and shards of bottles and hear the claws of cats leaping toward the hewn trunks. The tree that burst out of the house was seen from the corner where Boaz stood as if pickled in vinegar, maybe the house was merely a box.

The young man searched for a path among the shards of bottles and nails and suddenly felt a stream of water flowing from the next yard. In the window with the shallow light, a radio was heard and in his fantasy, Boaz could imagine the street going on even beyond the house that stood in the middle and cut it off. And farther on there was a building like a Greek temple with the municipal courthouse next to it and then the sea, whose breakers were heard even through the water rustling and the cats purring. On a small balcony latticed with crosses, an iron weave like an army range, maybe against snakes or other afflictions of nature, in a rusty can sprouted a geranium bush and its sharp smell, which surely came to him because of the water that had recently sprinkled it, filled Boaz's nostrils. Now he followed the young man and turned right toward the front of the house, a bare bulb hung there without a shade and a woman's robe on a peg that looked like a hook. On the hook stood a bird. The bird kept moving and its beak explored the source of the music coming from the radio and even in the gloom you could make out the gold color of its beak, maybe it was red and Boaz couldn't make the slim distinction. He thought: we had the barn in the settlement and now there's destruction there.

Then a scene flickered in his mind and he smiled. Teacher All's Well stands before the class in the settlement, excited, a dark spot starts showing at his fly, his pocket is puffed up from the cotton he bought at noon for his wife Eve, and put in his pocket, and the girls are giggling and the boys are weeping with laughter and Teacher All's Well is talking excitedly about Jacob's ladder . . . standing on the earth, the whole Land of Israel folded under the stone pillow of Our Father, the ladder facing up . . . Oh, what a wretched and sublime nation, he said, and Boaz now remembers the blush on the faces of the farmers' only daughters who had often seen bulls mounting cows and Mrs. Czkhstanovka standing next to the national flags and waiting for a bridegroom who never came, but they weren't used to seeing a teacher with wet trousers saying: Oh, what a wretched and sublime nation, struggling with God! Israel! An eternal struggle of the nation and its God, Nation and Land, Language and Fate . . . And the girls are giggling, the spot's spreading, maybe touching the cotton Margalit saw him buying with her own eyes from old Greenspan whose son committed suicide. And he said: Stiffnecked, struggling fateful struggles, disappointed but not ceasing to believe . . . maybe in order to lose! And that's something modern writers don't understand at all! And he looked at his flock, who had no idea who the modern writers were and what they meant and here, thinks Boaz, stands a young man, maybe I'm standing there, and thinking about spots on the trousers of Hebrew teachers. A garden of nails caught in a pale light and the smell of geraniums intoxicates and the crumbling stone fence and the tree inventing the house and everything here is longing.

And we're all of us acting in a Jewish Western, somebody will say later on, and then this moment will be remembered. The young man who may be he averts his face, Boaz knows it's impossible. The geranium, the longings, everything is mixed up here in a restrained essence. He didn't come to Tel Aviv to seek a new war, especially not against himself. But the enemy, it seemed to him, is shrouded in a smell of mothballs, I and not I, thought Boaz. When the young man turned to him, something forgotten flickered in Boaz's mind. He recalled that once he was in the battle the man in the café told him about, but he knew he didn't remember it, he thought then that the Boaz who went into the battle hadn't come out of it at all. Thirty-two killed. Menahem Henkin was killed there, too. But I didn't come out of it, somebody else came out of it, disguised as me. Now it was clear to him. The dark was such that as soon as the young man's face turned aside from the balcony and turned to him, he was blinded for a moment by the harsh light cast from the window when the light now came on. Out of a vague fear, he knew he had to choose, so there was a struggle between Boaz and the very tall mute young man. The light in the window went out and another light came on and a fire engine siren was heard wailing, racing in the next street, the young man was a cruel fighter, nobody could come out a winner in such a battle, thought Boaz. The nails stuck in his feet, the broken glass tore chunks out of his body, the geranium bush was abandoned. Its smell was forgotten in the smell of the cruel battle, blood flowed, and he didn't know if it was his blood or the young man's blood, the young man didn't talk, just groaned and roared, and Boaz tried to talk but no words were heard. Only afterward the young man groaned: You're all shit, what do you know. But now Boaz wasn't sure if he had really heard those words, he was just as struck as his enemy, the flight of the two of them was the most ridiculous thing Boaz could think of later on. How the two of us fled at the same time. He tramped on nails and glass shards and fled and saw another back fleeing from there and groaning and he groaned too, but now he couldn't know who was who, and Boaz imagined that that was all he wanted to know, who he wasn't, the bird with the gold beak flew off, the robe hanging on a peg before disappeared in a panic, a woman's hand was seen tugging the robe and maybe tore it, lights went on and off. Voices burst out of apartments where maybe they were trying to listen to a funny program at the end of the war, Hasidic music was heard in the distance, but what was clear to Boaz was that only one of them came from there and again he vaguely recalled that battle and he thought, Only one came out of that too even though maybe two of us were in it, who came out? Me or him, who comes out now: me or him, and he didn't know. And so, for a moment, when he stood in the street and people started appearing before his eyes, he could take pity on himself. But he was immediately disgusted with himself and stopped. Cleaned his wounds, but he recalled that he had gotten a tetanus shot some time ago and was protected from that harm; he wanted to be sure he wouldn't get rabies but that only embittered him even more.

The cats who were seen hiding between the fence and the house, where a tree was sprouting, were searching for a bend of the stones in the auto cemetery and suddenly they also fled all at once. The house couldn't be seen now. Who loses, who wins, the pain inside him, he hopped toward the tents on the seashore and wanted to get up and go to the settlement, to Grandmother, to be a live hero returning to the kindergarten teacher Eve and to her husband Teacher All's Well. Here, Eve, is a chick who did come back, your other chicks were left there. To see the gravestones, to forget. But he got up in the morning and went to the officer of the city. The office was humming with soldiers getting new uniforms or returning uniforms or requesting transfers. From the officer of the city he got addresses of those who had been with him. He tried to remember the battle he had left the day before yesterday and everything was mixed up in his mind, the battle, the movies, Laurence Olivier playing Hamlet, Goethe is better than Shakespeare. The girl he loved at night disappeared, maybe I dreamed all those things. He walked with the list in his pocket stood still in the street and saw an apartment on the second floor. On the balcony hung flowerpots and a gigantic awning covered it from the sun. He went up and knocked on the door. A woman opened it. She looked at him and tried to wipe away some tears seen drying in her left eye. Boaz said: I'm Boaz, I fought with Johnny. The woman brought him inside and gave him tea. He drank it and tried to talk, but he couldn't. She said, what are you seeking here, Boaz? He didn't know and so he left. Then he went to the cafe and sat for three days and waited for some parents to find him there. He bought a gigantic Bristol sheet and wrote on it in big letters "I know dead people," and hung the Bristol paper on the tree in front of Kassit Café, among the announcements of exhibitions and poetry books that were now starting to come out at dizzying speed. But only one man asked him if he knew Menashe Aharonovitch and Boaz said he didn't. People who knew him laughed and Minna appeared with the torn finger and said Boaz was out of his mind but she didn't dare approach him. He sat there at the table, alone, full of a new joy that bloomed in him, waiting to give testimony. The waiters served him beer or coffee. The money ran out and he left. The policeman who tried to tear the Bristol sheet off the tree couldn't do it because Boaz fought for his right to give testimony. Three days later he sat with a woman he didn't know and tried to explain to her how the woman he had slept with in the hotel looked. The woman he didn't know thought that was surely love and didn't understand him at all even though he talked about love as if it was a war you died in. He wanted to tell her, That's perfect non-love, but I'm searching for her. And only at the end did he start striding toward Menahem Henkin's house. Here there was already a problem, he knew Menahem well, he defended Menahem, and after he died they said maybe he had been all right. Then the "maybe" was erased. The street was flooded with light but Boaz walked in the shade and when he had to cross the street he leaped across. He believed he'd find the young man who beat and was beaten by him embracing the woman he almost succeeded in loving in the hotel, but he didn't. Courtyards swallowed up the beautiful and the good who tried to seem indifferent. People were already starting to come out and seek a new substance in their new state, which distributed food coupons and declared austerity. When he came to Henkin's house, he saw a dim light, loved the name of the street, Deliverance Street, near the sea, small, pitiful houses, tipping over, and clearly they had once been nicer and more festive. He wanted to tell Henkin that he had sat in Kassit Café three days and waited for him and why didn't he come, but he saw a scarecrow of a man drying himself at a dead castor oil tree. Henkin looked suited to the place. His clothes were dark, his hat was from another decade, the music that burst out of him was a waltz of slaughtered ducks. He looked avenged and defeated. With eyes full of sad cunning Teacher Henkin searched for his son at a fence covered with brambles, now wretched and neglected. A small garbage cart stood there, empty, rusted, and the enclosures of the port looked too bright in the sunlight. The intense blue of the sky swallowed up the particle of distance between him and the sea. The houses protected only themselves. Henkin didn't protect anything. Boaz stood there stuck and waited and Henkin looked at him. After about an hour, Henkin went into the house, opened the slats of the shutter a little and peeped outside. Boaz went on standing. A little while later, he came outside and gave Boaz a glass of cold water. Boaz didn't drink it and returned the water to Henkin. He saw Menahem playing in the yard and thought, what could I have told him, Henkin couldn't have recognized Boaz's face because of the strong light and he saw only the stunned silhouette in the afternoon light and then he dared ask, he asked: Who are you?

Just, said Boaz.

Just what?

Just standing here.

Henkin wanted to ask, but some skepticism had already sneaked into him, that sense of loss that, anyway, he wouldn't answer him. He muttered something and said, And doesn't the young man have a name?

I did have, said Boaz and then he started pitying all that life here and he went away. He took the kitbag from the tent, walked to the central bus station and got on a bus. He had soldier's tickets and rode free. The discharge would start tomorrow. Henkin waited a few minutes and went inside. He locked the door and tried to recall the young man's face, but he couldn't.

Tape / —

And then a wind started blowing and Teacher Henkin said to his wife: They won't understand, Hasha Masha, they won't understand, there's an undermined system of fares here, look . . . but she didn't want to read.

Tape / —

. . . And once again I recall the young man who stood here years ago. Now I think it really was Boaz Schneerson but maybe I'm wrong. Boaz never confirmed that he stood here and took the glass of cold water and didn't deny it either. The story of the Last Jew was also constructed from the end to the beginning, and only after I invested a few years in my investigation of the Last Jew did I meet Ebenezer completely by chance, even though he was here, near me, all that time. And after the meeting with Ebenezer, doubts about the hundreds of pages I had written stirred in me and I decided to think about writing the book with that German. Maybe that writing itself is an attempt to decipher, to uncover the things whose logical sequence is so strange to me.

My dear son Menahem I lost many years ago. Menahem was killed in two different places: he was killed in battle in the valley near Mount Radar where he lay among thirty-two bodies, and he fell in battle for the Old City of Jerusalem, at dawn on May twentieth, nineteen forty-eight. Maybe she's right, Hasha Masha, who maintains that the glory of mourners in front of a mirror is common in me. I'm trying to reconstruct things: I then felt that life stopped all at once, wasn't in store for me anyplace else, the energy in me was masked by the pain that was too splendid in my wife's eyes, but was all I had left. I sank into endless thinking about my son and my own life was only a setting for the sorrow I shaped in me; like somebody who creates life on the model of death. I looked at my little house on Deliverance Street, near the old port of Tel Aviv, against the background of the sea that sinks there a bit to the north, makes a kind of semi-bow, and at the undrained station is a small airport where small planes land or take off over our house. I looked then at the desolation of the forsaken concrete of the port, the abandoned enclosures, the creased houses, and the dusty trees, eaten by sea salt, and the sand that penetrates everything here, thickens holes, turns everything living into scarred desolation bereft of beauty. It's hard for me to describe the essence of that pain, they're the strongest yearnings for a person whose death is never grasped. That death is in you, lives in you, in the chest, the dream, waking, slumbering grown to somewhere you have no idea of, and then the wakefulness, the emptiness, the waking distress. Memories are nothing but nonstop poundings in softness, maybe a mute shout in a dream and you don't know whether you're dreaming it or it's dreaming you.

In the cemeteries for those who fell in World War II, the anonymous graves say: "Known only to God." On a check you write: "Pay to the bearer," so it can't be transferred to somebody else. Pain has no heirs, there is no imagination that can hold the empty space left behind by some anonymous person known only to God, if God knew him as I do, he would hold the whole earth.

All I had left of Menahem were a few school notebooks, a naïve scrapbook from the seventh grade, photos we took here and there of Menahem's grandfather and grandmother who have died meanwhile, of uncles, friends we used to meet sometimes. Photos in the drawers of our table or with Noga, who was still living with us then, before she went to live with Boaz. His mother hung Menahem's clothes in the closet. Our house is a closet for Menahem's clothes. A picture album, a few notebooks and that poem, enveloped by this house. Hasha Masha scoured the buttons, sewed on the ones that fell off, polished his shoes carefully, scoured the isolated objects

we had left and I, who had once worked for a tailor to pay for my schooling, sewed the rips, stitched together, then I ironed everything and we
hung them up in the closet and ever since then he's known only to God.
All we had left was to sit and wait. We had to make up a life to justify what
had ended.

Boaz Schneerson came and moved me out of my orbit, killed Menahem
in another battle, brought him back to life, and put him to death again, but
about that I'll have to talk later. Noga left us for Boaz and I went on teaching awhile, I was even principal for about two years. But when I figured out
that I was talking to students who had finished school long ago and maybe
were parents of their own children, when I figured out that in my increasingly frequent hallucinations I was talking to Menahem's friends who remained his age, on the day it ended, but in fact they had already graduated
and were filling the world with mischief, or teaching, or running factories,
and I called those kids by other names, when I saw that I was hallucinating, I resigned.

That was a few years ago, years after our son fell. The photos didn't
help, nor did the endless walks every morning between seven and seven
forty-five from our house in the north of the city to Mugrabi Square that
had been obliterated meanwhile along with the clock that had anyway
never shown the right time, but stood there like a clear sign of some sta-
bility that's gone now. Nothing helped, the emptiness was heavy as the
nothingness of Menahem's shoes in the closet. Polished, shining, destined
for nothing. At the end of every journey, thousands of kilometers in the
same orbit, I remained alone.

Until I met Ebenezer I thought my investigation of the Last Jew resulted from a conversation I once had with somebody who had been the
principal of our school, Demuasz, the teacher who had been there even
longer than I. I have to say that compared to what Demuasz built I didn't
contribute much and our school sank into a gray slumber of routine. What
I did contribute is a wall of memory and every year the graduating students
say with an embarrassed smile that the next reunion will be held on it. And
then they also see Menahem's name carved there, heading the long list.
I put up the wall by myself and there was some pleasure in beginning the
long list with my son's name and adding after the name, as ordered by
Demuasz, the words, May God avenge their blood. I didn't believe in those

words, but I gave in. Today I know that in those days when I talked with Demuasz about the strange man who lived in his house, Ebenezer was moving into the Giladis' house next door to our house, but since I was so involved with myself and my solitude, I didn't pay any heed to that and didn't even notice that the Giladis moved out of here and a real estate agent was hanging around here tired and sweaty and I didn't see that night when Ebenezer came with a truckload of furniture and closed himself in the house and slammed the windows. Demuasz, who helped me quite a bit in my work on the Committee of Bereaved Parents, invited me then to his house and introduced me to the guest who was staying there. The guest was paralyzed, waving his arms like a double-edged sword, I don't know why that image came into my mind, or a sword of the Lord of Hosts, in a Jew of all people a sword is like a shattered sanctuary, and that smashed shard muttered vague words that nobody understood but when he met my eyes, and maybe he saw there a pain that touched his own pain, he told me in a few sentences about the Last Jew, but then he didn't yet know who he was. In my house I was inferior in my own eyes and in my wife's eyes. The death of my son, if I can be forgiven the expression, was a few sizes too big on me. The embarrassment of the father looking at the forever empty shoes of his son was a definite condition of enmity, and in me at least, a certain glory of timorous but not undramatic grief. I wouldn't say I was nice to people, I had a certain bitterness I didn't like in myself, but I couldn't control it, the yearnings for my son were also yearnings for exchange, a death for a death. Questions of why him, and if there is a fixed number of dead, why did fate pick a fight with me of all people. I didn't ask anybody why fate hadn't picked a fight with his son, I asked why it had picked a fight with me. My wife almost forgave me with painful contempt. The destroyed Jew in Demuasz's house was still alive, from me he was dying, from me he was also drawing some consolation, I don't understand why, maybe my bitterness suited him since dying is a condition of the present and not of the past. Noga was still living with us then and she and my wife would look together at the photos of Menahem, at the notebooks, they loved and hated one another in a kind of shared plot where I couldn't set foot. They were locked against me, I had to meet a dying Jew in a strange house to glory in my pain.

At the sight of him, I could more easily understand the life that Hasha Masha and Noga inspired in the cobwebs of our house. At the sight of him

I understood how awful but also how encouraging it was to hear the breathing of my two women when I couldn't fall asleep and turned and tossed
helplessly. The man told me about the Last Jew, about his knowledge.
That night I dreamed I came home and killed Hasha Masha. She walked
from room to room in her underwear and kept me from thinking about my
son. Then I served Noga her blood in a glass. In the morning I wanted to
cry but my eyes had been dry for years.

What looks one way today looked completely different then. I was already a person less arrogant in his pain, less elegant, less portrayed by himself, more submissive to real pain who changed his self-image as somebody
who contains pain. Without the vitality that Noga imparted to our house,
the house looked like a tomb. The windows were always shuttered, my
wife in black, under the lamp that comes down almost to the table, the
shade creates a familiar shaft of light, a shade I bought many years ago from
a refugee who came to our house during the big Aliyah, and when I bought
that shade, I seemed to be buying the skin of that refugee. I remember the
crooked smile on his pale face, he also wanted to sell me a watch and rings,
all gold, he told me, and I bought the wax-paper shade that turned yellow
over the years. Its edge grew sharp as a clown's hat and it had burst now
and was sewn and repaired but we didn't change it, just as then I still
didn't take care of the yard or the house, we hadn't yet changed anything, we didn't buy any furniture or new curtains and beneath the shaft
of light in the dim room at the table once polished and now rubbed beyond
repair sat my wife, shrouded in a smell of moths and mints and tea with
lemon mixed with orange peel. A smell of mothballs and old paint. Maybe
because of that closed desolation, I accepted Demuasz's invitation and
that's why I could sit facing that destroyed Jew and instead of trying to
listen to him, I tried in my mind to compare one suffering with another,
one pain with another. A crooked game, my wife would surely have said,
and I would watch the man's silence, his dying eyes, his hands drawing
wild illustrations for me in the dense air of the room, and it was then that
he told me things.

Today when I reconstruct the things that led me to Ebenezer and the
encounter with the German, I recall that that morning, when I went to
Demuasz's house, I did see a stranger standing in the door of the Giladi
house with his profile to me, I remember a sense of panicky haste I felt at

the sight of him, something bothered me and at the same time erased the
picture from my mind, like that quality I developed over years to dream
that I'm late and then wake up with a start, a minute or two before the big
old alarm clock rings. And the man stood there in his shabby but elegant
clothes with some old humility, maybe even a spiteful clown but for some
reason I didn't think about him, didn't register him in my mind, maybe I
thought the man was a guest of the Giladis, maybe he inspired me with
some vague dread. I came to Demuasz's house bearing in the depths of my
mind a faded picture of Ebenezer, and the man in the Demuasz home was
in bed, as if he were waiting for me, I thought, maybe he intends a ceremony of death for me to gore me with his pain. To triumph over me. I
looked at the glass of water on the nightstand next to his bed, at his teeth
in the glass, his eyes were wide open but hallucinating, his leg twitched
under the thin blanket, above him hung an old picture of a butterfly surely
left over from the days when Demuasz was a teacher of the nature of our
Land and his lips started moving, gaped open and spread and were again
covered with a scrim of feeble violence, I took off my hat, my hands were
clasped in one another to preserve that measure of fitting courtesy I assume
when necessary. A snort like a phony chirp of a bird rose from the man's
nose and he said to me: Henkin, I want to say something, Demuasz was
stunned and I, my habit for many years, I mechanically thrust my hands in my
pockets and pulled out the square paper I always had in my pocket, and the
sharpened pencil I never left home without, and when he spoke I of course
wrote it down as if I were again Henkin-researcher, Henkin, one of the
tough young men who plies his pencil, as my students once used to sing.
And the man, still with his eyes shut (he shut them when he started speaking), his leg started twitching, and the false teeth in the glass, because of
the tilt of my face and the flash of light, looked monstrous, gigantic, he
said: The name of the company there is D. G. S., initials of Deutsche
Gesellschaft für Stadtlingsbekampfung M. B. H., an all-German company
of fighters. In nineteen forty-four it paid dividends of two hundred percent
to A. G. Farben, one of the three concerns they owned. The cost was nine
hundred seventy-five deutsch marks for one hundred fifty kilos of Zyklon
B. twenty-seven and a half marks a kilogram for one thousand five hundred
human beings. At that time, the mark was worth twenty-five American

cents, Mr. Henkin. That is, six dollars and seventy-five cents. In the summer of forty-four, Mr. Henkin, the life of a Jew was worth less than two-fifths of a cent. And then they said that was too expensive. They sat in Berlin in armchairs and wrote a report. They wrote that that was too expensive. It's all economics, Mr. Henkin. So, they said, the children have to be thrown straight into the fire. They were frugal, he said, and knew what things cost.

He was silent and I held onto the square of paper in my hand and didn't know what to do with it. It took me a few minutes to understand what he was telling me. For a moment he opened his right eye, which was shrunk in swollen orbits and looked like a bluish-green sore, looked at me defiantly, as if he had beaten me in an exciting but exhausting game of chess and said, You understand? I know a lot of numbers from the Last Jew. Everything is numbered in him. The new Bible, you're a Hebrew teacher, has to be written from numbers. And then he shut his eyes, wheezed, and didn't talk anymore. I thought he had died but he was only slumbering and didn't wake up, then, but, when he spoke I thought about an amusement park where I used to go when I was a kid and where there were terrifying toys and I told Demuasz, who came in now, the smile of an expert on his Jew, he told me shh. And I told him. He said Yes, he quotes him now and then but he won't hold out much longer. I told Demuasz that I had heard the stories about the Last Jew from a bereaved mother whose son had fallen in the Sinai campaign and Demuasz said, Yes, the distress they bring from there, to save two-fifths of a cent, Henkin!

I went back home and my wife was sitting there under the sixty-watt bulb I could never change for a hundred watts because of her stubbornness, her beautiful face was resting on the binding of my son's closed photo album, guessing the photos perfectly, and I went to my study, I sat down at the desk where I hadn't worked for years now, took a smooth sheet of paper out of the drawer, picked up my Parker pen, checked it as a scribe checks his quill, and wrote "The Last Jew" and a few minutes later, I drew a thick line under those words and added in small, even modest letters, I'd say, maybe for camouflage: "A Study by Obadiah Henkin." And then I looked at the page and I knew I had to investigate that Jew and I looked at the window and saw the emptiness of the yard and the Giladi house and I dimly remembered seeing a person there in the morning but I didn't really think about him, his image flashed through my mind and was immediately erased, and some panic attacked me.

And again I found myself investigating, interviewing people, going to Yad Vashem, the Holocaust memorial, to Kibbutz Lohamei HaGetaot, I heard that the man who talked to me in Demuasz's house had been taken to the hospice in Gadera and had been lying there like a vegetable for a few weeks, suddenly he opened his eyes and said: Did Obadiah talk to him? And they asked him who? What? And he smiled, shut his eyes, and died. I thought about his words, about the mission he seemed to assign me, I thought about my wife in the ravines of light, the very solitary house, the empty rooms, the old samovar still heating water for tea and a long time ago I'd become acquainted with the ironic malice of the solitude decreed by pain that has to be acted to live it, and I started investigating the life of a man and all I could know about him were trifles. And at that time we are still living in a certain regularization of organized hostility, my wife and I. She looks at me with transparent malice, sympathy, I'd say, and refuses to sleep in the same bed with me. At night I try to touch her, to reach out my hand, like a lovestruck boy, the two of us in our beds, tossing and turn-ing, trying to sleep, no tranquilizer or sleeping pill helps, I'm trying to caress her but she doesn't respond to me, even though she's not angry ei-ther, she keeps inventing hope for me for other times, or maybe a fabrica-tion for the past, you have to listen carefully to hear the quiet tears flowing on her cheeks, she never sobs aloud, she doesn't weep in the light, and she mocked my daily walks, my activity on the Committee for Bereaved Par-ents, my searching. After I brought home Boaz Schneerson and Noga was still living with us and what happened happened, her contempt changed to hostility, and her words became as sharp as a razor. She always wears black for herself, she doesn't share her pain with anybody, she doesn't go out of the house, my need to understand the lack of Menahem makes her suspicious, and she apparently has a need incomprehensible to me to be a perfect and unchanging enemy to herself to preserve some trace of close-ness, a closeness that's hard to define, as if a shared secret helplessness and a strong hatred unites two people not because of the past but despite the past. I'd say that a canned love prevailed between us, frozen in a deep freeze, a love that has to be assessed with webs of amazement, transparencies of the window through the heavy shades, furtive looks, stabbing sentences, the way each of us gets into bed apart but always together, at the very same time, and gets up separately but together, prepare without words for another day to live it together, but apart. We had no secrets, I told her everything and she was silent to me about everything. Love of Menahem was shared, but she saw one person and I saw another person. Maybe it was inevitable that like me, she too discovered she was cut off from the bond that bound us and yet she couldn't grant my request, forgive me for my behavior toward Boaz or toward myself or toward the Committee, she didn't forgive me for the life after death I tried in vain to grant Menahem.

Since she didn't leave the house, I'd do the shopping, pay the bills, collect the pension, take care of whatever had to be taken care of, and once a year, we'd go to Kiryat Anavim on Memorial Day. She'd do that reluctantly, with some distress, would get into a cab. Withdrawn into herself, on the path leading to the cemetery she'd walk alone, as if she couldn't bear any contact.

She wouldn't go to her son's grave, but came with me so I'd be sure my son was really buried there, since as far as she was concerned, he was buried there as he was buried everyplace else. The closer I went to the grave, the more exaggerated she became, maybe even magnificent to some extent, the place was so unimportant to her that a few times she missed some Memorial Days and refused to come with me. But when she did come, she'd stand there, enshrouded in herself, looking at me, and then she'd walk toward the road, sit stooped on the bench of the taxi stand, and wait for me.

At that time something else happened that only today I can connect with the Last Jew. I started working and fixing our garden then, cultivating it again. At the time, I thought resurrecting the idea of reviving the garden was accidental. Apparently I saw the buds of the renewed garden in the Giladi house and the sight of the graceful foliage near my window woke me out of my swoon of many years. On a certain day and I can't be precise about the timing, that man I described before as somebody who stood in the doorway of the Giladi house dressed like a clown with his profile turned to me started working the Giladi garden, which, like all the gardens on the street, had stopped blooming when my garden withered after Menahem was killed. Suddenly I began to neglect the mourning Teacher Henkin and to see a red-brown loam, a compost heap. To sense that wonderful, sweet, bitter, sharp smell, the sight of the trunk after years of looking out the window and seeing only gray and sand, and wind, and heat, and something neglected and stinking at the seashore and then, one day, the eyes light up at the sight of a new stem, at a spinning spurt of a sprinkler, at the sight of a rosebush and a bougainvillea starting to ignite, and the evening falling on it smoothes the ground and it doesn't fall anymore, doesn't drop like an estimated nothingness and a blossom that blooms for you evokes completely different longings, longings for life, for morning glories, and then I saw thorns in my garden, crabgrass, destruction, a heap of brown needles that fell from the pine tree, the ground covered with sand and dry leaves, and just like that, I started hoeing a little and then fixing here and there and suddenly I found myself working and hoeing and banging. Every day I'd work for two or three hours, in an undershirt and cap, I sweated, I fixed the faucet, I bought a new hose and sprinkler, and new life ignited, a life that died with the black villas. A lightness and lust filled me, my bones began to recover, not to creak, and how I loved that house I had bought in 'thirty-seven through the Hebrew teachers' organization at the time of the riots the Arabs call the great revolt, the remote neighborhood in north Tel Aviv at the edge of the city, and the new port born then and now dead and left barren and demolished and the street next to mine they called Gate of Zion, and I live on Deliverance, near the sea, nice small houses of teachers, union officials, and the neighborhood blossomed then, its gardens were handsome, the red roof tiles, the houses like little exclamation marks in the desert of sand near the sea, south of us stretched the hills and the Muslim cemetery, north of us forests to what my son called boos, Reading Station that was then small and insubstantial beyond the Yarkon River and then I planted a fine garden and Demuasz helped me choose its plants, and geraniums and climbing roses blossomed in it along with a fragrant jujube and mint and pansies, and in season lilies blossomed and a blaze of fine wildflowers and I planted a pine tree and two cedars and a purple bougainvillea that covered the front of the house after a few years and set fire to it with its sweet light and the castor oil tree that had been standing here for generations I didn't uproot and the soft lawn that needed a lot of watering and the sprinklers spun at night and made a pleasant intoxicating rustle and during the years of the great war, my son would take care of the garden and slowly it turned into his garden. He loved to prune, uproot crabgrass, tend the garden, good hands he had, he loved to work when nobody ordered him, not like in school where he had to work under the triumphant baton of Demuasz who also turned tending the garden into a national operation, here at home he was Menahem, master of himself, he'd frown capriciously and tell me, Henkin (he didn't call me father), go to your books and find me exactly how an Afghanistanian bamboo smells. That was almost our only point of contact, back then, but usually I'd let him work alone while I was locked in my room, investigating, correcting notebooks.

And at night, we'd set up a table in the garden and Menahem hung a lamp outside and we'd have supper on the lawn, yogurt, eggs, herring, salad, black bread and butter, or later margarine, near the bougainvillea with its cruel sweet colors and the breakers of the sea would be heard and the sirens of the ships and the launches sailing toward the ships, not to mention the crickets and the insects that would circle the lamp and Menahem loved to destroy them and I asked him not to kill them and his mother would look at him with some hushed sadness and say: Leave him alone Obadiah, after all he's a little boy. In her voice I could make out a complaint or submission, but back then I was too busy to have it out with her, and she'd say, Menahem is what we were, but I couldn't accept such an unpedagogical assumption that contradicted my craft that still lodged in me back then, imparting values.

A few days after we found out that Menahem had fallen there was a heat wave. We didn't yet know where they buried him and Jerusalem was still cut off from the coastal plain. I went outside, not yet understanding my self; I stood in the customary white shirt and shorts of those days, I picked up the hose by rote, turned on the faucet and aimed a jet of water at the roses dyed by the red and pink colors of sunset. The light was soft and the heat was heavy and the sea to my left was smooth and crystalline and suddenly I saw myself as a scarecrow watering his own grave, a teacher made of crystal, stuck forever in a conspiracy of death against my son, I tried to water for him the garden he wouldn't return to, I thought in terms of the grammar of nothingness, of the grammar of life, or nonlife, and a grammar of nothingness of my son suddenly became definite like the declension of a verb with no future and no past, and so maybe no present either, and the garden the nothingness of all things palpable like the declension of the verb "to die" was proof that Menahem became in this light, the numbing heat that blew as from a bellows, the foliage that in its wickedness wanted to live, that didn't long for Menahem like Yoash's dog that died of longings when he didn't return from the battles, but the garden didn't weep and didn't long, it wanted me to water it as if Menahem its owner weren't dead, the leaves were dropping, they had no grief, I hated that blossoming, the heat blew, the sea stretched to distant lands I could once have lived in, I thought to myself: What do you all want from me, you give birth to dead foliage. I wanted to take vengeance on somebody, the garden was the most convenient target, Menahem wasn't in it, shouldn't I have been mad at somebody, and I laughed at myself, Hebrew teacher, grammar of vengeance, watering gardens where wheelbarrows full of a son's loam won't go anymore, I turned off the faucet, the hose I left where it was (and it stayed like that for years until it rotted and was swallowed up in the heaps of sand that kept piling up), I went into the house and my wife looked at me and said: Did you turn off the water on the flowers, Obadiah? I said yes, and she said: That water, and I said: His garden and she said to me: His? She didn't ask, she said, and at the end of the word she put a hesitant question mark and so I neglected the garden, bushes of weeds began sprouting and I didn't uproot them and the faucet rusted and was blocked, sometimes I'd shut my eyes, I was waiting for him, expecting the evening, the table on the lawn, the herring, the—. "Henkin look up in the dictionary to screw a tomato in ancient Indian," I was expecting his joyous open laughter, humiliating me, the annihilated insects around the lamp, but everything is covered with nettles and yellowness and sand and obstinate callused melancholy shrouded our house and infected the other houses and the gardens ceased one after another, and maybe the Giladis were afraid to appear joyous with the hose next to our house, and slowly their garden was also humiliated and then it was too late to save it and anybody who could took heart and started all over, and then began a plague of dead gardens and it wasn't only Menahem who fell, Kuperman's son also disappeared and they didn't know where he was buried and Yehoshafat Neiya's son was badly wounded and was in the hospital, and slowly the foliage disappeared and only a few dusty stubborn trees remained and the street became dusty, lost

its charm, and no longer had even an old-fashioned elegance, only something forlorn, more scorched than parched, and the weeds wove themselves
into a new weave, as if death had its own interweaving, which is simply
another form of the verb *to be*, a sprouting in a different direction, and
something elite, distorted, miserable, but not without honor, took the
place of the charm and the capricious sprinklers and the rounded roof tiles,
the walls turned gray and it's true that in the house where your son grew
up from the age of seven to the age of nineteen you don't seek aesthetic
meaning at his empty shoes and his clothes in mothballs but I had a clear
need to seek formal meanings, real formulations as I was accustomed to
doing in the analysis of a story by Brenner or Genessin, something musical,
maybe a feeling that had lodged in me and now disappeared, that behind
every pain is a certain logic and that I had to decipher it for the students
and there's understanding behind the complexity of the instincts and a
wisdom woven in this or that pattern and grief and love have their own
grammar.

So when, maybe too late, I noticed the garden being cultivated next to
my house, when I saw a new rake, a new ladder, a hose, young virgin foliage and a sprinkler spinning, maybe then something penetrated my consciousness even though consciously, maybe as a defense from something I
was afraid of, I started working our garden and some audacious sickness,
certainly not acute, poured into me intoxicating letters of what I could
have read by myself if only I dared: furtive bliss, bliss stemming from the
fact that for a long time I hadn't yet succeeded in hating the garden because of the nothingness of my son. My wife then said to me: Obadiah,
what are you trying to do in old age? You'll start knocking nails for me and
knowing how they hang pictures on a wall, Obadiah, said my wife, you're
too old to be a human being—that she said now with a wickedness that
even she herself felt but couldn't stop herself, you'll start learning to long
for your son without the whole world knowing it, she added with a kind of
poison of love, maybe you'll even learn how to take out the garbage without spilling half on the floor and you'll learn how to make children who live
and don't die. Much as her words pained me, especially the last ones, I
knew it wasn't at me that she aimed her anger and even she herself was
sorry for her words and she said: The department of dead children is me,
you just watered gardens, children, a new nation, empty rhetoric, and my

thirsty body. I saw her, I looked at her sad eyes. And with a solid longing
that lodged in me from the first day I saw her, her little body wrapped in
skin soft as down, her limbs that haven't grown old but only softened with
the years, her frightening orphanhood, and I said: Not everything is locked,
Hasha Masha, and I went outside, I meant love, maybe hate. I ripped up
some crabgrass. I started tending a garden in my old age. I stood there, I
knew she was looking at me, I thought of the album, of the photos of the trip
to Caesarea that her innocent eyes see through the binding of the album now
closed forever, I thought of her inability to really hate, I contemplated the
bright but blurred photo of the tour, the picture of Caesarea, a few children
in bathing suits, rocks, an older girl with a wet skirt clinging to the hard
body and to identify him and Menahem's face in the middle of the photo, his
hands held out to the sides, oxygen ate part of the picture, and his hands are
trying to embrace the world with a love that maybe really did lodge in him,
for life, for the garden, for Noga, for the sun, and for the sea and he's there
linked to his mother's words, not mine.

   And so I discovered that the Giladis had disappeared and no longer lived
next door to us. Together we moved here, together we built our houses,
together we had children, Amihud their son and Menahem our son play
with one another, and then they fly kites and frolic in the bamboo nests
they called boos and look at the sea and swim. Here we came to live as a
national mission, to conquer another square of land for the nation, here in
the far north then, cut off, and now it's become part of a city with many
gigantic hotels and shops and cafés and restaurants. Giladi was an official
in the company to prepare for settlement and bought land all over Israel
from the old and spoiled effendis in Beirut or Damascus for the institutions
and he'd run around on his big motorcycle and there was always some big
secret on his face that he couldn't reveal and after Menahem's death, the
Giladis stopped coming and if they did come they felt uncomfortable and
fled, and so ties slackened and we were also cut off from other people we
knew and new ties were made that were essential, at least to me, and even
Amihud stopped coming and I dimly remember that he invited me to his
wedding or maybe some other event, and I couldn't go and then we didn't
see each other anymore and now I discover that they're not here anymore
and I didn't notice that they had moved. And I thought, funny how people
cut themselves off. The place took on a new form. The gardens I had de-

stroyed in my mourning, the Giladis whose secrets I had long ago not tried
to decipher in meandering conversations with Mr. Giladi, Ben-Yehuda Street
where I walk every morning is changing, tourists come to photograph ruins,
couples in cars on the seashore, petting or perhaps even copulating, and
Berla's kiosk has closed, the huts of the youth movement have disappeared,
and the sands have been concealed under the impetus of hotel building and
only Singer's little shop with an old sign advertising a brand of cigarettes
they don't make anymore is still here, and the sign hangs in the salty sea air,
rusted, groaning when the wind blows in winter, cobwebs of an old man who
was once the first one to wrap food in clean parchment paper and not in
newspaper, and we're left an abandoned island next to the closed port and
in the grocery they confirmed it, yes, a strange new neighbor lives there,
a refugee they told me. Comes to the store, buys, is silent, and goes, always
dressed for the theater, Singer's son told me, dragging a crate of eggs from
the pickup truck on the sidewalk, cartons of eggs in a crate, like all of us,
and so I paid attention to the garden that put an end to some gnawing
grief, some misery we all felt but didn't talk about, and there was fertilizer
there and suddenly piles of red loam and planting grass and you just don't
see who does it, he's solitary as a thief at night and working when everybody's sleeping maybe afraid of being seen and I work my garden and my
garden starts touching his garden and a kind of union is created here, I fix
and somebody else fixes, I uproot crabgrass and suddenly the street is full
of uprooted crabgrass and who the man is, I didn't know then.

And so we met, Ebenezer and I. When the pine tree looked green and
fresh and the bougainvillea started blooming and the piles of sand disappeared and the new lawn was planted and looked green and soft and
mowed and the geranium bushes started blooming I was filled with a kind
of pleasure, a plea for far-off days and the tombstone around my house was
shattered and my body stood erect, even my face took on color and at night
I could sleep from fatigue, and in my mind's eye I saw Menahem running
around in the garden I had planted for him, as if life has cycles and there's
a return from death, and he pushes a wheelbarrow as if it were a train and
goes *toot toot* and then I saw the walls of my house peeling and I bought
paint to paint them and I fixed the roof tiles and a carpenter came and
fixed the windows and I stretched new screens and I cleaned the gutters
and I made a new gate and I put Menahem's wheelbarrow next to the new

faucet and my wife refused to go out to see and peeped out the window, and who knows, maybe she smiled to herself, and I wanted to hug her and she avoided me with an almost virginal laugh of an old woman, and she even said: So what, Menahem will grow up in you to be a gardener. And she tried to wipe away invisible tears and ran to our room and I didn't say a thing, but then I saw my neighbor, he was pruning a rosebush that almost touched a vine that started preening wildly on the trunk of the cypress that looked green again and not dusty.

It was summer then, perhaps late summer, because of the heat I took off my shirt and stayed in my undershirt. A nice smell of a watered garden stood in the air, the cool of evening stood in the dark sky, and he stood also in an undershirt but without the cap I wore and I saw how blasted and white his body was, as if a dangerous malediction lodged in him, and yet in his behavior, the way he pruned, the way he measured and plucked tendrils, there was some authenticity, some solid standing on the ground that was his, surely this is how a person prunes a garden he longs for and is rooted in, this is also how a person hates his garden and this is also how he loves it, I was amazed at those phrases but they echoed in the back of my mind. We stood there, two old men, watering gardens, who just a while ago were tense, maybe we were safeguarding something, getting to know one another through gardens, through our almost naked bodies, each one holding the strong flow of water like mighty gods trying to make the harsh and obstinate earth fertile, I thought about the man's fractures, what holds him together, I could see myself, an old teacher, looking like somebody who stood for many years in front of children, teaching them why they would have to die, and behind me the pictures of Herzl, Ben-Gurion, Berl Katznelson, and Weizmann repeating Zionism that the children later realize on memorial walls that took the place of the pictures of the leaders and here he belongs and yet as if he belongs, to those same echoes that made me send Menahem from his first year to war, so those fractures would have a place in the sun, I thought about Tel Aviv, from here it looks like a city joined together obstinately and innocently, half its name Tel, mound, a place where cities are buried and discovered after thousands of years, and half its name, Aviv, spring, is blossoming, blossoming of what? I thought about a line from the words of the Last Jew, he quoted the Yiddish poet Itzik Manger on one of those tapes, who said: When they buried the last of the

Gypsy kings, thirty thousand violins came to play on his grave and I thought
of what he said, what he quoted from some person who may have breathed
his last right after he said that, and Itzik Manger surely meant that he was
the last of the violinists playing on the grave of thirty thousand Jewish
kings. And at that moment each one of them turned into two-fifths of a
cent.

The sight of my neighbor made me sad, like somebody who's used to
investigating a situation woven of words, two separate entities, two different disasters, the disaster of the Last Jew and God and the disaster of the
wars my son falls in and surely it's from that junction, I thought, that the
great and awful moments of our life are woven, the junction of celebration
and the junction of nightmare, an illness of malediction leaving smoke that
came here to ask for steps for feet they didn't have anymore, an echo seeking a foothold, and yet a foothold that knew what its echo was. . . . Maybe
Hasha Masha really is right and there's no need to talk and a man can be
silent with his fellow man and know things that many words don't know,
maybe it was his accent, when we did speak, an accent composed of an
ancient phonetic layer of the natives of the Land of Israel, the way farmers
talk, which once, when I immigrated here in the early nineteen twenties, I
knew as a worker in their yards, and along with that some foreignness, a refugee language, in short here I hold in my hands an enormous sex organ of
some ancient god, spraying water, talking with a scarecrow that sprouted
in my neighbor's yard, a scarecrow who came from two disasters, and wonders. We talked of the Giladis and he claimed he didn't know them and
didn't know where they had disappeared, I was impolite, maybe because
of the heat and I asked myself who he was and where he came from, and
he peeped at me like an old acquaintance. With some practiced smile at
the edge of his mouth that lacked suppleness and yet was quite harsh, and
I sensed that his eyes were mocking me, as if he were saying: Old Henkin,
surely we're old friends and surely I knew where I knew him from and he
said surely my name is Ebenezer and the name of the woman who lives
with me and is married to me is Fanya R. He pronounced the words carefully and I sensed that he had a special need to feel the words as if he
weren't used to speaking Hebrew, which sounded, as I said, both rooted
and foreign. I sensed that he had a need to say "the woman who lives with
me" before "is married to me," an amazing phrase in itself, surely I would

have said my wife and not the woman who's married to me as if she's married to him and he isn't married to her?

I thought about the Giladis, about his phrases, about the way he bent over and plucked out tiny crabgrass that I may not have noticed, and then he said: Did Boaz Schneerson come visit you yet? And I thought here it comes, like then, when I learned my son died, simple things once again start to take on a twisted meaning, as if everything was planned and he started taking care of the Giladis' garden so two months later I could come out and hear that name, Boaz Schneerson, from him, and suddenly a distant memory flashed in me, the moment when Boaz maybe really was standing here, still a young man who had just returned from the war, raging and furious, he looked at me, and when I asked him who he was and gave him some cold water he took off. I remember how he looked at me then, and I felt a strange envy of him because he was alive and then when I met him, years later, I didn't remember what I remembered now, and now of all times, when the stranger asks me if Boaz Schneerson came again, or perhaps he said "yet," to visit you, what does he have to do with Boaz? What does he have to do with the person who destroyed my life and stirred Hasha Masha's hostility, where does that stranger get a tie with us? I looked at him in amazement and he managed to smile, a smile Boaz would surely call the smile of a hunter of agricultural machines or something, Boaz's diabolical phrases. A pleasant wind now blew from the sea. The air cooled off in a cooling and graying space, a bittersweet smell of geranium, and the blue sea stretching beyond his back, an overloaded ship sails toward the port of Ashdod, smoke rises from the ship's smokestacks, and the man measures me, waits for an answer, or perhaps not, and I water, that's the safest thing. I don't let the hose slip away, I don't let the stream dwindle and then the man says: So? He doesn't come anymore, the bastard?

No! I said, almost reluctantly. His mouth was gaping open a little, a bird of death I saw, a spasm I saw, invisible blood flows. A blasted cheek, a bandage on an arm, the bold clear colors before sunset, spots of color on the back, was he hit hard? The sight of the scars reminded me again of the sight of Boaz. Back then, when I didn't recognize him, the sight of a captured jackal, and the man talked and straightened up again and I said what I regretted afterward and after you say it there's no way back, I said: This garden belonged to my son, Menahem, he fell in battles in Jerusalem, for him I replanted the garden. But he didn't pay attention to the seriousness I tried to give that moment and he said: Surely you're going to the party this evening, Mr. Henkin, Menahem's been dead a long time . . .

Before I could digest the words, I said: I'm supposed to go out this evening, but I'm not yet sure I will and once again I wanted to gain time, to understand how he knew what he knew, how he knew my son's name, how he knew I would go out that evening, was he spying on me; his face was shriveled now, as if he had just been taken out of the grave, his hands didn't shake, he held the hose with a certain cunning and only his torso was seen moving a little, as if he were praying and even laughing a laugh pieced together of tatters of pain and seeking a foothold, assembled, and stitched together again, he even demonstrated some insolent shyness. His ear turned red, and his cheek drooped toward a strong and handsome chin and a dimple was hollowed in the cheek, and suddenly out of the blue, in an improvised but wonderfully measured formulation he said: Go, go. It's important to us that you go!

And the hose surely granted me freedom of maneuver and I did aim it at another bush, I started filling the hollow and I thought: Is his pain really more than my pain, can pain be learned? Had he lost more than I? I recalled how Noga visited us suddenly, that was about two or three months ago. She came into the house as if she were hopping on air and not on the ground, as usual, so delicate and yet something solid in her as always. She sat next to Hasha Masha and was silent. Her eyes were fixed on the album of the one who had been her lover.

My wife got up, went to the kitchen, and brought tea. She put on the water in the kitchen in silence, her hands holding the kerosene stove and not seared. My wife touched Noga's forehead with a finger, maybe measuring her son by the love of his youth, by my total incomprehension. Noga sat, more beautiful than ever even though she looked scared that day. Uneasy, she put on her shawl and took it off again with hands that were almost shaking. Every now and then she looked in the mirror and sat next to my wife and then Hasha Masha gave her a black comb and Noga combed her hair and then she gave Hasha Masha some small tweezers she pulled out of her purse. The tweezers were silver plated and capered for a moment in the room whose light came between the slats of the slightly open shutters, and Hasha Masha plucked out two or three hairs from her left eyebrow and then returned the tweezers to Noga and went to the kitchen and put on another kettle of water and came back and let the water steam and when the kettle (I didn't dare do a thing) was empty and about to turn to carbon, Noga got up slowly, almost deliberately, put the hairs carefully into the ashtray, and the hairs that Hasha Masha had plucked were mixed in the water from the vase that was poured into the ashtray and Noga put down the ashtray, touched my wife's head lightly, walked to the kitchen, filled the kettle with water, and the kettle fizzed and groaned, and Hasha Masha, with a certain arrogance, took out her new reading glasses and sat frozen with the reading glasses on her face and then Noga held out a sheet of paper and said: That's what I wrote to the judge about Boaz, and I wondered how Hasha Masha knew that Noga intended to show her a letter she had written to the judge about Boaz, and my wife read the letter and nodded her head and glanced mutely at Noga and Noga didn't lower her eyes but smiled and Hasha Masha said: You know how to condemn scoundrels, Noga, and you also know how to sleep in their beds, and Noga didn't say a thing but took the letter from Hasha Masha and folded it up carefully and put it back in the purse and then with the delicate movement of a tame eagle, she took the glasses off Hasha Masha's eyes folded them up and put them into the case waiting for them on the table and Noga measured the room again as she used to do on hundreds of evenings when I sat with her here when she still lived with us, looked through me and saw a wall and on it, as always, still hung the yellow landscape by the painter Shor, a picture whose frame had been shattered for years now, and after she drank the tea and Hasha Masha put the glasses on Noga's eyes and measured her with a look and took off the glasses and Noga blinked like somebody who isn't used to reading glasses, Noga took out some chewing gum, folded the paper, delicately put the gum into her mouth, chewed it with her mouth closed for a minute or two, went into the bathroom, threw it in the toilet, flushed it, and returned to the table and sat down. Her hand reached forward and in it was the strip of paper that wrapped the chewing gum. Hasha Masha carefully folded the strip of rustling paper and put it in the ashtray, waited until Noga gave her a box of matches and lit a match, burned the paper along with the handful of hairs and then Noga got up, kissed me on my forehead and said, I love you, old

Henkin, caressed Hasha Masha, who shut her eyes, giving her face an expression of pleasure and regret, and left the house.

I went outside, I looked at the brilliant sea, I found an old teacher looking at a wall he had painted with his own hands and he was ludicrous in his own eyes, superfluous vis-à-vis the silence of Noga and Hasha Masha, I said to myself, utter a song! Hasha Masha lived the moment and every moment was final, a tumult that begins and ends. Menahem is a foundation, not a display window . . .

My neighbor is smiling now, maybe he's also reading my mind, this moment is his! The water flows in the hose and I watch the stream of water, blended in it, flowing with it and then I'm finished on my neighbor's contours of pain and my pain is suddenly opaque, as if a miracle happened to it. But it doesn't let me flee from myself.

Go, he said, go, Mr. Henkin, it's important for all of us.

Who's all of us? I asked.

He didn't answer. His stream was sharper than mine. His water was more concentrated, and he enjoyed the sight of the water flowing from him, absorbed in the hollows, mixing with the organic mulch, annihilating the desolation the Giladis had left behind. There was an arrogant and malicious meekness in him, I thought, as if he were protecting himself, even from me, as if he were connected to the deed he was doing and to a possible escape from himself, he was routed and protesting at the same time.

All of us is a lot of people, he said, all of us is me, it's the woman who lives with and is married to me . . . here in the north, he said, the wind is humid, rusts, in the south the air is dry and purer.

In the south?

He didn't hear my question. He said: I'm not used to the north, the air makes me sick. . . . I was amazed at the use of the word "north" applied to Tel Aviv. I didn't understand what south he meant, and then, to add perplexity to my perplexity, he said: Near Marar the smells of orange blossoms were preserved in the clear thin air for a month after they finished blooming.

Since I didn't know what to ask, I said, You were in the south? From my words you could have thought I was talking about Sudan or Ethiopia. I thought about Marar, it was an Arab village I used to pass by years ago on my way south. The village was destroyed in the war my son fell in. I hadn't heard the name of the village since 'forty-eight. Boaz surely passed by Marar on his way to the settlement where he was born and where he returned to see his grandmother. The village was destroyed and not a trace remains of it except for a paratrooper memorial erected at the foot of it years later. I didn't have time to think when he said: Yes, the sand sticks to everything, the wind isn't harmonic, sometimes it is, sometimes it isn't, degree of dryness against degree of humidity, here is not the south, Mr. Henkin, and Boaz should have known that and protested, my neighbor's stream of water was now sparkling in the bright light of approaching dusk, and in the extracted sword blade flashed a bold rainbow full of colorful impulsiveness. Who are you meeting tonight, Mr. Henkin, he said more than asked.

A writer, I said and added with a thoroughly inappropriate apology: I was invited to a reception and haven't yet decided.

An Israeli?

No, I said, anger rising in me now: a Hebrew writer doesn't hold receptions. Too bad, said my neighbor with genuine grief that filled me with wrath because naïveté, ignorance, and stupidity sometimes infuriate me more than simple belligerence. I don't know a lot, Mr. Henkin, said my neighbor, do you know what it means to be a person who has no life history? A man without a history? Not knowing anything but what you don't have to know. I ask, I don't mean to irritate. Now I really did pity him without knowing exactly why, I said, The problem is that I was invited to a meeting I don't want to go to. A meeting with a foreign writer, I added . . .

Foreign and hostile? he asked.

I laughed, a stream of water gleamed. He looked at me, even tried unsuccessfully to smile.

I said foreign, not hostile I hope, what does it mean that you have no life history?

I don't know, that's what they tell me, an important writer?

Yes, an important writer, I said.

I thought about the order of his words, the order of the questions, he was silent a moment, tried to read my mind and of course that incensed me, I shifted the hose to the bed of onions while he raised his eyes to the horizon now covered with reddish purple clouds and he asked, And where is that good and foreign writer from?

Germany, I said, swallowing the word, his roses stood erect after drinking
so much and now looked terrifying in their pleasant and venomous beauty.

And he's a good man? he asked.

He took off his hat. He had gray hair, pulled back with sweat. Drops of
water coursed on his cheeks.

I think so, I said, I read his books, in Hebrew translation, of course, he's
decent, no doubt about that, I felt funny apologizing to him, stripping
naked in front of him, while as for him I don't know a thing about him, but
I went on, what does it mean, decent? He takes dogs across the street? Old
women? I assume he's decent, that the self behind the words is decent and
honest. I think, I said, that he succeeds in doing what great literature
should do, which is to give birth to things that haven't yet been born, reveal what was invisible, give legitimacy to the absurd and surely our lives
are nothing if not completely absurd. His face was closed, he was listening
or not, I don't know. The roar of the water in the hoses was louder. The
silence of the approaching evening enveloped us. I tried to understand
what a man with no life history thinks, a man from whom nobody expects
anything. I thought about the Shimonis' apartment, where the Committee
of Bereaved Parents meets every single week. The thundering laughter
internalized somehow whenever Jordana from the Ministry of Defense
started chewing one of the plastic vegetables in a bowl there, as if by
mistake. She's a Yemenite, Jordana, her teeth are white, once when she
chewed the plastic vegetable she said to me: Too bad they put life into the
china statue I was meant to be. When was the last time I saw a china doll
in the form of a Yemenite woman? And I didn't laugh, and those sad parents laughed as if they'd fall out of their clothes and only Jordana and I
didn't laugh. They needed to laugh together, loathe together, live together, and those plastic vegetables they don't remove from the table of
the Shimonis whose son fell in the battle for the fortress of Navi Yehoshua
in the Galilee, which turned their house into a club, never did you feel that
you were disturbing there, that you were intruding on their privacy, and at
their house the meeting would be held this evening . . .

Mr. Henkin, maybe you can do me a favor, said my neighbor, his eyes
fixed on the sunset that now ran riot as usual, full of cheap splendor and
glory, purple clouds slowly joining together in the sky, turning gray and a
light kindled in them, like a last attempt at life, a small plane flew low,

intending to land in the small airport beyond Reading, its lights going off and coming on and it made a big circle in the sky where a flock of birds sailed in a hypnotic, geometric silence.

Maybe you'd do me a favor, he said.

Of course, I said. Not a muscle moved in him now. Sculpted against the horizon. A flow of blood toward the thorny rosebushes, a sunset full of arrogance.

Tell the important and decent German writer that the scion of Secret Charity wants . . .

Who? I asked.

Tell him the scion of Secret Charity wants.

I laughed, since I'm expert at doing the wrong things at the wrong time. My neighbor didn't move and I thought he didn't sense my laughter, maybe he didn't hear it. And then he said, the muscles of your mouth, Mr. Henkin, don't know how to laugh. That has to be learned too. I tried to protest because his words were sharp, too sudden, but he waved his hand as if driving off some pest, another plane circled now and started landing, the water in my hose dwindled a moment, as if in spite, maybe Hasha Masha was taking a shower, maybe she flushed the toilet, and then from the silence and my stream of water that had almost stopped, he said: Tell him I want him to give me back my daughters.

All my life I was a rational man. A realist-Zionist, as Demuasz used to put it enthusiastically, the infidel shall live by his faith. Pascal's statement that the heart has reasons that reason does not know was just as alien to me as Kafka's stories. But ever since the disaster, I have clung more and more to nonrational contexts. An amazing idea rose in my mind: the German will surely explain to me what my neighbor said and that thought infuriated me very much and also excited me. Everything was so unexpected for Henkin, who had done the same things all his life, loved one woman, one son, one house, one land, one language, one dream, taken the same route every single morning, hundreds of times, read one chapter of the Bible and one legend from the book of legends of Bialik and Ravnitsky and suddenly the reason that reason doesn't know . . . So I tried to put into my stance a pride he had robbed from me. A right I had toiled to cultivate, as my wife says, my right to suffer. The water returned to the hose, I thought about his semicolon, the semicolon between the last words, and because of that a

current of electricity passed through my spine, a semicolon I once tried to
teach my students and I became absurd to them. I thought about my wife
who despises me now when she maybe gets up from the toilet we put in
years ago and isn't white anymore, yellow and bluish snakes creep on its
sides, I thought of Menahem who would sit on the toilet or as Amihud
Giladi said when he used to come visit me: The toilet Menahem learned
to masturbate on and I then pretended not to understand, and Amihud
said: He taught me to masturbate, and I tried to imagine my son masturbating in the toilet, I, who dreaded the very thought of it. I thought of
Menahem, pushing a wheelbarrow, saying, Here's the train with a cold
bringing red loam, and then masturbating with Amihud, maybe that's the
answer to the daughters of that neighbor who suddenly have a garden of
their own?! My thoughts, like my torments, are overcultivated. And suddenly some response to my neighbor standing there waiting for his daughters bursts in me and illuminates my pain in a wretched light, so righteous
is he there facing me, facing me in the righteousness of his no-daughters and
I think about the one who from now on I'll secretly call Germanwriter, what
I'll say to him, how I'll talk with him, the bereaved father once again brought
me very low, that homonym, member of the Committee of Bereaved Parents, who doesn't laugh when Jordana of the Ministry of Defense chews
plastic vegetables mistakenly or not. I always measure dimensions by non-
dimensions. In the newspaper I first pause at announcements, Yoram and
Hannah Tsipori are pleased to announce the birth of their daughter Liat, and
I loathe with unbridled loathing the grandchildren born to children who
were even younger than Menahem and I see my neighbor, yearning for his
daughters, he didn't mention a number, but more than one, with that hose
of his in the light of sunset that already falls more than descends, what is
it to lose daughters, two, three daughters? A picture rises in my mind, I
teach Hebrew grammar, Teacher Sarakh knocks on the door, the picture
of King George behind my back, covered with fly droppings, the war of
Teacher Henkin against the British Empire and in our school, we also sang
Hatikvah as if it was a ritual of taking an oath to the Bar Kokhba Uprising,
we even had a socialist tendency some nationalist touch, the hands in the
classroom go up to answer a question and Teacher Sarakh knocks and I
open the door and see a hand holding an ear and the ear is stuck to a body
and the body is the body of Menahem, and it's burning with awful anger,

he broke hangers, your son! And I have to lock the door immediately so the students won't see, ostensibly quiet and restrained, inside me hums the strict father I have to play, as always, bereaved father, nationalist father, resurrecter of gardens, and my son stands there, his ear in the hand of Teacher Sarakh, a smile on his face and she's shaking, You're merciful with him, she says, I remember the word merciful, like a gracious lord, and that hatred of hers, for me, for Menahem who broke her hangers, he broke more of mine but I'm still silent, her anger from the days when we all met on the Tiberias–Tsemakh road and she and Hasha Masha quarried stones and I came to work and at night I lectured on Hebrew poetry and I taught Hebrew to those pioneer men and women, and she wanted Menahem to be hers and I wanted Hasha Masha for a wife, and not her, even though she was so educated and knew Rosa Luxembourg and they said that Trotsky had embraced her for three nights in a row and then was captured, and she walked on foot from Russia to Turkey and from there sailed in a ship to the Land of Israel and here I come, teaching, talking, hewing words in the glowing air of the Galilean nights, and I don't have a Menahem for her, I knew only one woman, and her eyes were full of doves that flew off and didn't return. And I told her: Not hangers, coat hangers, and she wanted to be choked or to choke because for such sad and loyal barbarian women it's all the same, hangers, coat hangers, what difference does it make, but back then precision was important to me, my neighbor is wait-ing, why is he waiting, I don't have any daughters for him. I then took my son to Demuasz and said Demuasz, here's Menahem, who broke coat hang-ers in the hall. And he repressed a smile and asked why did you break hangers, Menahem, and Menahem said that they were there and blocked his view of the wall. And I, I corrected him there, I said, the coat hangers blocked you, and Teacher Sarakh looked at me both excited and frighten-ing, and I think of the grammar as her weary face of the shout, how it shouts or weeps in correct grammar. Today I know that what is written has to be written despite grammar and not because of it, Menahem died with all the tables of tenses and verbs, pain isn't measured in commas, but my neighbor's semicolon was so precise, only a tongue can be precise like that, can describe something that's both awful and precise and so even scarier than the thing itself . . . And she waits there, Sarakh, for me to punish him, she wants to see the whipping, the gallows, only when she sees the blood of one who could have been her son will she calm down, understand the precise meaning of the flydroppings on the face of King George. And then they demoted Menahem to a lower class for a week, and he sat next to a little girl and pinched her, maybe he was looking for her breasts and pinched her behind. A shriek rose and they called us, and Menahem's mother said: You go, you're the pedagogue, not me, and I went and the parents of the little girl, I even remember her name, Hedda Topolovsky, her father it seems to me rolled cigars and her mother, her mother I don't remember, maybe she worked for him as a model, I'm starting to be ironic in old age. And that Mrs. Hedda Topolovsky, what's she doing today, the little girl my son pinched, maybe she runs the branch of the Merry Wives of Windsor in Haifa, or maybe she teaches in the school for the blind or maybe she's a high-priced whore, she's surely alive, the poor girl he pinched and maybe she hasn't recovered since then and searches for Menahem in dark corners, in luxury cars she rides in with her splendid pink behind, and surely all those little girls that I to my distress was the first to discover their breasts even before the boys hit their backs as evidence of the new bras they wore, every one of them had a pink behind in their youth and later they grew and the pinkness disappeared, and they don't have Menahem in the streets where their behinds rustle in pink panties instead of the behinds that turn white and yellow with the years and they say: Hello, Teacher Henkin, and I know them but their names I don't know and what difference does it make now, their names they sold for some name of a husband that Menahem could have been or not, hangers, coat hangers . . . Maybe they get into them all their lives with coat hangers, without coat hangers, all the officers, all the criminals that filled our land, and Teacher Sarakh, with legs that swelled up on the way from Siberia to the Land of Israel, hit the soldiers entering into the pink behinds to defend her from Menahem who could have been her dead stepson and not the son of Hasha Masha and then I scolded my son, stubborn and rebellious son I said, but deep inside me I tried to defend him, I knew I was a sinner . . . Why, Hasha Masha, why didn't you see how I tried to defend your son even then, when I was busy educating many generations for the state in the making?

And then my neighbor bent over and I heard a click, as if something that had been glued was freed.

We shut off the faucets. Darkness fell. You could have not died, I said in my heart to Menahem. Soon I'll go to Singer's store, as if years hadn't passed, as if my new neighbor didn't exist, I'll buy margarine, white bread, eggs, herring, and Mr. Giladi will be there with the smile full of a national secret on his face. And Singer will say to me: How are you today, Mr. Henkin, and I'll tell him everything's fine, Mr. Singer, oh these long summers . . .

My neighbor who remained mute and indifferent looked at me, I averted my face and went in my house, there wasn't even any point parting properly. My wife was standing in the kitchen washing dishes, she said, You stroked your little garden, Henkin? I told her, Don't start with me, Hasha, and she said, Masha, and I said to her, Hasha Masha. When we met on the road from Tiberias to Tsemakh her name was Masha, later on her friend Sarakh changed her name to Hasha. Now when I call her Hasha she says Masha, and when I call her Masha she says Hasha, so I call her Hasha Masha. You've got to know when to get into the grave and shut your eyes, she said, you're hurt, Henkin, what happened to you?

The neighbor asked about Boaz, and I told her what had happened.

She looked at me and smiled. I saw her appraising through me the lost character of Boaz Schneerson. I showered, put on my clothes, and stood there holding a cup of tea. I looked at the miracle of nature (as Noga put it) that was Hasha Masha, torments created some absolute unchanging in her. And once again a corrupt lust for her rose in me, a lust that at my age I was supposed to be weaned from, the teachers' organization had recently sent me for a routine examination and the doctor who was surely much younger than Menahem could have been gave me a thorough examination, put me on a stationary bike, measured blood pressure, blood, urine, heart, what-all, and then he said to me: You're in good shape, Henkin (as if he were talking about a used car), your arteries are the arteries of a forty-year-old, and I never heard about arterial stirrings but Hasha Masha evoked stirrings in me, arterial or not, I want her and every night she groans in the next bed, and I can't touch, and what should I do? Go look for some widow who'll have to get used to me and I to her? I could love only once in my life, give birth to one son, changing wasn't possible anymore.

I called the Shimonis and said I was sick and couldn't come this evening. My voice shook when I lied. My wife was putting up water and making more tea, the Shimonis said: No, out of the question. They spoke from both of their telephone extensions, from two rooms, as they usually did, they said: You've got to come, Henkin, he asked, and today he called again and asked to meet you. I told them I didn't understand why, I didn't know him, but they swore to me that he asked especially that I come and it was important and I mustn't dare not come, they said partly as a joke, partly as a hidden threat I had to discern. Hasha Masha is listening, smiling; I get dressed, a mildewed chill and a stifling of words on her lips she sits.

I came to the Committee of Bereaved Parents by chance, like all the things that had happened since my son fell. It was years ago. The garden was already destroyed, the house was wrapped in grief, the bonds between us and old friends were cut, I'd walk on Ben-Yehuda Street every morning, seeking, I'd teach, my heart wasn't in it. I'd be invited to circumcisions and weddings and I didn't go, I began wandering around aimlessly, and in an indifferent and alien human sea, I came on people whose eyes were perplexed and caught in my eyes, I sensed them, they sensed me, eyes staring, seeking something that wasn't there, vague, protected yet defeated looks, a gloomy pride of the vanquished, I smelled them and they smelled me, pain touched and engendered partnership, some necessary hold, I don't remember anymore exactly how it happened, maybe at the zoo where each of us separately used to take our dead sons to see the sights of their childhood. People feeding pigeons and pigeons flying calmly, feeling one another, and here's closeness, I had a son, we had, somebody comes to me in the street, carrying a briefcase, in it newspaper clippings his son had cut out for three years, surely there was some purpose in that cutting out, some goal, and what do you do with that, and the two notebooks he left behind and will the newspaper clippings explain my son to me, are they evidence he'll show to strangers, and who are the strangers, us, and so we started gathering not out of excessive love, not because of a common past, what remained between us was the heavy hatred of solitude, there was a need, maybe stupid but sunk inside us to introduce our sons to one another, each of us was amazed at the edge of his companion's pain, on buses, in parks, on streets, in cafés, stone butterflies trying to hunt their own shadow on the edge of the sidewalk, boasting of wings that became our dead sons, maybe that was an organized revolt against the life that gushed up around us, the new state, the national excitement, we wanted to be protected, together we could find the code words of our yearnings.

Hasha Masha didn't need any proof, she always had our son, not for one minute was he not with her, or more precisely, in her, she could long for him and not for somebody like herself. For her he wouldn't exist in conversations about him or in a reconstruction of the battles he took part in or measuring the road he took to the seashore in the morning, he was buried in her kitchen exactly as he was buried in the cemetery at Kiryat Anavim, he once lived so he's always alive, he once died, so he's always dead, she didn't need to translate him into something else as I did. If she wanted to, she could have known exactly how far he didn't grow. She didn't wait for his death to grant her life.

She seldom came to our Committee and later she no longer came even to important meetings. After years of chance encounters and tours to battlefields, the Committee turned into a fact, and I put my heart and soul into the activity of the Committee. The Shimonis made their house a regular meeting place that was quite convenient for all of us.

The meeting with Germanwriter wasn't something I longed for. The chairmanship of our Committee was ostensibly a technical matter, but I was the only one who always came by himself, and maybe the people sensed I was lonely not only for my son and aside from that I was an experienced teacher and even a school principal for a while, I knew quite a bit about printing and formulation, and anybody who wanted to publish a booklet in memory of his son could come to me and I knew what to advise him, close work relations were created between me and Jordana of the Commemoration Department, a harmonic system woven between us that considerably influenced the parents who joined us after Sinai and the Six-Day War and those who fell between the wars who were mostly attacked in some national corner that can't be pinned down precisely, and now I had to come because Germanwriter asked explicitly for me and the Shimonis explained to me that the German was a member of some committee of noble-minded Germans, who cooperated with our committees all over Israel and there was already a thread of a Committee of International Friends, and the group of fifty from England, survivors of Buchenwald, through the German group subsidized a splendid booklet marking twenty years of the liberation of the camp and the slaughter of those survivors in the Land of Israel. An American group got a grant from them to plant a forest in the mountains of the Galilee not far from where the Shimonis' son fell and echoes of our sons found a response in various lands, international meetings were even held in Switzerland, England, Denmark, the United States, but I don't go to them since, on the day I ascended to the Land, in the month of Nisan nineteen twenty-one, I swore I would never leave this land and I intend never to break my vow, but the meetings take place and I prepare the material, write, correspond, attach photos, edit, and the German committee of which Germanwriter is a distinguished member financed quite a few commemoration activities and therefore I'm obliged to meet that noble-minded man and I can't, something mocks me, my neighbor with his requests, my conscience. My poor dear, says my wife contemptuously, it's really hard for Henkin to meet the international glory of his son, the representatives of the Foreign Ministry of the power of death, why don't you go, Obadiah?

Hasha Masha drinks her tea. In the glass, her teeth look quite white and big. Gray hair falls on her taut forehead, caught in the light of the sixty-watt bulb, she says from her glass, maybe hisses: Clowns of bereavement, Henkin. Members of an operetta deceiving your pain, your children will never be any more than what they were in their lives, Henkin, and I tell her with repressed rage, Ours, ours, Hasha Masha, ours! She says I had one son, Henkin, and he won't be anybody else, not because of the Committee, not because of Boaz Schneerson. My death is preserved in dark rooms, Henkin. And then I recall the episode of Boaz Schneerson and am silent because what will I say? But the German issue had another touch. The writer was very famous, they were waiting for him here, and maybe it really is so important for us to know what those who were our executioners are thinking? Maybe we like to be photographed on the rope? Pictures of hell on the walls of Paradise . . . And Hasha Masha gets up and makes herself some vegetable soup on that kind of kerosene stove that hasn't been used for some time, nothing had changed in her house, she has some definite nonobligation to the present, no faith in the future I said to her: In biblical Hebrew there is no present tense at all, and she said: Obadiah Henkin, life is not Hebrew grammar. Life is Hebrew death, and I said angrily: But others die, too, all over the world people die in wars that are lost and not lost, and "others" is already grammar, because there is "other" and there are "other males" and "other females" and there is "they" and there is "we" and there is "you," I thought about that writer, about his words and what will I say to him and I talk about him with Hasha Masha, who turns her back to me and cooks vegetable soup for herself that smells wonderful but I don't eat despite my hunger, there's surely a meal waiting for me at the Shimonis and they're offended when I don't eat and I say: Maybe I won't go after all, what would Menahem say, there's also a matter of conscience and pride, maybe that's blasphemy, blasphemy of him, not us. She turned her face aside and looked at me for a long moment and next to her I saw a spot of oil that I notice at times on the wall, ever since that day many years ago when I threw the bottle of oil in anger at something she said, and she bent down and straightened up and laughed a mute repressed laugh, like weeping, and didn't answer, didn't fight, accepted my rage as well as my love with bitter and chilly sympathetic anger . . . How do you know what Menahem would say, she asked, on what authority do you struggle in his name? If he were a grownup today, maybe he would have gone there, maybe he would have imported gas stoves from there? Or color TVs? I shouted at her: No! No! No! And she said: Samuel Yankelevitch, who was your best student, to whom you regally granted very good grades when Menahem would come home with satisfactories and you said that's what you deserve, Menahem, didn't that brilliant Samuel Yankelevitch go there to buy gas masks he brought to Israel during the war, how do you know, did Menahem leave you a will?

Don't ask Menahem with that black magic, ask yourself, Henkin.

Outside was the fresh smell of approaching autumn. It was early evening. A time when the sourness of the air is clearly felt near the sea. When I was young I attended a German gymnasium, but when I came to the Land of Israel, I swore to read and write only Hebrew; my knowledge of English was superficial and almost inarticulate, I remember in 'thirty-nine, the ship *Patria* came to the shore of Tel Aviv, not far from our house, got stuck on a sandbank, and all of us went out to the beach to mingle with the immigrants and carry them to the beach and confuse the English. I brought to our house a pale young man wearing a rotten belt, his teeth yellow in his mouth and dressed in capes and I remember sitting in the evening and the young man spoke German because he didn't know any other language, and he told things the mind refused to believe, I understood every word but something in me revolted, I couldn't talk with him, only mutter something, in those days I used to sit with the big map that

Becker, the geography teacher, drew for me, my son helping me with pins and colored flags and I marking the fronts and the battles from the reports of the BBC and the Voice of Jerusalem. Menahem would laugh at his father even though he'd bring him the pins and flags and say: Henkin, beat the Germans on his map, the Jews are good for wars on maps. I was fascinated then by what the café experts called "the theater of war," and didn't pay heed to the contempt of one who would later be a real Jewish soldier, at least the double Menahem, the one who was and the one invented for me by Boaz, and now I can't tell them apart anymore, and I conquered Benghazi and retreated again to shape the border or to make a tactical retreat, years passed and I sat at the map, we conquered cities and we retreated, there were successful landings and less successful ones I accompanied the Red Army in its panicky retreat and then in its mighty victory procession. I was a strategic expert and at the Milo Club, where I'd stop to drink coffee with people who are mostly not among the living anymore, I was considered an expert in the information, but my heart was heavy, my family I had left there was destroyed, I went to the Jewish Agency with people and we knocked on windows, have to do more, we said, and they told us, we're doing, but that didn't satisfy us, and ever since then I've had a vague sense of disgust and offense that I wasn't there with them and this evening I have to represent a committee of dead youths to the hangman, no matter how many there are. I walk on Ben-Yehuda Street and turn toward Keren Kayemet Boulevard, lights sparkle, cars stop at traffic signals, cafés are buzzing as always, why, I wonder, did he ask to meet me of all people? As I was leaving the house, just a minute before I left the house, a window was opened in my neighbor's house, and I saw a woman's face looking toward our gate, maybe a painted face, as if her hair was blue and she was white, upright, glassy, and thus, pondering the sight of the woman who closed the window right after she saw my eyes staring at her, I came to the Shimonis' apartment and Jordana, our Yemenite, opened the door to me and looked wonderfully sweet and beautiful in the white dress she wore, maybe too sheer, but not offensive. Her dark, almost purple face stood out clearly on the white background of the dress and her hair was wrapped in two thin plaits that softly clasped her smooth head, her smile was open, her teeth were white, behind me the light suddenly went out and I was steeped in dark, and in front of me in the abundant light from the corridor stands the girl of our sons' dreams, gleaming in the flash of light, and I'm facing her, Henkin at the usual time, in person, my wife at home, alone, eating vegetable soup, the lost energy woven like a lordly and modest halo around the splendid hair of Jordana from the Ministry of Defense, a halo of the disaster we were all in, the enemy who comes to review the honor guard of dead youths.

In the doorway of the apartment of the Committee of the Dead stands Obadiah Henkin. A charred smell of his son rises in me. A German saving matches tosses my son straight into the fire, how much is two-fifths of an American cent in Israeli money? Sturmbahnführer of literature counts matches and I come to meet him, how do the bereaved parents of Jewish children look in his eyes? My neighbor sends regards with a poem. Marar, from Marar, he sends regards, south, there Arabs were expelled sir, surely you weep for their fate, I can imagine that, and justly, and unjustly, a Yemenite woman beams at me in the doorway of the sanctuary of the Shimonis who have never lacked money, filing pains, come in, shaking hands, smiling, everything's professional, organized, very formal, one of the veteran Hebrew teachers, and I thought about Jordana's devotion to us, about her beauty wasted on us. Of all the sons, she told me, I love Menahem the best. At first I was amazed at the phrase, then I got used to it, as if it were obvious that of all the sons she'd choose Menahem, I would almost have married them off to one another, in moments of nightmare, at night, maybe against Noga, between one dozing and another. And when she came to our house and Hasha Masha looked at her suspiciously but also graciously, with a certain compassion, but without contempt, she didn't give in, wanted to see the photos again, to hear the poem Menahem wrote, spoke angrily of Noga who was unfaithful to Menahem and went to live with Boaz, back then she surely didn't know Boaz. I wanted to say to her: Look, Menahem died many years ago, you were then four, five, six years old, but she'd fix me with a wild look, ardent and virginal at the same time, what's the difference? As if love or life really could be divided into periods, everything is one piece, and if I've got our Menahem, why shouldn't she? Maybe Jordana was his great love? And she smiles a professional, almost cold smile at me, surely I know her dark side, when she sits in my house and loves my son with a desperate love. Here in the Shimonis' house, she's on duty, frozen, modest, smiling, embracing her dear parents, who knows how many of them were previously her lovers, and she dropped them for Menahem, her great love, what do I know? I know that there were two men in her life, something happened to both of them, they said of her that she kills men. They're afraid of her. She brings bad luck, they said, and ever since then enclosed in the department of commemoration, letters, poems, memorial books, statues, always willing to help, to run to the printers, to study, to find material, to find contributions or grants, and surely Menahem her great love was a fake Menahem, not the one that was but the one I made up out of Boaz's lies. But she loves him and I won't rob her of him, what do I understand about love? When my only love is Hasha Masha sitting now and loathing me in her heart and yet loving me in her own way, as if her malice is a dim yearning of flesh . . .

Everybody eats, standing or sitting, talking, Germanwriter sits in a corner, in the green armchair, surrounded by human beings and he notices me and something strange, mysterious lights up in his eyes for a moment and goes out, I think of Jordana, look at her, I think of the German, of his look, is that regret? Is that vengeance? Is that an impossible measuring to see the condemned after what happened, to measure them for the death that is destined and withheld from them?

Here they are, all of them, the Davids, the Cohens, the Sackses, the Ilans, all the parents Jordana and I assemble, connecting their nights of terror to days of tours to the Golan, Sinai, Jerusalem, air force bases, to places where the great battles took place, I tasted the delicacies Mrs. Shimoni served me, naturally I was careful not to munch the plastic vegetables, not to open by mistake the pack of cigarettes from which a rubber doll jumps out with a sharp screech, the Shimonis' sense of humor was never to my taste, but I envied their ability to laugh even next to the picture of their son, to buy nonsensical objects together in all kinds of places in the world, to return to an imaginary and impossible childhood, and Jordana, as always, knows how to appease, to rout the pain, to organize a group dance of graves. They eat they laugh they drink, and I always inspire here the same respect everybody needs at special moments when a correct quotation of a biblical chapter or of Alterman or Bialik grants metaphysical meaning to a moment, to say solemnly: Maybe once in a thousand years our death has meaning, and to see how they become serious at Alterman's words, aware that they have lost beloved sons, to see a sublime vision beyond the yellowing bindings of the books they've issued in their memory and are now forgotten in dusty

cases . . . Mrs. Shimoni asked me if I liked the food, I said I never ate a
better mushroom pie and she smiled at me, tapped my back and so at
long last I could sit. Jordana finished a round of handshaking and hugs in
the enormous room, and I could see her stand alone a moment, belonging and not belonging, trying to be drawn out of herself, not to be seen,
with her eyes shut she stood, as if muttering a prayer that was foreign to
us, everybody was buzzing around her, and then she stepped toward me,
her back bent, sat down next to me, pressed her foot and thigh and carefully put her hand on mine, like a secret bride, gently crushed my hand as
if her hands were also muttering incantations, and then she opened her
eyes that had been shut when she sat down, or perhaps landed on the sofa,
and very slowly the flush returned to her face and the smile was stuck in
its place and once again she was charming and necessary to everybody and
lost to herself. For some reason, I recalled the first time we met, when I
came to her on behalf of the Committee of Parents, which was then in its
infancy, to help me finance a book about the son of the writer Aviram who
wrote heartrending texts about his son and we sat then for long nights and
pasted the photos and the writer Aviram compiled lines from various poems
and then, at the front of the book, he quoted Alterman: Don't say I came
from dust, you came from the stranger who fell in your stead! Jordana now
asked me how was Hasha Masha and I knew that in fact she wanted to ask
me how was Menahem, but she didn't ask, I said that Hasha Masha was
eating vegetable soup and loathing, and she understood, and then when
she started comparing my clothes to the clothes of her uncle who was
always dressed with splendid restraint and never as an actor in a play like
most Israelis, I felt for the first time, after many years, a physical attraction
to a strange woman, her body clinging to my body, her thigh to my thigh,
her foot to my foot, I can imagine what was going on through the dress,
where the legs led, as Menahem once told me when I asked him why he
peeped on the stairs toward the second floor of my uncle Nevzal's house
where a young woman went up with her dress flying. The secret of our
youth, Jordana, on both sides of life, is alien to Menahem, negates him and
something rose in me, something that for the first time in years opposed
Menahem himself, maybe envied him, not against myself, and the death
that led him away from me. Germanwriter still sat opposite, I could see
him through the bodies moving in the room. Corruption fills me beside

Jordana, she sees me as the father of her lover and I'm surely betraying both of them.

And then I heard her say in English: Yes, this is Mr. Henkin, and I raised my face, and a big man (now that he stood up I saw how big he was) stood over me, his eyes like two clear lakes, caught in a kind of thin veil as sometimes on the eyes of an aging dog, his face smiled a smile that was forced but also innocent and perfect, a wise smile intellectuals sometimes have, I tried to stand up but my legs became stiff and he said: Sit, sit, and Jordana stood up carefully so as not to cut herself off from my foot too forcefully and she chuckled, a chuckle that was a mixture of sympathetic complaint, See you, Henkin, she said in her official voice, and from now on, the picture of Menahem facing him is a group picture with a Yemenite girl, and the man stood over me, still smiling, a pensive second passed, Jordana was now smiling her saccharine smile at the drinks table, unsheathing fingernails of dry and charming purity (and I surely know her wild lust, her eyes staring at photos of Menahem, staring at his dead flesh) and she disappears now, mingles in the crowd, at the window the crests of the trees of the boulevard can be seen, a moon is shining on them a silvery light and a pleasant chill blows from the window. I didn't know what to do, my hand seemed to reach out by itself, I said: Yes, nice to meet you, my body still bound to the storm taking place in me before my son's fiancée vis-à-vis the bearishness of the German's full body, and then he sat, introduced himself, as if hangmen also have to be polite.

With his king-size body he completely filled the empty space left by the thin Jordana. His long legs rose a little, stuck to one another, even his head was higher than mine, although when he leaned his head on the back of the sofa and the soft fabric touched his hair, we were almost the same height and now I could peep at his profile. Before his face looked like a hybrid of a giant dog and ancient trees, something soft, kind, but his profile was different, harsh and sharp, his nose that looked a little squashed from the front looked aggressive from the side, arrogant, in his cheeks more existential suffering than real suffering was obvious, something serious, devoid of softness. His profile had some blend of innocent nobility but also soft earthiness, for a moment he even shriveled and became tinier than he really was and instead of Jordana's delightful behind there was now the giant ass of a German, solid, heavy, a man who looked sated but full of remorse, and suffering was stamped on his face, a suffering whose nature I didn't know, my mind was empty.

I didn't know what to say, I didn't know what not to say, maybe because of the picture of Amnon, the Shimonis' son, hanging across from me, thoughts were contradictory, so maybe I told him: When I was a child we had a sexton who would wait in the corner until the women got up from the bench and would sit down on the bench quickly so his body would absorb the warmth of their bodies, and I tried to laugh, even though he didn't succeed either, the two of us thought about Jordana who had been sitting here before, he tapped me carefully on the shoulder, his hand was manicured, delicate though very big, I spoke broken English and he looked forward toward the backs that were now wildly hugging the girl of our sons' dreams. Mrs. Shimoni walked around with a tray from one person to another, her cleaning woman served drinks, Mr. Shimoni in an amusing Tyrolean hat was standing at the bar and pouring drinks as if the whole thing were a big joke. The sons are laughing at them, I thought, and the German pulled a cigarette out of a handsome silver case, a pleasant smell of good tobacco wafted from it, he offered me a cigarette, I refused politely, he lit it with a gold lighter that seemed to be swallowed up in his gigantic hand, I was afraid he'd be burned but then he put the lighter back in his pocket, inhaled smoke and I could see how nice his suit was, the vest, once I was an expert in such things, an English suit, not stylish, solid, and yet, maybe because of the beautiful scarlet tie, maybe because of the sky-blue shirt, he didn't look like a prosperous merchant but like an artist who doesn't really want to look like an artist, a man of change but he also had the tranquility of clarity, which unites everything into a pleasant unity. And surely that's what we all aspire to, it suddenly angered me that he was such a good writer, as a gift to my son I wanted him to be a bad writer, but some sympathy was ignited in me, a closeness to the man, the expression of his eyes, when he heard my stupid story about the sexton he was gracious and not evasive, looked straight into my eyes, inhaled smoke, and was with me despite the great tumult around us. A picture of a Lag b'Omer bonfire rose in my mind, a gigantic effigy of Hitler was burned, Menahem and his friends sang, Hitler's dead your mother's sick a German submarine, and a woman who declares on the radio: To punish Hitler he shouldn't be killed, he should be brought to the Land of Israel and shown a kibbutz, and how children plant trees. I wanted to laugh but the innocence in his look was greater than the innocence I was thinking about, and that annoyed me, the smoke curled, we were still feeling each other out, a thigh touched my thigh, I thought about the bomb shelter on Halperin Street where my son used to smoke the first cigarettes he'd hide in the first-aid box back then when we sat in the shelters. I thought: I'm drawn to vengeance, maybe because of Jordana, a vengeance that doesn't suit me. The force that came from him, obstinate and cultivated, his hands clasped his knees and the cigarette burning in his hand next to his left knee, he looked at my hand, silence prevailed, and then he said: Maybe you're perplexed, is it because I'm a German? I tried to say something but the words stammered in my mouth, and he went on almost in a whisper, if so I can understand. I'm perplexed, I affirmed, but that's not the issue . . .

If you want me to go, I'll go, he said, over there, and he pointed to a group of people that included a tall handsome woman, there's my wife, you know, he added, and I gauged the resonance of his wife's whispers, "the Jews and the Germans, unlike the Latins, didn't seek or find the perfect form, but always some original amazement prevailed, if an abyss gaped at their feet they looked into it and found emptiness and filled it with hewn, new, cruel substance, some new reading of chaos in which is hidden something that wants to be discovered, some imperfection, a divine imperfectness," said the German and the emphasis of the connection restored me, it was precisely the somewhat awkward Gothic style that drew my heart to his fiction, I loved the practicality he wove from the devils that gushed in him, to which pain do I ascribe you, Germanwriter? Which side do you belong to? You're surrounded here with people, some of them came from your area, they listen to you, maybe you express them better than we do even though they've lived here for years, you express them better than we do, that's a certain failure of culture, of education, of vision . . .

They're incomprehensible, he said, his eye close to my face became watery, melted in the warmth now coming from him, obstinate, but disguised as pallor, I listen to the German of my readers at the Goethe Institute, they speak the German of my grandfather, of the writers I tried to learn from . . . And, without noticing it, we slipped into speaking German and even though I hadn't spoken German for about fifty years, my German wasn't broken, it flowed with a naturalness that was so fluent at first I didn't notice it, and neither did he. The florid language of my father, my educated teachers in Galicia, my uncles, strict teachers, everything came back to me, sat on my tongue, I thought, Culture! Language! He, German-writer, is surely the Bialik and the Alterman of thousands of human beings who live here, he's their real geography from which their longings, their loves, and their nightmares are woven, and they're said to be people who live in the past that never had a future and here is their future, somebody who can someday describe them, he lights another cigarette with the gold lighter, maybe Zyklon B, I tell him that sentence about our Germans, he smiles, Really? I don't think so . . . It passes . . .

And then I returned to the anger that had permeated me before. There was no closeness between the two nations, that was a one-sided love, the closeness of Jews and Germans, it's a lie, that's what they want to say today, the Jews lived in Cologne before there were Germans there. Ever since then they burned in desolation for fifteen hundred years. They stood on tiptoe and waited for kisses. That was a one-way struggle, sir, not closeness, the German your readers speak here is a language foreign to them, and they don't know, they're tolerated, no more, excuse me, but—

I know, he said, it's hard to understand . . . The Prussian state was founded by Teutonic peasants who came back from a Crusade and studied it here, in Palestine. From here they also brought the glass for the windows of their houses and the Bible and what I talked about before. But what was the switch? What was our eternal fortress? I'm seeking, searching, do you think there is really a chance?

He fell silent now. People's loud talking was heard, and more than talking, they were yelling at one another. Laughter was heard, somebody maybe munched on a plastic cucumber by mistake. On the walls, aside from the picture of Amnon Shimoni there was a picture of the Empress Theresa, pictures of snowy European landscapes, a photo of the River Zin in the Negev and an aerial photo of Jerusalem with the edge of the wings of the Mirage birds, a gift from the air force for bereaved families. All that was cut off from some possible answer to Marar, an answer to my neighbor whose request still presses on me, to wondering why he wanted to meet me, of all people, surely not to tell me how many readers he has here and how profound is the closeness between the murderers and the murdered,

I tried to calm down, I found myself speaking ardently, in a language I hadn't spoken for fifty years, I tried to find in front of me an empty strip of wall (something rare in the Shimoni house), between china plates, pictures, objects, the Binding of Isaac drawn on glass and a small portrait of Goethe next to a Bedouin ruin that may have belonged to Amnon Shimoni or maybe the Shimonis bought it themselves, I didn't know, an empty strip of wall suddenly glittered, split off from all the objects and grew bright, next to a reddish shade of chiaroscuro colors on the wall whose whiteness had long ago darkened to a kind of pleasant, old patina yellow, a splendid shade of rust, and there I could imagine my face, without a frame, in a light purple, striped tone, without a face, as if the fading graffiti on the wall blended into the wall and doesn't exist except in the vision I created on the wall, a gesture of the existent toward its image, there I was revised in that nauseating light that now started becoming hard inside me, not toward what was in me but for what I could have been if I weren't formulated by ideas instead of trying to formulate them, and there I found myself, my body clinging to the body of the German and I could understand that bear next to me, smoking the cigarette that turns leaves of elusive bright thin smoke violet and telling him: I've got something to tell you, that is, I was asked to tell you, and he then held the smoke in his mouth, exhaled it very slowly, pensively, ardent but restrained. In my body clinging to him I felt him shrivel, grow hard, a car passed in the street and illuminated the pillars of the boardwalk for a moment and the two of us could look at the bored back of the girl of our sons' dreams, so thin, swarthy, in the white dress, hear our laughter mixed up in the tumult, he stubbed out the cigarette in an ashtray and asked: What were you asked to tell me?

He didn't even know how to formulate the question. I liked that.

Staged regards, I said, embarrassed.

He said, Who? And now some tone of violence was heard in his voice, which Boaz would explain to me later, was in my voice when I told him to come to my house and bring Menahem's poem, a violence of those pressed to the wall who don't have any more words.

I told him: I've got a neighbor, he asked me, in fact he didn't ask but demanded, really, to deliver something to you and what he wanted to deliver to you is hard for me to deliver, courtesy obliges me to forget his request, while another obligation, a higher one, obliges me to tell you . . .

He smoked another cigarette and I knew I couldn't avoid it, I saw that in his eyes, the lighter was crushed in his gigantic hand, I thought of talking to him about lost wars, but I said: My neighbor said he's the scion of somebody named Secret Charity which means in German . . .

I understand the name, he said quickly, what did he say?

He said to tell you, that scion . . . He's the son of his great-grandson, he said in German, now he tried to smile, stubbed out another cigarette in the ashtray, and when he lifted his finger, I saw that it was stained with ash, he looked at me for a split second, took the lighter out of his hand, moved it to his other hand, lit it, I waited but he didn't take a cigarette out of the delicate case, and only raised his hand pensively and again tried to smile, like somebody caught red-handed he put down his hand put out the lighter and put it in his coat pocket. I said quickly: He asked me to ask you to give him back his daughters! I felt the blood drain out of my face. I was afraid to look at him. He gazed a bit, his eyes slowly shut, tense, a long time passed and maybe the time was short and I only imagined that it was long, and then he said in a voice that suddenly sounded as if it came from the other end of the room: Maybe that's why I came here, for somebody to ask me for his daughters.

For some reason I believed him, there was no pleading in his voice, no asking for forgiveness, no evasion. He said simply what, maybe, he had to say. I looked at the picture of the Shimonis' son, the room disappeared, I no longer saw the people. Our association was total, isolated, and then the German said to Henkin who builds castles in frail air: Ebenezer didn't have daughters, Mr. Henkin, like Samuel Lipker, his adopted son, he sells lampshades that weren't made from his parents!

Something in me revolted, even though I didn't understand the meaning of the words, I was filled with a vague longing to run away. I remember the first time we went to see my son's grave. When I stood at the gate of the cemetery I wanted to flee. As if my son was waiting for me there. I thought about circles; I go outside my room and there is no Giladi, a new neighbor lives there, works a garden, talks about north Tel Aviv, I then investigate the history of the Last Jew, and the Last Jew I investigate is named Ebenezer, why did he ask me for daughters he didn't have? Ebenezer, the one I investigated, didn't have daughters, he had a son, the

son's name wasn't Samuel Lipker, what's the connection to Marar, to Boaz
Schneerson, to Germanwriter? From what side does the sea die near my
house, an old man once asked me on the seashore during an evening stroll,
how are you sure that Hitler is dead? Did you see his body? How do you
know? Germanwriter is talking and I'm listening to him slowly through my
thoughts; they held a meeting for me at the Writers' Union, he said, it was
hard, what I saw that morning at Yad Vashem was still echoing in me, not
that I ever wanted to forget. They spoke, and something brings you close
but nevertheless an accusation was heard in their words, what could I tell
them? That I've already spent years investigating the history of the Last Jew,
the great-grandson of Secret Charity? No, don't say a word, Mr. Henkin, I
know what you do, so I asked to meet you, wait, maybe you don't know or
you didn't know that Ebenezer Schneerson is the Last Jew.

Schneerson? I asked and felt my legs growing cold.

Schneerson, he said, your neighbor! Look, Mr. Henkin, I'm so sorry but
he doesn't have and didn't have daughters! At that meeting with the writers one writer spoke excitedly; he said: We live in a world where people
walk around who at night dream dreams that terrify them, he meant me—
This is a land woven of nightmares of two hundred, three hundred thousand people and this venom of theirs is the texture of our life, he said, the
foundation of this tribe that stands with a flag in hand under eighty meters
of water, and then he said to me: Here's my friend, acquaintance I would
say, his name is Boaz Schneerson, he thought he lost his father in an awful
disaster, but his father, whom he didn't know at all, returned after forty
years, and they don't know one another. . . .

You understand Mr. Henkin, there are a lot of people here, not Ebenezer,
not him, who really believed that awful absurdity that I may be able to return their daughters to them, what I really came to do is to return Ebenezer's
daughters even though he didn't have any daughters.

I listened, I thought about Boaz, about my neighbor, I tried to believe
everything I was hearing, that I wasn't dreaming and indeed I wasn't
dreaming, he said those words and I was silent and listened. I tasted the
wine I saw in a glass standing nearby; it tasted disgusting but it cooled me.
And I sipped the wine again. And the writer said: Ebenezer who's the son
of the great-grandson of Secret Charity.

I said scion, I said.

Yes, the son of his great-grandson, he said without listening to me at all, he's waiting for me. In the special language of Samuel Lipker whom you may not know, he asked you, Mr. Henkin, to bring me to him. We should go, ah, this party is starting to weary me.

I poured myself another glass of wine. Jordana came to us and tried to smile, I couldn't respond to her, and the writer said to Jordana: Call Mr. Givon from the Foreign Ministry for me a minute, I want to tell him something, my legs are heavy and I can't get up. She looked at him and I looked in her eyes and they were empty. The man from the Foreign Ministry came and we, two tame dogs, we looked at him and didn't know him. I drank more wine, the Germanwriter also sipped and Mr. Givon, splendidly dressed fitting his position, bowed to us and my neighbor on the sofa said to him: I'm going with Mr. Henkin and Givon said to him, Fine, tomorrow morning at ten we'll come get you. Please don't forget the luncheon with the Foreign Minister . . .

From my perspective, the German's leg looked like a mountain. I looked at the fold of his trousers, which was sharp and precise, I saw a spear. Beyond the boulevard a light was gleaming and from some hidden window came rhythmical, distant music, I drank more wine until the glass I was holding remained empty and one drop rolled around on the glass and left a delicate trail behind, a small drop of blood, small as a miniature galaxy in the process of final destruction.

When I reconstruct today what happened then, I remember that I was amazed. I started drinking everything that came to hand, from half-empty goblets, from bottles on the table, while the German drank in a more controlled manner, like somebody who's used to drinking, munched roasted peanuts, and then I knew I was drunk. The writer begged pardon and said he had to go to the bathroom a moment, he wandered toward the corridor and I pondered something that had happened long ago, in my childhood. It was the night of the Passover Seder, I drank wine then and went out of the room, I went up to our attic, I found there the piles of my father's books, textbooks, reading books, sex books, forbidden stories including a small booklet titled *The Tale of Reb Joseph de la Rayna and His Five Students* by Solomon Navarro. The subject of it had a name that was destroyed, and I read it drunk and shocked, and later on, that story is etched so deep in

my memory—and that was the one and only time until that evening that
I got drunk—until I wrote the first study in the Land of Israel on the case
of Joseph de la Rayna. In that story I found some apocalyptic meaning for
our enterprise here. For the great spiritual revolt. As I said it was my first
study and as far as I know that study of mine preceded many greater scholars than I. And to this day I keep a letter of congratulations from Bialik
about that study of mine that was published in 1912. Once in a moment of
anger I even called my son Joseph, and when he wanted to know why, I
told him the story and back then I didn't have time for my son as I do
today, and he, for some reason, copied the story into his notebook and from
then on whenever he rebelled—and he rebelled so many times—he'd turn
to me with his refreshing and open laugh and say: Henkin, I bring salvation
and I ask him, how, by pinching a little girl's behind? And he told me something like: Why don't you say ass, Henkin, why behind or buttocks? And
how do you know I don't bring salvation? And I try to explain to him the
tragic, pathetic structure of the yearning for revenge the enormous need
for salvation, for breakthroughs and breakthroughs, talk about chains, about
the sense of impotence toward the creation and the sense of betrayal of the
nation but in vain.

Now I could have fun with my real son, not the Menahem Jordana is in
love with, not my son that Boaz Schneerson created for me, but the one my
wife shaped in her heart, impetuous, loving the sea, and I got up, my head
spinning, the teacher Henkin who placed thirty-four generations of students walks like a drunkard, my son is smoking in the shelter, I approached
the Shimonis who separated me from the wall opposite, the wall where
my features were still stuck between the Bedouin ruin and the etching
of Goethe. Gallantly, I took Mrs. Shimoni's pure, wrinkled hand, kissed
it, and said to Jordana: Eat a plastic tomato, Jordana, and Mrs. Shimoni
looked at me with measured, chilly defiance, she wasn't used to seeing me
lose my poise and here I am a fool in her eyes, mischievous, and she tries
to formulate something against me, something her son will transmit to my
son, that's what we always do, bring our sons not only for the sake of closeness but also for the sake of conflict, listing virtues in our sons they didn't
have, blazing up toward the dark death where our sons are cut up for a new
fabric, and they're exaggerated there immeasurably and Mrs Shimoni
smiles at me, we're too sad to be vindictive, guardians of sin or judges,

only wondering sometimes, and she smiles as if she understood at long last, everybody has his own apostasy, even Obadiah Henkin, and Jordana looks at me, knows me here and knows me in my house, half and halved, smiles an overly professional smile, and Mrs. Shimoni softens, forgives me, that awful need to remain loyal, Jordana glances at her, her hand held out in that same gallantry in which I kissed it, and I go to the wall, maybe, I don't see exactly . . . Contradictory thoughts in my mind and then the German's handsome wife appeared, introduced herself, a few words of parting were said, hands were shaken with exaggerated fervor, and the writer pressed on me with his outsized body and the wife said, My name's Renate, and I said Obadiah Henkin, he hugged my arm hard but gently and pulled me outside, Jordana tried to get to me, to catch my eye, maybe I saw a laugh on the lips of 'sixty-seven, but it was hard for me to create contact, and we left, Renate walked behind us, the door slammed.

My legs were heavy, I felt my body pulling me down and yet my head seemed weightless, in the staircase it was dark and I looked for the switch. And the German, even though he was such a well-known writer, didn't know how you illuminate Israeli staircases. With light legs, maybe too light, I searched for the switch with my hand stroking the walls. My hand came upon the doorbell of the neighbors' apartment, hit a bracket where a lamp or a mailbox may once have hung and then suddenly the light came on, and my hands on the wall were white with plaster, even my nose was white and the German lady was wiping the plaster with her finger. We went down the stairs and stood in the entrance hall, facing the gray-white brick wall that remained as a shelter from the days of World War II. I saw clearly—sharpened by my drunkenness—the soot of a cigarette crushed in a slot between two bricks. Renate also looked at the spot of soot illuminated by the dim light from the staircase so that those bricks, two bricks and between them was a spot, those bricks were lighted more brightly than the other bricks and when Renate stared at the spot next to the wall of darkened stones I saw how proper and handsome her clothes were: she wore a light gray Indian silk blouse, a faded scarlet skirt, a necklace of small delicate pearls, while she attached a restrained dark black comb in her hair. We walked slowly toward the car parked not far from there. The German opened the doors and for some reason I was glad it was an Escort assembled in Israel, and I, mocked by my son for knowing every article by Ahad Ha-Am and not knowing the difference between a tile roof and a DeSoto, I now know the names of cars, their virtues, from my incessant rambles I learned to know the capacity of a motor, what is a gearshift, whether the car is automatic or front-wheel drive and it was terrific of me to know for him not only *yearnnnnings*, as he'd say, or what difference does it make but what are Ford and Fiat and Escort. The German asked where we were going and I wanted to tell him: Ebenezer lives on Deliverance Street but I said: Go north here, and on Nordau Boulevard you turn left and . . .

The newly painted gate was gleaming in the silvery moonlight, I wanted to point to the rose and geranium bushes, my lightness was beginning to dissolve, the sea peeped through the two trees in front of our houses and somebody had already started grooming and pruning them, in that epidemic of resurrecting the gardens that had broken out in the neighborhood. I saw the shutters shift a moment, the flash of my wife in the cleft of the shutter, and when we went inside Hasha Masha was sitting under the sheaf of her light, forlorn, torn from the world, the light flattered her, I could see her beauty in the eyes of strangers too, Germanwriter and Renate his wife were bracketed in the door, next to the white spot I hadn't repainted, where I had once torn off the mezuzah in rage. The dull gleam in Renate's eyes grew even duller, I glanced at her, from where she stood, in the presence of the gloomy room she fished up the face of my wife and I saw how she was seduced by the beauty of Hasha Masha, how she warmed to her, maybe the wine sharpened my senses that I hadn't known before, and the light, more than flattering her emphasized her powerlessness, her clinging to a certain moment in her life. She looked at the opened door, at the two strangers, captured by Renate's eyes and suddenly she got up as if all those long hours she had been waiting only for them, slammed the door behind them, and was stirred to life. She held out her hand to the writer and his wife, and I wondered what had made my wife suddenly so calm, so domesticated, there wasn't a trace of the contempt or anger in her I'd usually see when I'd bring strangers home. She was glad, really glad to hold out her hand to Renate. She looked at her a long time and when Renate wanted to kiss her cheek she refused but with a friendly evasion, without challenge, as if it was a delaying tactic, the kiss grazed Hasha Masha's hair, and in her eyes a smile of sisters in sin ignited, which I couldn't understand except as a joke, since Renate looked at her and smiled too.

And as the two of them were looking at one another, the German was looking at pictures hung in our house, landscapes by the painter Shor, a small photo of my son, the heavy drapes, the old, simple furniture, and then Renate sat down. She sat on the front of the chair, her legs held tightly together, I wanted to tell her: No one will throw you out of here, but I didn't know what Hasha Masha had given away in her rare smile. The German was busy with some thought, as if he was and wasn't here at one and the same time, he smoked his cigarette, measured the face of my wife, his face became hard, maybe that was a challenge, maybe a measuring, I said in Hebrew: They're terrific and they want to meet our neighbor, but my wife wasn't listening to me at all, she hadn't even noticed my rare drunkenness, the German exhaled smoke from the cigarette and a cloud of smoke suddenly filled the room and Hasha Masha said to Renate in German I never knew she could speak, Come with me to the kitchen, I made cookies and cheesecake and there's also tea and coffee. For years she hadn't made anything for guests, the fact that she had clearly expected them to come perplexed me even more than her German, Renate almost skipped from the chair and the two women, who, despite the difference in their height, in a strange way looked like one another, were about to go to the kitchen but at that very moment Renate stared at the closed album, stopped a second, trembled, and Hasha Masha, who was attentive to her, came to the table, put a finger on the album and then on Renate's pale face, and then the two of them quickly took off for the kitchen, we were left alone in the room, the album was illuminated by the beam that always fell on Hasha Masha's head, shadows on the walls, my head was now light and elusive.

The German's hand began moving toward the album. He waited. A gigantic hand expecting, not asking but waiting, a hand hanging in the air, I said, Yes, look! He went to the table, stubbed out the cigarette in his hand and meanwhile I searched for an ashtray in the house where only Noga had smoked, and by the time I brought the ashtray the Shimonis had given us for our anniversary, that gigantic ugly seashell, the writer was already leafing through the album. He didn't pay any attention to the ashtray, just caught it in his big hand, without looking, crushed the stubbed-out cigarette with one spark still flashing in it, and looked at the photos with solemn slowness, page after page, and didn't say a thing, didn't ask, I wanted to say, Here's Menahem at six, here he is on a tour to the Carmel, but he didn't ask. I thought to myself, they and Hasha Masha know something, they know something about Menahem, about some life, and I don't.

Maybe because he was a German a forgotten picture from Romain Rolland's novel about Beethoven rose in the back of my mind. I recalled Beethoven's friend's description of the deaf genius listening intensely to music with his face impassive, as if, wrote Romain Rolland, the strength of the experience was too enormous to express in a look. I tried to understand what had been bothering me since the beginning of our conversation in the Shimonis' house, the sequence of accidents, the almost offensive circularity of Marar, Ebenezer Schneerson, Boaz, and somebody named Secret Charity and something that had now dissolved with the wine I had drunk and made me pleasantly dizzy, no, not the surprising link, not just that surprising closeness between Boaz and Ebenezer or the link of my investigation and the German's investigation, but something else I still didn't catch, maybe some fate I am to witness in the future no less than in the past, I said to him: Here is Menahem my son when he finished school, for example, the grammar school he attended, on his left is Amihud Giladi, the son of the owners of Ebenezer's house, before he moved here. He looked at me in *amazement*. His face was impassive, he was silent and in fact hinted to me that there was no need to detail those pictures and that the fact of Menahem's graduation from grammar school had nothing to do with what he was seeing now, as if Menahem's not-being had nothing to do with events when he was here, and whereas I knew I wasn't able to behave properly in such circumstances, that something theatrical and indulgent exulted in me at moments when I should behave in a precise and restrained way, I started telling the German who stood over the table and looked at the pictures in an unemotional silence, a story so characteristic of me, disgusting even myself but I couldn't change now of all times, before the photos of Menahem while his wife and my wife were developing a strange intimacy, I told him: A woman lived here on the street who recently opened a new shop, Salon de Pré she called the shop, once she was caught in the forest with a group of escapees from the ghetto, and Nazi soldiers—I said Nazis, not Germans!—caught them, the commander, she told me, was dressed very splendidly, wore riding pants, aluminum tags on his collar, a splendid silk hat on his head and in his hand he held a pistol and he shot,

one after another the children dropped, and when he came to her and
aimed the pistol at her son, on his finger pressing the trigger she saw a
gold wedding ring, the soldiers were gathering wood for a bonfire and she
stared at the finger, her child was pushed into her dress and with a vital
flash of a besieged mother (my words, not hers) she said to him: Someday my children will take revenge on your children! And the officer's hand
began shaking. At that moment maybe he understood, she told me, that
there's a connection between his children and those children he shot as if
they were an ecological nuisance, and he couldn't shoot that child. Throughout the war, he helped the woman. He'd show up from distant places, warn
her, and take off. She wrote a letter to the court in Nuremberg and told the
story. They wanted to know his name. She didn't know. They sent her
pictures for identification and she couldn't identify him. I looked at him,
he closed the album and looked at me, and then he said something strange,
he said: Mr. Henkin, I didn't save any children! I felt embarrassed and I
quickly moved the album to its place. Meanwhile the voices of our wives
were heard again, I heard their whispering, and didn't understand them,
they returned to the room with trays between them, for a second they
looked at the closed album, as if they sensed it had been closed a minute
or two before, I looked at the writer's face and it was impenetrable, a
mouth mute now, I felt remote, I recalled the memorial day we had held
recently for a commander when one of the government ministers said:
We're in deep depression, this is a hard time, and from the grave of our
loved one a beam of light bursts out to us and I stood there and something in me was revolted but I was also moved. Maybe both deceived and
pained, a beam of light bursting out of death! In the ashtray the spark of
smoke that burst from the stubbed-out cigarette could still be seen, my
wife wanted to say something, the tray in her hand, I said: I'd have to say,
he wrote a poem, I felt my legs buckle.

He didn't write any poem, said my wife in a soft voice, but Obadiah believes, she added in a voice that maybe for the first time in years didn't
have an echo of the contempt she felt for me. Obadiah believes that through
eternity the past can be improved. I preserve the album, added my wife
and said to the writer, so that Henkin won't succeed in taking new pictures of Menahem.

And then she said to me in Hebrew: They're mourning just as much as we are, Henkin, but they don't have a committee of dead outings and foreign relations, look at them, see how much they miss a son!

It's not our son they miss, I said in Hebrew, and she smiled warmly at Renate, who stood a bit embarrassed in a corner, the tray in her hand. No, not the son of your committee, Obadiah Henkin, their son!

And then she said in German: See what a little kitchen like ours can hold, and he wants a new kitchen! They put the cakes and the tea and the coffee on the table and there was silence in the room, not an embarrassed silence, but a silence of something pleasant, as if we had returned from a long journey, we drank, we ate crisp, tasty cookies, suddenly my wife stood up, looked at Renate who had lit a cigarette with the gold lighter her husband handed to her, took the cigarette from Renate's hands, a long brown cigarette that burned with a strange pale light, inhaled and swallowed smoke, gave the cigarette back to Renate, hugged her arm, went to the old radio in the corner of the room, a gigantic radio that looked like an abandoned closet that we had bought thirty-five years before in the teachers' canteen and after a long moment some tune started bursting out of the box and my wife started moving to the rhythm of the music.

I didn't know if Germanwriter and his wife understood how strange it was to see my wife dancing after so many years, but I couldn't tell them again about the Jewish woman in the forest that Germanwriter aimed a gun at her son's temple, the stories of my son standing against his assailants were finished in me, my wife returned to the Tiberias-Tsemakh Road, maybe she danced to win me, to wipe out in me the thought of Teacher Sarakh whom Trotsky had hugged for three desperate nights. My wife set her body free, came alive wildly, held out her hand until Renate got up from the chair, put down her purse where she had been rummaging before, and her hand caught the held-out hand of Hasha Masha who was dancing and together they moved with a kind of rare lightness, with a kind of oblivion, as if the music flowed into their blood and they were stripping off their clothes before a sun god that had vanished and we weren't important to them anymore, they were dancing for themselves alone, not for us, maybe not even for Menahem, the pale light of the lamp created a halo around their dance, we sat, the two of us, Hebrewteacher and Germanwriter, looked at our wives dancing as in some magic ceremony and on their faces a lost light coming from inside them, not the light beaming from the grave that government minister talked about but a white pale light of life that once was and maybe returns, at that moment it returns, and then, in the middle of the dance when Renate and my wife were almost embracing, the writer stood up, glanced through the window at the house next door then sat down and his hand started shaking, he stared at his wife and said as if he were talking to himself: You're a very wise woman, Mrs. Henkin, men like him are hard to know, we don't have a way to know through the body, we get data but the data aren't connected, after all we don't know according to unformulated dimensions. Our son didn't fall in battle, he committed suicide, why does a son commit suicide? He put his head in a gas oven, locked the doors of his apartment, and died.

They stopped dancing and the music coming from the radio was distant, and delicate, Renate looked at my wife, hugged her shoulder, and tried to assess me, to understand something that maybe connected me and Hasha Masha and Renate, and was released like my wife from all abstract thought, said: It wasn't a gas oven, it was an electric oven, maybe he electrocuted himself by mistake, my husband has already written the story. Life is simpler and more awful than stories. No, not electric, Renate, said the writer, gas, and Renate said without a trace of theatricality: There was no gas in his house, there was electricity there, maybe that was necessary because you don't commit suicide in an electric oven! And she went back to dancing, her face opaque with a mute expression. I looked at the expression of silent madness on the faces of our wives, and the sight was so pleasant, everything that happened could not have been different, and for some reason Hasha Masha could pity me now without loathing me, for the first time in a long time, without judging, and the two of us again, adjacent circles, maybe not yet connecting, with Menahem who died twice and Friedrich, their son who died in an electric oven and a gas oven at one and the same time, suddenly it was clear that every son died more than once. And maybe that was submission for the first time, without protest, in a long time, "known only to God," and the check that says: "Pay to the bearer . . ." The writer suddenly smiled and said: If they weren't our wives we could fall in love with them! And my wife went to Renate, who also stopped dancing, and they sat at the small table where once, a tortoise Menahem brought from the yard slept a whole night (and I then tried to coax him to put out his head and he refused and Menahem said something and suddenly the tortoise put out his head and wagged it) the memory was ignited and went out immediately, the sound of a plane landing not far from our house was heard, and Hasha Masha sat for the first time since my son fell and talked about him with a stranger.

Tape / —

And about ten minutes later when the writer dozed off and I counted the planes fearing some new preparation, the two women got up, Hasha Masha put a black crocheted scarf on her shoulder and gave Renate another scarf, a red one, with smaller, more delicate loops and when we went out into the garden we looked like four bent old people. The sky was illuminated by the light of a full moon, an intoxicating summer night, gardens washed and the sound of sprinklers as then, years ago, the dead castor oil plant was kindled for a moment by a silvery moonbeam and the extinguished streetlamp near our house was lit, the wretched houses of our neighborhood now looked beautiful, almost splendid in their poverty, the enclosures of the port looked connected to one another and enchanted, brightness touching the crests of the trees disappearing in the sky, the dark illuminated and transparent, airy, somebody stole the city, breakers of the sea rustle the silence in the garden, my wife nods, as if desperate to confront me, and the forgiveness was already devoid of substance, unnecessary, that same old love on the back burner during all the hard days of contempt, those long years, was lit once again. And then in that moment, the shutter in my neighbor's house was lifted like a warning and I surely wasn't thinking of how we'd approach him, how we'd get in, what I'd tell him, and now my neighbor said through the window: Come in, I've been waiting for you; he spoke German and Renate, who had previously separated from my wife, hugged Hasha Masha's shoulder again, bent over a bit, something softened in her even more than before, and on her face I saw a flash of a wild laugh like a rare bird that suddenly shrieks.

My neighbor was wearing an old-fashioned, unstylish suit (like a costume), on his head a gangster cap from the 1920s, some splendor devoid of beauty and full of innocence, he had paper lips, maybe cardboard, Hitler did die on the seashore, a Lag b'Omer bonfire of a man, Menahem dancing,

dancing, I wanted to burst out laughing if I hadn't recalled how theatrical I looked on memorial days and mourning ceremonies and in contrast I saw how comprehensible that was to the German, how much he expected to see Ebenezer dressed just like that. There was in that drama some contempt only sharpened by Renate's smile, the brazen pauper encountered the desired spectator, in the window he stood, asking us in, the light gleaming there, and Hasha Masha, without my saying anything to her, already knew what to say, what to do, how to go in, how to relate to the moment, how to live it from Renate's smile and Ebenezer's seriousness, and only an experienced teacher like me, who had stood all his life and observed life and thought he was teaching children how to expel the British in diversionary acts, could have watched not only a drama but even his son, seen everything as watching and being watched at the same time. And Germanwriter, like a giant thing bursting out of the dark, held out a hand to the window and said: Yes, yes, and as we approach the door the writer leaps into the room through the window, just like that, as if to lighten the moment, to grant it a certain unimportance—to reinforce its uniqueness. And now we're bisected, facing the reality of the room, Ebenezer declaimed by a jester from the street of the lost dejected and the magic of the enchanted moon in the sky in the window and I see the Last Jew whose sources I had been writing for several months, close to here, on my desk, through the window locked with the old repainted shutter . . .

The home itself surprised me enough. Not only because it was so unlike the Giladis' home but because for some reason I expected meager furnishings, as if Ebenezer's belonging both to Marar and the Holocaust required some obvious trigonometry, but in the room we entered through the corridor there were black shelves with birds carved of wood as if they wanted to fly. And a wonderful cabinet and a gigantic grandfather clock. And between the clean furniture made like ancient works of art and marvelously preserved, there was nothing but an emptiness emphasized more than appeased. As if the spaces of the house were deliberately filled with life, there was no dust, no spider web, no grain of sand, only a thin volatile smell of Lysol that had dried long ago, of scorching, of pungent sweets and flowers taken out of a vase. The white walls, the glowing neon light, everything looked like part of a stage set, like a home that has no life in it but is cleaned constantly and awaits some spectacle that's about to take place.

The grandfather clock struck now, a beautiful Gothic cabinet polished with purplish, maybe dark red, lacquer, some romanticism, some jest of the last creations of nonexistent worlds, my neighbor dressed like a buffoon stood there next to the giant bear and not far from him stood a woman, tall, her hair really bluish, her eyes leaden, her expression strange and yet painful, without a smile, as if she were trying to defend her buffoon. The German shook Ebenezer's hand and said, Oh, thank God, and Renate smiled at the woman, who didn't hold out her hand. Ebenezer smiled at me, clapped his hands without a sound, and Renate said: We came! And she sat on a chair whose back was covered with puffed pillows, and above hung two chandeliers, one beautiful, adorned with crystals without electric light, while the other, simple, only one strong neon light, illuminated the room, and Renate didn't look alone in her chair and blended in with the general atmosphere. Ebenezer went to the grandfather clock and when he separated the German from the clock, the writer sat down and pulled out another cigarette and lighted it and I tried to understand from my wife what was going to happen. On Ebenezer's face was a smile I had sometimes encountered on the faces of students caught red-handed, a painted pleading smile, and my neighbor suddenly shut his eyes, with the expression of a puppy dog, he stooped over a bit, illustrated on the wall, between the grandfather clock and the cabinet, and started reciting something, in Polish. When I raised my head I heard the numbers of the trains of Warsaw and their schedules, I was perplexed, I had read about the Last Jew, and yet, there was something so perverse in his appearance, so unsuitable, his wife stood there like an orphaned question mark, the grandfather clock swung its pendulum, the writer shut his eyes, inhaled smoke, tossed the unextinguished cigarette into the ashtray shaped like a ship's porthole, and Renate's embarrassed, Ebenezer crouched, a little Jew of contemptible humility, trying to please, and Renate yells: Enough, enough, and the writer says: Ebenezer, no! And he tries to continue but the writer yells, No, no! And I try not to look ashamed, try to sit, my wife looks at me understandingly, as if at long last cooperation between us has returned, some form of the shared and full Ebenezer's melody sounded like a prayer of the first part of the night, nocturnal Psalms in a study house, I didn't know what to say, the writer looked angry, and then Ebenezer stopped, his body shaking like an epileptic's, stopped shaking and he started laughing, he said: No? Not because of that? And I thought about the hours he had waited, about the days, about the daughters he asked for, I wanted to show the German that there was some picture album here of the daughters he claimed Ebenezer didn't have, and Ebenezer straightened up, pulled his clothes, picked up a bottle standing on the table illuminated by a strong light and drank from the bottle without pouring into a glass, and said: Excuse me, and took another swallow and gave the bottle to the German, the German drank a little and took out eyeglasses to read the label. The German said, I understand, I understand, and Ebenezer said: Fine vodka that, the best, and the German read the label again, drank again from the bottle (didn't wipe the mouth of the bottle) said: Good vodka, like a song, and Ebenezer said: You're quoting me, and the German said, I always quote you, Ebenezer . . .

When the two of them gave me the bottle I refused. I said I had drunk enough for one evening. I looked at my wife. For some reason she didn't react to my words but held out her hand, took the bottle, tasted it, and smiled, she didn't even grimace. Everybody accepted her sipping as obvious, the little radio played some tune and my neighbor said in French, What a sweet sin! The music will cover everything, and Germanwriter smiled, poured a shot glass, raised it said in Hebrew "L'Chaim," and drank. The eyeglasses he had taken out before to read the label were still on his nose, small ones, the kind worn by old tailors on the end of their noses. The two of them emptied the bottle in five or six glasses one after another in marvelous acrobatics, they made the shot glasses fly into their mouths, swallowed the sharp vodka without batting an eyelash as if they were trying to wet the kidneys and liver, I really envied their ability to drink like that. My wife now sat with eyes shut wrapped in the black shawl, I wondered what she was thinking about. When we stood at my son's grave I also wondered sometimes what she was thinking about.

And then the two men started talking, the two women and I were silent, Renate sipped a small glass of sherry from time to time and the tall blue woman gave us cookies and tiny tasty pastries and later some cold beet borscht. The two men talked about the German's investigation of the Last Jew, the book he wanted to write, and I, the "great" scholar of the man, was silent. I tried to ponder the chain of events taking place before my eyes, I thought of the stormy winter day when I came back from my daily

walk on Ben-Yehuda Street, not so long ago, it was raining hard, and I was
soaked, trying with all my might to hold onto my hat so it wouldn't fly away
and then I saw Ebenezer standing in the garden and watering. It was so
surprising that I forgot it, a person watering a garden in a downpour, maybe
that was the first time I saw him and I didn't yet notice him, and then the
rumors about the Giladis, the stories about the real estate agent sniffing
around in the street, I recalled how one day in a meeting at the Shimonis,
I thought of the new garden and then Mrs. Shimoni said something about
the science of widowhood and bereavement, she talked about a curriculum
to be proposed to the Ministry of Education and to be taught according to
her by widows and orphans. She said she had discussed that with a famous psychologist and the psychologist wrote a monograph about the
Israeli theory of bereavement, how "the togetherness" of committees like
ours dulls the pain and maybe people should be taught before the disaster
happens to them to spare them the hard years we all went through until we
found a way to live with the disaster. . . . I thought then about the garden,
maybe even then I pondered the Last Jew, I thought she was talking about
how (like her) you grow plants against solitude, how you buy dolls jumping out of cigarette boxes (or plastic vegetables), against pain, how you
move out of your house and start talking about the deceased—as she put
it—in the present tense! And then the poem written by Menahem was
mentioned and it was said that poems and essays and letters should be
filed long *before* death, children should be taught not to throw away things
like poems, essays, photos their parents can use afterward, and I was terrified and shouted but they didn't pay attention to me and yet there was
some relationship to me in those things since I was the person who found
a poem by his son and they didn't know that the poem wasn't written by
Menahem and how the sex kitten of our dead looked at us then and I
thought how that dark plot was hatched to blend us, to bring here a Last
Jew who would touch what was concealed in my yearnings, I thought about
Friedrich, the Germans' son, did he die by electricity or gas, suddenly that
was really important . . .

   In my house, about fifty meters away from that room, two hundred
typed pages were lying on the table. Everything was ready there for me to
continue my investigation, but now I learned things I had never realized,
things the files I had examined and the tapes I had listened to hadn't taught

me at all, like Menahem my son I didn't write my poem either, the German wrote it, I listen to the conversation between the two men, how close
they are to one another . . . still groping, as if that was a postponed life-
or-death meeting, and in the end I was the messenger boy. I looked at
Renate's eyes. They were damp but she wasn't crying. I saw in her eyes a
spark of understanding, as if she were saying to me, Look, Henkin, how
they're playing, how they're trying to touch one another, their eagerness to
play a game considerably obscures their ability to triumph over one another, there's no need to play now, Ebenezer, said the German, I shouldn't
have given a sign, I would have found you.

I needed a sign, said Ebenezer and poured himself another glass. They
drank, and then Ebenezer smiled: The daughters! You don't remember
things, said the German, everything was internal signs, what do you remember? You remember only your knowledge, so you didn't have to make
an effort, Secret Charity is also a memory you learned from somebody else,
you don't even remember who you are!

That's right, said Ebenezer. I'm a man without qualities, that's what
they said at the institute.

The German wanted to say something but stopped himself more for us
than for Ebenezer. He drank another glass and groped for Ebenezer's hand.
I was searching for you, said the writer.

He was searching, said Renate and my wife opened her eyes wide and
looked at her with a sympathetic smile. He asked and investigated said
Renate, they didn't know, even in the Foreign Ministry they didn't know.

Ebenezer is a small person in Israel, said Ebenezer and shut his eyes to
remember who he was, ID number 454322, no papers, only the health service and an election stub. The number there like a number on the arm.
One number more, that's all.

Ebenezer was silent and looked at him, he tried to imagine his mother
Rebecca. He couldn't remember, he tried.

And the son?

Here Ebenezer woke up, an echo of personal memory struck him, he
said: Ask Henkin.

I was silent and looked at my wife. A stub of a smile hung on her lips,
but even if she was thinking of Boaz Schneerson, she didn't say a thing.

And then the German said: When was that? 'Forty-six?

And Ebenezer who had almost shut his eyes, opened them wide and said: I don't remember, tell me, tell me why you were searching for me today, why did I want to see you. Before, when I wanted to recite, why did you stop me? You want to tell me something about me, about yourself, tell, what I remember I say, but I don't have a personal memory and what I do have is worthless anyway!

Yes, said the German, now more for us than for Ebenezer, who was listening intensely, it was in 'forty-six. I was living in Zeeland then, in a little village, about an hour from Copenhagen, I rented a neglected old schoolhouse among estates and farms, I renovated it a little, and in the big room next to the giant window, looking at the beautiful monochromatic landscape, I sat and wrote. In my youth I learned Scandinavian languages. My mother was of Danish extraction, I didn't want to live in Germany then. One day I had to go to Copenhagen to buy writing supplies and a coat for the approaching winter. I had practically no money and I saved on the trip, but I had no choice. I walked in the street whose name I don't remember today and a young man came to me, about seventeen years old, and introduced himself as Samuel Lipker the impresario, as he said, he spoke German to me and was the first man who knew as soon as he saw me that I was German. He said he was an American of Norwegian extraction who had been imprisoned in a Jewish concentration camp. I looked at him. He had eyes that were both awful and beautiful, enveloped by violet eyebrows, green mixed with gold, in his look you could perceive a bold Satanism but also some softness, he measured his words carefully, and something in the way he stood made you uneasy. He talked as if he were telling a secret: If you want to see a performance of a tremendous artist, a reincarnation of the magician Houdini, who was also, as you know, a Jew, come this evening to the Blue Lizards Club, and you won't be sorry. Then he smiled at me pleasantly, the smile of an accomplice in crime and said, So see you, Hans. I said to him, My name isn't Hans, and I started talking Danish to him but he laughed and said: Hans Kramer, SS. Dening. I know you, you've all got a fried smell of God in your pocket, and all the time he smiled at me, See you, Hans, and went off. A lot of swindlers were hanging out in Europe at that time, selling churches, nonexistent cities, whatnot, the boy was a broken vessel but his German made me curious, the page he gave me and that I held in my hand said in a broken language that Ebenezer the Great is the

Last Jew, scion of a family of rabbis descending from the Prophet Jeremiah and today he is the human calculator who can't be beaten or defied. That evening, said the mimeographed sheet, the Last Jew would perform in the Blue Lizards Club and everybody who came would leave intoxicated.

I bought what I came to buy, it was raining again, I walked in the rain and I thought: I'll go back to the village, the train leaves in about an hour, I'll go back and write, every minute's a waste. But a cold wind was blowing and I went into a small restaurant, ate something, and then didn't find a bus and I got into a cab and when I wanted to say: Take me to the railroad station, I saw a glowing sign in the distance: Jesus is the Messiah! I said to the driver: The Blue Lizards Club, and I dozed off.

I went down a few dark steps and entered a roofed internal yard. A short man in a suit smelling of garlic mixed with kerosene asked me for the price of admission.

Ebenezer now got up from the chair, went to the window and looked outside. His body was trembling. In the window the moon started setting. A pale glow rose from the street lamps along the old enclosure of the port. The writer took a sip of vodka, munched a few peanuts, wiped his mouth with a paper napkin stuck in a charmingly beautiful wooden triangle, and continued.

The dank hall was quite big and humming with people. I sat in the last row as if I had learned their theory of safety from the Jews. Always be close to an escape route. Two shabby musicians sat on the little stage and played. They played Hasidic tunes and their eyes were shut, and I wasn't sure they knew where they were, I thought at the time about what the English had said about Wagner, that his music was probably nicer on the ear when it wasn't heard. The tunes were shrill, not precise, without pain or laughter. Maybe there was some point to that revolting playing. A waiter wearing an apron came to me and even though I hadn't ordered anything, he served me a double shot of aquavit and when I finished drinking the aquavit two glasses of beer were brought to my table, along with a few pickles and herring with some small onions and a pinch of cheese in a copper bowl that wasn't especially clean.

Now that fellow I had met in the street climbed onto the stage, in the same clothes, and shouted Heil! And the people laughed and applauded flaccidly as if they only put their hands together and their laugh was also

definite but blurred. The musicians flowed to the back of the stage and fell
asleep sitting up and I felt some fraternity in the hall, as if everybody knew
each other from time immemorial and I was the only stranger there. My
being German filled me with dread. I looked behind, the doorway was
close by. The man at the entrance stood there, didn't look at the stage,
but at the ceiling, I looked at the ceiling and saw silvery cigarette packs
pasted to it. I thought about German soldiers who had spent time here and
that only increased my uneasiness, the fellow smiled, I looked back at him
when there was a hush in the hall, he said: I'm Lipker, remember? Danny
from America. Ebenezer and I are glad to return to beautiful Copenhagen.
Some of you suffer from ailurophobia, fear of cats, or androphobia, fear of
men, or optophobia, fear of opening one's eyes, or some suffer from the
typical American disease, archinutirophobia, fear of getting peanut butter
stuck on the palate, or even who suffer from phobophobia, fear of fear, all
those, said Samuel Lipker with a smile, are requested to leave now and
you'll get your money back.

He put his hand on his pocket. As if all the treasures of the globe were
in his pocket, nobody got up, he stopped smiling. If you don't laugh, said
Samuel Lipker, it means that we really have come to Copenhagen. And
that's good. Ladies and gentlemen, welcome in total silence the genius,
the man who possesses the most knowledge in the world, the memory of
all generations, on two feet, millions of words by heart, welcome the Last
Jew!

And then Ebenezer, you climbed onto the stage, you wore the clothes
in which you welcomed us tonight. You were pale, a hush was cast over the
audience, they were waiting for you, and when you appeared, Samuel said:
Birthplace—Palestine. Education—six years of grammar school. Loyal
remnant of the Third Reich, carpenter, you didn't listen, you stood there,
flooded by the spotlight shining on you, you shut your eyes, Samuel whispered a few words and only you heard, you didn't respond, didn't move,
stood as if you were praying, stooped over, you looked like a pauper, you'd
evoke pity and contempt and then Samuel said in a monotone that may
have been a signal to you: Ladies and gentlemen, set your watches three
years back, the time is seven twenty a.m., snow is falling, gray, smoke, two
cows are electrocuted on the fence, January, a train rumbles. And you were
concentrated on one point, stooped over, wretched, like an epileptic, and

the audience—that amazed me—set their watches, as if you really could
set watches three years back and a few minutes later, time no longer existed, and I say minutes and maybe it was hours, a voice sounded from the
audience: Einstein's theory of relativity. I waited, it was possible to hear the
dead herring in the onion sauce, and then you recited, you recited quietly,
in a monotone, in Polish, and then in Danish, the theory of relativity. When
you spoke Polish, Samuel translated, and I knew a little Polish, my father
was in charge of propaganda in Poland for a while, and my son, you don't
know, committed suicide after the conversation with my father, a conversation my father demanded and I opposed, he demanded that the grandson know and not wonder and after that you were asked to recite other
things, the audience knew what to ask, what to request, they knew you,
they loved you, maybe they hated you, I don't know, and yet it was so
touching, I drank my two glasses of beer, I ate the herring, and you recited Jewish knowledge, Danish was also Jewish knowledge as far as you
were concerned, you recited in great detail the annals and strange deaths
of Christian saints and the annals of their authentication, you quoted with
maximum precision (I checked it later) the love affairs of the popes up to
the fourteenth century. Then you recited the annals of the Jews of Spain
and the system of counting used at the time of the Talmud, and I listened
in despair, I enjoyed and was absurd in my own eyes, excited. You entertained, it was awful, you stood at your own end and you laughed, because
you knew things that shouldn't be known, that nobody can or should know
by heart. You were an acrobat of words, annals, history, and the audience
loved you, loved the disgust and the entertainment, they were tired, it was
after the war, hunger reigned, you amused them, they drank their beer, ate
the herring and the shreds of cheese, and listened.

Henkin the teacher, thinks Teacher Henkin, is sitting in a house that
is both familiar and unfamiliar, he is looking at the subject of his investigation and his ears are surely burning, Hasha Masha looks at him, does
she feel compassion? Henkin investigated the history of the Falashas.
The story of Joseph de la Rayna, Masada and Yavneh. Survival versus the
fever of revolt, wrote about the greatest heroic speech written in the history of Judaism, the patriotic speech every Israeli student learns by heart,
the speech of Eleazar ben Yair about Masada, written by Josephus Flavius,
that is, Yohanan the Traitor who commanded the siege of Yodfat, sur-

rendered, joined the Romans and wrote the history of their war against the Jews and with his own hands wrote the speech of great hope, the dying speech of Elcazar ben Yair. Only if you steal the victory from the Romans will you be remembered and that's how the Jewish memory was born, and the Last Jew is its last product, or perhaps not the last . . .

Some time ago I read in the paper that they were seeking soldiers at a salary of two hundred pounds a day for the Roman army. They were making a movie about the Masada revolt. And they really did set their watches back. In the Land of Israel, written time didn't exist then, Henkin, Hebrew time has its own logic. That attempt of mine to write about Ebenezer is my last attempt. And now it was stolen from me, too, a good writer doesn't have to be a commander of a bad camp.

I look at the big cabinet to the left of Ebenezer. Three squares constitute the center of each door of the cabinet. Made of veneer, so many shades of brown and beige and yellow and black that isn't exactly black but isn't brown either, woven into one another, etched with wonderful acrobats, winding and cunning, lacquer backgrounds, delicate work of stripes and slats, some intelligent musicality, for with his own hands Ebenezer had built that cabinet just as he had built the grandfather clock, and all the other furniture of the house, and had even carved the birds.

Who would have wasted days and nights to bring the wood to such a charming and complex decadence, to rinse the lacquer to lechery like some artificial rain, like a sweet psalm to wood, subdue the tones to a marvelous harmony, and he stands here before me, the father of Boaz who destroyed my life and recites not to me, nor to his great investigator, but to a German who tossed into the fire the last of the blacksmiths, the last of the carpenters, the last of the great artists, the last of the kings where a single violin played on the millions of their graves, Jewish entertainers in Warsaw, the electricians, the physicians, the great adulterers, that sadness that was thrown into the fire, two-fifths of an American cent, I look at the cabinet, who will still build such cabinets? You, Ebenezer? The world that wanted you to disappear comes to applaud you in nightclubs . . . And soon it's morning, they drink tasty, cold borscht, with a little sour cream, chilly, a pleasant wind blows from the sea, and the German says, Henkin brought me, he doesn't even know who you are!

I knew and I didn't know, I stammered pensively.

He knew and didn't know, said my wife with a laugh that was not devoid of warmth.

And Boaz, said my neighbor.

A fine dog, said my wife, a purebred, green and gold eyes, charm and devilishness.

A purebred, said my wife, son of a father who fled from him to be a Last Jew, took a great lust to kill a Jew, took Noga and Menahem Henkin, and Obadiah, my dear doesn't understand, the love that was suddenly kindled in her.

Renate got up and gave Hasha Masha a cookie. Hasha Masha gnawed on the cookie from Renate's hand. The German was silent, took a pack of papers out of his pocket and leafed through it, then he said: These are letters you wrote me, Ebenezer, and Ebenezer scanned the letters in the glow of the neon light and my wife fell asleep or perhaps only shut her eyes with a cookie in her mouth. Renate stroked my wife's head and started conducting an invisible chorus as if we were now to hear the singing of dead angels.

That was an awful night, said the writer. Three hours you spoke, in the Blue Lizards Club. You hypnotized yourself, and then I heard the melody, the rhythm. You prayed a distant prayer I didn't know. Then we talked. You knew exactly who I was. Then I didn't yet understand that you didn't have what the experts call "self-consciousness" and I didn't know you were a man without a history. For hours I interrogated you in the small hotel where you and Samuel were staying. I paid Samuel two marks for every half hour. He sat with a watch in his hand, and every half hour he asked me for money, and I paid, even for one minute not more, did you know then that Boaz Schneerson and Samuel Lipker were born on the same day at the same time? Did you know then that Boaz your son, whom you abandoned in a settlement, and Samuel, whom you found in a camp, were two sides of the same coin, almost the perfect image of one another? You told me then that Boaz was your bastard son! That Boaz and Samuel were identical twins born in different places to different mothers and maybe, maybe also to different fathers! Here's another irony. Here sits Obadiah Henkin, who meets Boaz who brings him a new son, Henkin investigates your history, and you live next door to him while I'm in Cologne, today I live there, no longer in Kanudstrof in Zeeland in an old schoolhouse, I live in a nice house and write a story, the title of the story is "The Last Jew."

I've got a new typewriter, no longer a shabby typewriter, a perfect IBM that can almost write by itself like that fish that once started singing to itself on the Baltic shore and we threw stones at an unseen enemy and warships cruised along the frozen shore toward Norway and then thawed the ice there on the sea, and we carved names in the ice . . . And you, Henkin, what's with your investigation? Are you able to understand? In an investigation there is no retrospective prophesy as in fiction, no poetic license! Henkin investigates and doesn't know that Ebenezer is Ebenezer, that Boaz is his son, and Samuel Lipker today is Sam Lipp and adopted in America by a Jewish poet who wrote laments on the death of the Jews, he betrayed you, Ebenezer, from the pile of corpses you pulled him out, supported him in nightclubs in Europe, led by him like a dog and today he got rich from you and disappeared and left you Boaz, Henkin, and you don't know what to say to Boaz, who lives with a girl named Noga who was Menahem Henkin's lover, what would have happened if my son had lived and came here to feel remorse, as he used to do in the not-so-distant past, what would have happened to him if he had met Noga? Would Jordana from the Ministry of Defense have matched him with her? My wife was dancing before to distant music from an old fashioned radio, and I understood, suddenly I understood the German's lost rage, that was our book, Henkin, yours and mine, he'd look at me and his eye wandered a moment, each one by himself alone can't write it, together, maybe . . . I was maybe supposed to write about my father, not a bad man, didn't throw children into the fire, didn't shoot children with a gold ring, Henkin, all together he was in charge of propaganda. He photographed the burning Warsaw Ghetto, photographed for history. You know what he once said, he said: They didn't want to hear. He meant the world. He said, We took one step, he said, and we waited, there was no shout, and we took another step and another, and then we thought, in fact they're waiting, that whole big world was waiting for us to succeed, and my father photographed the silence, photographed propaganda films, wrote a few monographs on the Jewish race, who didn't write? My son Friedrich didn't forgive. Maybe he agreed and so he committed suicide? Maybe he found too much understanding in the depths of his heart? Can I guess? Through Ebenezer I thought I'd find an answer, but I haven't found anything yet, my father told me: six days the destroyed ghetto burned and it was possible to read a newspaper two kilometers from the ghetto, maybe three, with a father like mine, a grandson commits suicide.

Who knows why your son died, said Renate without raising her head.

How can I write the story I can't not write? I asked you then, Ebenezer, why Denmark of all places, and you said there's a reason, my stepfather, that's what you told me after Samuel looked at you and you shut your eyes a moment, my stepfather, that's what you said almost loved a woman here who died on him.

Joseph Rayna maybe wasn't my father, said Ebenezer.

Maybe?

Maybe, yes, he said.

I remember, then, on that night, in the club, you recited the books of the disappeared Warsaw writers, the stories of Kafka, the poetry of a poet named Idah ibn Tivon, I tried to understand, there was no relation between things, everything was desolate, shrouded in some stinking glory, I'd say, and then you came down. The musicians crept to the stage, and played again. Samuel distributed baskets, in perfect order, as in church, and everybody passed the basket left or right, depending on the number of the row, and they contributed their funds to the basket and Samuel looked at them with his magnetic charm, that was a shameful drama, Ebenezer . . . And I want to read you an interesting document. In my father's cell was a man whom three countries wanted the right to kill. In his favor it can be said only that, as for him, he loathed all three countries to the same extent. When I went to see my father, right after I met you, he asked me what I was doing in Denmark and I told him I was writing. He said to me: Don't tell them too much, they won't believe you anyway. Then that man was extradited to Poland and hanged there. Before he was hanged he wrote his journal. I want to read a part of it now.

Kramer?

Kramer, said the German, SS Sturmbahnführer Kramer, he muttered. He muttered something about a cunning race and my father said, Why write about people who can't create and I slapped my father, not Kramer, he told me that Ebenezer Schneerson was his dog. He was born in Willhelma and then moved to Sharona. Today your capitol hill is located there, said the German, but then it was a village of German Templars! No?

It was.

Kramer and Ebenezer were natives of the same land. When Kramer came to Germany he was considered an expert on Jewish matters, along with the Mufti of Jerusalem who was to establish the army of the Greater Third Reich. But he didn't get to that.

Tape / —

And I thought about Sharona. It was there I saw Menahem for the last time. He came then from Caesarea. They gathered them in one of those beautiful gatherings. I went to him. I sat facing him and my son sat there and drank cold water. His face was tanned and a glimmer of apostasy flashed in it. He knew where he was going, but he refused to tell. I told him to be careful, and he said: Henkin, I'm a big boy now and I know how to kill and to be careful. He didn't offer me a drink from the canteen of cold water as if I too were part of the enemy he was about to fight. We didn't know what to say to one another. On the rifle he held, a new rifle he had just cleaned from the oil and kerosene and that wafted a pungent odor, a swastika was etched. Those rifles meant for the German army were produced in Czechoslovakia before the end of the war, from Czechoslovakia they came here. I resented that. My son was indifferent, he said: It's good for war like any other rifle, you can't choose your enemies just as you can't choose your friends, I prefer to fight the Swiss, but they aren't shooting at me. The Czechs sent me a rifle, he said, what do I care who it was meant for before? I told him, There are myths, there are words, that has a value, and he said, No value, no symbol, you're too old to understand, Henkin.

After he died you understood him, said Hasha Masha, who opened her eyes wide for a moment.

I was silent. I was thinking, we all were thinking. The light in the window was bittersweet. Bluish, a pleasant wind blew, a fragrance of sea and lemon trees.

Germanwriter asked for a glass of water, Fanya R. who lost two daughters for Ebenezer brought the writer a glass of water. The German wore deerskin shoes. Renate looked as if all her stars had died, what happened to the chorus of dead angels she had conducted before, why isn't she singing? Ebenezer sits and waits. The writer puts on his glasses and reads . . .

. . . I met Ebenezer Schneerson in the winter of 'forty-three, it was after Christmas. I remember exactly the argument between me and SS Übersturmbahnführer Weiss. I told Weiss I was destined to establish a splendid Arab army, or else to fight on the front like a hero and not to serve throughout the war as the deputy commander of a camp, and he told me: You were wounded in the leg, my dear Kramer, you were stationed in a place that suited you. No matter how sad and conservative my feelings were, my scale of values had always been consistent and stable and so I was silent. I knew that as deputy I had to supervise my commander. Weiss and I would watch one another, as they once said about the Germans and the French on the front in World War I, like two china dogs on a cabinet and on the prowl.

Being a patriotic worshipper by nature, strong yearnings were rooted in me for my ancient homeland, I was graced with a stubborn aspiration to be the heir of Heydrich and Müller, but the world didn't have to know about that. After a long and stormy struggle in which I was demoted to a position of a covered scarecrow with an aluminum lapel on his coat collar and wearing shiny boots, what I had left was the ability to detest. I did that abstractly. Solid and hidden carefully. Hence, my manners were perfect and thus I also hated Weiss. Commander Weiss's work forced him to stay in his office late at night. The food in 'forty-three was still good, our cook, at least, was French. The French did steal the Italian cuisine but they improved it immeasurably. And so, on my way to his office at seven twenty in the morning I often had the privilege of seeing Weiss tired from his sleepless nights in his bed in the office.

His nights, he told me, were a constant tour of hell. I loathed his use of the story of the distinguished poet in the context of the solution of the Semitic problem. I also suffered quite a bit from the fact that I had to put the rare and only copy of the *Divine Comedy* in a closet next to haberdashery, between suits and shirts. But authority as we know goes down while responsibility goes up, and so I had the honor of obeying one whose words disgusted me, and I had to listen to confused and meaningless speeches about the descent of the Muslims, whom I wanted to lead in our war against the British and the Russians, vis-à-vis Dante. The word Muslims rises here in my mind in view of the fact that they started then, to my displeasure, to call worn-out Jews Musulmen. Weiss claimed that the Muslims wouldn't forgive the distinguished poet for putting Mohammed and his son Ali in

hell while he hung their intestines at the entrance. As somebody who saw
pigs like Captain Roehm who lusted after men—in a moment of drunkenness, Weiss had the nerve to tell me that it was he who recruited the Führer
into the party—hanged on hooks like butchered meat, I had to rise above
myself not to challenge that claim. I told him, But Salah-a-Din was put
along with "infidels" like Homer and Virgil in a corner of infidels who had
a great soul, and he said, Yes, yes, but Homer wasn't a Christian and I said,
And us? We're different Christians, we belong to the SS Reiterstandarten,
sifting the nobility from the filth, burning the dirt, our faith dear Weiss, as
Rosenberg put it, is pure chauvinism; Jesus's mother served as a temple
and with the support of an important priest, she bore a German soldier
with fair hair and blue eyes from the tribes of the Germans in the Roman
army who moved north from the Carpathians, and we became *Gutgläubig*:
people with pure German faith of Nordic origin and not talmudist Yids
filled with remorse and when we drive in our shining Horick and Maubach
cars, we present a powerful future and not some primitive and frustrated
Christianity, but Weiss didn't answer me. In his heart I know he detested
me, I could see his mousy eyes looking at me with distrust, he knew very
well that every word he said to me would be reported to Berlin, in his own
heart he feared our illustrious Wotan customs that bore us in sublime excitement to the pure German soil to ancient altars or to the light of torches
in a strong song of brotherhood. He was and still is a traditionalist, he com-
mands death that smells Christian. My obedient nature often impelled me
to those clashes with Weiss despite the fact that I was almost anonymous
in our hierarchy while he— the miserable Christian—was called by his first
name by Göring and Goebbels, Dr. Frick, Ley, and Kerl who knew him
from the days when the Führer was in prison. His SS card had three dig-
its, two or three numbers behind the Reichsführer. But I already said, my
obedience was my first nature and not some random careerist blindness.
We'd sniff each other all the time, each trying to discover his companion's
secrets, "his companion," from my point of view should be written in quotation marks. I wrote before that I had a special privilege of seeing him
sleeping at seven twenty in the morning and so I could also see the special
way he woke up. The servant on duty who was usually a Pole, with his always delicate and beautiful hands—Weiss knew how to select handsome
young men to serve him—would remove the blanket and stick a cigarette

between his master's lips. And then he would carefully light the cigarette, wait until his master started sucking the smoke a little and his eyes would then express buds of waking. When he got out of bed he'd do it with a concentrated and frozen and maybe even savage leap. On the way to the warm bath, prepared for him in time, with the cigarette in his mouth, he'd open his old book of Walter von der Poloida or the poem of Ludwig and would read the book through its binding. He would immediately sink into recitation and by the time he entered the bathroom, the water was luke-warm. After a year he was able to repeat word for word what he hadn't read that morning. But to the same extent he was able to shout at me that he didn't consider the attempt plausible to restore to the modern world of the Third Reich the old-fashioned exalted aura of ancient German gods. Those gods too, he told me once with typical sincerity—sent word for word to my superiors in Berlin—impose infinite chains on man, impose too great a burden on a pure organism that, more than it loves or is enslaved to the gods, is enslaved to ritual. What we are trying to create, he said, is a ritual and not a myth. And I of course was filled with honest, maybe even patri-otic, grievance.

After one of Weiss's endless one-way arguments with me (I was silent then with outstanding nobility) he showed me as a gesture of reconcilia-tion—he apparently detested the instructions sent from Berlin as a result of my letters—a small wooden box and asked me with a jocularity steeped in horrifying transparent malice, what I thought of that box, I looked, the box opened to the opening notes of Beethoven's Fifth Symphony. I felt the box in my hands, felt my eyes fill with tears, I said to him: I haven't seen such a marvelous creation in many years, and that was truly true.

He lit an Egyptian cigarette whose delicate smell blazed up in my nose, drank wine from a bottle he used to keep in front of him. Those expensive cigarettes he used to chain-smoke and would put them out on his hand. For some reason he wouldn't crush the cigarettes in the many ashtrays heaped up in his room. I looked at the box again, outside, through the windowpane hazed with gray smoke. The landscape was gray, desolate, monotonous, and gloomy. This was not the proper place to show a rare creation of art. I asked Weiss if he had bought that box on one of his tours of duty in the East where he had served many years earlier as an agent for oriental objets d'art, something he'd do between his frequent appearances as an understudy opera singer in provincial towns whose names were known for not appearing on maps. He chuckled at me and said—something I of course understood immediately was not true—Mr. Beautiful People, those works are created here!

Then he told me about some ludicrous Jew who could do magic with wood. My friends in Berlin, he told me with a smile and a hint that didn't escape me, compete, after knocking themselves out about certain letters that come to them from here about ideological instability, institutional instability. Kramer, brotherhood of the leaders, for who'll get a box, who'll get a grandfather clock, who'll get an intricate frame smeared with endless lacquers and the secret of their blend isn't understood by the most famous experts.

And I'm there . . . Perfection evokes in me a dreadful sense of quiet bliss. I told him excitedly, without responding to his hints: Goethe said that the greatest virtue a man can reach is amazement, and I, I feel now a mastery and modesty of endless amazement, that's an enlightened and special work of art, can that be done by a blind man?

Can a bloodthirsty Jew, a perverse mutation, create that work? Weiss smiled and went on sipping the French wine and immediately, as an answer characteristic of him, with red eyes of drunkenness, started reciting to me the *Niebelungenlied* shrouded in tragic fates.

I went outside, the gigantic courtyard was empty. I had to find the Jew. I didn't ask Weiss, I knew he'd despise me too gracefully. I'm capable of smelling them from afar. And he was indeed sitting in the small storeroom under the guardroom that was never used, under a bare bulb hanging on an electrical cord at a table heaped with tin boxes full of liquids, pieces of wood, paste, planes, hammers, nails, and other objects scattered in imploring disorder. My look was apparently especially bold since he looked aside, froze on the spot, and stayed like that. With my supple cane I signaled to him to go outside. He obeyed immediately, blinked his malicious eyes, and from far away in the gray air, smelling the approaching odor of a Yid, two hundred purebred dogs started barking in their kennels.

He didn't look flaccid and faint like the other Jews but there was no pride of a human being in him either. He wore tatters I wouldn't have given to a pig. He maintained a distance of a meter and a half from me, as if that measure was natural to him and not just a form of obedience. I told him to come close to me and he didn't. I saw his body stiffen; closeness to us was forbidden and he knew that in his body, as a genetic code, but after I raised my voice and waved my cane, he came close. I wanted to discover his image. When he came close I whipped him, he bent over with a typical Jewish dexterity but didn't make a sound. The first blow struck him, but his evasion of the second blow almost made me stumble. He straightened up and said a sentence to me that I shall never forget, he said to me: My name's Ebenezer Schneerson, Herr SS Sturmbahnführer, and there is no acceptable reason for you to hit me, by day I'm the carpenter of SS Öbersturmbahnführer Weiss, at night I'm your Jew! And then you can hit me. I noticed the tone of the words. He knew how to emphasize the fact that Weiss's rank was higher than mine but he also knew that I had more power than Weiss. That Yid knew how to play Berlin against our camp, and if somebody needed proof of the force of cunning, that was a smashing example, and if my blood didn't go to my head that was because of the strict education I had obtained in my youth when I was sent to the homeland to complete my schooling, and because my father didn't spare me a decent education worthy of the name. Think before you hit, my father told me, and hit them so that the blow will evoke respect, more than strength, the memory of the blow is more important than anything. But there's no denying that at the sound of Ebenezer's words I was stunned. "My poor puppy ran away from here," I quoted in my mind a line from some forgotten song, and at that time I also saw before my eyes my sisters, Lotte, Sylvia, Kaete, and Eva, I saw my sweet mother in her new house in the homeland, an exact copy of our house in Palestine, in my thoughts I saw them listening to a sweet melody notes bursting from those beautiful music boxes, I saw them putting in a handsome cabinet the pearl necklaces and the beautiful objects I used to bring them now and then from organized tours in the liberated areas of France, Poland, Holland, and Belarus, and I said: Stand, dog, and he stood, I ordered him to make me a box like the one I had seen in Weiss's room but with a different tune, and he said, With your generous permission, and after I didn't say anything else, the dog waited a while and then without turning his face, as was customary, he walked to his kennel, his back knew the way, he didn't stumble, he didn't slip, but he walked backward as if he were born to walk backward. His eyes fixed on me the whole time, weren't lowered. He was frightened, he was very frightened, but he also knew not to show that fear. What a silly demonstration of courage when all I had to do was hang him on the hook and let his guts rot. His face was familiar to me, his name struck waves in my mind for some reason.

I couldn't shut my eyes that night. A scene from the recesses of my youth rose and bothered me and wasn't clear. I heard the sounds of the night, the orders of the guards, I was restless, those eyes of his, I knew them, I got dressed and went to the office to check what block he lived in. There were about a thousand creatures there lying on bunks. None of them paid any attention to me. What could hardly be called human beings were twined into one another like leeches. In the light of my flashlight, some of them were seen chomping breadcrumbs, their faces full of mad lust, hungry, some were rubbing the breadcrumbs on the damp boards to moisten them, others were picking lice out of their heads and swallowing them, others were scraping the sweat off the wall with their tongues, the Latvian and Ukrainian guards huddled around the small stove were amazed to see me. The wooden boards groaned, people muttered in their sleep or in dying that spared us the need to destroy some of them with our own hands every night. He looked straight into my eyes, as if he were waiting for me. I ordered him to get up and he got up. His rags now looked as if they were wrapping a scarecrow. I ordered him to stand on all fours and he obeyed. I was so stunned by it that my grief and offense increased. I was mighty and at the same time the deputy of a fool, a powerful and noble cog in a dark machine of strict and necessary laws. To preserve my honor I had to act as I demanded others act, the chain of orders I was part of created divinity, not vice versa, when I ordered him to recite the prayer *Adon Olam* sitting like a dog he told me he didn't know the prayer by heart, that infuriated me not because of what he said but because of the fact that when I attended the Hebrew course in my training as an SS Reiterstandarren I was almost the only one who knew anything about Judaism. And when we were told that every Jew knew the prayer *Adon Olam* by heart, I said there were many Jews today who didn't know it. And they laughed at me. The course was superficial and short, we could have succeeded much better if our knowledge had been much better. When I asked my commander, who was an ignoramus about Jewish matters, to read to the students, all of them loyal commanders and good Nazis, the important pamphlet "The

Catholic Faith against the Jews" by Isidor of Seville, and I claimed that that was one of the most ancient German works even though it was written in Roman, the commander said: We don't need to learn from the Catholics who the Jews are! As if that was what I meant. He said, and I'll never forget this: An ancient pamphlet a hundred years old shouldn't interest us when we have "The Myth of the Twentieth Century" by Rosenberg. I said, Commander, this pamphlet is more than a thousand years old and it explains to us how ancient and rooted our loathing is and even how justified it is, but instead of listening to me he became hostile to me and it wasn't only because of my wound in the first battle I participated in that I was transferred to the camp, but also because of the enmity of that commander who later participated in the revolt of the generals. And I was denied the bliss of serving the Führer with the courage I knew was in me, because of the miserable jealousy of a person who was later hanged on a hook and died very slowly dripping blood and kicking.

And so I stood facing him, I yelled: Pray *Adon Olam,* pray what you don't know. And he muttered something in Hebrew and then I opened my fly and urinated on him. The need to trample him was denied me, I could only insult him.

About a week later, special relationships between him and me started to take shape. Not deliberately at first. I wasn't proud of them then, and I'm not proud of them today. Weiss claimed correctly that I was confusing aesthetics with ethics and we sank into that eternal argument. I sank into a gloomy despair. I was the prisoner of my enemy and I loathed Weiss's perverse ideas. I wrote about the argument between us to my superiors in Berlin. And once again, as in the past, I was answered with a harsh and quarrelsome laconicism and even when I wrote them how Weiss composed a strident oratorio based on the song of the birds whose chirping he could imitate very well (integrating his life as a merchant of oriental objets d'art and a singer in coarse opera), intertwined with selected quotations from the speeches of the Führer, even that letter received an almost amused answer. In the letter I wrote how Weiss would sing his oratorio when he was sitting in his easy chair, an Egyptian cigarette in his hand that was filthy with ash, his face thrust in a dreadful picture of pastoral slopes as a background to a dance of phony satyrs, a footnote of painters puffed up with self-importance and devoid of talent, and next to the picture, dirty and with a broken frame, hung a picture of the Führer. The landscape was framed for him by a Jew—I wrote them—while the picture of the Führer had stood desolate and ruined for two years. In reply to that letter of mine, I was told I would do better to pay attention to the decreasing portions of hair that were essential for our manufacture of mattresses. And that was maybe because the exaggerated interest of certain deputy camp commanders in irrelevant oratorios and their inattention to what required attention was increasing, and the camp commander, it said there, who works to the best of his ability deserves the support of his deputy since he cannot supervise everything.

. . . I, the letter also said, had to continue to supervise but to worry less about the education of the commander, not to go easy on him at all, but to remember that there are people whose SS document is among the first five hundred documents and ideological problems of the Reich are solved now by thousands of professors and experts in famous universities like Göttingen, Berlin, and Heidelberg and they do excellent ideological work. Nevertheless and despite all that, they thank me for my devotion and loyalty and are proud of me even though, because of the burden of work in the service of the nation and the Führer, they cannot answer me except at certain times.

Therefore I went on with my deeds because my education imposed an obligation of honor on me to serve the homeland even if it involved danger or even a personal sacrifice. From that point of view, there was something in common between me and Ebenezer, the two of us were condemned to freedom and exploited by people who lacked nobility and imagination. And I could not get to the truly great men up above, because of the ignoramuses that stood between them and me, like Weiss, for example.

I talked about relations between me and Ebenezer. I was of course a volcano against a mosquito. But Ebenezer, unlike all my cannons, had a pair of intelligent hands, I was drawn to them. As a dilettante of the noble sort, and out of an infinite yearning for beauty, I learned to understand the perfection that is totally useless. When I listen to Beethoven's "Jesus on the Mount of Olives" or to Schütz's "Seven Words on the Cross," I can feel the unshakeable greatness of the German idealistic nature, that controlled boldness, sharp and original, some painful and tormented closeness full of bliss for perfection, an attempt to touch the untouchable, a wise and imaginative thoroughness along with a visionary penchant, a pure and virginal ideal, a struggle of man against himself and against others at one and the same time, with joy and disappointment necessarily intertwined, and not because of those circumstances or others and together they light a fire that is both ardent and burning, blood that is both beautiful and terrifying. If they left me here, in my cell, between one death sentence and another, yearning for something, after the defeat and the betrayal of the grateful liberated nations, these yearnings are not yearnings for life, but for a great culture we were about to rescue but didn't succeed, because the rescuers themselves were always unfit for the greatness of the mission. The Jewish culture of remorse once again ruled us and I can sense that in the things I read in prison. In the camp I saw behavior that didn't deserve the word "cultural," but my distinguished teacher was the monk Daniel who wrote "I gather spirit and hunt a hare with a bull and swim against the stream" and an ancient and noble taste fills my veins when I hear those things whose opposite are written now. The German person has some notion, even though it's often denied by him, of necessary worlds, and it some-times seems imperative as a means and not an end. It is the Jews them-selves who will suffer again someday, from the totality of our imaginary remorse and morality. German pangs of conscience will punish the Jews for their very existence, whereas our punishment was only for the quality of their existence.

I loved the way Ebenezer worked with wood, building boxes, the wis-dom of his hands. His idea of "the Last Jew" I thought a dubious joke. But today many admire the parts of his memory in seedy cafés and cheap night-clubs. Like one of the innocents was this man. One of my friends, Sonder-kommando SS Lieutenant Sheridan, once invited me to the camp where he worked. At dinner I met an officer I remember as even more splendidly dressed than we were. I remembered him from my schooldays in the home-land as the son of a distinguished and coarse farmer, whose father's estates stretched over a gigantic area near the duchies of ancient and historic Schleswig-Holstein, not far from the Danish border. All he could do in the camp was to become an absurd trickster who managed to get apples or bras out of villas or a pair of pants out of nostrils but was unable to get a decent living from his father's estates or to demonstrate the boldness of a German commando. I always knew he would sing the arias of *Aida* off-key but with ridiculous gaiety, while the celestial melodies of Bach or Buxtehüde imparted such mighty boredom to him that he was able to sing them without being off-key in the slightest with practiced pleasure only because he was bored. I told that because we tend to exaggerate our excitement about things outside the realm of nature as it were, like Ebenezer's tricks of memory and the incomprehension of his boxes and frames. How remarkable that a boob like him learned knowledge he thought was Jewish knowledge. Did he understand what he remembered? When I was in Paris years ago (I was given a Christmas leave from the camp) I met an old woman, half German, who had once been married to an Argentinean colonel. She introduced me to a young and handsome woman who loved to hear my stories and the songs I'd sing when she sat at the piano and played. Maybe that really was the love of my life. She once told me that she and the old woman—she called her noble—loved to hypnotize, and that sounded amusing after the quantity of wine we had drunk, and I succumbed to their pleas and was hypnotized and she wrote word for word what I said while I was in a trance and what I said was the precise history of the annals of a life a hundred fifty years before I was born. I piled up instructive and almost unknown details and the old woman who had inherited memories from days when somebody from her family served in the kaiser's army, burst into bitter weeping since I remembered places that no longer exist and battles nobody remembers. We checked in the SS library in Berlin, and in forgotten books we confirmed every single detail. In my youth I didn't know a thing about the man I described. Was it because of the hypnotic pleasure of that charming woman (who was later slaughtered brutally by barbarians of the French Underground), was it because of that that somebody had to admire me? If I deserve appreciation it's because of my love of beauty and because of my service to the Reich. And Ebenezer was a minor prophet of ideas that others expressed. It was the Duke of Wellington who said that great nations aren't capable of appreciating small wars. The opposite is also true . . . their memory is also their curse, Ebenezer captured knowledge, but his hands, his hands knew something else!

I'd come to Ebenezer's chamber and sit there. That life I had left was not the life I aspired to. He was afraid, he knew that unlike Weiss, I was a real enemy. But I was captivated by his creation. With thin knives he'd slice strips of veneer, put them together, twine them into one another, carve birds or portraits, spread lacquer whose secret ingredients and composition were known "in his hands." On the first nights I'd flog him but he never mentioned that to me, he made the kind of frames you don't see anymore, built grandfather clocks, more beautiful than anything I've ever seen in my life. A small kerosene stove would burn there and after a while I came every day, I brought a jug of coffee and by necessity we even drank together, he and I, I couldn't not come. Something enchanted me; I hated him but I couldn't take my eyes off his work.

I didn't like only the above-mentioned works, like Weiss, but also and mainly the act itself. That man knew wood in its distress.

I loved his hands, his fingers hypnotized by the big German magnet hanging over the altars of Wotan. I could be only me. The things I said in the courthouse in Nuremberg were only partial. When I was reading my words from the written text the bored Russian officer's snoring was clearly heard. Fortunately, I didn't have to pay attention to what I was saying then. One day, when Ebenezer was mixing lacquer, he turned pale and started talking. His words were a kind of recitation. I heard in them a distant, familiar, Jewish melody. He spoke without excitement. His hands were then shaping an eagle on a frame that looked both very ancient and new. He spoke and I wrote. Why did I write? Today I can no longer understand. Maybe it was an internal compulsion to know what caused the sordid creation to be noble in his hands. He spoke about the contracts won by some Neumark and Berl Shmuel in a contract of leasing salt and delivering it to merchants and Jewish suppliers named Simon Isaac Rosen, Isaac Shonberg, Jacob Lederman, and Michael Ettinger, and they got rich. When the Polish bank borrowed the sum of forty-two million zlotys in eighteen twenty-nine, the loan was financed by the commercial house of S. A. Frankel and the Berlin bankers connected with him in business contracts and even contacts with noble families . . . in eighteen thirty-five Jacob Epstein and Samuel Frankel were granted a loan of a million rubles . . .

Germanwriter stopped reading. His hands shook when he put the pages down on the table. Ebenezer looked at him. Renate shuts her eyes and stretches in her chair. My wife looks at the sea starting to turn blue in a pale and distinguished dawn. Fanya R. serves us coffee. We drink without a word.

Ebenezer said: And I recited those things?

The writer was silent, sipped the coffee and smiled.

Apparently yes, said Ebenezer, and also looked to the sea.

You were sleeping among the dying, said the German, you don't remember, you thought even Palestine was already conquered. That the whole world was German, that somebody had to preserve the knowledge. Geniuses were dying next to you, you said. Homer's poetry was Jewish poetry to you. But Kramer loved your boxes. I can understand. That's an astounding table, he said, and pointed to the table. And it was indeed astoundingly beautiful.

Germanwriter is now drinking Israeli Elite instant coffee, stirs in a spoonful of sugar and a little milk and is seeing a Land of Israel sunrise, like the one Ebenezer fled from to the barbed-wire fences, to Kramer. Renate says: I want to hear more and then not to hear any more ever again, and he, Germanwriter, smiles: To sit with Ebenezer, he says, and with Henkin, to read what Kramer wrote . . .

He was a pig and still is a pig, said Ebenezer shutting his eyes as if he were trying to remember. No anger was heard in his voice.

You mean what my husband wrote, said Renate with a smile, and reached out her hand and embraced my wife's hand, which moved to her. Ebenezer smiled again, tried to understand. Fanya R. gave Ebenezer a few pills, which he swallowed quickly and then drank a glass of water; you don't sound angry, I said with my characteristic foolishness.

My wife peeped at me, was silent a moment, became serious, and said: Anger and hatred are too narrow to include, Henkin. No response is possible. Impossible to investigate hatred or love, that you'll never understand. So your German invented a camp commander for himself.

I think he was! says Ebenezer.

Now he remembers, says Renate.

The German didn't respond. He was waiting for that, acted as if he were expecting all those words. My wife said: Can I hate those who killed Menahem? I'm too small to hate them, or to understand, or to love, or to forgive.

Time moved slowly. The light was already full when the writer put his glasses on again and went on reading. Ebenezer curled up in a corner and looked like a toy bear. On his face an old, refined, unnecessary pain was crushed.

. . . The amazing thing was that Ebenezer, who carved and recited, knew practically nothing himself. Once I made an interesting experiment. I said to

Ebenezer: You told me about Goethe's poem "Peace above All the Mountain-tops," and Ebenezer stared at me a moment and went on working. I said to him: You told me that the big beautiful tree where Goethe wrote that wonderful poem is in Hessen and around it you said a concentration camp was built. I said to Ebenezer: You're the one who said that every burger-meister felt a need to have some little camp of his own and the burger-meister of Hessen wanted a camp but didn't give up the tree. People were dying there but the ancient beautiful tree wasn't cut down. He looked at me and muttered something. I looked at him and then he said: Right, I said it. I laughed because he hadn't told me those words, I said. But he didn't remember what he had recited and so he thought those words had also been said by him. I tried to think about that wonderful tree, about that mighty spiritual strength endowed by that race that doesn't cut down an ancient tree where an admired poet sat and wrote the pinnacle of his lyric poems but neither does it give up a small concentration camp, maybe not an especially important one, around it. He was silent, what can I learn about his strange nature?

I wrote what came out of his mouth. Today I'm able to relate to those things as to my great foolishness, because that was how I also turned into a product of Jewish knowledge. A small payment and a debt of no honor. What do I have to do with the tractate on Jewish innkeepers in Polish jour-nalism? He quoted and I wrote down, a famous essay (according to him) by a person named Christof Hilyavski, "Project, or a New Light on Sorrowful Expressions that Accuse the Jews and that Is Found in Seven Paragraphs (Kramer) for Increasing the Income of the State Treasury at the Conclu-sion of the Days of Freedom Stated in the Articles of Confederation Pre-sented to the Honorable Delegates of the Confederation of the Republic in Warsaw in 1789"!

And here is a part of the libelous document (apparently I was selective):
How to correct that—
That is the remedy,
We have enough trees,
Too few hanging trees.
Hang Jews every year . . .
And Makolski's writings on Jewish innkeepers who exploit the peas-ants and enslave them, and testimony on who exploited whom and when.

Ebenezer knows names, dates, indictments, and what he calls with characteristic arrogance: "A few gentiles with a conscience" like Bartolomei
Djakonski, whose essay he quotes: "Principles of Agriculture, Craft and
Commerce" of 1790, which is simply an analysis (expanding the words of
one who fed Ebenezer) on the difficult economic situation of that time,
and devotes his writing to the Jewish tenants, explains the reasons for
their so-called tragic situation, their being surrounded by drunken peasants owning small farms, who are always guilty toward them, and the problem of forced superintendence, flaying the peasants' skin by the Polish
nobility (which the Jews, of course, are accused of) by means of their contracts with the tenant Jews and I hear names of those with nailed ears like
Jaczek Yszrszki, representative to the Sejm Mattheusz Tupur-Butorimowicz,
spokesmen for the liberal Polish aristocracy . . . And the growth of the population of Warsaw from eighteen sixteen (see the adjustment) 13,579 Jews
and 65,641 non-Jews. Later (eighteen twenty-five) 28,044 Jews and 98,399
non-Jews, and by the end (nineteen fourteen) 73,074 Jews and 547,470
non-Jews—the rate of residency, the rate of books of traitors. The rate of
left-handed writings—what wonderful knowledge!

Sometimes I wanted to stop. I was so full of wrath then. But I restrained
myself. I can imagine here in this prison cell, when three countries want
to hang me on their rope with the claim that they aren't fascist countries
like us and the flag is no longer a value but only an asset, but it's important
to them to hang me on a local rope full of values, they need the myth of the
rope wound around my neck, those colors! I can think with perfect equa-
nimity about the white, northern night of late summer in Copenhagen or
Jutland, people drinking beer, outside a white night light, clouds and rain
streaming, a beautiful and gloomy city, canals, ships past the old port, the
stock market building of Copenhagen crowned with giant snakes. Domesticated Viking savagery. And Ebenezer, a jester of death, tells them about
a Polish nobility, teaches them a Polish or talmudic song, the number of
matchboxes sold in Belarus in the nineteenth century, how many depres-
sions can be counted in Tolstoy's *War and Peace*, how many Jewish witches
were burned at the stake by bored priests in Frankfurt . . .

Germanwriter stops reading a moment, he peeps at the bright light
outside, his tired voice, the venomous light stroking the waves of the sea,
the port appears now in its ugliness, the old enclosures reveal their real

poverty. And he says: I'm reading because I had to read these things to Ebenezer. And I wonder why? Why did he need me, why was it necessary to read this journal to me too? Is there somebody that I, Obadiah Henkin, can ask for my son?

I want to know how I met Samuel Lipker, said Ebenezer suddenly.

Renate smiled and I looked at Ebenezer. Suddenly he was like a young boy, his eyes were illuminated, some wild freedom danced wildly in them, and his skin grew soft, became thinner, transparent. Read, he said, read from your story.

From Kramer's diary! said the German, unable to hide a thin smile that capered for a second in his eyes.

Tell me about Samuel!

The writer put his glasses back on and scanned the papers.

. . . Once we played chess. And I beat Ebenezer in five games. Sometime later he asked me to play with him again. I said to him: We played and I beat you but you don't remember anymore. We played a little and he beat me four games in a row. After I racked my brain I discovered that all his games were copies of the games played by famous grandmasters. Somebody transferred some more "Jewish knowledge" to him and I laughed. I liked to look at him, at his hand, at his spirit that moved it. An earthly technical link to a celestial melody. I didn't know but I wanted to be a witness to creation. A witness to the emergence of art. An exalted character is the character of the spectator. Who knows how to see. I called him by name. I also knew Samuel's name and that was almost strange. For us they were numbers, every single one was a number, and nothing else, just like the woman who cleans her house, and—here I quote the Reichsführer—doesn't call the vermin she burns by name. But I couldn't sit for long days with a number without a name. My generosity to him was so simple in its ardor that I couldn't aggravate its rarity anymore. Ebenezer met Samuel Lipker on the day a German civilian, a worker in the camp and a rather decent man named Hans Taufer, shot an apple he held in the mouth of a girl they called Bronya the Beautiful. That was at a discharge party for one of the commanders who was afflicted with a serious liver disease, and in those days, the days of the shameful and unnecessary retreat from Stalingrad where the generals betrayed the Führer and brought upon us the most awful disaster. In those days a party was a plausible excuse to dissipate the amassed gloom a little. It was a lovely dusk, drawn out and reddish, proper and wild in equal measure. Samuel Lipker was part of the Sonderkommando. He was burrowing—that fact I don't know from my own eyes but second-hand—in the mouth of a corpse, found a forgotten gold tooth and hid it. At that time, Ebenezer was standing next to the wire fence whose pillars curved in (I once told Weiss it would be good to create pillars that would look like they were crying outside and not inside) and then the shot that killed Bronya the Beautiful was heard. Hans Taufer didn't kill her on purpose. He was drunk and his hand shook. Ebenezer bent down and Samuel, who was burrowing in the teeth of the dead, also bent down low. Everybody knows how Jews bend down when they hear shots. Their famous survival is ultimately a bovine fear. When they bent over and looked at the window where Bronya the Beautiful was shot each recognized the other. Maybe they smelled, as a trapped animal smells its companion. Samuel crawled to Ebenezer. He gave him a piece of greenish bread, spat on it, and Ebenezer chewed. Samuel evoked longings in Ebenezer, as he told me later. When he saw that evasive and cunning lad he understood he wouldn't be the only one who would give up his life. A terrifying sense that surely also excited him. When he told me, I felt a kind of envy I was forbidden as an SS officer. I envied the love of the beetle for the flea. And because I write only truth I have to examine that. Maybe in Ebenezer's relation to me I was seeking something denied me, I was always flooded by the chill hard hatred of those around me. Even the last sight of the Jews wasn't especially likable. Weiss was busy with his miserable oratorio, drinking wine, and his endless meditation on the distant landscapes. The Ukrainians and the Germans with us were dreadfully simple and coarse. None of them had hands that could shape a box like a Grünwald drawing, a declaration of celestial disbelief in the cosmos and also a disappointed praise of God, and Ebenezer's love was kindled at the sight of a lad who was constantly busy rummaging in the mouths and testicles of corpses that were later burned. Their attraction to one another was for a past that was fictional but absolute as far as they were concerned. The spark that engendered love was, as I said, the sight of the dead Bronya.

And she died very slowly. In the window the sergeants' girl could be seen bowing as if she were made of iron. Very slowly she bent down, very slowly she died, when I wrote to Berlin about that whore, a few months before that (she was indeed the most beautiful girl I had ever seen except for some woman I once saw in a settlement in Palestine, and today I know she's Ebenezer's mother but then of course I didn't know) I didn't get a real answer. The reply I did get stated that I deserved praise for strict preservation of the exalted sexual practices of the German race, but . . . somebody wrote there, a fuck from behind or in front doesn't matter so much in certain cases of pressure, it said there, an SS sergeant is permitted to relax in one way or another (without specification) that letter was written to me at the height of the contemptible air attack of the Americans, surely of Jewish origin, who didn't understand what their leaders did, that what we were doing here was not only for the Third Reich, but for the whole civilized world. A testimony to their leaders' reconciliation with our acts and vice versa, how hypocritical the way we're punished now, when there are no more Jews in Europe and they may roar in public. When there were a lot of Jews alive they were afraid they'd knock on their locked doors.

They saw Bronya the Beautiful bleeding. The apple (as I understood) had dropped out of her mouth. She stood naked and the apple was supposed to look amusing in her mouth, and the shot was supposed to pass by her upstretched hand, but Hans Taufer missed. What amazed Ebenezer, as he told me later, when he quoted the story from Samuel who saw it along with him, was that after the shooting Bronya was still standing, even though she was surely already dead. A soldier started photographing her, bent over and photographed her from below, an officer named Kassinpoppinger who once called me "a dark and handsome man," photographed her from the top of the window where he had climbed earlier, Samuel told Ebenezer: She's disguised with blood, and Ebenezer remembered those words as "Jewish knowledge," a wise saying about the disguise of blood, she couldn't even die as a human being but had to stop time and drop very slowly, permeate with dread the brains of sergeants who fucked her from behind. She stood, Ebenezer told me, as if the officer who photographed her from on high was a magnet pulling her up, as a kind of revolt against the law of gravity of the earth, as if it wasn't possible for her to fall. And only after she froze in her death did she land and disappear from the eyes of the two observers, Samuel smiled wickedly and said: Bronya the Beautiful. He loved her. He didn't want to waste tears where the death of Bronya the Beautiful was a technical error of a German soldier who, despite everything known about him, was liable to miss his aim, a disaster happened, Ebenezer thought then (and Samuel remembered and told him), and Samuel doesn't know who the disaster happened to.

And then Ebenezer took Samuel to our alcove and showed him our birds, the boxes that were almost done, the grandfather clock, the frames, and for the first time since the boy Samuel had come to the camp, he said to Ebenezer (who told me), he felt life inside him, something dim bubbled up in him, agitation over Bronya's death and joy over the possible flight of wonderful wooden birds, as if he understood for the first time, he said, that there was something in imagination to fly away from here, and that there was someplace to fly to, that is another realm, beyond the fences. In other words: hope, the last thing somebody could have expressed, was starting to bubble up in him.

Ebenezer now said: He loved her. And they were shooting pictures all the time. I recall, that was scary, how much they shot pictures of her dead, and Samuel loved her. She loved him, too. Wildness, real wildness and joy. The soldiers and guards also loved Samuel. He had demonic eyes, like a phony gold ring. When he saw a phony ring he'd get excited and angry. As if he were looking in a mirror. Like a panther he'd stride there, bury and burn corpses, and seek in the bodies and find gold teeth or diamonds in rectums. Even there he bought and sold! As he did with me after the war when he dragged me to nightclubs and would sell my memory . . . When he got to the camp, maybe a few months afterward, maybe not there but in Birkenau, he saw his parents. They were naked. He never saw his parents naked and he was scared. He couldn't believe he'd see them naked. Their nakedness was too deep a betrayal. They were glazed and always dressed, impermeable, not connected to their bodies, to toilets, to jokes, to sleeping together, he thought they slept like two glass statues. On his father's face was a frozen smile as if a split second before his death he still thought, Ah, what a stupid joke! And so Samuel turned into a cat of corpses. Between his dead father's testicles he found a diamond. That was a strange gift of a strict father. Samuel knew how to plot, to walk between the drops, and the guards loved to touch him, he didn't care. Until he saw my birds. Sometimes they did things to him, he didn't see and he didn't hear. So they didn't kill him because of their rage, as usual, didn't crush him with an ax as they did to one child I saw, after they abused him.

Ebenezer stopped all at once, looked at the German who sat with his glasses still on his nose and the papers in front of him on his lap. The German wanted to continue, now he'd have to finish. He smiled at Ebenezer as if he were giving him a grade, as if he loved how Ebenezer filled in the crossword for him with a small square of knowledge, of words, and he continued . . .

. . . Samuel found one of his mother's dresses under the ass of a Polish guard. The guard was sitting in an armchair in the yard, next to the gate to the latrines and fucking a little girl who looked like a skeleton. Then he got up and Samuel slipped away, cut out a strip of fabric from the dress, and hid the fabric in his pocket. I loved—or perhaps the word "love" doesn't suit this journal—I sympathized with the way Samuel knew how to play the poor Jew and the soldiers loved the game, too. He knew you had to live another day. Another day, another two days, and that's how he got to the end. Chaos reigned. The radio didn't tell us the truth until the last moment. Documents had to be destroyed, burned, purged, and suddenly everything was over. So it wasn't Samuel's humble and disciplined attitude that saved him, but the disorder that ruled during the destruction of the camp. But when he did play it was a beautiful game. I loved to see his downcast look, his eyes running around like the eyes of a trapped mouse. No, he wasn't afraid, he wanted them to think he was afraid, it was just as amusing as the small and doleful choir in torn shoes that came from the eastern front to entertain us and the people in it stood shocked, split, hungry, and tried to make us laugh, and they dropped to the ground out of fatigue and hunger and Samuel stood there, I saw him, and peeped at them. He examined their acting ability, that beautiful bastard . . .

Germanwriter, who had stood and read for some time now, fell asleep, knocking his head on the paper. I thought of Samuel Lipker looking for diamonds in rectums. The writer's glasses dropped off and fell to the floor. Fortunately for him the lenses were plastic. The light in the room was soft, and outside laborers were heard on their way to work. A car passed by in the empty street and made noise. Ebenezer gave me a long and vital look, as if he never slept, Renate wanted to go to her husband but couldn't. Ebenezer said: Poor Henkin! Samuel the great actor! Came to you and shuffled the cards for you, played your son, I wanted daughters from the German and you'll ask him for him. Samuel's not a bad man, just amoral, born without a mother and an evil grandmother raised him. I know her, she's my mother. The German's journal makes me laugh. Only a journal like that can make a man like me laugh.

No Samuel came to me, I said, tired, and part of me was already asleep. Did Boaz come to me? Ebenezer looked at me a long time and turned his face away, maybe I really did hurt him. Renate asked: Was there really a commander named Kramer?

He knew a little bit about the poem of wood, said Ebenezer, your husband is a good writer, maybe too good. What in fact happened to us, I met him years ago, didn't I?

Years ago, mumbled the German either asleep or terrified and then he stirred suddenly, with a kind of sharp and panicky waking, picked up his glasses, stretched his slightly crumpled clothes. He said: So many things ago!

What things? Ebenezer looked amused again. A puppet acts, I thought to myself. A person who builds gardens in the dark. An enormous need to know who he was stirs in me and gives no signs. He said: We sat and talked, I remember. I remember, more and more I remember who I am and why I am. And so the knowledge was forgotten and that's good. A human being will come from me yet. You wrote to me. Then the contact was broken. The scholars who studied me at the institute told me, He writes, he writes, and what did you write? A fictional journal. Listen, don't make me what I'm not. And we searched for one another, why? Can I know? You should know. Or Henkin who Samuel came to and stole his daughter-in-law Noga from him. Mrs. Henkin, I wanted to tell you words of an old man who loved only one woman in his life, you're a very handsome woman!

She thanked him, my wife, and smiled at me. That was her first smile at me in years.

I was terrified.

Who was Secret Charity? I asked.

The two of them looked at me and wanted to answer and then Ebenezer said, You'll know everything, Henkin, everything you'll know, what was over long ago is starting over . . . Look, it's morning now and before it was night. Maybe a new millennium is starting?

We went outside. The sun was already beating down and Renate was supporting my wife. We walked to the car. Ebenezer fell asleep on his feet.

His wife dragged him inside and started lowering the shutters. Before he disappeared, his hat slipped off and he picked it up with some tired and clownish acrobatics. Renate sat behind the wheel and the writer fell asleep next to her. I shook the old man's hand. Renate kissed my wife, who bent over to her, she started the car, and drove off.

We went into the house. The heavy curtains preserved the night chill and for the first time in years we got into one bed together, dressed, but hugging, still silent. She kissed me softly and fell asleep. I wept but she didn't see. We woke up in the afternoon. We were hungry; we felt like two kids. We ate something Hasha Masha warmed up and we fell asleep again. This time we took off our clothes. We hugged, if we had been young we would have given birth to a son. The son would die afterward. But we were too old to give birth. It was beautiful to return to my wife's dark and fascinating openings. She hugged me and dug her fingernails into me. I thought to myself, She's become a cat, the mother of my dead son. We opened the windows and Hasha Masha made good coffee. A knock was heard on the door. I opened it and in the door stood Germanwriter and his wife. He was holding a big bouquet of flowers. We drank coffee, we looked at Ebenezer's house. The German said: Now he'll pretend to be sleeping. And indeed the windows were shut.

We got into the car and drove off. The road to Jerusalem was exciting as always. The German looked at the trees and the mountains and after the ardor of talking the night before the words seemed to have died out and were no longer stammered. Renate told how her son once took his sock, wiped his nose, and then put the sock back on. She laughed. Hasha Masha also laughed. The writer was tired and pensive. When we arrived, he said suddenly: What a beautiful place. We parked the car and walked on the path toward the cemetery. The light was savage but the trees soothed it. Their thick crests covered us. The path was full of dry and wet pine needles, the graves were lined up like a military parade. We stopped at Menahem's tombstone. His name was engraved in stone and so was his army number. I wanted to say something. And all I could say was, Here, next to Menahem, Yashka is buried. Yashka fell in one of the two battles in which Menahem was killed. Nothing is known about him except his name, he came to Cyprus in a ship of illegal immigrants, from Cyprus he came to Haifa and from there he went to the last battle he took part in. They weren't even sure of his name.

Meanwhile night fell. We stood there a long time. The moonlight that now beamed tried to save the horrifying sight of the dead lined up under the hewn stones. It all looked like a cheap stage set for something with no name, the pain, for some reason, maybe because of the passing night, was also fuller and more divided, desolate, and so I had nothing to say. I looked at my new friends, they guessed me correctly, I knew that from their faces. On the way back, the writer said: Who remains there, you or him?

I didn't answer, I thought. And then I said: Funny that Ebenezer thinks you wrote the journal. He didn't answer.

We saw each other twice more before they left. We sat a long night in Ebenezer's house and he told us, as in a dream, about Secret Charity and his mother Rebecca. Some things I knew from my investigation of him and some the German knew. We smiled at one another like two conspirators. Then the Germans left and we went to the airport with them. I had never been there before: the noise, the turmoil, the giant planes, all that was new to me.

Hasha Masha and I went back to playing World War II games. I corrected the old map. Jordana came and went, Noga came sometimes. In the game of old battles we came to the Normandy landing. Now I used more perfect flags, with pins with round colored heads. I bought a television set and I started cooking. It's hard for me to understand how a strict and harsh teacher like me turned into a cook. I love the smell of cooking and that activity whose purpose you see immediately. Ebenezer gave me two carved birds. I bought flowerpots and planted cactuses and the garden is growing beautiful. Hasha Masha found some soothing that allows us to go on living, she even started playing the old piano I bought her. She plays Russian and Israeli folk songs and a lot of Chopin, Brahms, Mendelssohn, and Schumann. There's so much romanticism still in those old bones. At night after we hug we dream of Menahem. Each of us with his or her own dream. But we're together now and only the dreams are apart and come together again. A month later, our committee received a big contribution from Germany to plant a forest in the name of the fallen of Brigade G. I was chosen to speak on behalf of the bereaved parents. At night Hasha Masha told me: I hate sacrifices to the dead, but you spoke well, Obadiah. I thought about Boaz, about his father who calls him Samuel, about his grandmother Rebecca in the settlement, near what was once Marar, near the vineyards, near the

almond trees. I thought: When will the German and I be able to write together the book about the Last Jew? Or perhaps that will be a book about
ourselves?

I didn't know.

Tape / —

Samuel Lipker of the Sonderkommando. What do you mean some grave-
digger of the dead. Eitdatius was Bishop in Shaybes. He wrote the continu-
ation of the memoirs of the world from the year three hundred seventy-eight
AD to four hundred sixty-eight. He continued the tradition of Jerome and
Eusebius of Caesarea. Aaron ben Amos, of the tribe of Levi, Aaron Amora of
Babylon, Aaron head of the court in Pombaditha. Aaron head of the court in
Zelikow (the glory of Uziel) Aaron rabbi of the city of Knishin (author of
"Jacob's Coat)" . . .

Aaron Rav ben Rabbi—not the author of "Oil of Myrrh" but the grandson of the author of "Name of the Great" . . .

Tape / —

With a good bottle of orange soda to be thirsty. Henkin hadn't been
seen for a few days now. The sea ranges from turbulent to billowy. When
I came to the Land of Israel, Samuel appeared and called me father. I
said to him Samuel, and he said, I'm Boaz. And he despised me. Maybe
he wanted to cry. Me too, old mother Rebecca laughed a hissing wicked
laugh. There was a rage in her because I returned after forty years and
didn't explain to her why. Maybe the jackal who raped her in her youth
laughed in her. Ever since, my dear Samuel, I've been waiting for you!

Tape / —

Maybe that's the preface to the Last Jew by the director of the solar
system who's based in Berlin, thinks that television antennas are arms asking heaven for salvation, sees wonderful people writing letters to one another and finds a small music box in abandoned houses where they listen
to innocent melodies and say, Oh, what beautiful work. And the lord of the
solar system sits and tries to restore the history for me, I want to get to
Boaz who returned from the war at another time, hit a woman on the boulevard, coveted her phony gold ring, then invented Menahem for Henkin

and killed him one more time, the director who writes a book like a shop lifter in a piano store; a deep sense of frustration. God had to create the world, but after He created it He changed His mind but by then it was too late. The gods of the solar system can indeed create or perhaps even have to, but they can't participate in running the world they created, since it's their night, in the morning they wake up from it and it's like a shadow. God created the world out of His waking. His point of view is different from the point of view of what are called human beings. He destroyed a world and created a mixture of chaos, storm clouds of gas from explosions in space, all those were the awakening of the world when his moon hit it. But for what are called human beings that was an event that was yet to happen. For God it had already happened.

In the beginning was the destruction. Hard to understand that in light of the ethical findings of God on the face of the earth. The time has come to tell the truth and to disappear. It bores me to see people who died a thousand years ago born and thinking their torments have meaning. For God, the aforementioned Boaz and Samuel and Ebenezer died long ago. The world no longer exists. Five hundred frightened travelers stuck for a few months now in a sophisticated spaceship on its way to the stars of Andromeda are freezing. When they reach their destination the ape will begin to resemble man and three billion years later Abraham the Hebrew will go to the land of Canaan. The words "ethics" and "forgiveness" remind us, slaves of the directorship of the system, of the words "ice cream" and "treason." The origin of God is from a green and yellow moss that grew in the depths of space. The Jews turned God into what never could have been; an imaginary and arid god. The real God knew about the grief brought on Him by His believers and the creators of His imaginary image. The grief of those Jews chilled his wrath at their stubbornness a bit, and so He fell in love with the smell of Jewish grief; the grief was a real challenge and only thus did the tragicomic encounter between God and His chosen people take place.

The first Adam lived in two fictional versions. One was with Lilith and the other was with Eve. I'm an expert on the creations. I live in the solar system, sit here in Berlin to teach you wisdom. All of that is still to happen. And Cush will beget Nimrod, a mighty one in the earth. The Pathrusim begat the Casluhim, Arphaxad begat Salah, and Salah Eber, Serug begat

Nahor, and Terah begat Abram. Abram will beget Isaac and Ishmael. Jacob
the son of Isaac will beget Simeon, Levi, and Joseph, the sons of Judah will
be Er and Onan, Tamar the daughter-in-law of Judah will give birth to
Pharez with one stroke of strong and splendid passion. Ram will beget
Amminadab, Amminadab Nahshon, Nahshon Salmon, Salmon will beget
Boaz, Boaz Jesse, Jesse David. Generations will pass. And somebody will
invent the wheel and will domesticate wheat and prophesy. Then Avrum
ben ha-Rav Kriv will beget the Vulgar of Vilna who will beget Praise of
Israel who will beget Unworthy in His Faith May He Live Long. Who saw
the light and his eyes were extinguished from sight. Unworthy will beget
Secret Charity. Secret Charity will meet the messiah Frank riding on the
horse of a knight with a naked woman rabbi. Rebecca Secret Charity will
be the daughter and wife of Secret Charity. Her grandchildren will be
Joseph Rayna and Rebecca. Rebecca will give birth to Ebenezer. Ebenezer
will beget Boaz. Joseph Rayna will beget another hundred sons and daughters. Samuel Lipker's betrayed father, the son of Joseph, will bequeath a
diamond in his rectum to Samuel, Boaz will be the adopted son of his grandmother Rebecca and the stepbrother of his father.

Wanderings, hostility, and unimaginably vast expanses of grief filled the
life of the Hebrews with yearning. From their place of birth they learned
the price of foreignness. They were forced to invent a god and heaven even
before they had ground to walk on. That is their ancient curse. Their roots
long for the air, their treetops for the ground. Only people who understood
heaven before they understood earth could imagine a universe and a creation as punishment or reward. In their flight to their savage pride, out of
a passion for vengeance, hatred of domestication and lusts for uncompromising rebellions, they clung to one thing that had no foothold in any reality, to words. They had a language before they had houses, they had a
grammar before they had a land, so they could create a future even when
they didn't have a past. They created for themselves a creator god who
judges the future according to what was. The desert was imprisoned in
their soul, the wanderings were their homeland. God was more important
than man. With the Hebrews, imagined glory turned into denial of life with
unbridled lust for it. An inconceivable yearning was born in them for something even the very old people, who remembered everything that never
happened (and invented in exchange a changing past) couldn't formulate

explicitly. The times were wild. Tribes and tribes joined forces in ancestral homes. They captured cities and burned them. Desperate ones went to the land whose wine is good, whose women made merry in the vineyards, its villages happy, whose gods were small, nice, and cunning, and they brought with them a jealous and rough God. Thus they learned desire and curiosity instead of learning domestication and obedience. Bereft of annihilated temples, what the Hebrews measured all the time because of the words that couldn't defend their stubborn savagery, was invented time. Hence the torments were necessary. And thus God knew there was a people who created Him. Others had ceremonies that belonged to a place, not to yearnings, God saw the disgrace and laughed. That was the one and only time He laughed. Ever since then He has been indifferent and gloomy. He's still waiting for the beginning of time flowing from its end, there are no more people in the world, there's a black hole in the sky from the place where there was a world and He's waiting. Only five hundred passengers in the spaceship going to the stars of Andromeda remained. It won't get any place, its time is borrowed from a nonexistent clock. It doesn't fit divine time. In the invented past of the Hebrews there were fathers and poets who called themselves prophets. Inventors of sublime words for a people who captured words and were captured by them. The land the Hebrews longed for was hard, lordly, capricious, hating lords, incoercible, loving ephemeral lovers, hating wild lovers who sing her songs of beloveds. The Hebrews had to surrender to their most awful passions to know better than all others how lost wars are won and so they invented defeat as a sign of their life and survival as a code of life. The Hebrews always knew the grief of extremities, therefore they were so stubborn, and with their own hands they created for themselves the instruments that always brought destruction upon them. The wanderings begat Torah and intentions of purity, the laws—the punishment; the punishment was God. From the frying pan into the fire, like splendor. That is how we were born, always to be burned, they said, and the angels heard and wept. Only God remains indifferent. He meets the people on their way from their end to their beginning. How can He grieve at the torments of man if His first encounter with him is after all his descendants have already died? In that walking backward, He has no ethics and He has no sorrow and the anguish alien to Him is left only to them. Fate is not a law of nature. It's inanimate nature. There's a need for that splendid invented past. What they always knew about God was the distance of time they invented and it is the opposite of the imaginary but imperative divine time between their unnecessary universe and the realm of their impossible yearnings. To belong to a place that doesn't belong to you. To serve an indifferent God out of a disappointed passion for His love, I can understand that here in Berlin better than any other place. This is their great contribution to current events. They brought God to armed revolt against the laws of the Milky Way, in their extinction the Hebrews were kings of a proud and invented past, in their flight to the past they laid the foundations of their mass grave.

Tape / —

Ebenezer was born five months after Rebecca Schneerson came to the Land of Israel. He didn't know who his father was. Rebecca Schneerson married Nehemiah Schneerson a year and a month prior to that. Before that her name was Rebecca Sorka.

Tape / —

When Rebecca Sorka, who came to the Land of Israel as Rebecca Schneerson, was born, the sun refused to shine. A Hasid who fled from a city of which nothing remains but a few traces, and who was padded with a blanket of feathers flying in the wind, then sat in a cellar and shouted. Rebecca Sorka was born but she refused to open her eyes. They shook her hard and she started breathing and when she opened her eyes she saw her mother. Her mother looked at her and was scared: on her daughter's lips was such strong contempt she was afraid to raise her to her breast to suckle her. The baby started flowing toward her mother's breast and caught it in her hands, she was strong enough to grab the breast and seek the nipple. Her face was full and more pale than red and a lovely down covered her head. As she suckled her, Rebecca's mother felt, maybe because of the darkness in the room, that the baby refused to suck, that all she wanted was to hold the breast. She was even more frightened, and waited for the sun, but the sun didn't shine that day. The baby fell asleep with her mouth stuck to her mother's breast. She didn't bite it and the midwife touched her forehead and her sweat was cold. Outside, Jews gathered who had stayed in the synagogue and were waiting to return to their destroyed city, and shouted, What a city with no sun! And in the yards when deaf Yossel's rooster crowed, Yossel went to the woods to search for the sun and bring its light, at that time the Hasid who shouted in the cellar died and Rebecca Sorka chirped and a drop of blood appeared on her upper lip. Furious peasants lighted a big fire at the synagogue to appease the cross, and when the fire started spreading, the baby smiled as her eyes stared at the flames capering on the windowpane. That night deaf Yossel slaughtered his rooster and when the fire was finally extinguished the rooster was found safe and sound under the embers of the bonfire the furious peasants had set. An old woman who claimed she remembered the children of Israel wandering from the Promised Land and saw the Temple in its splendor dreamed that from the belly of Leah Sorka came a witch. But Rebecca was too fragile and delicate, according to her father, for them to bring three rabbis to take the demon out of her. A Hasid stood outside at the gate and shouted: Damned reincarnation, damned reincarnation, but at that time everybody was concerned with the rooster that emerged whole from the fire and they forgot Rebecca. Rebecca's father, who had already dreamed of expanding his business outside the district, said: Over my dead body will they bring rabbis to talk about the newborn baby. And Rebecca's mother, who nodded to her husband in compassionate silence, prayed with restrained devotion disturbed only by the sound of the crickets. The crickets that shouldn't have been in the house that day chirped incessantly, and in the morning, when the sun Yossel had sought in the forest decided to return to the city, two scholars brought up the body of the Hasid from the cellar, his face was wrenched in a contortion and under his eyes three holes were seen clearly. The midwife claimed he was crucified. Many thought the holes were such strong pleas that they broke through and erupted and brought upon him the tormented death that bears a hint. After the Hasid was taken out of the cellar, the midwife got up and fled the house.

That night, the tombstone of Rebecca the daughter and wife of Secret Charity cracked, the Rebecca who was the mother of the grandmother of Rebecca Sorka who would come to the Land of Israel on the first day of the twentieth century and be called Rebecca Schneerson. Deaf Yossel, who went to the cemetery with his hands stained with the blood of the rooster he had slaughtered right after they found him safe and sound from the fire, saw the tombstone of Rebecca Secret Charity bending over and straightening up again.

When a crow swooped down on him, he tried to flee but couldn't budge from his place. Yossel, who contemplated Rebecca's birth, understood that the devil came back to lodge in the city and Rebecca Secret Charity accepted the birth of Rebecca Sorka with a blessing. That was the anniversary of a bold struggle remembered by only three men, the struggle between the rabbi of Lody and Rabbi Israel of Koznitz.

The fate of Napoleon Bonaparte at the siege of Moscow then hung in the balance. The rabbi of Lody, nine hundred kilometers from Moscow, feared the secularization of the Jews that would come with the destruction of Moscow, while the rabbi of Koznitz thought the fate of the Jews would be better if Napoleon won. After a bitter struggle between the opponents, the two decided that if neither side overcame, the war would intensify and a bitter fate was in store for the Jews. Hence, the question was not only to bring the war to a quick conclusion, but also which side should lose. On Sunday, the eve of Rosh Hashanah, Rabbi Israel immersed in the ritual bath, prepared himself for prayer, and wanted to get to the blowing of the shofar before the rabbi from Lody started praying. When he put the shofar to his mouth his heart grew faint and he felt that the rabbi of Lody took the blasts from him without taking the shofar from him. And so he shouted: He came before me, snatched the blasts and won! The device of snatching the blasts, brought Napoleon his immediate downfall. The rabbi grew excited in private and at night they said they saw tears wandering around his room seeking to return to his face. Meanwhile, deaf Yossel returned to the city. He told how the tombstone of Rebecca daughter and wife of Secret Charity had gone for a walk; the refugees in the synagogue interrupted and called yearningly to their city and the smell of burning stood in the air and Rebecca Sorka sucked slowly and important things that should have been done were forgotten. Leah Sorka, Rebecca's mother, didn't forget and said, They should have taken the demon out of Rebecca and now it's too late.

Avrum ben ha-Rav Kriv begat the Vulgar of Vilna. The Vulgar begat the Prayer of Israel who begat Isaac Unworthy in His Faith May He Live Long, who saw the fire and his eyes grew dim. Unworthy in His Faith May He

Live Long begat Secret Charity. Secret Charity met the messiah Frank riding on a horse with a naked woman rabbi. The messiah carried a torch and coined phrases good for all times. Secret Charity stood at a window on a winter night and saw the messiah get into his daughter's virginal bed. That was after he carried the Torah in a splendid ceremony whose cursed origin is remembered by the old people. In those turbulent years visions were seen as sunsets or rain are seen today. Secret Charity saw the *Shekhinah* in Exile and his heart broke at the injustice and he wanted to repair. He knew the world had to be purified to fit the letters of the Torah that were created before it was created. Because the messiah Frank converted, Secret Charity understood that messianism was a secret to be hidden and not to be revealed, and that there was an urgent need to be ravished, to confound the world to restore it to its origin. After the death of the convert messiah he stopped the moon for two whole days and the moon didn't set. Profoundly contemptuous of his ability to change the creation without knowing if that was the right way, he married a woman, went into the cellar, and lived buried there his whole life. He performed rituals, made calculations with the letters of the Torah, and discovered that in a certain order the words of the Torah sound like a melody that subdues all grief. From the rabbi of Lody, he learned to snatch shofar blasts and even groans of Jews who didn't know their groans were snatched by him. He decided to tell his fabrications only to himself; that way he could not believe them. Upstairs in his house, his wife sold bread, challahs, and bagels, and refused to admit the existence of her husband. She raised the sixteen children he'd beget in brief but very joyous sorties to her room, and there he also told her about his ravishment in the cellar, about the repairs he made in his solitude, and his children now and then were exiled to the cellar to take part in rituals where they saw their father connecting phrases. Then Secret Charity died full of yearnings for the messiah, and the most beautiful of his daughters was Rebecca Secret Charity whose grave shifted the day Rebecca Sorka was born a hundred years later. And Boaz Schneerson, the grandson and son of Rebecca, eighty years later, when he'll return safe from the war, will shout at his grandmother: Why didn't I die? I could have died, I had no reason to live when my friends died, why did you say Psalms for me all the days of the war and save me? and he hit her.

When Rebecca, the most beautiful of Secret Charity's daughters, was twelve years old and sister to eleven brothers and sisters whose number was to be great, the baker whose wife sang in the room next to the bakery died and the house collapsed on them. Rebecca went to the study house and asked some well-known saints who were steeped in prayer to tie themselves to the incense bowl and rise to heaven with it. They had to do that to challenge the Holy One Blessed Be He, she said, they tried to bribe heaven with anger, not supplication, their tears flow in vain and aren't seen there. Anger had always nested in her and the old men in the study house weren't embarrassed and tried to go back to their prayers. When she stood there her womanly fear was a soft and cunning loveliness and even the saints in their time couldn't resist the temptation and they thought forbidden thoughts about her body rustling with gloomy joy shrouded in dark ancient mold and steeped in passion. Rebecca's mother, who was busy selling challahs and bread and bagels, wanted to rid her daughter of the anger with a quick marriage. After refusing thirty-one fellows, some of whom even fled from her because of her venomous tongue, she saw her mother weeping. Her father had recently died and was buried standing up as he requested in his will, in a Christian-style coffin, and around her sat her fifteen brothers and sisters waiting to be married and she said: There's no point crying. Times were hard and because of concerns for livelihood and fears nobody went out then to pull out messiahs and Rebecca remained alone with signed and unsigned excommunications and declarations, many written by her thirty-one defeated suitors.

One day her mother took her to a distant city and gave her to some childless relatives. The old couple were dying in their room and Rebecca nursed them in their illness, started sewing in their workshop, and when they died, on that day and at that hour, she inherited the house with the little workshop next to it. Sitting in the workshop, Rebecca met one of the descendants of the converted messiah, nobody dared to get close to him even though he had returned to his faith long ago and grew cherries in a distant orchard. Rebecca betrothed herself to him and the city made a fuss. He was a quiet and strong fellow and was called Son of the Prostitute. Two days after the betrothal he vomited blood in the middle of the street and collapsed amid incomprehensible shouts. In death, his face was green and his eyes turned around. Rebecca carried him home on her back, took the washing implements and the shrouds from under the old folks' bed, washed his body, purified it, and wrapped it in a tallith. And then she wanted to marry her fiancé. Nobody had heard of marrying a dead man and so they called for Rabbi Kriegel, Rebecca's uncle who went from the Land of Israel to a place called America and stopped on the way to visit his family and was an expert in Jewish customs in Yemen, North Africa and Persia, and Rabbi Kriegel, who would later come to Providence, Rhode Island, brought evidence and proofs and when the marriage canopy was set up in the cemetery the men trembled and the women hid behind the trees and the rabbi stood there, his face grave, and married the son of the prostitute to Rebecca. She broke the glass herself and then said to the rabbi: In exile we married the *Shekhinah*, said my father, my father your uncle, married, in the cellar, a dead nation to restore her to life, and the people said: Behold, here lives a seamstress whose wedding speech is bewitchingly beautiful and she's a virgin and a widow and a divorcée.

Then Rebecca sold her property and disappeared. Once again these were times of riots, and aside from the singed smell of Jews, thirty four witches were also burned in the city square. Rebecca stood and looked at the fire. The women's eyes were laughing and when they burned they cursed and shouted, but they weren't afraid. A vindictive cold overflowed from them and singed the fire. What Rebecca saw, as she put it, was divine disobedience, she loved that sight, and felt as if she were looking in the mirror. Rebecca Sorka who came to the Land of Israel as Rebecca Schneerson would know that look inside her and would live with it all her life. Rebecca Secret Charity had curved, rounded cheeks, lips and some mysterious expression stamped in her gold-green eyes. She has a mute and ancient look, said one of the fellows who tried not to think of her body, she inherited that from the place where time was before it was created. In the cemetery she would eat her daily meal with her dead husband and feel close to her father, Secret Charity, with whom she could talk. He'd stand in the coffin and she'd sit on the edge of the grave and converse with him in a whisper.

She didn't stay very long in our city either but took off and opened a sewing shop in a nearby town. She learned to weave and embroider in a form that would match her father's phrases. She captured the melody for which the embroidery could have been a mantle, as if she was wrapping webs of dream on tree trunks. One day a Jew came to the city who was neither young nor old. Around his neck hung a sign that said: "Jew son of Jew, tortured and saved, please help this mute man who saw horror and returned from it," and it was signed by five well-known rabbis. Rebecca saw him walking in the street from the door of her workshop and the Jews read the sign, looked into his eyes where dread was frozen, tried to approach, and he repelled. Rebecca put on one of the wedding gowns she had just finished sewing and went outside with her assistant. Her dress dazzled the man's eyes. He came to her as if some force were drawing him to her. Tears flowed from his eyes and melted immediately. She saw Secret Charity and took pity on her father. The gown she wore was the gown of the daughter of Rabbi Yakub the Mountain. The stranger entered her workshop and the assistant brought him a glass of water. He looked at Rebecca and she felt he saw through her. The rhythm of his movements was like the melody that would bubble up in her when she sewed. Thus she understood that the man knew the melody of the holy books and the combinations of letters he may have inherited from her father. Since he wanted to speak he opened his mouth wide but no sound came out and then he again drank the water he'd been given. Rebecca, who had put on the wedding gown that wasn't hers, said: I'll call you Secret Charity after my father, his memory for a blessing, and the stranger nodded as if to say: that was, is, and will be my name. As a sign of gratitude, he fixed on her a tranquil look whose dread was dimmed for a moment; the look had a boldness that shook the folds of her gown and for the first time in her life she felt her body cling to the gown she was wearing, his look was demanding, soft and without pressure, and she saw his bitter despair, quiet and sure of himself. After they married they moved to our city to be close to her father's grave. She left as Secret Charity and returned as Secret Charity.

On the day she returned the man started speaking. He stood at the grave of Rebecca's father and suddenly words came into his mouth. At first he stammered, then he spoke fluently. Since for many years he hadn't talked, he couldn't tell exactly what had happened to him and after he mourned for the fate of the nation, he started seeing his wife with the same eyes others had seen her and he started longing for her. But he knew how to muffle his longing to intensify the malice and terror she sought in him. She gave him two living children and two dead ones. The two living ones were Rebecca and Joseph de la Rayna. She got special permission to name her daughter after herself, and she named her son Joseph de la Rayna. She wanted her son to be named after a bold sinner. Her son studied fervently with the persecutors of the messiah, refused to think of messianism that still filled hearts with savagery, lusted for the restrictions he imposed on himself and changed his name to Joseph Rayna and after he touched his mother and felt that like everybody else he also saw her as a naked woman, he went to another city, studied with a strict and handsome rabbi who spat whenever the name of those abominations was brought up by one of his students and forbade Joseph to mention his grandfather Secret Charity and his mother. Joseph married a young woman who brought a considerable dowry and a debilitating kidney disease and served as rabbi in a small town where he almost reluctantly inducted young men into the army of the Lord, put sticks in their hands, and even though he knew he was committing a grave sin, made them swear to wage heroic war and also added a formula of miracles he had learned from his rabbi; they had to learn to be defeated heroically, he said, but in his heart he dissented. When he was scolded for the sticks he gave the lads, he claimed he had a dream and in it he was told what to do, and he repented and to the day she died he didn't see his mother who poured into his soul the savage passions he wanted so much to suppress in himself. His wife groaned in her illness, his children were thin and pale, and he'd go to his sister Rebecca, sit with her, hold her hand, and fervently speak evil of his mother and his grandfather and say, Mother's damned sorcery His sister bore in her heart the memory of the nights when they would adjure angels and devils and call on Satan. Since she was also afraid of his passions, she married a man so short and anonymous she could barely have remembered his name if he hadn't been killed a year later by a group of bored priests when she was in the last months of her pregnancy. She gave birth to a son and sat with her brother who had meanwhile become a widower and asked on what day did Our Rabbi Moses die? When she found out that Moses died on the seventh of Adar, she measured the days and the hours, went to her mother, asked her to sew her a beautiful wedding gown and her mother didn't ask a thing and sat down and sewed her daughter a wedding gown, and on the seventh of Adar at one o'clock in the morning, Rebecca, daughter of Rebecca Secret Charity, died wearing the wedding gown her mother made her and that looked like a shroud more than a gown. Rebecca Secret Charity lived many more years, her husband died as he stood at the window and saw somebody who may have been the messiah Frank whom Rebecca's father once saw at that window riding a horse. Even as she was dying, Rebecca looked as beautiful as in her youth. A thin channel of malice was stretched on her face. She didn't die like other people but became transparent, and one day she smiled to herself, lay down in bed, and died. In her death she looked like a dead butterfly stuck with a pin on white paper. That was a winter day and rain sprayed and her son, who stood next to her, wept, and when he wept people saw the tears stop and stand still in the air between his eyes and the open grave. Jews said they didn't remember such an event since Secret Charity stopped the moon for three whole nights. The tears, said the Jews, looked like wooden birds; both birds and fixed, not moving. From the grave rose a tune. People thought it was the song of the choir of the Temple. Not far from there, Secret Charity was buried standing up. On his tombstone stood a crow, and that's how Secret Charity could have seen his daughter's grave.

Tape / —

Joseph Rayna grew up and didn't know his forefathers. His father pondered ancient books in secret and his mother was a thin; bright-eyed woman. Joseph was the sort of child you see sometimes at the entrance to Paradise: beautiful children, sorrowful and cruel, who serve as minions of gods who amuse themselves with them. His curls weren't shorn and his eyes were green-gold like the eyes of a demon and wrapped in ovalish ellipses like the rustle of a butterfly's wing.

When he attended heder, the children would make fun of him. He'd fix them with his serene and arrogant look and they'd be awed. Later one of the children said that Joseph had a green halo around his head and sometimes he'd turn himself into glass and you could see through him. But his eyes, said the child, remained opaque with savagery and they penetrated me and I saw dogs and wolves preying on humans on mountains I had never seen in my life.

Afterward Joseph's father moved to the other side of the city. He read ancient writings left by Secret Charity the father of his grandfather, who had to be willingly ravished to bring repair, and he converted.

Joseph's mother, busy with her embarrassing love for her son, followed her husband. Joseph was baptized and given a name nobody remembered anymore. Like his grandfather's father, her husband sat in a cellar and made kiddush secretly to keep the commandments of God in secret. Once when Joseph fell asleep in the park a group of young girls passed by him. They were shaken at the sight of him, stopped and looked at him. He woke up but didn't open his eyes and they couldn't resist the temptation and touched him, they shrieked and fled in panic. He opened his eyes slowly and looked serenely at their panicky running. Some man who stood there and caught them red-handed scolded them, one of the girls who feared the rage of her father, a district officer, said: He tried to play with us, and so a policeman appeared at Joseph's house and took him to prison. In prison Joseph was beaten and the police called him filthy Jew, and asked why did you do that, and he said quietly: I'm not a Jew and I'm not filthy and I didn't do a thing. The police were scared when he talked because he laughed as he spoke while they beat him harshly. His demon's eyes were shrouded in a harsh and indulgent dusk and they were forced to put him in solitary confinement. The girl who told her father the officer the story had a nightmare that night, repented, went to church and confessed, and the priest told her forget everything and say eighteen Ave Marias but she went to her father and told him. Her father, who was a person who had a conscience but also a position in the city, went to the prison and released Joseph. Outside, he slapped Joseph's face and said: I don't know who's lying and who's not, but you get the benefit of the doubt. Joseph looked at the hand that had hit him and said to the district officer: Some day you'll find that hand outside your body and whether there is a God or not, your punishment is already prepared and is found in the air, I see it and it will strike you. The man was stunned, and by the time he finished thinking confused thoughts that ran around in his brain, Joseph left. About a year later his hand was lopped off and then he was afflicted with a serious illness and when he searched for Joseph, he was no longer to be found. Then Joseph started writing his poems.

To get around himself like his grandfather Secret Charity, he wrote the poems in Hebrew, which he remembered from his days in heder. He would illustrate his poems with stylized drawings and his mother would hang them on cords around her bed. His father joined a group of monks who wanted to prepare the Holy Inquisition in the Ukraine and Poland. In those monkish rituals, Joseph's father was tortured with richly imaginative instruments of torture the monks tried to copy from old books brought from Spain two hundred years earlier. He sensed that by that humiliation he woke hidden forces from their slumber. Then the father disappeared and in a letter that came to Joseph's mother two years later the father wrote: Ever since I read Karl Marx, my world has changed. I abandoned the flayers who sell opium to the masses. The future is latent in the class war that will come and in which the working man will defeat the parasites, in the new world there will no longer be the exploiters and the exploited, no Christians, no Jews, no Muslims, but only workers and those who stand in the way of the revolution have to be burned. Yours always. Joseph's mother went on praying to the old gods, but her passion for her son made her feel very guilty and the fact that she didn't yearn for her husband sharpened those feelings and so, to justify her life, she joined a group calling themselves messianic Christians.

One night, Joseph's father appeared in workers' clothing, wearing a cap, and didn't ask to see his son at all. Joseph heard him come in and was filled with yearnings for his father. He put on his favorite clothes and all night long he sat on his bed and waited. He murmured Father! Father! But his father didn't answer. He was too proud to get up and go into his mother's room, he tried to cry but he couldn't. At dawn, he heard his father silently leave the house without telling him good-bye. Joseph buried his face in a bowl, poured cold water on himself, and stayed like that a long time, hardly breathing, and then he sneaked off, changed clothes, and went to his mother. He sat at the table, hit the tablecloth, and said: That man is no longer my father.

Joseph's mother told him that his father was confused, called her "Mezuzah," prayed in an embarrassing way, slept on the rug, didn't approach her, said he didn't remember if he had ever had a son, and looked lost and desperate in his new faith. Joseph said: There is no salvation, all those salvations have different names but all of them are nonsense, this life is what we have, not what doesn't exist. She wanted so much to hug her son but her hands didn't obey her. Afterward, she started bringing home her friends, the drunk old messiahs. They cultivated forbidden love with clamorous and wild lust and the children told Joseph, Your mother's a whore!

Joseph's poems became more and more glorious and the sight of his mother in the arms of old drunks eager to bring the messiah, stirred a strong impulse in him to honor the world with poems devoid of all connection with reality that would describe a nonexistent world. The house began to fill up with birdcages and every night one of the old boyfriends slaughtered one bird.

One moonlit night, for six straight hours Joseph's mother watched a slaughtered bird whose blood froze on the floor of the cage. The cage was gilded and the dead bird's mouth was sunk in a tiny saucer of water. When an old boyfriend came and started taking off his coat, she shifted her eyes from the cage and looked like a woman who had gone mad. The man was startled and threw his coat on the floor. Because he started cursing her, she spat on the coat, when he attacked her his foot hit the gold cage and the water spilled, he tried to steady himself, he touched the head of the bird, stumbled with a kind of swoop because he tried to keep from falling, his head split open and he died on the spot. Joseph came in and saw the chameleon of blood gushing from the old man's mouth. He went back to his room, took off his clothes, and fell asleep. In the morning, he didn't look at his mother. She hadn't budged all night. When she held out her hand to touch him, he started shrieking like a bird. She was very beautiful and pale then, at her feet lay the old man's body. His face was shriveled, his skin was yellowish, and his tongue was coiled outside. His wide-open eyes were gaping in an expression of extinguished amazement. His mother stood up, went to her room, and returned wearing a beautiful dress. Her face was serene but a spark of apostasy flashed in it. She giggled and Joseph saw her madness and thought: a demon entered her, even though he knew that demons don't enter human beings but live in them from birth. She said: Joseph my love, my old father is lying dead, I promised him to marry you off. She drank a little wine, looked at the old man, and said: I'm queen of the Hasmoneans. After they went down to the cellar she asked her son to lie down on his father's sanctification table where he'd perform his mysterious Sabbath rituals. She carefully placed four lit candles at the four corners of the table, looked at Joseph, held her hand out to him, and said: I'm the queen and I marry my lover. Joseph, whose wrath burned for his father, grasped his mother's hand and felt a mighty current of heat passing from her hand to his body. For a moment, the dress looked like a bridal gown and Joseph thought: maybe the moment of my death has come, when she asked, he broke the glass of his father's kiddush wine.

Joseph took the body of the old man wrapped in rags down to the courtyard, put it in a wheelbarrow, and took the corpse to the river. The municipal clerks came and asked him to help burn the cats because the plague was spreading to all parts of the city and the cats, they said, ate the mice the Jews burned in their houses to ward off the epidemic. After the cats were burned, he went down to the cellar and read the writings his father had left, read the "Words of the Days of the Lord" and felt vague but not intangible yearnings for the messiah Frank. He thought about the venom infiltrating his blood, about his mother, about the sorrow of his beauty, about his life, about his father, and thus he found out about Secret Charity and Rebecca Secret Charity. He went to the cemetery and searched for the tombstones. He found the graves of Rebecca and her father close together. He sat for hours and looked at the tombstone on the grave of Rebecca Secret Charity. He heard a tune coming from the grave and without moving he followed the tune and without moving his body he encountered daydreams that led him to realms where he had never been and on the tombstone, Rebecca's face began to be marked. At first the picture of her face was rough but it became clear. He burned a few branches in a pit, turned them into charcoal, and went over Rebecca's features with the charcoal, she looked a lot like him and didn't look like him at all. A painter of amulets came and copied Rebecca's face on paper and then went to his workshop and made Joseph an amulet of the face of Rebecca Secret Charity. And then came a letter from Russia with a curl of his father's hair. His father's will was addressed to his mother. Joseph wasn't mentioned in it. The letter said that Joseph's father plotted against some aged colonel and was sentenced to death. Not to be accused of devotion to a despicable religion, he hadn't said the *Shema Israel* and refused to accept forgiveness from a priest. When he was hanged, a writer wrote in the letter, he muttered words in Hebrew. He died as a revolutionary, said the letter, even though he was a troublemaking Jew all his life. Joseph went to the rabbi of the city and asked permission to be a Jew again. The rabbi blessed him and Joseph said: In fact, never was I anything, not a Christian, not a Jew, but the rabbi questioned him and received him back in the bosom of Judaism. Joseph's mother went on embroidering new royal gowns for herself that were just as beautiful and splendid as the arrogant words of her son. Joseph was sometimes her son, sometimes her husband, and sometimes an old adulterer who came to have sex with her. She tried to return to the Land of Israel and in her madness she began to recall her childhood there more vividly. She described Bethlehem, Jerusalem, and the Dead Sea to Joseph, and only years later, when he toured the Land of Israel, did he see how precise her description was and how correct were the details she painted and had never seen, and then she began to die and Joseph lay her in bed dressed in a royal gown, brought her hot tea and cookies, lay down next to her a whole night and hugged his trembling, weeping mother, who wanted to return to her homeland, and when she died, there was on her face a smile of bliss that Joseph had never seen there before. And then he wept. For the first time in his life, the handsome lad wept. He found a picture of his father, hung it on the wall, found a whip his father had kept in the cellar against the enemy who would come in the war between Gog and Magog and flogged his father's face until the picture was shredded. Joseph put on a splendid suit, shiny black boots, the black broad-brimmed hat of a Spanish grandee, picked up a short stick, and after arranging his mother's grave, he set out on the road.

In the women he found in his wandering, he sought the image of Rebecca that he wore as an amulet around his neck, but the only thing the women wanted from him was to be impregnated in his honor. When somebody in a tavern in Paris quoted a German philosopher who said that in vengeance and in love, women are more barbarous than men, Joseph said, and in life in general, and thought about the bold and roguish beauty of his great-grandmother.

Tape / —

In those ten years of wandering, Joseph Rayna begat fifty-two sons and daughters. Women saw him (as one woman put it in a letter preserved in the Nazi archive, titled: "Female claims concerning the imaginary virility of individual Hebrews who abused the innocence of Aryan women and bred with them with impure blood (A) Hebrew gestation, (B) contrition of Aryan women, (C) example of Francesca Glauson who delivered her son to the Gestapo in Bonn in 1942 and after the boy died, in an incident that took place in a camp, she described in detail the cunning of Hebrew wooing and taught a class of girls in Haan and later in Hamburg how to escape those and other errors, Heidelberg, 1944") as a harsh and deformed angel noble as beggars can sometimes appear: delicate and sensual. Women, says the letter of that woman, Frau Helma Rauchsfinger, loved the arrogant indulgence of Joseph Rayna, his self-confidence demonstrated in a generous and light manner. By submitting to that man—like other Hebrews—they thought they were fighting sins that wanted so much to be committed and overcoming themselves to be worthy afterward for somebody who would compensate them for all the suffering mixed with tormented joy, a person who would grant them bliss and safety and would wipe away the disgrace they had to experience in their flesh to know it up close. There's nothing like carnal experience to grant a woman what a man can get from abstract thought, maybe, writes Frau Helma Rauchsfinger, a woman can't even think an abstract thought, only abstract hating and loving are allowed both men and women.

When I read that material years later I laughed also because all my lovers were sons of Joseph and also because all my life I had been searching for Joseph and didn't find him and even though I thought he was my father, I was the only person of all the descendents of Joseph who couldn't really have been his son.

Joseph remembered all his offspring and all his women. He loved them no more than they loved him, but he understood their lust for him, just as the flower surely understands that not every butterfly is in love with it, but needs its smell and its pollen.

Joseph treated his women with a chivalry that many people in the late nineteenth century said had disappeared from the world. After wandering in many countries, he came to Denmark. In a fishing village in northern Jutland, where the Baltic Sea and the Atlantic Ocean meet, at different water levels, in a restrained dreary and bewitched light, the most enchanted light he had ever seen, he met a good-looking painter, fair and sickly, she sat in the strong cold, wrapped in a yellow wool shawl that glowed in the distance and painted purple waves where a scarlet hue poured a sense of ancient death and a boat, abandoned by gray-faced sailors who would never return, was bobbing on them. In the enchanted light, the painter looked like a goddess carved from rock. And she said: In that boat sits my brother, who disappears every winter and someday will return. Later on, she told Joseph that her mother brought soil from the Holy Land and her father was buried there, I think, she said, that he was a wandering Jew who came upon Jutland as a youth, and lived his whole life as a Dane but before he died he recalled his origin and asked his family to bury him on the Mount of Olives. She expressed no opinion on the subject and didn't care if her father was a Jew or not. She was a painter and painted the strong light.

As the winter intensified, they wandered to the Netherlands, went to Paris, from there to Italy, sailed to Alexandria and from there to the Land of Israel. Those were good times in Joseph's life. He listened to the painter's story about the paintings she was to paint, loved her exciting asceticism, her lack of lust for him, and her sharp and unique love.

She also feared he would fall in love with her as she loved. Her belly swelled and when they came to Jerusalem, she died in his arms in the seventh month of her pregnancy. Joseph buried her next to her father's grave. Then he toured the Land of Israel and saw the vistas described by his mother who was the last queen of the Hasmonean line. On Mount Tabor, he met a German aristocrat, Adorno von Melchior who wanted to establish a Jewish kingdom in the Land of Israel. When Joseph met Sarah, the wife of the German aristocrat, he felt he was liable to sin against his great love hung around his neck as an amulet. Joseph became the secretary of the aristocrat von Melchior. He wrote his letters in a florid handwriting and the woman he loved almost more than all the women he had met slept like an animal with mustached men who would beat her, Druses in white kaffiyehs with sullen eyes, and she said: I do that to forgive you for your errors, and the aristocrat said: She doesn't sleep with me because she's my wife and she loves me. Joseph understood the profound bond between the two queens he had met in his life, his mother and Sarah the wife of the aristocrat, and when he saw how much she yearned for him, he tried to touch her but she rejected him even though her womb began to stab and she wanted to give him children. After she told him things in that vein, Joseph wrote seventeen poems, each a description of a part of her body he didn't know. In one of the poems he described Frau von Melchior's neck as it looked in the transparent and strong Jerusalem light when her collar fell down and the cleft of her bosom looked like the winding of a beloved snake. The Frau loved the poems and he read them to her standing at perfect and absurd attention. On his travels for von Melchior he met the Jewish Pioneers who

were establishing the first settlements. He pitied their hard life and suffered the pain of their enslavement to Baron Rothschild. He liked to feast
his eyes on the handsome daughters of the settlers in the burning afternoons
of the Land of Israel. They were full of yearnings for their dream from the
moment they started building their miserable houses. With gloomy expressions, they tried to celebrate, contracted malaria, and wept.

A year Joseph Rayna stayed in the Land of Israel. He wrote in one of his
poems that the discovery of God among the rocks of the wasteland is testimony to the destruction of the nation. He parted from the farmers' daughters who, having no other songs, sang his songs as if they were hymns. He
parted from the wife of the German aristocrat who loved him so much she
fled for a month to some Druse sheikh who kept her tied to a rock in the
mountains of Transjordan. After leaving a bouquet of flowers on the fresh
grave of the Danish painter who had carried his son in her womb, he left
the Land of Israel, went to Alexandria, wandered to Persia, came to India,
and on a gloomy day in the winter of eighteen ninety-eight, he came back to
our city. He went to his mother's grave, and then to the grave of Rebecca
Secret Charity, the wife and daughter of Secret Charity, and closed himself
in a room and wrote elusive songs about the splendid, pedigreed, and desired
Land of Israel, and then he was discovered by a group of young people who'd
gather in the forest, wave flags in secret, and dream of a settlement in the
Land of Israel. In the exhausting cold, around a bonfire, the young people sat
and sang songs brought by an emissary. They sang Joseph's songs without
knowing it. Nehemiah Schneerson, the leader of the group, met Joseph in
the cemetery when he went to say kaddish on his father's grave and invited
him to tell his group about the Land of Israel.

In the group of young people craving salvation was one girl, a close friend
of Rebecca Sorka who would ascend to the Land of Israel on the first day of
the twentieth century and be called Rebecca Schneerson and would be the
mother and grandmother of Boaz Schneerson. Joseph looked at Rachel and
she trembled at the sight of the gigantic organ that was like a beam between the eyes of the well-born prince who told about the Land of Israel,
without emotion or yearnings. Shutting her eyes, Rachel Brin gleaned a
little of the light Joseph had taken from his great-grandmother's grave. The
light balled up into pain in her womb. When Nehemiah heard Joseph's
songs, which he had sung before without paying attention to their words

(Joseph read the poems despondently but unashamedly), the blood drained from his face and at that moment Joseph would look at Rachel. Nehemiah was furious at the songs without knowing why. He was a genius in the yeshiva who had disappointed his rabbi, who had expected great things from him. But when Joseph read all his poems and Rachel felt stabbings in her belly, at that very moment, on the other side of the city, at the entrance to the forest, Rebecca Sorka got up, and far from her friend Rachel, whom she had recently abandoned, looked out the window of her room and saw a light glowing in the forest but she didn't see its reflection in the windowpane. In the forest, naked winter trees awaited her. It was evening and she didn't leave her house. These things are the absolute truth. When she woke up in the morning, at the sight of the ceiling above her, she said to herself: My death canopy! In the shadows of the chiaroscuro, in her eyes black dogs were depicted slicing a person's body. The person she didn't know but for some reason she thought she should know him. After she dismissed the maid who came to brush her long delicate hair, she crossed her legs, sat up in bed, and thought about the man she had seen before in her fantasies, which were still too tormenting for her to think about now. So she formulated them to herself with fake indifference and wrote *Yeshua*, deliverance, on the wall of the stove bulging into her room.

When she came out of her room, she brushed her hair herself in the kitchen over the simmering skillets and pots and when she saw a fish fluttering in the sink she threw her hairbrush to the floor, wrapped herself in a coat, and went out. Her mother's eyes followed her from the window and then the fish was destroyed by a blow that shook the table. Rebecca's mother said to the cook: They've gone crazy, the young people, they just go to America, to the Land of Israel, got no manners, what a world! The cook didn't understand what she meant and so she didn't answer her. Rebecca wandered around aimlessly. The light she saw in the window still distressed her, but guided her steps. Even now, in the stinging cold, she knew precisely how beautiful she was. Her beauty was the source of her yearnings for herself. The taste of the night hadn't yet vanished and Rebecca hugged herself without emotion and her hands shook. She didn't shout because she knew that nobody deserved to hear her shout. Now the wind flew snowflakes to her. The houses flogged by the wind were wrapped in a dull glow of frost from the squashed sun flickering between the heavy weary clouds.

Rebecca took an apple out of her pocket, polished it on the fabric of her coat, and bit into it. The bittersweet apple pleased her. Snowflakes started sticking to her coat, she tasted in her mouth the jaws of the dogs preying on the man of her fantasy. Before getting up in the morning, before she opened her eyes, and as usual she counted the dead children she envisioned, she lost her reflection in the window and saw the dead in the obituaries plucked off the synagogue wall and hung over her bed. The dogs' teeth smelled like perfume. She put the dead children into a gigantic suitcase clasped with leather straps.

The suitcase exploded and eyes burst out of it. The eyes were words plucked from the obituaries, they flew in the room and sought a hold in the paper where they had been written before. The words would stroke her and torture and all the time she would think quickly: How many dead do I really know, and would count the dead and make a list on a scrap of paper and look at the list and say: There were more and I don't remember.

Rebecca spat an apple pip and trembled. A thin layer of ice covered the wooden boards that had been laid next to the houses. People passing by were so wrapped up that only their eyes showed. A carriage harnessed to a pair of horses wrapped in blankets passed by and sprayed mud. When she entered the copse, the top branches of the trees were already touching the shreds of sky sailing quickly under the heavy clouds instead of over them. By the time she climbed up the hill, the charm of the flying sky was extinguished and the air was layers of heavy, hostile gray. An unseen hand played with the sun that was seen flickering now and then, heavy, and immediately extinguished. At the moment of flickering, the top branches of the trees would move in the wind like sparks and she saw that as a sign that everything was crushed and broken and so she could blend more easily into something as hopeless and stupid as she. And then, as if by accident, she came to a river. The river was frozen and white. From the shadows of light she imagined she saw a cow munching snow across the river. Then she understood that those were linden trees. On the bank of the river, she stood still; I'm darling and wicked, she said, threw away the rest of the apple, took hold of the hem of her skirts, and lifted them.

Her naked skin was notched now by a strong burst of wind from the river. The cold was crushing and came with a blow of wind, and stabbed her. She felt a lust she had never known before. The wind ripped into her

body, through her groin gaping to it, and she felt the cold penetrate through
the veins into her innards, enter her belly, up to her throat and choke her.
Her nipples hardened and her body sharpened. Blissful now as never before, she was disgusted with herself, started smiling and the cold changed
to downy warmth. And again was sharp as a razor. Her heart beat hard. The
stone that had lain on her chest for many days began to melt. I won't have
to search for my other half anymore, she said to herself, if I stand in profile, they won't see me. The razor cut her, she put her hand on it and felt
the warm blood. She collected the blood in her hand and licked it. Across
the river, once again a linden tree disguised as a cow munched snow that
now turned black. She felt licentious and wonderful and wanted to marry
a woman. Threshold of my violated honor, she said with a splendor just as
false as the sudden bliss before that, I'm done with sadness, eighteen useless years old, the blood now flowed from her mouth, not from her groin.
Inside her, something refused to pity her and so she felt grateful. The kingdom of naked trees around her was a pierced slave to her, lords of cutting
down, glorious in evil, she said. An indifferent aristocratic and frosty wind
blew toward her. And then, on the verge of her bloody defeat, she undid
her skirts, let them drop, gathered her hair in the kerchief she kept in her
pocket, rubbed her hands with ice, put her frozen palms on her face, wiped
the blood of her groin from her mouth, and stepped back as if the river
were a lord and you couldn't turn your back on him. She thought: nothing
can ever again endanger my beauty, and the solitude filled her with joy and
the joy created tears that weren't tears of sorrow, they were red in the
extinguished and kindled light and they dropped onto the ice.

The tears of blood resurrected a passion in her she didn't remember
being in her, to know what would happen to her after the stone in her chest
melted.

Rachel Brin came to talk with her. She saw Rebecca light and hovering.
Rachel was her only friend. Maybe she pitied her. Later on, Rebecca would
say that Rachel was simply a necessary device to be saved at long last from
the need to know how unnecessary love is. New winds were blowing in the
land then, new books were read, people fled to distant places. The riots
left an unprecedented rage. In the attic, Rebecca found books her father
had inherited from Secret Charity, his great-grandfather. Rebecca saw
the world in translation. But as in translation, she couldn't pity the dead

people she collected in her boxes, not even her aunt who died near her.
Her grandmother's dying was a poem in a foreign language for her. So she
created her own language of syllables and taught it to Rachel Brin. Rachel
believed Rebecca that there were enchanted trees and when they'd lie in
bed under the obituaries and the words would fly in the room, some ancient anger that Rachel didn't know would slowly pass from Rebecca's
body to Rachel's. At the age of seventeen, Rachel Brin was what Rebecca
would never be, a love that came from Rebecca's body and disguised itself as a body. So, Joseph Rayna's unborn son burned so much in her.
With her good common sense, Rachel understood what others never did:
that Rebecca was able to love only a love that others loved for her. What
was strong in Rebecca turned dreamy and loving in Rachel. You've got to
learn how to stumble in order to triumph, Rebecca told her, but Rachel
found in her room only dry tears and wept them for two days. She looked
at the tears and saw the beautiful rainbows and couldn't appease Rebecca,
and when she started to weep the weeping of Rebecca's world, the letters
flew into Rebecca's eyes and she laughed. Rachel was startled and felt a
stab of a son in her womb. So, Rachel turned Rebecca's truths into a game,
and would help her cut out obituaries just because she didn't understand
why she did it. She spoke the language of syllables with her and didn't
know why. You have to learn to build yourself a coffin and live in it, said
Rebecca, but Rachel thought about beauty and about life. Rebecca learned
about her great-grandfather who was buried standing up, she wanted to
understand who was Rebecca Secret Charity who bought herself a shroud
at the age of fifteen, measured it, and kept it under her bed. Till the day
she died, she slept in bed as in a coffin, under the mattress, the shroud, the
soap, and the brushes hidden. She prepared her grave and wanted to live in
it. Nehemiah Schneerson, whose girlfriend intended to ascend to the Land
of Israel, saw Rebecca for the first time when she was gathering obituaries.
Nehemiah, the hope of the Gaon Rabbi, then fighting the struggle of the
gods against the prophets of Israel who, in his opinion, were bringing disaster and destruction onto the nation. He wanted to ascend to the Land of
Israel to restore the kingdom of David and Solomon, to grow Japhets and
Boazes and not to cultivate prophets and mourners anymore. Maybe that's
why he hated Joseph's embellished songs so much, even though they were
filled with freedom and love of the Land of Israel. He loathed the ethics

that brought a heavy disaster onto his people. Between Elijah and Ahab, he chose Ahab; between Saul and David, he chose Saul. He was born in the destruction, the prophets prophesied me, he said, I'll prophesy their disgrace, and the old rabbi wept.

So deep was Nehemiah Schneerson's grief for the destruction of Jerusalem that he couldn't understand that what he wept for was the image of Rebecca Sorka tearing down obituaries from the wall of the synagogue. He studied math and engineering and history and prepared himself to extinguish his wrath in decadent exile. When Rachel Brin wanted to join Nehemiah, the boys were embarrassed, but Nehemiah said: We're creating a new nation and woman is part of that creation, no more separation between men and women, together we shall strike the decadent exile. He didn't yet take off his hat, but he did stop wearing ritual fringes. And so Rachel met Joseph Rayna, who came to tell about the Land of Israel. They weren't scared by the stories of malaria and torments. What did scare Nehemiah were the songs, and when Rachel gazed at Joseph Rayna, who decided to drop anchor and stop moving, Nehemiah felt betrayed. That didn't excite Joseph, and when Rachel watched disaster approaching her body, Nehemiah saw songs that poured a cunning sweetness and didn't touch distress. As far as he was concerned, the songs were artificial fire dreamed by the locomotives he saw at the edge of the city. What does a locomotive dream? he asked. Saints weep in cellars, he said, they don't seek a locomotive's dream. And when three hundred Hasids stood on the roofs and shouted "Our God is the Lord," and tried to mediate between the nation of Israel and its Maker, Nehemiah felt betrayed because of the shouting on the roofs and because of the songs and because of the disgraceful beauty of Joseph Rayna, who told more about himself than he told about the Land of Israel. He doesn't belong to her, thought Nehemiah. The shudder in Rachel Brin's body infected Nehemiah and he didn't understand that what he felt was fear. The Land of Israel of the songs looked like a fraud to him. The rattle of Purim noisemakers mustn't be adorned with yearnings. He of course didn't understand then that he was jealous of his wife's lover.

When Nehemiah spoke of the weeping eye of God, Joseph said: I thought you killed God, and Nehemiah thought: Maybe I did, but your songs, he said, they're words about nothing and Joseph said: So what? Why should they be about something? I don't yearn for anything, Nehemiah. And all that time, Nehemiah didn't sense the electricity between Joseph and

Rachel Brin. He thought: There's no grace, there's no messiah, there's no
real foe, only words and anger. He didn't know those awful words flying in
Rebecca Sorka's room and seeking a foothold in a reality they didn't deserve.

Tape / —

Many years later, when Ebenezer sat in Rebecca Schneerson's room at
the settlement, after forty years had vanished, he'll tell his mother about
what I heard from a dying Jew in Block Forty-six. The dying Jew told me
the history of a monk he called "our pauper monk, crown of the gentiles,
our noble brother Avidius, man of dreams, flint, and humility." In a letter
Avidius wrote to a woman he had loved many years before, and now she
was forbidden him, he tried to describe his feelings in the eight years he
had sat bound to a stone pillar in the Sinai Desert. He described his torments, his endless gazing at the heat, the wind, the rain, the birds, the
desolation, and after five years, he wrote, the silence passed, the flesh
passed, leaving delight spinning rustling and unseen webs, both dark and
pure. As if the dread were tamed to silk of stones that dropped and melted
in the heat and were heavenly dust on the earth disappearing under the
stone pillar and throughout the expanse, silence reigned, and love sprouted
from the heat and the silence, unbearable, independent love, without flesh
or spirit, generous love without slander, a rare touch of a butterfly's legs in
a fire that doesn't destroy but flickers, taming sorrow to scan silently the
reality you're part of and it is no longer in you, only a prayer prayed by a solitary angel for you and strong and wonderful bliss fills the heart, and Rebecca
will then tell Ebenezer: I know, for eight years I wept for Nehemiah, the
nonlove I found in the river, and then I came into being without compromise
and it's impossible, isn't it, Rebecca will say then, impossible to try to extinguish the force of love in love!

Tape / —

The love Rachel Brin saw in Nehemiah's eyes was alien to her passion and
yet like it. She pondered the imbroglio she had come upon and thought,
Rebecca is busy rambling after herself and so I'm left alone, I came here as
her emissary, Nehemiah is probably thinking of her but saying the words

of Joseph, Joseph is looking at me, while I'm giving birth to his sons, maybe Nehemiah hates in Joseph his nonexistent love for Rebecca?

When she walked, she heard steps behind her. The rain that fell earlier had stopped. She felt silence. There was a bridge there and she stopped on it. Joseph approached and clung to her. They started flowing with the ice floes in the river that looked as if they were striking one another and stopped flowing separately. A hot, round ball took shape in her. That was her first kiss, and even though she was trembling, she didn't feel love. She was scared by how much her body longed for the man and how empty her heart was. On her retina she could have described his body to herself through his clothes. Later, they would meet in remote barns or secretly in Joseph's room, at night, and he taught her body to love delicately, but also when they were together they felt that some alien hand was playing with them. When she became pregnant, she went to her sister in the big city. Her sister took her to a doctor. The doctor only confirmed what she knew. She returned to the city and suggested to Joseph to run away. But he said: I've run away enough.

When it became known, Rachel's mother summoned Uncle Zelig, whom the Russians called the Bear, and the Jews called him Secret Glory. Broad-shouldered he was, with a mighty body and little eyes like the eyes of a mouse, watery and blue, he lived alone in a distant garden, guarded it, prayed a lot with the few words he knew. For twenty years he served in the Czar's army and it was said that he slaughtered people in the wars and didn't forget whence he came. His niece Rachel he loved more than anything. He came to the city bringing with him a goat that he said was touched by a peacock's feather. The golden fleece will soon be found. The newborn will be named Secret Glory after me, he said, but he went in vain to Joseph's house: Joseph wanted to marry Rachel. The city concocted rumors and everybody accused Rebecca whose grandmother's grandmother was Rebecca Secret Charity. Rabbis wrote bans but when Zelig asked them to stop they did because for a long time Zelig Secret Glory had considerable strength, was simply one of the Just Men. Rachel's parents came out of their quarantine, and a Russian sorcerer brought by Rachel's mother to sprinkle sulfuric acid on the threshold of Joseph Rayna's house looked like a scared vulture, and the house seemed wrapped in flames, but Joseph told them: Why are you

acting like fools, I'm marrying Rachel Brin and nobody will stop me especially since there's no need to try to persuade me. When Rachel was with
him, she learned to shut her eyes and think she was Rebecca. Now, when
there were no more passions left in her, she went to the wedding canopy
as the mother of Rebecca's son. Rachel's mother agreed to invite Rebecca
to the wedding. Rebecca came with her parents. The house was already
humming with people. That was a disaster everybody watched joyfully. Mr.
Brin was rich enough to evoke envy. Two days before the wedding drunken
Cossacks had beaten two Jews in the street. The police who came six hours
later seemed to be searching for hens and beat Jews at random to distinguish
between their profound contempt and the Cossacks' enraged drunkenness.
In Rachel's house, nineteen of the twenty Klezmers were playing, one of
them lay dead in the cemetery. But the celebration couldn't be postponed.
Rebecca's father looked at his daughter and said: You're dressed as if you
were the bride, and she answered him: Maybe I really am?

Rebecca embroidered her gown with her own hands; her mother envied
her. In Rachel's house, brandy, food, and baked goods were served mag-
nanimously, everybody started hugging one another and guests came from
far away in carriages and Rebecca looked at her father. When she got her
period at the age of fifteen, she thought the blood gushing from her was
the blood of her parents, and now that it came out, I'm not anybody's anymore, she said then to herself. She recalled that now, as she walked to
Rachel's house. Rebecca's father said: That's nice, what you made, and Mr.
Brin wrung his hands and said: They killed the flute player but what, if we
wait until they don't kill Jews, we won't be able to get married and there
won't be new Jews to kill. Nehemiah stood with his group of lads. When he
saw Rebecca he trembled a moment and suddenly understood his anger at
Joseph. From far away, Rebecca saw her bridegroom's back. The position
of his back was brittle, tense, and yet Rebecca could discern, reluctantly,
the nobility and remorse in it. Rachel kissed Rebecca, whom she hadn't
seen for a long time, and burst into tears. From far away, Joseph's back was
still taut. Rachel tried to say something in the language of syllables, but the
syllables flew away from her and she couldn't find them. She was wearing
a beautiful and ancient wedding gown whose tassels and fringes were made
of gold embroidery. Rebecca asked where the beautiful gown came from
and Rachel said that her father found that old gown in the home of a poor

sage, who told him that in that wedding gown of Rebecca Secret Charity, the daughter and wife of Secret Charity, Joseph's grandfather, had walked to her wedding canopy. Secret Glory stood next to Rachel's father. To Rebecca his eyes looked like small chameleons. When he looked at her, like many others, he too felt some uneasiness, because he was embarrassed, he started moving here and there and after she looked straight at him, he lowered his eyes and somebody said to him: That's Rivkele, Rachel's friend and Rebecca corrected angrily: Rebecca!

The young people said: An anarchist poet entered the kennel and will bark! And they laughed when Rebecca came back to the room, one of the men looked at her who laughed at Joseph brashly and said: Look, a wild man is tamed! She took out a demon who was with her from the river and waved it at him. He stood still, and the glass of brandy in his hand was emptied without him drinking from it. The fellow looked at the emptied glass and was terrified. Rebecca turned away from him and once again her look was drawn to the taut back of the bridegroom. Rachel's kiss and weeping were additional proof that maybe the river didn't stop for the disaster. The stone came back and lay on her chest. With her kiss, Rachel stuck Joseph to Rebecca's lips. Joseph, who felt the sudden silence, turned around and saw the glass that was emptied and then saw a woman's back slipping out but when he wanted to understand what happened, new guests entered and started hugging him with clumsy wildness. Nehemiah came to him and congratulated him. You're very polite, Mr. Schneerson, said Joseph. Once, Joseph added, I saw a wedding in your Judea, the bride was covered with dust. In your holy books didn't you read about dust? Will love of Zion wipe out the dust? A destruction isn't only demolished palaces, a destruction is also endless misery. Then came a rabbi riding on a donkey. In his modest coat a radish somebody gave him. He smelled of garlic. The bride curtsied in the dust and her eyes were yellow. They threw rice at them. The donkey brayed instead of the musical instruments they didn't have, the canopy was put up in the field. The bridegroom smashed a glass but was afraid to break it for real. I wrote them a song and they still sing it to this day.

Rebecca went to Rachel in the next room. In the mirror, Rachel's mother was seen putting a pin in her hair. Rachel fell into Rebecca's arms and wept again. Rachel said: This is your son, Rebecca! Not mine, we've had a disaster! Rebecca shook her head angrily and said: This is your coffin, Rachel, not mine. He's got fifty-two sons and daughters, said Rachel. He's a pedigreed little god who spawns and begets all over, and Rebecca said: You're a fool, Rachel Brin, you're a foolish and contemptible little girl. Love your husband! What else is left for you to do? And Rachel who was offended, said with a wicked smile taught her by recent months: See what a disaster the emissary from the Land of Israel your Nehemiah has brought on us!

Mine?

Not yours?

Rebecca was amazed at the new strange phrase, but she cherished it in her heart and didn't say a thing.

She mingled with the crowd. Nehemiah tried to fish out her profile. The musicians played with fake gaiety. Rebecca saw a back hugged savagely by uncles and cousins and relatives. Violins ripping. Outside, it started snowing. In the big room there was a sour smell of human beings, and wine and pots of delicacies and flowers. On the wall hung a charity box of Rabbi Meir Ba'al ha-Nes and underneath it was a flowerpot with a bush in it. Rebecca was pushed to the wall and stood with her head next to the box and her legs touching the bush. Now Joseph and Rachel stood close to one another and four men held the wedding canopy over them. One of the men was Nehemiah. When she looked at Joseph, she knew him from her dreams, that was the black man sliced by dogs. As her lover was pledged to Rachel, Rebecca saw the tears Rachel tried constantly to wipe away, and then Joseph noticed Rebecca. He noticed her when the rabbi talked and he put the ring on his bride's finger and said: Behold, you are consecrated to me, and then for the first time in his life, Joseph Rayna fell in love with his grandmother's mother's mother who stood and looked at him now with a gleaming smile on her lips. Because he turned pale, Rachel held him up, she looked here and there, and saw Rebecca. As soon as the ceremony was over, Joseph was cut off from his bride.

Rebecca left the room a few minutes before the end of the ceremony. She passed through various rooms, crossed the kitchen, and went outside. Beyond the paved square stood the old house where she had sat years ago with Rachel and talked about bewitched trees. Outside there was an intense chill and all she wore was a thin dress. She climbed the stairs of the old house and everything was empty except for some old pieces of furniture and objects tossed here and there. She went into the frozen sewing room and sat at the window. She picked up a few old bags and cloths basted coarsely, reeking of an old summer, and wrapped herself in them. She was warmed a little, but the stone didn't melt in her chest. She put her face against the windowpane and looked outside. Snow fell and a rooster came out, pecked in the snow, and pranced back to his shelter. Clouds touched the chimney of the new house and from the windows you could see the festivity through the mists coming together and parting again, when she looked at the rooster, she recalled how she held Joseph's hand before she was born. When the rooster came out again, Joseph was standing in the door of the room and she didn't even turn her face to him; in advance, she knew every movement he'd make. At that time, Rachel said: Apparently he's scared, he'll come back soon, he's not used to getting married, veteran libertines don't get married every day and everybody laughed and drank and she left the room. Joseph dragged a broken chair and sat down behind her. He took a bottle of vodka out of his pocket and started drinking. Downstairs in the yard Rachel appeared in her bridal gown. Her eyes looked around until she raised them and her look met Rebecca's eyes in the window. Trembling with cold, she hugged her shivering body. For a moment, her look froze, then a painful smile crept over her face, her hair scattered in the wind, her gown was covered with sticky snow, and she turned back to the house.

Joseph Rayna's lips were seared, he couldn't think. All he had left in the world was painted on the amulet around his neck and on the back turned to him. Rachel went into the house, asked the musicians to stop a moment and announced with a choked and giggling laugh that her bridegroom had apparently drunk too much and with all due respect to the guests was already in bed and snoring like a slaughtered bird and please excuse him, and the musicians started playing again and Nehemiah looked into Rachel's eyes and was silent and pale and Rachel went up to her room, shut the door, locked it, lay in her bed and instead of crying, she burst out in a laughter that was quite different from the laughter that choked her before; she laughed so wildly she had to bury her head in the blanket.

In the attic of the old house sat Rebecca Sorka. For one moment she turned her face and looked at the handsome man sitting there. She found a sooty old lantern, Joseph gave her matches, and she lit it. He held out the amulet to her. She looked at it a long time and said: That's me? And he said: Yes. She touched his hand and said: You've got a wife in bed, Joseph, and we're brother and sister. Because she knew Joseph's face so well and he knew her face so well, there was no point talking. When they held hands, they felt the guile of the loving couples who had toiled for generations to permeate the two of them with that longing, destruction, and disgrace, the profound and sublime loathing they felt for themselves. The lamplight moved in the wind winding in the frozen room. Outside the snow went on falling. Rebecca said: Now go to Rachel, tomorrow night I'll wait for you at the bridge.

The next day she waited for him wrapped in a coat. The cold was intense. Rebecca told Joseph about the river. Holding hands and walking along the path covered with blackened snow, they felt that their distress didn't humiliate them enough. I don't want any child from you, Joseph, said Rebecca, why did you come and kill the river for me?

Joseph returned to Rachel, who knew how to accept him with untormented betrayal. And the next day, Joseph and Rebecca went to the small station on the outskirts of the city. Trains would slow down when they passed our town, only one small train a day would stop at the station that didn't even have a name. After the big curve, beyond the poplars, the trains would speed up and fly to unimagined distances that Joseph knew and Rebecca didn't. When Rebecca was a fourteen-year-old girl she saved the son of the stationmaster from being trampled. She didn't mean to save the child. The guard was a drunken lame Ukrainian called Jewish Death. The ant has five noses, said the Ukrainian to Rebecca and Joseph who had come to the station and gone up to the room of the bats, upstairs, and lovers he said, have only one limb. Then he sat in his chair, laughed, and drank his brandy. Joseph and Rebecca sat upstairs and held hands. Downstairs, the slow trains moved and the Ukrainian would bring them cookies and wine. A few days later, Rachel came. She found the two lovers holding hands and looking at one another. To translate the distress of the silence, she moved toward them stunned, hunched up in the pincers of their hands holding one another, and said: What dependence, Rebecca! That silence! And she put her head on Rebecca's lap and stroked her own womb and looked into Joseph's face and her cold heart was calm. Rebecca looked toward Joseph's son in Rachel's womb and thought of the dead children she had packed in the suitcase. Joseph looked at Rachel trying in vain to remember who she was. Rebecca pushed Rachel off her and said to Joseph: If you really love me, give your wife what she deserves, I have to know . . . Joseph said: I want you, but she laughed in his face, felt Rachel's womb, and said: First be a father of your son, beget him for me, too, and she left. Rachel got up and stood facing him. She said to him: You don't have to pretend anymore, Joseph. But to save something that died in me, at least embrace what you left in me. They hugged and then Rebecca shouted: I've got to see love, and they hugged again and then Joseph saw Rebecca in front of his eyes and was with her. Rebecca stood in the next room in the window bay overlooking the tracks and the avenue of poplars and looked at them. With all her might, she pitied Rachel's love for Joseph, but along with love a profound contempt was anchored in her that had always been embedded in her and now found a correct spelling. She said to herself: an ancient contempt came to me from a distant grave, and then the river laughed in her.

And the city concocted rumors. The mothers of Rachel and Rebecca locked their houses, put down the shutters, sat in Rachel's house, and wept. Together they sent their husbands to the rabbi of the island, delegates went out urgently to sages in other cities, and Nehemiah Schneerson leading his group of youngsters would try not to hear, not to know, to console himself with love of the Land of Israel, and at that time the three would walk in the forest, pick blackberries and red berries, and in an abandoned hut that Rebecca knew from her torments in the forest, Joseph and Rebecca would love in silence, Joseph trying to embrace Rebecca, press her to him, kiss her, and she let him but only a little and Rachel pleads with Rebecca to give Joseph herself and Rebecca despises Rachel and says, Why? Why?

One night, Rebecca's father came into her room and hit her; she slipped away from him and escaped. Rabbis wrote excommunication decrees and Rebecca returned to her hut. Rachel sat outside and Joseph was inside and made a fire of pieces of wood he had previously gathered. Rebecca let him undress her and stood before him naked. The fire enhanced the beauty of her body. She shut her eyes and let him stroke her. She didn't want to see the sight of her body in his eyes. I won't allow any love to confound the high price I set on the beauty I feel, she said. Shutting her eyes she could have been destroyed by gods Joseph said were in another location, and returned to the grave of her disappointments that were always her life itself. I'm part of the night, witches burned in fire, sleep, dreams, the pallbearers

of Rebecca Secret Charity, she said, and Joseph was willing to die just to be
borne by her, but he was afraid of the lofty words buzzing in his temples.
Rebecca knew there wasn't even one corpse who would be ready for love like
Joseph. Suddenly she abandoned her body, a wild joy she didn't know except
from dreams came to her, Joseph's hands came, his body came close to her,
blood started flowing when he came close to her, seasonal blood, she said,
seasonal blood, Joseph, and he didn't see a thing, a forbidden woman, said
Rebecca. And suddenly a tremor went through Joseph, Rebecca laughed in
his face, he saw the laugh, hit her, and she dropped down, laughing, Rachel
looked on hypnotized, and the blood still flowed and Rachel thought to herself: Who do I love, Joseph or Rebecca, and she knew that the hatred she felt
for them was a kind of irreparable love. So she didn't know who she wanted
to kill, and she hugged her son in her womb and called him to herself Secret
Glory and Rebecca dreams, despicable in her own eyes, hugged in Joseph's
arms, looked into his eyes and he is in her and her blood flows, and she
gives birth to dead sons, all of them in her suitcase, and he still doesn't see
the blood, and then Rebecca gets up and Joseph is still writhing on the
ground, and she says: You're a fool, Joseph, you're the most beautiful man
I ever met in my life, you kill you in me, and she started getting dressed.
When she was dressed, Rachel came in and Joseph looked at her with the
pain of his tormented body. Rebecca looked at Joseph and Rachel and they
looked so distant, so threatening in their soft words.

In that longing, she was afraid she'd be a mirror there and see herself.
In her eyes, they were so full of a future she didn't want to be in. Such a
love mustn't be fostered because it's against all possibility of real disgust,
she said and left. Joseph ran after her, pleaded, but Rebecca strode quickly
and without turning around. From the windows of the city, frightened faces
peeped out and contemptuous looks were hung on her and on Joseph running after her. Rebecca's mother put her head in the oven and Rachel's
mother took her out of the oven, poured water on her, called the doctor,
and Rebecca's father sat cross-legged and started praying, even though he
hadn't prayed for years, and Rebecca walked to Nehemiah's house, and
Nehemiah Schneerson's mother was knitting a shawl and looked outside and
saw Rebecca knocking on the gate of the house. Nehemiah had dressed
ahead of time, as if he were waiting for some sign. A few days before, when
he saw Joseph walking around like a blind man, he wanted to mourn and

then he went to the forest and vowed revenge against Judea for preventing him from avenging the cursed Exile, and said: In blood and fire Judea fell, in blood and fire Judea will rise, and now, dressed in warrior clothes he stood in the door he opened to Rebecca.

From his mother, Nehemiah inherited the intelligence of the quiet defeated people who fabricate small consolations. Rebecca said: If you want you can marry me, Nehemiah, I'll be your wife all the days of my life, and only yours, but if you don't want to, tell me now.

Later on, she told Nehemiah what had happened to her in the three days since Rachel's wedding. He was silent, sipped the tea his mother served, and his eyes filled with unshed tears. He didn't say a thing. Then they drank wine and the two of them were gripped by some spasm that united them so profoundly they had to embrace. And Rebecca felt peace for the first time in her life. For a moment she loved Joseph with an impossible love and hated him with an impossible hate, and that was the last time she thought about Joseph with that passion and disgust that had filled her from the moment she saw him at Rachel's wedding, and until her grandson Boaz was born she no longer yearned even one minute for the handsome man who was her brother, her cousin, and her only lover. When she felt peace, Nehemiah stopped being afraid of her. She drank wine and began talking gaily, she said: Does my educated lord know why God lays tefillin? Nehemiah looked out the window. In the window Joseph appeared. She said: Because it is written, The Lord hath sworn by his right hand. Does my young lord know that King David, like Joseph Rayna standing there outside, sang a song in his mother's belly? It is written that he sucked from the breasts of his mother and looked at her breasts. Don't blush, lad. And then he started singing. And it's written, Bless the Lord O my soul and forget not all his benefits, said Rabbi: that's because he made teats instead of intelligence. Not I, Nehemiah, the rabbis said: That's so he won't look at her groin. Don't blush! Nehemiah, who had almost not listened to her, said: You'll love me Rebecca, and she said: Maybe, maybe. I told you about David because of my violated honor, we'll go to America and start a new life. And Nehemiah said: No, to the Land of Israel, and she thought: We'll go there and from there we'll go to America. She didn't like to argue with him.

Joseph and Rachel asked for compassion, but she banished them. I'll bear the hatred that hates the only love I could have had, she said. There

were pogroms then and people hid in their houses and Nehemiah went out
with his group to defend the lives of the people and they were forced into
exile for fear of the authorities and Rebecca followed him, and after the
ransom was paid, people said: Something new happened to the Jews, and
Rebecca laughed, it was because of her hatred that those things had come,
and then Rebecca and Nehemiah got married with a haste caused by the
time and the dread. Hasids again went up to the roofs and shouted to God,
Secret Glory died choked by a drunken Cossack who beat up a Jew, and
two wrinkled old women died holding onto one another in terror. A house
was burned and the smell of its smoke filled the street and a child was
thrown into the fire. Only relatives were invited to the wedding of Rebecca
and Nehemiah, there were no musicians, people were busy fixing their destroyed houses, and Nehemiah told them: Why fix what will be destroyed
again, go to the Land of Israel, and they laughed at him. But Rebecca's father came at night, hugged his daughter, touched Nehemiah's arm, and said:
Maybe that's a vision of death, maybe this nation can't be revived, but go and
erect a house for me there. Rebecca's mother stood on the side and didn't
say a word. Something deep and old rested on her beautiful face. They had
to slip out of the city at night. An old carter took them over the border. The
new arrest warrant against Nehemiah had been delayed in a tavern where a
clever Jew deceived the officials with cheap brandy. The Ukrainian who
wanted to reward Rebecca for his melancholy kept the drunk until morning.
After wandering a lot, Rebecca and Nehemiah came to the city of Trieste.
Rebecca went to the coffinmaker and told him of the coffin she wanted for
her husband and the splendid coffin of her husband, when her stomach
swelled up, she took with her on the ship. As the distance between her and
Joseph grew, she could love him like a shadow blended with who she once
was. Now Rebecca Schneerson was taken to the land she didn't want to go
to with a fetus in her belly and a husband in a coffin.

Tape / —

The journey to Jaffa took ten days. The sea was strong, and near Crete,
the stairs broke and the sailors stretched ropes along the moldy corridors,
and in the crowded halls people lay groaning. Rebecca sat on deck and
knitted a scarf. The waves would break at her feet and didn't touch her. A
Russian officer, splendidly dressed, brought her a cup of tea and said: For

a brave and beautiful lady. She looked through him and saw the breakers stopping at what could have been her steps. Twice a day she would go down to the belly of the ship and sit at her husband's coffin and then would go up and sit on deck. Looking with meticulous indifference at the Christian pilgrims, the Hasids in black caftans, shouting and screeching, and the Pioneers who would recite the moldy poems of Joseph Rayna and long for a place they had never been.

The morning they left Alexandria for Jaffa, the storm stopped. The seagulls danced dances woven of ancient and stylized geometry over the two masts where endless banners in various colors waved in the wind. Rebecca wondered if the seagulls didn't see an ancient Phoenician ship now, and then, as she was stroking her belly, she wanted to sacrifice to the god still remembered only by those eternal birds. But the times of the birds and the times of the passengers were different. The phenomenon of the ship would pass against the eternity of the celestial fabric and the sight only filled her with yearning for another reality, for a place you don't long for and where you don't return. America, discovered by her grandfather's grandfather, Rabbi Kriegel, on his journey from Hebron, was the realm of her dreams when she went to Nehemiah's house and asked him to marry her. She wanted to be reborn. Even though she had never seen Rabbi Kriegel, she remembered him as a disillusioned man who married Rebecca Sweet Charity to her dead fiancé. Thinking about America, she understood the Hasids and pilgrims coming to the Land of Israel to visit the graves of the dead, but she couldn't forgive the Pioneers for the insolence fostered in them by yearnings as if that place hadn't died two thousand years ago. The seagulls were an ancient sign that the time of the Phoenicians and the raging gods still existed despite the dreams of the Pioneers. The birds tried to bribe the sky with their satanic and delicate flying but her husband's coffin was launched precisely because of the hidden wisdom of the seagulls. The sea grew calm. Her belly seemed too heavy. The eternal glass of tea brought her by the Russian officer was too sweet and in front of her was the saltiness of the water that almost touched her feet, but stopped just before her. The shore approached. The pilgrims sang excited songs whose words they read in ancient books smelling of dank gray they held in their quaking hands. The Pioneers donned berets, white shirts, and coats. Wrapped in bliss they looked toward the light strewn on the long sandy shore. When the ship dropped anchor opposite the hill of Jaffa, Rebecca folded the scarf she had knitted, straightened up and stood at the ship's railing, and her gigantic belly touched the steel cables. In the distance, boats were seen rowing toward the ship. In the boats sat sailors with thick mustaches and big bodies. The sky was clear and waves struck the sides of the ship that dropped its anchors and hooted. The light was clear but shrouded with a certain stiffness, which even now, on the first of January, in the year nineteen hundred, looked both pungent and clear. Rebecca looked at the hill. She saw mosques and churches, and beyond the mosques and the churches sands stretched to the horizon. A caravan of camels raised clouds of dust and a few distant treetops sweetened the bitterness of the yellow desolation. A smell of lemons and sea salt rose to her nose. She felt no sense of returning home. Never had she felt she had come to a more foreign place.

The sailors carefully put her down into the boat. Then the coffin was brought down and placed next to her. Her swollen belly and her husband in the coffin awed the sailors and they were afraid to look straight into the beautiful face of the woman to whom the Russian officer offered a flower before she was taken down from the ship. She despised their fear of the evil eye but in her heart she appreciated their pretense of indifference. She always loved events devoid of value that were played with too much importance. Someday she would tell Boaz that in the end a state is a flag with a land.

The sailors rowed vigorously toward the port and when she came to the shore, a Turk in a green uniform with a red tarboosh was waiting there, and behind him stood a barefoot Arab lad holding a somewhat torn parasol over the head of his master. The Turk was holding a truncheon in his hand and tried to smile at her. He stood in a vacuum strictly preserved by both Turks and Arabs. Wherever he walked, he was surrounded by that reverential vacuum. Behind him, near the wall of the big mosque, sat Arabs smoking narghilas; not far from them stood skinny horses whinnying and stamping their feet. A gigantic pile of oranges was seen, and behind it, against the background of a small shop, two skinned oxen were hung on hooks. The blood poured down to the ground, but because of the blinding light she didn't see the blood. Her slippery jumping made the Turk under the parasol bend down a bit, and he leaned aside with ostentatious exaggeration. He said in Arabic: A beautiful woman for a dead Jew. The Arabs who couldn't come close to him laughed in the niche of the mosque and one of them laughed and started choking. The smoke of the narghilas flowed into them like snakes. The Turk, maybe he thought they were laughing at him, hit one of the Arabs with his truncheon. The Arab fell, his legs got wound up in each other, and his white tongue twisted out. Two coals sprayed on his dress and somebody crushed a sharp-smelling lemon and put out the sparks. The Arab tried to laugh in his fear but the Turk farted in his face and the Arab swallowed the moldy air, lifted the sole of his foot, showed it to the Turk who was no longer paying attention to him. And he shouted: I'm your sole! And through his lifted foot and the truncheon that very slowly returned from its blow, Rebecca's skirt was visible to the Arab. The Turk withdrew, made room for the beautiful lady, and two barefoot sailors carefully put down Nehemiah's coffin. The Turk said with philosophical restraint, in French: We're born and we die. And he stared at Ebenezer who was still in the sixth month of his gestation.

A Jew in a white suit, and only when he got close did she see how dirty its cuffs were, approached and called the two sailors. From the distance, Rebecca had seen him wiping the sweat from his forehead after he took off the straw hat, and his watery eyes trying to hint something to her. When he started playing with coins he took out of his coat pocket and bouncing them one by one, she caught the lust the coins evoked in the eyes of the sailors and so she could calm down.

The Jew with her concluded the negotiations and approached her. Once again he took off his hat and said: Don't worry, madam, a room is waiting for you, if it can be called that, in a hotel, and tomorrow, the funeral will be held. And Rebecca said: I'm not worried, sir. I'll stay a while and then I'll go to America. The Jew wiped his sweat again, took out a chain of amber beads, played with them a little, and muttered: I don't care where you go, madam, or when. Jews come and Jews go. For me it's the same money. Permission for your husband's coffin is just as expensive as the return ticket you're going to buy from me. He didn't wait for her answer. Then he laughed. His laugh lacked symmetry and so it sounded thoroughly superfluous to her.

Joseph's hands rested like cotton on her body and were wiped out with the passing of his laugh. Now when she felt his sweat, she felt a certain closeness to him, maybe because he wasn't part of the wild vista of Nehemiah's longings either. If you need something, he said, don't hesitate to call me. Mr. Aviyosef Abravanel, everybody knows me! Scion of the house of David. When a kingdom is restored to Israel, after these ragamuffins, my son won't have to stand here and greet ships in corners bearing impending disaster, and his eyes flashed now, his pain changed into bliss. He didn't notice her contemplation or the change in her treatment of him, he was looking at Jews lying near the enclosures, waiting to board the ship depressed and despairing of the land, looking at the Pioneers who just came and who looked too excited and hungry for love of the Land that has no love to give, and he said: They don't know the laws of the exhilarating corruption of these Turks . . . their savagery, you've got to know how to make that baksheesh look delicate and cunning. When my son is king of Israel, guards will stand here in scarlet and silver, with flashing swords in their hands and the birds will sing verses from the Song of Solomon in Hebrew. The Turk with the truncheon now approached Mr. Aviyosef Abravanel. Mr. Abravanel put the string of amber beads in his pocket, lowered his face a bit, stooped over, and yet—and she saw that clearly—precisely measured his rigidity and the power of his money against the truncheon in the hands of the authorities. The Turk's look was both covetous and wicked. Mr. Abravanel's stoop was measured and the obsequiousness was precise. She didn't imagine how much she would enjoy that, she also felt stabbings in her belly, the pain passed and of all the names that rose in her mind, the last of them was Ebenezer. But Ebenezer was the only name Nehemiah intended for his son. She felt no love for the fetus in her womb. The stabbing belonged to Rachel's belly. The son who was to fill water jars for beautiful women of Bethlehem and to plow the land of his forefathers was only a proper and undesirable pause for her, for the disgrace she had brought on herself with her love for Joseph Rayna and her marriage to Nehemiah, two things, and she knew that well, that shouldn't have happened. Many years later, when she'd sit at the screened window with the flyswatter in her hand, looking joylessly at the almond groves she had cultivated, at her good citrus groves and vineyards, and Ahbed, the grandson or great-grandson of Ahbed, would put the big old fan in front of her and try to turn it on even though the generator was broken, she'd think of Boaz who was both her grandson and her son and would say to herself: How come Boaz, Nehemiah's grandson, would be the spit and image of Joseph Rayna? And the dark plot in her blood would then be poured into the tune that never let go of her, the tune of her secret unknown even to herself.

Moshe Isaac was born in Bukovina. In Poland he married Sarah, daughter of Rabbi Where-the-Wind-Goes-Down. After he moved to Galicia and begat five sons, his last son Jacob was born, and then he died and didn't move the rod even in the wind. Jacob who moved mountains with his eyes that went blind from thirst for salvation begat Joachim the Dane, who went to seek the traces of the Dane who saw the Sambatyon River circumventing the realms of Sabbath, found a wife in Russia, and became enslaved to her compassion for him. His son Sambatyon the Dane begat Nehazia the Dane, who was also called the Genius of Tarnopol, who returned his forefathers to the soil and annulled the observation of the sky not through books. Nehazia married his cousin Miriam, daughter of Elijah, and begat Avrum the tavern owner who taught children, and hid creatures who saw sights they shouldn't have seen and showed them the straight path. From many torments, he died while walking and was buried in a small cemetery where a two-headed cow was later seen. Avrum begat Moshe Isaac who learned a little math, wrote three books, and in his dreams would see a city named Berlin and knew the names of its streets by heart even though he had never been there. He married a wise and modest woman named Leah. Leah raised two daughters who died of typhus and a young son named Nehemiah. Moshe Isaac died young and had time to hear his son Nehemiah learn Talmud. Nehemiah left the faith, taught and studied the Torah of the Land of Israel, married Rebecca the daughter of the great-granddaughter of Secret Charity, husband and father of Rebecca Secret Charity. Nehemiah begat . . . The ship emitted a long siren and then a short one. The birds circled above the church that looked like cardboard from here. The light was blinding. Ebenezer stabbed the womb of his mother who was looking at the sands of the Land and didn't come to it.

Tape / —

Rebecca followed Mr. Abravanel's Arabs, who led the coffin on the back of a donkey. Behind her, the sea ended and now she was walking in dark moldy alleys. Niches that may have been shops swarmed with dusky human beings with burning eyes, beyond there the honking of a train was heard whose locomotive tried in vain to bestow an importance on the city

but the palm trees had beautiful shapes and thin trunks. Rebecca calculated precisely the delusion in which she followed her man's coffin, and if
there was any beauty in the shabby outposts of the ancient east that hysterical women sometimes used to exaggerate and glorify, she knew how to
protest that misleading vision with smiling rage. The tears that would later
flow from her eyes for eight years in a row were already waiting for her
through her eyelashes. The new and ugly hotel was teeming with noisy
Jews. Outside vegetables and flowers were sold and the smell of charred
meat stood in the air. The fragrance of lemons and the sea only intensified
the smell of charred meat revolving on spits as if human beings were being
roasted. The coffin was put in her room. After the door closed behind them
and the Jew in the white suit arranged everything and even hinted to the
Turk who had followed them all the way to wait for him, only then did she
calm down. When she decided not to weep yet, her eyelids almost swelled
with tears. She went to the coffin and looked outside. She saw houses closing in on her from all sides. She looked here and there, lowered the filthy
shade, opened the top of the coffin and Nehemiah got up, stretched, and
hugged his wife. He said he would never again lie ten days in a coffin, even
if he had to die for it. His face beamed with joy that didn't fade because
of what he could see through the window or from the cracks of the coffin.
When they looked outside through the transparent and filthy shade, Rebecca
and Nehemiah saw two completely different landscapes.

The hotel was in turmoil. Jews who wanted to board the ship honking
in the harbor sought buyers for their miserable belongings. Arabs haggled
cunningly and the dignitaries among them would spit at every Jew heading for the ship, and Nehemiah, who was watching his wife's face, didn't
see the Jewish lords wearing suits and smelling of perfume who came to
take care of the new immigrants, to arrange their papers, if they had any,
and talked with the Pioneers as if they were recalcitrant children who
came to embitter their lives. Nehemiah said to Rebecca: I swear to you,
Rebecca, I've come home and I won't leave here. And she, who longed with
all her soul to leave here, was too stunned by the solemnity of his words to
respond. She thought: I've got his son in my belly, he'll learn. From the
window, on the other side of the room, a little square was seen with a carousel spun by a donkey and a camel. An Egyptian dancer in red and bright
scarves danced there to the cheers of mustached men who cheered and

applauded and thrust money between her breasts. Her eyes were painted, and even from the window they looked bold. The donkey spinning the carousel with the camel stopped, and a man in the uniform of a retired emperor whipped him and cursed in Italian. At night, they put into Nehemiah's coffin the body of the man who died of typhus, Rebecca took from her trunk a black silk dress and a black silk scarf, and the next day she went to the funeral with a sweet expression of modesty steeped with charm on her face.

The tears she had wanted to weep the day before now flowed, cultivated, proper, and foreign to her. They were meant for a man she didn't even know, and another man she didn't even know praised Nehemiah, a cantor recited the prayer for the dead and somebody volunteered to say kaddish. The Turk who stood there all the time and stared at Rebecca wanted them to put up a tombstone immediately. And the tombstone was ready that very day with the engraving: Nehemiah ben Moshe Isaac Schneerson, born in Ukraine in 1880, buried in the Land of Israel in the month of Teveth 5660 (1900). The Love of Zion Burns in his Heart. The Turk asked the translator to translate for him. The translator read: "Nehemiah Schneerson born in Russia in the year eighteen eighty, buried in Palestine in the month of January nineteen hundred. The love of his wife will accompany him." Rebecca whispered to the Jew in the white suit: What is he saying, and he translated for her. She said, Why did he say Russia, and the Jew said: For him, Ashkenazi Jews are born only in Russia, for the Turk it's all the same, anyway he doesn't know where that is. The Turk smiled, received what was coming to him, and left. Later on, what was written would be corrected and the document signed by two rabbis along with the photo of the grave against the background of the Mount of Olives would be sent to the family of the dead man in Aleppo, Syria.

Nehemiah wasn't thrilled by the sight of Mr. Abravanel, who came to talk with him in the locked hotel room about the wretched settlements. An empty suit, he said to Rebecca who made tea and served them. A pleasant wind blew from the sea. Nehemiah wanted to go immediately. Rebecca wasn't thrilled, but the hotel wasn't her heart's delight either and so it was decided to leave the next night. Mr. Abravanel, whose son would rule Israel after those ragamuffins, arranged everything and the next day a cart waited for them at the door of the hotel. Nobody peeped out the windows. The streets were dark. The Turks were already beating one another in their dark rooms. The cold of the night before vanished in a dry chill. A wind blew from the Libyan deserts. A precarious smell of cardamom, raisins, and droppings rose in Rebecca's nose. Nehemiah smelled lemons and honey. The road was deserted and the sky was strewn with stars.

On the day Nehemiah and Rebecca came to Jaffa, the settlements were transferred from Baron Rothschild to the IKA Company. The settlers knew the new company wouldn't soon fire the staff. The carter who brought Nehemiah and Rebecca said: It'll be bad! Everything will go down the drain, and Rebecca asked him what could go down the drain and he didn't answer, but cursed his horses.

Despite the worry, Nehemiah felt a quiet bliss. In the shadows of the mountains in the distance, he saw the sights of his childhood, the carter began singing melodies and one of them was Joseph Rayna's sad song about the rivers of the Land of Israel going to the Temple to ask forgiveness. Nehemiah longed for his wife, touched her belly, and said: That son, let it be mine! And Rebecca, who knew what he wanted to ask, didn't say a thing.

By morning, the jackals' wailing stopped and a clear blue light began filling the world. Nehemiah didn't shut his eyes and Rebecca dozed off. In the distance, as on a saccharine color postcard, the Arab village of Marar was seen, all of it like a beehive. Dogs barked and a smell of droppings and sweet basil rose from the village turned by the sun now rising fast into a kind of ruined ancient city. Later, the heat intensified with the eastern wind from the desert, and a struggle of forces raged between winter and the hot wind and when they passed by some fig trees and sycamores, the sun already blinding their eyes, the settlement emerged in the distance. A few neglected and cracking houses, fleeing, maybe eluding, thought Rebecca, limestone fence trying to unite the houses into one block, a few young trees, and some desolation that wasn't created or dissolved. The heat was heavy now and Rebecca felt dizzy.

Nathan, Nehemiah's old friend, rode up on a white mare and even in the distance he hugged the image of Nehemiah in his empty arms. Nehemiah roared with joy at him. Rebecca was amazed and said: At night he learned to talk with wolves? And the carter said to her, Those are jackals, Madam, not wolves, and she said: Jackals, wolves, same pest. When they came to what Nathan called the center of the settlement and what Rebecca privately called that miserable hole, the sun was beating down with its full force.

Near the synagogue, whose second story was still under construction, stood the miserable-looking men who were trying in vain to stand proudly. Nathan, who used to sit with Nehemiah in the forest and was his teacher before he ascended to the Land of Israel four years earlier, was wearing a dusty beret and his face was scared by the sun. He hugged Nehemiah, looked at Rebecca, and a forgotten smile rose up and crept over his lips. The people whose clothes looked to Rebecca as if they belonged to another climate surrounded them, there was great excitement, for some reason everybody thought that what had been broken in those years would be fixed with Nehemiah's coming, that his good sense and integrity were a hope they had cherished for days and nights. They said: Everything here is sold to the Baron, but we won't be dependent on his charity. Nehemiah smiled, some of the men he knew, others he knew only by rumor, their letters he had read several times, moldy water flowed along the ditch where they stood, Nehemiah thought of Abner ben-Ner and his heroes, and saw Arab children, barefoot, splashing in the moldy water, dragging piles of straw on their backs. A pesky buzzing of flies struck his ears but he tried not to hear. Nathan said: Soon our community will be blessed, and riots of agreement rose from mouths that were parts of faces that tried to adorn the moment with a smile that was stuck years ago to old valises. The young vineyards, crests of trees that were planted, and the limestone wall touching the houses, everything made Rebecca clearly suspicious. Nathan took off his shoes, looked at his old friend, and in the blinding light that had no corners, no ends, struck by a hot wind sharp as a razor, he started dancing with his arms spread out to the sides, and everybody stood as if they were turned to stone. The carter unhitched his horses and gave them something to chew from the crib, and Nathan, (very) isolated now, danced with a slow, hesitant movement as if he were groping in an invisible space, with his eyes shut, with great devotion, and Nehemiah put his coat on the ground, took off his shoes, too, and with the devotion of Hasids standing on the roof and yelling The Lord is God, he hugged Nathan and together they danced while everybody looked at them without budging.

Tape / —

Then the things were taken off the wagon and moved to the house that had stood empty ever since the death of the woman nobody had known and by the time they tried to ask her she was unconscious and died. She was buried in the nearby settlement because the idea of death could still be fought and a cemetery of Pioneers looked like a superfluous demonstration of failure. The ruined house was moldy and in the middle of the combined kitchen-bedroom lay a dead dog. Rebecca tried to fix the house and Nehemiah to tile the roof with the help of his friends. The smell of the dead dog remained there a long time. At night, all the men crowded onto the roof, held a bottle of wine they drank because of the sudden cold that replaced the hot wind, and to the sound of monotonous, quiet singing, they finished the roof Nehemiah tried to tile. The Turks who slept in their tent next to the settlement came at dawn with the dogs but the roof was done. Furiously, they tore down some vines, lit a bonfire, and made coffee. When the coffee was ready, one of the Turks poured coffee on his friend. His friend got up and shot him. The corpse lay there with gaping eyes. Rebecca passed by with her swollen belly and saw the dead man. Suddenly she recalled the smell in the ruin and thought, Is that smell the smell of a dog? Then, she said to herself: Now I know who the dead woman was. She hurried to the cart standing there, asked the driver to take her to the nearby settlement, came there about an hour later, went to the Baron's official who was sitting there with a young girl on his lap and listening to music played for him by two pale little girls dressed in white, on flutes, and she said: The name of the woman you buried here was Jane Doe. The official saw before him a splendid woman filled with a fetus, lusted for her but was also disgusted by her, and he said: Who's the woman? And Rebecca said, She lived in an orchard near our city, she was crazy and saw visions, her father was a cobbler who was murdered by rioters, she saw her mother turned into ashes, please write her name on the tombstone, and then she returned to the settlement and with a fluttering heart she wondered why she had done what she did. A jackal who fell in love with one of the bitches who came with the Turks wailed at Rebecca's house, she blocked her ears and tried to return to the river and there was nothing around her but desert and jackals and a smell of Turks and the blood of one Turk still close to the maw of the jackal who had approached the blood and sniffed it eagerly. The yard was full of thistles and thorns and in the summer the snakes would come rustle among the stones. The rain came down and the wind broke the roof tiles. Rebecca said to Nehemiah: Look at the limestone wall of the settlement, you've built a ghetto here. And Nehemiah twisted his face, which was already seared by the sun and was sad like the faces of his comrades and wrinkles were beginning to be plowed on his forehead, and he said: We need a defense, Rebecca, the Land isn't ours yet. And she said: And it won't be, and she turned her face and went to the yard and dug a pit and didn't know why she dug a pit. In the morning, Nehemiah came out and saw the pit, deepened it and said: I'm building an outhouse. He didn't know how to pull up crabgrass any better than to dig a pit. The outhouse he put up collapsed in the first rain. The crabgrass covered the vegetables he planted. The vineyard he was given was the property of IKA. In the summer the grapes would be taken away from him and he would get only a partial payment. Then Nehemiah thought of citrus fruits. The members heard that Nehemiah had an important idea and wanted to assemble, but the synagogue wasn't finished and the members said: How can we live here without a cultural center? They went to one of the abandoned huts and fixed it up and the next night, they called it the "Community Center." They assembled in the "Community Center" and even Rebecca, who was in the last week of her pregnancy, came. Nehemiah talked about citrus fruits, how it would be possible to grow them and market them, how it would be possible to be independent of IKA and the Baron. Nathan and his friend Horowitz went to Jaffa, bought saplings, returned, and planted the first citrus grove, but a deluge came nonstop for three days and three nights and the saplings were crushed and destroyed.

When Rebecca felt the labor pains approaching, she went to Jaffa, A few hours after she came, Ebenezer was born. It was a warm day in early spring and a few days later, Nehemiah came, his face was joyful. He looked at his son, the first son of the settlement, looked at Rebecca and saw her chilly smile and looked at his son again. Doctor Hisin refused to let him hold his baby, but when he looked at his son, he perceived, not how much he looked like him, since the infant didn't yet look like anybody, but how much the baby didn't look like Joseph. He examined every centimeter in his baby's face and was then appeased, kissed Rebecca, and said to her: Suckle the young lion, Rebecca, and she shut her eyes, picked up the infant, and reluctantly began suckling it.

About a month later, her milk was still flowing but her heart was cold. She was returned to the settlement on Saturday night and the next day, the rabbi was brought from the nearby settlement and circumcised Ebenezer

Schneerson, and Rebecca stood there and watched the rite of circumcision as if they were circumcising a stranger's child. And around Ebenezer, the first in Judea, stood barefoot houses charred by the beating sun. Rebecca hadn't imagined such a shrill light. She searched for corners of shade and found a baby running around between her legs. Nehemiah's sublime ideas didn't withstand malaria, typhus, and robbers. Heat waves would blaze and the hot wind plowed furrows in the ground that hadn't been worked for hundreds of years. The water was drawn from a nearby well, and when the well was destroyed more wells had to be dug. Trees born beautiful and green looked withered and weary. Rebecca observed her son, her house, and began weeping the tears that had stood behind her eyelashes the day she came to the Land of Israel. Eight years, Rebecca wept nonstop. A very little bit of the ardor of Nehemiah's speech clung to his acts. The house he built listed to the side, the nails would come out on the other side of the wall, the saplings were never planted in time and were never trimmed in time, the water came late to the ditches he didn't know how to dig properly.

The Baron's official, smelling of eau de cologne and wearing charming clothes, came with the Arab workers and the workers uprooted what was left of the citrus fruits. Instead they planted more vineyards. For some time, the synagogue turned into the official's residence. Little girls from distant settlements played a piano there that had been brought on a cart and the playing filled the broad street of the night with a dull melancholy. The flies multiplied feverishly, the pipes rusted, the roofs didn't stand in the wind, two girls from the Galilee went to live with the official in the synagogue and didn't come out of the house for a week. Drunken shrieks were heard even in the distant fields. One night, a flock of vultures was seen waiting for corpses. People were scared and started praying, but there was nowhere to do it. They prayed in the street, in the field, on the carts, in the barns where the cows refused to give enough milk. Nathan went outside and yelled: Not yet, not yet, and Nehemiah went to drive the vultures away with a stick he had cut from a hollow old fig tree that collapsed and died. The vultures didn't flee. Every morning, one of the farmers had to clean the house of the official who kept spitting black watermelon seeds all over. At night, the men gathered and Nehemiah persuaded them to rebel against the official and throw him out. The official discovered that Nehemiah was fomenting a rebellion and incited the farmers against him.

At night, Nehemiah was called to the official's house to clean the latrine. Nehemiah refused to go. He was ordered to leave the settlement. Everything was mortgaged and he had no grounds to claim his plot of land. The Arab police came with the Turkish modir and the white-clad official accompanied them. He tried to smile in French. The Turk was hypnotized by the splendid French and kissed him on the mouth. One of his choked girls groaned, Rebecca laughed through her tears and went into the house, looked around, and said: This isn't our house, Ebenezer. Nehemiah and Rebecca packed their belongings, the members stood ashamed but didn't lift a finger. Anybody who dared help Nehemiah could expect to be expelled. At that time, Nathan was in the nearby settlement in the middle of an argument with the local rabbi about the year of *shemittah* when the land must remain uncultivated and the pointlessness of following its commandments. Nehemiah walked with his belongings to the edge of the settlement and at the collapsed dead hollow fig tree, he built a hut. Nehemiah called the hut Secret Glory after the son of Rachel Brin, and only later on, when the haggling was over and the official dismissed, did Nehemiah return to his house and Secret Glory was forgotten and turned into an area overlooking the path of the cemetery, where the first members of the settlement who died were buried, even though the first dead woman was buried in the nearby settlement, but then Nathan still fought the idea that death could live with the builders of the new Land of Israel. Rebecca went on weeping and in her mind's eye she saw the splendid carts of America and a future full of baskets of flowers and American officials equal to her beauty. Her tears didn't stop even when Nehemiah drove away the vultures, and their improved house was nicer this time and Ebenezer started crawling on its floor.

At that time, a new official came who was more audacious than his predecessor, didn't spend time with young girls, but hated what he called those ignorant farmers with a blind hatred. He had big plans to bring ships up to Jerusalem to ram its wall and make it a big and fine open city, but nobody heeded his ideas. He came to the Land because he heard songs of a man who would sing in the cabarets of Jewish intellectuals in Poland and his name was Joseph Rayna. In *Ha-Tsefira* he read that the Crusaders had brought a ship up from Jaffa to Jerusalem and used it to ram the wall, he also read in a Russian newspaper that Jesus was then seen on the Mount

of Olives, and after a week-long procession around the city, the wall fell.
The official hired fifty Arabs who tried to bring a rotting Greek ship up
from Ashkelon to Jaffa and from there to Jerusalem, but in Ramle, the Arabs
ran away and because he was left without a ship and without employment,
he was sent to the settlement that embittered the lives of the officials. He
was chosen for that purpose by an official who met his orphaned comrade
on his way from Jerusalem to Jaffa. He was so bored by the monotony of
the road that he refused to look at it. The official heard Nehemiah lectur-
ing at the community center on the citrus fruit that was to make the place
flourish and discovered that, in litigation over the land of his hut, differences of opinion were revealed in favor of the Turkish side. He brought
police from the splendid house of the Kamikam in Wadi Hanin and arrested Rebecca and Nehemiah and a few other people, put them in handcuffs, and took them to Ramle. Three Arab mukhtars, who had previously
received a decent bribe, swore honestly that Rebecca Schneerson had
whored with them in the fields near Hakhnazarea. The Arab mukhtars,
who received a decent gift from a Sephardi Jew from Jaffa, who was urgently brought in a wagon hitched to four horses along with a drunk old
German doctor named Dr. Kahn, tried to change their testimony, but were
beaten in the courthouse and testified again what they had testified before. Rebecca looked straight at them, stopped weeping, sharpened her
beauty, and they were filled with a fear that chained their body and they
felt they couldn't move. Then, they opened their mouth and, in the eyes
of the witch, they said: We were wrong, kill us, but we were wrong, that
woman didn't whore with anybody, we lied. The big governor who came
from Jerusalem didn't want to roil the waves and acquitted Rebecca. The
Arabs were afraid but he also acquitted them. He delivered a venomous
speech, but since he was tired and weary from a pleasant leave in Beirut,
he delivered his speech in blunt words but with eyes shut with fatigue. He
said that Zionism is a crime, that the Jews want to banish the masters of
the Land, and why all of a sudden did they come to a land that wasn't
theirs? Did they decide to crucify messiahs here again? he asked. Since
most of those in attendance had no idea that the Jews had ever crucified
messiahs they looked at the governor's moving lips with vague awe. The
Jews, he said, were a superfluous people, wherever they were they caused
trouble and wanted to start a world revolution. They are ruled by the El-

ders of Zion who sit in a secret house in Jerusalem and direct the world. They want to rule the whole globe, he said, and Rebecca woke him from his fantasies and said: Maybe the whole cosmos, but since he didn't understand the word and was very tired, he laughed. And when the governor laughs, all the Turks laugh too. Before he left, the governor told Rebecca: After all, that Jesus was also one of yours, and only Mohammed came in the desert and not from some hole of a Jewess. But then a rich man from the Jaffa center arrived with a Turkish modir, whose bribe amounted to a fortune and the matter was settled, and Nehemiah's lands were returned to him and he built a hut on the land, and the house that remained empty was turned into a chicken coop that Rebecca fixed up afterward.

Tape /—

To bring order into things, a famous tea agent was brought who would write fiery articles about Zionism as a spiritual center. And the wise old man, who was the first Jew who saw Arabs in the Land, wrote a fiery article and for the first time since Nehemiah killed prophets in his room at night, he hit a beloved and admired person. The matter was forgiven. People said that Nehemiah suffered enough when he saw foreigners vilifying his wife, who hadn't stopped weeping. A Jew from the committee argued with the agent and the official who wanted to bring a ship up to Jerusalem. They stood next to the well the official had taken for himself and distributed its water according to his own malice. He stood there wearing an officer's uniform unidentified with any known plan, a woman held a parasol over his head, but the argument ended to everybody's satisfaction. The water was transferred to the authority of the committee, the house was sold, and Nehemiah won the official tenancy of his house. One youth slaughtered himself at the well in torments of malaria. Those who came to his funeral were arrested and taken in handcuffs to Ramle. Rebecca saw a Turkish *shavish* approaching her as she went to visit Nehemiah, who was one of those arrested. After a hefty ransom was paid, they were all released. Rebecca didn't forgive the *shavish* who looked at her and lusted for her. When he approached her in the garden of the Russian church and tried to lift her onto the mare, she kicked him. He chased her to her house in the settlement. At the house Rebecca shot the mare and the *shavish* thought he had been shot himself and lay on the ground a whole day without moving. The fellow who slaughtered himself lay dead in the community center, and the men decided to cancel the excommunication of Rabbi Nathan and mark the plot of Secret Glory as a cemetery for the settlement. Horowitz said: If Yashka died (that fellow who committed suicide), we're all liable to die and it's impossible to bury everybody in another settlement, since we can't have one settlement all for the living and another all for the dead. And after they dug the first grave, they put a fence around the plot. Nehemiah delivered an excited speech about the torments brought by the purification of salvation and resurrection. Excited by Nehemiah's impressive words, the men sat and argued what to call the cemetery. The names "House of the Eternal" and "Cemetery" and "House of the Next World" didn't appeal to them. Nehemiah thought there was no need to give it a name. It's enough that we know, he said, that we'll be buried there. But Jews yelled and somebody suggested calling the place "Roots." Nehemiah said: Absolutely not. Anybody who calls his first cemetery "Roots" calls the Jewish state that will rise here "Hill of Graves" and that's forbidden. But his words fell on deaf ears and the name remained.

The official left one day and didn't come back. The synagogue was renovated and was once again a place for prayer. The citrus fruits were also planted and flourished. The new authority was more enlightened. The Turks were busy with the Young Turks' revolution and were bound by secret letters that would come in the middle of the night from anonymous and veiled emissaries. Nehemiah again gave speeches in the community center and in Roots. Rebecca didn't stop weeping, and between her and Nehemiah grew Ebenezer. The Turks, who were waiting for the end of the revolution, said: The Jews will kill each other all by themselves and that will save us gallows and expensive bullets. From pogroms we came, Rebecca told Ebenezer, who didn't yet understand the meaning of the words, and to pogroms we shall return. Between the speeches, Nehemiah had to fertilize, chop, plow, and sow. He was delicate and fragile. The climate of the Land was hard for him, and he struggled with it in a silence produced by a lover's envy. The farmers did win a certain freedom but still felt like slaves. In Nehemiah's house, Rebecca's depressed spirit prevailed and a foolish child got underfoot. The drought that year was worse than the last year and some of the new citrus groves died, but in the winter the new saplings that had been planted grew as high as a child and the rain came in time and then came the Bedouins and started grazing their flocks on the young saplings. When the farmers resisted the Bedouins, they attacked at night. The Arab guard ran away and appeared the next day accompanied by Turkish police and asked for the money he was owed. Within a few days, the area was devoured by the black goats. The carts that went to the distant fields were attacked by the friends of the guard who didn't get his gold, even though the Turks got what was coming to them to ignore the place. One day the young farmers hid in the cart, with sticks in their hands, covered themselves with straw and sacks, and when they were attacked by the Bedouins, they burst out of the cart, about twenty of them, and beat the Bedouins roundly. The next day, Nehemiah made a long speech into the night: our force is our reply, he said, blow for blow.

A young Arab woman from the village of Marar cooked and laundered in Nehemiah's house. His fields flourished because of the help of his experienced friend Nathan. He now had a small dairy, a chicken coop, a vegetable garden, there was a quarry whose profits the farmers shared. In the nearby settlement bigger houses were built. The women played piano. The men drank tea or coffee and smoked cigarettes. The officials vanished, replaced by various committees and representatives of institutions. In the Jerusalem newspaper with a circulation of five thousand readers, they called the nearby settlement Little Paris. At night the girls sang a Puccini opera and an eminent man from Poland applauded so enthusiastically that everybody refused to join him for fear of offending him. He contributed money to the settlers to buy gramophones. The disease of music increased the appetite of the cows the Arabs milked in the nearby barns. Nehemiah's comrades, who heard him talk about the new "Hellenizers" in the nearby settlement, envied the inhabitants of the settlement and the delightful girls in splendid clothes and secretly brought fine fabrics from Jaffa, gorgeous *abbiyas* from Damascus, silk from Tadmor, carpets from Aleppo, and kerosene lamps from Gaza, and the mosquitoes, said Nehemiah contemptuously, now had to stick to choice silk, because they didn't like the sacks anymore. There were more Arab settlers who came from Egypt to spread rumors of the Jews' gold. As the way became harder, Nehemiah's love for that Land grew greater. Logic and facts of life had no place in his considerations. He grew roots at an alarming rate, and Nehemiah would give speeches that were not forgotten many years later. He would swallow quinine against malaria and see visions: behold, Rebecca stopped weeping and is bringing up an ancient Hebrew shepherd for him. Every week he would examine Ebenezer to be sure he didn't look like Joseph. Rachel Brin, who went to America with her son Secret Glory, wrote Rebecca a long remorseful letter. She told that she had divorced, married a shirt dealer from Long Island, moved to a place called Connecticut, and Secret Glory, now called Lionel, would go to an American school next year. Rebecca wept more bitterly when she read the letter and then she crumpled it up and rubbed her son's face in it.

Ebenezer didn't understand what was said to him. Because of the Hebrew, the Yiddish, and the Arabic that were spoken in the house, he seemed to doubt whether there really was any language that suited him and was silent in all three languages.

One night Nathan was arrested and nobody knew why. Nehemiah defended him and later, when he came back home, Rebecca had to take care of him. He said: Kiss your son, and she said: In America love your son, Nehemiah, and then Horowitz's brother returned from some distant village where they grew silkworms, and when he tried to interest Nehemiah in the big silk production that could be developed here with the ancient mulberry trees in the grove near the big cave, he was bitten by a sneaky snake and died, and then Nehemiah spoke in Roots about silk production. Rosy dreams of those who buy damascene silk, he said, and even spoke again about distress and hope, but because of Rebecca they expelled him and because of Ebenezer they pitied him and the child who grew up without a language would wallow in the fields, murmuring vague words that weren't like a human language, and Nehemiah kept fading while his love for his son grew with Rebecca's tears. An Arab woman raised his son. A screen of tears separated him and Rebecca. Nehemiah, who now spoke of a Jewish church and of masses of Jews coming on big ships, had to see his son grow up like an Arab dog with a cropped tail and mute. And then new Pioneers came to the settlement, whose coming Nehemiah wished for. They were quarried from a different rock, strong, desperate, and focused in their belief. They established two labor parties, and sought positions for their war. Since the only capitalist they could find who was even willing to wrestle with them was Nehemiah Schneerson, they went to foment the revolution in front of his house. Since they believed that the future was in their pocket, their obstinacy was dismal and deadly serious. In their eyes the Arab woman who worked in Nehemiah's yard was an exploited proletarian. When they yelled at his house: "Death to capitalism," "Long live the world revolution," and "Long live Hebrew labor," he came out to them in his tattered clothes, tried to stir yearnings in them for what he yearned for, and they thought he was trying to divert them from their righteous opinion. Rebecca, who never looked at them, had to drive them away because her Arab woman wanted to sleep, and in the nearby settlement a woman still stood with a parasol, but the official who had been under the parasol had gone. And the laborers tried to engage the Arab woman in conversation and explain to her in excited Russian how exploited she was.

When he went into first grade, Ebenezer was the worst student in the class. He refused to read and was bored with the books his father read him with desperate assiduousness. He'd chomp on vine leaves and gaze at the trees and fields for a long time and find a small measure of solace in them. Only when he started playing with the logs in the yard did the desolation vanish from his face. Then he started carving. He was eight years old. He carved a bird and suddenly he was quiet and happy. He learned to carve human faces and birds before he knew how to write the words bird and man. The Hebrew hero who would grow here on his native land found tranquility. He'll be a carpenter like that fool from Jaffa, said Rebecca between one tear and another.

Tape / —

One night, after Ebenezer sat all day in the yard and carved a bird and sang, Nehemiah thought: Maybe my whole life was a mistake, Rebecca is weeping, my son is carving birds and can't tell the difference between see and sea. He put on his clothes, went outside, saw his son bent over a piece of wood, kissed him, hitched up a cart, and went to Jaffa. There he bought a plow and returned in the morning. Two laborers arguing fervently about Plekhanov's theory were sitting in his yard and eating grapes. Rebecca sat in a chair and tears covered her like a curtain. Nehemiah was covered with warts and sunburned and his hands were suddenly weak. Ebenezer was sleeping with his mouth gaping and looked like a bird he had carved the day before. Nehemiah walked in the fields and a full moon was hung in the sky and an intoxicating aroma of citrus blossoms filled him, he saw his mare and stroked her and let her gallop home and went on walking along the hedges of prickly pears and acacias. Suddenly he heard a rustling, saw his friend Nathan dressed in tatters and looking like a madman. In his hand he held a bottle of wine, which he offered to Nehemiah. Nathan was distraught, his mouth sprayed foam, and when he tried to talk he couldn't. Nehemiah didn't know what to do with the bottle in his hands and so he started drinking from it. When he drank he started thinking of Joseph Rayna, his songs, his hatred for him even before he knew who Rebecca was, he thought of the fifty-two sons Joseph begat with women he chanced upon. He thought about his love for Rebecca and more than he understood it, he felt for her that feeling like the beloved moth in the kerosene lamp. He thought he was thinking of Joseph out of loathing, but he also felt some admiration of a man betrayed and despised. Rebecca will never be mine here, he said to himself, this land is foreign to her and as long as they sing Joseph's songs here, she'll remain the lover of that noble pampered rogue and because of that I'll never be able to let her leave me, he said, and he understood the labyrinth of his torments as a circle with no exit.

Some time later, Nathan managed to say something that had been swallowed in his mouth a long time. He vilified himself, the settlement, Ebenezer, Rebecca, Nehemiah, the Zionist Committee, the Lovers of Zion, the new laborers, he looked at Nehemiah as if he had only now discovered him, kissed his face and vanished into the night. Nehemiah returned home. Rebecca stood tied to the mare, alarm on her face. When she saw him she went back to weeping the tears that had previously stopped on her cheeks. He went down on his knees and told her how much he loved her. He grabbed her by the waist, dragged her home with a force she didn't know was in him and she yelled: I thought you went to America without me! And then he locked the door and lay with her furiously, and the delicate man who was Nehemiah saw hostility in Rebecca's eyes, got up and started beating her and from her tears she burst out laughing. But she also loved the suddenly strong hands and his desperate embrace and they lay together in silence and he stroked her and penetrated her like preservative and kindled in her some spark of children she had once buried in suitcases. Afterward, he sat naked and asked forgiveness and she said: In love there is no forgiveness, Nehemiah, I'm yours, and that's it, just let's leave here, and she stroked his face and kissed him and then they lay like two young

people who didn't know what love was and talked and Nehemiah said to
Rebecca: Our strange child, I love. And she said: Maybe you'll tell him, and
Nehemiah said he couldn't. And she remembered how Joseph Rayna waited
for his father who didn't come and in her heart she wept for the awful days
in store for her son she couldn't love and her husband couldn't understand
and couldn't get up and tell him how much he loved him. After he fell
asleep, Rebecca looked at him and said to herself: We will leave here, my
love, we'll build a life in a place where you can make a future and not only
a made-up past.

His love for Rebecca intensified so much in those days that he had to
scrunch up his face to recall the reason for the eternal quarrel between
them that had made Rebecca weep for seven whole years now. Nehemiah
almost stopped giving speeches, spent less time in the community center,
wrote fewer letters to Zionist leaders, and didn't stop trying to seduce his
wife, who looked at him with a delight that once alarmed her when she discovered it herself. Nehemiah would look at his son and think that maybe his
son was happy in his ignorance and that shamed him. He was now working
a few hours a day for a Hungarian who built wine barrels and was an expert
in sawing trees, polishing them, and cutting them and mixing lacquer and
other preservatives. Ebenezer was willing to lie around his place all day,
refused to go to school, and the Hungarian would look at him through his
pince-nez, laugh, and say: They want educated Jews, but only ignoramuses
will build them a land! And he laughed. And at that time, after the Arab
pogroms and the great theft of the Bedouins who emptied the barns came
the Wondrous One on a noble white mare, with thin legs and a long delicate neck. He sat on a tufted saddle built like a kind of dwelling and was
dressed like a high priest with a breastplate and emeralds and a silk gown
and a sky blue kaffiyeh, he was girt with a sword and two rifles and belts
of rifle bullets, and everybody was sure a distinguished Arab robber had
come to the settlement. As they stood in tribute to his impressive appearance, the Wondrous One got off the mare, who whinnied and stroked his
supple back with her head, and he said in an ancient Hebrew accent:
Hear O Israel the Lord our God the Lord is One. And when everybody
was stunned and even awestruck, the man said: Joshua conquered Canaan
by sword and storm, you won't conquer it by planting vineyards. I live in the
Arabian Desert. Who I am doesn't matter, I heard about Jews who came to

renew a kingdom and I said to myself, I'll teach them war against the Arabs, you see the Bedouins and you don't know their dignity and malice and
cunning, you fight the wrong enemy with sticks.

He pitched a tent for himself on the edge of the settlement and would
cook his meals with his own hands. Women from all around came in carts
to see the prince of the Jews. A new wind started blowing in the settlement, backs that had been bowed for years suddenly straightened up. Even
Ebenezer's wood carvings stopped interesting folks. The Wondrous One
taught them savagery and speed and surprise and night raids and aggressive defense and outflanking maneuvers. He taught smells and winds and
seeing in the dark and how to tell an enemy horse from one that isn't by
its droppings and how it creases the leaves and branches, and everybody
became eager for war. And once again a light shone in the beautiful faces
of the men who had come to the Land to build. The Wondrous One was
cruel, fast, mysterious, and decisive, but after the training and fabulous
nocturnal sorties he would close himself in his tent in silence. One night,
when the men stayed in the fields on a test sortie beyond the settlement,
only he and the women were left, the Wondrous One entered Rebecca's
house, sat on the mat, politely dismissed the Arab woman, and the Arab
woman fell on her face and wept to hear the flowery Arabic in his mouth
and said that was the Jewish messiah, and left, and then the Wondrous One
drank a cup of coffee Rebecca served him and told her she was a beautiful
woman and belonged to the desert. And for the first time in seven years,
Rebecca stopped weeping. Long afterward, Boaz, Rebecca Schneerson's
grandson and son sat, and his yellow-green devil eyes will stare at her
with a wicked smile and will scold her serenely for reciting Psalms in the war
and saving him from the death he deserved more than Menahem Henkin,
Yoske, the naked Nahazia, and Yashka, and would ask again as before what
the Wondrous One said that night the old people had been telling about for
fifty years now, and she will say: Nothing, Boaz, it's all legends, he wanted
me to come with him to the desert, they're all like Joseph Rayna, words,
words.

After he left Rebecca's house, the Wondrous One went to his tent. And
after the men returned, he blessed them, spoke of future wars, tried to
hint at the essential missions, packed up his tent, and at night he vanished
and nobody knew when or where. The next night, the Bedouin herds came

onto the fields that had just been planted. On the Sabbath morning a man came to the synagogue and yelled: Herds in the fields! The rabbi wasn't in the settlement that Sabbath and an argument broke out about whether war against the Bedouins was a life-saving act that canceled the Sabbath. Nehemiah jumped up, mounted his mare, and started galloping. When the others saw him, they also mounted their mares and donkeys and still wrapped in prayer shawls, they dealt the Bedouins a crushing blow, as they had learned from the Wondrous One. After that, Nehemiah never went back to the synagogue. Then Rebecca started coming to the synagogue. Malicious rumors spread, but Rebecca sat in the women's section and smiled at the Ark of the Covenant as if she were conversing with the Holy One Blessed Be He. The tears were seen again in her eyes. She didn't pray but sat and stared at God in the Ark of the Covenant and was silent. After she returned from the synagogue she saw Nehemiah pulling up crabgrass. Bitterness filled her. Nehemiah tried to kiss her but she slipped away from him. So beautiful she was in the morning light! Ebenezer sat in the corner of the yard and carved a bird's face. And then the sound of the locusts was heard. Everybody ran to the fields and made bonfires. Some tried to get rid of the locusts with prayers and others by banging on cans. One of the bonfires spread and burst into a conflagration that reached Nathan's cowshed. Rebecca, who saw the fire, ran and stumbled into a pothole. An Arab galloping by her whipped her. She tried to pull the whip and bring him down from the horse, but the whip slipped out of her hand. She was hit in the face and covered with blood. There were no paved roads and water flooded from the gutter. The roof of Nehemiah and Rebecca's house burst and a week later, when the first rains of the season began, the strongest the Land had ever known, the roof Nehemiah tried in vain all night long to reinforce with a pole collapsed. The clothes in valises in mothballs, waiting to go to America, were flooded, everything turned into pulp in one downpour and Rebecca saw all the tears she had hidden among the clothes and they melted right before her eyes. Your tears have brought destruction upon us, said Nehemiah bitterly, but she didn't think he deserved a reply. The cows were terrified by the torches, the horses whinnied, and Nathan's donkey burst into the house and crushed the ladder Nehemiah was standing on and holding up the roof. The Arab woman fled in panic and five days later the cracks took on a brown-yellow tone and Rebecca sat and looked at the destroyed house and at Nehemiah, whose body and spirit were broken and then suddenly, he turned pale, dropped, and shut his eyes. A few days later, the doctor was called from the nearby settlement. He examined Nehemiah and brought another expert from Jaffa who came riding on a brown horse and the two of them told Rebecca that Nehemiah wasn't suffering from any disease they knew. Rebecca knew what Nehemiah's disease was, but didn't think the doctor would understand. As far as she was concerned, her husband's shriveled face, his shut eyes, his burned skin, and his broad forehead constituted authentic proof of the disease of despairing love that Rebecca, as somebody who had never loved except through somebody else, knew well. For many days, Rebecca sat at Nehemiah's bed and nursed him in his illness. And Ebenezer, the first Sabra in the settlement, would carve wood and be silent and Nehemiah woke up one day, stared wearily and dully at his son and his wife and whispered: Stop weeping; extinguish the tears, you won. We'll do what you want!

She didn't know how you think about going to America without tears. There was a heat wave and a strong wind blew and people seemed to be walking like shadows seeking a foothold in corners that were like shade, but didn't stop the wind. The sky was heavy and brown. An intoxicating smell of thistles rose in her nose. She pitied Nehemiah for not leaving her and now he had to pay the price of her stubborn war, but she didn't know how to tell him that. When he recovered from his illness, Nehemiah looked like a different man. A puerile rashness seized him. He put on a light-colored suit he had bought from Hazti who came every week in a cart loaded with luxuries, and something that had always been stormy in him was now appeased. He'd walk around the settlement like a hopeless lover of it, talking with his neighbors, making new plans, preparing an irrigation system, a new community center, a paved street, planting almond trees, building a sanatorium for asthmatics. His friends looked at the man whose fields and farms were failures, whose citrus groves suffered more than others, whose wife had been weeping nonstop for eight years now, whose son carved wood, and recalled the stormy nights on the threshing floor, the dreams he tried to inspire in them and were so in love with him that they were forced to invent in their common past things that never had been and never were, to increase his image and love even more. In Nathan's house a few people gathered to celebrate Ebenezer's ninth birthday. The boy sat in a corner and didn't want to talk, just looked at them and showed them a carved bird and when he laughed he looked like a jackal. Rebecca rubbed her face and was silent. Nehemiah looked outside, drank a little wine, raised his glass and said: To a hundred and twenty Ebenezer, looked outside and through the window he saw the darkness descending, lovely roofs, citrus groves, vineyards, ornamental trees, cypresses, cowsheds, chicken coops, a suppressed smell of hay stood in the air and he told them how much he loved them and added: Doesn't Ebenezer look like me? And Nathan said he doesn't look like you, Nehemiah, but thank God, he doesn't look like anybody else either. At night, Nehemiah said to Rebecca: Let's leave Ebenezer with Nathan and go on a trip. Rebecca put on a yellow dress and wrapped a scarf and in the autumn of nineteen nine, nine years after they came to the Land of Israel, Rebecca and Nehemiah left riding on two donkeys to part from the land of Nehemiah's dream. They rode along wadis and ancient riverbeds, met groups of young Pioneers quarrying rock in remote places and living on farms in the mountains. Nehemiah said: They will succeed where we failed. They yearn less for the past and more for the future. They would conquer the Land because it's theirs, they didn't come to ask for pity but to rape the Land. In Jerusalem, Rebecca prayed at the Western Wall and Nehemiah watched her from the distance. They crossed the Jezreel Valley, rode among desolated swamps, toured the Galilee, and after a journey along the Jordan, they came to the Dead Sea, lay there on their backs, and the salt bore them and the mountains around were a shadow of something that didn't exist at all. Rebecca said: I'm looking into a mirror, and she laughed, and he loved to hear her laugh. At night, they slept embracing. Never had they loved one another so much. She almost forgot her body's longing for Joseph. Nehemiah's courtesy was only salt poured on the violent and seductive sweetness. Something is dying in him, she said to herself, and something else is maybe lit. She began to be filled with hope and regret at the same time.

They returned to the settlement and Nehemiah delivered a speech that lasted from six in the evening to three in the morning, and the farmers sat lit by the halo of light, and there was still a distant echo in it of their dreams. Six hours Nehemiah talked and nobody budged. Even Rebecca sat fascinated to hear the visions Nehemiah spoke of and she really didn't know that she saw them. In the middle of his speech, Nehemiah looked at her and understood sadly that Rebecca's mind was made up. That night he parted from every corner of the farm, kissed his son for a long time, and like thieves in the night, Nehemiah and Rebecca left with their things hastily packed and after another farewell from their son who didn't understand a thing, they rode to Jaffa. Ebenezer watched them from the distance and didn't weep. Rebecca said to him: I'm going with Father and you'll join us as soon as we get settled. She didn't want to bring Ebenezer to America but she didn't want to say that, neither to Nehemiah nor to her son. Ebenezer sat and etched the face of an owl on wood. Even when Nehemiah wept for a long time and hugged him, he didn't say a thing. He just tried to understand what was happening to the piece of wood when you carve it like that so the face of the owl looks as if it burst out of the wood and is also destroying it, shattering it to pieces and at the same time, honoring it.

Nehemiah was silent all the way to Jaffa. Rebecca, who didn't know what to think about, was still dozing and trying to dream about the last days, and when she woke up and they were close to the citrus groves of Jaffa and saw the palm trees at the entrance to the city, she recalled the small details that had joined together into some picture that was not yet clear to her, and when she looked at Nehemiah she saw on his face the expression that had covered his face on the day of Rachel's wedding. His hatred now for Joseph was so strong that Rebecca almost fell in love with him.

And suddenly from the dread that filled her, maybe because of remorse, she wanted so much to save Nehemiah, to give up, to be somebody she never thought she could be, to take Nehemiah back to the settlement to his son and to his lands and to his friends, but she didn't know how to do that and was silent. Jaffa was now a different city. Jewish shops were opened in the narrow streets. Carts from settlements in Judea and the Galilee came to the city, people bought agricultural machines and seeds and sold farm products, and the city was teeming with life and they were already starting to build the new neighborhood of Tel Aviv on the sands north of the city and Arabs were still smoking narghilas next to the mosque and Turks were standing barefoot and listening to an orchestra of ragamuffins from Egypt and slapped their faces whenever they fell asleep while playing and ships anchored in the port and two locomotives were added to the railroad junction whose tracks already reached the edge of the desert and Nehemiah and Rebecca stole into the hotel.

Nehemiah didn't go out the door of the hotel and Rebecca bought a few souvenirs for her friend Rachel, met Jews she thought she had known before, and saw an elderly consul stroking the body of an Arab boy on a dark streetcorner, and then she drank tea with mint with the Jewish agent Joseph Abravanel, who reminded her that his son would someday rule the Land and didn't mock her, but quietly arranged the tickets and the cabin on the ship that had already tooted and the toots were already dancing on its masts and the ship looked menacing and beautiful among the little waves capering on the shore and then she sat next to her husband and said: I smell fire, and he said in a hollow cracked voice, You smell the future, and she felt stabbings in her womb as if there were a child in it and she wanted to give birth for Nehemiah to all the dead children she had once known but she was silent and said to him: What did I do to you, Nehemiah, and he said: You were Rebecca, you were what you were, don't cry, I love you more than any person in the world and I won't tell you again how much I love you because you won't believe me. She smiled at him and hugged him, but he put her off and as she was falling asleep, she seemed to hear the sound of weeping, but since she had never heard Nehemiah weep, she thought somebody else was weeping in one of the rooms.

Early the next morning they went to the port. The valises stood at the jetty with the boats, Nehemiah said some harsh words to Joseph Abravanel, who was dressed in white, and paid a few cents less than what was demanded. He haggled and Rebecca had never seen Nehemiah haggle. Afterward—as agreed in advance—he put her on the boat, since he had to load the valises on another boat. Rebecca stood on the boat, she couldn't sit down. Something in her was still steeped in an incomprehensible dread. The ship tooted and she trembled. She wanted to weep, but she had no tears. She wanted to go back and couldn't now. The sailors raised their oars and pushed the boat. They jumped on a big wave and Rebecca saw Nehemiah standing and looking at her, but because of the strong light, his face was clearly seen despite the distance. And even though she was scared, she didn't yet know what she was scared of.

Banners and flags rose and fell on the masts. Rebecca thought for a moment about eight years of tears. Nehemiah stood on the shore, the rising tears on his face were incomprehensible in view of his erect and aristocratic stance. Something was ruined and she didn't know what. He looked so bold and tense that in a little while he would leap and rush to battle. Nehemiah vanished behind some shed, and right at that moment she grasped what was liable to happen and started yelling, but the roar of the sea swallowed her yells, she started hitting the passengers and they were alarmed and the sailors rowed her back to shore and she jumped off and ran in the shallow water and everybody looked at her and silence reigned and she came to the corner of the mosque just one minute after Nehemiah, with eyes wide open, but without seeing a thing, took out a gun, aimed it and shot his temple.

Very slowly Nehemiah collapsed onto the ground he had sworn never to leave. When Rebecca came to him he was still trying to touch the Land and his body was already dead. People gathered around Nehemiah. And Rebecca lay there with her mouth stuck to his, trying to make Nehemiah breathe, until they separated them and dragged her away from there and carried his body to one of the sheds. The ship tooted again and Rebecca looked one last time at the ship waving its flags, and very slowly she started walking toward the dead body of her husband. Clotted blood was stuck to his lips. The gun was still in his hand. The Turk wanted to write down something, but she told him: There's nothing for you to write, he's been buried here for nine years.

She touched his forehead and said: You shouldn't have done that to me, Nehemiah, and an awful anger, an anger steeped in love, rose in her and overcame her, and she gave into that anger and let it twist her face, and the Turk who saw her was forced to fall and then to run from there as if he had seen the sun coming out of a hole in his pants.

At the funeral, in Roots, she stood silent. Nobody dared approach her. Ebenezer, who stood not far from her, was also silent. She didn't shed a tear. They don't deserve that, she thought, but she also knew that there were no more tears inside her to weep even if they did deserve them. Ebenezer said the orphan's kaddish and Rebecca went back home, closed the windows and the doors and said: No mourning, nothing. Nobody will come in here.

On the last day of mourning, Ebenezer finished carving two heads of wood. He called them Father and Mother, one of the heads was Rebecca while the second was Joseph Rayna. And then Rebecca assaulted Ebenezer, broke his carvings, and started a successful farm.

My friend Goebbelheydrichhimmel.

Tape / —

About two weeks ago, I returned from a visit to Israel. Because of the heavy fog in northern Germany, we were forced to land in Copenhagen. A freezing rain was falling and it was impossible to see a thing. We took a cab and went to a small hotel near Herdospladsen. I called Inga, who by the way sends you warm regards. She came immediately and as usual didn't leave us alone. She fed us at a small, and I must say excellent, restaurant not far from the hotel. Then she informed us she was taking us to a party at the American ambassador's. When we got to the ambassador's house there were only a few guests left, including an Israeli, a native of Copenhagen, who fought in the war of independence in Israel, returned there in the fifties, lived there, worked as a journalist for an Israeli newspaper and for a Danish newspaper and was now the editor-in-chief of *Politikan*, his name is Pundak, a pleasant and wise man of principle who can formulate things in a way that isn't harsh, doesn't place perplexing full-stops, a cultured man in the old sense of the word, an excellent editor and a fascinating conversationalist. His wife Suzy is a woman with a profound bubbling in her, whose rare common sense, existential perplexity with a thin patina of a smile that's liable to be broken any minute spread over her face. There were also a few writers there who are familiar to you, too. Herbert Pundak saved me from an unnecessary conversation with an American colonel who thought that now that I returned from Israel we had a lot in common. He and I, thought the colonel, understand those Jews. I didn't want to quarrel as soon as I came, and the ambassador, who, by the way, is a German Jew, came to us, and looked too cordial for me to cause a diplomatic incident. I felt tired. The trip in the morning to Lod Airport, parting from the friends I had made there, the flight, the trip to the hotel, the dinner with Inga, and now the party, all that dropped some heaviness that I couldn't yet get away from for some reason. So we sat in a big pleasant room and sipped punch. I sat in a big comfortable fine leather armchair, across from me above a fireplace was a big black wall. I turned the chair around a bit, the color of the black wall turned blue a bit, and then, when I heard the editor of *Politikan* explaining something about Israeli foreign policy, and the

ambassador trying to argue with him, I saw the face of the Führer looking at me above the fireplace and I shuddered. Inga, who sat next to me,
asked what happened, and I said: What's missing on that wall is the picture of Hitler! My knees buckled, I felt as if my blood ran out. I was sorry
for what I had said, but I really did see the Führer looking at me in that
splendid room. The ambassador got up, stood over me, Renate sipped
punch, he looked at the wall in silence, and said: Were you here then?
When I said I had never been here in my life and didn't understand why
I had said what I did, the ambassador came to sit down next to me, stroked
my knee, chomped on a cigar and then lit it, and also lit the cigarette I
took out of my coat pocket, and said: You're sure? I said: I'm sure. Funny,
said the ambassador, this was the house of the governor Werner Best. A
decent navy man, and his assistant Diekwitz, also a navy man, who informed the underground of the expected expulsion of the Jews, and afterward the house was transferred to the Americans, and here, on that wall,
until forty-five, was a picture of the Führer, and the armchair you're sitting in was there at that time, only with different upholstery, of course.
Next to it is a trap door, the governor was sensitive to explosions and
under this room, which is an addition to the original house, a big shelter
was dug. He'd sit here, smoking, drinking wine, with the opening next to
him leading to the shelter . . .

On the way back to the hotel I saw a crowd of Wehrmacht soldiers
marching along those ancient and beautiful streets in the winter gloom. At
the hotel, I drank more wine. Renate wept at night, wrote a postcard to a
woman she had met in Israel, fortunately I love Renate too much to give
my opinion on her foreignness. After thirty years of marriage she told me
that night of all times about her youth in those days when you and I would
shoot at low-flying planes, did you know, that when Renate heard that the
Führer committed suicide she wounded herself and had to be put in the
hospital, and back then the hospitals were crammed to the gills, weren't
they? The next day, the sky cleared up and we flew home.

I had a strange dream. I was waiting for my father at the railroad station.
Renate came arm in arm with an old Jewish woman. A man who may have
been a Jewish pimp from a Stürmer cartoon asked me what side the snake
pees on.

I'm sitting at home now, in the room you know well. Behind me is the beautiful picture of the black horse. You write that my last book sold three million copies. I was glad to get the nice articles you sent me. The depth of the article from the *New York Times* amazed me, I never heard of the author of that article, Lionel Secret, but the name does ring a bell only I can't decipher or locate it on the map of my memories. I loved the thin irony of the article seeing my book as my most successful suicide attempt, the one you can photograph and go on looking at it. I remember my father telling me that the film he took in the Warsaw Ghetto was a beautiful film. When I saw the film afterward I understood what he meant. The book I've been trying to write all those years about the Last Jew doesn't interest you. But in addition, it also refuses to be written. I'm now rewriting a novella I wrote a few years ago but my heart is given to "The Last Jew" that's stuck in my craw. In Israel, I met Ebenezer. The meeting didn't do me any good. I met a man named Henkin who's also investigating the Last Jew (he's not a writer) and his wife is the woman that Renate loved in Israel. Ebenezer's mother, Rebecca, I didn't meet. She's very old, they say she's still beautiful. For some reason, I was afraid to go visit her in her settlement.

Since you're not only my editor and publisher, but also my close friend, I must explain to you clearly where I stand now. I know, you've worked hard for many years to promote me. You published my books when nobody else wanted them, you believed in me despite the bad or indifferent criticism or the thousands of copies you had to bury because nobody wanted to buy them, and I, I of all people, now sit and write what our reader won't want to read and our critic will trash, and the most awful thing of all, what is hard even for me to write. The book can be written by two different people, my dear, by me and by that Henkin. And then it won't be the book you wanted, will it? I am my father's son and Obadiah Henkin is the father of Menahem Henkin, who fell in Israel. Someplace, an ancient battlefield is stretching between us, and in that battlefield is a person devoid of memory of his personality who is also part of me and part of him. It's like two men trying to beget a son together. There's a nice saying: The best poem is a lie. What is the German lie and what is the Jewish lie that can create on paper the existing character, painfully existing, of Ebenezer Schneerson, son of Rebecca and father of Boaz Schneerson, stepfather of Samuel Lipker, a man who hoarded knowledge to remain a last Jew in a war that you, I, and he were in together on both sides of a death that's now being forgotten?

Grief is banal. Life is banal. Death is banal. Everything is banal. The tormented and monstrous words. What to do? I have to prophesy Ebenezer through Henkin and he has to prophesy him through me. What will come out of all that may be bad but necessary. I know how much these words upset you.

What I can't grasp in that banality is the symmetry. Boaz and Samuel Lipker are the same age, born the same day, one in Tarnopol in Galicia and the other in a settlement in Judea. They look alike. When Ebenezer met Samuel in the camp he didn't know that Samuel was the last son of Joseph Rayna whom he went to Europe to seek and came to us. He didn't know that Samuel and Boaz are alike because he had left Boaz when he was a year old and hadn't seen him since. So isn't it funny that, when Ebenezer returned to Israel forty years later and met Boaz (and Samuel whom he hadn't seen for many years), he said: Samuel! And Boaz was offended to the depths of his soul. I have to understand Ebenezer, his mind, the words he hoards and then sells to foreigners in seedy nightclubs. I understand that you want another book, you want a different story, but I, I have no other way, I have to live in the stammering attempt to write a book that doesn't want to be written . . .

Tape / —

Attached below, another chapter of the draft, the third copy. If you compare it to the previous copy (that you disliked so much) you'll see that in principle I didn't change things, I just cooled them a little, I distanced myself, I let people shape themselves a little in view of the words that didn't stick to them. And so . . .

Bent over he was at the barbed wire fence, maybe more than bent over, he was leaning forward, and his whole life would pass in that second like a flash with nothing except memories of others, and he won't know if what passed through his mind was his life.

A woman in rags passed by on the other side of the fence. She said: Are you all right, Schneerson?

I'm looking at you through a fence we haven't passed through for years, he said, I look and I see. He didn't know how he knew they hadn't passed through it for years if he didn't remember who he was and what happened to him.

I'm eating, said the woman.

And then a slice of bread she held in her mouth dropped. The bread fell on the ground covered with bone dust that flew in the wind. She bent over in alarm, picked up the slice, cleaned it with her hand and put it back in her mouth. At that moment, Samuel appeared, touched Ebenezer, and said to her: See how much food they brought, sausages, cheese, bread, and she smiled, the slice of bread in her mouth, and then she fled wildly.

Ebenezer stood still because he had nowhere to go. Everything was in motion. Bonfires were lit. A tank was slowly squashing the drooping roof of a gigantic block that had previously collapsed. Imagined shapes of human beings, staggering, dressed in pajamas or tatters. A soldier vomits. Hands of a dead man leaning on a wall, like a skeleton who started walking and stopped, the hands are stretched forward, clenched into fists, the skin is flayed. A Spitfire was circling in the air and dropping paratroopers full of food and medicine and uttering a purity of distances no longer unimaginable. For a moment Ebenezer sensed the stench that had been with him for three years.

April fifteen, nineteen forty-five. Five hours and five minutes after noon. A long twilight, whose long faded shadows, twined with fiery hues, create calculated uncertainty and solid vagueness, an hour with no boundaries, until the dark that may really descend again. On the horizon blue mountains, treetops and silence. A gleaming gold of a tank tramps to the block. Behind Ebenezer the blocks still stand in a long line, a ditch perpendicular to them, its banks concave. A second glimmer of a passage from one planet to another. In the distance, SS Sturmbahnführer Kramer is seen. Tied with a coarse rope. Two British soldiers guard him. One of them touches him, almost pushes him, and Kramer tries to wave his hand, as if he wanted not to wave the white flag, his eyes keep revealing contempt and at the same time keep surveying the destruction, the tanks crushing his blocks, their sloping roofs, and those people in pajamas. The impulse is mechanical, his hands are bound and he can't wave them, he drops his hands and once again straightens his hands behind, Ebenezer sneaks a look at him from the distance, and very slowly turns his back to him. Ebenezer feels a stab in his back, as if he were shot, but Samuel's hand is stroking him, Samuel doesn't see what Ebenezer sees, he's already far away from here, in a future that's almost solid and bound to reality, Kramer doesn't interest him anymore. Ebenezer wants not to see the humiliation, he didn't want it. A British officer who had previously been seen chatting with the tall, ruddy Red Cross representative then asked Ebenezer something and Ebenezer said: It's true that I was almost the first one in this camp. But I'm not the last! And he blushed at the sound of his words. The "but" sounded arrogant and coarse. The architect Herr Lustig made them a stylized roof, Kramer requested, Weiss approved, and so he got sloping roofs with a unique angle for that camp. The originality of their slope is an interesting modular plan, said Herr Lustig. Concentrating vertical force. The arc on which the roof is set doesn't have to be a concrete support but only its bottom half, you can learn from these dimensions in the Alhambra, for example, he added. A city isn't houses, Herr Lustig then said, camp and city, town and future concentration of human beings will constitute a planned texture and not some accidental combination of beautiful or ugly structures, streets or squares, it will be a unit in itself!

The officer who sees the corpses all around wipes sweat from his brow and thinks he has no choice but to bow to Ebenezer and he does, as if he were viewing a natural force, gallops on a horse, Jehu King of Israel a chariot too fast, and Ebenezer stands up too fast, pickling for four years, and yet too fast, and he thinks, Toward what? They lived in those blocks? He has no satisfactory answer. To what? Hard to know. He has to organize a journey of dying people. To bring them quickly to some sanity. So they won't eat with their fingers and won't be so alarmed. Kramer is sitting there, he could have shot him.

A waste of a bullet, thought the officer.

I'm a carpenter, aren't I? said Ebenezer as if continuing innocently, I understand wood, huts, screws, nails. These are excellent huts but they're not meant to accommodate a thousand people in one hut without heat or toilets. I'm not complaining, he added, and the Red Cross man tried to laugh.

Why not? asked the officer.

I don't know, said Ebenezer.

Beyond the grove appeared people in civilian clothes. Their faces furious, led like a rebellious flock, kicking and cursing. Farmers brought to German Poland at the beginning of the war, one of them dressed like a rich man, bags under his eyes, tall and pale. British soldiers are leading them. A few of them stand still and the soldiers urge them on. Then they stop and wait for instructions. A mixture of orders from a microphone in English, German, Yiddish, makes that unreal moment concrete. The orders are barked out unreliably, thinks Ebenezer, they haven't imagined where they're going, they should put Kramer in charge! The civilians, who had lived in the area for years, are expecting a salvo of shots that will destroy them. They're shaking before the rifle barrels in the hands of the soldiers. Nobody bothers to explain to them. They're led to the giant pits that were dug a few days before and they think that here they'll be shot here. But instead of burying themselves they're assigned to bury those they didn't have time to burn. Abomination appears on their faces, so some of them were filled with indifferent heroism; not to yell or plead. In silence they worked, in silence they vomited, in silence they understood the respect-inducing sight of Kramer. When they passed by Ebenezer Schneerson they saw the first person in their life who lived in peace on an alien planet. Until today, they hadn't seen such human beings up close, but only as miniaturized geometric shapes. They had to lower their eyes. Kramer didn't hesitate to sneer at their look. Ebenezer still thought they were only lords with bad timing. That was a perplexing moment from Samuel's point of view, who's the stumbling block here and who would change places with whom?!

Ebenezer thought: Never did they know a real shame of humiliation, if they had known they would go into those graves and not come out. But Kramer knew them (and Ebenezer) very well, thought Samuel, Ebenezer is trying to locate himself: I'm the memory of things. I'm a crapper of the Poles. I'm a hidden light Gold told about before he died. I'm an electro-magnetic equation. I hover in the wind. A music room of symbols. The culture room where Bronya the Beautiful was shot with an apple in her mouth. The girlfriend of entertainers from the east. Barefoot, almost tired, they fell asleep trying to make Kramer laugh. He stood, in his hand a gun aimed at them and they tried to sing comic songs. In the scaring cold of the evening, in the light of the nearby glow of the explosions, but then Kramer fell asleep standing up, the gun in his hand and bliss on his face. How do you understand that sight?

A week before the end, Sturmbahnführer Weiss agreed to fix the Führer's frame. And Ebenezer was assigned to fix it. Ebenezer tries to locate things.

The entertainers were killed in an air raid on the way from the camp to Hathausen. Everybody kept Jewish prayer books in their cases to sell after the defeat. Like Samuel, they're also living in the future already. Ebenezer hasn't yet moved, Kramer is sitting and watching his Jew. Samuel is lusting for the wallets of the British soldiers. Kramer's Jew doesn't understand why they tied the commander's hands, Kramer isn't used to being tied. And then a Jewish soldier of the British army barked, at Kramer he barked, to emphasize the gravity of the moment, to defend himself with hostility, because of the need to disguise himself as a dog, and Kramer smiled, calm, he knows Jewish dogs, an inflexible and inelegant race, the soldier can't see what Ebenezer saw, the twilight darkened now and only Ebenezer, who had learned in childhood to see the eyes of jackals in the dark, saw Kramer's glowing eyes.

You and I, he said.

Then he looked at the darkening horizon. The charm in it earlier vanished. A reddish winding spark looked threaded like a shoelace. Two poplars were still seen blurry in the distance, beyond the grove that was no longer seen, and further away the small church was seen. Look at the new church, said Ebenezer.

It was here all the time, said Samuel.

I didn't see it until now, said Ebenezer.

You didn't look, said Samuel.

And it was here?

All the time, said Samuel.

Funny, said Ebenezer.

But Samuel also understood that Ebenezer was now thinking about the railroad car that brought him here because then, in the railroad car, the years he had had before ended. Then the church was seen and afterward was wiped out like all the memories and now it was new. Samuel smiled at the food now brought in open railroad cars. A plunder of food lighted by hurricane lamps and spotlights. A fresh lemon fell to the ground, and when a German tried to pick it up he was kicked by a soldier who tried to laugh and didn't laugh. But the German didn't want to straighten up now. There was no point. Somebody yelled: Get up, and Ebenezer said to the English captain: You really think I'm a joke about an elephant?

The Englishman said to him: I don't think you're a joke about an elephant, Mr. Schneerson. I do, said Ebenezer. They brought me and I remember now. Who am I who remembers? Don't know. There was a floor. And German soldiers and Jewish forced laborers from Vilna were still alive. The first hut they built around me. I arranged the joints, I put in the nails, I supervised the work, from inside, and they built the walls around me. That's how you trap an elephant, isn't it? You draw a trap around him and he's inside. Maybe I'm still building the hut the tank is destroying. And what now? Go know, my back is turned to Kramer, who sees me in the dark even if his hands are tied.

You're not alone, said the Englishman, who had known something about psychology before the war and once in London saw Sigmund Freud get into a black car driven by a young woman. There was no joy in his voice when Ebenezer tried to stitch the tatters of dark with leaps of words. The glowing light of the hurricane lamps and the spotlights covered the area and distanced it from him. The man on the microphone almost pleaded: You've got to be free! You've got to be free! Free? Without Kramer? That's absurd, said Ebenezer.

It will cost a lot, he said afterward to the officer. Women were still hiding in the huts, peeping out, scared. Skeletons in pajamas dropped after eating the first time, typhus will eat them, he said in English, officials and doctors ran around here and there. DDT showers operated vigorously. A tank fed the motor of the generator that operated the electricity. The Germans who had been brought to Germanify Poland dug in silence and buried the dead in the dark. Nobody paid attention to them anymore.

Weiss wasn't found. He's worth a lot, Weiss, said a German soldier who sat tied up in a wheelbarrow. Ebenezer gazed in wonder at the sight of hunger and thirst that split his lips. Did you ever see hungry Germans? he asked Samuel, who wanted to sell food to the German, but the German only had marks and pfennige and that didn't satisfy him and the Englishman was starting to show signs of impatience and the Red Cross man thought that was disgusting. Then another German rummaged in his pockets and found money. Samuel helped him search, went and brought food and water. He took the watch from the German in the wheelbarrow, he told Ebenezer, who looked at him sadly: I piss on the Englishman, what do

I care what he thinks of me! And they devoured the food. The Germans
don't have diamonds in their rectums, said Samuel, and there's no point
searching. He's got a watch, and that one has a camera, here it is. Everything's for you, Ebenezer. I'm taking care of you! The German's face was
red, he was eating bullybeef and overcooked fruit and vegetables. The
English officer averted his eyes. The Germans burying the dead in the
pits looked mutely at the German chomping in the wheelbarrow and their
mouths started chomping air.

Got to find Weiss, yelled the English Captain Wood. He yelled at
Kramer: Your commander has gotten away from us! Kramer didn't answer.
He was staring at Ebenezer. The wretched stance was an instance of offense to him, Ebenezer had to remember that moment, he even wanted to
take pity on Kramer, not Kramer the commander but Kramer the prisoner,
Kramer who even now was Weiss's deputy, but he couldn't. No feeling
throbbed in him. He thought maybe they were members of the same band
of grave robbers. Got to spray, yelled the Englishman, and find Weiss.
Coarse eating, typhus, lice, more DDT, less eating. You've got to be free!
Germans to work. The smell is awful, got to bury and burn as fast as possible, otherwise they'll die of plague. Destroy the blocks! And maybe
Ebenezer said: Leave something for a memory, otherwise they won't believe us. Kramer should be given to a circus, let him be taken from place
to place and tell. The Englishman looked at him with open animosity and
Samuel laughed. He feels uncomfortable, that Captain Wood. He sees
death and Kramer feels something, he doesn't know what. What world is
there outside? asks Samuel and tries to sell food to the Germans in exchange for watches and rings. Memory is Jewish science, scoffs Kramer, and
a young Australian who replaced one of the guards pushed Kramer and in
the process hit him in the ribs. But he didn't show them the pain, not
while Ebenezer was standing in front of him. The German in the wheelbarrow finished eating and started shaking. A jeep sped by and sprayed
thick dust. The German who was covered with white material tried to wipe
it off his face, but his hands were greasy from the food and Samuel said: It's
bone dust, and the German shook even more and tried not to see the skeleton of a woman in pajamas who stopped not far from him and held an
apple, her mouth was toothless, she spat at the German and in terror she
wiped the dust off him with her hands. I wipe myself on all of you like

paper, said Samuel. The German waited for his tears to flow and wash away the spit but they didn't flow. He doesn't like the taste of our spit, said Samuel, and a salvo of shots was heard in the distance, the microphone went on barking.

The improvised white flags were waving by ten. The tramping tanks stopped on the fences. Why didn't you think of a decent and splendid defeat? he asked Kramer, who blocked his ears. White panties instead of flags, that's a disgrace, isn't it? Fat Frieda, for whom the French chef would make fish heads, stuck a white ribbon to her sleeve and ran outside when she heard the tramping tanks. An enormous wolfhound burst out of the guardroom and chomped a hand that had previously been torn off, dripping thick material that may really have been blood, thought Ebenezer, the dog sat down on Frieda and she yelled: She's here! The dog loved her and lay on her to protect her and licked her, and she yelled: Get off of me, monster, but he didn't understand the orders and licked and Frieda was crushed, turned pale, turned blue. What love, said Samuel afterward, and the tanks split the fences and people in pajamas peeped as if they didn't believe. Skeletons who came to life walked on the ground padded with bone dust and the dog was called Brutus. Until they shot the dog, somebody said: Those were barks permeated with ideological awareness! And then Weiss was seen fleeing for his life with a bottle of wine in his hand and the picture of the Führer he managed to throw at the dog who was shot. The dog licked the Führer as he died. Not exactly a heartwarming picture when Frieda was crushed to death. The funniest thing of all, said somebody, was that Weiss looked shocked but was afraid to throw his cigarette on the ground so as not to litter the yard. And they didn't know where he was. Those bonfires, the food that came, the British officers, Captain Wood who took a position next to Ebenezer all day. Eat! Drink! You've got to be free! shrieked the microphone.

Then they die in DDT showers. Final solution of life, says a man who swallowed too much food and he turns pale and drops, his hand outstretched, still managing to trap a slice of sausage and chokes. And tranquility reigns, at long last tranquility reigns. Imaginary, not imaginary, one toilet for four hundred German workers. Stench mixed with an aroma of a distant meadow. Captain Wood a crumbled empire with medals on his chest. Historic spectacle, he says to himself, St. Bartholomew's night, and

Kramer doesn't budge. It's to his credit, isn't it, thinks Ebenezer, he
didn't ask for food. When he was given a glass of water, he held it in his
tied hands. And then he poured out the water. Some time has to pass, time
that will grant these moments their meaning, and the moment hasn't yet
come. Kramer is trying to give his sitting that proud solidity he saw in the
propaganda films that were wasted on him. He looks at his last battlefield.
His soldiers are in wheelbarrows or graves, tied up, pleading for food and
water. A momentary ritual nightmare, he said to Ebenezer, who couldn't
hear him. In a little while we'll know what to do, the Führer has surely left
instructions, there's something to be done, but we don't yet know what, got
to gain time, a retreat for some time and then we'll attack again. Kramer is
seeking some sign, why didn't he devastate the land along with the traitors.
It all has to be started over, says Kramer. And Ebenezer is amazed at how
he can read Kramer's mind, even today. Kramer says to the Englishman: I
beg your pardon for the water I spilled, I'm talking now as one officer to
another, but without getting any orders what can I do? The Englishman
didn't understand Kramer's splendid German, and went on drinking his
beer, and spitting. The sight of the splendid death of another officer who
was mistakenly shot by an English soldier cleaning his weapon pleased him
quite a bit, even though it was incorrect in terms of military protocol. The
gravediggers also saw in the death the nobility they were denied and didn't
yet know how to be despised properly. Weiss the fool is hiding under the
dead Jews, thought Kramer, I'm still secretly recording things about him,
as long as I haven't received an explicit order to report what Weiss is doing.
And the dead officer dropped masterfully. And in contrast to his splendid
death, Weiss was now taken out of the corpses and, shaking in terror, was
led to them. Some of the skeletons he lay under were still breathing, his
mouth dripped the remains of wine he had drunk in hiding. They sit him
down next to Kramer and somebody kicks him too, he bites his lips, wails
until his hands are tied. Don't blindfold him, says Samuel, let him learn to
see! And the English obey Samuel Lipker. Weiss asks for food and water
and the soldiers bring it to him. He holds out his tied hands, chews hungrily and drinks water. He tries to wipe his face but he can't. Finally he
manages to wipe his face with his forearms. Kramer points to the dead
officer and says: There died a manly officer, you sell yourself for a slice of
bread! Weiss doesn't answer and looks around. Something isn't clear to

him. His eyes run from Kramer stuck to him to Captain Wood, he's trying to know where the power is. Maybe there's some mistake here. There was no mistake, says Kramer. Weiss doesn't get it yet. People are passing by him with wheelbarrows full of cadavers and he turns his face aside. Only when Kramer challenges Weiss and looks at him with restrained and tranquil contempt does Ebenezer understand that maybe the war is over.

Samuel understood that by nine in the morning when Frieda started looking for linens to make white flags. Ebenezer is slower. An enlightened camp, Samuel Lipker says to Wood, an enlightened camp with electricity, water, and a French chef.

Night falls. Samuel falls asleep. He earned enough on the first evening of life. In the morning a new sun breaks forth. Somebody took pity on the Germans digging and filling gigantic graves and gave them food. They swallow hungrily. Kramer sits without moving in the place where he sat yesterday. Maybe he didn't shut his eyes either. Weiss is transferred to the improvised interrogation room. Kramer says contemptuously: Now he'll sing them oratorios, but his voice is hoarse. Ebenezer approaches Kramer, touches him. Kramer looks at his Jew. A long meaningless look. They no longer have anything to say to one another. A whole day, the one and only day in their lives, each looked at the other. Kramer doesn't want to smile. Cold, hunger, and obstinacy have done their work. He waits for the secret orders.

Avenues in light Ebenezer sees. Near him they're still digging. He thinks: When did I meet Samuel Lipker, when did I leave Palestine, is it still there, what happened to the beautiful bougainvillea, did I ever really have bougainvillea? Maybe there really is a horizon near the church I saw yesterday for the first time. For three years I didn't hear its bells. What do I remember? I've got to learn my life.

Then Ebenezer leaves the Red Cross hut. Somebody had already managed to draw a Star of David on the hut. Kramer is still sitting pensively. A woman is standing over him and yelling: Say where they killed my children. Where did they kill them, there were three, Haimke, Ruha, and Shmil, where did they kill them? Not far from here is a fine camp of officers, like a pastoral painting. It was here all the time, says Ebenezer, and Ebenezer didn't know. They talk about distributing ration cards, updating, registering, spraying, about food portions and medicine. Captain Wood is rather busy today. The blocks have almost all been destroyed. Old Jews set up a synagogue in a tent. Look for a Torah scroll in the garbage. At night a psychiatrist in a sailor's cap arrives. A woman stands above him and looks at him. She's amazed at how he can sleep in that noise. Look how he sleeps, he hasn't got dreams! And Captain Wood says: He'll understand, he at least has to understand, got to find a way to separate between total disbelief and reality, between life in London after the month of the blitz we came out and found the fog, the street, that's what saved us, they've got to start finding something and understanding. Ebenezer doesn't understand that the church exists! What are the Germans burying, asks the Red Cross man, can I really examine every body? And how many bodies are here? Ebenezer shuts his eyes and says: Abramovitch five, Avigovitch three, Anishevitch two, Baborovsky three, Bennoam two, Bronovitch . . . What is he doing? asks Captain Wood and Samuel says: He's counting for you how many there were here in the three years so you can examine the corpses from the list. There's no need, yells Captain Wood, suddenly flushed, as if the number of dead is meant to indict him, and he stops Ebenezer, who opens his eyes. He looks and sees that the numbers he was about to deliver are registered with surprising clarity on Kramer's face. Ebenezer tries to maintain the barrier, he looks at the sky, a small plane lands not far from here, he tries to find the sky as Captain Wood once found a street and fog. Grass, cows grazing not far away, when did we see cows? He doesn't remember and isn't sure he really didn't see. Samuel is making deals with soldiers, selling souvenirs, already inventing himself the lampshade made from his parents, and selling it to them, and they weep quite a bit hearing Samuel Lipker's story. By the end of the day, the story was practiced and recited properly, without mistakes, from now on, he'll easily find the place where the soldiers' tears of remorse flow and will make a deal that's not bad. He understands that there's money in tear ducts. Kramer has now turned into a landmark. Two steps from Kramer, on the right, there's a psychiatrist who has gotten up and is trying to understand, to help. Let him hold white underpants, says somebody. Why are they making a picnic of all this? says Captain Wood in a moment of perplexity. The barbed wire fence is already starting to totter, strewn with dead dogs who fled and were electrocuted. People are washing, scared of the light. A little girl asks a

soldier for candy and next to her stands a table full of candy. Hard to understand, thinks Ebenezer, but possible to peep, Fraulein Klopfer sits tied up
next to Kramer, lowers her eyes, and Samuel says to Captain Wood: When
they threw babies into the fire she took a baby, tossed it up and aimed
it so it would fall straight down, like a rock into water. You'd be amazed
how much a year-old baby wants to live and how he leaps and shrieks.
Look at her! That's how you'll find the street and the fog. A sunbeam
prances on the Germans digging. A blond boy with blue-gray eyes stands on
the edge of the pit and hands his father a sandwich. His face is transparent,
so fair. The father chews hungrily and mutters something, and the little girl
at the table, to the right of Kramer, swallows some chocolate and her face is
smeared, and an American soldier takes a picture of a little girl brown with
chocolate next to the DDT showers. Clouds float in the sky. How do you
guess, Fraulein Klopfer, thinks Captain Wood. She lifts her face and looks at
the dim glow of the horizon, valiant Germans are digging pits and filling
them with the dead, that destroyed harmony shatters in her a vital force that
Kramer is trying to suck out of the air as if he were waiting for dispatches,
the Führer won't forsake us, he says confidently. Does Captain Wood understand the meaning that I'm not the Last Jew, that a disaster happened and
Samuel doesn't know who the disaster happened to? This is how a very powerful system is devised, says the psychiatrist.

Who will arrange the battle Ebenezer is now shaping in his memory, his
chronicles, thinks the psychiatrist sitting with Ebenezer in a special tent
set up for him.

I knew I'd be the last to give up!

How did you think about that?

I didn't think. It came by itself.

And in the previous camp?

There I didn't think, and don't remember exactly.

Will you hypnotize yourself to remember?

Samuel can help me.

Samuel, come help him.

Samuel approaches, stands next to Ebenezer, says: Shut your eyes, set
your watch back. Kramer stands up to come see the box you made for him
and then . . .

I came to Birkenau. For years I searched for Joseph Rayna. Here I was almost the first one. They built the hut after I was inside. Three years here is the climax!

And what did you do?

Don't remember . . . at night they didn't shoot me, but they told me, at first there were no chambers here.

Gas?

Gas.

And what did they do?

They tried with a diesel motor and heavy oil, says Samuel, that took an hour to suffocate thirty people in a closed truck. Weiss came and saw my box.

Then you made boxes?

Yes, says Samuel, and that's how he remembered.

How?

He heard people murmuring. They were finished and were dead. They were hungry, stunned, groaned at night, talked, he started remembering, doesn't know how, he said: I'll be the last one who will guard everything they know.

Humiliated?

Maybe he didn't say humiliated, isn't humiliated too strong?

Perhaps. I wasn't there. You come from another world, Mr. Schneerson.

But he's here.

Yes, he's here, but look, he isn't anymore.

I don't know, if he was, he'll probably remain.

No, he isn't.

I didn't have the strength to remember the other things, so maybe I could not know how awful it is to live here.

To ignore?

Yes. And not to think. Just remember things I don't understand anyway.

There were geniuses here. Do you know what a mine of knowledge was lost here? Only a little of that he remembers.

Why?

Everything came according to a certain music, the words came one by one, incomprehensible but etched. You think I'll ever be free of that?

I don't know.

Let's say, I thought about Wittgenstein's theory, there is such a man, isn't there?

Yes.

I thought about it, don't understand it, but every word of his I know. I remembered his words and I forgot what I did before.

Everything comes at the price of something, says Samuel.

Apparently, says the psychiatrist.

I'm a superficial man. I thought I'd hide and they'd come and then I'd tell them. I loved a woman. I left everything, but I don't remember now. I remember their words. Got to be freed first. I already remember Captain Wood and you, sir, a sign that I'm not the Last Jew. A sign that I'm also starting to remember things that are happening to me.

Then they passed through small cities, slipped between closed borders, and the money Samuel earned was enough to slip from place to place. Samuel said: The dumb psychiatrist thought you're a sorcerer and not a poor soul who drills from the words of others. In one city they met a woman who knew Ebenezer. During the war she had sewn uniforms for armies that had passed through there. He asked her to tell him what he had searched for there fifteen years before and she didn't want to remember. When they came to the destroyed street of the Jews they met some Jews who were standing and feeling the ruins in amazement. Samuel and Ebenezer stood on the side. They had no concrete memories here. Poles came out of a nearby house and started beating them. Samuel spat and Ebenezer looked on in astonishment. He thought: Kramer was right. Then he started talking with Samuel about Palestine. Didn't remember much. Remembered his mother, the settlement. Remembered dimly, he had to make an effort. Samuel didn't want to hear. What will I do in a savage land? There they won't throw stones at you for coming to feel destroyed stones, said Ebenezer. Everywhere there are pogroms, said Samuel, I'll teach you to hit them where it hurts. Why did you leave, asked Samuel, but Ebenezer didn't know anymore, something about Joseph Rayna . . . I was ultimately an echo that picked up echoes, says Ebenezer, Captain Wood, who attended Eton and Oxford, doesn't hold a stick in his hand, doesn't understand, I'm with Samuel, where to?

Echoes touch echoes, pain touches pain. What a gigantic sky like a canopy of death.

My dear Goebbelheydrichhimmel, that's all for now. Second draft. The words aren't yet stuck together precisely. Imagine writing *achtung* today when the meaning of the word in the dictionary is: term of respect!

I remember back then, in Denmark, when I sent you my first stories. Those were different times. We tried to understand what had happened to us, you were also steeped in dread then and tried to investigate. I wrote you the story about myself, a soldier who created contact with the enemy and was sent back in shame from the occupied land to command children shooting at low-flying planes. You wondered then, you were even afraid that what I did in Denmark would disturb the publication of my book. Then I came back and you supported me, I'm grateful, if not for your help, who knows where I'd be today? You want Germany without remorse because in the end remorse doesn't help. An artist, a boy, a magician, not a Jew . . . a Jew in a story sounds too simple, to write about Jews means writing not only about Wasserman, Walter Benjamin, Gershom Scholem, Buber, and Einstein—we're allowed to talk about them, in articles and lectures—but also about moneylenders, wretched street musicians, a schmaltzy wedding orchestra, knitted skullcaps, ritual fringes, and you think, Ah, literary *judenrein* is after all a certain enlightenment. Symbols? Yes: fish, midget, architect, only not Mr. Cohen who lived in Cologne and has been burned on our bonfires for one thousand five hundred years, looks like a caricature, sells kosher salami.

Samuel Lipker now blows up Arab villages and so we can erase him from literature, what do I have to do with him, you ask, what do I have to do with the story of Ebenezer? Who's interested in Ebenezer? I understand, for you he's superfluous, for me he's hard, because with Ebenezer I'll be a stranger in the literature and the cinema where I'm one of the central pillars. And I'm not talking about the literature and cinema that are *judenrein*! All of us knew some Samuel Lipker, didn't we, in school, on the street, we had a common biography, and where are they? Ebenezer didn't know he couldn't enter great German literature. Human tatters here and there, and nothing else. I can invite my translators from all over the world to a splendid conference, lecture to them, and maybe a translator will even come from Israel, they'll all sit, and I've got money to do that, don't I, and I'll explain the subtleties to them, but none of them will be bold enough to ask me where in my fiction is Hans who once lived in the house where we're meeting. He's just some Ebenezer, some carpenter. See how much more interesting Kramer is than Ebenezer? Why do we need Ebenezer in Kramer's story?

Kramer grits his teeth when the Jews are involved in a revolt against themselves and us, he knows how to keep his mouth shut and not say what he once said in awful words, and he's right, dammit, they've got no right to blow up quiet villages, but maybe I have no right to tell them that. I should investigate Kramer, and not only against the background of Wilhelmstrasse, but also against the background of Walter Benjamin, or his family who maybe played in the women's orchestra of Auschwitz. How enlightened and beautiful we are today. They gave us European manure, six million graves, and we gave them an extension. Now we're right again and again they're not. Act nice, we tell them, and then we'll talk to you. You destroyed the Arab village of Marar, so why are you still talking! We buy eternity with sublime conscientiousness, with measured words, without mentioning names. And Lipker sells and buys cigarettes. Ebenezer sells knowledge in nightclubs. Not nice. A literary Jew is Freud, not Lipker! What you want is a nice story about a carter's ass. He pees and sees through the prism of urine the fisherman and the farmer's wife kneeling. You want indifferent, estranged words, mother died on Sunday, was born on Posen Street. You want a thin literature in a world where literature has nothing more to say. But look, we're successful, they read us. Maybe you're right and I'm not, but your rightness is starting not to interest me, my friend, Ebenezer's rightness is more perverse, incomprehensible, but more important to me.

Meanwhile until I can write what you and my friends will sneer at, I will write my novella, I'll finish it, I promised and I'll keep my promise. Afterward, we'll sit, Henkin and I, and together we'll write a book, from both sides of the absurd, from both sides of death. I'll describe everything, every single detail, there'll be a pissing snake there, and Hitler who didn't die, and Jews who aren't literary, maybe even without qualities, love is a banal issue, like hate, like death.

That's it so far, because soon I'll start being banal again. The words don't scare me anymore. With a bitter sneer I'll write the prologue to what you call an epilogue. I'll write my lament, along with Henkin, an old investigator who lost a son in the war with the Arabs, and you'll have to publish a book that won't gain you anything, that critics will desecrate and not celebrate, that people won't read and won't buy.

Tape / —

Joseph Rayna died, appropriately, on his birthday. Sixty-two years old he was at his death. He stood at a wall, his hands raised, his body blighted, bereft of the spirit of life even before he would die. Until his final days he had walked around erect with a crooked indulgent smile on his lips, as if everything happening before his eyes was known to him long before. Maybe it was the smile of schadenfreude. Beautiful was Joseph, as old angels are when a tired and bored God stopped taking an interest in sugary young men. A man in whose arms a Hebrew queen had died, whose father was hanged, and for whom a hundred women got pregnant. I searched for him, I knew he hadn't gone to America, but I didn't find him. His hollow songs Joseph had burned in his mind long before his death. Samuel Lipker was born from an almost absurd coupling between Joseph and a lustful woman who acted heroines she loved in a locked room all her life. Samuel's father didn't know that Samuel wasn't his son. He left Samuel a diamond in his body. He and his wife were too decent to accept the truth and admit it, so they learned how to live alongside it, to console themselves with the silence between them. They refused to admit what deviated in them.

Tape / —

When Samuel's mother went to the store to buy bread and flowers, she'd look at the trees or the display window as if those too were paintings by some genius artist. Her devotion to the beauty and glory of art was so great that she was afraid to deal with them in public. So as not to shame what she secretly called: that muse!

The universe, as she revealed to Joseph later on, chose to crush in herself her own great talent, a talent she was forbidden to waste for the pittance of small inauthentic theaters with an audience smelling of popcorn and fried onions. If only I had been born in Paris, she said.

The great love affair of her life began like every war, quite by chance. It was of course a moment that would later be described as unforgettable, and was preceded by steps that of course could not be changed. She was stand-

ing there in a flower shop and, as she put it, smelling the aroma of the
distant rivers that watered those delicate flowers when Joseph Rayna, the
aging lover of women, saw her reflection in the window and began wooing
her with a courtesy that was splendid, wicked, but so tired it looked elegant and theatrical to her. He bought her all the flowers in the display
window and five boys had to carry home the baskets of flowers and at the
sight of them she laughed a wild laugh, which this time—uncriticized—
came from within herself. The boys bore the flowers with lockjaw disci-
pline. The secret had to be equally elegant and concealed. After acting
Electra and Antigone all her life before walls crammed with plates and
pictures, now she stood at the flowers and waited for a love letter from
Joseph Rayna. Abrom Mendelstein, who would later be shot and laid diago-
nally on top of his two brothers and his father, with whom he would dig the
grave, lent Samuel's mother his room. Since he couldn't carry on a real
affair, he loved to see love flourishing in his friends. He was a teacher of
Akkadian and Aramaic and his wife Frumka was such a free woman that she
had had three lovers by then, and she didn't make love to them because of
firm reluctance to yield to feelings that didn't throb in her. She belonged
to a small progressive and stormy faction that seceded from the central
section, and she also seceded from the general party in the Warsaw committee, whose sixty-two members split into six different trends and once
a week, Samuel's mother was lent the small apartment and Joseph would
arrive gasping from all the stairs he had to climb.

With him, Samuel's mother could declaim in French drenched in ancient and sweet idioms the ancient Medea, full of evil and passion, and
plot against herself. In her late youth, as the mother of Samuel, whose miserable father was Joseph, she began to sing, and was cheerful even though a
bit vague from so much life that had landed on her and she thought quite a
bit of things she had seen as if they were written in a book and not really real.

Searching his father's naked body before he put it on the heap of
corpses to be burned, Samuel was amazed at the sight of his parents' surprising nakedness. He succumbed to the profound feeling of disgust and
gratitude when he found the diamond.

Lionel Secret once asked his mother Rachel: Who was my father? And
Rachel Brin, Rayna, now Blau, said: I was married to a man named Nathan
Secret, he died, I came to America because my friend Rebecca kept talking

about the trees dripping gold of America. They didn't drip gold and she
went to Palestine. Until I married Saul Blau who started selling his shirts,
I worked hard. Today our trees are all right, she said.

Tape / —

Lionel Secret, who was once called Secret Glory, was a frightened child
and at night, to fall asleep he would sing Schubert lieder to himself and
until the age of eleven, his voice was thin as a girl's. Rachel had two daughters and two sons with Saul Blau and Lionel grew up to be a tall fellow with
an ascetic handsome face, his hair was black, somebody said he looked like
a butterfly trapped and proud at the same time. A dimple of eternal pondering was set into his right cheek and made him look determined, but also
thoroughly confused.

When the war broke out, Lionel enlisted and after training in England,
he was sent to Europe and for seven days he shot at an enemy whose precise location was confused by the maps. When the mistake was discovered,
half his battalion was taken prisoner, and the remaining soldiers stopped
shooting at the empty hay loft and waited for Lionel, who was familiar with
the impressive parades of the brown shirts on York Avenue, near his house,
and he called to his comrades to flee. Three deigned to join him. They
slipped away, lay in the rotten hayloft, and when the Germans came in
with their prisoners, Lionel prepared an attack like the game he had once
played in summer camp where he was assigned the role of the Indian.
More soldiers who had previously thought they had no chance to escape
came to help them, destroyed their captors and made their way to brigade
headquarters, which had gone astray and was tramping in a direction not
only imprecise, but also unknown. Lionel managed to deliver his prisoners,
earn a salute of honor from an old commander who yearned for more successful and chivalrous wars, fight a few weeks in battles better prepared
but still lost, see a British plane brought down, hear its pilot yelling *Shema
Israel* under the parachute the Germans peppered with bullets, engage in
diversionary operations in which he taught an aged commander how to
smell Germans by the smell of beets and potatoes, and lead a unit of Aus-
tralians and Canadians to a town completely different from the description
in the briefing. In that operation, a British soldier was shot who lobbed a
hand grenade and knocked out an armored car with a German brigade com-

mander and his Polish adjutant, the Pole tried to shoot and in his death throes, he hit a little girl standing there playing with her two dogs, and on its way to the little girl the bullet also passed through Lionel, who managed to destroy the armored car completely and to shoot a last bullet at the Pole, and at the end of all that he was taken to the hospital.

Lionel won two medals, which were awarded him by a brigadier general, who still remembered his fury at the sight of a Jewish tailor bent over in a small street in Liverpool.

By the time Lionel, the fifty-third son of Joseph Rayna, returned to America, he was an officer in the British army. After Pearl Harbor, the United States was forced to enter the war declared on it by the Germans. Lionel commanded a training school in the southern United States. After toiling for half a year training young men, he was sent to Europe to take part in the great Landing. After he was wounded again, this time by shrapnel, he was transferred to intelligence, to the division of interrogation and liaison. Aside from English, Lionel knew Yiddish, German, Polish, Russian, French, and Sanskrit, and those languages, at least some of them, along with his profound knowledge of Latin and ancient Greek, helped him considerably to be considered an excellent interrogation officer. And indeed, he was promoted, and in 'forty-five, a few months before the war ended, he attained the rank of major, and General Eisenhower, in a letter of an efficient secretary, thanked him for his contribution to the war effort and awarded him a special medal for outstanding service, bravery, and model behavior.

There was a moment when Lionel, who still thought of himself as Secret Glory, thought that the stories he hadn't yet managed to write were also the only stories he would write. He even thought of choosing some death of honor. The novel he thought of writing about Joseph Rayna, whom his mother had told him about with her eyes filled with youthful mischief, refused to be written. He published some short stories in important journals with small circulation. And once he wrote a letter to Rebecca Schneerson in Palestine. Her answer was matter-of-fact: if you're really a mature person, you will probably understand how much your fate can't touch my heart, you're in America with your mother and I'm not, I'm busy in the cowshed and with the almond trees, the war didn't pass over us, Nehemiah died on the shore of Jaffa, you asked about my son who's wandering around Europe. I don't know, I think he was killed, the adulterer Joseph Rayna didn't make me children, but on the other hand nobody can know for sure who was the father of my son, yours, Rebecca Schneerson.

When Lionel was thirteen, he loved a twelve-year-old girl who lived on the other side of the city. She lived in a big house surrounded by a fine garden, planned by an English landscape architect especially for her father, the main Ford dealer in the area. Lionel would bring her flowers he picked in the fields, wrote poems to her, and told her about the stories he would write when he grew up. The girl's name was Melissa and she had bright and beautiful oval eyes and sparkling brown hair. One day Melissa threw away the flowers, turned her face away, and said in a voice choked with weeping whose subtleties he didn't understand: My mother told me I'm big enough not to be a girlfriend of some Jew from Poland. Lionel returned home, sang lieder to the toilet, and wept behind the locked door. Rachel said: That happens in Poland, not in America. He listened to her and said: Maybe it shouldn't happen here, but it did. A month later, Melissa got sick. The doctors couldn't diagnose her illness. Melissa asked her mother to call Lionel and he came. By now she had little breasts and her eyes became more white than bright and Lionel shut his eyes which were almost weeping and saw the angel of death sitting between Melissa's eyelashes. Later on, when he would come out of the hayloft and fight the Germans he would do that to save Melissa and her parents, he would feel that he was returning them good for bad. Lionel wanted to pray but didn't know what God they prayed to in the elegant house of the main Ford dealer. He stroked Melissa and told her how much he loved her. She showed him pictures of movie actresses filled with sweet smiles and he told her she was more beautiful than they were. Her sweet eyelashes and her face were now full of something he knew was death. But Melissa's parents, who tried not to see Lionel, said: She's got the flu and in a few days she'll get better. Lionel pleaded with them to send her to the hospital in New York, but they said angrily that the doctors of New York were no better than the doctors of their city. He told Melissa: I think of you, I'll always love you, and she told him she'd always love him and in secret they signed a lifetime contract. The contract was hidden in Lionel's pocket and Melissa asked him to forgive her for what she had once said to him. After I told you what Mother told me to say, I wept all night long! she said. Her eyes dimmed, he saw how close death was and called her mother in alarm, and her mother told him: She's tired and you should go now, Lionel. He told her: My name is Secret Glory, and she looked at him, saw the flash of wrath burning in his eyes and something primeval and ancient made her tremble even though she didn't even know what it was. Her parents brought young Brook to read her the history of the struggle for the Connecticut River from the journal *Our Connecticut*, a bimonthly and a source of pride for many buyers of cars from Melissa's father. Melissa lay with her eyes shut, pale and transparent as a butterfly and with a slight effort she managed not to listen to young Brook.

He didn't go to Melissa's funeral. Two years later, he went to New York to school. His mother and her husband moved to New Jersey. In New York, he clung to a girl who talked about class warfare and her cunning and elusive body wasn't at all like the purity in Melissa's eyes. Lionel wrote a few more stories, and to descend to the masses, he tried to live with the woman who cleaned his father's house, was unfaithful to her with a girl from Radcliffe, went on a long trip around the world, a trip that lasted six years, and then he spent two years closed in a room and wrote a novel that wasn't accepted by any publisher, and then he went to a small city, started teaching in a college, and for three years he collected old cars, ambulances, locomotives, tow trucks, and buses, and parked them in a lot he leased and would walk among those cars and think, Why do I collect this garbage? I don't even like to drive and detest every car and every bus I collect.

Saul Blau expanded his business and opened a few shirt shops. Lionel met the woman who had once been an elusive girl and talked about class warfare, now she took Lionel to her old parents' house and during the Kiddush, she raised her glass to toast the Molotov-Ribbentrop Pact, which, in her words, liberated the toilers from the malice of the capitalist war. Lionel scolded her, he yelled that she was Jewish filth, words she treated with such abysmal tolerance and contempt that she almost burst out laughing. Then Lionel went to enlist in the Canadian brigades at the Canadian consulate in New York, and went off to fight as we said, because of that woman for the lost Jewish honor. He of course couldn't tell her that he was going to fight for Melissa, for Melissa's parents and their Ford cars. The lot of cars, buses, and ambulances he sold. His stepfather told him: Don't worry, Secret, you're all right in my hands, I'll invest your money and add as much and more, you'll be both a hero and rich.

Saul, Rachel's husband, liked to pound his hand on the table and say:
Oh, just be healthy! He conquered the field of cheap shirts with diligence,
guile, and restraint. He said: I push the shirts on them so my parents who
were murdered in a pogrom will lie in warm shirts in their grave. Rachel,
who didn't understand the connection between his dead parents and the
shirt stores spreading over the city, loved in her husband the lack of
Joseph's madness. At night, she secretly longed for the forests, Rebecca,
the language of syllables, and one day, she said: Someday I'll visit Rebecca
in her forest in Palestine.

When Rachel heard the Nazis singing on York Avenue and saw their
goose-step marching, she locked the shutters of Lionel's apartment right
over a big bar whose owner was passing out wine and cakes to those in the
parade, and she asked Lionel: What will be? He told her he would fight
them for her too. She said: Lionel, you're not a child, you're a grown man,
forty years old, not married, not settled, without a serious profession, and
they're strong. Watch out for them, and when she looked into his eyes she
saw a smile capering in them, some weary and glowing splendor of dignity
that reminded her of Joseph Rayna's face and she was sorry, so sorry, she
had had to grant her son a father like Joseph Rayna, which would surely
bring destruction on him in the war against the Germans now shouting in
the street below. Weariness and life did their work and she had neither the
strength nor the will to tell her son who his father was. Suddenly she said:
The words of Joseph Rayna could have been a reply to those satanic parades. After Lionel enlisted, Rachel waited for him behind the locked shutters. Every week she went to his apartment and would arrange his books.

Lionel came to Cologne as an interrogator of prisoners. He came there
on the same day that Ebenezer Schneerson and Samuel Lipker came to
Paris, where they started performing in a small nightclub. In Cologne,
Lionel met Lily Schwabe. When he saw her he understood that Melissa
hadn't died, and children who had once shot at airplanes near the destroyed factory now stood almost naked in the street and pointed at Lionel,
who strode to the temporary headquarters. The city was destroyed. Lionel
helped a local Jewish committee find Jewish children hidden in monasteries and other hiding places and weren't told that the war was over. After
thinking about Lily, he made a decision to give her up from the start. He
was also afraid that another Melissa would die on him.

After he gave up Lily, he went to the river. He sat at the river and drank juice from a can. Near the place where he was sitting, workers were digging under a destroyed house and taking out corpses of prisoners of war killed in air raids. In the river he saw moss and oil spots and scum, but fish he didn't see. He didn't see fish because even the dead fish were fished out by the hungry Germans. He was disgusted with himself for being sad at seeing hungry Germans. That thought brought him back to Lily. She looked too hungry to be Melissa. Everything metamorphoses into everything, everybody lives again and again, death is a cease-fire, he thought. He went back to the city and found himself in an army canteen. He bought kerosene, clothes, oil, soap, sausage, canned milk, wine, cheese, cigarettes, dairy products, and other groceries, put everything into a kitbag, and went to Lily's house. Lily touched the groceries, tentatively, and, with her eyes shut, her hands stroked the canned milk. She smiled shyly, nervously smoothed her faded dress, and started cooking. Music came from a soldiers' café not far from there, and then she set the table and after everything was perfectly arranged—the gleaming, old dishes—she burst into tears. Lionel got up, went to her, stroked her and then licked her tears. She stood without moving and let him lick her eyes. Then they sat at the table and ate. He looked in amazement at her ravenous eating. They drank some wine and sat at the window where bonfires were seen. Two whole days they didn't go out of the house.

Later on, Lily will tell Lionel that the blood shed then was the blood of her virginity and that he was the first man in her life. When Lily saw Lionel, almost twenty years older than her, standing in the door of her house and holding a kitbag in his hands, she felt for the first time in her life an enormous need to belong to somebody. A day before, as she sat in the office among disgruntled women and waited to renew her temporary ID, she saw Lionel walking in his uniform. She remembered that, when he passed by her, there was an innocent dismay on his face, and only then did he discover her and start talking with her and she smiled, even though she didn't know she was Melissa, and then he said: What is this Lily Schwabe, and she said: Lily Schwabe is a woman who lives in a destroyed house, and she gave him her address—something she had never done— and he went off and she was afraid she'd never see him again, until he showed up.

Two days later, Lionel stood in the little bathroom, facing the mirror that had cracked long ago, and cut his face with a razor blade. Lily, who thought he was trying to commit suicide, yelled and ran to him and tried to take the razor out of his hand, and then he told her in German: I'm not committing suicide, I just cut myself. She was amazed to hear the German, and said: Why didn't you tell me you speak German, and then he said: Don't worry, Melissa, and she said: My name is Lily and you speak German. Suddenly the sight of the people he interrogated rose in his mind's eye, the convulsions of laughter, the attempt to be cunning, but still strong, the endless deceit of those who didn't know anything, always they knew nothing, and he said to himself: I shouldn't have found her here. His hands shook and he slapped her. He said: I know how to say that in German, too, and she sat down on a broken chair, stroked her face, and said: Take the child, too! And he said angrily: There is no child and there won't be any child, and she said: Then take the no-child. And then she told him about her father taken prisoner by the Russians, he tried to trap her, to know if she was lying to him, but after a while—and he was an excellent interrogator—he understood that Lily Schwabe really didn't know why that war had raged. She knew French, German, literature, and history, but because of her reason and some profound wisdom in her, she didn't know why that war had raged. She didn't know that people died in camps. That offended Lionel. He knew that everybody said that, it was convenient for him to know that they said and recalled things and tried to pass on to the agenda. But to meet somebody like Lily, and to understand, to understand that she truly didn't know, that was beyond his understanding. He told her: You're not guilty, *In sinne der Anklage—Nicht schuldig*, as the war criminals then claimed. She wasn't angry at him for hitting her, and he said: You taught yourself to be devoid of moral judgment, but neither did she understand why Lionel's Judaism constituted any difficulty in their relations. She understood only that he shouldn't have German children. And she said that. She tried to understand what happened, to explain how she had shut herself off, maybe against her will, maybe because of some indifference, maybe because of a fear that she couldn't hold out, she lived on the periphery, and the war passed by her, the city was blown up, people went away and didn't come back, but she didn't ask questions, maybe she feared the answers, she only remembered that near the end of the war, she saw the

young children, she'd see them on their way to the nearby school, shooting at low-flying planes and being killed, and older prisoners of war, bound
with ropes, loading sandbags to defend them and being killed too. Lionel
said to her: You're the wrong product of the Third Reich, everything was
wasted on you!

Lionel got up, walked around the room, and for three straight hours, he
delivered a speech to her about the continuity of the Jewish fate, about the
lost echoes of their footsteps, and he left. Two days later he came back.
He'd bring groceries, and she would cook. You're learning to eat, he told
her, envying her hunger. All the time he would talk about his shortcomings,
his advanced age, his failure as a writer, his life as a superfluous journey
between nothing and nothing, and Lily who began to understand that her
name was not only Lily but also Melissa, began to learn English, and one
day she sat among his dirty clothes and laundered them and thought about
a certain word she had learned that day, and shouted it to Lionel who was
in the bath, and he opened the door, saw the young woman sitting there
lovesick with his clothes and gave her some answer about the word she had
uttered, and then he understood the meaning of his love, he understood it
from her concern with his clothes and with words, understood what sensu-
ality a woman could grant to the pants of a man she loved, and how far she
could go to speak a language that is the soul of things and their formulation
before they were in the world. Now he saw Lily imprisoned in a world that
for some reason didn't take vengeance on her because it didn't know what
profound rebelliousness was buried in her, how she could betray herself,
her parents, all out of a total dissociation, out of a rare ability to be like a
wax statue in a legend in which a prince appears and grants her life. Her
life is my sad echo, he said to himself, and loved her as much as he was
disgusted by her and by himself, loved her more than anybody else he had
ever loved in his life.

Tape / —

When Ebenezer and Samuel Lipker came to Cologne, Samuel stood in
the street and distributed announcements about the performance. He had
no guilt about dragging Ebenezer to that place. As far as he was concerned,
the enemy should also enjoy. Lionel heard about the performance and
decided to take Lily. When they entered the small wretched nightclub

they were greeted by the owner, a very thin man with smoky eyes, holding rattles to be shaken, and when they sat down at a big wooden table where people had carved their names for years, two gigantic glasses of beer were already standing before them and in front was a small lighted stage. The place was crowded, the smoke of cheap cigarettes spiraled up from all sides, and whenever Ebenezer declaimed, the room thundered with the excited rattles. Next to Lionel and Lily sat five hugging men who wept all the time. For some reason, the tears the men wept were so big that when he looked at them, Lionel could see how the space left by Ebenezer's words, words with nothing behind them except borrowed memory, stirred laugh ducts in five men who came here to demonstrate disguised laughter. Ebenezer looked to Lionel like a repulsive Jew who wanted to look like a repulsive Jew, rather stooped, and Lionel wearing the uniform of an American officer felt uncomfortable, he was amazed not only that that man was amusing people who would have tortured him a year ago, but also at his own amazement. Lily understood that Ebenezer was reciting things he didn't understand, but as far as she was concerned, there was something in that fact itself that justified what she had tried to explain to Lionel without much success, that she too had lived ten years in a recital and didn't understand that she was reciting, didn't even want to understand.

And then Lionel noticed Samuel Lipker. Between the excerpts, Samuel praised the Last Jew who was appearing here before this distinguished audience, as he put it. He spoke like a person reporting on percentages of interest or a rise in stocks, restrained and aloof, and all the while his face was thrust at the audience, he had to know who his real enemy was, he had to overpower them and Lionel understood his look better than he understood Lily's enthusiasm at hearing the things Ebenezer was reciting. Lionel hated the covetousness he discerned in Samuel's eyes. He saw in him something that reminded him of the awful moments of his life, when he saw in the mirror a person he himself didn't know. And then Ebenezer said: I now list essays on the history of the hostility to the repulsive Jews (he didn't say that mockingly, he said it dryly, as if he had no opinion)— Distinguished gentlemen, set your watches a thousand years back. I'm trying again, I said then boldly: the news according to Benbas, the dialogue with Trifo by Justin Martyr, the pamphlet against the heretics by Iraeneus, I'm sorry about the whisper, reading from a distance, dead letters torn in my mind, a smell of a distant church, a ringing that deserted the bells and remains hovering in the air, torturing Jews by Tertullian, calling God by Lactinius, and that fool Kramer thought only about the essay by Isidor of Sevilla and his pamphlet against the Jews. A great expert you had there! Kramer . . . removing all the heretics and an explanatory essay against Jews by Hippolyte, tasteless kinds of flesh of Jews by Novatian and a selection of testimonies by Nissa and testimonies from the Old Testament against the Jews, proof of the Good Tidings, history of the church by Eusebius. Eight sermons against the Jews and proof to the Jews and the Christians that Jesus is God by Chrysostom, a pamphlet by Saint Augustine, his Heavenly City . . . Rhymes against the Jews by Ephraim the Syrian, Sergei de Abraga: the Torah of Jacob and the proofs against the Jews by Ephrat, the sermons of Masrog, the Sabbath against the Jews by Isidore . . . Something is omitted here, and the book of Orthodox faith, a dialogue of Jason and Papikies, a dialogue of Timothy of Aquilla, a dialogue of Asnasius and Pepsicus, and Philo, and Lily thought Ebenezer was singing. When she said that, Lionel looked at her and suddenly couldn't recognize her. Inside him, a melody he knew from childhood began singing in him. Melissa is listening to my father's melody, thought Lionel, who was my father? But when Ebenezer started quoting poems by eighteenth-century Polish poets, the ruddy-cheeked old man with the red flower in his lapel was moved to tears and frenziedly wrote down every word in a big notebook in front of him. His hand flew over the paper, his eyes were almost shut and some coquettish smile spread over his face. When Ebenezer moved to the stories of the Cadet from the *Zohar* and then to the stories of the Brothers Grimm, the old man said: Forty years I've been investigating forgotten Polish poetry, both of us, he and I, the only ones in the world who still remember. I sit in London, sir, investigate, encyclopedias empty of that poetry, no books, there was a man who remembered and passed it on to Ebenezer, in his mind he holds onto that sublime poetry, I copy it to publish it. Is there anything more awful than a nation forgetting its songs, Lord! Of all the dozens of poets he knows—I follow him from city to city—only three are still known to scholars of Polish literature. Who was the man who taught him that poetry? Could it have been a Jew? How does a Jew who died know that poetry? And the man wept and Lionel didn't know exactly what he was weeping about. He covered the notebook so the tears wouldn't melt the words he wrote and he started shaking the rattle. I don't know, if he'd ask me I'd be amazed, do I really know those poems? Maybe German-writer knows. The man stopped shaking the rattle and again wrote something. Lily swallowed a piece of orange Lionel gave her.

And then Ebenezer stood up to the cheering rattles. A bitter smile flickered in the corners of his mouth. Those who didn't just want to shake the rattles applauded. Ebenezer looked tired and pale. Samuel Lipker gave him a glass of beer. Lily said: That lad looks like you! Lionel, who had known that from the first moment, glared at his venomous beauty, he shifted his eyes to Ebenezer and thought: Ebenezer and I are the same age. I'm with Lily Schwabe and he's with Samuel Lipker, and he envied Lily's beautiful eyes that saw that beauty.

Anger at himself made him shiver and he diverted his hostility to war against Lily.

And Lily was an easy enemy, thought Lionel with his characteristic bitterness. And then a murderer who had been dormant in him ever since Melissa shut her eyes was kindled in him. His hands reached out to Lily to strangle her. There was a lot of noise. A flush rose onto Lily's cheeks. She saw the hands reaching out to her. Samuel Lipker stared long and wantonly at Lionel, who felt his look. He dropped his hands and buried his face in them. Lily sidled up to him and caressed his hand, shook the rattle exaggeratedly, and sipped the beer. The Pole stood up and went to sit someplace else. Lionel wanted to get up. Ebenezer was standing on the side of the stage and looked like a grasshopper stuck to a blackboard in a biology class. Lily is watered by an artificial rain, he thought, and Melissa, my angel, you died before my eyes. Samuel Lipker now told how he had met Ebenezer, how Ebenezer learned his knowledge. He told how they had crossed borders and countries, and said: This performance is designed to collect money for our families, we glean pennies to save souls from death. He didn't expatiate on what death and only the smiling expression of Ebenezer's eyes clarified for Lionel the disgrace of the moment. When they passed the baskets among the audience, Samuel's eyes examined the room carefully but kept coming back to Lionel. When the basket came to Lionel, Lily wanted to pay, but he caught her hand, held the basket for a whole minute, looked at the money heaped up in it and passed it on. Samuel looked at the basket that dropped out of Lionel's hand, and his eyes expressed some contempt and then Samuel said, his eyes staring into Lionel's eyes: Ebenezer has to save his daughters! But Lionel knew and didn't know how he knew that Ebenezer had no daughters. Now he wanted to see Samuel's defeat but maybe even then that love for that bold and attractive lad stirred in him, and the closeness he felt for Lily made him shiver even more, he had to kiss or die, her or him, he went outside and threw up. Then, he took the rattle and shook it in the street until they came to Lily's house. People dressed in rags sitting huddled at bonfires next to what once were their houses looked with characteristic loathing at somebody who had lost them their palaces, and he yelled: I piss on you and the dream girl of the Third Reich also laughed. At home, Lionel said: I'm forty-four years old and I weep without tears. And you, a daughter of the thousand-year Reich—and you laugh! You're an ad for Ritesma and Simon cigarettes, a painting of the great German school, sitting with a kike born in Poland and wanting children he doesn't have to give you.

Lily made tea for the drunken Lionel and then she lay down beside him and was Melissa with little nipples who killed angels of death with her soft eyelashes.

What made you Lily made Himmler Himmler, said Lionel with his eyes shut. And thus he started writing her a farewell letter in his mind. She told him: What's simple about love? You were the first man in my life and you'll be the last. She didn't understand how Lionel knew that Ebenezer had no daughters. She wanted Ebenezer to have daughters. Lionel got angry, but couldn't explain why Ebenezer had no daughters. And so maybe he felt she was immune to him, maybe because of her love, maybe because of her youth as a wunderkind of the Hitler-jugend maybe she had never been a member of, and they talked about the resemblance between Samuel and Lionel. Lionel got angry, as if the heavy blood coursing in him truly had a voice and a shape as the professors and sages in this city had taught for ten years. A scene of a dream she had had arose in Lily's mind. In her dream, she told him, her father, who was now a prisoner of the Russians, was stumbling in a forest and she was a baby bird. Her father picked up the baby bird and decided to cook it. Then he would shoot at birds who came to ask for the baby bird. He put her into a basket, and walked, and that's how I was adopted, she said. Lionel thought of Joseph Rayna. Once, when he had heard about him, he had wanted so much for him to be his father so he could kill him. He thought of how his mother had told him about Rebecca Schneerson who would translate people into an eternal texture of contempt like copy paper that transmits things and serves as a fluent copy but preserves the original. Those thoughts begat in him an almost regal lust that was translated into a tormented and enormous night of love and copulation like some whorehouse of angels, he thought, and when he woke up and saw her sleeping, he noticed how white and clear her eyes were. Don't die on me, he said in a panic. And then he sank into sleep and when he woke up he saw her eyes wide open and looking at him. The responsibility filled him with a bitter taste. She'll look so beautiful on York Avenue, she'll dry the tears of the world, she has no right to wonder about Ebenezer's lost daughters, and he said to her: When Samuel Lipker searched for diamonds in corpses, you sat and drew sunsets with flags at the Baltic shore and a heroic and bold race lusted for you with avid eyes, but she didn't answer him. She tried to remember how beautiful it was to fall asleep in his arms, and she said: But if you decided that I'm Melissa, then let me be Melissa retroactively, too. The vanishing figure of her father didn't grieve her. In her dream, she remembered, she dreamed that somebody pointed an accusing finger at her, but since she never knew what guilt was she didn't know what the finger meant. You know, she said, you're now all the memories I have, I came to you from total darkness.

That night he said he had to go away for a while. He brought a lot of groceries and two pairs of nylon stockings. She was silent and looked at him, and whispered: I'll be here, Lionel. Soon, they'll finish repairing the house across the street, the apartment there belonged to my grandmother, she died in the war. The phone number in her apartment is 46655. If you don't come back and don't call, you'll find me behind Himmelstrasse, in the new cemetery, in the northern part where they're now burying people. Look for the letter S. I'll die secretly even if you don't come back, but if I die, Lionel, all your women will be dead in my eyelashes like the eyelashes that filled Melissa's death. If there's life after death, and if Germans are allowed to enter there, I'll wait for you there, too.

For a whole year they didn't see one another. At night, he called her from distant cities, had long conversations with her and once wept into the phone for two whole hours and didn't say a word and she listened. Once she told him about the house she had moved to, told that she was working in the committee of DPs and people were coming back from Poland and

Czechoslovakia and other places and searching for their families and she tried to find the addresses. Lily told that an American officer sent her a package of food every week and he whispered, It's me, you fool, and she laughed, he wasn't sure, and she said, I know my dear, and I'm waiting for you. And he told her: You're naïve, Lily, and she said: Maybe, I eat little, don't look bad. I bought two new dresses, also sewed you a coat of thick cloth I found in an excavation under a house they repaired and I made myself a shroud, Jews die in shrouds, don't they? Thinking about your eyes and Samuel's. About your oval ellipses, demons have green-yellow eyes wrapped in oval ellipses!

Lionel, who was interrogating prisoners in various cities, got in touch with Jews who were busy sneaking across borders and ascending to the Land of Israel. He got them cigarettes and food and for a long time he'd hang around in places where roads converged of Jews fleeing from northern Europe and flowing south to get to the Land of Israel. Lily understood who he was seeking and once told him, When you find him come back to me.

Tape / —

That year, the wandering of peoples began, my friend Goebbelheydrich himmel. People, like little ants, slipped across borders, through mountains, in forests, slowly slowly came to gathering places near Marseilles or Naples, in the forests of Yugoslavia, in many places they gathered. And I searched for Ebenezer.

Tape / —

Lionel travels. People start setting real clocks, no longer covering up sin. My mother was a lampshade, said Samuel, and Ebenezer now performed in a hundred and sixty nightclubs. Now he appeared on a list of professional nightclub entertainers. And one night in Marseilles Lionel Secret sees a long line of Jews. The Jews are waiting to board a small ship named *Redemption*. A small ship, like a Mississippi riverboat, says an American standing not far from it and goes off. A young man comes to Lionel, too short to be the thug who taught ourselves to be, his arms strong, he clasps Lionel's hands and thanks him for the cigarettes and food, asks Lionel to get weapons too. Emotionally, it's still hard for Lionel to smuggle weapons they'll use to fight the British. The British medals still flutter over his shirt pocket. The line to the ship winds around along a deserted and forgotten quay. The people sit or stand, buy, sell, hold onto their miserable belongings, scared of every stranger, and Lionel notices Ebenezer and Samuel. Ebenezer is sitting on a suitcase. At the sight of Lionel, Samuel takes off and Ebenezer points to an empty place and says, Sit down, take a place in line, we're going.

Samuel told me to go, he added, and I'm going. Samuel says I was born there. One of the Israelis announces on the loudspeaker that the boilers have broken down and there may be a delay of a few hours. Tea will be distributed to you, he added, but nobody got up, they're afraid to lose their place. There's room for four hundred people on the ship, and there are seven hundred people standing here. Sounds of strife are heard in the distance. Behind a destroyed enclosure, a battle rages between Samuel Lipker and another man. The man bought a defective camera from Samuel and is demanding his money back. Lionel leaves Ebenezer gazing at the water of the port striking the concrete wall, and stands not far from the enclosure, Samuel hits the man and then wants to go back to the line and then he looks at Ebenezer's back, Ebenezer is sitting up and dozing with his eyes wide open, Samuel discovers Lionel looking at him, shifts his eyes from Ebenezer to the American officer. The power coming from him annoys him, he says: You think you're an important person because you've got a house and money, I remember how you saved a few pennies! I've got a few francs, maybe you need a little money to buy some ice cream or chewing gum? Lionel, who looks from Samuel to Ebenezer, feels some calm, as if his whole life had been aimed at this moment, some moment when he had to know well how to act, and he said: Looks like I hoped you'd come back.

You don't sound sorry, said Samuel.

Give me the money you said, Lionel suddenly says furiously.

Samuel seeks in his pocket and gives Lionel a few pennies. Lionel takes them, counts each and every penny, and tosses them into the sea. The pennies are swallowed up in the water, and Samuel says: I worked hard for that money, sir!

He worked, says Lionel, and points at Ebenezer.

You're helping these miserable Jews? asks Samuel. You're an old miser who got medals of dead soldiers, I know guys like you. Lionel didn't answer. For a moment, he looked to the side, fog started moving toward the port, people started making bonfires from tree bark they had gleaned.

You don't answer, said Samuel.

No, I don't answer.

Why didn't you give me money then?

Because you sold things that weren't yours, he said, and Ebenezer had no daughters.

Samuel looked to the side and he also looked at Ebenezer now. An amazement he didn't understand flooded him. He felt animosity and softness at one and the same time. Ebenezer looked like somebody who was finished here, on the edge of that water. Samuel, who started acting the poor soul, bent over a little and said: I've got something here that they made from my parents, this lampshade, you can't know what was there!

Lionel was tense at every word. Samuel's cunning stirred old memories in him. A boy standing at the window of Melissa's house and waiting for a signal. For some reason he was less furious now than he thought he'd be. Maybe suffering does have some reward, he said to Samuel, but I'm not the man who will give it to you. That lampshade you sell to the soldiers who believe you isn't your parents. You deserve a lot more, but you also deserve less than what you demand! Don't try to lie to me. I'm fond of you because of what you are, not because of what you can sell me.

I'll sell the truth, said Samuel angrily. In his mind's eye he now succeeded in seeing his naked parents.

You're lying, said Lionel.

Samuel measured Lionel, looked again at Ebenezer, and said: If we leave here, they won't let me back.

If you want, they'll let you, said Lionel. And he felt like somebody who steals a piece of bread from a pauper. And they started walking in the fog that thickened and covered the port and Ebenezer who sensed something, turned his face, saw Samuel's back far away in the fog and wanted to run after him, but he was afraid to lose his place in line and by the time he made up his mind, Samuel and Lionel had disappeared in the fog.

Tape / —

I don't remember, I sat there. Somebody who was me, he thought. What was he thinking about? About somebody he loves, he thought. Some yearning, to love somebody like that, without conscience or regret, and they would have destroyed him if not for my boxes. Bronya the Beautiful with an apple in her mouth, she connected us, held us, on what authority did he go, I didn't know, but I didn't know who's thinking what I say now, confused, lost and alone, without myself, my memories, no, his image in me, a lust to embrace him, to hold the hand, forgiveness from him for asking about all the things I didn't do.

In the cab, Samuel was silent. Lionel looked at the gray houses and next to them the bay spread out, gleaming in the dull light. They got out of the cab and climbed the stairs of Café Glacier, the big balcony was closed. They sat at a little table, the place was almost empty.

Now tell me, said Lionel and offered Samuel a cigarette. Samuel lit it with a little lighter Lionel handed him, he looked at the lighter and Lionel said, Keep it, and Samuel held onto the lighter, wanted to give it back but couldn't, buried it in his pocket, and started talking with the cigarette in his mouth. That American officer looked naïve to Samuel, but also bold. For a moment, he thought about a possible love affair between his dead mother and the officer and from the recesses of memory rose a picture of his mother, dressed in festive clothes, next to a statue of a bearded poet and Samuel is eating candy wrapped in gold foil and afterward he would straighten the foil and bury it in his pocket. If only I could really understand his suffering, he thought. Lionel said: Look, man, for a long time now I've been interrogating people, I read you and you think, Ah, how naïve is this Lionel Secret and don't know that my name is Lionel Secret, but I know that your name is Samuel Lipker, I don't know who your father was, who your mother was, I don't know exactly what world you came from. He bent over a little, the cigarette dropped its ash on the table, the place began to fill up, beyond the locked balcony, the sun began to set, the sea was transparent and gleaming.

What did you get the medal for?

I fought.

What did you do before?

I wrote stories.

Why?

I don't know, said Lionel.

So don't write them, said Samuel, and began drinking the wine they were served. Lionel tasted the wine. In the distance, fogs thickened even on the nearby boulevards, haberdashery salesmen seemed hidden in niches, he felt like hugging the fellow, stories that should be written—are written, he said, the rest don't matter, and you're right.

I'm not so sure I want to be right, said Samuel. But then the moment became soft and pleasant and Lionel looked confident sitting across from him, Ebenezer is simple and pure, said Lionel, you're not. You always divide everything into black and white, said Samuel, that's why I can defeat you.

Not me.

You're also them.

That's what I wanted to write about, said Lionel.

And do you have a car?

I have a lot with buses, cars and tractors, fire engines and pickup trucks. I used to play with them like toys.

I'll have a Mercedes, said Samuel. Part of my wealth stays with Ebenezer. He'll need it. The rest is with me. I'll wear nice clothes and drive a splendid car. Lionel advanced his hand and stroked Samuel's head. Samuel's eyes were glassy, he looked in despair at the stroking hand. Lionel wanted to explain to Samuel who he was and what his life had been. But Samuel kept his distance and when Lionel understood why he had waited all the time, why he had been searching for Samuel and didn't know he had been searching for him, why he was sitting with him now, he wasn't able to explain, he got up, begged his pardon, and said he'd come back. He found the telephone and Samuel called the tall maitre d' with watery eyes who was looking at him with wicked indifference, and said quickly: Pad the bill! Afterward we'll split it fifty-fifty! The maitre d' smiled, a gold tooth danced in his mouth. Samuel suddenly had a dreadful erection. Some tear duct he'd forgotten started pressing on his eyes, tears of people he didn't know wept in him, he didn't want to be caught again by those maitres d', and the maitre d' hissed between his teeth: It'll be fine, and he went off. Samuel sat and looked at the food he'd been served and for a moment it seemed to him that he was loved. He just didn't know by whom.

Lionel called his hotel and the old woman at the reception desk said one minute, Mr. Secret, and transferred the call to his room, where he had an extension because of his high rank and even from here he could smell the old woman's sly smile.

On his bed sat Lily. She wore a bathrobe she had brought from Cologne and was shaking with cold. She closed the windows but the cold didn't stop. She didn't know how to turn on the heat. The phone rang and she was afraid to answer. She had gone through a lot of trouble to get a travel permit. She even promised one of the officers she'd go out with him and that was how she found out where he lived and went to him and the old woman at the reception desk now became fussy, and Lily had to bribe her with the last of her money, and now, when she wants to surprise Lionel with or without his lovers, the phone rings. Her hand reaches for the receiver, but the hand doesn't manage to pick it up. The phone stopped ringing and she picked up the extinguished receiver and heard beeping. Then her eyes starting shedding tears and she tried to talk to the dead receiver. Lionel tried to dial again, but his line was busy. Lily dropped the receiver, put it on its cradle and stood up. Her body trembled, the window was covered with mist. She hugged herself. And then the phone rang again. She picked up the receiver and didn't stop weeping. Lionel recognized the sound of Lily's tears. He said to her, Don't cry, little girl, but she didn't stop. She tried to talk but only fragmentary syllables burst out of her mouth. All those tears piled up in her for years, she later told Lionel, at long last I was Melissa, maybe I died and your voice talked to a dead woman and I didn't know what to say. Only after a few minutes did she say, Yes my dear, I'm here, sorry.

I know you're here, he said to her.

His laugh was calming and offensive, but she had already learned what was in store for her, a whole year in a closed room she had acted at night the wife of a child thrown into the fire, learned in books what she could have known if only she had opened her eyes earlier while acting herself in another garb, and learned to hate in herself what Lionel loved in her. She knew he was searching for Ebenezer to try to forgive himself and she couldn't take part in the forgiveness. She had nothing to complain about. He called her. He heard her body rustling in the distance. She asked where are you and he told her, and she said: I need you here, and she blushed. And she told him she blushed. I'm dining with the fellow who appeared with the Last Jew in the nightclub, he said, Boulevard Canbière, Café Glacier, upstairs.

I'm coming, she said.

And now Samuel Lipker is looking at her. The light in the hall dims, the erection still prevents him from standing up. A torn ad for Ritesma cigarettes waves on the wall. He knows the ad hung in the room of the guard who'd hug him and give him candy. On the ad for Ritesma or Koli cigarettes was a photo of a typist, maybe it was a drawing, the drawing was Lily. Now he could know how German guards' cigarettes create for him the Melissa that Lionel tried to tell about earlier. The guards in the camp loved her too, and that strengthened her unimaginably, now he could sit across from her, loathe her, understand her, he already teased Lionel who probably beat and tortured her to teach her what love is. She was and still is the girl of all our dreams he thought. Even of Leibke who was shot by the guard, and the man who castrated himself after Bronya the Beautiful refused him. Bronya the Beautiful with the apple in her mouth. No, they didn't look alike. Bronya looked like his mother, Lily was a wild song in the Tyrolean Mountains. With her he could capture stars or hunt electric rabbits. Beautiful only for herself. And the love she showered on Lionel made her forbidden. Like death, he thought, to sleep with her is to sleep with cancer, she looks at Samuel and at Lionel and recalls the frightening lad she saw in the nightclub, and when Lionel looked at her and caressed her with his eyes, Lionel thought: She may not know that a disaster happened, but she knows exactly who it didn't happen to. Lionel pronounced the names of the dishes he had ordered for her in a charming French accent that made Samuel measure Ebenezer against Lionel again, he also wanted to understand what they wanted from him and how much he had to pay, and what he would have to pay. The ships in the port hooted, the noise in the café grew louder, waiters tried to please Lionel, Samuel imagined himself sleeping with Lily and stroking Lionel's hair, and for a moment, his parents appeared to him walking arm in arm in the street, houses began falling on them and they vanished along with the pain in him whenever Ebenezer would recite the past that none of them knew. Lily tried to eat but had no appetite. Her lips were shaped like her eyes. The lines are clear, a slight flush rose on her cheeks, something in her image recalled not only ads for Ritesma cigarettes, but also pale northern twilights. Some total defeat melted in her. The struggle between himself, thrown into the fire, and the pallor of her face enchanted him, and he could understand things in her face that Lionel couldn't. Her hair was especially fair in the light of the lamp above her. When she fixed her eyes on Samuel, his erection stopped and he calmed down, as if he had met his mother's lover. He said: My mother was an actress in a house full of carpets and she'd act for me. Ebenezer's memories were enough for me, my mother also had a husband. He was an unsuitable lover for my mother, she wanted opera generals. I'm a corrupt angel and look like it. So do you. In her late youth, after she finished being a communist, my mother seriously thought of going to a convent or into international prostitution—I imagine from Ebenezer—her lover was an old man by then, made hundreds of children with weary women, Ebenezer sometimes recites some of his poems, once I was in love with them.

I know, said Lionel.

Samuel glanced wearily, laughed at Lily, and said: So will you marry me, Lily?

And she looked at him and decreed, No! and turned pale. He tried to pretend to weep, but he burst out laughing and they looked at him. Suddenly, maybe for the first time in years, he didn't know how to act himself.

And then he started telling Lily about the lampshade they made of his parents. He said those words while his eyes, where a rusty gray flash now sparkled, were fixed on Lionel. She stopped trying to eat the duck wing and Samuel measured her movements like a panther waiting to pounce. Lionel's hands moved, the smile was a mask for tension, Samuel smoked another cigarette and didn't want to light it with the lighter he had taken from Lionel before. He was afraid she'd recognize the lighter and despise him. The ash straggled until it dropped. When the ash dropped, Lily felt as if her belly were shriveling.

People wearing clothes too big for them, with berets and caps or shabby Hollywood hats on their heads, entered and sat around the tables and ate eagerly. The waiters ran back and forth. A woman in a sparkling red dress sang on a small stage, lighted with a beam that turned her face into an overcultivated mask. At the piano sat a pianist with a thin beard who looked bored and tired. Now and then, he sipped from a bottle standing on the piano. American, Swedish, and African sailors came in with their temporary, dyed women. They would all order cognac or calvados and slurp fish soup. The Bay of Marseille was lighted, a motorboat groaned rhythmically, drunken sailors banged on the tables and shouted demands for food. The light outside was growing dim, and the locked balcony was full of cigarette butts and papers flying in the wind. In the distance, the sea looked like a black mass.

Ebenezer, now looking for Samuel in the city, said to the investigator years later: I didn't look like a Muselman because Samuel Lipker and Kramer would bring me thin beet soup and bread.

Dear Renate,

You asked me why, back then in Marseille, that is, what impelled us, what exactly happened, I didn't know what to answer you then and today I don't either. Aside from my love, I don't find words that can convey the precise experience. But since you asked, I'll try. I sat facing the two of them, Lionel and Samuel Lipker, and longed with all my soul to die.

Lionel then looked toward the balcony, I don't know if we saw that sea. Samuel tried to steal me from Lionel. He also got up and recited to the diners an excerpt of Ebenezer they knew by heart, but they didn't applaud him. They were furious that he had disturbed their eating, and had disturbed the fat singer's singing. The sea was locked in the distance. A balcony full of cigarette butts. I wanted to go to the movies. They were then showing *The Arch of Triumph* with Ingrid Bergman and Charles Boyer, who sat like us in Café Glacier, on Boulevard Canbière and drank Calvados. Lionel sketched something on the white paper on the table, sipped the wine that Samuel gulped, and said sadly to Sam (Samuel): If you think you have to go back to the line you can. The two of you can open a war souvenir shop in Jerusalem named for Joseph Rayna. I heard that his songs became national anthems there. Sam looked at Lionel and Lionel looked at Sam. Those two men suddenly looked like two dead men fighting over me. I wanted to express my opposition, but I didn't know if I had it coming. I knew I had to perform Gretchen for them and not talk. I don't know if you've ever been for sale in the Jew market, Renate! I was an essential enemy to them, maybe (and this is ridiculous) a desired enemy, and Sam was so sunk in the moment, in the happening itself, that he had to measure it carefully since he wasn't used to it. I wanted so much to return things to their simple and human concreteness, to deviate from the tragicomic event, as Lionel put it later. Those two poets, great-grandsons of messiahs, didn't see me with flesh-and-blood eyes, maybe not only with those eyes. They saw me as some substitute for an argument in order to gore one another. The singer sang in a nasal voice and Sam mocked her, maybe that was a certain response to his failure to make the drunken sailors laugh by reciting things Ebenezer remembered and that weren't important to them. The sailors tried to defend the play of their love with the wretched streetwalkers and would hit and shout and kiss, and Sam thought, I read his mind didn't I; I can't swindle this man anymore. Precisely in his weakness, he's strong! A weakness of supple and tense softness and Lionel said to him: But on the other hand, you can also stay with Lily (he didn't say "you can stay with me," he only uttered my name).

Then the haggling started. I was the payment, so they didn't ask me. Lionel said something about the possibility that Sam would live with me, and he said: Lily will be a mother to you, and Sam said, Mother? An ad for a fucking cigarette will be a mother to me? I've got enough dead mothers and fathers, and Lionel said: You've got a dead mother and two dead fathers, you'll have a new father and mother and I'm still not mentioned by name. Renate, nobody talks directly to me or with me, doesn't ask anything, but I deserve it, why did I come here? They were discussing payment and I'm hanging in front of them on a hook, unkosher meat in a Jewish market. They have to triumph over one another in a defeat that will of course be all mine and mine alone, I was silent, Renate, I was silent and suddenly had an appetite and I tasted the dishes Lionel ordered and that I couldn't eat before. Lionel talked about the fact that I wouldn't have children, the level of the execution of the castration had been so high that for a moment, I felt how all the children I was supposed to give birth to flowed out of me and died on my lips, and I felt blood between my lips and I licked them and they didn't know what I was doing with my lips, and Sam said: She's trying to be sexy like Hedy Lamarr. What children? asked Sam, and Lionel said: She won't give birth to children who will later have to defend the lost homeland of lampshades, and Sam said: There was no lampshade, and Lionel said: There were, but not yours, and then he laughed, and the singer was also offended, she turned her face away and sang in another direction, and a drunken sailor hit a whore, who dropped onto the floor. There was a thud, the bored pianist burst out laughing and played more excitedly, and the waiters ran and brought drinks and food and I was sold there, a few kilograms of Lily, a few liters of Lily juice is there juice of Lily? I was silent there. No Ingrid Bergman sat on the balcony of Café Glacier with yearning eyes and a great melancholy love for Charles Boyer. In the end, I was miserable German mincemeat, good for swindling themselves that I was somebody else, I shot them at low-flying airplanes.

And that's how he bought a German streetwalker, Renate. I should have been more than I was or perhaps less, maybe an amorous girl, weeping after the death of the Führer in the bunker, something made me transparent, bereft of location and caught in a maze, they talked about some life in America, about me, about Sam, about me and Lionel, and I wanted to shout, What about me, and they knew, the two of them, that I wasn't important anymore, not out of wickedness, out of love that the two of them even then had to share, and I didn't yet understand what glowing hell I now got myself into, go home I said to myself, buy yourself a poor little husband, cook potatoes for him, let him flourish on the holy ground where you were born and where you'll be buried, but I couldn't, I was born in the air, and above, above everything, faced off, like two knights, my two men fought a desperate war for the heart of an imaginary aristocrat, who no longer lives in a nonpalace where the big, splendid and superfluous duel was held. I wanted to say, You're in love with a shadow, but I knew not to talk, maybe I really was somebody and didn't know it.

I disguised myself as an abandoned queen, I was to them what they wanted me to be. Later a past will be created and I'll be able to make a defense pact with it, for war or peace, I was packed, virginal, an invisible blood flowed from my lips, I gave myself to them and they were genuine lovers, so dreadful, so innocent, Jews trying to buy their dream in a world that wiped them out. Maybe I was what was necessary, everything was a provocation against the world, I was pathetic, possible, and eagle-y.

I applauded the fat singer who tried to thank me so much she almost stumbled. The contempt on her face wasn't hidden by the smile she wanted to direct at Lionel's pocket, which was supposed to be opened for her. The lights of a motorboat looked like embers in the fog. Outside, Ebenezer looked for his dear one. I thought, Could I ever have saved Samuel?

I knew I could save Lionel. But Sam and I were too alike. I, the Ukrainian guard, and the German who hugged him and killed his mother, all of us were too alike. A whore broke a bottle on the table next to us and with the broken bottle, she threatened the drunken sailor with tattooed writing on his hands and he tried to burn her nipple with a cigarette. And that's how that preserved moment was born when we all fought to make each other lose. Our lost honor. I'm trying to describe to you, Renate, a lost moment of anguish and bliss.

Did I have permission to warn them that underneath the mantle of serious transparent and beautified merrymaking, I'm a hard woman?

When we went outside we saw Sam get the money from the maitre d', maybe we were ashamed, to a certain extent we were also a little proud. The maitre d' smiled obediently and gave Sam (Samuel) the money. I think he swindled him, but Sam didn't haggle. It was too late now to go back to the starting point.

And we walked along the boulevard. Love and hostility in equal parts, I thought, where will I get the strength to cope with these two Jews, with a man who buried his mother and father and sells them to every soldier, and Lionel, forty-five years old, seeking himself in sewer images. When we came to the hotel we were so tired that even the dark contemptuous look of the old woman at the reception desk had no effect on us. We couldn't talk anymore. Between me and Lionel was a lust that could be smashed with an ax, I hugged Lionel, he smiled at me, shut his eyes, like a licentious sailor he put his hand on my crotch, turned his eyes to Sam, and fell asleep. Sam fixed his eyes on Lionel's hand and very slowly shut his eyes, then I fell asleep too. The next day, we went to Cologne. Lionel said: What's this about converting to Judaism? We made a deal, you don't have to involve God in such a matter, but I said to him: I have to cut myself off, I want a circumcision, and Sam didn't say a thing but murmured thanks to me for knowing how to kill my parents and not only my children.

I improved my English, which had become an obsession for me. I bought dictionaries, I learned words by heart. Everything had to be formulated correctly, so I would have to cope with Lionel in his and Melissa's words, to understand him in his own words. And the rest you know, somebody remained behind, I don't know that Lily, drawn on a faded ad for Ritesma cigarettes they don't smoke anymore in your country . . .

Tape / —

Dear Mr. Henkin,

Your letter reached the Department of Investigation of the Missing a short time ago. As for your issue I recall that before his death, your son, may the Lord avenge his blood, served for some time under my command. I decided to examine your questions both as a sign of my devotion and my emotions, since Menahem, his memory for a blessing, fell many years ago and I still remember him well. You wanted to know if a man named Samuel Lipker had ever come to Israel, and if he served here. I went through the old files, and I found the following details (they don't appear in chronological order, but merely as fragments and I copy them as they are). When we asked him (Lipker) what he would do now, he said he'd finish the war and go to drain the Amazon in Brazil. They pay good money to drain the swamps and cut down the forests, he said. He took part in the diversionary battle at Mount

Radar. Thirty-two men were killed there. Three played dead and at dusk, they got up and ran away. One of them was Boaz Schneerson, the son of a man killed in the Holocaust. The name of the second one I don't know. The third apparently was Samuel Lipker. Before that he took part in the battle of Latrun. He joined a brigade without being registered properly; it seems there wasn't time. He came to Latrun straight from the port of Haifa. As far as we can tell, he came to Haifa after being caught on the ship *Salvation* (*Paducah*) and was in a British internment camp in Cyprus. The ship left Marseille in 'forty-six. Contradictory evidence exists concerning his boarding the ship. A number of people who were on the ship claim that Ebenezer Schneerson, Samuel's companion, was last seen keeping his place in the line to board the ship, but Samuel didn't come back and was seen talking with the American officer who would bring food, cigarettes, and weapons he managed to smuggle out of the nearby American army camp. Three men testify that his father, that is, Ebenezer Schneerson, disappeared but he himself did return to the line and boarded the ship. At that time, there were no detailed lists, but my investigation shows that most of the ship's passengers I talked to don't explicitly remember if Samuel Lipker was on the ship, except for two who claim that he was there and came to Cyprus with them. When the battle occurred between the little ship with two smokestacks and the British Royal Navy, Samuel fought along with them. They remember that he guarded the deck and with a hose of salty water he sent the people back to the hold of the ship so that a new shift of people could come up on deck to eat, go to the toilet, and get some fresh air. In the battle with the British, three Jews were killed, a little girl who was born and died that same day was called Salvation, and was buried at sea. The commander fought with the one gun he had.

Outraged he was. He tried to run away from Cyprus and was beaten. Later he started his commercial deals and with the fortune he had he continued to make money. Those deals flourished until May seventeenth, nineteen forty-eight. Then Samuel Lipker was put on a ship—even though there is no exact list of passengers, and some claim he wasn't there—brought along with five hundred other young men who were trained secretly at the port of Haifa, were trained two days more and sent to the battle of Latrun. At night, Samuel found a way to escape and came to the other side of Bab-el-Wad. At the Arab village Bidu he met the members of the fifth battalion of Harel. He was transferred to Kiryat Anavim. Nobody remembers him, except for one woman, a medic, who said that a quiet fellow came. He was apparently a handsome young man, she said, but sported a dirty, bristly beard, and it was impossible to recognize him. He joined a division of sappers sent on a diversionary operation near Mount Radar, and as I said, many were killed in the action, while he played dead and was saved. When they came back to Kiryat Anavim, one of them went to try to kill the commander who had abandoned them, while Samuel disappeared.

After the war, he apparently came to Tel Aviv. Walking in the street, seeking what he (later) termed before the investigating officer a new biography he could live in, he ran into somebody at a kiosk who was his age and it seemed to him they had been in a battle together, and that man hit him in an empty lot near the house where Samuel Lipker thought he found a young widow, to whom he was sent by a member of the battalion. The blows were apparently serious and he was wounded and hit back at the person who apparently looked like him. Afterward, he changed his name to Joseph Rayna. And after a certain period for which I have no testimony, he was called Joseph Ranan. When he found out that he was considered killed and that a grave was dug for him in Kiryat Anavim, he said that was fine and let them think that Samuel Lipker had died in the battle of Mount Radar. He was sent to an officers' course where he claimed he was born in Israel and even described his parents' home. He changed the money he had apparently brought with him for valuable objects, traded in them even during the officers' course and then bought himself an apartment, and rented out the apartment the army gave him. Then he was sent to train recruits, suffered a failure in a battle he went to with his recruits. He didn't go drain the Amazon, because the sailors on the Greek ship he was supposed to board looked like white slave traders. Disguised as somebody else whom he himself apparently didn't know, he taught himself basic Hebrew. He got entangled in lies that he couldn't get out of or perhaps he did get out of them and I don't know, he had a plan he devised that nobody would be good enough to hear. And he wrote songs that one girl, whose parents were killed in the Bialystok ghetto, claimed were surprisingly similar to songs her parents had sung in the Zionist club, Young Judea. The girl was afraid of him and ran away and by then he was called Joey Gold and many legends were spun about him. He fought a personal war against an unreal army, and at night after bloody battles he sat in his house and wrote songs that were said to be composed of adjectives and overly exalted words and they smelled moldy, abandoned, and obsolete. After he killed a prisoner in the Gaza operation (the details aren't clear enough because the killer of the prisoner also appears under another name), he was punished, but in the Sinai campaign, he was called back into the army. He commanded a unit that parachuted behind enemy lines. The flanking operation he commanded clashed with the original plan and even though it succeeded, he was rebuked for his rashness, won a medal for heroism but was demoted, which he apparently resented. Then he sold his house, bought an abandoned house in Jaffa, cultivated a beautiful garden, but people who call him by different names aren't sure if it really is the same person. He looked for the man who wounded him when he came back from the war, but didn't find him. He was violent and soft only at times, said one woman who wished to remain anonymous. The investigator at the trial held for him said: Maybe that man doesn't exist, he's both alive and dead. He killed and somebody else was punished. Who is Joey Gold, asked the investigator and added: I can't swear that he exists. The documents say you were killed, he said to Joey Gold, and Joey Gold said, Maybe I really did die.

At the trial, apparently, he said: We don't go like sheep to the slaughter. Here there won't be another Maidanek. The judge reprimanded him for those words and said: You belong to an arrogant generation that was born in Israel and isn't able to understand. After a jail term, he returned to his house in Jaffa. He learned how to play seventeen different musical instruments, wrote poems nobody reads anymore, and very slowly faded away, as if the earth swallowed him up. I can't describe that any better, but there are almost no milestones after that.

Tape / —

I, Ebenezer, what do I know?

Alphabet—Sandwich Islands; the number of letters is twelve (Jewish knowledge!). Burmese alphabet—nineteen letters. Italian—twenty. Bengalese—twenty-one. Hebrew, Assyrian, Akkadian, and Sumerian—twenty-two letters each. Spanish and Slavic—twenty-seven. Arabic—twenty-eight. Persian and Coptic—thirty-two. Georgian—thirty-five. Armenian—thirty-eight. Russian—forty-one. Muscovite Russian—forty-three. Sanskrit and Japanese—fifty. Ethiopian—two hundred and two.

Miracle of the passive voice in Hebrew: We were passed over, lamed! We were torn asunder!

The Bible (in English)—thirty-nine books in the Old Testament. Nine hundred twenty-nine chapters. Twenty-three thousand two hundred fourteen verses. Five hundred ninety thousand, four hundred thirty-nine words, two million seven hundred twenty-eight thousand one hundred letters.

In all languages the name of the deity is composed of only four letters: Latin—Deus. Greek—Zeus. Hebrew—Adon. Aramaic—Adad. Arabic—Alla. The same is true of Parsi, Titi, and the Jadga language. In Egyptian Oman or Zaut. In east Indian, Asgi or Zagl. In Japanese—Jain. In Turkish—Aadi. In ancient Scandinavian—Odin. In Croatian—Duga. In Dalmatian—Roni. In Tyranian—Ahir. In Etruscan—Chur. In Swedish—Kodr. In Irish—Dich. In German—Gott. In French—Dieu. In Spanish—Dios. In Paroani—Leon.

Tape / —

At a formal luncheon on the ship, the captain asked Lionel who was the boy he had adopted, and Lionel said: His name is Samuel Lipker, and Samuel said: That's a grievous error, sir, my name is Sam Lipp, and I was

born in Boston. They sat on deck. Soldiers served iced tea to the returning heroes. From the Statue of Liberty, an escort rowed out to the ships
that sprayed jets of water and colored balloons were flown on the piers.
Samuel looked and said: A whole city is waiting for me. He said that without any emotion.

Tape / —

When Mother built.

When Rebecca Schneerson built her destroyed farm in the settlement,
a spark of apostasy flashed in her. Enraged by Nehemiah's death, she built
a model farm. She erected a modern cow barn, built a dovecote and a
chicken coop, planted citrus groves and vineyards, her vegetable patch
was big and well-watered, she had fields of clover, corn, and barley, she
built an incubator for chicks, the first incubator in Judea, and in the annual
milk production contest, two of her cows usually won first place. One day,
when Ebenezer was fifteen years old, and the Great War was in its second
year and Turkish and German officers would stop in her house on their way
south, Ebenezer was hit by a stone thrown at him by an Arab. Ebenezer,
sitting on a piece of wood and carving it, was concentrating so hard he
didn't see a thing, but Rebecca came out to hit the son of the Arab who
stood near his father. The man came to defend his son. Rebecca shaded
her forehead with her hand, and said to the Arab: I would curse your father
if I knew which of the ninety-two lovers your mother had was really your
father! And the Arab enjoyed the curse more than he was offended by it.
His donkey deposited droppings next to his feet. Rebecca laid the stick on
the ground and wiped the sweat off her brow. The Arab said: You're an
angry woman, I'm Ahbed. She said to him: Listen, there's a good farm here,
there's a garden, there's food, come with your stupid son, work here, and
I'll pay you more than all the seedy dignitaries in Marar, and that's how
Ahbed started working for Rebecca and living in the old cow barn Rebecca
fixed up for him. After the war, when locusts and hunger destroyed the
rage in the settlers, Rebecca was the first one to restore her farm. Then
Captain Jose Menkin A. Goldenberg came to the Land with the British
Service, as it was called then. The captain, who edited a French periodi-
cal in Cairo, before that had been an officer in the Argentinean army, an
American citizen, with a name he claimed was Swiss, and belonged to the

Greek Orthodox church. Captain Jose Menkin A. Goldenberg came to the
Land to prepare, as he put it, a tombstone worthy of the Italian poet Dante
Alighieri, which a young officer in His Majesty's army in Jerusalem thought
it fitting to erect. The young British officer was excited by the return to
the land of the Bible and thought the Captain planned to erect a memorial to the prophet Jeremiah, and only later did he realize his error. The bureaucracy was still in its infancy, the Arabs sharply attacked the Balfour
Declaration, the government appointed a Jew as the first commissioner in
Judea, and Captain Jose Menkin A. Goldenberg, known as an international
expert on Dante Alighieri, claimed that the series of incidents described
above was a sign that the desired memorial would be erected. Nobody
understood the logic of the series of incidents, but since the idea was so
confused, they thought something was indeed hiding behind it. Some
claimed that the whole issue of the memorial was simply an optical illusion
and the Captain was a spy, but nobody knew who he was spying for or why.
The Arabs, who then began to fear that the Jews had come to steal the
land from them, were afraid that the Jewish commissioner would divert
the water of the Yarkon River to London and the water of the Jordan to the
arid plains of England. That was the time when a young engineer in the
military service came up with an idea about ships to bring icebergs from
the north to the Mediterranean, and the Arabs also saw that idea as a Zionist plot to steal the desert from its eternal inhabitants. They heard that
there was a Jewish river in Asia, where Jewish kings and princes lived,
headed by a queen as tall as a two-story house, and the river stopped flowing on the Sabbath. They were afraid the Yarkon and the Jordan would also
stop on the Sabbath and then the black goats would cross the Jordan also
on winter days too. They demanded that if the Jordan really was stopped
it should also be stopped on Friday, their day of rest. The river (the
Sambatyon) was invented by Jewish liars who Captain Jose Menkin A.
Goldenberg thought were his ancestors back when they lived in the eleventh century, of whom, he said, not even one trace remained of the survivors. So the Captain was able to invent a family tree for himself going back
to the eleventh century, dream of memorials, and come to the Land of
Israel disguised as whatever he wanted, and after the Arabs finished worrying about the fate of the water, they started getting anxious about the idea
of the memorial. And all that happened before the Captain would come

to the settlement. First, they claimed, they never heard of the poet. Second, the editor of the Jaffa newspaper, Nasser, wrote Dante was a fanatical anti-Muslim, while it is a Jew disguised as an Orthodox Greek who wants to build the memorial, and we've got enough of our own imposters and spies, and dignitaries hastened to hold ceremonies of reconciliation in proper houses overflowing with charred meat and steaming coffee but nothing helped. Nasser wrote in his newspaper that no tombstone would be erected to Dante in the land that was holy to Muslims because Mohammed's legendary horse rose from there to heaven. The Captain, who came to the settlement at the height of the struggle for the memorial, sat in the community center erected by Nehemiah and read a Hebrew newspaper from Jaffa, and saw Rebecca and her son in the distance, walking in the street. Ebenezer was now a lad of nineteen and held in his hands a sawed-down tree trunk. The Captain got to his feet, pressed his sword to his thigh, and followed Rebecca from a distance, which he privately called a distance of decency. The young staff officer who was reprimanded for confusing Jeremiah with Dante was seeking an outstanding Arab poet to pacify the Arabs, and the Captain who moved between the monasteries and the churches in the Land in an attempt to bribe the abbots of the monasteries and the priests of the religion to support the idea of a memorial to Dante encountered a firm and hostile refusal. The Captain had instructive theories, which nobody he met was interested in, like the theory about the site of Moses's grave, and without knowing about the melody of the Psalms that Rebecca later taught herself (maybe she knew it from her childhood) he taught himself the book of Psalms, so he could recite it by heart from beginning to end and from end to beginning. The Captain really didn't get excited when he heard the idea that he was a triple spy and that he had also been a spy in the war, he didn't even get excited that under the aegis of the British government he continued, according to the slanderers, to write sharp and satanic articles against Great Britain in his French newspaper in Cairo where he hadn't been for months. When the Captain saw Rebecca walking with her son, as he put it later, he was filled with that longing that a self-respecting South American (or Mexican, according to Rebecca) captain feels one moment before he's executed. He followed Rebecca, and Ebenezer, who turned around, saw him, and said to his mother: A man in a uniform is following us, and she said: A fool with a sword, like Joseph with his songs. Rebecca had plans for the new government and, as she told Ebenezer, she somehow counted on the certain folly of the Mexican buffoon who would follow her home, knock on her door, and stand at attention, and when he did indeed do that she opened the door to him, and his sword struck the post and the Captain saluted chivalrously, or as she put it, like every dumb Turk when a beautiful Jewish woman passes by, and she brought him into her house, let him sit alone for a long time, sent Ahbed to him with a glass of cold water and then with a tray where a carafe of coffee and small cups wobbled and only then did she come in, dressed in an elegant gown, and they chatted about the weather, government upheavals, locusts, typhus, the banishments the Turks had enforced, and she told how she had fostered irrigation when people were tortured and killed and the Arabs then raised their heads and said: The Jews under our feet, but me, she said, they didn't touch, they'd come and look at me and a poor German in an officer's uniform played melancholy tunes for me and would moon after me. All the time, Rebecca was devising her plans and now and then she peeped at the face of the Captain staring at her with a savage intensity so shrouded with respect that he couldn't see her.

And then the Captain saw the row of Ebenezer's birds coated with black lacquer. The birds stood on the cabinet, and when the Captain looked at them they looked so wonderful he almost forgot why he had come to that house. He stood stooped over, conspicuous by the sudden change in him, and the birds looked as if they were trying to fly. Only later on, when he had sipped the fine wine Rebecca had gotten from the manager of the winepress with every shipment of wine grapes, only then, perhaps as a response to the bliss that flooded him at the sight of the birds and Rebecca's beauty, only then did he start talking about the life and bliss possible for strangers as for relatives, and after all, he said to her: Every husband and wife were once strangers to one another, and she said: And that's how they remain, Captain, and he tried not to hear what she said, expressed his admiration of the birds, and Rebecca said: Those rare birds are carved by my Mongoloid son. And Ebenezer, who was sitting in a corner cracking sunflower seeds, said: She means me, sir, and the Captain said: It's impossible to carve birds wooden and metaphysical at the same time without a Jewish brain! And Rebecca said: But as far as I can tell, you're not a Jew, Captain, and he said: I am what I am, according to a preformed model, made to change with circumstances, and Goldenberg is indeed a Swiss name, but my father, who wasn't Swiss, could also have been called Goldenberg. She didn't understand exactly what he meant, but she didn't think it was important enough to rack her brains over. He said to her: There is no reality, honorable Mrs. Schneerson, there are only distant memories, real hatred, and unrequited love. Rebecca asked: Doesn't unrequited love have to start at some requited point? and he thought she was joking, but for some reason she enjoyed the conversation, and he said: No, unrequited love is the beginning situation of a dream that realizes reality. There's a certain opposition here, he added, but in time everything becomes clear. I'm cursed by everybody, Jews, Arabs, English, Christians, Shiites, Sunnis, Alawis, and that's how I can defend myself. If I had one friend I was fond of, or one nation I could cling to without prior conditions, and respect, maybe I would lose the right of criticism and shorten my honor and my life. Did you notice, dear lady, that I said "honor" before "life"? If I'm not honored, I live in a cloud of fake and unnecessary honor. Only somebody who has his own friend or group is truly in danger, so I'm safer than everybody and tremble with love that is not yet realized as unrequited from the start and so is full of opportunity never to be realized, but that love is very close, and I am more protected than endangered as many thought.

The Captain excitedly felt the birds. He claimed they were wonderful creations, maybe the most wonderful he had seen since the bronze, stone, and wood statues he had seen in the museum in Cairo, and suddenly he spoke with no real connection to the birds, said that Arab children had to be taught how to paint the eyes of a dead fish to look as if it had just been caught. He even tried to learn from Ebenezer the secret of the lacquers and the sort of metaphysical geometry, as he put it, of his works. Ebenezer spoke slowly and Rebecca gazed vacantly at the ceiling. He said: I mix lacquers and carpenters' glue, solutions, I invented a spray, resin, I know how to wound trees without hurting them, know flowers with colorful pollen, and I hear the wood by its weeping and laughing, carve faces and birds, sometimes I recognize the faces and sometimes not. Rebecca said her son wasn't exactly a great scholar and had only gone as far as sixth grade in the settlement school whose level of education was as high as its ethics. And

if his father were alive, he would have taught him something. Only after
the Captain had gallantly proposed marriage and an impressive dowry and
had been turned down with a politeness that really wasn't characteristic of
Rebecca did he clutch his sword to his thigh again and hear Rebecca talk
about what she wanted to talk with him when she saw him following her
in the street. She talked about the complicated network of canals to transport the water of the Jordan from its sources straight to the Negev and the
south. That way, she said, we can buy miserable desert land for pennies
and then, secretly, transport water and work the land and establish the
agriculture my husband dreamed of but I realized, and we'll be rich as the
Jews in America. The Captain was excited to hear the words, in his mind's
eye he already saw the big canal, the dams, the dike, and the twisting,
state-of-the-art pipe. Soon after, he promised Rebecca to convey her ideas
to the authorities, who sounded like his cousins when he mentioned them,
he recited to her the book of Psalms from beginning to end and from end
to beginning and Ebenezer fell asleep in his chair even when two members
of the settlement whistled to him in the window to come with them to
beat up an Arab who stole Horowitz's mare.

The Captain stood in the middle of the room Rebecca had built in
memory of Nehemiah and recited. A murmur that reminded her of
Nehemiah's look when he spoke about the Land of Israel now rose in her
ears, Ebenezer woke up, listened a moment, and then fixed in himself
some memory of reciting words that were the same as a very certain music
and he tried to think of the birds flying in his mind and he had to cage
them in wood, for he had never invented a bird but caged the birds of his
mind in the wood he carved, and he let the wood follow the prepared
shapes and Rebecca saw Ebenezer open his eyes wide and shut them
again and she pondered the melody sunk deep in her heart and didn't pay
any heed to it, and some tune that played with Nehemiah's old excitement
and her weeping on his last day, those were yearnings that turned into a
melody more ancient than those yearned for and talked about and observed, something ancient that rose in her and overcame her, and she pondered the history of her family, pondered Rebecca Secret Charity, and said:
It wasn't in vain that those awful people lived and dreamed and shouted,
and she thought about the profound and hidden connection there seemed
to be between swindlers like her and the Captain and God. Suddenly she

understood that if she uttered aloud the chapters of Psalms, whose mysterious melancholy she always knew, but hadn't dwelt on, the chapters would
turn into a force that would reach the farthest place she could imagine,
and the touch would turn the impending death into something that could
be directed. Her legs grew light her head was suddenly empty, light and
flighty. And out of an anger that gnawed at her against Nehemiah she
started forgiving him now of all times because he had managed to hurt
her so perfectly, and she thought about her relation to herself, that is to the
God of her fathers, the God played as a clown by her fellow farmers in the
Land where there is no shade or corners, and night falls suddenly black and
ruddy. Ebenezer panted. Poor orphan, she said to herself. The Captain's
solidity was splendid, she had to admit that he was a noble man with no
purpose or homeland and that the strip of light gleaming on him was both
his geography and his biography. What worlds woven in the force of the
words could start revolutions in the cosmic order, she thought, a thought
foreign to her. And deep inside her, she could feel how she once again
gathers corpses in the suitcase, writes "Deliverance" on the ceiling, her
virginity cut off at the terrorist river, some threatening and frightening
force caught in her words about the Land, building and with the word
destroying, and she said to herself: There's a connection between circum-
locution and circumcision, a Mount Nebo of words, words that bring rain
in due season and not in due season. Rebecca knew that those Psalms or
the melody heard from them have no connection with belief or nonbelief,
just as her life with Nehemiah and her nonlife with Joseph Rayna had no
connection with love or nonlove. And so she returned to the room where
the Captain was still reciting. Her son dozing in his chair dreams of birds
in shining lacquer and in her a barrier was now planted that would later be
fixed, between her and her milieu, and a melody of the Book of Psalms that
would be the meaning of her life. When the Captain finished reciting he sat
down to drink wine and his face was pale from the effort, his nose looked
red and his cheeks looked gray, but she applauded him, and at that moment, long before he was born, Boaz Schneerson was saved from the death
lurking for him in the war.

Ebenezer then built his hut in the citrus grove near the water tower, not
far from the hill of the Wondrous One and nobody knows anymore why it
was called that. The hill overlooked the fields and the desolation from the

east to the distant mountains on the horizon, and a deaf girl who lived in
the nearby settlement came one day and stayed there, sitting and watching for long hours as he built boxes or carved birds and she watched in silence. Ebenezer didn't miss his father, whose disgrace he had had to hear
for years from his mother, he only yearned for Rebecca and she wasn't his.
To herself she admitted that she had never managed to love Ebenezer
more than she had managed not to love him, or to love his father. But
those rare moments of affection for Nehemiah that increased after his
death didn't touch her son. He didn't look like her, he didn't look like
Joseph or Nehemiah. He didn't look like her father or like Nehemiah's
mother, he didn't look like anybody she knew. Rebecca started reciting the
book of Psalms a week after Captain Jose Menkin A. Goldenberg erected
his tent, which reminded her of the Wondrous One's splendid tent, and he
started digging the rock of Hagar wife of Abram, which, according to his
calculations, was buried there. He had ancient maps showing him ancient
places long forgotten. That day in the citrus grove, Ebenezer carved his
father's image on a wooden board that he planed and filed and covered
with lacquer and the deaf girl wept. And then, for the first time in his life,
Ebenezer knew the taste of love. The touch was nice. The deaf girl's face
was twisted like a captured bird, but her voice wasn't heard and that scared
him. When he lay in bed afterward and looked at the tin ceiling above his
hut he felt exalted and didn't know why. His mother, who had started sitting in the big chair at the screened window with the book of Psalms in one
hand and a flyswatter in the other and Ahbed and the laborers working the
farm, imposed a considerable yoke on him too and he had to go out to plow
and harvest, to take care of the chicken coop and the cow barn, and among
the laborers who worked in the yard he met a Jew wearing a *kippah* who
didn't believe in the resurrection of the world according to Marx and
Engels like the other laborers in the other yards, prayed devotedly, and
waited patiently for the messiah. He was a humble man and not unpleasant, who loved the deaf girl with a quiet and restrained love. When he'd
see her coming back from the citrus grove with a light gleaming on her
face, he was filled with longing and thought: If only I could grant her a soft
and dreamy beauty like that. Ebenezer he privately loathed, he called him
an idolater. Later on, Ebenezer explained to the deaf Starochka why he
couldn't really love her and how much he yearned for somebody he didn't

know who and she wanted to tell him something about her love but her inability to talk saved her from an absurd plea and she walked to the settlement, sat in the yard, and the Hasidic laborer brought her a glass of water, looked at her a long time until she grasped how strong his love was, took his hand, and kissed it. Then she started going to the synagogue and praying devotedly, smeared her crotch with red, and went to the wedding canopy with all the laborers standing around and calling out Mazal tov, Mazal tov.

His wife's silence, the laborer said later, was the grammar of messianism. He said that against Ebenezer's idolatry, but they didn't understand his words anymore than he himself understood the decree of his life and his marriage to a virgin whose wild shouts he saw in his mind's eye a thousand times when she came out of Ebenezer's hut. In those days, the Captain stopped digging for Hagar's rock and started seeking the stones of Jacob's Ladder in the mountain opposite and people who hadn't visited her house for years once again knocked on Rebecca's door and talked with her about agricultural matters on which she was an expert as she often said, reluctantly, and in the settlement rumors spread about her impending marriage.

The rumors were premature, but the Captain didn't despair and went on proposing marriage, money, travels to distant lands, and a pedigree from the eleventh century, and so when Rebecca brought up the idea of traveling south with him to find out whether those lands in the desert could be bought until her plans for the canals would be realized, he saw that as a sign whose plausibility nobody of course would understand, that the memorial to Dante Alighieri would be erected and on the other hand his desired marriage to Rebecca was already sealed. Ebenezer was left to manage the farm, the Hasidic laborer went to the Hasid village in the south, and was replaced by another laborer who wasn't a Hasid, but didn't want to foment revolution against the capitalists, Ahbed the son had long ago replaced his father who was about to die and milked the cows and the Captain and Rebecca rode in a carriage hitched to a pair of horses to the lands of Ruhama.

It was a fragrant spring day after a stormy sudden rain and flowers appeared blooming in places that were always arid. They came to a squashed hill where she had stopped on her journey with Nehemiah on their last trip. Everything was desolate and hills and hallucinatory yellow expanses stretched to the horizon. Rebecca was furious at Nehemiah that she had to travel to these distant places instead of him, with a Mexican stuffed animal who could be set as a scarecrow against planes, and then an Arab came to them who popped up from the ground wearing a suit and behind him— between the rows of prickly pear—walked some short Bedouins.

The Arab greeted them and Rebecca gave the customary reply and then the Arab sat down and she and the Captain immediately sat too, and the Bedouins sat not far from them, and the Arab fiddled with some amber beads in his hands, and asked: So you're suddenly here and why are you suddenly here, maybe you've got family here? Rebecca smiled and said: My family is three clods from the right and the Arab laughed and the Bedouins laughed too and the Captain, who didn't understand Arabic, or pretended not to understand, tried not to laugh and looked at the horizon, something Rebecca wanted him very much to do, because the horizon was in the west and there was Gaza City, and she said: I'm just touring for no good reason, empty and wonderful, why not, and the Arab, whose *misbakha* in his hand began moving nervously, said: For no good reason? By my eyes, people don't come here for no good reason with a chariot and generals. Later on, Rebecca explained to the Captain that since the truth is not accepted literally in the Land of Israel, the Arab understood that the distinguished lady in the chariot and the general who surely commanded big armies came here to sniff land and buy it for some secret army that would destroy the holy places of Islam, which, as everybody knows, are south of here, about twenty days away. And since he knew she was a Jew, he also knew the exorbitant price. She waited. The Arab muttered something to himself and went off and half an hour later he returned with two more Arabs. The Bedouins were ordered to gather branches and twigs for a bonfire. They made sweet black tea; Rebecca and the Captain drank it very slowly with the Bedouins, who smacked their lips to impart to the scene the honor due it. The two men who came with the Arab were even more eminent than he was, dressed more splendidly, even though a smell of sheep dung and fragrant wormwood rose from them. They whispered together, their faces darkened and they whispered together again and excitedly offered Rebecca a hundred English pounds if she'd get out of there. She said: With all my heart, I thank you for your generous offer and appreciate your magnanimity and your ignorance of Arabic numerals, which you gave to the world along with the alcohol you don't even drink, one hundred English pounds is a hole in the penny of the hair of my late grandmother who is buried so far from here that I don't remember her name anymore and so I am not left without a mother to thank for your generosity and with the necessary modesty of a woman with a thousand soldiers at her disposal not far from here, to tell you to leave me and my friend the field marshal alone before the armies come who are now on sixty-six English warships at the shore of Gaza and peace on Ishmael and on the holes of all the pennies. Not only did they listen to her tensely, but the Captain was also listening. He thought he should smile, but he understood from her trembling and her tension that he better not take his eyes off the point he was staring at.

Then, since her splendid words only confirmed their suppositions and even sharpened their cunning, the Arabs announced, even without consulting anymore among themselves, that when they said a hundred pounds they didn't mean a hundred pounds, but the wind distorted their words and when she looked at the Arabs with ostentatious ennui, and peeped surreptitiously at the place where the harbor of Gaza was likely to be, and sixty-six warships had already started raising smoke in her eyes, the price went up to a hundred and fifty and then to two hundred English pounds, and then Rebecca took the money with generous weariness, got into the carriage, called the Captain to get in with her, and said: *Yallah,* let's get out of here, we'll buy the lands for your army someplace else.

When she came back to the settlement Haya Horowitz and Frumka Berdichevski saw a smile on Rebecca's lips. The rumor spread like wildfire and the farmers wearing clothes taken out of mothballs began coming to her house with bouquets of flowers and bottles of wine. They said, Congratulations, and when is the wedding? And Ebenezer, who was summoned from the citrus grove, appeared holding a new bird that had almost managed to fly out of the wood in which it was carved, saw the laugh on his mother's lips, and the laugh frightened him. The farmers were insulted when they heard there wouldn't be a wedding, not now—as she said—and not at any other date, and they went off disappointed and then Nathan, Nehemiah's old friend, began dying and Rebecca, who hadn't seen him for some time, went to visit him. She sat next to him, held his hand, told him not to be afraid of death because there's nothing more awful than life, and then she told him about the Arabs and how they had given her two hundred English pounds for land she hadn't intended to buy. He burst out laughing and didn't stop for three days until he died with a smile on his lips. The settlement forgave Rebecca for all her insults over the years because of the laugh she gave Nathan on his deathbed. At Nathan's funeral in Roots, Rebecca recalled the first day she had come to Israel and wept. But they didn't see the first tears Rebecca wept since she went to Jaffa with Nehemiah.

At night, she lay in bed with her eyes wide open and thought about Nathan. She thought that twenty years had passed since she married Nehemiah. She tried to grasp her life and to understand what she had meant to do with it if people like Nathan died while others grew old and her mongoloid son sat in the citrus grove with a deaf girl and sculpted birds. Ebenezer came to her. She smelled his smell of resin and wood and lay still in bed with her eyes shut. He sat on the stool not far from her bed and wanted to know if the laugh he saw when she returned from the trip to the Negev was the laugh of Joseph Rayna. She told him, Maybe, maybe, but don't hang too many hopes on that. The next day, after many years of not doing that, he carved the portrait of Joseph again and she looked at the portrait and didn't say a word, suddenly Ebenezer seemed so unworthy of the gigantic and splendid war waged inside her by two valiant and desperate men like Joseph and Nehemiah, that all she could tell him was: There's a resemblance in the face but there's no resemblance in the spirit of the face.

Ebenezer was ashamed, he went outside and hurt himself with an almond branch and had to go to the doctor. Rebecca said: Nathan's wife saw you hurt, so watch where you walk, your girlfriend is only deaf and not blind, and he said: She hasn't been my girlfriend for a long time, she's married to a laborer and lives far away.

The new doctor's name was Zosha Merimovitch. Even as a child, he had known the legends about Rebecca by heart. The legends began to be embroidered back in nineteen ten, two years after Rebecca buried Nehemiah. She went back to Jaffa then to buy a plow and stayed in a small hotel.

It was a hot day, Zosha Merimovitch was told, and Rebecca went out in the morning to buy a plow and old Michael Halperin, filled with the fury of many languid Jews, stood at the circus that had come to town and saw

Jews wearing white suits, with delicate hands, smelling of perfume. He tried to excite them with the idea of a Hebrew army of ragamuffins that would conquer the land of his fathers from its robbers, bring it to life, and restore it to what it was and they nodded fondly at the barefoot ancient prophet splendid in his oriental garb, but their eyes were fixed on the beautiful Egyptian dancer, shaking her buttocks to the sound of the drum and the oud, and on the caged lion. An Arab knife-sharpener stood there and sharpened sickles, knives, and swords for all the wars Halperin said were coming. And then Michael Halperin entered the lion's cage, and the crowd held its breath. He stroked the lion's mane, stood facing him, sang Hatikvah and the *modir* didn't know if it was forbidden to sing it even in a lion's cage, and the lion lay on the ground, fixed watery bored eyes on Halperin, and fell asleep. The lion's grating breath and Halperin's singing were the only sounds. The lion's hair looked like Halperin's.

Halperin's singing in the lion's cage stirred memories in Rebecca of the songs of Joseph Rayna. She said to herself: Heroes in a cage of a tame lion, a cheap stage setting, a stupid attempt at would-be salvation. The words of Hatikvah always made her feel melancholy. Words full of longing for artificial horses and visions of returning from a hunt in a nonexistent forest. She despised Halperin because no Hebrew army, she thought, would spring up from his shouts and the bombastic song in a cage. And, unnoticed, Rebecca went into the cage, locked the door behind her, and then there was a silence people had never heard before. You could hear, said Zosha Merimovitch's mother, the sound of the oil in the bottles on the stand of the old oil vendor, whose knife stopped being sharpened at that moment by the knife-sharpener.

Rebecca opened the lion's maw, managed to look into its mouth, and saw how big its teeth were. The Turkish *modir* now stood up and started lashing himself with a *turbatsh* and Rebecca, who didn't know what language the lion spoke, ordered it in Arabic, which she thought was closer to its language than any other language she knew, to roll over and play cat for her. The lion did as she ordered and to the spectators, who may have invented some of it, its movements looked like coquettish rotating movements and some versions have it that even its roar sounded like a cat's meow, but Zosha clearly remembers that in the conversation about that subject, various opinions were expressed about the purring, since a Turkish

cat whines *yeow* and a Hebrew one *yooo* and an English one *meow*, so there
was no consensus about whether the poor lion whined like a cat, and the
lion, who apparently smiled at Rebecca, lay on its back and then got up and
roared and she didn't budge until it walked in front of her, knelt, turned
its face, and she stroked its mane, straightened her dress, wiped off a few
pieces of straw that had stuck to it, and said: No blood and fire, no hope,
this is a place of circuses and Jews, there's nobody to erect a kingdom of
Judea for here, Michael Halperin, there's no reason, and she went out of
the cage. The doctor Zosha Merimovitch, who was then a little boy,
trembled with fear when he heard the story and people told how Michael
Halperin then went to Rebecca, bowed to her as he had once bowed to the
lion, and she said to him, The lion of Judah bows to a miserable lady of
exile? And in a mocking voice, she went on: You're a funny Jew, Halperin,
go save another nation in another place, but never mind, you're the clos-
est thing to a lion I've seen since the Wondrous One was here and taught
the fools in the settlement how to smell the feet of robbers who went
through the field. Grand pianos they've now bought for their daughters,
and she left.

The doctor, now a grown-up, waited for Ebenezer. Now and then he
peeped at her house but never managed to see her. And she refused to go
to doctors. He waited for the bold fellow, the hybrid of Michael Halperin,
Rebecca Schneerson, and Nimrod the hero. His contempt for Ebenezer
was perfect, he treated him without looking at him.

The Captain moved to the nearby settlement, which was big and rather
close to both Jaffa and Jerusalem, and the door of his house said: Captain
J.M.A.G., Citizen of the United States, Argentina, French Editor, Please
do not visit on Sunday and Wednesday. The Captain's trip to Cairo was
postponed again and again and every Wednesday he would ride to the
settlement to visit Rebecca, sit in her house, tell her about his plans, and
give her a most discouraging account of the irrigation plan for the Middle
East she had devised and still expected to realize, even though for some
time now she didn't remember why she had ever devised that plan. The
Captain didn't give up his idea of marrying Rebecca. He listened patiently
to her tribulations, the story of her weeping for eight years, the story of her
life with Nehemiah and her tribulations with her stupid son, who goes to
a doctor who probably studied horse doctoring in Beirut, to put iodine and

a bandage on his face. For some reason, the Captain saw the story of her going into the lion's cage as overwhelming proof that she would marry him someday. Because she could never understand the disposition of the Captain's ostensibly logical connections, she took the words literally and learned how to go on refusing him politely. She would say her "no" pensively as if she meant "yes," while gazing softly at the Captain's increasingly pale face, and so she could keep his hope on a back burner and know that every Wednesday he would come visit her to propose new ideas to her and some of them really weren't bad, like building the airport years later.

While Rebecca was pondering how much alike were the Wondrous One, Joseph, the Captain, and the German officer who played songs for her during the war, new settlers came to the settlement. The Turkish *modir*, who was banished from the Land by the British, sent her a love letter from Istanbul and the manager of the wine press started sending love letters with shipments of brandy he would send to her home. The economy improved, new rest homes were even built for rheumatics since the air of the place was good for them. Roads were paved and the settlement was enveloped in thick green foliage, and there were corners where the sun never penetrated, and Rebecca went on protecting her son at a limited distance of time and space. One day a young teacher came to the settlement from Tel Aviv whose name was Dana Klomin. She brought twelve little children to show them the pit of the first settlers, which they had started digging next to the synagogue some years before. In the community center hung pictures of the early days and one of the farmers took the children on a tour of the community center and showed them the pit, Roots, and told about the tribulations, the torments, and the malaria. He told about Nathan and Nehemiah and the Wondrous One who came riding from the Arabian deserts to teach war. The teacher Dana was short, round, handsome in the unaccepted meaning of the word—as Rebecca put it—her eyes were gray, and when she twisted her ankle on a tour of the Hill of Tears, she was taken to the home of Zosha Merimovitch the doctor, who knew her father in Tel Aviv, and when he fixed her heel and bandaged it she saw on the windowsill a bird made of wood that Ebenezer had brought the doctor as a sign of gratitude for his cure. She looked at the bird in amazement, and said: That's a bird of paradise, it almost flies and doesn't fly, like me, who carves such a handsome bird? The doctor, who never caught on that there was anything special about the bird or Ebenezer, refused to see and turned his face away when he'd come to him, put the bird on the windowsill because he didn't know where to put it, said: That bird was made by Ebenezer Schneerson, who sits alone in the citrus grove and carves.

The children were resting in the Horowitz home. Dana Klomin limped slowly to the citrus grove. It was a beautiful day, and she deluded herself that she was going because of the beautiful day and the charming and pleasant view, but what led Dana Klomin, whose ankle hurt, was the rare sight of the bird. Dana's father believed in one thing only—in the charter. He thought he was the only one who still followed in the path of the greatest Jew of our generation, Theodor Herzl. He was excited by the Hebrew kingdom modeled on Rome, with a senate and an enlightened king, and for him Zionism wasn't only a solution to the distress of the Jews—or returning them to their homeland—but also an act of legal and historical justice. Mr. Klomin thought the Land was empty of people, the Arabs who lived in it were accidental wayfarers, no one ever called that land by name except the Jews, he said excitedly. It wasn't the homeland of any nation, no city was a capital for them, only the longings of the Jews preserved the Land from total disappearance, he claimed. He quoted Disraeli, who said in his book *Tancred:* "The vineyards of Israel have ceased to exist, but the eternal law enjoins the Children of Israel still to celebrate the vintage. A race that persist its celebrating their vintage, although they have no fruits to gather, will regain their vineyards."

A plot of land without declaring a historic homeland, without a flag, an anthem, or a legal system, was merely an aftermath of nothing. The emptiness of the Land was the implementation of an essentially ahistorical political mishap that demanded legal correction, a kind of leadership fraud, and the proud Israeli nation had to accept the charter for the Land of Israel and establish a strong and enlightened kingdom there on the European model and not on the savage Asian one, establish a supreme court there, a parliament, a decent and consistent constitution, enact a law of languages allowing only Hebrew and ancient Latin and the Hebrew army that would arise would establish those points of Zionist settlement that Jewish poverty had established so far without any real vision or proper planning. Zionism had to be made into a profitable business, he argued with the fervor of a person incited by an idea that nobody can or will take seriously. He was just as disappointed in his daughter as Rebecca was in her son. Like Rebecca, he also hoped his grandson might follow in his path. He had ideas about breeding his daughter, an expression he himself adopted, with a scion of the house of David, but the only scion of the house of David, Mr. Joseph Abravanel, seemed cheap, Levantine, and devoid of greatness, and the son was even dumber than his father. Mr. Klomin even thought of trying to marry his daughter off to some European prince, but since he didn't know who to appeal to in the matter, he didn't do anything. Dana, who had lost her mother, attended teachers' college and all she wanted to do was dry flowers, teach, and give birth to her own children so they would also love to smell flowers. She loved the settlements, hated Tel Aviv, which had grown and was noisy and pretentious now, she read old novels in yellowing bindings and dreamed of the simple and beautiful life in the lap of nature. She loved everything beautiful created by man or nature. She hated her father's big words, but she loved the solitary and stubborn man who raised her after her mother died in childbirth. When he furiously argued to her that what we need are warrior engineers and chemists and jurists and not teachers, Dana said to him: But I love flowers and the smell of rain and a grape harvest, and he twisted his face and shouted: From romanticism you beget stupid children, not a Jewish state after two thousand years, Dana!

What angered him especially was her collection of smells. She'd collect leaves and plants and blend them with liquid and seal the smells in jars and call every smell by its own name. She had a bottle of lust and a bottle of the smell of humility, and a bottle of a pauper kingdom, and a bottle of Tyre and Sidon, and a bottle of licorice essence, and more and more bottles whose very sight stirred gloomy despair in Mr. Klomin—who, of course, was always dressed to be taken to some king or high commissioner. Her friends went up to the Galilee and sang bold songs, sprouted mighty mustaches, and tapped each other on the shoulder. New settlements were set up at night and Dana's friends guarded them, but for her they lacked the poetry she was seeking, the sadness, the shame, her smells sought birds like the one she saw on the windowsill of Dr. Zosha Merimovitch, whose father once argued for three straight nights with Mr. Klomin about the squadron leaders he wanted to command the future Hebrew army. She dreamed of a heavy pensive man who would spare her the need to choose between her father and her friends.

For three days Dana Klomin stayed in the citrus grove. The students got a short letter brought to them by the grandson of Ahbed. In the letter, Dana wrote: Forgive me for staying, give warm regards to the teachers and don't judge me harshly, I can't leave, yours in friendship and love, Dana. The students returned to Tel Aviv with the janitor of the school who cursed the teacher who fell in love with a carpenter, and on the way they saw a man wearing a strange uniform driving a wagon loaded with splendid furniture and sporting a sword. That was Captain Jose Menkin A. Goldenberg, who after a sharp argument with the committee of the nearby settlement in which he tried to explain for the hundred and first time why his name alone was a guarantee of his being Swiss and that the Greek Orthodox church is the desired answer the Jews were waiting for, while they claimed against him that he was a fantasizer, a traitor, cheating his nation and his religion, and they said: How long will you stay with us? He put on his fine clothing, wanted to go to Rebecca, but since it wasn't Wednesday, he did what he would have done if it weren't Wednesday and he had no words. He went for a tour and when he came to Gaza he saw an Arab wearing rags and selling antique furniture, who claimed it was furniture of Modo-Louigo fifteen, or in another language: in the style of Louis XV, he bought it as an imaginary wedding gift for Rebecca and was now driving it in a cart to her house. When Dana entered the hut, Ebenezer lifted his face, smiled at her, and went on working. Then he looked at her injured heel, took the heel in his strong, rough hands, looked at it, and for the first time in his life felt that he belonged to something bigger than himself.

He gently twisted the heel, stared at it long and hard, and felt so close to the heel, loved the skin, the way the heel coiled into the foot, looked at Dana, and said: I think I've been waiting for you for years, but I'm not good with words and I have to go back to carving, wait. She waited a whole day. Her eyes were veiled with a grief that may have always been in her and turned into tense expectation. At night they lay down beside each other on the mattress of leaves outside and the sky hung above them, peeping between branches, the sky was starry and black. Three days and three nights they stayed there. When he looked at her she felt that all the smells she had caged in bottles were now one person she wanted to pity and take care of his strong hands that were gently creating a bird or a portrait, out of a joyous intoxication, a dark sadness, and a disguised heaviness.

The two of them were no longer children. Ebenezer, who many years later will be the Last Jew in seedy nightclubs of Europe, was then an eccentric fellow of twenty-six and a deaf woman had once loved to touch him. Because he didn't know many words, he didn't clearly think love; he bit Dana's earlobes and thought "doves." She said to herself: Maybe that's not love, but that is what I was looking for. He thought: Got to give her a house, give her a child, and her own pepper tree. They laughed, something Ebenezer couldn't do without recalling his mother's angry face.

Dana didn't understand why she yearned for a person who wasn't exciting, who made her feel heavy. Years later, when Ebenezer would sit in a little city in Poland and think of Dana, he'd say to himself: Why didn't I tell her I loved her more than anybody in the world and never could I love anybody like that? But he recalled that when he was with her he didn't even know he loved her. All he knew was that he had to be with her.

The wedding was held right after the harvest. Most of the farmers dressed in white brought gifts. Rebecca, who sat in a house full of antique Louis XV furniture, looked at Dana as if she were seeing the greatest fraud of the century. What did she find in my son? She pitied Nehemiah, whose dreams of Abner ben-Ner and Yiftach begat a pensive and foolish man who touches a short, plump woman, smiles as if he were a mechanical doll. Beyond the fence of the settlement the house of Dana and Ebenezer was built. That was the first house outside the wall of the first settlers. Rebecca built the house because Ebenezer had to stay close to the farm; somebody has to protect what I established, she said, even if he does carve birds. The house she built for her son was handsome, abutted the vineyard with the ancient pool still in the middle, whose bottom was Crusader and whose turret was Mameluke.

Mr. Klomin, who came to the wedding furious and betrayed, was wearing a light-colored suit with a flower in his lapel. He was amazed at the sight of Rebecca Schneerson's elegant house and happy above all to meet the Captain in his official uniform. The two of them whispered together in Dana's new kitchen, among jars full of flowers smelling like jujubes, wormwood, mint, and citrus blossoms mixed with the smell of fresh paint, and after a long talk each hugged the other's shoulders, shook hands, and looked excited.

And on the day he parted from his daughter, Mr. Klomin increased his party by one hundred percent: it now had a leader and a single member.

The Captain was appointed deputy squadron leader responsible for organization and indicating avenues of financing, activities and political empowerment, preparing strategy and tactics, and in addition the Captain was to train leaders of the army of gladiators, lieutenants, and pashas that would be established someday when the old-new constitution would be shaped and the nation would recognize its three hundred Gideons, and then the Argentinean with American citizenship and the Swiss name, who belonged to the Greek Orthodox Church, was responsible for protocol, military, taxation, consolidation, building and general strategic forecasting.

Pleasant smells blew from the citrus groves and the fields. Dana's schoolmates came from the Galilee on horseback; they tapped each other on the shoulder and yelled. They danced bold and "awful" dances, as Rebecca put it, until the wee hours of the morning. The splendid kingdom is realized here by a carpenter and wild people shrieking, said Mr. Klomin sadly, and he gazed yearningly at the nobility of the Captain and Rebecca. He saw them as a symbol of his dream. Rebecca agreed to describe to him what she felt when she entered the lion's cage. Mr. Klomin looked at the Captain's padded visor, ostentatiously hated the roars of the wild Pioneers, saw his son-in-law standing on the side gazing, and said: They should have begat Rebecca and the Captain, and not vice versa.

The feast was made from the Captain's recipes and the farmers drank and sang and recalled Nehemiah and his beautiful words, and late at night, when the Pioneers were still singing around a bonfire, the aging farmers sat on the side and yearningly sang old songs they had once learned from Joseph Rayna and wept when they recalled those distant days, and said: Here we married off the first son of the settlement. After they left, Dana sat and looked at the sky. Ebenezer sat next to her. Rebecca thought of men who see the features and don't understand the essence. She thought of Joseph, of the Wondrous One, of the Captain, of Mr. Klomin, and then she thought a thought that was so strange to her she tried to get it out of her mind and couldn't. She thought: Maybe we nevertheless did something important here; maybe this settlement and that whole deed aren't as small as I thought, maybe there was something in Nehemiah's vision that hasn't entirely vanished and wasn't in vain? But then she saw in her mind's eye the great war that was coming and the Pioneers shooting at the enemy and the Arabs sharpening knives in Jaffa for all the future wars and she feared for Boaz, whose image she could already discover in her.

In the morning, two Arab women cleaned up the destruction and Rebecca looked at the new house and thought, What can those two fools do at night? and she wanted to laugh despite the scattered leftovers, empty wine bottles, and the flowers eagerly pulled up. In the room, the lamentations of the old-timers still echoed. In the sunlight, it was hard for her to see last night's thoughts as real. And so she could almost forgive her son. In the house next door, the gramophone Mr. Zucker had recently bought started playing Beethoven's violin concerto. The speaker was aimed at Rebecca's house and she linked the music with the pleasant fields of morning, the dew, the almond grove in the distance, the mountains on the horizon, and again she saw the impending storm of war and started reciting Psalms to try to change something in the world, and if she had thought of that deed in real terms, she would probably have burst out laughing. Afterward Ebenezer and Dana went for a walk. Ebenezer sewed a handsome tent, they loaded the burden on one mule and Dana rode on a second mule and Ebenezer got off and picked flowers for Dana, who put them in a bag tied to the saddle, and thus they went up to the mountains and down to the valleys, crossed wadis and rivers and at night, they looked at the stars and felt an intense closeness, some longing for one another they had a name for and didn't know how to call it, and they'd lie like that, clinging desperately, breathing each other's breath, and Ebenezer wanted to say things, but didn't know how to say them, and his hands would knead her strongly and gently. He carved birds for her, built boxes for her, crowned her with portraits, and she lusted for him, touched him in surprising places, and they would laugh wildly, like hyenas, listening to the jackals wailing in the distances and answering them.

On the third evening, they came to the crossroads of the desert. Above rose a mountain and on was it the holy house of the Shiite priests. In the distance, dawn illuminated the mountains of Moab and a profound serenity reigned over everything. Birds began chirping, when they came to the top Dana didn't find flowers but thorns, thistles, and nettle flowers she was afraid to pick because they blossomed only one day a year. They were ordered to say *Sala'am aleikum ya ahl el-kubur*, which means Greetings to you who dwell in the graves. And at the same time, Ebenezer began blessing with head bent: *El-sala'am aleikum ya ahl el-duniya,* which means Greetings to you people of this world. And then the old man there told them that if they forgot those words their only son would die within three months, their house would be destroyed by fire, and their name would be wiped off the face of the earth. Dana said: We don't have a son, and Ebenezer said: We will have a son and his name will be Boaz. Dana asked why Boaz, and Ebenezer said: Because he will be the grandson of Nehemiah. And when she asked what would happen if they had a daughter, he said: We won't have a daughter, we'll have a son.

From the moment he was born, Rebecca claimed that Boaz was her son, that she had held him in her womb as a pledge. Dana held the baby, suckled him, and was afraid to let Rebecca touch him. At night Rebecca started whispering her Psalms angrily and furiously, prayed to a lord of another world, a strange, hostile one, who once lived with her forefathers in cellars. Dana wept and told Ebenezer that Rebecca was praying for her death, and Ebenezer tried to calm her but didn't know how to say that in the few words he used. He said: I'll protect you, Dana. She hates me, said Dana, and wept. I'm so scared, she loved Samuel, I wanted to understand, I couldn't, I looked at my son, he doesn't look like me, not like his mother, he had green-yellow eyes like the eyes of a demon, he laughed, a laughing baby he was, he touched his mother and would turn his face away from her, and Ebenezer went to his mother and said to her.

Tape / —

You're praying for Dana's death, said Ebenezer. And she said: I'm praying to who I want and for what I want. You're not even the son of your father, not the grandson of your grandfather, you didn't come out of me, you came out of the coffin of a Jew who died of typhus and was buried in Jaffa under another name. Give me the only son I deserve. At night Rebecca yelled at the fence so they would hear: Ebenezer is the son of Nehemiah! Who else could be the father of a mongoloid who begets sons of a king if not a man who died on his wife at the shore of Jaffa to punish her for a life she didn't want to live? No Joseph would have begat a silent bird carver who tries to sleep with the daughter of a eunuch from Tel Aviv who begat his daughter from a charter translated from ancient Latin.

Dana heaped up pillows and boxes and blocked the doorway and
Ebenezer paved a new path around the old house and Rebecca sat at the
fence and wished for her grandson and couldn't see him. At night, no light
was turned on in the house. Ebenezer sat in the house holding a rifle.
Every noise made Dana jump. One day, one of Dana's friends was brought
who had a stomachache and volunteered to guard the yard and whenever
he saw Rebecca approaching he aimed his rifle at her and said: I'll shoot
you, and she giggled and said Shoot, fool, and he aimed, trembled, and
didn't dare shoot until one day he crossed over the barricade and hired
himself out to work in her yard.

Tape / —

Boaz was born in the nearby settlement, in a small hospital, on April
third, nineteen twenty-eight. On that day and at that hour, in Tarnopol,
Galicia, Samuel Lipker was born. Samuel's sire then wrote a great poem on
his unrequited love for Rebecca Schneerson. Then he wrote a lament on
the death of Jews that would be written again later on by a man named
Lionel Secret. The lament and the love poem to Rebecca were the only
two successful poems ever written by Joseph Rayna. But they were left
with his clothes before he was shot to death. No one remains who will
remember them except for one man who recited them to Ebenezer and
then died with a piece of bread wet from the damp of the wall stuck in
his mouth. Joseph wrote about the most horrible disaster as if he envisioned it. The words walked among ruins of Jews and a path strewn with
human obstacles who didn't know what they hoarded in their minds, came
to Ebenezer, who stood in Cologne and recited the lamentation and the
love poem. In its words, Ebenezer heard a distant melody reminding him
of his love for his mother. And Joseph Rayna didn't go to America to save
himself because he thought that if he went there, he would betray
Rebecca. And so, without knowing, Lionel Secret learned from Ebenezer
the melody of the great lament he would write years later, and would restore the first love of his mother Rachel, her love for Rebecca Secret Charity and the great-granddaughter of her daughter, but by the time he wrote
the lament, his mother was dead and buried in New Jersey under the name
of Rachel Blau, faithful wife of Saul Blau.

Those are the annals of Israel. Abraham begat Isaac. Isaac begat Jacob, end.

Tape / —

When Mr. Klomin came to the settlement to see his grandson, Dana claimed that Rebecca had sent him to spy. Mr. Klomin came with the Captain, who had just returned from Rebecca's house. Rebecca stood at the fence separating her house from her son's house, and Mr. Klomin, who knocked on the door, didn't get an answer. He wanted to read to his daughter the six-hundred-page letter he had written to the High Commissioner. The Captain also considered that letter the pièce de resistance of the life of Mr. Klomin, who started believing the rumors that had been making the rounds of the *Yishuv* for some time that the Captain was secretly inciting the Arabs to revolt (he didn't know exactly against whom) and therefore Mr. Klomin believed that that inciter should be used to remove the foreign government from the Land by means of his loyal or hidden servants. The Captain's generosity enabled the recruitment of about twenty new members into the party, but the source of his money became more suspect when Shoshana Sakhohtovskaya returned from Egypt. Shoshana was the daughter of Nathan, Nehemiah's old friend, and married a Jewish officer in the British army who was stationed in Cairo and he was said to own two factories for holes in pennies (one for the hole of a penny, and one for the hole of a tuppence). Shoshana told with a fervor that almost made her face bearable, that the Captain's newspaper sold only thirty-four copies, was merely a deception and behind it, she said, hid a secret, international, maybe even religious body, she almost shouted, a body whose purpose is to convert the Jews of the Land of Israel to Christianity and keep the Land from turning into a Zionist base. The Captain was too polite and in love to try to refute those accusations, which seemed exaggerated even to him, although he did see something in them that was fair to some extent. In his opinion, the accusations were partly correct, but imprecise, maybe even malicious, and he pledged himself by his nobility, which he occasionally called "South American nobility" and "Swiss courtesy," to silence and would wring his hands, and say: I said what I said out of love, I don't go back there, that's a fact, I'm no longer friendly with the

English, I live in the settlement, and the proof was so dubious that every-body almost tended to accept it and Shoshana Sakhohtovskaya sat at night, gobbled up all the oranges on a tree she had planted with her own hands as a child. She heaped up the peels in a pyramid and when a black bird with a yellow beak stood on the tip of the pyramid and nodded its head and an owl screeched at night, Shoshana burst into bitter weeping, and called out: At least I have someplace to go back to. The Captain didn't explain what places he didn't go back to, and people wondered about those places, for a person generally isn't born in Argentina, Switzerland, and the United States. He has to choose, said those who were considered experts in the ways of the world. The elders of the settlement, who were grateful to Rebecca for Nehemiah and for Nathan's happy death, said: The Captain's Greek Ortho-doxy is not exactly the religion that prevails in Argentina, the United States of America, or Switzerland, so when the Captain went to get his things that would come three times a year in a ship to the port, a few members of the settlement watched him and with their own amazed eyes (Mr. Klomin stood with them, even though he was ashamed of it) saw a gigantic trunk taken off, placed on the shore, and a British officer loaded it on a cart and took it to the shed, where the Captain was waiting. An aged consul stood next to him, eating an apple. The case was opened, there were new uniforms there, medals, and hats with padded visors. They also saw how the Captain was granted new insignia, which the aged consul pinned to his epaulettes, and he shouted unambiguously in a loud voice so they too could hear that the Cap-tain was now promoted to the rank of colonel and the adorned scroll in the consul's hand was seen even from where they were hiding. The insignia were made of gold, the new visor was woven of silk fibers, silver and gold.

Later on, when Rebecca wanted to know more details about the event that had been described to her in great detail, she asked Captain (Colonel) Jose Menkin A. Goldenberg to read her the scroll. One paragraph in the scroll seemed to her to suit the Captain to a tee. The paragraph said: Colonel Jose Menkin A. Goldenberg valiantly defended the homeland, destroyed, captured, burned, smashed, split, sliced, trapped, penetrated, attacked, surrounded, crushed, broke, overcame, breached, caught, re-pelled, cleansed, cracked . . . And Rebecca listened to the words, was si-lent, and then said: It's nice of you that after all those deeds you're willing to waste time with simple people like us. They sat, drank a little brandy, the Captain smelled of imported flowers, and she said: Here you are with us and we're fond of you, Captain, and for us you'll always be Captain, they suspect you, respect and esteem you, you buy us gifts, but who you really are we don't know and maybe we won't know.

Rebecca, who was too busy with her attempt to capture Boaz, was really not surprised that not only the Captain and the manager of the wine press were wooing her, but also the Jewish husband of Shoshana Sakhohtovskaya, who owned two factories for holes, who came to visit. She told him: You should be ashamed of yourself. You're married to the daughter of my distinguished friend Nathan.

The war for the fate of Boaz was then at its height. The fence between the houses was thickened. For more than a year now, Rebecca hadn't seen Ebenezer or Boaz, Boaz would cry at night and she would yearn for him. Ebenezer started having nightmares he wasn't used to and Dana claimed that Rebecca was casting spells on him through the fence. When he woke up, he looked at Boaz and hated him. He said to Dana: He looks like Joseph, and she said: Ebenezer, this child is your son and I'm not to blame for who he looks like. Rebecca spread the rumor that the child was brought from Joseph to her through Dana's womb, and Dana grew melancholy and made bitter claims against the mother of Ebenezer, whose nightmares thickened with her dread.

One day Ebenezer burst the barriers, punched the guard he had once employed and who worked for his mother, stood at her chair, and pleaded with her to leave them alone and not harm Dana. She's all I've got, he said. I had nothing, Father died, you weren't there, I've got Dana! And she said: You two don't interest me, Ebenezer. Not you and not your Dana. You've got my son, give him to me, take your Dana and go to hell. You pray for her death, said Ebenezer. She laughed and said: I've got no control over what the Holy One Blessed Be He does. I filled my part of the deal with your father, he wanted you and I have Boaz. And until he's mine, I won't shut up.

Rebecca turned her face away and through the window screen she saw Ebenezer's back as he went off and a longing she had never known passed through her, a longing to bequeath to Boaz her life and her property. For the first time in her life she felt that she had surrendered to the most ridiculous of feelings, to pure unconditional love. The yearning flattered her but also scared her.

A few weeks later, when Boaz reached his first birthday, Dana went out to look for Ebenezer, who hadn't returned from the citrus grove for three days. He sat in his hut and tried to discover his father's real face in a tree. Suddenly, the sky darkened and a heavy rain poured down. The drops fell savagely on the ground and looked gigantic, a wind blew and the sky turned black, a haze filled the air, the foliage looked purple, the sun that flickered for a moment between the clouds was almost green and a thick dust from the desert grew turgid in the eddy. Lightning flashes struck the ground and cut the air with a loud whistle. Two Arabs driving a load of spices on a donkey on their way from the desert to the village of Marar saw Dana lit in the light of the flashes. She was wet and her dress clung to her body. One of them attacked her. Her wet hair fell on her face and his old friend grabbed it and her when she tried to defend herself from the rain. The first one grabbed her with his hands, stretched over her and tried to rape her. She fought him with all her might, bit and kicked, but the mud was moldy and she couldn't see a thing. When she fainted from swallowing mud the old man said to the young one: Come on, let's get out, we've killed her. He tried to give her artificial respiration but her body was cold. Out of dread he took out an aluminum cup and started digging a pit. They buried Dana, but she was still alive. She tried to get up but the earth crushed her and broke her clavicle. She tried to move, and her head bumped into a rock. Ebenezer heard the roars, put on the old raincoat hanging in the hut, and went out. He walked in the rain, soaked to the skin. And then he saw, he didn't yet understand what he saw, he thought of going on, and turned around. He tried to listen to Dana's heart, but her heart wasn't beating. He sat next to her, looked at her trampled body and didn't shed a tear. He picked up her body, cleaned her face and body, straightened her dress, and carried her in his arms. He came to the settlement where all the inhabitants were sequestered in their houses and looking out the windows at the rainstorm and the windswept street. They saw Ebenezer carrying his wife's body. People came out of their houses and started following him. Old Horowitz came outside and bowed his head, tears gushed in his eyes. Ebenezer didn't say a word. He took Dana to the threshold of his mother's house, put her body on the doorsill, and called out: Here you are! You wanted her dead and you got it.

He took a knife from the hiding place in the cowshed and went to the nearby village. An old man for whom he had once carved the dead faces of

his daughters told him: Go to Marar, you'll see a donkey with a damaged
saddle at the house of Abu-Hassein, and you'll know. Ebenezer climbed up
to the village. The inhabitants were hiding from the storm. His smell was
blended with the downpour and the dogs didn't smell him and didn't bark.
He came to Abu-Hassein's house, saw the donkey at the next house, examined the saddle and called the Arabs to come outside. They came out,
the old man started trembling, but Ebenezer whose hands were strong,
grabbed the young one, smelled Dana's odor on his clothes, and killed him
with two stabs. The old man started running away, men from the settlement ran up, and dragged Ebenezer back to the settlement. In the yard,
they washed the blood off Ebenezer. All night Ebenezer sat on the doorsill of Rebecca's house next to Dana's body and watched it. Rebecca looked
outside and saw her son and his dead wife and wanted to go to them, but
Ebenezer warned her not to come. The rain stopped, the sky cleared up,
and a fragrance of spring filled the air. There was no trace of the storm
except for the lightning damage, split tree trunks, and a lot of sand piled
up wet and sticky. The next day, the funeral was held, Rebecca stood on
the side, between the Captain and Mr. Klomin. Mr. Klomin, gazing, tried
to understand the meaning of the empty space that filled him. With his
great expertise in the charter and the illegality of the British Mandate, he
had never noticed how much he loved his daughter. Now when he felt love,
he didn't know what to do with it. At the open grave, Ebenezer told his
wife: You were a gift given to me and taken from me, this morning I looked
in the mirror, there was nobody there. And then the cantor recited the
prayer for the dead and they filled the grave with dirt and Roots grew by
one more corpse. He returned from Roots alone. He sat a long time and
looked at his son. He wanted to touch him, but he didn't. The child's eyes
were wide open. For a moment Ebenezer thought the child was smiling.
His eyes were mocking, and Ebenezer got up and slammed the door. He
stood next to his house, looked at the path where Dana had planted roses
and geraniums and at the pepper tree he had planted for her and at her
herb garden, and he yelled: Rebecca, I'm going to find who cursed us.
Rebecca approached the child and looked at him. Her son's bowed figure
was seen from the myrtle tree on the path. He was twenty-seven years old.
The year was nineteen twenty-seven. The month was April. The air was
drenched with the intoxicating smells of spring. The Captain moved to

Ebenezer's house. The paths and flowers went on blooming every year. The dried flowers in the books and the sweet smells in the jars and bottles stayed where they were.

Forty years, Ebenezer Schneerson didn't see his mother.

Tape / —

Your blood Dana. Your Dana blood. Blood blood. Your blood Dana. Dana Dana your blood. The blood of Dana. Dana. Blood blood blood Dana. Blood of Dana, blood. Blood your blood Dana Dana. Your blood Dana. Your Dana blood. Dana blood. Dana Dana. Your blood Dana. Blood.

They said I went to Marar to kill an Arab. I don't remember. I tell how I went to kill an Arab in Marar and I don't remember. An empty space I am. Stories of others or of others about me. Who am I? Forty years searching and don't know.

After forty years I came and saw him, and I said to him: Samuel! I was so happy that Samuel was here. But that was Boaz. He was offended. What do I know about Boaz?

Tape / —

Teacher Henkin met Boaz years after Menahem was killed. When he retired, there was nobody to say good-bye to. The teachers had changed. Damausz sat in his house and embroidered his old dreams over and over again. Old Teacher Sarakh with her swollen legs didn't even bother to come say good-bye to him. She grows silkworms and gazes at the sea getting blocked across from her house. Teacher Henkin bought a new overcoat and a broad-brimmed hat and every morning as usual, he went on walking from his house on Deliverance Street to Mugrabi Square, which had meanwhile been destroyed, and then back home again. "Grief of the world," Teacher Obadiah Henkin would say to himself at the new hotels, crushing the handsome hills at the seashore, the new houses, the discotheques, the banks popping up like mushrooms. Here and there, a few veteran teachers still live, Histadrut members, who now add a second story to their little houses and will soon sell the houses for accelerated development. Only the corner of Henkin's street remained lost between the new building sites closing in on it. They're wiping out the sea, dammit, said the baker's wife to Mr. Henkin, and he said, Yes, yes, too bad about Noga, thought Henkin, what's she doing? She lived with us, Hasha Masha and she, like two conspirators. A bare bulb over my wife, the garden hasn't yet been renewed, the paint is peeling. Unlike Hasha Masha, Teacher Henkin doesn't know that relations between Noga and Menahem—what he privately called their engagement—ended a few weeks before Menahem fell.

How many years does Teacher Henkin walk in that set route? He stopped counting. Ten, fifteen years? He's not sure anymore. The years are accompanied by demonstrations of hesitation, partial juggling of retreat, attempts to understand death from a new, unusual angle, getting to know the bereaved parents, the Committee of Bereaved Parents, the Shimonis, all that happened while he walked every single day, at the same time, on Ben-Yehuda Street to Mugrabi Square and back. Later on, after he'd meet Boaz, it became clear to Teacher Henkin that his son didn't fall in the battle of Mount Radar, but in a battle that would stir heroic feelings in him at first, that battle for the Old City. Teacher Henkin, who had had many illusions shattered in his life, was angry about the battle in the Old City, which might have been won if not for the order of Ben-Gurion, whom he had once thought great. But he wouldn't get his son back in either case, Hasha Masha will then say, and he'll stare at her, but then he won't be angry anymore at her hostility.

And so he also learned the battle for the Old City: the weary fighters of the Harel Brigade (and Menahem, he thought then, was one of them) bombarded Mount Zion every night from Yemin Moshe whose residents had previously been evacuated. And the mountain was captured. Menahem was in the armored car that climbed the mountain from the Valley of Hinnom. The fighters met in the Dormition Monastery, next to King David's Tomb, near the place of the seder the Christians call the Last Supper. After a short rest, the fighters were assembled in Bishop Gubat's school next to the monastery, and in the shadow of Byzantine acacias, they ate grape leaves stuffed with dry bread. From the other side of the narrow path separating the mountain from the Old City, on the splendid Tower of Suleiman sat the fighters of the Arab Legion commanded by British Colonel Wood. Colonel Wood, who graduated with honors from Eton and had a degree from Cambridge, had previously served in Europe, was one of those who liberated Hathausen concentration camp, fought in the Pacific, and then volunteered to help his old friend Glubb Pasha organize the army of the grandson of the Sharif of Mecca. Now he held a stick in his hand, which once, when liberating the camp, he refused to hold.

In the besieged Jewish Quarter, a handful of Jews remained, whose ammunition and food were running out. By order of Ben-Gurion, the governor of Jewish Jerusalem refused the offer of the rescue battle made by the members of the Harel Brigade. The governor claimed he didn't have reinforcements that the fighters of the Harel Brigade were exhausted and a considerable part of their fighters were killed or wounded. The commander of the Harel force decided to carry out the operation despite the governor's refusal, and that was a historical moment, thought Henkin excitedly. Ben-Gurion, who feared the rage of the fighters, approved the operation but at the same time he ordered the governor not to assist it. We need a historian, said Henkin, who will come and arrange the data, so that battle can be summarized properly. The commander said: We have to strike the enemy while he's stunned from the battle on the mountain. The night before, a hole was made in the roof of the Dormition Church by a Davidka shell that tried to hit a target far away from there and missed. The enemy had tanks, armored cars, and artillery. Colonel Wood relied on his weapons and his loyal soldiers. At dawn, an armored car approached the wall of the Old City and poured fire on the nearby Jaffa Gate. Seven Iraqi and British officers were taken prisoner. On Mount Zion sat Menahem along with Boaz. He wasn't thinking of the international conspiracies, of Ben-Gurion writhing in the torments of his decision, of the governor and his struggle with the commander of Harel, he was waiting to finish the war, go back home, live, then he got a cone of explosives and crawled toward Zion Gate. Over the gate were two heavy machine guns, whose range covered the narrow path and you had to slip under it. The explosive was connected to a wire and to the cone, and you could push it with a pole under the coil of the barbed war fence stretched there. At three twenty AM, on the twentieth of May nineteen forty-eight, the cone burst the fences, a mighty explosion was heard, shots were fired feverishly, and Zion Gate was breached. In the smoke of shooting and explosions, Menahem and his comrades burst into the city that previously, in a brief and laconic but emotional ceremony, the commander had called the Eternal City. In the short ceremony, the commander said in a restrained tone: One thousand eight hundred seventy-seven years ago we were exiled from here, you are the first to climb the wall of the Eternal City, hold on and embrace it. When Henkin will tell his wife about that, she will say to him: Is your pain less because of that?

Ra'anana ran first, followed by the rest of the fighters. A soldier who had laid explosives at the gate with Menahem lay wounded; later on they would pick him up. Menahem ran behind Boaz, shooting at the wall on which Colonel Wood's terrified officers and soldiers were fighting boldly. The Armenians, in the winding street to the Jewish Quarter, watch in awe, the fighters hold explosives, rifles, submachine guns, and food. The commander says on the walkie-talkie: They're losing control, complete surprise, send fighters to replace us, we're bleeding, if you send them fast, the Old City will be in our hands by nightfall, over and out. From the other end, there was no answer. Bearded, weary fighters burst out of the besieged Jewish Quarter. A brief but joyous encounter. Shells land on all sides. White flags start flying over the houses of the Old City. The Arab fighters are losing control and starting to flee, Colonel Wood can't hold his fighters. They're fleeing. *Havaja* Wood, they yell at him, nothing to be done, and he, stunned, waves the stick he's holding. You have to learn from the enemy, he'll say later on, and he doesn't mean Kramer, but Menahem Henkin.

Complete chaos. Menahem attacks, says Boaz, and then, during the battle, he's wounded by a stray bullet. His brain is pierced and he dies on the spot. If I had caught the bullet, it wouldn't have been a stray! Menahem didn't suffer, Henkin . . . The governor didn't heed the request for help, the besieged people went back to the Jewish Quarter with food and a little bit of ammunition. They found out that new fighters were coming to relieve Boaz and his companions. They pulled out with the dead and wounded. The new ones who came were old men from the corps of elderly who weren't fit to fight and didn't know why they were sent. The retreating Arabs saw the wheel turn, girded their loins, and drove out the old men. The exhausted inhabitants of the Jewish Quarter surrendered by waving a white flag. At the same time, Henkin discovered later, in the headquarters on Schneller sat a hundred armed fighters who weren't sent. Menahem fell for nothing, said Henkin to Hasha Masha. The liberation of the Old City was postponed for nineteen years. Meanwhile, Menahem came back and was killed in another battle, a battle that didn't get into the history book.

Did my son fall for nothing? Henkin will ask.

Did he fall in an unknown battle there, or in the Old City?

He fell, says Hasha Masha, even if he died in a traffic accident, he didn't return.

The merchants on Ben-Yehuda Street set their watches by Henkin. They're building a new city around him, and only the sea remains stuck to itself. And he doesn't know, they say. Henkin took down the mezuzah on the second day of the Six-Day War, when the Chief Rabbi said that the Israel Defense Forces won because of the will of God. Hasha Masha thinks: Why did fate connect two such different people as Menahem and his father? Menahem was impetuous, friendly, loved the sea, didn't believe especially, didn't not believe, tied cats' tails, smoked in shelters, a simple boy, I loved him, but Henkin needs a hero and a poet.

He searches for his son on Ben-Yehuda Street as if Menahem is no more on Shenkin Street than on Ben-Yehuda Street. The Committee of Bereaved Parents, what a feast they make there with the plastic vegetables. What does Jordana who loves my son want from me? What an insane nation . . .

Noga understands, knows, and only he, Obadiah, sets the watches of those miserable merchants. Your devotion, Noga, is a noble trouble. I understand, know that you stopped loving Menahem and stayed with us, I don't bear a grudge against you, but to love you for that I can't and you know that. Let Henkin think what he wants, ponders Hasha Masha.

Years later, Hasha Masha will write to Renate:

> My dear,
>
> You asked how those years passed. They passed. I sat and waited. For what? For nothing. Noga wrote Menahem a letter telling him she had stopped loving him. He was killed before he got the letter. She stayed with us. She rejected suitors out of hand. Men don't understand death, Renate.
>
> Here is a description of a tour of Teacher Henkin: On the ruins of the Turkish fortress, between Nordau and Jabotinsky Boulevards, which used to be called Ingathering of the Exiles Street, they've built a new building. Instead of the Moses and Shapiro families new people now live there who closed the balconies with sliding shutters. Atom Bar, teeming with Jewish

whores and Australian soldiers, changed its name and now its clientele are old Poles and women with weary faces. Then there was a club of aging artists there.

The bicycle repairman says: He's wearing a hat again. The perfume shop that used to be a grocery is now on the way to being a women's shoe boutique. The Czech shoemaker, who couldn't forgive himself for choking his sick wife in the bunker and brought new machines from France, died from missing his wife, and left the store to two young men who sold it to a used car dealer. What had been a vineyard until 'forty-eight turned into a big shapeless building with a turret facing the sea. A splendid victory for a lot of seasonal change, says old Damausz, who lives above the perfume shop, next to the grocery of Halfon of the women's shoes who later opened a paint store and even later a small restaurant with a sign that said: "Original Ashkara Mélange from Jerusalem." And Mrs. Yehoyakhina Sheets of the flower shop looks at the "Original Ashkara Mélange from Jerusalem" and says: How beautiful it used to be here. The German tobacco vendor whose wife ran away with the Great Dane dog and his son who wasn't killed in the explosion of the bridges in 'forty-six now manages the new branch of Bank Leumi. Henkin walks in a maze of changes. They know him, Renate, he doesn't know them.

What was once the bulletin board where Menahem used to post declarations against the White Paper is now a marble building with an office for modern matchmaking, as if there is modern and nonmodern matchmaking. Well-packed white buildings on the next corner take on a Mediterranean patina, rust in the iron, in the cement. A slow destruction gnaws the chill beauty, among the ruins walks Obadiah. The owner of the store on the corner was once a women's hairdresser named Nadijda Litvinovskaya. She sits in the window of "Sex and Beauty." They blink their false eyelashes, and manicure men too. A state of dying sycamores, she says, water flows in the winter and in the summer is an awful light. My daughters married contractors from Herzliya Pituah, children go to school with diplomats' children. How are you, Mr. Henkin? Thank you, he always says, how many years?

Maybe five, maybe more. A small country with falafel, without
opera, with Sabras, come to me to be beautiful with black on
the seashore on a body like Negresses. And I say, Here's
Teacher Henkin walking, how's the missus, and he says, Thank
you. After the barber shop, I had a salon, after the salon a boutique. Then Sex and Beauty. His son is still dead, poor soul.
And the soda vendor who now sells "modern beverages" says
carrot juice for women goes well now. And Mrs. Pitsovskaya,
five streets past Mugrabi, Mrs. Pitsovskaya says: Thank you,
he'll say to me. My son's teacher, he'd learn and forget what he
learned, and now he's money and knows what the teacher never
knew. That's life, no? One with sense is a poor soul, one without sense makes money. Rich people have sense, too, says
Halfon sadly. All poor men aren't wise and all rich men aren't
fools, he adds. And the husband of Zipporah Glory-Splendor
stopped selling eggs on the black market, will import instant
coffee, now imports rare clothes from Hong Kong at the other
end of the world. If all the Chinese jumped at the same time,
the world would move and we'd be in Saudi Arabia and we'd
have oil and they'd be in the sea, says Halfon. His boy sometimes kills in wars and then goes to Bezalel to be an artist, says
Marianne Abramovitch. And Mrs. Lustig from the candy store
died of cancer of love, they say in the next shop, she played the
piano, forgot to sell candy, it was hard to digest, and the son of
the neighbor upstairs, who died of an inflammation of the uri-
nary tract, was once a naughty boy who tried to trip Henkin who
said Thank you, didn't see, looked, tripped, didn't see. When
will there be peace, Mr. Henkin? asks the man who sells
purses and cases. Henkin doesn't know, smiles with the contemplation of a bereavedfather, Renate, that's the wisdom of
that man, maybe cunning, maybe a lifeline, and he says, What
do I know: Abravanel's pharmacy on the way back turned into
a travel agency. The messiah who used to sit in the street and
smoke twigs sells carpets and in exchange forgot the redemption we expected so much. They sell gifts and souvenirs.

Shops for watches and windowpanes that used to sell radios and phonographs.

Tape / —

And this is how Teacher Henkin met Boaz Schneerson. It was a nice day and suddenly the first rain of the season started falling. Teacher Henkin struggled with the wind, but the rain fell in front of him, didn't yet get to him. He rowed toward Mugrabi Square, passed by Sex and Beauty, Mr. Nussbaum was already setting his watch and then he entered the rain, raindrops whipped him obliquely, touching the sidewalk like dancing magnets, the dust was erased, beyond the display windows wrapped in mists Teacher Henkin looked like he was rowing in the sea. From an opening in the clouds a prancing sunbeam slices the well-trimmed hedge for a moment and wafts a fragrance of jasmine. Across from the German bookstore on the corner of Idelson, the rain stops. Teacher Henkin looks at the visual illusion. The rain falls up to Idelson Street, and from then on, to what was once Mugrabi Square, rain doesn't fall and the sky isn't cloudy. The border of the black cloud is right over him. The bookstore owner smiles at Teacher Henkin, who doesn't heed him today. Nor does he peep into the display window to see the beautiful wrappings he looks at with love and pain. Old books bound by aged binders, how many of them are still alive, I don't know, but today he doesn't look. Behind him, the rain is seen in the display window as a geometric disaster, both tame and wild. Facing him on the dry curb stands a young man. The young man isn't especially tall but isn't short. Pinioned in a raincoat that comes to his waist, the young man stands and looks at the rain on the other side of the street. The young man sees Henkin and his yellow-green eyes, exaggerated to a certain extent by a prancing sunbeam, look as if they're trying to penetrate that miracle that facing him stands a man in a black coat and hat in a strong oblique rain, while he stands on dry land. Henkin isn't able to think logically and tell himself: If you walked ten, fifteen years on Ben-Yehuda Street to seek traces of a dead son and a familiar person came to you standing on dry land as if obeying your secret intentions, an event happened, certain wishes were answered, but the rain was too pesky for Teacher Henkin, who was seeking Boaz without knowing that he was seeking Boaz to understand what he was seeing.

(I don't know if these things were written in Hasha Masha's letter. I recite them and now I don't know, maybe they were in the letter and maybe I'm quoting another source, what do I know?) The young man dropped his hands with restrained nervousness that didn't cover impatience and anxiety, and then Henkin thought: Maybe he's waiting for me, and understood, and the young man turned his face aside, took a pack of cigarettes out of his pocket, those hands were familiar to Henkin. The slight tremor, the slight restraint of the tremor, the young man takes out a pack of matches, lights a cigarette and bends the match, looks here and there and doesn't toss it to the ground, which amazes Henkin, the street is whipped by wind and the young man puts the extinguished match in his pocket, exhales smoke, turns his face again, and he says to himself, Teacher, here's a teacher, and he knows he's thinking about something else, but he doesn't know what he's thinking. The cigarette is a shelter, the rain on the side of the teacher is also a shelter. Between them stands the ruin, will the teacher cross the street?

Teacher Henkin waits until the little car that burst out of Jordan Street passes by him, its left side is already whipped by rain and its right side is dry. He looks at his watch as if it's important to know what time it is now. Music comes from a locked apartment. He knows it's a Bach piano concerto. And then he crossed the street and stood on the dry land, looked behind him to make sure he has come from the rain, the cloud hasn't yet moved, Henkin is leaking water, while the young man is dry and wearing a raincoat, the cigarette held for a moment in his hand and then he thrusts it back in his mouth. And his mouth takes on the shape of a question mark. Therefore, the encounter became like most important encounters, through small misunderstandings, through alternating rain and dry, through a cigarette that should herald a change. The roof of Mugrabi Cinema was open, and the roar of its closing was heard. From the window above peeps the face of a worker closing the roof. The young man flicks the cigarette into a niche, the match is bent in his pocket, the cigarette in a niche, the time is eight-oh-five, and then Teacher Henkin has to cope with some uneasiness that fills him, shuts his eyes, says: Hello, and the young man tries to look surprised, hesitates, wrings his hands and separates them as if they bothered him, and says: Yes, hello.

My name's Obadiah, says Teacher Henkin, you're familiar to me, were you my student and I forgot?

As he said that he thought: Did a student wait for him here in the dry part to toss a cigarette into a niche?

I wasn't your student, said Boaz, I had a kindergarten teacher who knows us even when we grow up. She says the features of the face don't change.

You're familiar to me.

You're familiar to me too, says the young man, but he says the words warily and then they understand. The moment the rain crosses the street, both of them see the same picture in their mind's eye: years before, Boaz stands in front of Henkin's house on Deliverance Street, measuring it, observing, not saying a word, refusing a glass of water, and Henkin goes into the house and looks at him through the shutter.

My name's Boaz Schneerson, he says, you're Menahem's father.

After they went into the café, the worker came out of the kitchen, closed the windows, and stretched the covers over the chairs on the sidewalk. Boaz and Teacher Henkin sat down at a table and a weary waitress got up from where she was sprawled, chewing gum, slowly came to them and they ordered coffee, one roll, and cake for Boaz. Teacher Henkin also ordered a glass of soda. He tries to sit more authoritatively, as if it were important to set the balance of power and know who was more important, who had more rights. And Boaz understood and didn't resent him. He understood that Henkin had to win where people like him always lose. Recognizing his look blended of reproach and envy, he decided to ignore it. I have no other line of defense, he said to himself and was amazed at the words "line of defense," which he had heard from Rebecca. The conversation flowed while drinking coffee. At first there were gropings, Henkin took off the hat, asked Boaz if he really was the young man who once stood in front of his house, and Boaz tried to evade but his face answered yes, and he couldn't explain why, he just said, I was angry then. Why didn't you ever come to us, asked Henkin. I didn't know, said Boaz, for some reason I didn't know. His death was too much for us, we didn't manage to live afterward, maybe the next generation will be more successful. He wanted, he wanted so much to tell Henkin how he once saved Menahem from death, by mistake, when they shot at them from the village of Koloniya and Menahem shot through the peephole of the armored car and he suddenly was pushed to him, took him down, and a bullet penetrated the armored car and bounced around in it and hit one of the guys who was slightly wounded, and Menahem was saved. For how long? What will he tell him? I saved your son so he could die a month later? So, from the hopeful eyes of that handsome old man, dignified in the enjoyment of his loss, Boaz told how Menahem had saved him from death. He also put in suddenly's, as if there are suddenly's in war. Very slowly, the scene changes, the story changes, the image of Menahem grows bigger, Henkin's eyes demand more and more and Boaz talks from the man's desires, it's sad for him to sit across from that man, who seeks Menahem and finds Boaz, so he tells him stories of Boaz as if they were stories of Menahem, what difference does it make, he won't die from that again, thinks Boaz and Teacher Henkin swallows every word, a strong wind flies dust, the rain whips down, the waitress shivers, winter's coming, leaves fly in the wind, cars look elusive in the oblique downpour that fills the street with spraying water, and he tells Henkin his son who was Boaz, he tells and exaggerates and he doesn't care, good luck to him, he thinks, from the things he tells he even starts loving Menahem, a national hero he creates, Menahem who would tell him about the English in the Muslim cemetery and who would peep at them screwing Ruthie Zelmonovski's sister. Single-handedly, Menahem now conquers Jerusalem for Teacher Henkin . . .

And there was also a moment of no return. And maybe all those tapes were meant only to describe that moment, so I know, my son said what he said and from then on everything was obscured, it's hard for me to understand how, because of one song, such a strong revolution takes place, Boaz spoke, maybe it was an indifference coordinated with the fears, the eyes of Teacher Henkin demanding more, pleading, dictating, Boaz reads in them things he has no time to discern precisely, to decipher, he has to talk, he restores the dead Menahem, magnifies, turns his death in a diversionary action near Mount Radar into death in the Old City, there was a mistake in the recording, he said, the reports were confused, another Menahem fell near Mount Radar, I was in both battles and I know, Menahem saved me, helped the wounded, they don't know what happened to him, he became so human, something in him started to pity, the opposite of what he tried to be, he sat in the courtyard, says Boaz, the guys were killed on Mount

Radar and he waited for us to decide what unit he belonged to. We held a discussion, it was decided to accept him, that was the moment he showed me the poem, he quoted a poem then and I write too: and it was written in Henkin's eyes: Poem! Poem! And Boaz reads word for word: Poem! Poem! As if he were first learning to read, and Teacher Henkin is silent, drinking thirstily, unable to conceal from Boaz his other son, the one Hasha Masha mourns, the one Noga loved, was another Menahem and Boaz discovered him, but he knew all the time that Menahem was different, they didn't know, he knew. A poem he wrote, Boaz reads on Menahem's father's face, and that's how the poem was sold to the teacher who had thought all his life in the ancient skill of his profession, systematically, around and around, and the poem will bring redemption to men who are so in need of the right word, the proving word, the knowing word. And Boaz now forgets Menahem who, between battles, took him to the movies to see *Fiesta in Mexico,* the one and only film showing in besieged Jerusalem and the owner of the movie theater sat outside and waited for somebody to come and watch it, and the divine Esther Williams jumps every night, at the same time, with the electricity from a private generator, into a beautiful blue pool, and Ricardo Montalban with splendid sideburns and brilliantined hair sings with a Mexican accent and Estherke swims in a shiny bathing suit and her teeth are white, and then he took him to the twins and one of them was a little hunchbacked and had a wounded look in her eyes and they sucked lollipops he had brought from the black market. A bereaved father wants a Menahem he dreamed about at night. As if imprisoned in the hands of that teacher, Boaz sells heroism and a poem. He'll love me, Boaz says to himself, he'll love me, and a deep wound inside him all his life gapes open. They drank another cup of coffee, something becomes clear in Teacher Henkin's face. One eye still pondering, he finishes sipping the coffee, looks at the new cigarette in Boaz's mouth, even hands him a match from the box of matches on the table. The rain outside stopped for a moment and then intensified, and then Boaz lopped off the match on the table, looked at the heavy clouds in the window, somebody drew a rabbit on its steam, and a little girl sitting there sang: Come to me, butterfly grand, come back to me, sit on my hand, and she said: I love my rabbit. And there were also faces she had drawn, and the waitress wiped the table with a gray rag, trying to gather up the cigarette butts and Menahem grows stronger,

his image is opened to a new biography, a salvation of the wounded, the
battle for the Old City, explosives in the Wall, after all, Hasha Masha said
afterward, after all why should you blame Boaz? He sat with Henkin and
Henkin wants to be worthy of his son, wants his son to be worthy of some
ideal so he can love him, what did Boaz do? He told Henkin Menahem as
if he were Boaz. What Boaz did in the war was copied to my son. And Boaz
erased himself, was he looking for a father for himself? I don't know. I
loathe the fellow, but I also understand him. The devil in him, that innocence to read in Henkin's eyes what he longs for.

But while Boaz was completely sunk in his new creation, Henkin suddenly gaped out of the thoughts from his starched suit, became serious,
grave, the teacher I met on the Tiberias-Tsemakh road, that gentle savage
who read us poems and quarried and knew how to love this body of mine
with hands full of softness and honor, and he said: The poem, Boaz, what
about the poem?

What poem?

The poem Menahem wrote.

Oh.

I want it.

But . . .

No but.

Boaz came back to reality and once again found himself sitting in the
café. The waitress was sitting in a corner humming to herself. The rain
subsided and strips of blue sky appeared between the clouds.

The poem disappeared.

Find it.

Where?

You'll find it, Boaz Schneerson, and you'll bring it. You know where I
live, you came once, and now I know why.

Henkin leaned forward, his eyes cold, Henkin's dead son, says Boaz with
restrained fear, is indifferent now, his dead son wrote him a poem. What
does he want from me, fucking Henkin?

Bring it!

I'll look for it, said Boaz. Henkin observes him seriously, Boaz is terrified in the chair.

You will bring it.

A teacher's grammar: I shall bring, you will bring, we shall bring, where shall I bring it from?

Bring it from wherever you bring it, says the teacher of Hebrew language and literature.

I'll look for it.

You'll find it, says Henkin and starts to get up, and then he turns to Boaz: Tomorrow afternoon. I can't, said Boaz.

Tomorrow afternoon, said Henkin and all the softness disappeared, no poet was written on his brow . . . a father's acquisitiveness, Boaz didn't take it into account. Tomorrow afternoon. Deliverance Street, near Singer's store. I'm waiting for you, his voice is cruel, rigid. He wants to pay, but Henkin doesn't let him. I'll pay, says Henkin. He counts the coins, puts the wallet back in his pants pocket, puts on his coat, his hat, repeats: Tomorrow afternoon. When Teacher Henkin goes outside the wind scatters the fast-sailing clouds. Across the street, on the wall of the house, gigantic wet spots appear, the street is gleaming with the sudden sun, Boaz remains on the corner, lights a cigarette, puts the match in his mouth, and tramples on the cigarette.

Tape / —

Report 5/677—E. S.—(The Last Jew)

By 1946 we found out about Ebenezer Schneerson. We had been tracking him for about a year and in January 1946, we created an initial contact with him. His impresario—as Samuel Lipker was called—presented us with unacceptable conditions. He demanded that the material to be published be recorded in his name, and that in exchange for every hour of debriefing the aforementioned (Samuel Lipker) would be paid ten dollars. Our then modest institution could not have accepted those demands and henceforth the meeting with Ebenezer was postponed until the year nineteen fifty-six 1956. When he came to us, Ebenezer was fifty-six years old. He suffered from pain in the pelvis, his fractures are patched up but are abnormal, his body is scarred from the blows he received, and even though the scars have healed he urgently needed treatment. His heart is abnormal, his pulse is too rapid, his blood pressure is high, he was borderline diabetic.

This report does not constitute research but is an introduction to research that will be documented forthwith, and is to be seen only as an interim report. When Ebenezer Schneerson came to us, we discovered that during the years since his release from the camp his intellectual activity had been reduced to a minimum. Only after long conversations did he become free for what he himself called "the need to do something in this life." He could not say explicitly "this life of mine." The word "mine" wasn't clear to him. His life was reduced to words he guarded. The body was only a tool to protect what his brain preserved. In conversations we held with him at the time of awakening (seventeen recorded conversations) when he was in a non-alert condition, he talked a lot about being the only survivor of the Jewish nation. In sixteen of the conversations, he repeated the sentence: "All the Jews died and I have to tell the world what they knew."

In the period he stayed with us, he created a genuine and first contact with a stranger. Traveling to the nearby hospital to treat his burns, he met Mrs. Fanya R. (Debriefing File Number F.R./6/444). Fanya R. was hospitalized in various institutions and when Ebenezer met her, she was in the small hospital then financed by a fund called the Fund for the War-Damaged, whose origin is not clearly defined. These were people sent to the camps for obscure reasons, or whose postwar status is not clear. Mrs. Fanya R. was sent to the camp because she was the lover and mother of the daughters of a Jew named Joseph Rayna, and later it turned out that Ebenezer thought this Joseph was his father. Joseph Rayna was shot to death in Dachau. The aged Joseph Rayna met Fanya R. under circumstances that the abovementioned is not interested in telling. She gave birth to twins named Danka and Toleda. When the girls were five years old, Fanya R. learned that her mother, Käthe née Prausen, married her husband Mr. Prausen when Fanya R. was a year old. Before that, her mother lived for some time with another person. To make a long story short, note that Fanya R. discovered that Joseph Rayna was her mother's lover and that she was not only the mother of his daughters, but also their sister. Her emotional condition, which was bad in any event, grew even worse and in the camp she cleaned latrines. Her daughters were taken away from her and when the war was over, she went in search of them. They were killed by Dr. Mengele, whose experiments on twins are widely known. Only when she met Ebenezer did something stir in Fanya R. that had previously been dead. After a certain period, her condition improved, her attempts to hurt herself almost stopped, and in March nineteen fifty-eight, Ebenezer Schneerson and Fanya R. were married in a modest civil ceremony.

Ebenezer claimed that he was the stepfather of both his wife and her daughters. As far as he was concerned, he was the brother of his daughters, his own uncle, and even his mother's brother. I'm almost my own father, he smiled at us. In a ceremony held in our institution, Ebenezer adopted Fanya R.'s dead daughters, and, the two were retroactively named Danka and Toleda Schneerson.

Ebenezer claimed to us that he had married Fanya R. out of sympathy. He loved, he said, only one woman, whose name was Dana and his mother murdered her. Samuel Lipker, he said, was searching for him because they had gotten separated from one another in a heavy fog in the port of Marseille.

After he started opening up to his past (for example, his recall of Joseph Rayna and his relation to him), it became clear from things he dredged up from inside himself with difficulty (we spent several days on that) that he had wandered in Europe and searched for somebody he thought was his father and on his way he came to Russia. After the signing of the Molotov-Ribbentrop Pact and the division of Poland, he was expelled (as a Pole) from the Polish territory that had stopped being Russian and was then expelled to Russia as a Ukrainian. In the struggle between the Belarussians and the Ukrainians for German sympathy, he was caught in a maze of schemes and this is not the place to describe them, and in the twists of the cosmos he discovered that the Jews were glad when the Russians came, but were bitterly disappointed. The Poles in the area were landowners who had previously been moved there by the Polish government to hinder the progress of the Belarussians who were expecting the Germans, while as for the Germans, they disappointed them too after they came. Crossing the border to German Poland (along with a group of Jewish youths returning to organize the Pioneer Youth there), he was captured by the Germans. He managed to run away and came to a Polish village. The Poles who thought he was a Ukrainian turned him over to the Belarussians who judged him for what they called "despicable Polish subversion." Naïve and uneducated, he didn't understand the delicate subtleties in those relations of nations, and in Operation Barbarossa he was captured again. When he ran away (he was swift and strong), he was tortured by Yugoslavian partisans who were searching for a way out to the Russian forests and thought he was a hostile Jewish-German spy. He was caught in a tight net—and this is not exactly the place to go into detail—of Lithuanian, Russian, Jewish, Belarussian, Ukrainian, and Polish schemers, and at any rate, his Judaism was only one more pretext for abusing him, and a millstone to hang accusations of identity on him of which he was ignorant. Lacking an ideological background, it was easier for him when he was captured by the Germans as a Jew. The Sonderkommando caught him and this time he couldn't run away. Now his pedigree was clear. No importance was ascribed to the fact of his birth in Palestine.

What stands out in Ebenezer is the lack of individuality in the accepted sense of the word. One of our investigators called him "a man without qualities" from Müsil's well-known book. But that of course is only one aspect and does not characterize his personality. His love for his wife Dana and for Samuel Lipker is not the love of a man without qualities. His life is made of too many libels for him not to be aware of some of them. After he spent time in several camps, he was taken to Hathausen and was the first prisoner there and even helped build the camp. From what we know, it was his skill in the art of carpentry that kept him alive.

For a few weeks we observed his work and although at first he refused to get involved again with carpentry, he eventually agreed to show us his handiwork. He was ordered by our investigator to build a small pipe rack. For two weeks we observed his production. Clearly the final shape wasn't clear to him; the rack resulted from a need called in this report "particular," that is: to be this rack and no other, and that a metaphor of a well-known concept. Ebenezer built drawers for pipecleaners, matches, of various sizes, he lined the concavity with green cloth, he used forty-two different lacquers he created from solutions of glue powder and other materials. He skillfully planed tiny pieces of wood and interwove them in a marquetry: the rack was the product of many combined details (things Ebenezer apparently imagined, but didn't know) and the product was a rack of restrained beauty and uniqueness. We sent the rack to four different museums (in Amsterdam, Vienna, Berlin, and London), and the unanimous opinion was that this is an excellent rack, the handiwork of an early nineteenth-century artist. Dr. Rosenberg of Vienna, the greatest expert in European cabinetry of the period 1795–1838, mentioned the names of only two artists who were capable of building that rack and claimed that we had presented him an absurd riddle, since he knew every rack made by those artists, while an imitation of the rack of those artists was impossible. Thus it is hard to argue that Ebenezer Schneerson is a man without qualities.

After we collected other works by Ebenezer, in the homes of former SS officers, we made a small exhibition of his works. The exhibition was presented only in our research institute. We wanted to print a modest booklet in honor of the event, but Ebenezer refused, saying that only Samuel Lipker had the right to do that.

His story in the camp (and his survival as a carpenter, if what he produced can be called carpentry) is told in the expanded research. What can be said positively is that there was a certain moment when Ebenezer decided to give up being the Last Jew in the world. Out of an empathy he developed for his imprisoned companions, fear that many geniuses and scholars, writers, and researchers would die without leaving a trace of their knowledge. In our work with him we have penetrated to only a certain area of investigation of his memory. In his hallucination under hypnosis he told us how he once sat in a woman's house, a woman he apparently respected and maybe even had relations with, and hated himself for what he called his betrayal of Dana. At night he sat in a little room, he told us, and tried to recall Dana. Her precise image eluded him. All he could remember was a vague form of a woman. He felt a need to remember her exactly as she had been, something that's hard for the human memory to do. He had no photos. So he sat, stared at the burning oven, concentrated and very slowly remembered a small dimple in Dana's right cheek. He meditated on the dimple for a long time until it was completely clear in his memory. Then, he left it and meditated on her nose. When the nose was clear, he left it for a while and the mouth began to be drawn in his mind and only then he connected the dimple in the cheek and the cheek to the nose and the mouth and did he connect the throat to the orbits of the eyes and come to the hair, which at first was separated from the other parts of the face and joined to them, and so, very slowly, Dana's image was drawn like a crossword puzzle that became a precise photo he'd see before his eyes. Her legs, for example, he recalled when he thought about the hike they had once taken to the desert and Dana tripped and he smeared the wound with medicinal leaves he had learned from the Bedouins. Ever since then, he said, Dana appears whenever I need to remember her, he shuts his eyes, thinks of the stove and Dana's image rises in his mind. He claims he has many keys he remembers dimly but when he needs them they appear in the back of his mind and through them he remembers things. For example, Einstein's theory of relativity depends on thinking of the smell of roasted coffee. A pince-nez raises before him the entire Pentateuch.

Did he learn to photograph knowledge? It's hard to say since he didn't read the knowledge and if he photographed it, he photographed the voice that recited the knowledge. If so, the word "recorded" will be more appropriate. But that doesn't explain anything. At most it can describe a process whose source remains blocked. According to a representative sample, we measured about nine million words that Ebenezer knew orally. For instance, in nightclubs where he appeared with Samuel Lipker, he often recited lists of those killed in the pogroms of 1915–1919. The knowledge was divided by towns (the key to that knowledge was drummed out by the fire department orchestra in Livorno). Many of the towns he mentioned were wiped off the face of the earth and there is no longer a trace of them on maps. In a forgotten Jewish book titled *The Scroll of Slaughter,* we found one section he recited almost completely. Of the two hundred pages we copied of our tapes I shall present a few examples: Garbatishi, Kortivo district, Minsk Gubernia, six Jewish families. Granov, Haysen district, Podolia Gubernia (attack of Petlura's Cossacks) eight families, etc. . . .

Or an alphabetical list of the murdered: Golobibsky-Haim Austoroy, forty-five years old, his son Jacob, seventeen years old, or in one town: Klibanov, Elijah, seventy-one years old, along with his wife Hayke. Israel Zvi Goldenberg, forty-five years old, Israel David Klayman, fifty-five years old, murdered along with his two sons-in-law, Isaac and Samuel . . . And then: Hanna Gradover, Simha Feinstein, his son Nahman. Lev Austoroy, his wife Sareke, his daughter Rebecca and his son Elijah. Abraham Lapolski, Moshe Kalike, Yosef Krayz, Leah, daughter of Arye Hoykhman. Her husband Yanek and her four children (their names are erased from the tape), Isaac Posman, Meir ben Arye, Parnes Hadash . . . Joseph Joffe . . . Benjamin ben Elijah . . . Toni daughter of Haim Serberiazsek, Pisanoy Baruch Beamer . . .

The number of killed in those towns and villages (only to the letter C) amounts to two thousand one hundred.

The lists of Jewish communities we found at Yad Vashem and other institutions include some of the names mentioned by Ebenezer. We discovered that *all the names that appear on tombstones or in lists, in books, in the scrolls of slaughter, also appear in Ebenezer's recital, but there are many names he recites that have no alternative indication.*

In one town—fortunately for us, the register of its Jewish community has remained intact—were names of all the Jews who had lived there. Ebenezer recited all their names. After this timing and what was said above, it is clear to us that what he knows, he knew precisely. And there are things only he knows or that we cannot know more than what he knows. Meanwhile, of course . . .

What made the research even more difficult is the disorder of the knowledge of the illogic in the logic of memory. For some time, we entertained the idea that there was a logic unknown to us in this illogic, but that remained an intellectual amusement. You do know that his encyclopedic knowledge is not systematic at all, books in five or six languages, the Bible, and suddenly brilliant lies about astrophysics (made up by a mad genius), a long solid study refuting Einstein's theory, an atomic structure of the world according to the order of the letters in the Book of Genesis, annals of the world according to a person named Pumishankovitch who argues that God was created after the world and the Torah of the Jews is nothing but an attempt to combine the annals of nature with the annals of antinature, a book about the world as a fallen planet in a system of stars that were extinguished long ago, a rather bold theory about the influence of the battle of Albania on technological development. A hundred and fifty pages of *The Jewish Wars* by Josephus Flavius in reverse order, books of mythology describing unknown myths documented with knowledge and skill, even though they're apparently fakes. Books of religion and science, journals of three people who tried to measure their love for one another by writing hasty lines in the depths of the earth until they passed out, the stories of Kafka, stories of the Hasids, journeys of the emissaries of the Land of Israel to future generations of the eighth century to the end of the nineteenth century, family trees going back to the first generation, calculations of the end of days according to the books of Daniel, Ezekiel, and Nostradamus, and documents of wars, mathematical theories, the poetry of Homer, the poetry of Virgil, Dante, and other writers I attach in a separate appendix.

Ebenezer doesn't understand the material he knows, he doesn't discriminate, doesn't judge, doesn't know the material isn't Jewish knowledge. The number of twins who studied in orphanages in Lodz between the two world wars is no less important than Kafka's letter to his father. What is important to us is that everything he knows seems important to him because it's somehow knowledge and so the thoughts or nonthoughts of an ant are important and so is the length of the road between Marseille and Bordeaux. As far as he's concerned, everything is Jewish knowledge because it was conveyed to him by Jews. What happened is that like everybody who remembered more important (or unimportant) details he had to carry many more keys with him, and that was to be done by turning his own ego into something even more unimportant. In other words, he learned to remember by learning to forget.

We all remember millions of unimportant details about ourselves. Every such detail had to be forgotten in order to be substituted by impersonal knowledge.

The memory, as we know, is somehow a chemical instrument. Ebenezer's handiwork helped him quite a bit in amassing knowledge. A piece of wood was for him what for others was life, utopia, hope. As a craftsman who understands wood, his brain cells, or some of them, turned into sponges of knowledge and at the same time also into extinguishers of themselves. Therefore, the key of the "keys" is buried in the substitution of physiodynamic materials (if we can use that terminology). The memory of one day in distant childhood, a day a normal person can contemplate for hours and find in it images, smells, feelings, exchanges of words, surprises; in Ebenezer, that turned into the key to a book, to a system of stars, to what didn't happen to himself and thus the memory cell changes its purpose (we talked above about a chemical instrument), and instead of remembering things that were, he remembered things that were not. And in this case, there are and there aren't are all the same. Just as a rack or a cupboard turned from an unclear idea into what can be called "rack reality" or "cupboardness" from the need of the details to harmonize. And that is really how the knowledge Ebenezer acquired was photographed or recorded. They piled up and Ebenezer's brain turned more and more into an instrument alien to himself and unlike other brains, also cut off from itself. In other words, into a sick brain that distinguished between knowledge that knows for the person himself and knowledge that is alien and destined for others. Thus Ebenezer's individuality could be more and more forgotten and hence his great dependence on Samuel who was to Ebenezer what a normal brain is to another person—both guide and leader. Ebenezer's consciousness of knowledge was in fact a total unconsciousness of himself and also one aspect of the forgetting of his individuality. That is: Ebenezer's remembering was the opposite of nonhuman. Maybe in that the Germans succeeded to a certain extent: a subhuman turned into a nonhuman to survive and to defeat the commandment to be like that.

In the brain that was alien to him, Ebenezer knew there were no more Jews in the world because he decided to survive. A person who knows Einstein's theory by heart can understand that if there was Samuel, then not all the Jews were dead. But things are more complicated particularly in this point. The survival of the Jews (those who did survive) his brain could not absorb. Something deep inside him knew, and still knows, that he is the last survivor. So even now he records everything he says, hears, and sees in order to remember.

Hence your conversations with him that night you described to me, in his house, along with the Israeli teacher Henkin, were recorded by him and remembered by him now as Jewish knowledge along with what he learned in the camp. In his rare consciousness, Ebenezer constantly reconstructs life at one point in the eternal and unchanging present, and prophesies (if we can use that unprofessional term) his past he didn't experience, while what he reads no longer is. As the god in the composition of the madman Ebenezer quotes on behalf of the director of the solar system who describes God as creating from the end to the beginning and merciless, because all life has already died and He meets them on their way—from their death to their beginning. That's how he himself is. As far as he's concerned, they all died and he recites knowledge about something that no longer exists, and not only of those who no longer exist. What I'm writing to you now and will be given to Ebenezer as a copy to keep will also be read by him and recalled as Jewish knowledge. I mean these words literally, the words you're reading now . . . What Ebenezer knows, he knows because the words were recited to him. Even the words he recites about himself. Even what he knows about himself. Hence he's deprived of judgment about the value of information, of a book or any system of knowledge dormant in him. He paints the world he wants to guard on the walls of his consciousness. There is a sentence by Professor Sharfstein (an Israeli philosopher) that may be able to describe this situation precisely. The sentence appears in a book titled *The Artist in Western Culture*. There he says: The god Siva, without a brush and without paints, drew the world on the walls of his own consciousness.

We tried to investigate according to known experiments, for example the experiments of Professor Alexander Luria. Following his example, we urged Ebenezer to recall something that happened in his childhood. We told him about something that happened to him that we found out from a source other than him. When we talked to him about that memory, connected with his dead wife, and we measured his pulse, the pulse speeded up and then fell back. When we asked him to recite a forgotten memory also connected with Dana, a memory he dredged up from what he himself had amassed from things he had heard about himself, from others, the pulse rate was much weaker (seventy-two beats as opposed to a hundred twenty). We tried many other experiments enumerated in the full report and this is not the place to go into detail. The process was repeated several times. The memories that were *not* told to him did not change the pulse rate. They were alien to him, even though they had happened to him and were a considerable part of the web of his life.

Comparisons with people whose memories are as phenomenal as his did not help us either. We questioned A. G., who now appears all over Europe on television screens and defeats sophisticated computers with quick and correct answers. That gave us no help. Those people were conscious of what they knew. They learned when they were in distress and did that to remain alive, so that in the meantime they would not be impaired. They did not erase themselves to fill the empty space of their brain with knowledge. They learned equations or books by heart because they had to triumph over nothingness and fear.

I attach the tapes. I understand from your words that the book you and the Israeli teacher want to write will be composed or woven mainly of our tapes. Keep in mind that the life of Sam Lipp (Samuel Lipker), for example, is known to Ebenezer only when he was in a trance of indexing his memory. In his real life he doesn't know. In his real life Samuel may also be dying. The Jews are still all dying, and always will die. Hence, we in fact

did not succeed in deciphering the secret of Ebenezer's memory, but
only in documenting the nature of remembrance. Just as Ebenezer builds
racks, so he builds a world of knowledge. The conversion and shoe sizes
of a group of Warsaw writers. For us at least the mystery remains. Are we
witnessing a kind of spiritual suicide? Vengeance? Escape? I said before:
Ebenezer doesn't judge. As far as he's concerned, the Germans are neither
bad nor good. Not those he meets today, and not those he met before. The
shadows in his brain have no concrete reality. The shadows have no judgment, no past and no future. Fanya R. is his wife. Does Ebenezer live with
her or does somebody Ebenezer imagines as Ebenezer live with her? We
have questions that only a metaphysical and historiological pathology could
solve and therefore science, as in many cases, remains helpless. Art may
indeed grant legitimacy to the absurd. Existence is absurd. Ebenezer is
absurd and there's no possibility of granting him legitimacy, maybe it's
possible to tell him, not about him. As for us, we shall send you the full
research, but if our research adds to the perplexity or enlightens it, only
Ebenezer's God knows.

Yours truly,
Alexander Twiggy Henderson Levy

Tape / —

Got to bring Henkin the poem, thinks Boaz.

Thinking poem,
Menahem poem.

Boaz remembered how they brought Menahem Henkin to the school
gym. The commander looked at the three corpses and said: So Henkin got
a summons? And he wrote: Menahem Henkin, Palmah, Harel, the fourth
brigade, headquarters company, to inform the parents, Deliverance Street,
Tel Aviv.

Fuck it, he said, soon I won't have any live soldiers left! From Tel Aviv,
a soldier went to inform the Henkin family that their son had fallen. Boaz lay
under a tree and smoked. Years later, he would part from Teacher Henkin
on Ben-Yehuda Street. The sky is blue and the clouds float quickly. The
vendor of German books crossed the street and walked past Hayarkon
Street. Boaz started walking to the central bus station, stood in line,
boarded the bus and fell asleep. An hour later, he came to the settlement,

it was afternoon. Rebecca expected him as always. She didn't measure, she
didn't complain, she didn't pressure, she sat at the screened window and
waited. For some years now, Captain Jose Menkin A. Goldenberg had been
living in Ebenezer's old house. The house is rented to him with a lease
renewed every year. If Boaz wants to live here someday, he'll have someplace to live, said the old woman.

A month after Ebenezer disappeared and boarded the ship that took
him to Europe, Rebecca Schneerson went to the offices of the National
Committee in Jerusalem. She asked to speak with the head of the committee. They told her that the head of the committee was abroad on a mission.
She said she wanted to adopt her grandson as her son. She was told that
wasn't possible. Rebecca tried the chief rabbinate and the various district
offices and deigned to meet with people whose existence she once
wouldn't have been willing to admit. The Captain's connections with the
British Mandate authorities weren't any help either. A grandmother can
adopt her grandson, she was told, but to state explicitly and officially that
Boaz is Rebecca's son by birth was not possible. She wrote a long letter
explaining her request. According to her, there was no proof that the person called his mother did indeed give birth to him. In another letter, she
claimed that Boaz was her son from a marriage she had never disclosed. She
quoted a well-known and reliable Russian newspaper that told of a woman
who got pregnant in eighteen twenty-one, while her son was born thirty-
two years later. But even this quotation, which, after a visit from the Captain, was authenticated by three old Russians in the Russian Compound in
Jerusalem, didn't make the required impact. When serious arguments were
raised against a retrospective pregnancy, she deigned with the courtesy of
a desperate woman to refrain from hearing the explanations and whispered
to the Captain: They always were and still are fools. Later on, she'll tell
Boaz: I was impregnated by a river. Don't turn up your aristocratic nose,
even a distinguished mother like me sometimes gets pregnant, the river
lusted for me and I for him, all your life you've seen streams, what do you
know about a river. Do you know that the Americans bought the Dnieper
and transported it to America? And Boaz said: You find a way to say
America every chance you get. How do you transport a river? He was ten
years old then and she was his mother.

I love him, Rebecca said to the Captain with uncharacteristic candor. I love him like the clods of earth love the dead. Like the riverbank loves the river. I love him as you could have been able to love if you were as false and splendid as Joseph Rayna and as innocent and beautiful as Nehemiah. When I fell in love with Boaz I gave birth to what I didn't want to give birth to all the years, and Ebenezer who's wandering around in Europe didn't come from me, Nehemiah brought him to me and I reluctantly nursed him. If your god can make a virgin give birth to a son, Boaz can be born from a grandmother who loved him before he was born. At last, the Captain gave in and with two Arabs from Marar and Mr. Klomin, they went to visit a friend of the Captain who lived in an ancient house with a wooden turret in a tropical garden on a hill crowned by cypresses and palms, near Jaffa.

The road to the house passed over a small wooden bridge. Years ago a small wadi flowed under the bridge, and even the ancient water had stopped flowing in it. Between geranium, jasmine, rose, and violet bushes the gentle chirping of rare birds was heard and in the small pool in the center of the yard crowned with thick evergreens, gray and white ducks floated, and one swan who looked arrogant and strange in the musty dank garden.

The Captain's friend was old, wrapped in a cloak that may once have been white. The man put on a pince-nez and his face looked like ancient parchment. For a long time, the two of them walked, hugging, among the bushes and whispered together in a language none of the guests understood. Then they stopped, the Captain put his hand in the old man's sash, hiccuped, thrust a paper-wrapped package into the sash, which the old man took in his hands, sniffed like tobacco, smiled, and then the two of them hugged with masculine savagery, the old man's face was so glowing and joyful that even Rebecca felt a slight stab of bliss in her belly. The old man came to Boaz, called an Arab boy wearing an *abbiya*, who had stood all the time in the shadow of the ancient marble pillar swathed in ivy that climbed up it to a locked window whose recess was more imagined than visible. The boy entered the house and came back with a tray and handed out cold juice and tasty ice cream. After they listened to the bird, which the Captain claimed was called a bird of "the real opposite," which repeated the same chirp one hundred fifty times an hour, without the slightest change,

the old man, who was holding Boaz in his clasped hands, said: I've got a
document that will suit him, Mrs. Schneerson, and he hugged Boaz's
shoulders and Boaz smelled a smell he later knew was the smell of death.
Rebecca wanted to say something, Mr. Klomin straightened up and his
face turned gray, but the Captain put a nervous but agile finger on her lips
and whispered, so Mr. Klomin would also hear: Everything's fine, there's
no baptism, let me take care of things, money and God are my business . . .
The old man disappeared into the house. Boaz and the Arab boy threw
stones at the swan, and as Rebecca was trying to assess the brigades of
Klomin's Hebrew army against the odor left by the moldy old man, a peacock sallied forth from the bushes. The peacock proudly bore a gigantic
colorful tail and it looked to her as if it were desired by the sun and the
trees, indulged and arrogant, and the birds stopped chirping and then she
thought about Joseph and about Boaz and her insides cramped as if she
were giving birth to Boaz, and then the old man came back, hopped on his
feet that touched and didn't touch the pebbles of the stream scattered on
the paths, held out a parchment scroll to Rebecca, grabbed Boaz, who approached him with the Arab boy standing on the side and smiling with
teeth that were almost black, and then he turned to the Captain and said:
I do this because of our Lord the Messiah and because of the great patriots who fought in the bold battles of our homeland, and to Rebecca he said:
Dante Alighieri Boaz Schneerson of the house of Tefanus, in the name of
an ancient hero, Elia the Tyrean, who delivered his mother from the claws
of a cruel potentate and granted her his eternal youth and his delicate
manhood and appreciated her as a slave of the church and an angel of
the hosts of the Lord, Dante Alighieri Benedictus Boaz Schneerson, hal-
lowed by being your legal son and the fruit of your loins. And you Rebecca
Schneerson confess here and now before me and before the living God that
there was never any doubt in your heart that this child is your son, your
flesh and blood! And this lad will be your son from now on forever. Amen.
Rebecca, who had never been eager to say words of prayer in the Promised
Land, said "amen" in a soft voice, and the man said, If there is anyone here
who wants to protest or who does not agree let him now raise his voice or
forever hold his peace . . . And then Mr. Klomin yelled, all flushed and
fervent: I, I object, and the old man smiled at him, tried with all his might
to hear Klomin's yell, and said: If so, I see there are no objections? And

Mr. Klomin now shoved the Captain closer to the old man and yelled into his ear: I, I'm his grandfather! And the old man delayed a moment, a moderate atrophied smile caught at the corner of his mouth, and said: Since there are no objections, I hereby declare Boaz Dante Alighieri Benedictus the legal son of Rebecca Schneerson. May it be His will.

Rebecca looked at the old man. His serenity in contrast to Mr. Klomin's yelling became foggy and then his eye was covered with a cold metallic glint. Klomin tried to yell, but he too fell mute at the sight. The two Arabs from Marar bristled where they stood. The old man sank into the ground until he was no longer seen. Later on Mr. Klomin (who then filled his mouth with water) would say: The ground was loose because under the building there was certainly an ancient excavation and he sank into it, maybe it was a graveyard from the period of the kings of Judah, Mr. Klomin would add, during the summer they lived in the coastal plain, maybe it was a center of magnetic heaviness, and Rebecca's hungry look turned to a spear point of the yearnings of two thousand years united in her and she didn't know and sold her grandson to the bosom of foreigners and her ancient blood was then roused to avenge her and foreigners who plot evil against us and the magnetic center turned into an archaeological incident because of the forgotten grave of a Hebrew king. Rebecca laughed, and said: He seeks kings everywhere, simple Jews also lived in this land, Klomin, kings lived in palaces. And Mr. Klomin, sunk in glowing contemplation of the future of the new old Israeli kingdom, said in embarrassment and longing for the great moments that had all apparently been before he was born and he had already despaired of finding them in his life, that if a person understood the great moment in which he lived, he could experience things beyond time and place.

Rebecca didn't want to hear about the graves of ancient kings. She saw a gentile sinking into the ground. The Arabs were willing to swear to it with a thumbprint. She still remembered Nehemiah's war against the prophets. In her heart she laughed at the poor men who always fight wars that were decided long ago. Boaz remembered the peacock and the old man who disappeared into the ground. Never did he accept his adoption by Rebecca as more than a sufficient reason to torment her or love her as the only person he knew whose loyalty to him he never doubted. She was mine, my mother and my father betrayed me, he said to Noga.

The next day, Boaz had to stand before a big crowd at the community center and tell how the old gentile sank into the yard and disappeared. Some of the founders who limped to the community center shook their heads. Rebecca didn't come. Horowitz's daughter shouted: She always was a witch and always will be . . . Nehemiah knew that and so he died, she taught Aryeh to play the piano.

Tongues began wagging freely and used what Boaz told. There was no television back then, Noga, Boaz will say later on, and there was still fantasy in the air. She killed the mare of the baron's official, yelled an old woman whose false teeth fell out of her mouth from enthusiasm and her son had to search for them among the feet of the old people that smelled of powder against prickly heat and cow dung. She killed Nehemiah and Dana, she hates us, she lives in the settlement and closes herself up. Germans played for her on the piano during the war when they burned cowsheds of All's Well and Meshulam, her Captain is a spy for the Armenians and Americans and he's a Greek like we're Turks. She injects milk hormones into her cows so they'll win the contests. Her chickens are bewitched and lay eggs nonstop and don't even have time to eat. When the bull sees her he immediately mounts all the cows in the barn. Boaz burst out laughing and the others also felt they were talking nonsense and laughed, in fact nobody was really afraid anymore. Even the exact description of the old man sinking into the dirt wasn't very scary, Rebecca no longer aroused in them more than an enormous need to describe their life as a certain miracle in which she was the leaven. They remembered the Wondrous One and Nehemiah as if they were her lovers. Lately, they were filled with yearnings for Ebenezer. After all, Ebenezer was the first son of the settlement who had changed in their eyes into a mysterious and miraculous tale. As they looked at the birds he left behind they began to be filled with forgiveness for the child they were never able to understand. They didn't forget how he walked in the rainswept street with Dana's body in his arms. His image grew to dimensions it had never had before, and as his death grew more certain, his qualities became more refined. A wood carver turned into a wondrous sculptor. And then it was also decided unanimously to call the community center built by Nehemiah in the name of his dead son and they put a wooden plaque up at the entrance and carved on it: Community Center in Memory of Ebenezer Schneerson Who Knew Wood in Its Distress.

Boaz, who grew up in Rebecca's house, didn't resent the facts of his life, which changed with the years. He succumbed to the essential quality of the settlement, a quality that turned into an incurable disease, to create the past according to the givens of the present and to live in a fictional past as much as possible. His age changed. Later on, when he tried to correct the date of his birth, he couldn't anymore and he remained the age written by the Captain in the document given him by the old man who sank into the dirt, and the Captain's retrospective godfatherhood turned into a fait accompli. Boaz was the only lad in the settlement who had two birth dates, two godfathers (Klomin and the Captain), two mothers, a father in heaven, and three grandfathers: Klomin, Nehemiah, and Joseph Rayna. One of them, and he didn't know which, was also his father or perhaps wasn't, as he used to say afterward. A woman named Rachel Brin who grew shirt trees in America is his aunt, her son Secret Glory also called Lionel Secret is his cousin, the world was created when Secret Charity went down to a cellar and started sallying forth at night and made nineteen children with his stunned wife. There they shouted in cellars, said Rebecca, and not in ridiculous community centers . . .

Boaz was a taciturn lad. In a small settlement like that one, it's hard to guess the force of hostility and jealousy children feel for somebody who has three grandfathers, a mysterious father, and two mothers who gave birth to imaginary fathers. What the children of the founders didn't know began to be added to what the founders themselves had now forgotten, and their children's children added the rest. Horowitz's son opened an institute for the improvement of seeds that were marketed in many countries. The hothouses they started building were the first of their kind. The produce of the citrus groves, the vineyards, and the fields was good and the yield of the cowsheds was high. The eleven sons of the settlement who fell in the riots of 'twenty-nine and 'thirty-six were joined by heroes who fell in other places and were adopted after their death. Roots, which started as a small handful of graves, turned into a national parade ground hidden by pruned trees from the hot desert winds. Florid speeches were delivered in Roots on memorial days, some of which were invented as needed. Even the death date of the Wondrous One began to be commemorated among most of the nation, children in uniforms carried bouquets of flowers and stood with wooden spears in their hands and swore loyalty to the nation and to the future of the settlement. Choral singing was an integral part of the ceremonies. Throughout the Land of Israel, there wasn't a settlement whose choir sang only in the cemetery. All's Well, principal of the school who was also the husband of the kindergarten teacher Eve, sat in Rebecca's house and tried to learn from her the melody of Nehemiah's speeches from which, he thought, Nehemiah embroidered his "historical" speeches. And she would make up new melodies for him, which he tried unsuccessfully to imitate. Very slowly, he learned the fictional melodies. The Captain, who knew melodies from distant lands, taught him the art of measured grief, the words of the hymn of death, and even the consolations of the old man, who for twenty years was tormented by a damaged heart, succeeded in his premature death, at the age of eighty, to be eulogized as a Pioneer and a hero rich in deeds, who at his death bequeathed us life.

The rabbi of the nearby settlement was now beginning to enjoy coming to the settlement. He knew that here, God was the one Rebecca Schneerson conspired with, but he no longer had enough strength to fight the war of the Lord. A late spring would grant the settlement more spring than the nearby settlements. Old Horowitz told the journalist who came to interview him that the marvelous sculptures of Ebenezer, who was almost Boaz's father, were the most beautiful artistic creations he had ever seen. The aphorism about Ebenezer on the wall of the community center was contributed by the Captain. The farmers helped Boaz overcome the enmity of the children. The yearning looks of the girls he learned to accept as he had to accept his grandmother's Psalms or the mysterious whispers of Mr. Klomin and the Captain about the national-royal party. They still plotted stratagems. Every Wednesday, the Captain still asked for Rebecca's hand and got a negative reply. There was no reply from the British crown even after five letters of five hundred pages each. That was the great imminent war that granted Mr. Klomin the possibility of preparing an innovative strategy, using a short-range tactic to solve the problem of British rule. The royalist party won the settlement (with the Captain's modest support) a contract to sell citrus fruit to the British army, whose troops increased. The best agricultural deal since the beginning of the Jewish *Yishuv* in the Land was buying the land for a big airport. At a time when the rumor spread that the settlement was infected with the disease of death and old people were dying at the rate of one a week, the sons of the founders, with the aging

Captain as agent, sold lands at an exorbitant price to build an airport. Some
of the founders were fictitious in any case, and so only the local historians
were interested in bearing witness to the disease of death, especially since
the price yielded such great wealth. At the eulogy of old Horowitz, who
wept at the sight of Nehemiah dancing with Nathan on the day he came
to the settlement forty years before and followed Ebenezer when he returned Dana's body, it was said of him that he was a Pioneer not only of
Hebrew agriculture in the Land, but also of aviation in the Land of Israel.
From here, said Principal All's Well, the airplanes of Judah will fly to strike
the enemies of the Lord. A third of the land for the new field, whose airplanes Horowitz prophesied, according to his eulogy, belonged to Rebecca.
While Ebenezer was wandering from Poland to eastern Ukraine and to Russia and from there to the camps, Boaz and the other children of the settlement were working to build a new airport. The adult workers learned to
appreciate his silence and the quality of his work. Boaz was then thirteen
years old, strong with a solid body, and after only two weeks he was appointed supervisor of the work of his older comrades and his salary was
raised. That, of course, was without any connection to his special relations
with Captain Jose Menkin A. Goldenberg, whom the British discovered
was a great air force expert. Boaz didn't ask how the Captain or even Colonel (for he was promoted), who had never fought in any war that anybody
had ever heard of, knew how to build airfields. But when he saw how the
field was built and the planes started landing, and even more marvelous,
taking off, and how satisfied the British were with the field, the row of
concrete antitank structures, the way of sheltering airplanes against an air
raid, and building decoys to mislead the enemy, Boaz said to himself: What's
to ask, maybe in Argentina they fought with airplanes in the last century.
But he wasn't even sure the Captain came from Argentina. The British
looked at Boaz and said: He's clever like all the Jews, and he laughed. His
yellow-green eyes caused incomprehensible excitement among the officers'
wives, who sat around a lot in chaise longues topped with parasols held by
Arabs from Marar and looked at him. They didn't know he was building a
future airfield for Mr. Klomin's royalist party. They would look at him excitedly, giggle, long for children in their wombs, and didn't know it. They
were too delicate to express what every one of the children of the settlement understood; but Boaz didn't care.

He walked around among the intersection of the looks of the English women who drank cold juice, as Rebecca said later, as beautiful angels walk around at the entrance to Paradise and try to bribe the gods with their beautiful eyes. She took that sentence, although she messed it up a bit, from a description of Joseph Rayna, who she knew sometimes was Boaz's father. Where could such a resemblance between them come from? she asked herself with a pain she didn't reveal to anybody, not even Boaz, how can it be that Joseph Rayna and Boaz Schneerson were one person born at different times?

At least he doesn't fall in love with those women, she said to herself, at least he doesn't get ugly women pregnant. And then she clapped her hands and Ahbed, the grandson of Ahbed, brought her a cup of tea.

After twelve months of war, in 'forty-eight, after he wandered around for a while and didn't know how long, he met somebody who was his double. He took a fake gold ring off the finger of Minna, the building contractor's daughter, and came to the settlement. Autumn made the descending evening silent and dangerous. The threshing floor wasn't there anymore. Instead of the threshing floor was the big house surrounded by a garden. A black DeSoto was parked next to the house. He thought of the chicks of the kindergarten teacher Eve that had died so they could build a new house here with a DeSoto. He recalled the car he had stopped in Tel Aviv, and thought maybe he shouldn't have banged the heads of those two people together. A woman wrapped in a shawl stood in the glow of evening and pruned a rosebush. In that soft, splendid hour she looked like a firefly. The light glowed on her, flitted and returned. Somebody inside the house was playing with a flashlight. She stood out against the background of the summer ground that had drunk the first rains of the season that morning. On the way, in the bus, he saw two Arabs in the field. The sight of them calmed him. They weren't an enemy he had to shoot at.

The Arabs in the field allowed him to think of Rebecca. They were sheikhs; planted in the landscape like scarecrows, cut out of it, without challenge, without the affection or longing of All's Well her husband or Eve whose chicks didn't all return and some were buried in Roots to her husband's florid speeches. The Arabs in the field were domesticated in it. Nor did he resent it, because he thought about his grandfather Nehemiah who couldn't be like them. I'm the wrong man who returned from the war, he thought, and it's her fault! No threshing floor, no Menashe, no Menahem Henkin, no double, no redhead, in the end there's me. On the porches, in the chill evening wind, sit the old women, Grandmother will bury them all and when my turn comes, she'll bury me too. And then she'll go back to Joseph Rayna somewhere in the green moss at the end of the solar system.

He saw children at the bougainvillea bush and thought about a little girl he had once known. They spawn like fish, produce Hebrew soldiers in an assembly line for Eve the kindergarten teacher. I've come back without your chicks, Eve! The soldiers died for you, proudly they carried to their graves the exalted words you instilled in them. Did that help them? So you've got a flag! In the bus, a woman sat next to him and read a magazine. She wore a purple dress and her lips were painted. She didn't know that Marar no longer exists, she didn't even know there ever was a village here named Marar. She read indifferently about the homemade ink flag hoisted in Eilat. The picture shows a person climbing a pole and hanging an improvised flag. The Arabs don't draw flags with ink, Marar was destroyed, they killed Menahem and they go on plowing. The woman in the bus smiled at him. What? Marar? You didn't know, new in the Land, you lived in Beersheba, a new housing project, in the war, it was bad. She talked about another war when Ebenezer died and we built an airfield for the British. A radio is open to the evening, the old women sit listening to music, the wind blows silently, the trees move in restrained splendor, the old women don't recognize Boaz, they don't know that Ebenezer's son brought them the state. Boaz returned intact, not wounded, no woman stood up for him in the bus. All's Well won't make a speech for me, he thought bitterly, no flag will wave, no enemy will be arrested for my dead body. That "togetherness," which started in Eve's kindergarten and continued in the threshing floor when they all sang "there was a young woman at Kinnereth" and I sat on the side, I prepared the next wars with Jose Menkin A. Goldenberg. I helped him woo Rebecca. I told him how she looked without a bra and without panties, and he blushed. He clutched a sword he no longer wore belted at his side, stood gazing, the girls sang about the threshing floor, and I sang and didn't sing. The truth is that what oppressed him most was that he couldn't get killed. I have nothing to come back to, he said to himself, and those who did have where to come back to and what to come back to, didn't return. That's not glory, Eve.

From the day Boaz was mobilized until the war was over, Rebecca Schneerson sat pinned to her chair. My men die too much, she thought. She wasn't really interested whether Boaz wanted to or not, she decided he would return and she recited Psalms. Some nights she shouted the verses and other nights she whispered them. Today she got up from her chair. She knew Boaz was coming back home. And Boaz is walking on the path, evening has fallen now, the no-threshing floor in the distance. One summer when he worked in the Burial Society to understand "what life is woven of," he sat with Tova Kavenhazer on the threshing floor. She was quite beautiful then. They hugged and he pressed against her and she felt his eyes penetrating her body through her dress, and then he told her about Nimitz's body, how they embalmed it, washed and wrapped it in a tallith, and Tova Kavenhazer jumped up in alarm, pushed his hands aside, and yelled: With the hands you embrace dead bodies, you embrace me? And he thought, With the hands I embrace her I embrace dead bodies, and ever since then he often pondered that sentence. She ran away. I was left with the thoughts, embracing dead bodies and embracing Tova Kavenhazer . . . She yelled: Don't you dare touch me, Boaz Schneerson! Later she married a shopkeeper from Akron who sold bootleg vodka.

When he entered the house, the Captain stood up, saluted, hugged Boaz, shook his hand, and left. Boaz put the kitbag on the ground and looked at Rebecca. She moved her hands a little, almost said something, but didn't. Behind her, through the screened window, the skeletons of almond trees were seen and the moon was starting to light the roof of the cowshed. They looked at one another and her mouth became soft and yet it was firm, and then he took a step toward her, his body rigid, stuck to the center of gravity in a space he didn't know yet, regulated by glory, and hit her hard. The accumulated rage pitched the old woman aside, dropped her to the ground, and Boaz trampled on her and from the window of Ebenezer's house, the stunned Captain peeped out. In the distance music came from a radio, the Captain who was afraid to interfere, tried to move so as not to see anymore. Rebecca lay on the ground, her body heavy and shrunken, her lips rounded, and a strange smile on the opening of her lips. The lips seemed stuck to her mouth. The lamp moved from the blow and then stayed still, murmurs of pain were heard, Boaz kicked her again and she shrank up and growled, but the smile didn't depart from her mouth, a thin slit of abomination popped up and vanished, and then the slit was filled with blood that flowed like a chameleon, and in the pain a groan of laughter was heard. The old woman lay shriveled and laughing; jets of blood burst from her face and her wide-open eyes.

Boaz went to the window, hit it, and yelled: That's not for you, Captain! And when the Captain took off, he made out the curbstones of the path and for a moment something the Captain had once told him flashed in his brain: Your mother built the path, and he asked then, Who, Rebecca? And the Captain said, No, Dana, and for the first time in his life he felt a longing for a stranger and hated himself so much. Boaz turned from the window, an oppressive compassion lay on him, he picked Rebecca up off the floor, sat her in her chair, brought a bottle of cognac, washed her face, and then kissed her wounds. She sat silent, blood still gushing, smelling of flowers, cognac, and sweat, she picked up the flyswatter that had fallen, wiped her dress, and since she couldn't yet talk, she pointed to her purse on a small chest of drawers next to the door, and Boaz handed her the purse, she opened the purse, rummaged around in it, took out a brush, undid her long hair from the pins that were trying to hold it, and started brushing it. After her hair was smooth, she got up, went to the bathroom, turned on the faucet, and let a stream of water flow on her face for a long time. Then she wiped her face, went back and sat down in her easy chair, and Boaz looked at the beautiful woman who had smeared a little powder on her face, stretched it, put the black scarf on her back, and said: A new state you've got, every Negro's got a state, Indians in movies have a state, Charlie Chaplin has a state, my grandfather's grandfather didn't have a state, but he was wise and didn't stand at attention every day at flags, like stupid Eve. I came back, said Boaz and didn't know what to say.

I waited for you. I went to the settlement. There's a new watchmaker there, came here a few years ago. Hung up a blue and white flag, stood there in the sun and sang one of Joseph's songs. They've got ministers in top hats, like Stutberg's automobile! Nehemiah knew when to die and where, on the border! They made themselves an army of Mr. Klomin and the Captain, won a state from some Arabs who didn't know the shape of a pogrom and don't know on what side you write what they never could read and made a state for Ben-Gurion, Princess Elizabeth, and Shirley Temple! So what? Did you fight for them too? You look tired, it was hard to bring a state to the people of Israel? Maybe you're hungry. Eat something, Boaz.

But what does all that have to do with Stutberg's car? he asked.

His automobile, when he brought it, everybody came to admire. It was a first auto. He opened the hood of the motor and everybody, Horowitz the dummy, Nathan Nehemiah's friend, and even Holtz who later married somebody who was almost your mother and didn't talk, even he stood there with a *kippah* on his head and admired, and they said: A motor that drives a cart like ten horses, ten kilometers an hour! All the insides of the auto were outside, now they look at the insides of the Jewish state, what a wonder! The Jews have a state too.

Eat something, she said.

She made a theatrical gesture that amazed Boaz. She stretched out her hand and her last word rang like a period and not a question mark, not an answer, not a suggestion—a gesture. She reached out her hand, her face became tender, and yet, as always, some thin thread of chill malice was stretched on her face and the blood still flickered from invisible scratches and Boaz felt his feet stagger, went to her, sat down on her solid lap and she hugged him, laid his head on her chest, and when he tried to weep, whimpers blurted out of his mouth like the whimpers of the jackal in his childhood when the settlement was girded by whimpering jackals and at night he would listen to them and try to understand their shrieks.

She stroked his face with her thin hands, kissed his neck, and whispered: I had to, Boaz, it was one night, I sat here in the chair, it was dark, the generator wasn't working and the civil guard walked in the street wearing berets and yelled to put out the light. In the distance, machine gun shots were heard from Negba and I felt in my flesh how Boaz in the mountains, is stabbed, shot, almost dead, eyes shut, I saw vultures, vultures with your eyes, Boaz, vultures, beaks of death, I aimed the words into the sky, to the river that throbbed, to Secret Charity, and I recited Psalms in an ancient melody, and you walked between the bullets, and you lay down and didn't die, I stopped, I stopped short, the vultures wanted your flesh, the eyes, the words stuck to you, you lay in my words, and a few hours later, something happened, I don't know what, I fell, as I fell before when you hit me, I drank blood, and Ahbed, the grandson of Ahbed, was scared, he didn't leave with the other Arabs and stayed, he yelled: You fall,

Madame, they see blood in the dark, too, the window was open now, I was full of blood, I said to him, Shut up, Ahbed, and you ran, and you fled into the mountains, I had no choice, Boaz.

I know, he said.

Later, they told me there was a battle in the Old City and you died. I said you didn't die. People came from the settlement. They said, I have a grandson there, recite Psalms for him, what could I say? My Psalms don't belong to their grandsons. Hillanddale and God's Joy lost a grandson, what could I do? My Psalms weren't meant for their sons and grandsons . . . In our city there was a woman who went mad. People came and tried to get the madness out of her with fire and sulfur and they couldn't. She was possessed by the spirit of a heretic who ran away to Germany. They tried spells and it didn't work. She shrieked and her eyes burned, they raised heavy smoke and it didn't help. Need connection, they said, need connection. They said: a false messiah is eight hundred and fourteen and Joshua son of Miriam is eight hundred fourteen, but it didn't work, not even Shabtai Zvi. Didn't work, they blew the shofar, and said Lord King and pass away and the spirit didn't leave. They shouted, Out evil one, and then they said, There's Rebecca there, bring her. They clothed me in a gown and scarf so they wouldn't see my face and they took me. I used to sleep with my eyes open back then. I said to the man, Out evil one, come to me, I was beautiful, come hug me, the rabbi was scared and blocked his ears, didn't want to hear, I said I'm yours, I thought about the river that would make me pregnant some day, and the spirit left, I felt it strong in my body, a piece of him stayed in me, didn't leave, I spat and then he was scared and part of him ran away. They saw the window opened and he flew, you think those are tales, but he flew, then I left, they wrote his name on an amulet and the man came back, because they didn't write the name of the woman on the amulet, but by then I wasn't there and after eight days of the circumcision, she died foaming at the mouth.

I hit you because of the Psalms I don't even believe in, said Boaz. I don't either, said Rebecca, and she got up and warmed the meal she had made every single day for two weeks.

And he ate. He was even hungrier than before. He swallowed the food and drank red wine. She said: All the old people are finished, young people die in wars and you remain. The disease of death is raging here.

The Captain and I remain in the meantime. He stands outside and envies. I'll let him wait until tomorrow. Your godfather, don't forget. The Captain had a plan to conquer Egypt in one night. The army is here, he said, got to send soldiers to Egypt and conquer the whole land at night and the sources of the Nile and then Farouk's soldiers won't have anyplace to go back to. But he did build an airfield for the English and the English won.

Where do I get a poem?

When Boaz came home, Rebecca was sitting at the window, he recalled that night after the war. Since then she bequeathed me everything, he said to himself, but something in him was worn. Rain fell and drainpipes whimpered. The leaves on the trees stood erect, straightened up, the dust left after the watering was routed, the vines Dana had planted years ago were opened to the falling rain, illuminated in the beams of electric light from the windows. Never does she ask Boaz where he came from and why. He stands, looks at his father's carved birds still trying to fly.

She said: Still sitting in the café and wasting time?

Yes, he said. In her hand she held a bouquet of flowers. The sense that he had once had parents perplexed him again.

Rebecca looked at him. He came to her and kissed her on the mouth. She shrank. In the distance, the face of the Captain was seen waving to her. They sat and looked out the window, the rain fell, he said: I've got to find some poem, I told somebody his son wrote poems.

Take Joseph's poems, said Rebecca. The words there are a space between things, that's what they want, don't reveal too much, it was like Joseph, bold in bed and a liar on paper. He rummaged around in an old desk and found a big envelope. He chose a few poems Joseph Rayna had written to the German noblewoman named Frau von Melchior on the beauty of her neck, her face, and her legs, took eight poems and read them and started laughing. Three poems he knew from school skits.

I didn't know they were his!

They don't know either, she said.

The rain stopped and the wind dispersed the clouds. Boaz passed by on a neglected path, the rain has just stopped, the black sky is strewn with stars, and he walks like a snake, eludes, even though nobody is pursuing him, in his pocket the poems of Joseph Rayna. From the opening in the trees, he could see people eating supper, he could guess what they were eating now. The radio played music from the war—Don't tell me good-bye, just tell me cheers, for war is but a dream soaked in blood and tears. He threw a stone at a window and went on. The window shattered before he disappeared and a shrieking woman came outside, her husband apparently holding a dog's leash, but Boaz was already beyond the prickly pear hedge. In the distance he could see Nathan's son tracking him with a flashlight and the woman screamed: Come here, you hero, let's see if you've got any blood! And her husband said to her: Don't waste your strength, the dog growled but didn't bark, he was an old dog, about thirteen years old, he knew Boaz even before Nathan's son, at the age of forty-five, decided to get married. Between the prickly pear hedges, he found wood sorrel. The wood sorrel shouldn't be there now, he chewed the wood sorrel, crushed it and sucked fragrant, wet, and bitter jujube leaves. From there he slipped off to the citrus grove, in front of him stands a water tower and behind it Naftali's farm is lighted by the light of the night milking, from Dr. Zosha Merimovitch's house came a weeping woman, next to the no-threshing floor he stopped. In the distance a tractor could be seen leaving the lighted dairy. Empty milk buckets clinked. He walked along a path where young people once marched to future wars in front of All's-Well's flag, a scent of washed earth was a restrained reply to the silence of the jackals that had disappeared. In the dairy sat old Berlinsky, reading Spinoza as usual. Next to him, milk jugs were heaped up and a sourish smell came from the dairy. Boaz walked in back, found an empty can, emptied a little milk from the jug standing there, and drank. The taste of the fresh, unfiltered, unpasteurized milk, pleased his palate, he licked, and could see old Berlinsky amazed as ever at the absolute but surprising beauty of the refined logic of Spinoza's ethics. He could imagine how in a few moments, the old man's eyes would be veiled as he again ponders the injustice inflicted on such a great spirit. And that was a blatant injustice, he'd yell at them when they'd bring the milk at night, he was a prince of the Jews, why don't they forgive him now that there's a state, why don't they go down on their knees and beat their breast for the sin. Even Rebecca would blurt out a few good words now and then about the old man, and nobody knew where he came from or what he had done before he came here at the end of the war. After he drank some more milk, he came to the house on the no-threshing floor. He could see, even at that hour, how beautiful were Mrs. Ophelia's roses. In the house of the firefly, the phonograph played Fauré's requiem, he knew the music from Tova Kavenhazer's house. He remembered Tova's father trying to point a menacing finger at Rebecca's house and saying: She fights us as if we sinned when we ran away from Germany, and then he'd play for Boaz the requiem of Fauré or Verdi or Vivaldi, and would say: What does she know, a savage from the dark of the ghetto. Boaz broke into the old DeSoto, hot-wired it, released the handbrake, and let the car slide to the foot of the hill. When he came to the foot of the hill, next to Noah's house, he started the motor and drove off.

The radio didn't work, but the car's lighter was fine and Boaz was filled with respect for the old car. He lit a cigarette and hummed a song to himself. The road was almost empty. Fresh smells of virgin land rose to his nose, a smell of just fallen rain, of night, windows were open, for a moment he completely forgot that tomorrow at one in the afternoon, he had to bring a poem.

After he entered the city, he ran out of gas at the corner of Shenkin and Ahad Ha-Am. Boaz pushed the DeSoto to the side of the street and saw a bored policeman. The policeman was feeling his gun and looking at the dark display windows. Boaz asked the policeman if he had a pen. The policeman said he did and gave it to Boaz. He asked, Why do you need a pen? Boaz said: I stole a car and I want to leave a note. The policeman said: You've got a Sabra sense of humor, and he laughed. Boaz took out a scrap of paper and wrote: I took the car because my ass is shaking in buses, in America there are more Jews, but on the other hand, there are buses at night there, too. A state isn't all of the dream. There's no gas in the car. Return to Mrs. A. name of the settlement . . . Signed, Generous Contaminated.

He thanked the policeman and the policeman went on his way, Boaz waited a little, pinned the note under the windshield wiper and heard a rooster crowing. He didn't know there were roosters in Tel Aviv, and when he looked at his watch he couldn't see the hands because the phosphorus had worn off long ago. He walked along Ahad Ha-Am Street, came to Ben-Zion Boulevard, sensed people slumbering beyond the walls, and if they had been made of glass, he could have seen them weeping. Near Habima Theater, he saw the end of the boulevard and thought of Minna, sometimes when he'd think of her, he'd come to her, bite her, an affair of many years, where to, where from, for whom, and in the middle she got married and divorced and was now alone again, the bleeding finger. He saw people drinking coffee at the kiosk, most of the sycamores here were torn down, the sands covered with unfinished structures, somebody started building a gigantic parking lot next to the old streetlamp, on Chen Boulevard there were little houses, their lights out, and Boaz climbed a tree, came to the top branch, pushed himself, touched the window, pushed it, and landed in a room. A small lamp hung over Minna. She was reading a book. She looked at Boaz, who stood up, and said: Boaz Schneerson, where do you come from? He said: Where do I come from? There are no doors in the house anymore, said Minna, in his free time Boaz takes off fake wedding rings or plays Tarzan. Then he got into her bed and hugged her. She said: After all these years either you love me or you're going to hell. You take off my ring in the middle of the street, come, go, come back, disappear, I've had it, I'm a big girl, want a real life with a husband next to me, I'm not just for sleeping with when you get a hard-on, Boaz.

Then they talked about her nipples, and he said: I let you get married and I didn't tell at the rabbinate, you'll teach me how to love, and she said either you know by yourself or it's not important. They kissed one another with serene passion, shrouded in the past, everything flowed slowly now, he calmed down inside her and she reached out, her hand took a flower from the vase and laid it on her chest. Then, rage stirred in him, he thought of Menahem that he was screwing for him, and about the poem, he fucked her and then he lay on his back, struck, and his eyes began shedding tears. At first she thought it was the water flowing from the flower, but when she saw the tears, she was scared. She sat up straight and said: Never did I see Boaz crying! He bent over, put on his shoes, and said to her: I have to invent for somebody who's dead, I'm going and don't make yourself beautiful for anybody, you don't know what pain will be on your father's face the day you die. She took a thermometer out of the drawer of the nightstand and put it in her mouth. He looked at the book she was reading and saw that it was a report of an income tax evader. He asked her if she read that book a lot and she shook her head and didn't take the thermometer out of her mouth. He wrenched the thermometer out and she said, Yes, mainly because my father is one of the main characters, he put the thermometer back in and she shook her head and he didn't know if she was really laughing. He asked,

What's with you? You'll sit like that until morning, and she nodded. He went up to the window, caught a branch and once again pushed himself and was on the tree and when he crossed above the street, a motorcycle roared by underneath him. The streets were empty and he walked to the tents where he had once lived. The tent that was his was lighted by a hurricane lamp. A worker was sleeping there. Boaz went in and the worker didn't wake up. He looked under the bed and found an old carton. He picked up the carton and went outside. The sea stretched before him and two people were seen walking on the boardwalk. A dog barked, the hotel where he had once stayed with a woman whose name he didn't know was dark. He walked to his hut, went upstairs, opened the door, a few minutes later he sat at the small table and the lamp was lit and he tried to think of Menahem's letter, and what he would do with it. When Menahem died, Mr. Henkin, said the commander, he received an order to move, soldiers were lacking, every death was a national annoyance, not like today.

Boaz Schneerson

I checked your Thompson, it's dirty, I cleaned it. They say you'll be active tonight, they're going up on some crappy hill, I didn't mention to you that you look tired. I owe you my life. A moral obligation, my father would surely say. I found a saboteur's knife in Amnon's clothes—he stole the clothes from the horse. I'm going up to Jerusalem to see *Fiesta in Mexico* for the tenth time, crazy about Esther Williams, she's all there is. I wanted to tell you something important, Boaz, I wasn't able to save your life. Thinking only about how you get out of all that. I'm drunk on the champagne you all brought from Katamon. You bathed in champagne, I drank. I'm thinking about home, father and mother, mother's all right. And Noga? She's silent. I belong to her as you belong to orphanhood, but maybe I love her, and she? There's no contact with the plain and I don't receive tele-pathic messages. And here's the list you asked me for: in the platoon, twenty are left not wounded and not dead. There are four shirts in the warehouse, not too clean. There's also an over-coat of Yashka the partisan, who may really have had another name. Possible to mend and wear. There are two torn flak jackets, five black undershirts, a package of Fishinger bittersweet chocolate, three stocking caps, one with holes, and a few coats, I think—five. In Mapu's *Love of Zion,* there are nicer descriptions, ask my father. There's one girl in Jerusalem, not the prettiest, but at night you don't see anyway. Her parents were stuck in Tel Aviv and couldn't come back to their dear daughter, who puts out and also puts out omelets with eggs she bought on the black market. Her address is Love of Zion Street 5, 3rd floor. If you get by there, go to her. She knows you from the stories. Eat an omelet in her warm bed. The twins asked about you, thank you for my life and I hope you die a true national hero.

Yours, Menahem Henkin

Tape / —

I could have composed the letter in short, poetic lines, Henkin, but you won't want that, eh?

Boaz sits at the table. It's four in the morning. The roof is burning in a black silence. Menahem wouldn't have written: Clods of dirt mounded up/I will shelter my soul in yearning . . . The poems don't get women pregnant anymore, Boaz thought, but their innocence is exciting, how was the illegitimate father of a hundred offspring able to write such innocent lines? An ancient smell of a starched collar rises in Boaz's nose, an aged, old-fashioned adulterer, with flowers in his hand, chocolate in flowered paper, roses. He had learned Menahem's handwriting before, now he tries to shape a poem. Very slowly the rhymes are constructed and he sharpens, edits, I need another Menahem, trees, groves, Tel Aviv, peeling houses, burning sun, and annihilated jackals, sunset, melancholy—a beautiful word, melancholy. And so dawn breaks, breaking dawn! I laugh. Boaz copies the poem, in three places he writes *k*'s not like Menahem, maybe to give himself away, he scorches the paper a little, scrunches it, pours tobacco and sand on it, tramples it, straightens it, wets it and dries it. Turns off the light, disconnects the telephone left by the former owner of the house, and falls asleep.

At exactly one o'clock, Boaz is standing at Henkin's house. The house is still neglected as then, the yard is a weave of crab grass and thistles, the trees, like corpses, without foliage, trampled in some disaster that befell

them. The sea is seen through two houses, in one of them a woman is beating a small dusty rug. Over the little grocery is an old sign, SMOKE MATUSSIAN.
Mr. Singer in a wrinkled shirt, beyond him the enclosures of the port, and
Boaz knocks on the door and Teacher Henkin in a white shirt and gray
trousers opens it and lets him in. For a moment, they look at one another,
then Henkin drops his eyes and without a word leads Boaz into the gloom
of the chilly house.

The shades block the light, a bulb is lit above a silent woman in a dark
dress, the woman raised her face, looked at Boaz with a long and weary
look, and without getting up or turning her face, she said: Will you drink
something? Coffee, juice, tea?

He looked at her, the closed photo album lay in front of her on the table.
He said: Thanks, and followed Teacher Henkin who led him with ostentatious impatience. But at the same time as if he also wanted to defend
himself against something. In the other room, he saw the library Menahem
used to joke about: books up to the ceiling, manila files, big notebooks, a
mess, a table lamp with a hexagonal, old-fashioned shade, peeling a little,
on the wall documents of the Jewish National Fund. Boaz sat down in a
chair across from Henkin and waited. The woman didn't even knock on
the door, she entered and put a tray with two glasses of juice, cookies, and
a steaming glass of tea with a slice of lemon next to it. Boaz said: Thanks,
but she had already slammed the door and didn't hear.

Boaz took out the poem and put it on the table, for some reason he
couldn't put it in Henkin's shaking hands.

Henkin picked up the poem, put on his reading glasses, felt the paper
and with his other hand, started stirring the tea and squeezing the lemon
slice. He took a handkerchief out of his pocket, wiped his fingers carefully,
put the handkerchief back in his pocket, and once again held the paper in
both hands. Boaz took a glass of juice and drank. His eyes wandered over
the shelves and he tried to read the titles of the books, what he wanted to
see was *Love of Zion*, but he didn't find *Love of Zion* among the books near
him. Henkin muttered, This is his handwriting, it's exactly his handwriting, a poem . . .

And then he sank into reading that lasted about an hour. Never had
Boaz seen a person read a poem so devotedly. Henkin forgot that a person
was sitting across from him. He forgot the tea he had stirred and hadn't

tasted. His glass of juice also remained undrunk until Boaz gulped it too. The pale light through the cracks of the shutters dimmed for a moment, maybe the sky was covered with clouds, Henkin didn't move, his lips stammered, his eyes blinked through the glass that emphasized their pupils, from the other room came the sounds of water boiling and a fly buzzing, somebody opened a door and locked it again, the sea breaking was heard clearly and a car honked. Boaz felt disembodied. The light glowed on Henkin, but Henkin wasn't there. On the horizon between two cracks of the shutter a line of sky or sea was seen, he didn't know which, a dim light that slowly darkened his eyes, a hand unattached to his body started hurting, he tried to feel the hand but couldn't, the pain wasn't his, suddenly he was in an unfamiliar landscape, a name echoing in his brain: Baron Hirsch Street, Tarnopol . . . mountains wrapped in white savagery rising over him, birch trees, in the distant mountains time goes backward and they become different, bald, in a desert, high, rising to the sky, bright, Boaz thinks names he never knew before: quartz crystals, orthoclase crystals, ancient granite rocks, red and brown, even black, tiny gardens, like grooves of blood in the expanses of wasteland, yellow flame, slopes hewn by ancient gods, perforated, stone beasts of prey, gigantic, in a gnawing expanse, sky hanging obliquely, as if falling, crag crown, a cliff over a wadi wide as a person and high as the sky, a plant called round-leafed cleome, a person he knows but doesn't know who he is, somebody very close to him drinks tea with desert wormwood, and Captain Jose Menkin A. Goldenberg stands wearing a uniform gleaming in the awful light, and says: Here the golden calf is buried! And a person finds the place of the golden calf from an ancient map, and says to the Captain: Here a memorial to Dante Alighieri will be built. The Captain says: He's not dead, Boaz isn't dead, he found a golden calf, what an historiosophical find! Gibal Mussa, near a prairie crushed with rocks, between snake and heron, raisins of sun here, the eagle eye that's the innocent eye, in wadi channels that are the face of God, the face of man, and there the nation was created.

When Henkin started talking, Boaz looked at his watch. An hour passed, he knew he was in a place where he had never been, and now he also knew what his father looked like, something that embarrassed him with Henkin who now addressed him. You won't understand, Henkin spoke in an excited but quiet voice (you didn't discover the three k's, thinks Boaz sadly)

unbelievable, really unbelievable . . . I always believed, they laughed at me,
I told them, you don't know, you don't know him, his special qualities will
come out, I knew! And he had to rebel. This poem, Boaz, could have been
written only by one man, only by Menahem, that's what's special in the
poem, not its nature, others will testify to that, but its specialness, it's the
clear expression of a man who revealed himself and said something of his
own. Here's the house mentioned here, you surely won't understand, it
was destroyed to plant the boulevard. How angry he was then, he said:
They're building a wasteland, Father, and I remember, a little boy he was
before we moved here and that sycamore on the corner of Dizengoff and
Arlozorov, they cut down . . . the Gilboa! We went on a field trip with the
school, a Passover outing it was, we stood on the top of the mountain, and
in the sunset I recited to them marvels of poetry: The beauty of Israel is
slain upon thy high places: how are the mighty fallen! And Menahem then
laughed at his father, here's the allusion to that poetry, to that moment, to
the fear at sunset, is that the food of our fields, an eternal curse or a momentary distress, what did we know, and the dead ant, in the fixing of facts
with a water meter, that is, a word meter. The magic of the poem is hypnotic, deciphering the lad, and his mother didn't believe, a son fell, she
said, another son in the cruel world, I knew that before he left us, more
precisely, when he left, I knew he'd set some nail, that he'd leave me some
sign from a concealed inner world. And the poem . . . A poem that reveals
a person so much! That will be so personal and yet general, human, and I
waited.

And then Henkin yelled: You could have brought it before!

I forgot I had it, said Boaz.

That's some nerve, he said angrily. That's a violation of every moral
law . . .

And then he was silent, looked at Boaz, and tried to smile, for some
reason he didn't have to maintain his coolness now, his heart told him that
everything he wanted to know about Menahem was buried in this man.
And Boaz Schneerson wants to stop him, to put the clock back, but it was
no longer possible . . .

You don't think the poem is wonderful? Henkin suddenly whispered.

I don't understand it, said Boaz.

That a boy writes like that, the only thing anybody ever asked of him was not to walk on the lawn, says Teacher Henkin, to respect his elders, to be proud of his wildness, new Jews riding horseback, and then comes a moment of softness, of withdrawing inside, and the boy stops the enemy with his body, silent words tell the horror of the stories, coming from him, and he writes them letter by letter, and pulls out a submachine gun, goes out to the last battle, fights for the life of his parents and friends, and is killed, a bullet hits him, is mute and silent, and death flows from him, he flows death and death flows on the mountains and leaves a hidden corner, invisible to his father, the beautiful boy who was and they didn't know, didn't know him, Hasha Masha, they and you, you thought, you're the poor boy, you didn't understand, you didn't grasp! You too, my Hasha Masha . . .

Dear Renate,

It's been a long time since I managed to find the emotional strength to answer your letter. Last night they said on the radio that the cold in Europe had passed and the snowstorms were subsiding. I was glad. You ask me if Boaz came to us to defeat us. On the word of a wounded lioness I can say: No! He came because Henkin was looking for him. It was me he was afraid of. He knew I don't believe. When he left the house, the day he brought the poem, Henkin came to me with trembling hands, holding the poem. I told him, Obadiah, it wasn't Menahem who wrote that poem, Menahem loved the sea, he didn't write a poem, he wasn't a hero like Boaz . . . And he shoved me out of the chair, that man who never killed a fly raised his hand and brought me down. Then he went outside and hanged his head on the wall, I brought him a towel filled with ice cubes and held it to his brow until the swelling went down. For twenty hours he sat with me, Renate, twenty hours straight he talked about the meaning of the poem, how that poem couldn't have been written by anybody but Menahem! I fell asleep and he went on talking. He didn't even know I fell asleep. Then he fell asleep sitting up, muttering. I cooked, and made coffee. I waited for him to wake up and he talked again. And so he gained not only a poem he read to his friends, printed and copied it, but also a son who before—and it's awful to say—he didn't have.

And Boaz started coming. Henkin needed him. Can you imagine a worse place for a sympathetic family atmosphere than a house of mourning? But it was in the house of mourning of all places that Boaz wanted love and forgiveness. That's what I couldn't give him. Noga could.

If we had written our husbands' books, maybe we'd know on what side of life death is found and so we'd have given birth to stories and not begotten them. But I'm just an old Jew who sits alone and thinks, not particularly profound things, I've got my own contempt, I see a sea and Menahem still swimming there, I can even still love Henkin . . .

I'm a former quarry worker who married a teacher and raised a dead son. You write to me about metaphysical visions and about the Last Jew and your husband is seeking a story so as not to write it and I understand, the abstraction of our men needs to be turned into female concreteness, and then maybe a suddenness will be born that is not only foreseen but is even a vision, like a son who bursts out of you, to give birth is to produce concreteness, to become a point, a house, and earth and water to irrigate, to give birth is also to dig a grave. Maybe someday the books will write the authors and not vice versa.

I raised a son and I did know who he was. Menahem didn't want to jump beyond his navel. He wanted a good life and a sea, not to do anything, just to live. That's all he wanted. Maybe that's not sublime, but it's human. And Henkin sat and kept on drinking the stories of Boaz, who told, and everything that happened to Boaz he projected onto Menahem. Everything he experienced, Henkin now experiences from the fictional life of Menahem. And he wanted me to believe. I closed myself in the room. Boaz would try to catch me with his charms, his charming smile, his voice, he didn't know I'm impregnable. No Joseph Rayna would get me pregnant.

Noga and I pretended. I needed her in some way that's hard for me to grasp. Menahem was dear to Noga, she was tormented by what was happening. Only later did she understand that he didn't get the letter ending their relations. Henkin was mourning too much, his committee, and we remained together, I and he with Menahem because he stopped consoling us. Noga has a noble firmness that Menahem was the first to discover. And effortlessly, completely naturally, she played Henkin's daughter-in-law. She had one love to give that she exhausted on Menahem. Maybe only somebody who invented a new Menahem could have penetrated her armor, that secret I never understood. Only somebody who pretended he loved her before, saw her picture that Menahem had in the war (Boaz told her that story and she didn't believe it) and fell in love with her there, maybe even caused Menahem's death out of love, only he could have touched her so deeply.

For a while, Boaz thought he would be the last survivor of his regiment. Like his father he thought he'd be some Last Jew, and he went back to the settlement. Then he was idle. He thought, Who were my parents? He was searching for something, didn't know what. He had money, he didn't have to do anything. He wanted the days to pass and to pass with them, he met Henkin and got a borrowed father, he sold a borrowed son, he stole Noga. He pressed and she gave in. I told her: In my house you won't sleep with Boaz! I couldn't bear it, I was afraid of what Henkin would say and how he'd respond, now, he thought, Noga could be proud of Menahem. She stroked me with her gentle hands and said: You're right, Hasha.

And Henkin didn't see. A new son he discovered and nothing interested him. Only later on, two years later, when Boaz and Noga were living together and Boaz came to Henkin and told him: I faked the poem, why didn't you see the three fake k's, the land mines I buried for you, why didn't you notice? I saved him, he didn't save me! When he said that—and he said that because he thought Noga was beginning to love Menahem

again because of the stories he created—only then did the tumult take place that I told you about, Henkin's decline, Noga's
suicide attempt, and then Boaz turned into a vulture.

Even in all that he's not exactly guilty. At least with you, I
have to be honest. We were living in hell. Noga got pregnant. She
couldn't see Henkin, she had cheered him with long walks along
the Yarkon River, she couldn't see that proud man ridiculous as
he was in the days when he read his poem to every bereaved father and mother at the parties at the Shimonis. In some way that
may not have been clear to her, she pushed Boaz to tell Henkin
the truth. Indirectly she shattered Henkin's delusion. That was
a second death of his son, Renate, and that was hard. Boaz then
believed purely and simply that he did kill Menahem, the more
she refused to believe, the more he believed, and when she
talked about Menahem's beauty and his virtues, he yelled at her
and hit her. When Noga found out what happened, she came to
Henkin and told him: Boaz is lying, Menahem did write the
poem, but Henkin whispered to her: Why didn't you tell me you
were Boaz's girlfriend? We were close, why didn't you tell me?
And he looked at her, he had known her for years, loved her, and
said to her: Noga, you don't know how to lie! And she thought he
would do something, came to me trembling, I told her, Look,
little girl, he's a strong man, Henkin, an old-line Zionist, he was
in the Labor Brigade, he experienced hard things, he'll recover,
she talked to him some more and he couldn't answer and threw
a chair at her. She was hit and went outside. Then she brought
him flowers. Boaz came and said to her, What right do you have
to talk to Henkin about me, why do you interfere in my life, you
want Menahem back? He's not with me anymore either, and
Henkin heard, Boaz went into his room, all night long they
talked. She sat with me and we drank sweet vermouth. Two big
drunks. In the morning Boaz came out and slapped her face. In
the room Henkin sat with the poem, more broken than I'd ever
seen him, and then Noga got up, and said to Boaz: You know
what, you can go to hell, and she left. After she had gone, I sat,

my head splitting from the drinking at night, Henkin got up and walked to the seashore and went into the sea with his shoes and clothes, and it was winter then. In the morning Boaz came back and Henkin woke up and asked with a weary face, anxiously: Where's Noga? He said: She died, Boaz, she died. I told him: Stop, the two of you suffered blood, and the two of us went out to look for Noga. Then I recalled the cave. In the world war, Menahem and his friends, especially Amihud Giladi, who lived in the house where Ebenezer now lives, would hide tea and rusks and stones there to be partisans and fight the Germans who were then in El Alamein, they wanted to build a fortress on the hills where the Hilton now stands. Noga knew the old cave, she called it "Menahem's cave." I told Boaz: She's surely in Menahem's cave. That was a mistake, he was offended and said, What do you mean, what cave, we've got our own places, what do you mean, Menahem's cave. I told him: At least she can be there, but he didn't want to believe it, wanted to go to other places, at night he looked in all the places and didn't find her and there was nothing left for him to do but go with me even though he didn't want to believe, I dragged him to the cave and he didn't even know where it was, and Noga was there, had swallowed pills, we dragged her to the corner of Jabotinsky, took a cab and went straight to Hadassah Hospital, they pumped her stomach, and she aborted Boaz's son, the grandson of the Last Jew!

We sat there, Noga and I, Boaz was miserable, more miserable than I had ever seen him and he told me that he didn't kill Menahem, but he should have killed him, and who did he tell? He told me that! And Noga said: I'll never give birth now, and then I wept too. And then Boaz's business developed and she helped him. She told me: He is what he is, and I love him. And she helped him, but everything began with Henkin, he went to his committee, years before, read them Menahem's poem. And then he brought the Defense Ministry into the picture, and Jordana the Yemenite who fell in love with Menahem, and that business that flourished.

Tape / —

A few words about words. A vulture is an artificial bird, with a broad wing-span, a twisted beak, the vulture is the hawk, the falcon, the bearded vulture. Vulture is a general name for all birds of prey and also the name of a specific bird, the precise identity of the vulture is not known, I, Ebenezer, what do I understand about vultures? In that winter, among corpses, didn't a man stand there named Hans Kritacal who is today a teacher in Hamburg? Five Ukrainians with axes beheaded thirty-two children, and he didn't stand and recite a poem?

What sadness is spread over everything here.

Tape / —

From the letter of Obadiah Henkin.

> . . . And I don't know whether to be glad about your offer or to be sad. For a long time I've lived beyond gladness or sadness, so let us say that I accept your offer, or perhaps it was my offer? To cooperate in writing the book between two experienced writers, each on his own, something that may never see the light of day. In your last letter, along with Renate's beautiful letter, you write me that you wrote to Samuel Lipker (Sam Lipp) in America and about the answer you got. I think that answer is indeed important and I translated it into Hebrew.
>
> You wanted to know what exactly I call "the external additions."
>
> Among the books Ebenezer knew by heart (aside from those we've already talked about and catalogued), is also a treasure that can't be known exactly. In addition to the report of the Institute there is material (about a million words) whose sources are not known and yet are quoted from books. In other words, this isn't personal knowledge by this or that person, but knowledge taken from books (through people, of course) whose identity I can't verify. I shall list some of those books that may be most important to us:
>
> 1) "Travels of the Tribe of Menashe," by anonymous, in manuscript, copied in 1454 by Rabbi Joachin Eliahu, Amsterdam.

2) "Tribulations of the Sad Knight Kabydius, His Journey to the Land of Israel with Peter the Hermit and his Love for Judith." The name of the author isn't mentioned in Ebenezer's words, but the transcription is from the year 1343, Paris.

3) "Sources for the Burial of Moses, Story of the Golden Calf and Its Location." Written by Reb Yehuda Ber Avram ben Abraham (maybe a convert?), printed in Leipzig in the year 1984 (*sic!*), a year that is still far from us—Ebenezer insists that the date is correct and doesn't remember if he saw it or is only quoting.

4) "Kinds of Jews" by Sergei Szerpowsky and his son, Warsaw 1745.

5) "History of the Nation of Israel According to the Creator," by anonymous, printed in Tarnopol in 1767.

6) "Source of the Animals and the Creation, God as a Chariot that Was," by the Divine Kabbalist Ahmed Abidion ben-Haalma Downcast Eyes, printed in Istanbul in the year 50 after the death of the Messiah (apparently meaning Shabtai Zvi).

There are of course more books, but I haven't yet investigated. The books I listed above are not found in any library or known collection of books. Nor are they mentioned in any other place (I checked with the librarians in Jerusalem, Tel Aviv, Copenhagen, Paris, London, New York, and other archives), nor are they mentioned in any other book, and that may be the major problem, because if they are not mentioned, are they knowledge or fiction? And if fiction, whose?

Considering what we know about Ebenezer, he couldn't have invented those books. The books I examined constituted (each in itself) a conceptual, planned and formatted whole, sequences of facts that can be checked, and cases that really can be checked sound authentic. The material is on its way to you so you can review it more carefully, but the story of the Sad Christian Knight Kabydius can serve as an example. His tribulations in the Holy Land match other writings we're familiar with. Even the description of the siege of the city of Trier, where

Peter the Hermit was helped by the Jews (who were then slaughtered), is similar to descriptions we have from other sources, even though Kabydius himself is not mentioned in any other source. The story of Judith sounds quite authentic as we now discover more and more details today about the existence of many Jewish settlements in the Land of Israel during the time of the First Crusade and later.

Tape / —

The wandering Kabydius was the son of one of the Hungarian tribes. In his youth, in a little village in the Carpathian Mountains, he met a Jewish family. The family celebrated a holiday that was alien to him. After he was banished from his lands by his father, whom he tried to kill, he wandered to Rome. For some time he stayed there with a group of monks and along with another monk, he loved a twelve-year-old girl who died in their arms, and so he called himself Kabydius the Sad. The other monk went outside the city walls and was devoured by dogs. After he learned that his father had died, Kabydius went back to his homeland. In the mountains, he met the same Jewish family. The father of the family was an old man whose tongue had been cut out by some riffraff on its way to join Peter the Hermit. One of the old man's granddaughters was a handsome lass with a swollen belly. The village where they had lived before was burned down. The girl was pregnant from the one who had cut out her father's tongue. Kabydius wanted to kill them, but changed his mind and hugged the handsome girl and her mother fell to her knees and pleaded with him to wound her and not her pregnant daughter.

Kabydius, who was confused by his hatred for his father and his disappointed love for the twelve-year-old girl, sought "a bandage" for his soul full of sadness of the world, as he put it, and approached the mother. When he asked to marry the daughter and be a father to her son, he was banished by a group of audacious Jews who burst out from a distant place at night. Kabydius wanted to go back and take vengeance on the Jews, but it had

started snowing and he went to seek his estate and discovered
that, in his absence, his father had bequeathed it to his brothers and they banished him. Ashamed of his lust for that Jewess,
he searched for the riffraff that had cut out her father's tongue
and was introduced to Peter the Hermit. Peter made an indel-
ible impression on him. He was ugly and strange, but a real
leader of knaves and belligerent men. In the hermit's eyes, he
saw light. The crusade to the Holy Land was at its height and
Kabydius didn't join his peers but went with Peter the Hermit,
as his servant.

The great battle took place in Antioch and only afterward did
they descend along the shore toward Jaffa. The knights, writes
Kabydius, mocked him and said: What is a man like you doing
among streetwalkers, thieves, and rapists? and he said to them:
Peter is the leader and I wash his feet for the sake of Our Lord
the Messiah. They called him Peter the Dark and were afraid of
him. The knights teased him—he doesn't give his pedigree in
the book, but hints that the others knew it—and he had to fight
a duel against one of the knights and even to run him through
with his sword. Kabydius provides a detailed description of the
battle for Jerusalem, the ship they dragged from the port of Jaffa
and turned into a ram to batter the wall, how Gottfried of Bouillon knelt at the sight of the Holy City, the siege of the city, the
bloody battles, how they circled the wall of Jerusalem for seven
days and seven nights, and how the Savior was revealed on the
Mount of Olives and they burst through the walls, and the
blood, he said, as is also mentioned in other sources, flowed up
to their knees, and cursed Jews were entrenched in the last
tower, fighting along with the Muslims and were burned alive.
And then he heard a voice: The holiday you saw on the mountains was my holiday, you're here and I rule over you, and
Kabydius was angry and his heart filled with dread and he told
Peter, who commanded him to be flagellated. He accepted his
punishment in stoical silence, he wrote, and when the whip was
laid on his back, his head was bald, he felt a genuine regret and
exaltation he had never known before. After the coronation of

Beaudoin as king of Jerusalem, Kabydius went to the Galilee.
Along the roads, they built fortresses then. In the blazing heat
of August he scaled a high mountain and joined a group of
monks and Muslim prisoners, who were busy building a fortress.
He began hewing stones. They told him not to hew stones because it was contemptible work meant for slaves. He said: I
committed heavy sins and I must atone for them. They listened
to him as a hewer from far away. They said he could grant to
stone the charms of both European and Eastern art.

Three years later, his memory began to break down. A cloud
shrouded his soul; he could remember only the stones he had
hewn the day before. Peter was not seen again, counts and bar-
ons were appointed to the estates of the Holy Land, a struggle
raged between the priests and the royal house of Beaudoin, but
Kabydius remained far away from those events. The Count of
Accra, who was brought in a sedan chair to see Kabydius the
hewer, looked at the stones and said: I want Kabydius to build
my castle. And so it was. Then, he wandered, went up to Jerusalem to see the Kingdom of Jesus on earth and in the streets of
Accra silk cloths were stretched to hide the blinding light, ships
from Genoa brought delights from the East and glass from Tyre
was brought and used for windows, something that had not yet
been seen in Europe. From the Arabs he learned the theory of
the arch to allow for high ceilings in their buildings, he went
down to Caesarea and built there too, he participated in building halls for knights in Accra and fortresses in the Galilee, the
Golan Heights, and Bashan, and within ten years, Kabydius was
one of the great builders in northern Israel.

Kabydius was in the prime of life, and was sated with wars
and excommunications when he met Judith in a small Jewish
village not far from the fortress he was building. At night, said
Kabydius, Judith would fly off, in the morning she'd come back.
Like everybody who desired her, she abused him too. When he
wanted to beat her, she slipped away from him. Her family plotted against him and he wanted to burn down their house. At
night, bitter people came and beat him until he bled. He

wanted to tell Count Montfort about that, but a crow followed him and tried to poke out his eyes. Judith was picking flowers. It was after the rain. When he raped her she laughed and when he swore love to her she spat in his face. When her belly grew, and his son balled up in her, he wanted to marry her, his memory returned to him, he remembered the lass in the Carpathian Mountains, and he said: Maybe she's the same woman or I'm cursed by Jewish witches. Judith refused to marry him. He dimly recalled when he lived in Rome with the monks and loved a little girl. All my life, he thought, I've been caught in ropes with a curse and I can't get away from it, where is the whip that will take Jews out of my insides. He came to Judith, tied her to a post, whipped her, kissed her, and all night long he talked with her. She sneered at him, her hands tied, her eyes flashing, and when he asked again and again to marry her and be a father to his son, she laughed. When he castrated himself before her eyes and felt them taking him on a stretcher as he was bleeding, he recalled seeing a spiteful joy sparkling in her eyes. He came back to Judith with his face burned and emaciated and was a eunuch in her yard

He was allowed to play with his son. Kabydius was old now. Judith was called mistress of the village where a knight served as her slave. She didn't marry anybody, and he hewed stones and built her another house more beautiful than the houses of the Galilee. There he sat and wrote his history, his shame, his regret, his sorrow, and his love of a woman who was once a little girl in Rome, then a woman in the Carpathian Mountains, and then a mistress in the Galilean Mountains. At night he would carve birds for his son.

. . . That's only a collection of fragments from the story, and you can peruse it when you receive the material. After I read, I asked myself how and why did this story, fictional or not, get into Ebenezer's hands? Is bird-carving coincidental? Those questions will remain without an answer for the time being. I can assume that bird-carving is Ebenezer's addition, but if it is an addition, why did he add it here and not someplace else?

Why is bird-carving not mentioned in the nine million words investigated by the Institute? And the story of the Golden Calf and the place where Moses is buried, for instance . . . the area of Santa Katerina in the Sinai was barred to Ebenezer.

Now that we can get to it, it's easy to think of his descriptions. But when Ebenezer recited that book (which I listed for you at the beginning of my letter), the area was hard to go to and was in the hands of the Egyptians, when could Ebenezer have been there? In my humble opinion, he never could have been there. I don't know if traces of this ahistorical or even historical myth can truly be found, but the descriptions of the place, the geography, the names of the crystals, the stones, the rocks, the various areas, the climate, the lifestyle of the Bedouins, the monks, all that is precise. It is true that people visited there throughout the years, but it was surely not Ebenezer who invented what they saw or didn't see. The date of writing this ancient book is in another few years. What does that mean? Why did Ebenezer insist that the book be written like that, that the secrets in it are things that happened so long ago? According to various calculations (see appendix) I found in the Book of Salvation, which Ebenezer quotes and copies of it are also found in other places, the year 1984 will be the year of destruction. Also according to the prophecy of Astronomus, the decline before the annihilation begins in that year. The place where Moses is buried isn't clear, according to the book, but when I went with the members of our Committee on a trip to the Sinai last year, I was able to follow Ebenezer's guidelines and I found monasteries that even the Society for the Preservation of Nature didn't know about, I discovered waterfalls, wonderful oases, and sights were revealed described precisely in the book to be published years later, and recited by Ebenezer!

What else can I tell you? I'm sorry I can't respond to your request. When I ascended to the Land of Israel in the early 1920s, I swore I would never leave here. Why did I swear, why do I keep this oath? It's hard for me to answer. Jordana keeps coming. Her love for Menahem touches my heart. Maybe the mean-

ing of Kabydius's book is that love may really be only between
the dead and the living? Maybe that's the meaning of the story
of Ebenezer, Boaz, Menahem, Rebecca, Joseph, Nehemiah,
and Friedrich? I'm not a literary scholar, I'm a tired old
teacher, but there's surely food for thought here. The love
people are afflicted with like a disease is a relationship between
naught and aught. Maybe later, life began to envy death and
imitated impotence.

Maybe everything that was didn't have to be. As I write these
confused things to you, Jordana is sitting in the other room and
looking at an album of pictures of Menahem. Hasha Masha is
drinking coffee. Boaz is wandering around in his jeep and im-
mortalizing the dead. You write me that Samuel Lipker claims
that Lionel doesn't know that Samuel is his brother. It always
seems to me that Samuel is here and hasn't really gone to
America. Something of his spirit sometimes sits on my neck.
When Ebenezer called Boaz Samuel, I knew that was more than
a mere coincidence.

Yours . . .

Tape / —

When Yazhik was three years old, I had, said Yazhik, three hens. I fought
with Petlura in 'nineteen. Ever since then I learned why hens have a red
comb, Ebenezer, the blood was soaked in chewed grass, in berries, the
woman my father slaughtered I saw in my dreams night after night for four
years and two months, except for one night when I was drunk and couldn't
dream. Then I counted the poplar trees in a radius of seventeen kilometers around our house. There were twenty-six thousand, five hundred
thirty two trees. They were cut down at a rate I tried to understand and
couldn't. Meanwhile, the farm grew and two hundred eighty hens were
added—and three new roosters. The number of trees decreased in the
snowstorm of 'twenty-six, I found a woman whose mother was a Jew. She
almost loved me, but I was tempted to tell her who my father was and she
remembered poor Nakhcha, her uncle whose hand was cut off in that pogrom I couldn't tell you about. Seventy thousand Jews died in that pogrom
under cover of the great revolution. Maybe since then my hostility has

sprouted for people with squashed noses. What am I doing here? I hid a little Jewish girl, the woman I found dead, I stopped counting poplars, the hens went to Berlin in a freight train, the little girl lay under the stairs, upstairs my mother was dying with a candle at her head, night after night I went down and talked with the little girl and she was scared. And only later was she not so scared. In the dark she sat for three years, until the bent legs were stuck together, shin to thigh, I went to fetch a doctor to separate the shin from the thigh, under the stairs smelled of rotten flesh, I brought her cabbage and potatoes, her eyes were burning and her forehead was blazing. They killed the little girl with one blow, without separating the shin from the thigh, they left my mother to die alone with the crucifix hanging over her bed. The Sturmbahnführer from the Generalgouvernement stood and preened in the mirror in my mother's room, he wore oak clusters on his collar, his boots were gleaming, the guards would spit and a slave would rub them, me they tied to a cart and the Ukrainians pointed at me as if they had reasons, and said Yazhik the Jew-lover, I tried to count the reasons and discovered that in the end they were only one reason, and I stopped, I always liked to count, I saw bodies, arms cut off, I wasn't one of you, I didn't have to die but to live on the border of death and starvation, I saw them bring the people, scare them with clubs, blows, undress them and then straight to the showers and lock the door, they were more confused than scared, and then that revolt broke out with one hand grenade that barely killed one soldier, a machine gun from the tower shot and it all ended as it had begun, outside next to the mass graves stood people and searched. Later, years after the war, came the Poles, opened graves and searched for diamonds in corpses and that's how they found out what was under the ground. It once belonged to my grandfather, his name was also Yazhik. You won't die, Ebenezer, and you didn't die. I saw your box when I worked cleaning the home of the General Gouverneur. On the walls they hung pretty pictures, I counted a hundred and thirty-two pictures, two hundred etchings, a hundred tapestries, forty-nine easy chairs, twenty-two carpets! Once I brought champagne and milk to their party and then they discovered the little girl when I went to get a doctor to separate her shin from her thigh, there I saw your box. The box played "Silent Night." Once I counted ships in the river, I wanted to dream of how I'd go to Canada, I had some uncle there who didn't write a word, but was there. The ships sailed without me, I remembered Petlura, my uncle was his soldier, now in Canada, you remember how a ship looks: masts, cables, chimneys, flags, and here I'm drawing you a ship, Ebenezer.

Tape / —

I look at what he draws, try to remember and can't. It seems his name was Yazhik. Where did they all go?

Tape / —

Among the hundreds of women standing at the ropes stretched by the marines was Rachel Blau. When the ship anchored the sirens' wail sawed through the port and flags were raised and lowered at a dizzying pace and then the gangplank was lowered and the first off were the coffins. Then the wounded were carried on stretchers. On the dock stood tense young marines in polished uniforms, saluting. A band played marches. Lionel disembarked with the wounded officers who received a noisy welcome and women shrieked hysterically. Rachel discovered him between a young woman and a back turned to her with his eyes fixed on the ship. Only when he turned around did Rachel see Joseph Rayna and trembled. If she hadn't been pressed among the hysterical women, the wife of the Shirt King would have collapsed, but they pressed her and she didn't collapse. The young Joseph Rayna, gazing at the city, looked as if all the women waving their hands had come only for him. He smiled at them, and Rachel saw Lionel hold on to him and with the young woman they came down the gangplank.

When she looked at Joseph, Lionel said: Mother, meet Samuel, and he said: Sam, my name's Sam, and she smiled, and what once she couldn't do she now did in the arms of her son, she pitied herself, forced a smile, and shook Lily's hand.

Lily glanced at Rachel and saw how Samuel and Rachel looked at one another. Lily kissed Rachel's face.

The band went on playing and Lionel muttered something to a young officer who limped toward him and slipped away from there to the open arms of a young woman holding a baby. Lionel was the oldest officer of the group, his hair was gray, carrying the kitbag he looked like a military commander in propaganda movies. Genghis Khan he isn't, said Rachel doubtfully, like her husband, she too thought Lionel would never excel at selling shirts, but neither of them had expectations. Her husband maintained with a trace of envy that Lionel was meant to hover through life as an artist, and Rachel said: But he was a brave soldier, and her husband said: A good soldier is a luxury, I have to sell them shirts and our younger son will carry on my business, Lionel will be fine, I'll take care of him, let him just be healthy, in a family like ours we also need poets, he said with an understanding whose generosity evoked contempt in Rachel's eyes. She loved her husband with a quiet love full of regret for the life she had once cast away to gain what Rebecca had taught her not to want.

Sam saw the tall buildings, a train passed overhead, the ships wailed and an airplane was seen landing at LaGuardia Airport. The might he saw before his eyes terrified Sam, but he remained calm and tried to understand how much Rachel understood about who he was, and when he understood that she understood, he relaxed, that was a victory over Lionel, and he needed that victory.

Outside the fenced area the cars were parked, and in the distance Saul Blau appeared in a checked shirt waiting for his family and listening to a baseball game on the radio. Next to him stood three youngsters who waved at Lionel, who kissed each of them, shook hands warmly with Saul, and Saul shook everybody's hand and tried to hug Lily who was almost swooning and after they got into the station wagon, and started driving, Saul carried on a conversation all by himself. He asked about the war and answered his own questions. He explained where they were going and asked if they knew where they were going, Sam meditated and sank into a doze and thought about the flag that had been raised, and the trumpets, he saw a gray sky touching the sharp roofs, and Saul said: They fucked the Germans and the Japanese, now they'll have money to buy shirts. Sam looked at the street, Lily sat pressed against him, silent. The bustling streets changed to bridges winding into one another. He felt his erection secretly oppressing, wanted to rape a bridge or shirts, to rip the words from the mouth of the man who raised shirts and talked about how it would now be hot in his parents' grave.

In the house of the Shirt King, they consumed with exaggerated ardor the supper that Rachel had cooked. They drank Coca-Cola and sweet wine and the host wasn't compelled to try to talk for them all, nor did he know that his wife's first lover was sitting here. He told Lionel about his war experience. Lionel was silent, looked out the window, and ate slowly. Saul said: I transported machine gun shells for the howitzers. My father fought alongside the Ukrainians and I fought alongside the Austrians, we stood and shot, and then I saw Father, his memory for a blessing, shooting at me and we stopped together. We were in one city and in two different armies, that's how it was to be a Jew back then! Our synagogue was besieged. Always ready, what remained there, what remained? Nothing! But to shoot your father, you didn't have that in this war, Lionel. Lionel didn't answer and looked at Lily. At night she shook in his arms and the shaking went through the wall and touched Samuel. He forgot he was Sam, thought he was Samuel, and started shaking too. Rachel lay with her eyes wide open next to her husband and saw Joseph and didn't know if she yearned for him or if it was once again Rebecca who yearned inside her. The house was surrounded by a fine garden and Lionel explained to Sam that the garden was supposed to be like the garden of the Ford Motor King in his hometown in Connecticut. Samuel saw a moon that looked like a splendid coin and shone like cold metal, the trees moved in the wind, the house was overheated, and Samuel had to open the window and a cold wind penetrated the room. Samuel thought: I'll teach that Shirt King, and when the rage subsided a little, he whispered: Fuck her, Lionel, put your Jewish prick in!

They found a nice apartment on Morton Street in Greenwich Village. When they finished furnishing it, Rachel came to visit them. She looked uneasily at the apartment, which looked more like the apartment of a beggar than the apartment of an heir to a shirt kingdom. There were a few modern lamps and one cabinet that wasn't especially ancient, but the chairs, the easy chairs, the tables, and the cabinets looked strange to her, the paintings were full of some mold that depressed her. She looked painfully at the world she had fled, while Joseph walked around the house looking at her as if she were an old whore selling her wares in a display window.

Her thoughts about Joseph were confused and depressing. She simply didn't know how to think of Joseph, facing his son. Sam left the room, passed by Rachel, who was looking at Lionel. And in the small yard squeezed between gray walls, Lily sat on a wicker chair amid the old wet fallen leaves and thrust a needle into embroidery. Sam looked at the locked windows above the small gardens connected to one another, but no one was seen in the windows.

You're sitting on my mother's dress, said Sam. She raised her face and looked at him. She put down the embroidery and without a word moved aside to the chair. The chair was empty. She looked at the empty chair, shrugged and went inside. Her face remained impassive. She waited until he'd disappeared and continued embroidering.

When he looked at Rachel, her look was dreamy, perplexed, when he felt he disgusted her, he also disgusted himself, went out to the street, walked to Seventh Avenue, and turned north. In a small square, he discovered a luncheonette. Through the window, big empty tables were seen, he went in, ordered a hot dog, slathered a thick layer of mustard on it, ate, drank a cup of coffee, his English was fluent by now, but nobody noticed his accent. Not far from there, he saw a man carrying an aquarium. He followed the man. The man turned into a side street, stopped at a restaurant, and started going down the stairs. The sign on the door said: "The Five Tightrope Dancers." At the entrance, there were no tightrope dancers, but an aquarium. In the aquarium were elusive rare fish. He loved the bold cunning colors. A person in a white coat said to him: Beautiful, eh? Dangerous and very poisonous! Everything beautiful is dangerous, and vice versa! Sam said: A city of philosophers, and continued looking at the fish. In the distance cars were heard honking, a subway train passed and the building shook. He wanted to lead a dog named Ebenezer and take the money out of those people's pockets. Lionel is a lifeline but also an obstacle, he thought. When he went outside, the sky was rounding. Two people in overalls were hanging ornaments over the street. The wind moved the wires where the workers were hanging the ornaments. A woman who passed by said, What a nice Thanksgiving it will be. The cold increased, and the workers finished hanging the ornaments. And then he saw his first funeral in America. The coffin lay in an open car, embellished with wreathes of flowers and behind, in a gigantic black car sat people dressed in black. A mounted policeman passed by him. A dog stood tied to the fish store and barked at the coffin, the workers crossed the street behind the cars, one of them genuflected, the other ate a sandwich of four slices of bread with white saliva dripping from them.

He went back home and when he passed by Rachel, he tried to pretend she didn't exist. He went into his room, locked the door behind him, stood silently shaking, and through the window he saw Lily's back.

Lily got up, her back disappeared from his view, the yard was suddenly full of moss and greenery stuck to the old crusted stones. When they entered the apartment, the landlord said: Sherlock Holmes stayed here for two whole days when he was in New York. He said that with an impenetrable face, and Lionel said: That's nice, did he also sit in the garden? And the landlord said: There he solved the murder, and didn't expatiate on what murder. A woman now stuck her head out one of the windows, gaped open her mouth that swallowed wind, and Sam could see the firm teeth in the distance, he thought about her thighs, about the juncture of her legs with her thigh and felt warmth inside him. He didn't sit down and read the books he should have read, but slipped through the yard and entered the room. The voices of Rachel and Lionel were heard dully from the living room. Lily lay in bed and stared at the ceiling. Sam went to her, undid the button of her shirt, grasped her breast and looked into her eyes. Her look was cold and distant. She put her hand on his erection and he squeezed her breast, and said: Tamed eagle! And she was silent, and when her hand touched him he smiled, moved away from her, and she didn't even bother to button her shirt. He went to Lionel's desk and started burrowing among the papers. Lily lay and watched him calmly. The drawer was neat. Sam said: Secret Glory is with his stepmother and I'm with the ad for Ritesma Cigarettes . . . Lipp is lip in English. I'll buy a Mercedes and Maubach and Horick. Whores of public remorse, Lily.

She didn't answer him, shifted the embroidery she had been holding in her other hand, and put it on the cabinet and buttoned her shirt. He took a bundle of papers out of an envelope and glanced at them. What are you looking for? she asked.

I've already found it, he said. Then he wrote something on a scrap of paper, put the papers in the drawer, and said: Tell your man he shouldn't have taken me, I'm not worth his beauty or your beauty. Look, he added, I wandered around with a Jewish dog, I sold condoms and lampshades, I had it good. Sam took his mother's strip of fabric out of his pocket and put the fabric on Lily's face. She didn't budge and didn't move the fabric off her face. He waited, picked up the fabric, looked at it, shrugged and put it back in his pocket. He waited but she didn't say anything. He noticed her tears trying to tear the scrim of her eyes. But she didn't weep, and he said: I saw an American funeral and venomous fish in an aquarium. They've got a hard life here in America, give me money, I've got to go, I'll come back later and don't let them try to be rebuilt with my money. She stretched out her hand mechanically, opened a drawer, took out a bundle of bills and coins and gave it to him. Sam picked up two coins that fell on the ground, and examined the bills in the light of the lamp next to the bed, and said: They must be counterfeit! He counted the money as bank tellers count money. You sit here and sew corpses, he said, you sewed corpses for women mourning in gigantic cars, you really think you can be my mother?

Self-pity doesn't suit you, Sam, said Lily and turned her face away.

That's right, said Sam. What do you know? You're just a filthy Jewess, and he left.

On the way out, he yelled at Rachel: Stay well, Grandma! She tried to see him in the opening of the corridor, but couldn't say a thing, her mouth was dry, and when he went out she said: You made yourself an apartment of rage, live like artists, stay well. Lionel served his trembling mother coffee as Sam's back was seen on the sidewalk, striding quickly.

The wind blew harder, workers were still hanging ornaments over the windswept street. In twenty-six minutes and thirty-two seconds—on the new watch Lionel bought him—he arrived. At the information window he asked for the bus to Washington Depot. The woman said mechanically in a very clear, hasty, nonhuman voice: Have to go to . . . to arrive . . . at . . . and from there . . . from . . . to . . . and . . . the price is . . . And she was already talking to somebody else. He went down the escalator to Platform Fourteen. Not many people were in line, and those who were seemed to know one another, even though they practically weren't talking. A little girl with yellow hair asked him if he really was the Brooklyn Bridge. He whispered something to her in Polish, and she apologized and ran to her mother, who was laughing aloud at the comics section she was reading and chewing the end of a pencil that was crumbling between her teeth. Then he got on the bus, waited until the doors were locked, and shut his eyes. Calm enveloped him. He thought, these wouldn't get on the trains, at most they'd work guarding and burying corpses. He issued precise orders of burial and opened his eyes. The tunnel was over and the light was strong for a moment, they rode along a street whose houses seemed to be dying. Then they entered another tunnel, a single policeman stood in an alcove chewing gum. At the end of the tunnel, light was seen at last, then everything was gray, isolated houses and fields. Sam saw cows and a little church and hills. The sun peeped out for a moment between the low rounded clouds. The bus was overheated and Sam opened the window, but people asked him to close it. The little girl was sitting at the back of the bus, her mother was still laughing at the comics she was reading. Sam signaled to them that he was deaf and couldn't hear. They said: Poor thing, but he's got to close the window. A man in a yellow suit and one of Saul Blau's colorful shirts, smelling of cheap perfume, got up and tried to close the window. Sam started struggling with him, the man was surprised and didn't know what to do. The others were silent and indifferent, wrapped themselves in their overcoats and looked as if they were freezing in the strong wind. The man said: Must not be an American, doesn't understand English. He was amazed to hear his own words, something wasn't right. He stood up, his hands intertwined in Sam's, and said: What I meant was that he's deaf in English. Sam kept the window open, but two men coming back from a deer hunt, dressed in gigantic hunting jackets, got up, overcame him, and locked the window. Then they laughed and passed a bottle of whiskey in a brown paper bag from hand to hand. Sam burst out laughing. A woman sitting in front of him turned to look at him and turned pale. The man next to her was reading a newspaper, and said: They come here like flies, got to know how to behave with those who come, got to show them who's boss here. The woman slapped the man and he yelled: Whore! When she turned her face again, she hadn't yet answered the man's yell and he went back to reading the paper. Her face was full of amazement and then suddenly innocence. Sam smiled until she blushed. He pointed at her breasts and drew enormous circles with his hands. Even though she stopped blushing the man with her was afraid to look. The headlines of the evening paper looked threatening through his eyeglasses.

Isolated farms were now seen, frost stuck to them, the trees were naked, cars were seen driving on paths dwarfed by tall trees. About two hours later, the houses increased, the farms gave way to more elegant houses, and then an industrial area belching smoke and taverns, little signs, blinking at their doors, well-tended gardens attached to one another, another hill and naked treetops, and then the bus stopped. Sam looked at a woman who looked monstrous with her face stuck to the windowpane. She gaped her mouth open and blew on the window, her nose was smashed against it. Even in the strong cold, she looked despondent and forsaken. He waved his hand at her and the bus started moving.

For a long time he walked in the forest in the stinging cold and then in the fields, he saw houses with red roof tiles, haylofts, cowsheds, handsome rustic churches in domesticated groves, in the distance a hill was seen and on it a sweet, gray little town, with a gilded clock on its church steeple and then, when he came to the house, he opened the gate and a gigantic dog assaulted him. Sam climbed up on Ebenezer's tail and pulled hard, went down on all fours, kissed the snout of the dog who gasped heavily, hit him, petted him at the same time, and by the time the little woman hurried to the gate at the sound of the barking, the dog was lying next to Sam and wagging its tail, its mouth drooling and its face thrust in Sam's hand. Facing him was the old house surrounded by a big garden. The windows were shrouded in shades, the entrance was like a Greek temple, the chimneys belched thin smoke scattered in all directions by the wind. The dog didn't move at the sound of its mistress's hasty steps. Sam noticed the woman's antique beauty and looked at her calmly. She asked who he was and what he wanted. He told her that first he had to pee and then he could talk with her. She swallowed wind, her look passed angrily, maybe even more, offensively, over the dog's swooning back, and she said: This is a private house, sir, not a public lavatory. She used the professional terminology, and even that neutral name sounded coarse in her mouth. Her lips clamped righteously.

I come about Melissa, said Sam.

Now, when she looked at him again, she saw him through a thick cloud. He saw the blood drain out of her face. Her anger at the treacherous dog lying next to her young enemy increased, she banged her hand nervously on her thigh, and said: Melissa? Melissa's dead. The fact that Melissa had died so many years ago and suddenly she had to say that, embarrassed her immeasurably. Maybe for the first time in years, Melissa's death was so needless and yet painful. She dropped her eyes and saw the shoes that had walked in the fields and forest and the spots and the flickering of the trampled leaves, and she said pensively: Thirty years ago, and then she was scared and said in a voice almost shrieking at itself: What do you mean about Melissa?

I have to pee, said Sam.

She shrugged and yelled furiously at the dog: Come here, Smoky! The dog straightened up, looked at her, wagged its tail, and Sam hit his thigh and the dog clung to him as if it feared for its life and started shaking. Sam kicked it until it whined. She yelled: Why do you kick him? And Sam bent down and kissed it. She hissed furiously: A dog is supposed to guard the house from strangers! What are you here for?

To pee, said Sam.

Not you, him, she said, and she felt her position in the doorway of her house turn into a farce she didn't want to take part in. Sam said: I'm not a stranger and he understands, and then he noticed her sweet wickedness, an orphaned warmth, some old yearning on her face. Now he didn't know if she was a guard in the camp or the NCOs' housekeeper, so he could smile at her and say: Look lady, he won't bite me, he knows who's the master and who's the bitch, where do you pee in this splendid house?

The gentleman talks funny, said the woman. Her anger was more for the dog than for him. Her mouth gaped a little, she had to pluck up a properly shaped humility. Who are you? she asked again. Why . . . But now she also saw him more clearly, and a forgotten memory rose for a moment and extinguished in her, as if a forgotten picture was drawn and she didn't know what the picture was. Now she also looked scared.

Sam said: You've got no choice, don't let me pee in your beautiful yard. They walked inside. A maid in an apron who had just been shedding tears over a bowl of slaughtered onions came running up with her eyes red and dripping. You should have been here before, said the woman in a voice with a threat aimed for later.

I tried, said the maid with extinguished awe.

Trying isn't enough, barked the woman.

Let the dog bark, said Sam, it doesn't suit you, you were born delicate and only later comes life and makes us dogs. Believe me, I'm an expert. When she raised her hand she looked surprised at herself for almost striking him. His charming smile spread over her face. That only increased his dependence on her. Let me pee and then we'll talk about Melissa, he said.

The maid genuflected at the name. He passed through the room, went into the corridor, turned right, and found a toilet.

Afterward, he looked for a towel. The maid who ran after him stood next to the door rubbing her hands on her apron. He went to her and wiped his hands on her apron and went into the living room, whose walls were covered with mounted animal heads. The woman was sitting in a straight-backed chair and looking at him. He felt close to the iron that came from her, all of her solid in a wonderfully shaped posture, he could feel the hatred in her eyes. A pleasant smell of spices crept into the room and was swallowed by a fragrance of roses. The drapery looked more beautiful from this side of the room. The woman could categorize corpses with model precision, he wanted to tell Kramer.

The thoughts were messed up in his mind, his mother acting Ophelia in a room closed with drapes, a smell of spices in a house they lived in for many years.

The dog who was clinging to his leg all the time growled and the mounted animals looked at him with flashing eyes.

Why did you come, she said.

I love her, said Sam. He smiled a smile of condolence and on the piano he could see the faded picture of Melissa in a white dress, a bouquet of flowers in her hand, and behind her a grown-up man holding a cigar in his hand. When she got up the dog growled again.

He knows you?

Dogs know me, said Sam.

But he can't know you, she said and was immediately embarrassed because she knew she had asked the wrong question.

That's love, said Sam. You know how beautiful she was, Melissa?

Her body shook, she dropped her eyes, shook her head and muttered. Why? Why? Why?

Don't know, he said. My name's Sam, I loved her, they took me to the fences. She came to me and said: I'm yours, she didn't even know my name is Sam, I came to ask for her hand and you said she's still dead.

The woman who was shaking got up, very slowly she sought a path between the carpets, the chairs, the easy chairs, the heavy electric lamp standing on an ancient pedestal, above her the stuffed animals watched. He got up and walked behind her. She stood shaking in the corridor. Her hand moved to the telephone. The maid appeared and Sam dismissed her furiously. He went to the woman, kissed the back of her neck, waited for her to hit him and then, when a jet of blood burst from his mouth, he hung up the phone, kissed her hard on the lips, wet her with his blood, and said: No need, I'm going, why do children die in such Paradises? It's not fair.

Maybe I'm dreaming, said the woman, maybe I'm really dreaming, maybe this isn't happening, I'm calling Smoky, come here Smoky, and he doesn't come, maybe it's not happening, maybe I'm dreaming, it was quiet, more than thirty years it was quiet.

I'm sorry, he said. He pushed her into the living room and sat her down on a chair, she buried her face in her hands and waited. She looked like somebody who doesn't know what to wait for anymore.

I don't know you! said Sam. I'm not willing to accept Melissa's death, I absolutely will not accept it.

You're a wicked cruel man, said the woman and stood up, sturdy now. The maid came in and tried to help her mistress get up and he pushed her until both women fell down. The dog rolled around on the rug and waited for somebody to applaud it. Sam broke a buffalo horn and tossed it on the floor. That's all, only slight damage, he said, why not? You'll pay for my visit. He pushed the two women into a little room whose door was open, jumped out the window, and ran. The dog ran after him, jumped over the fence, and went into the grove. He ran along the fields and the grove reappeared. He barged in among the trees and came to a small cemetery. It was dark now. It was barely possible to read the names. He searched for a tombstone with her name and didn't find it. He kissed a tombstone he thought was hers, saw people with flashlights searching for him, nodded at their innocence and said: My dear woman, I have overcome Kramer and Weiss and the German and Ukrainian guards and then the Soviet police and the occupation authorities and the Yugoslavians and the French and the Italians and the Danes, and those fools think they'll catch me with pitiful flashlights. Dogs barked in the distance and he understood their longing for him and barked back at them. The people with the dogs looked at one another and yelled, but the dogs stopped and wouldn't go on. Sam came to the bus stop, waited in the gloom of the thick trees until a bus came, he darted inside, paid, and fell asleep on the seat.

When Lionel asked him where he had been, he said: I went to visit Melissa. She doesn't love you anymore, Secret. Then, he went into his room, locked the door and fell asleep standing up, leaning on the door.

Committee of the Survivors of Hathausen/Division to Celebrate Liberation Day

New York,

Dear Sir (Samuel Lipker):

Attached is the questionnaire we informed you of. Please fill it out and send it to us as soon as possible. Erase what is superfluous.

Full name.

Parents' names.

Are they alive?

Other family members.

Their addresses.

Dates of internment in the camp.

Do you recall what you did? If you had a job, what was it?

Did you live in the blocks? Did you live in the Sonderkommando Services camp?

Detail why you think you survived.

Where did you go after the liberation?

How did you come to the United States?

Do you remember people who were with you in the camp?

Do you remember outstandingly cruel incidents?

Do you have a profession?

A brief history of your life, personal details, memories (if possible), experiences, songs you sang, dances. Do you have plans for the future? Do you remember Frieda Klopfen?

Please send us the form as soon as possible.

Yours,

Most sincerely.

To the Committee of Survivors of Hathausen,

Greetings,

My name is Sam Lipp. Frieda lay under a dog that crushed
her. When they threw me into the fire, they remembered that
I was fourteen years old and took me out of the fire. Then I
chewed bones to understand the sky, which was mostly cloudy.
I and my father live outside the planet earth. Why didn't you
celebrate your entrance into the camp instead of your exit? You
don't interest me and please don't send me any more material.

Samuel Lipker was killed in Hathausen and I do not know
the place where he is buried.

Yours, SS Stürmbahnführer Kramer (Samuel Lipker)

Later on, when he told Lionel of his trip to Melissa's house, Sam was
smiling and Lionel was silent and pensive. He looked at Sam's face, lit a
cigarette, outside it was pouring rain, and Lionel said: How did Mrs. Brooks
look? And Sam said: She asked about you! Lionel laughed. Sam said: They're
sending me letters for a celebration of the liberation, if they call, say I died,
and he left. Lionel came back from his room where he'd help Sam with his
homework. Because he had learned from Ebenezer the craft of remembering, he learned well and fast. He finished high school in a year. At first, they
teased him because of his age, but the other students quickly learned not
to get smart with him. Then, he went to NYU. Rachel said: He'll give you
trouble, and Lionel would answer her: Mother, he's my son!

The stories Lionel wrote weren't bad, but they weren't any better than
the stories he had written before. The sense of defeat was much less bitter than it was. By the time he started writing reviews for *The New York
Times*, Lionel was close to fifty. The editor, who loved his stories that were
printed in little journals and that granted him a certain cachet in marginal
literary circles, asked him to write an article. Then he wrote more articles
and soon after, he became the regular critic for the paper. When he was
afflicted with melancholy visions of his life, Lionel said: Everything is past,
the future is now behind me, the lad I was created a man and the man has
lost the lad, the hopes were disappointed, even if they weren't very big,
average men lead lives of quiet desperation, he quoted Thoreau, I exist,

write, I'm a draftsman, not a creator. To take Sam's lampshade. The number of lampshades in the hackneyed kingdom of the eternal. To make a
poem. My words grope in vain for a story others will write better than me.
Watches Lily, sees the devil in Sam's eyes, and dies for another night. A
year is three hundred sixty-five dogs. Sam Lipp is now twenty-three years
old. Lily sat at home and read dictionaries, vocabularies, and the more
precisely she learned English, the more she thought she forgot her native
tongue. She taught herself with an anger she never imagined was in her to
flee from the language she had grown up in, and she thought that in an
idiomatic and fluent English, and that was how she could forget she once
had parents and the more her children continued not to be born, the more
her roots were erased, until she was forced to think for a long time to answer Sam who asked her the name of her father, who may still have been
a prisoner of the Russians. Her life was a small ghetto protected from an
insult she never felt, but his eyes were a witness to it. One night, when the
snow piled up to the middle of the window and a strong wind blew outside,
Sam came and lay next to Lily. Lionel whispered: Lily, he wants you, very
slowly she turned her face, looked at him, let a tear pearling in her eyes
soak the pillowcase, stretched out her hand, gently stroked Samuel's face,
and Samuel said: You sleep with every filthy Jew, you don't even know
what a gentile prick looks like. He pushed Lionel onto his side, pressed
Lionel's eyes until he roared with pain, Lily felt his body choking her. She
tried to crawl to Lionel, held her hand out to him, but Sam grabbed the
hand, clasped it hard, and when she looked into his eyes she could see the
snow piling up in the windows with eyes that once saw a forest on a hike
with somebody who may have been her father. She laid her hands on his
eyes, shut them, and he stroked her back until she shuddered, but now
Melissa laughed inside her and Lionel, who felt pity for Sam and knew that
tears covered his eyes, talked to her and when she raised her face she saw
Lionel looking at her, the tears remained on his smooth chest, and even
though she wanted him now, she could do nothing but defeat Samuel in
him and her lips were caught in his watch chain, and she was so confused
that even five years later, she could remember that the time was then one
twenty-one in the morning. Samuel flipped her over, lay on her, slipped
the pillow out from under her head so that Lionel's head was now higher
than hers, put the pillow on her face, didn't press, straightened up a little

so he could look at the three of them, and said: I love her, Lionel, but she loves you, don't worry, I'm trying to steal Melissa from you, but she's dead all the time too, and Lionel whispered. That's all right, Sam, and Lily tried to say something, but the pillow over her face didn't let her talk and Sam pounded on the pillow until it dropped off and fell on Lionel's chest as he lay there now, squashed the pillow with his head, and when Lily saw Lionel's face, she clasped Sam and at the same time pushed him off her. The snow kept piling up, Sam hit Lionel's leg to get him away from him, he grasped his father's face with his hand, hugged it hard and Lily thought she was cut because his hand was in her crotch. When she started crying, her face turned red and she touched Lionel pleadingly. She turned over, hugged Samuel. As he was above her, Samuel kissed Lionel on the lips, jumped out of bed, stuck Lionel to Lily, ran to the kitchen, banged his hand on the wall, poured water, brought a glass to the room, poured the water on them, pushed them closer together, and started singing a song a Ukrainian guard had once taught him as he hugged him from behind. Then, the three of them lay on their backs and looked at the snow. The dark was lighted by a streetlamp.

The stories you write, said Sam as if he were continuing a conversation he had started years ago, are still lifes, beautiful and dead. You're too respectable, Lionel, you're not young, your words have no proper story and you're waiting for a story in all the wrong places, and you let every fucking Jew fuck your wife.

Not everyone, said Lionel.

Everyone, Sam repeated.

This is a fascinating city. See how arrogant its snow is, added Samuel. You're searching for humiliation, Lionel, you're selling Samuel Lipker to a German woman. Look at your city, there's no melancholy eaten by moss in it as in the city where Joseph Rayna begat Samuel Lipker on a miserable actress, you measure others' pain with a yardstick. What do your tears know except what they have to glean from a city where everybody passes through like a Cossack in a pogrom? You searched for a son in the wrong place, you dismantle the enemy into elements, produce with your hands—or Lily demonstrates to you—a disaster that was supposed to happen to you and happened to me and her. And without you, Lionel! That yardstick! Grasp. Like loving Lily through me. I read in a book that Paul Klee the artist said that creation is to turn the unseen into the seen. Ebenezer would perform with me in nightclubs. I led him on a rope like a trained monkey. He really was the last survivor of the Jews and they really did all die, they don't know they died, but they died. He recited the words and they thought he was talking about something that once was. They didn't understand that he was talking about what maybe wasn't.

Tape / —

On a Wednesday shrouded in a doughy dust in the air, Sam left the house and walked as if he had some purpose. Lionel and Lily sat and read an article that appeared that day in the *Atlantic*. Lionel sat with his eyes shut and Lily read him his own article. He wasn't smiling and was listening intently. Tired birds were seen dying on branches heavy with dust. He met Riba-Riba at the corner of Thirteenth Street, next to the weaving machine shop. Riba-Riba's neck looked thin, her head was crowned with a splendid mane of hair, and when he told her how beautiful was the back of her neck in the distance, she giggled nervously. At the sight of her smile, he could sense that the end of the story that hadn't yet started wouldn't be especially pleasant, but since he was waiting again for a funeral that hadn't passed, something in him longed for a well-done rite, and Riba-Riba, with the embarrassed and defeated smile, may have been the proper answer to the sight of the birds that weren't birds of gold at all and looked as if they would land in a little while and die from the heavy heat. Riba-Riba said: When I presented the evening of Irish songs at the university, I waited for you, Sam, I waited awfully, and you fell asleep. Sam said: I was tired. When she said she was going to see a matinee performance of a Tennessee Williams play, he told her he'd go with her. He asked her to buy him a ticket for the seat behind her. Since her father owned a nightclub and her mother was a well-known Irish Gypsy, it wasn't hard for her to get tickets. She said: It's awful sexy to sit like that, so he chewed on her ear and kept her from seeing the play. Through her hair, he saw his mother acting on the stage. Outside stood Joseph Rayna with a bouquet of flowers and seeds of Samuel Lipker poured on his eyelashes. The actors were well-trained, they raised their voices in the right places and knew how to structure the pauses precisely. The critics' florid words hanging on the walls of the lobby suddenly began to be possible. But something rebelled in him, and he may have fallen asleep or chewed Riba-Riba's ear again if he hadn't sensed that all those days, all those years, he had wanted to do something those people were doing now on the stage, but not like his mother, or those actors, to do that as Joseph Rayna acting the lover, at the house where his mother acted for the indifferent walls. What he wanted more than anything in the world was to stand there and stage Ebenezer, himself, Weiss, Kramer, Lionel, and Lily. In other words, to stage the world that almost was and only Ebenezer remembered it.

When they went out, it was raining a warm spray. Sam pushed Riba-Riba to the entrance of a dark office building and fucked her standing up. She bit her lips and because she felt both humiliated and blissful, she asked Sam for a cigarette, stuck it in her mouth and acted as if she were in a silent movie. After he snatched the cigarette butt out of her mouth and threw it toward the entrance, they broke apart, she combed her hair, and then they went into a cafeteria. Sam glanced indifferently at the gigantic Camel cigarette belching smoke rings at the news making its way around the old *New York Times* building. Opposite was a gigantic Paramount ad showing Duke Ellington smiling along with Frank Sinatra.

When they went out, the misty rain was still falling. Sam started talking about death as a gesture. She wasn't sure and saw a church altar and Sam raising her up before God with white skin and blue eyes. Sam said: They indulge with embellished words. Try to depict life as if it's possible to resurrect life. Riba-Riba shook with some vague fear and hugged Sam. She said in a voice that was too loud: We started from love standing up and we'll end with a true feeling, and he said: Say "we screwed," and she blushed and said the word and then Sam became serious and kissed her face. Her mouth tasted of mint, toothpaste, and potatoes. They passed by a funeral home and Riba-Riba was afraid to go in with him, but he insisted and they went in.

In the splendid and darkened room lay a well-dressed corpse, painted and made up and even its shoes were polished. Soft, melancholy music with something metallic was heard in the background. A woman dressed in black and enveloped in a delicate black silk scarf raised the hem of the scarf a little and looked at Sam. She didn't look at Riba-Riba and she immediately dropped the scarf. Sam smiled at her sympathetically, but the woman only shook her head with a domesticated sadness and looked at the dead man. A crushed odor of flowers that may also have been artificial rose in his nose. A person in a costume that looked like a blend of an official uniform and a frock coat entered, stood next to the woman, and with profound and gloomy understanding looked at the body. With a hand that almost succeeded in trembling, he brushed two hairs off the dead man's brow and with careful gentleness he brushed the patent leather of his left shoe with a handkerchief he took out of his pocket. The woman, who was still staring at the dead man, whispered something none of them could hear. And then more people in black came into the room and stood next to the woman. One of them wiped a tear from his eye and put the tear in a handkerchief and the handkerchief in a pocket that was apparently reserved for tears. The person standing next to the man with the tear took a scrap of paper out of his overcoat pocket, put on his glasses, and read a poem in a monotonous voice. The poem was written by the deceased before he died, he emphasized sadly. The poem was a trade balance of a small company called A. B. Lin, in Long Island. It said that life is a conglomerate of big joys and little events. The last words of the poem were: "Melina, Melina, go in your Caddy to the sea and see for me the scene of sunset I haven't seen in twenty years." The woman didn't budge. Sam smiled but the man didn't smile back. They looked at Sam and Riba-Riba and tried to recall what side of the family they belonged to.

Tape / —

As far as I know (I'm reciting now), Sam Lipp went back to the theater he had been sunk in forever and didn't know it, so maybe the words "went back" are superfluous, like the word "deceased" mentioned above.

Tape / —

From a letter written by the prisoner (Number 3321/A) Kramer, to the PEN association of writers in the city of Cologne, a few weeks before he was turned over to the Polish authorities:

> The letter and the journal I gave to your distinguished society, but as far as I understand, it used them adversely. Since they have not yet hanged (or shot) me, I am permitted to express my amazement that the writers of our nation are capable of distorting things like that and betraying the belief of a commander who

served our homeland loyally. And as for Samuel Lipker, whom
you ask about, I must say that when he associated in the camp
with Ebenezer, I knew that his bestiality would someday be
translated into troubles for us. Nevertheless, he remains alive.
There was no decision on the matter. I remember Samuel once
told me: Commander, maybe all of us betray something more
sublime than we are, and judging should be a blissful act, right?
Those were words on the tip of my tongue. I must state that if
Samuel Lipker does something in his life he will appeal to the
dark alleys of our great spirit, and not like a great many of you, he
will not be afraid to ask why he betrayed our nation with his
Führer, will not be afraid to touch what the Americans call in
weather reports "the eye of the hurricane."

Tape / —

Lily sits and combs her hair while Sam looks at her trying to understand.
The beauty of her movements, holding the comb in the hair, the head bent
above and behind to right or left, fill him with a dim sense of joy he never
knew before.
Sam and Riba-Riba at the Easter service in church. The sorcerer is about
to don garments of authority, his face is white and pale. He dons a gigantic hat that looks like a miniature church building. With his terrifying magic
the sorcerer stops a great erosion of force that becomes thin and pleasant.
The pulpit is high and gilded. Music bursts from all sides of the church,
people in their best clothes, looking like they're embalmed, kneel at the
altar of colored lights and a smell of incense rises into the air. Sam thinks
that a temple like that can imprison divinity, speak in its name, tame it,
and at the same time not let it in. The words whispered there are important and unimportant at the same time. The service isn't about life, but
death. He thinks of the synagogue where he'd spent Yom Kippur and Rosh
Hashanah eve in his childhood, its low ceiling, the poor God with a white
beard sitting in the locked Ark with a few meager ornaments, and facing Him
men wrapped in prayer shawls and a charred smell of tobacco rising from
them. Sam stands at the mysterious service held in the pulpit and thinks
that God has a place only through the mask, since only there is He truly
strong and false. The confessionals furnish feelings with institutionalization

that turns into a linguistic inquisition, a rule of power and force for a gossipy human mumbling, and like that, an ancient and savage Torah can become noble, full of splendor and so sexy. Sam didn't really know how close that notion of his was to the opinion of SS Stürmbahnführer Kramer, to whom he once bowed whenever he saw him passing by.

One day, after Lily wrote two hundred words on his body starting with the letter A and drank fine rosé wine that had been chilled in the refrigerator before she went to abort a German child at an abortion farm in the mountains of Pennsylvania (at that time Lionel was sitting offended with himself and imprisoned in guilt feelings and trying to write a story while wearing new house slippers he claimed sharpened his ability to think and Sam was trying to write for himself the nightmares of the past night), Sam looked at Lionel and said to him: Statistics, Lionel, write statistics in crappy rhymes! Make a ceremony. See a church. See a sorcerer with words in Latin. And Lionel said: She went to abort a son, Sam, and Sam said: Blessed be the just Judge, and went to Riba-Riba. She wanted to take him to the village, to her parents' house, to lie with him on the soft green lawn, introduce him to the cows and horses of her childhood, but he wanted to celebrate mysterious ceremonies and understand to whom the disaster truly happened. He introduced Riba-Riba to a fellow and told him, with premeditation (because he knew that the fellow was in love with Riba-Riba and would tell her what he would tell him) about their sex life and he did tell her. And then, he told Lily with a savage laugh, she was offended and phoned, and I hung up. She went with that Trevor and lay with him on the damp lawn near her stinking horses and cows and they got wet and came to the little church where a bored priest married them, and after that Sam tried to rape Lily in the kitchen and she said: They took a child out of me, Sam, don't touch me, and he slapped himself instead of slapping her.

Tape / —

Question: Have you ever known a person named Sam Lipp?
Ebenezer Schneerson: No.
Question: Where did Samuel Lipker disappear?
Ebenezer: He went for a moment and disappeared . . .
Question: Did Samuel Lipker have any connection with the theater?

Ebenezer: I was his puppet. He took money. He's also my son.

Question: What year are we living in?

Ebenezer: The clocks and calendars were set by Samuel. He doesn't come now. I need him.

Question: Thank you.

Tape / —

At night he'd wander around the city, to hear jazz at Bop City, Minton Playhouse, Birdland. Sam loved the organized improvisation, the celebratory sadness they made from New Orleans funeral music. He'd sit in a little bar on Eighth Avenue and order drinks for girls who would giggle at the sight of his eyes. "Awful eyes," one woman called him. Once he sat next to a girl with unstylish gray eyes, who reeked of perfume. The short hair no longer symbolized any regret and was deliberately miserable, cheap dye poured from it. When they drank, she mixed whiskey with water. Then they went to a small hotel, and when he fell asleep after she took pity on him and he called her: Crystal Heart, and she told him he was a darling wolf, she stole his money. The gonorrhea started two days later. The doctor gave him penicillin injections and then he went to see a play in the Village and fell asleep. On the fourth evening, he passed by the bar and saw her. He went to Washington Depot, came to the gate of the house, and the dog ran to him wagging its tail. He yelled: I love Melissa. Through the window Mrs. Brooks saw him and ran to the telephone, but he yelled: I've got American gonorrhea now! He kicked the dog and ran to the boulevard, where rain was falling on the thick treetops and didn't get to the lush ground full of the moisture of crushed leaves. He lay on the edge of a small field, between pines and oaks, and thought of why he had kicked the dog. He went into the forest and yelled: Melissa, Melissa, until he became hoarse and then he kissed a cow lying on the ground chewing. A person passing by said: Cows lying is a sign of rain. Sam wondered if the cows also knew that there really had been rain. He took the bus back to the city, and even though he was soaked to the skin, he fell asleep. When he returned to the bar to look for Crystal Heart, he was thrown out by the bartender in an apron, who had little eyes with a cold metallic glint in them. At dawn, he lay in wait for the bartender near the parking lot Mr. Blau had recently bought to build the biggest store for colored shirts in the eastern United

States. He knocked down the bartender, wrapped him in a bag, and beat him until he heard his bones grow faint. Sam whispered to him: I wasn't born yesterday!

The man groaned but nobody heard. Later, the police found him. The cops who got a weekly payment happened to be at a crash course in Virginia and the substitute captain didn't want to reorganize the area. The bar was closed despite the damage to the police car and over the protest of the sergeant, who got forty dollars a month and came back from Virginia to get his take. Sam deigned to testify in court. He had received threats by phone and he wrote down every word that was said and told Lionel he was studying theater from life instead of vice versa, and Lionel looked at him and recalled how he fell asleep at the beautiful play they saw in the Village, tried to understand, but was tired and fell asleep. When they tried to stab him and missed—he didn't retract his complaint, even when a policeman who came back from the crash course tried to persuade him not to testify. After the sentence was declared, he felt relief, but also abhorrence. He looked cheerfully at Crystal Heart and at the kicked bartender. There were no marks on the bartender. Sam didn't admit to any attack. They looked at him with cold, flashing hatred, but he said: You're terrific. Everything exploded then, everything he had kept inside from the day he had left the camp was now a ring of suffocation. The play he went to see with Riba-Riba opened the dam. Now he didn't know when he was dreaming and when he was daydreaming and all the time the SS men were beating him and he was shrieking, No! No! And he saw his mother naked and his father expecting him with a diamond in his rectum. Everything was woven in his mind with dark and humiliating ceremonies carried out on lighted stages.

Tape / —

> Dear Lionel,
>
> For some years now, I've been following your son. You asked me to help him, you told me to try to advise, you're a senior member of the university, you said, and I did keep my word. Sometimes it's hard for me to understand, Sam's past is a sealed chapter for me, while you refuse to tell me. When he dropped out of regular school and registered for the theater department, I was afraid, but his talent is impressive, and I thought to my-

self: Well, you also maintained that he should do whatever he
wanted. But when day after day he wandered around cemeteries and seduced women to come with him to their houses and
performed plays for them that later damaged them emotionally,
I thought I should do something, but I didn't know how. What
Sam could say in his defense in the case of that woman, Mrs. G.,
which you yourself were involved in: "She put on a striptease
for me, because she thought men are aroused by black panties,
and afterward because she thought I had a sexual disease—I
told her about the gonorrhea I picked up—I kissed a boot and
acted for her how I'd fuck its mate. And then she laughed,
what's she complaining about all of a sudden?" It was hard for
me to explain to him, the anger in him is incomprehensible to
me. What attracts him is the human sewer, or magic. I don't
understand what all that has to do with theater. In my opinion,
he's playing with fire and that fire is buried inside him. He told
me that on one of his visits to the cemeteries, a woman saw
him, took him to her room, undid his trousers (these are his
words), and when he penetrated her, he fell asleep. When he
woke up, he said, she was naked and smoking a cigar. He said
he turned on the radio. I'm reconstructing the details that coa-
lesce into a picture you should be aware of. He said he com-
bines tidbits in his mind like a man named Ebenezer did.
Women in cemeteries, religious ceremonies, music he hears in
jazz clubs—all that, he said, is intertwined, into one equation.
And he can, he told me, recall who a disaster truly happened to.
What disaster, Lionel? When he left the theater department
and joined a theater that traveled throughout the state, you told
me to persuade him not to go, but you know how much I tried
and the result, nil! What I do know is that instead of studying
theater in our department, one of the best in the United States,
he worked in lighting, sets, as a stagehand, and learned to sew
shrouds (his words) and to be a stage manager you claimed then
that I should persuade him to work in what he really wanted to
do and not in stage management of an amateur theater that
traveled from one small town to another, but I didn't succeed.

Look Lionel, Sam recently came back. He came back to the department and I accepted him. What you may not know is that he doesn't study but is preparing a play with three actors and has even managed to persuade me to help him. I'm writing to you because if there are complaints about my behavior, know that I tried, but he has some charm that compels you (me) to give in to him; and so it happened, Lionel, that people who studied four years in the department, successfully finished and did all their assignments, are waiting to put on their play while Sam, who didn't study in a regular way, who hit a teacher, who slept with, or in the words of one witness, raped two women directors we brought to the department, is producing a play and I, I am its sponsor. And as for the rest—

Yours . . .

After Sam's premiere performance, there on the stage covered with thousands of pairs of shoes while a gigantic heart pounded metallically and three actors fought some war against themselves, Rachel Blau decided to reveal to her son who Sam Lipp was and who Lionel's father was. Her husband told her: Why is that so important? I'll take care of everybody and if Sam wants theater and Lionel wants to write stories, let them. Rachel didn't argue with him. She took the subway because she didn't know how to drive and didn't want to waste money on a taxi. When she came out of the station, she fainted. People who from now on would look alike to her took her to a nearby hospital. Nuns dressed in white laid her in a narrow bed, above her hung a big crucifix and below burst the melancholy cold sound of the nuns' singing. When Lionel came, she smiled at him and thought he was all the people she had seen before. She was transferred to Mount Sinai Hospital but her condition didn't improve. Lily took Lionel's hand and then touched Rachel. Rachel didn't know who they were anymore. She turned to Sam and spoke Polish. She muttered and suddenly fell silent. Her face contorted and Sam told her in Polish: Regards to Rebecca Secret Charity. Lily said: She'll recover, but everybody knew she wouldn't.

A week later, the play of the shoes closed and the reviews came in. Sam listened and was silent. Then he said: The play was no good, but I know what I want and what I want will take time, but it will be better. He came home and saw Lionel and Lily sitting with dictionaries in their hands and Lily was editing an article for Lionel for *The New York Times*. Sam looked at them and glanced again at a story that Lionel published in *Harper's*, and said: I'm a wretched creature, Lionel, a creature others die for, Ebenezer recites them, I'm not an expert in writing stories, in your articles you're wise and smart, so you succeed, but the heroes in your stories aren't wise like you, and that's not good.

The next day, Lily found a letter. Sam had sent the letter with a dog he rented in a shop of postal dogs. The dog knocked on the door and Lily opened it. There was also a bill and she paid it, patted the dog, and it wagged its tail and left. The money was in its mouth. The letter said:

> Lionel, here's a list of materials to weave your poems; twenty-one thousand synagogue curtains, seventeen tons of brown and black hair, six tons of blond hair, two tons of silver and gold teeth, eight million pairs of shoes, one million six hundred thousand pairs of earrings, two million three hundred thousand silver candlesticks, two million little Havdalah towers of silver and other metals. Two tons of diamonds, thousands of kilometers of train travel, coal for the trains, track repairs, employment of train workers. Thousands of kilometers of barbed wire fence and coils, thousands of tons of gas, bullets, spades for burial, crematoria, one million five hundred thousand used beds, factories, shops, research institutes, fur hats, granite hats, felt hats, cloth hats, wool hats. Dental crowns, phosphate from bones, fat for soap, cooking ovens fit for use, cars! Silver, dollars, marks, zlotys, francs—together, more than three billion dollars, machines, presses, stockings, overcoats, carpets, works of art, luxuries, etc. . . .

> I hired the dog who brings this letter from a shop on Fourteenth Street because he looks like Ebenezer. Calculate the burials, the killings, the fear, the frozen feet, the time wasted rewriting and writing every execution, spying, axes, chamber pots. Does the energy really get lost, Lionel, if all that is later turned into a book of tears hidden by Jews in cellars?

Tape / —

The Lament for the Death of the Jews was written over a year. Lionel revised, corrected, rewrote, and then, when it snowed nonstop for three straight days, the first chapter of the *Lament* was published in *The New York Times*. It was based on statistics. Reactions were immediate and excited. By the time the snow melted, Lionel had been interviewed on television and had signed a contract with Harper and Row. A few days before Christmas, Sam brought home a fir tree he bought on the street. Lionel, who was concluding a phone conversation with his new agent, said: Why on earth a tree, Sam? Got to be, said Sam, I'm fed up with cemeteries. I searched for life in zoos and I studied beautiful and natural death in the Museum of Natural History, I know how living creatures turn all dread and hostility into ceremony. A Christmas tree is also a ceremony. They hate together, love together, forgive together, kill together. Lily said: A beautiful tree, Lionel, and everybody has trees.

Not me, said Lionel. Rachel is still dying in the hospital. Saul Blau would bring shirts, and in pain at his wife's condition, he started in his mind's eye to dress his hungry children in all the shirts their parents, may they rest in Paradise, didn't have. Sam already had seven hundred sixty-seven shirts and didn't wear even one of them.

In London, the section that appeared in New York was published. Criticism was excited there, too. Dead Jews are excellent material for artistic success, says Sam, the death of a Jew works today, and Lionel who had turned into a success story, written up in *Time*, felt crushed, borrowed from Sam, incomprehensible to himself, humiliated.

Lionel didn't think all that was happening to him, he said: Jesus was a tremendous success story and he started believing that things were again happening to Sam, and Sam—dammit—won't put up a fir tree in my room.

Sam came out of the subway station. In his hand he held the hand of a tall girl. Her name was Licinda. Once they had studied acting together. When they acted an improvised piece and he called her Melissa, he was filled with a wave of warmth he had never felt, and then he mocked her and said how tall and shrewd she was. Maybe that's love, Licinda said then and he laughed. Licinda had long hair as smooth as silk. It was light brown and looked like a cascade. A rather nervous laugh was sketched on her open face by tormented nerves. Sam and Licinda walked in the dirty melting snow and bought wine and flowers. Loaded with shopping bags, they went down the steps and entered the house. Lily said: Sam brought a girlfriend with flowers and wine. Lionel saw the shy but aggressive laugh on Licinda's face and wanted to hug her as an old acquaintance. Lily took off Licinda's wet coat and gave her some hot wine and together they stood in front of the fireplace. Big logs wisped thin smoke and spread a pleasant warmth in the room, and Sam asked Licinda to help him. Lionel sat down in the brown easy chair, put on the new eyeglasses he had started using a few months earlier and wasn't yet used to, and Lily asked, What are you doing, and Sam said: Trimming the tree for Santa, Lionel. Lionel said: That's stupid, and Lily said: Lionel, your son wants a fir tree so let there be a tree, and Lionel said: He's a grown-up now, my sons die in private hospitals in Pennsylvania and don't put up fir trees in my apartments. They didn't respond, even though they saw Lily turn pale but recover immediately and they stood the tree in a box of sand, reinforced it, Licinda took out the ornaments that Sam had bought before and the chain of small lights she had hidden in her purse. Lionel asked: What exactly is your full name? And she said, My full name, Mr. Grumpy, is Licinda Eliot Hayden. Lionel said: His grandmother is dying and he puts up a fir tree! Licinda tried to help Lily put up water and make coffee, but Lionel got up from his easy chair, took a bottle of scotch out of the chest, poured drinks, added ice, and gave one to Licinda. She understands that better than coffee, he said angrily. Sam hung the chain of lights and plugged it in. For a moment the lights shorted out. They saw themselves as demons in the light of the red stumps of wood blazing in the fireplace. Sam fixed the broken light, fixed the short, and a pleasant light spread in the room. Lily went to Sam and gave him a cup of black coffee. He stood next to the tree he was trimming, drank the coffee as Lionel, Lily, and Licinda drank scotch and turned on the radio. Christmas songs were playing on the radio. He hummed the songs to himself, and Lionel said: Lily, light Hanukkah candles. Lily said: Not me, and not you either. I'm just a wasted father, said Lionel, I didn't teach you anything. Sam laughed and said: What I've forgotten you won't have time to learn. And then he added: You're too sentimental, Lionel. You're able to yearn for things that never were. I'll tell a story: A man married off his son to a woman. He made a banquet for his friends and

when they had eaten, he said to his son, Go up to the attic and bring us
wine from the barrel that's kept there. The son went up to the attic,
went to the barrel, was bitten by a snake, and died. The father waited
and the son didn't come down. The guests ate and the father went up and
saw his son thrown dead between the barrels. He waited until the guests
had eaten and drunk and finished reciting the blessing, and he said to them,
Gentlemen, you didn't come to recite the blessing of the bridegrooms today,
but the blessing of mourners. Not to bring my son to the wedding canopy
did you come, but to put him in the grave.

Lily said: That's not Sam's voice, that's Ebenezer's voice. Licinda, who
didn't want to understand and was frightened, said feverishly: What difference does that make? And Sam said: Christmas or Hanukkah, the main
thing is that we're happy because I found myself a nice and wonderful
woman and so cruel that her name is Licinda Eliot Hayden.

Licinda went to Sam, kissed him on the mouth, and said: It seems I love
this man, and then she sat down in a chair, stretched her legs to the fire,
and let the warmth enter into her until she felt the warmth suffocating her
crotch and she started weeping. Sam asked her why she was weeping and
she didn't answer, waited until the tears dried, and then asked if it really
was allowed to sing Christmas carols in this house. Lionel said, No, but
Sam said, Of course, and started to sing himself. Lily softly hummed "The
Star of Bethlehem" and Licinda tried to sing but couldn't, because the
tears moved from her face to her throat and Lionel, who wanted to lecture
to her about the history of the Jewish people, decided to give up, shut his
eyes and sank into a doze of weariness, which he later claimed was a characteristic result of his advanced age. Sam said: Safer to sing the songs of
the winners, Lionel! But Lionel was already asleep, and Lily said: What the
losers never understand is that there really aren't any winners in the world
. . . And Sam looked at her, put on his coat and went out. Licinda watched
him go, and Lionel who woke up saw the door shut, and said: Don't pay
attention to every word he says, and he fell asleep again, but Lily said:
Listen to him, he knows something none of your friends knows. Licinda
shut her eyes, licked the little bit of whiskey still stuck to her lips, held her
hand out, and Lionel, who opened his eyes again, held out a tired and shaking hand and poured her another drink. She poured the whiskey into the
fire and brought her hand back to gesture a request.

No, no whiskey, she said and covered the mouth of the glass with her other hand. Lily went to the bedroom and came back from there in a white dress. Her hair was disheveled now. Sam, who came back with two bottles of wine, saw two angels standing next to the fireplace. He uncorked one bottle, poured into Licinda's empty glass, and also poured for himself, and after they drank, he said: Blessed art Thou O Lord our God King of the Universe who commanded us to light a Christmas tree, amen.

And then, when Licinda sat down, he ordered her to stand up, his voice was metallic and coarse. Lionel poured himself another glass of whiskey, this time without ice, and drank it without putting the glass down until he turned pale. Church bells were heard in the distance and Licinda started humming "Silent Night." Sam hugged Lily, put out the colored lights, and said: Lionel, sing something. Lionel asked: Sing what? His voice sounded of blood with an edge of whiskey. A song of thanksgiving to the god of Licinda and Lily, said Sam. Lionel said: I'm too drunk, and he fell into the easy chair. Sam said: Too bad I don't have nails. Lionel opened his eyes, took off his glasses, and looked at Lily. His face was impassive; Licinda looked drunk. Sam turned off the light again and plugged in the colored lights, Lily glowed against the dark tree. The branch moved, the electric lights went off and on, and Sam said: We're celebrating today one thousand nine hundred sixty-two years of His birth. Licinda tried to applaud, Lionel wanted to get up, and when he did, he slapped Sam's face, but Sam didn't react. Licinda said: That's beautiful, God! That's beautiful . . .

Advertising jingles were played on the radio. Lily released her hands from the tree, and Sam said: Two demonesses, he laughed and was sad at the same time. Lionel suddenly looked sad and gnarled. Sam said. The hangwomen look beautiful in the home of the hanged. Else Koch had a dog, his name was Man. Lionel, who muttered vague words, looked at the two women.

Licinda said: I met Sam when he did the play with the shoes and I'm scared . . . Lily said: Welcome to the home of the urban hangwomen. For the sake of argument, I'm Else Koch and you're the woman named Frieda with a white band on your arm trampled to death by a gigantic dog . . .

Two hours after the birth of their messiah, when heavy snow started falling in the window, Licinda fell asleep in her chair. Lily stood fascinated at the tree and her eyes measured its beauty unlike the snores of Lionel, who firmly refused to admit that now that he had become a well-known poet, he started snoring. The light goes on and off. Sam pees sitting down on the toilet and forgets to get up, and then begins the event that Sam later called "the four lost years." None of them remembered exactly how it happened or what caused the years to disappear, but four years passed. Life flowed on the side, as if on another planet, Lionel published more and more chapters of the gigantic poem (seven hundred seventy-five pages) about the death of the Jews, Licinda came and went, there were months when she was apparently not there and Sam missed her or perhaps didn't, none of them remembered exactly. And then she came back and maybe she really wept as it seemed later. Sam hugged or hit her that time she remembered extremely unclearly as the day she broke the glass where Lionel collected the tears of angels. He was drunk and slept hugging the scrap of cloth of Sam's mother's dress and Sam was watching him. Other events took place: international or national, elections, one president fell and another was elected, thieves were arrested and one murderer drank the blood of his victim, the newspapers with Lionel's articles or articles about his poems were published regularly, none of them filed the oblivion precisely. Somebody, maybe Lily, said: Maybe we invented a machine of oblivion, but then they forgot they said that. A fortune teller Licinda may really have visited said: You're in love with a shadow; the man you live with doesn't exist, or he lives far away from here and Licinda was scared and ran away from the fortune teller's dark house and Sam staged plays, chose a group of actors and somehow, along with oblivion, as if in a dream everybody dreams together, united a troupe of actors, an auditorium was found at a university, they worked on the body, soul, and dialect of actors, Lily managed the house and the lives of Licinda, Sam, and Lionel, discovered in dictionaries words that were also forgotten, Sam was so immersed in forgetting that he once spoke for a long time in Yiddish with Licinda, and after years when the invention of time stirred ancient echoes in her, Licinda said: That's funny, Sam, and she started dreaming about people she had never known and who maybe really were her forefathers. The invention of extinct time wasn't a secret. An important poet claimed in an interview he granted one of the newspapers that Sam Lipp dictates his poems to Lionel from documented dreams filed by a Jewish magician who learned nine million words by heart and would recite them in seedy nightclubs.

Near the end of the long period of forgetting, Sam staged a play for two actors, closed the play because the words written by the playwright bored him. He wanted the Bronya the Beautiful to hold an apple in her mouth, he wanted to see his mother in the empty room, and he wanted Ebenezer, the camp, Kramer, the smell of bodies, he wanted to create a world nobody still believed ever existed. Licinda, who had long ago forgotten, stopped asking herself if she was in love with Sam and accepted her life with him as natural and started feeling children in her womb and was afraid of green-yellow eyes. She taught Sam quiet ceremonies of love, restrained lust, softness, and said: If I'm four years older it means they passed. Sam said: Ebenezer assigned me to be a witness, but how do you witness? Testimony has to be lies and by that to describe truth. The first time he produced Lionel's *Lament for the Death of the Jews* (an excerpt of the second cycle), the play was harshly criticized. He read the reviews calmly and said they were surely right, but he was more right. He taught his actors to be animals, to steal, to devour one another, to survive. They crawled and licked and hit one another, fought and learned to speak out of need and not desire. And Licinda sat in Sam's studio and took care of the wounded and offended actors, brought coffee and beer, mended, organized, supplied every detail, for long hours she talked with Lily, and at night she'd let loose.

Sam taught his actors and himself to act Darwin's theory of evolution, and started supporting them from the money Saul Blau would bring him from the shirts, five percent of their income belonged to him and he didn't know why. Rachel died alone quietly in a room full of flowers in a private hospital for incurables, and even at the time of her death, she didn't know who was who and didn't know that Sam Lipp wasn't Lionel and Lionel wasn't Joseph and Saul Blau was her husband. She smiled, shut her eyes, and from so much sadness and weariness she forgot to open them.

At his mother's funeral, Lionel stood and tried to remember his youth, and suddenly he grasped that all he had left were Samuel and Lily. He talked about Samuel's plays, and Lily said: He's not doing theater, he's creating the Fourth Reich! Then he put in a new door and the carpenter, who remembered Sam from the camp, said: Where's Ebenezer? And Samuel said: He died and I died too. The carpenter who remembered how Samuel used to bring him a slice of bread from the kitchen of the Sonderkommando, said: You know what's really awful? That we are alive. Lionel wrote a poem about that. The poem constituted a kind of end to the four extinct years. Critics started talking about Samuel's plays. His new theater evoked strong and contradictory reactions on both sides. At his birthday party, Sam sang a jolly song in Yiddish to the daughter of one of the actresses. Six of the actors could have been the baby's father and Samuel sang the song and started weeping. They saw the tears and Licinda ran away. And thus ended some camp with barbed wire fences, where they acted and dogs were sicced on them and he stood and whipped himself. In the morning when he got up, his leg was broken. The doctor couldn't explain the meaning of the phenomenon and put a cast on the leg. Samuel went to Licinda's parents, played chess with them, and taught them how to cheat at cards. In the small town in upstate New York he learned the annals of Licinda and connected her to the parents of his parents. And thus Licinda started having nightmares about the parents and grandparents Samuel knew from other places.

Among the salvations Licinda's grandfathers sought were salvations like the ones his parents' parents sought. And thus Samuel came to the story of Joseph de la Rayna and started adapting it for the theater. He told Licinda: You're my great love, you'll be what you always were, you'll be Frieda and Lilith. A German author wrote to Sam and Sam answered him. He wrote: I know who I am and who my father is and who Lionel's father is. Next time you'll be Weiss, but I'll be Kramer. Lily said: He's creating the Fourth Reich!

Tape / —

I've been talking for a few days now. Quoting. I didn't register the number of the tapes. Registered on the boxes. I'm tired. Are you a doctor, sir? Is it true that I masturbate into tapes? An unpleasant word for the first son of a settlement in the Land of Israel. Who lives in me and I don't live in him? You wanted to cure me, you make me talk, don't remember. Who taught me to hypnotize myself? The light is dimming, love that dream, the window, the ceiling, the gushing words, what else is left. The walls will fall. The treachery of mother, Joseph Rayna and Samuel. A garden is watered by Teacher Henkin. A dead son he raised. Boaz came. Said he was my son. Who's my son? I'm a pen that wrote a story, a story wrote a pen. They write about me, not worth a word. A tired carpenter of boxes for whores of SS

men. Bad climate. One day a heat wave and then rain. Dana was soft as a
caress. Mr. Klomin, friendly and lost. Mother? Her hatred. Walking to Marar
to beat an Arab. Maybe I killed him. They said I said.

> *At the hems of a shepherd's cloak*
> *I found a lover*
> *Haughty near a stream near a stream,*
> *A bird passed by a dream*
> *The song a feather above*
> *Is that love? Is that love?*
> *Is that a song I remember?*
> *Is this me?*
> *Is it me speaking?*
> *Who's speaking?*
> *End.*

My friend,

I attach here a report of Boaz Schneerson's lawyer. I hope
you'll be interested in it. Incidentally, yesterday Ebenezer appeared at my house. He was wearing the kind of white suit they
used to wear in Tel Aviv in the twenties. He knocked on the
door and in his hand he held a bouquet of flowers, red chrysanthemums. I opened the door and he held the bouquet of chrysanthemums out to me and said he had come to wish me happy
birthday. I told him, What's this, and he said: Isn't today your
birthday? I thought a little and said: Right, and Hasha Masha
and I had forgotten. I invited him in, he entered, sat on the
sofa, and was silent. Then he got up, took a little tool out of the
pocket of his white coat, and asked permission to fix our cabinet. Hasha Masha, who had come into the room a few minutes
before, said: What's this? Why? He said: That's what I can do
when I don't have my words, I've got information for the wood.
Your cupboards and cabinets are dying, Henkin. He fixed the
cabinet and then the easy chair and the cupboard and the chest.
He went to his house and came back with a case full of bottles
of lacquer in various shades and brushes and sandpaper and he

smeared, filed, and smeared again. I loved to see him at his craft. He worked for many hours and stopped only once to drink a cup of tea that Hasha Masha gave him. This morning he returned to my house and looked at his work, fixed here and there and then I saw a smile spread over his lips. I said, Ebenezer, who knew wood in its distress, and he said, Nonsense, that's not what was, today it's nothing, and he left.

Yours, Obadiah Henkin

And here is the report.

To: The Assessing Official

For the Department of Investigations, Misgar Street 3, Tel Aviv.

In re: Income tax file of S.L.A. Company (Boaz Schneerson) No. 34/4654/8

From: Attorney Gideon (Janusz) Kramer, Ben-Yehuda Street 128, Tel Aviv.

(S.L.A. Inc.) Director: Boaz Schneerson, Tel Aviv.

Dear Mr. Mahluf,

As you know, my client is employed by the paratroopers of the Israeli Defense Force, heroes of the underground, saints of the Holocaust and ghetto fighters. My client's assistance to the bereaved families is widely known (See Appendix 1—letter from the branch of mourning—Ministry of Defense, letter from the branch of widows and orphans and letter from the branch of the bereaved). From 1952 until today, inclusive, the company (S.L.A.) has helped publish hundreds of memorial books. The company gathered material, helped directly or indirectly to publish other memorial books, helped establish district, local, brigade, family, and regimental memorials, initiated and established memorial barbed wire for Holocaust and heroism (including memorials), took care to locate, establish, maintain, populate, and decorate dozens of memorial rooms in public institutions, together with the Memorial to Sons it established meeting and unity houses, put up memorial plaques in schools, kindergartens, universities, and along with construction and repair companies (see appendices 2, 3, and 4) advised and assisted in establishing memorial monuments, signs of battles (including living reenactments of battles), public parks to the memory of the fallen and missing, and libraries in the name of those who fell. The S.L.A. company organized memorial conferences of brigades, battalions, the underground, official (132) district (245) military (334) ceremonies, and as aforementioned established the society of thirty-one (31) various memorials in various locations in Israel to commemorate the Holocaust and heroism. The company organized sixty-four assemblies and conferences to commemorate the fallen with subjects set in advance by the company in close and active cooperation with the Ministry of Defense, the (Israel Defense Forces) IDF, Yad Vashem, the Philharmonic Orchestra, Beit Berl, Beit Ze'ev Jabotinsky, and others.

In sum, those conferences (mentioned at the end), less the number of closed conferences of the Intelligence Institute—number two hundred twenty-one.

In Appendices 6–10, you will find the names of hundreds of lecturers, paid consultants, payment for flag-raising, renovation, washing and maintaining memorials, care of tombstones, parking arrangements, payment for the Composers' and Authors' Association, orchestras and choirs, announcers, speakers, eulogists, poets paid royalties and/or one-time grants by the Company.

The Company also collects objects left on various battlefields, purchases objects that fell into unreliable hands, locates pieces of clothing, accessories, personal effects all over Israel.

Ever since listing for income tax purposes began, nine hundred fifty thousand kilometers of travel were listed. As for the value of the cars and jeeps, see Appendix 8a, which deals with the problem of attrition of cars and jeeps on battlefields and in the desert, and landmine insurance. The value of the insurance, amortization, small construction of barbed wire fences moved from their places—and in that matter, also see the judgment of the district judge in Jerusalem, A. Jacoby, in District Court Case 6/678 1961.

To calculate the correct value, it is necessary to add eighty-one flights to Eilat and Sinai (for the aforementioned purposes), twenty-four trips abroad (financing activities of commemoration and fund-raising in Denmark, Germany, England, Holland, the US, South Africa, etc.), for contribution, consultation, commemoration, demarcation, and investigation.

Between 1952 and 1972, the Company employed for payment forty-six sculptors, two hundred craftsmen (carpenters, tinsmiths, ironworkers, painters, speakers, cantors, burial society, flagmakers, artists, graphic designers, chauffeurs, researchers, interviewers, tape recorders, maintenance workers, etc.).

A consultant from the Bergen-Belsen Society was employed by the company for two years at full payment and there were also royalties for printed material—all that in the sum of one hundred thousand dollars. Maintenance—two hundred fifty thousand pounds. Memorial for the Holocaust cost a sum impossible to detail here. The average sum for a reasonable calculation is one hundred thousand dollars, but the final sum has not yet been set.

Until '62, and in general, many documents are missing. The Company was then the private business of Boaz Schneerson and was not listed properly according to corporate law, but it paid its taxes as a private person. The sum of taxes was calculated and the difference was paid afterward according to a judgment (see Appendix 11).

Exchange of foreign currency was done according to the usual rates. Nontaxable contributions were calculated separately, they are listed in Appendix 12.

There were problems of publicity. The statue by Tamarin, who specialized in various trends of commemoration, constituted a problem in itself that is illustrative of all the problems. The great nuances of artists like Tamarin pose an especially difficult challenge to an attorney trying to prepare a report like this. There are memorials whose purpose is no longer known. Tamarin's fame grew because of the memorials and his fee also rose, because some of the agreements with the committees of parents and ad hoc committees were made prior to that. Cataloguing fame in the context of the fervor of those concerned with the issue casts doubt on a proper investigation of the expenses. Sometimes the date of concluding the memorials is so important they no longer calculate the signed contract and pay whatever comes to hand, and then S.L.A. has to bear financial responsibility, while its taxes are set according to contracts and memoranda of agreement, or receipts whose evidence is contradictory. There are memorials that were paid for, even though they were not erected because of stubbornness, or a public scandal. Merely dismantling memorials cost the Company about three hundred thousand pounds, moving memorials from place to place cost a great deal (see Appendix 16). Shifting the border, correcting mistakes, all that was not brought into the first account, and now has to be corrected.

Clearing rubble cost a fortune, but the tax is not valid in that matter, since the tax law does not take account of dangers of fire, war, etc. Payment to the army for burned tanks for memorials is calculated according to a price list that does not correspond with reality. In the case of operas of grief, bereavement, and plays of mourning, there is no precedent in the income tax legislation, while the value-added tax is high. Memorial conferences of underground organizations or regiments of the War of Independence are calculated differently from conferences of existing regiments that the IDF still refers to by name.

I want to mention a few numbers as an example of what is written in Appendices 17 and 18. Five hundred forty-five pamphlets for schools were printed and distributed by the S.L.A. Company without cooperation with other bodies. Pamphlets for kindergartens (544); songbooks for youth (134); pamphlets for preparing assemblies in grammar schools (524); pamphlets for junior high schools and vocational high schools were printed in hundreds of thousands of copies. Pamphlets such as "What to Sing on ____," "How to Arrange Flowers at the Ceremony of ____," were printed in thousands of copies and distributed free. Pamphlets for young people in the Diaspora were printed in sixteen languages. The price list was high because of the costs of translation, editing, and printing on quality paper. Records, help in writing musical or dramatic works, radio and television programs, ninety-six films for the Diaspora in cooperation with the Foreign Ministry and the Absorption Ministry. And if you add to all that the postponed payments, an unstable calculation of the rates of inflation and the cost of living, you will see the impossibility of a precise listing.

All the aforementioned does not take account of the personal contribution of Boaz Schneerson, his private expenses with regard to those activities and others are enumerated in the appendices. His activity on behalf of the committees of parents, the commemoration rooms, swimming pools in soldiers' homes, seminar rooms, youth hostels and their upkeep, mobile libraries in memory of the missing, and on this subject, see the letter of Jordana Etzioni of the Ministry of Defense and the letter of Mr. Obadiah Henkin, chairman of the Committee of Bereaved Parents and another letter of his vice chairman Isaiah Shimshoni.

Additional expenses with regard to lawsuits with artists, creators, craftsmen, committees of workers, the union of painters and sculptors, the union of engineers and architects were more than ten times more than a rough estimate. I attach to my letter the affidavit of Boaz Schneerson, given to attorney Bohan Tsedek, the letters of Henkin, Shimshoni, Jordana Etzioni, and others, and as a sign that these words are written innocently, three letters are attached above by members of the Committees of Bereaved Parents of World War II, the War of Independence, and the Six-Day War, separate from the central and national Committees of Parents. A letter from the Society of Bergen-Belsen in New York is also attached here, along with one from the Union of Fifty in England, a letter by Professor Israel S. Shauli on the sociology of bereavement, a letter by Mr. Nahum Naftali who teaches widowhood in three high schools (experimentally), and letters from three well-known intellectuals who have never taken part in any assembly or memorial book, and whose material has never been printed in this context and thus they have no axe to grind, and they are A. Galbovski, Avinoam Ha-Hini, and D. N. Avigdor.

See also Appendices numbers 20–25 —Commemoration, What Is It? (Jarushka and Aviram). "Bereavement and Insomnia," published by the Institute for the Study of Contemporary Judaism. "Poetry of Mourning, Revenge for Bereavement," by S. Nahmiahu. "Songs and Hymns for Holidays and Celebration," by Even Hen and Atara Shaked, etc.

Sincerely, Gideon (Janusz) Kramer, Tel Aviv

I have translated the contents for you, not the appendices. The trial took place before a judge in the district court. Boaz pleaded guilty. After you judged in his favor, Boaz wrote a letter to the judge thanking him, he said he was writing on behalf of Menahem Henkin, may the Lord avenge his blood. And I? I was silent.

Tape / —

Rebecca Schneerson's house, afternoon. On the table stands a steaming samovar, on either side of the table sit an old woman and a man in a uniform, decorated with medals and sporting an unidentified military cap. They're drinking tea. An Arab boy named Ahbed brings a plate with pistachios, sunflower seeds, halvah, biscuits, dumplings, and goat cheese; he serves a pitcher of water and two glasses. The old woman puts a sugar cube into her mouth and sucks the tea through the sugar.

Captain: Excellent tea.

Rebecca: Thanks for saying that, Captain, it's excellent even if you don't say so.

Captain: I say the tea is excellent because it's excellent and also because I think it's excellent.

Rebecca: You've been saying my tea is excellent for forty-five years now, Captain, you say it's excellent when it is excellent, and you say it's excellent even when it's not excellent. And always on Wednesday. I'm starting to doubt if I can believe your honesty, Captain.

Captain: I say the tea is excellent on Wednesday because only on Wednesday do you invite me. I say the tea is excellent even when it's not excellent for three reasons: One, I can't bear tea and I drink tea only because of you, so whether it's excellent or it's not, it tastes the same. And the second reason, I say it's excellent is because I know only one kind of tea and it's the tea I drink with you, and so it has to be excellent even when it's not excellent. Another reason is that I've been drinking tea with you for forty-five years now and you still stir strong feelings in me, if I were allowed to marry you, I would start drinking coffee also on Wednesday afternoons or continue drinking tea, and that would surely amount to the same thing, because I would be too happy to distinguish, just as the hope that you'll still deign to marry me allows me to enjoy your tea even when I loathe it. In South America, we're used to drinking coffee.

Rebecca: And when were you last in South America, Captain?

Captain: To be precise, I'm a colonel. And second, you're evading again.

Rebecca: I'm now over eighty, Captain. You won't be a colonel to me now, children you won't make me now, what good will it do you to marry me? Money you don't need and even if you did, I'd leave everything to Boaz and not give you a cent.

Captain: You don't appreciate the force of my love, Madame.

Rebecca: I'm not fond of that word, Captain.

Captain: I know, but I also know you wouldn't have drunk tea with me for forty-five years if you hadn't found something in me.

Rebecca: You didn't stop amusing me, Jose Menkin A. Goldenberg. You remind me of Michael Halperin in the lion's cage. You remind me of the of the splendid and absolutely needless way my husband died on the shores of Jaffa.

Captain: May he rest in peace.

Rebecca: As a Christian you don't have to say such things.

Captain: I also have memories.

Rebecca: Years ago you didn't have memories. You've changed with time, once you didn't have a childhood because you couldn't have been born in all the places you said you were born in. You're Argentinean, Jewish, Christian, Swiss, American, and you're also a spy and write for a French newspaper in Cairo.

Captain: The newspaper was closed thirty years ago. I've always admired you, Madame, and your late husband, too.

Rebecca: That's because you didn't know him, he wronged me.

Captain: He was a brave man.

Rebecca: He was innocent and beautiful, not brave. I'm brave.

Captain: You're very brave, Madame.

Rebecca: I'm also beautiful and lately you've been forgetting to say that.

Captain: You're the most beautiful woman I've ever known.

Rebecca: You say that so I'll agree to marry you. But this week is out of the question.

Captain: I've been waiting forty-five years now, Madame.

Rebecca: Another few days won't change anything.

Captain: At our age, it can change a lot. But I told you twenty-five years ago, in February, if you change your mind on a day that isn't Wednesday, you can always wake me up, I'm a light sleeper and I hear everything.

Rebecca: You're a light sleeper in my grandson's house.

Captain: In your son's house, Rebecca. Didn't you adopt him?

Rebecca: In your church and that's not legal.

Captain: It was legal in your eyes then and it's legal in the eyes of God.

Rebecca: God doesn't live here.

Captain: But you talk with him.

Rebecca: That's because of something else, not faith.

Captain: Your grandson or son worries me.

Rebecca: My son.

Captain: He worries me even though I love him.

Rebecca: My son died in the Holocaust. Boaz doesn't have to interest you.

Captain: I'm his godfather.

Rebecca: You're right, will you have some more to drink?

(She pours him another cup, he drinks with polite reluctance.)

Captain: Good.

Rebecca: What worries you?

Captain: He sells poems and monuments. He refuses to build me the Dante monument and he's got a girlfriend.

Rebecca: He's got me!

Captain: He's got one. She was the girlfriend of somebody who died. He killed her boyfriend. That's what Mrs. Hazin from the grocery store told me.

Rebecca: Her father was also a fool. I didn't know you went to the grocery store.

Captain: Once I went, I don't go anymore.

Rebecca: You insult him, Captain. Ever since he's been working in the burial society he hasn't been the boyfriend of any girl.

Captain: Yes he is, and I'm worried.

Rebecca: Stop worrying, I know everything, he's my son and my grandson.

Captain: Maybe he's also your father and husband? What about me?

Rebecca: You're starting to be sentimental again, Menkin. Now you'll start weeping on me. You're eighty years old now.

Captain: Even old men are allowed to cry, Rebecca.

Rebecca: Not to us.

Captain: I'm going now. Take it under advisement, I'll wait for you all my life, but my life now isn't something that will take much time.

Rebecca: I'll think about it. (Smiles sweetly.)

He gets up, kisses her cheek, salutes, exits. She sits, and the great-grandson of Ahbed enters with a tray. She looks at the window and sees Jose Menkin A. Goldenberg's splendid back walking proudly toward Ebenezer's house.

Rebecca: That fool Dana!

Tape / —

Frustrated, unkempt and crimson, reminded, a whiskey in his hand, how to forget, in a bombastic letter to a judge consulting with a serial thief who sat with him in a bar and said an apple no longer symbolizes joy, Boaz. They lend envy today with interest, I'm drunk. The thief climbed on the balcony to make love to two lighted trees that had been brought here from civilized countries. A thick-bearded Anglo-Saxon from North Africa drew partitions on a map of a city that had been invented that morning with a joy that looked to experts more bored than it was supposed to be between three wars in which sympathy for Israel was almost uprooted along with the knowledge of forgotten courage. People were already drawing maps of cities where they were almost born and which had been annihilated long ago and they did that with chilly amazement, and then with a thief of flowerpots, on the balcony, above a ticking tranquillity, a fabric of tan tones and crumbling, filed in a nailed file cabinet with sorting tags that look like the homemade jam of a woman of a soldier's dreams, stood Boaz Schneerson and wrote a letter to the district court judge, chief judge, and an account of the days with him, and on him, and under him, and the thief forgives him and says: The arrow, sir, is no longer a symbol of regret just as the apple isn't a symbol of joy, and Boaz asks what is regret, he doesn't know, and then he recalls. He always recalls that there were days when he gave his temples the importance they craved, well-shorn temples, the best Middle Eastern tradition here on the shore of yearning. Shower, laced-up dresses of local charmers, lacking the lace of laciness for a person like me, a system in himself, hoodwinking eye and sin, a sin that isn't his sweet crimson air flowing and glowing, poets, and I am for the judge and he is for me, leather case with silk leather case of wild lexical mélange of a lecherous word-thief, never let it be forgotten, he said with a glass of liquor in his hand, the face of a judge you can see only on unnecessary waking, yours, Boaz Schneerson! Women will stand in line, will learn birth and death in retrospective reconstruction, waving a smell of sour balsam who rises in that house of quarrels to die with me drink himself to death, and here, after they turned the maps into scattered tombstones and the present to an arrow sent to what almost was, his mind was swallowed up, his tongue was glued to the table of an overly enlightened woman's lap, Noga's here, Noga's there, Henkin will bite, Henkin will sing to me, to exclusivize the root and uproot the exclusive, the gray ancient preserved and choked, everything was spilled out, destroyed like the riddle of cities that don't exist, will here become the intercity mourning with drivers attached to the index, sucking the marrow of stone, we will die in a noontime nap, shame on the meek, horrible and terrible, a record of nothingness, the last rain abundantly and I rain from my own abundance, in the language of darkness, grace of whisper plowed and traps drought, this is how the sum of all roots routed in you, son of a bitch, was born . . .

Noga, Noga. Noga, who was a stranger to the hut on the seashore even before Boaz Schneerson moved to the attic apartment, she sat—and this is something that happened long before that—padded in a sheaf of light that shone on her, and she defended herself from her feelings. She didn't know what to do when they knocked on the door: to open, not to open, she worried, the sea spread out through the window, and she waited for Boaz to tell her. He didn't tell and she got up, hugged her shaking body in her hands, stretched them, went to the door, was a little amazed, and opened it. There stood a solid man wearing a beret who said something about how Boaz knew Menahem and maybe he also knew his son who fell in Ramle and loved to read the poems of the poet Ratosh. He wants to know if Boaz can arrange a meeting for him with the poet Ratosh. The poet Ratosh can explain to me, said the man, and Noga trembled because she knew that Boaz would bring him Ratosh the poet, to explain his son to him, then he showed the letters of the son and asked for an expert opinion, maybe to make a pamphlet of them? Letters full of names, Ratosh and the poems of his black wedding canopy and the night road from Mesilot to Sadeh Nahum and Beit She'an at night when the Arab dogs are barking and he quoted an excerpt from the book *Pampilov's Men*. The man measured the rectangle of sea in the window and smiled. Then, maybe about a month later, a child also came with a letter and Boaz said too loudly: If a woman comes here, give her coffee, I'm going down to swim in the sea.

But the woman was already on her way to him and the man whose son loved Ratosh's poems met her, but didn't know where she was going, and Boaz thought: Somebody said we have to find a moral equivalent of war, what's the equivalent of that nothingness, that dreadful, heartbreaking lust? Meanwhile, he put on a bathing suit and over the bathing suit he put on his pants and shirt. Noga looked at the sea. The woman walked past the hut. He'll search for the poet Ratosh, said Noga, what do I tell Menahem from Menahem, to Boaz from Boaz? But Boaz didn't go down to the sea. He sat down on the windowsill and drank the coffee Noga gave him before. Outside the wind raised leaves and papers and sand in the wind and yellow limestone flowers didn't budge. A ship sailed north and Noga stood up and facing the small mirror tried to put on a new belt. In the mirror, Noga saw Boaz's half-shut eyes and also the ship. What began as trying on the belt turned into being a game. She stretched the belt and released it, and said: I've got a riddle for you. A bagel distributor walked on Mapu Street and distributed four bagels to every apartment. When he came to the last apartment he saw he had only three bagels left. He panicked and thought: Where did the fourth bagel disappear? He reversed direction and searched for the bagel. He came back to the bakery and understood that he had lost the bagel on the way, but didn't know where. You know where the bagel disappeared? Boaz didn't open his eyes and his face was stuck to the rim of the cup and she knew he was measuring her with his eyes shut, that he was expert in looking with eyes shut and she played with the belt again, her face frozen, the man seeking the poet Ratosh still between her lashes and Boaz was silent and waited for the woman who was now walking in the street and he was still wearing a bathing suit under his clothes. Noga emitted a brief laugh that shriveled her cheeks and suddenly made her lost, burned, he wanted to get up and hug her, but he didn't know how much, sometimes, it was forbidden to touch her. And then Noga whispered: A fat man and a beautiful woman sat in a train compartment. The fat man was smoking a big cigar, and the beautiful woman was holding a barking dog on a leash. The beautiful woman said to the fat man: Sir, your cigar bothers my dog and so he's barking. The fat man with the cigar said: Your barking dog bothers my cigar. Finally, the beautiful woman rips the cigar out of the fat man's mouth and throws it on the platform. The fat man picks up the dog, removes its leash and throws the dog outside. The dog runs after the cigar and you know what he found?

Boaz didn't know.

He found the bagel the bagel seller lost, said Noga.

Boaz didn't respond and looked at the ship that had almost disappeared beyond the Sheraton. A sudden rain fell on the sands that scrunched up as if they too were ripples of water. A woman in a transparent raincoat approached the hut. That is a war ground and you don't see blood, said Boaz and looked at the sand. The woman passed by the German who was still selling suitcases here so that some day he could go back to Europe and he didn't know how to cross that cruel sea that erected a barrier between him and the landscape he yearned for. The woman thought: For two weeks now I've been trying to get here and have been afraid, and Noga heard the knock on the door even before the woman knocked, and she straightened up, took off the belt, Boaz didn't budge, and said: That's the woman who wrote to me. Noga said: You should have known where the bagel was, but Boaz stared at the door and Noga opened it and the woman came in out of the rain and sprayed water on the floor. Noga helped her take off her coat. She lit the stove and the woman stood between the stove and the door and when she looked at Boaz, she was no longer sure why she had come.

Boaz saw a child running along the sand in the rain. The woman was blighted, but her breasts were full.

After she spoke with her eyes almost shut, Noga went to a corner, sat and folded her legs and decided she was a statue. Menahem's poem, she said: "So charming, Teacher Henkin said to write to you, you have no idea how many times he read the poem to us, and my Yoram is also in that poem, they were all boys who gave birth to themselves, a poor generation, they tried to be answers to their parents' dreams which they themselves had to kill. Surely you'll forgive me. My late husband used to say: Take care of him, I won't hold out and he really didn't. Didn't I take care enough? Noga didn't budge and said: He forgives you, and she stared at Boaz hunched up on the windowsill. Boaz performed an experiment he had tried in his childhood after he read *Yotam the Magician* by Korczak, he tried to be invisible.

Yoram fell in Iraq-Manshiya. You must have known him! Everybody knew him in Tel Aviv. He'd walk on his hands on the shore from Frischmann to the pool in the north and back. Here's his picture, she said, and held out a hand with a picture suddenly, Yoram Pishinovsky, you're sure you didn't know him?

Boaz takes the photo and looks. Curly hair, serious eyes, soft thin cheeks, deathphoto. The serious and saccharine puppets with gigantic pompadours who left class photos that were too professional, he thought. Noga offers the woman coffee, but the woman doesn't want to drink. She can't sit either. Hidden treasures went down the drain, she says. Here, this is what we have left of him, and she takes a few drawings by Yoram out of the leather case and gives them to Boaz and wants to know where his Australian hat and Parker fountain pen disappeared. Sorry about such nonsense, but what's left of them? A fountain pen, and even that's lost! The Negev was cut off, and I searched, she said, and how do you know where to search for things like that? And something was needed? Then they showed me a grave, but there was no hat there and no Parker fountain pen, and I asked, and I'm a member of our club aren't I and every week, I come to the Shimonis, but nobody knows and then that poem and you . . .

We walk and Teacher Henkin explains. He also speaks nicely. But at least he's got a poem, no, Yoram didn't write poems. Now she said pensively, sadly, hunched up inside herself: I stand here and look at you and the young lady and the stove and I think: What folly, what am I searching for, you must think I'm a fool. And in the middle of her words, she stopped, picked up her coat, and started putting it on too hastily. Her defeat was total, in the depths of her heart she knew she had come in vain and that whole two weeks, she muttered, that whole two weeks, a vague hope lodged in her, now it's not! In her face Boaz saw that mysterious charm of pain when it's disguised as shame, what a patched-up fragility is life itself, from that human crease life burst forth that terrified him, he couldn't imagine it and thought about himself, about Menahem, and then he got up and took off the woman's coat, sat her in the chair, the rain stopped, the clouds sailed quickly and the blue sky appeared and he said: It will be all right, Yoram's mother, it will be all right. And a few days later, he brought the woman a Parker fountain pen and an Australian hat. Her house was full of plants. She grew them as if she wanted to hide in a jungle. Now she was practical, asked where to put the things, and Boaz built her a corner, hung the drawings from school, the letter from the Ministry of Defense, the map of the battle for Iraq-Manshiya that Boaz had brought her, the hat and the fountain pen he put on the cabinet, with an enlarged picture of Yoram framed in black. She stuck some money in his pocket, and said: You had expenses and I don't think you should bear them. He pushed away the money, but when he saw how she thrust the money into the pocket of his coat hanging on the hanger, he didn't say a thing. He also bound the compositions for her, and that's how, that's how it all started, said Noga—

Tape / —

For three days she didn't talk. And then she tried to talk and a choked moan burst out of her mouth and then they went into the other room, and he said: Noga, they need that and I bring them what they want. I didn't search for it, it found me. And you too, it happened unintentionally.

Tape / —

Noga sat in bed. She posted her legs like two shapely and tented triangles in the light from the lamp. Wearily her arms hugged her raised legs and her head rested on her knees. In the room the small electric heater burned, spreading a reddish light. Boaz was seen walking toward the water. Only wrinkles of sand and spots of damp remained from the storm. She smelled death and thought maybe the ceiling really had fallen on her at night. Her face was red from the light. The room smelled of cigarettes, rain, and wet sand. Boaz's supple body was seen solitary and gallant at the empty sea. She thought about the frozen water slowly warming his body, the light dwarfed distances, the opaque and airy sea, filled with a supple body of a snake. The crystalline swimming was more ancient than she, a thousand-year-old woman, death in her womb, everything was so unreliable: the woman with the money, those people who come, the trips, the notebooks he was starting to edit, that foolish man. She didn't move until she saw him come out of the water, spraying sea jets, in the cold he ran. She put on an old bathrobe she had brought from the Henkin house long ago and decided to brush her teeth with her fingers, to rub the gums with cold water and char a hem of the robe. He ran along the shore, maybe where Yoram Pishinovsky had walked on his hands and everybody would admire him. After she brushed her teeth with her fingers and burned the hem of the robe, she drank four cups of cold water, and gnashing her teeth as a betrayed woman she could wait for him again with such great lust.

Tape / —

>To the Court, Tel Aviv
>Re: Income Tax File No. 34/17656T. S.L.A. Company, Ltd.
>Dear Sir,
>My name is Noga Levin. For six years I have lived with Boaz Schneerson, director of the S.L.A. Company, Ltd., and I love him. I mention that detail even though I know the court does not consider issues of emotion, or even concepts of morality and justice, but law. Love and law do not necessarily overlap. Maybe loving means breaking the law? While there is a law of justice, there is surely no law of love. By the letter of the law, I also think Mr. Schneerson's acts are not to be faulted, as is clear from your correct and reasoned judgment. On the other hand, if I had to judge Boaz Schneerson, and my love would serve as some measure—just as admissible as the testimony you heard and the papers you read—I may have judged him differently.
>
>And again, I do not mean to cast doubt on your ethical integrity or your judicial talents, Judge. It is not you I'm judging, but myself.
>
>I don't think I will be able to sleep quietly or look at myself in the mirror if I do not give vent to strong feelings of shame that fill me. Love, unlike the law, is relativity seeking cover.
>
>With my own eyes, my dear sir, I saw a marginal issue in Boaz Schneerson's life turn into a flourishing business. The very fact

that the death of strangers turns into a "business" in the usual sense of the word is not monstrous in my eyes. On the other hand, I am aware of the objective need, if pain can be called that, which turned the S.L.A. Company Ltd., into a business. That is, I am judging the situation of which Boaz Schneerson is only a symbol. Yet for me, he cannot be a symbol, but a man, a man I love.

I was not a mute witness, sir, but also a reluctant partner. In general, I can insist, but in fact, the business flourished and I helped. I was drawn into Boaz's wild adventure, first as a spectator and then as an advisor. It wasn't possible to stop the cart. Pain was driving the cart. I mean what people felt, yearnings for their sons, their husbands, their dear ones. When the cart came to the bottom of the mountain and I told Boaz Schneerson what I thought, and asked him to stop, he said he couldn't. What started as bad luck and then was inexorable, turned into ambition. And it was all innocent: first Henkin, then a man, then a woman who wanted an Australian hat and a Parker fountain pen, and then? Then it snowballed. Boaz brought together a bereaved father with a poet whose poems his son liked to read, so the poet would explain to the father who his son was. And Boaz even started getting interested in his acts because they contained some reply to the burning in him, a challenge, maybe it was a mercy killing, after death, of the best of the youth, to lose everything, maybe it was a reply to the fact that his grandmother saved him from death when he didn't want to come back. And by word of mouth, his name became famous. Anybody who needed a notebook came to him, anybody who needed a monument came, the personal need of every single one of those people was human, but the address was now an office with a telephone and a secretary and jeeps and cars and such, income tax files, and calculations of losses, and expenses, and an accountant and a lawyer.

There were real poems and letters, and there were also fakes. They need that, said Boaz, and I provide them with what they need. Isn't that a picture of a real situation? Surely, its ethics are definitely dubious, its relative morality—isn't. The death of others cannot be a source of resurrection. That death, sir, took his friends, him it didn't touch, what a revenge!

And then we had to move. The hut on the seashore was now full of portraits, objects, parts of burned tanks, maps, and in the penthouse apartment on Lilienblum Street, the rooms were now turned into offices and there was a secretary there and two typewriters, a Hebrew one and a foreign one, and file cabinets. The number of temples grew. Hundreds of booklets were written and edited. We became a company of gravediggers.

In the war, Boaz Schneerson lay among the dead and played dead. Two or three hundred times he was condemned to death because all the shots aimed at the dead could have killed him. Maybe that's how the notion of a vulture was stamped in his mind. It all started in the house of Mr. Henkin of the Committee of Bereaved Parents. He brought a poem there. He brought hope after death there. Menahem Henkin was the fellow I had a relationship with and some days I thought I was in love with him. Maybe that was the most awful thing of all, the sense of betraying love, revealing it in a true light, too late. Or perhaps in a late light, too true? We were mobilized then, we'd meet for a few days and part, I was afraid of him, I pitied him, and maybe I loved him, because a latent fear lodged in me that Menahem Henkin was destined to die, but then I also discovered that I didn't love him. I was alone, I had nobody to talk to, I sat with Menahem's mother and looked at her, at the locked seal on her handsome face and I didn't find solace, I couldn't say a thing, everybody knew that after the war we'd get married. His mother was worried, she didn't even try to admit the existence of my allusions, she wrote him letters that didn't get to their address, and knitted him socks that nobody wore, and I sat and wrote a letter to Menahem explaining to him why we had to part, for a moment I forgot the vague lodged fear in me, the fear that Menahem was destined to die. I sent the letter, and then we found out that he fell. I didn't know if he got the letter and I was still his girl. Uncles from Switzerland sent chocolate and gold earrings to the fiancée, the fiancée was me. Suitors were afraid of me. I sat in the Henkin house. Everybody wanted me to be the model widow. They didn't want the happiness of those who come back to their lovers, marry, and disappear into the gray everydayness of rationing and the new state, they wanted the little bit of splendor, the pain and bereavement that stuck to me and I sank into a slumber that lasted years. Menahem's mother understands now. Later on I understood that all the time she knew the love affair had ended long ago. She felt more than I knew, but she also thought I had betrayed her. Henkin was compelled to give concrete expression to his pain, I was his refuge. I divided myself between them, Henkin and his dead son. I recorded in the album, in a fluent handwriting, the names of the places where he was photographed. On the day Henkin brought Boaz Schneerson home, I knew that Boaz came to take me.

He wriggled and waited. I waited too. Menahem's mother sat and looked at me contemptuously. Death blended me with Menahem, through Boaz. In fact, after I loved Boaz, I could return to loving Menahem. Boaz, who didn't know I had stopped loving Menahem even before his death, tried to put a hand on me and then changed his mind and didn't. I waited. I didn't say a word but I wanted to. They always think they defeat me, both Menahem and Boaz, while I, I chose the two of them by myself. Boaz decided he had in fact killed Menahem because he saw a picture of me with Menahem, he loved me and came to take me away from him. He described to me how he killed Menahem to get me and I tried to pretend I believed. He was attached to me even though he tried to live without love. But he wanted Menahem's mother to forgive him for being alive instead of Menahem. And Boaz went on building a stage set for the dead. As a judge you must know: He didn't kill Menahem, Menahem died long before that, but . . . I told him, come on, let's start a new life. He fled but he didn't want to. There were meetings with army officers, parents, engineers, writers, poets, sculptors, planners, lighting experts, printers, I served coffee, tea, peanuts, wine, I was there, I saw him weeping as he sat and wrote fictional love letters, it was a humiliating spectacle. I told him: You're reducing them; what kind of victory is it that nobody will remember? And the apartment grew.

And everything was full of fabricated death.

I'm writing to you because I want you to know that no matter how reasoned your judgment was, it approves, as I do with my life, a serious act that may in truth not be judged. Like many people I know, and you too, without any premeditation, Boaz turned the nightmare into a celebration and then into a profession. But to the same extent, you can say a prison warden deserves punishment because he keeps under lock and key a person whose nature is to be free, or that you yourself sentence people to severe punishments when the natural law is that life precedes everything, you judge the person by the laws of society, not the laws of nature or life. I understand those considerations, I accept them, but because of those very reasons I must protest, at least to you, because you judged in favor of a man I love, and so you were the only person to whom I can address these words. I go to the Ministry of Defense and see thousands of notebooks. I peep. Oblivion is a medicine that, like life, is intended to circumvent death.

I thought then in court that maybe you would condemn something rooted so deeply here, so awful, but you made a judgment and a judgment didn't make you, you didn't indicate the root of the problem, I wasn't disappointed, I understood, I have no complaints. I attach a letter I wrote to the Levinsky Teachers' College on the night I got drunk for the first time in my life and Boaz raped me when I would have defended myself with a broken bottle in my hand and I didn't hit him.

Yours, Noga Levin

To the Administration of the Levinsky Teachers' College, Tel Aviv

Dear Sirs:

I was very interested in your announcement in the newspaper. You ask the students who attended the Teachers' College who lost their husbands (or) their fiancés (your word!) to send one page with the events of our life for the anniversary of the Teachers' College, and here is mine—

My name is Noga Levin. I finished school in nineteen forty-seven. My parents died two years before I was born in a small town near the Zxanten Gulf in southern China. We were the only Jews on the street. All my husbands died of the cancer of war. The last one was in his death throes on the way to the cemetery, but it wasn't possible to change the custom, and in the middle of the funeral, he died. If you're preparing a class reunion, please do not include me among the bereaved girls. Death terrifies me. I live with a man who refuses to marry me, because he loves me. All my love affairs were with dead men. Now that I live with a hangman, I weave a new rope for him. He kills my husbands and every time he succeeds, he brings me a black flower. So, it's not true that there are no black flowers—they should be grown in beds for memorial days and days of mourning and that could even have been a branch of export. On memorial days I sing sad English songs. I know somebody who sold a hundred thousand armored cars for days of mourning. With the money he got from the armored cars, he bought me a white dress and real pearls. Please take me off the list of volunteers for teaching widowhood, bereavement, orphanhood, and commemoration. I intend to live in Denmark with a dog close by and a thin man who smokes a pipe and works in a bank close to home and goes to work on a bicycle. I live with a man who lends his acts of heroism to all kinds of dead people. I think he's teaching me something I don't want to learn even when I was a student the Teachers' College. The main thing you didn't teach me. You taught me to live with death, you didn't teach me to live with life. And that's now a national phenomenon. Now I'm drunk and I feel how much I lack something called a hunger for life.

Respectfully, Noga Levin

Judge, the letter was returned to me, the director came to visit me. He found a cold, silent, and apparently handsome woman. That's what he said. I told him somebody wrote the letter in my name. After he left, Boaz Schneerson filed that letter under "trivialities." You do know the file "trivialities," the one that isn't taxable.

Yours, Noga Levin

I want, said Noga, for somebody to finish me off and Boaz. To destroy the devil in him that lives in me. To release us from the dependence on ourselves and on death. But the years pass. I'm here. I learned, Noga thought of driving a jeep, they collect parts of burned tanks and rotten berets, etc., etc., etc. . . .

Tape / —

I got off the plane shrouded in foreignness. Ebenezer Schneerson got off the plane shrouded in foreignness. Around him was a state he didn't know. When he got into the bus from the plane to the air terminal with Fanya R., he tried to think, but he couldn't. he only said: When we come to Israel, there will be Israeli buses at the airport and Hebrew police. And Fanya R. said: Ebenezer, we've already come.

The clerk stamped his papers, the suitcases came on the baggage carousel, and he stood outside, facing the yelling cabdrivers, Fanya R. leaning on him and he looked at the turmoil.

They took a cab to the settlement. The driver was listening to a radio program and Ebenezer looked at the landscape he thought he was imagining. When they passed the tombstone of the paratroopers, Ebenezer asked to stop. He asked: Where is Marar? The driver turned his head, looked at the strange couple in amazement, stopped at the barrier of prickly pear that still remained here on the border of the citrus grove, and said, What? Marar? What Marar?

The village that was here, said Ebenezer.

Don't know, said the driver, that's the tombstone of paratroopers.

There was Marar here, said Ebenezer.

There was also Sodom and Gomorrah, said the driver, but the tourists don't find them and come to Tel Aviv, which is almost the same thing, and he laughed. He was smoking a pungent cigarette. Ebenezer looked for the houses sliding down the slope, like dovecotes, and didn't find them.

Maybe there was no village, he thought, maybe there will be, I don't know, what do I know, maybe that's part of the things that are going to happen like my trip to Israel that is still to come. Something in him bothered him; there was Marar, there was Dana, they weren't, and a dull ticking of old lust stirred in him.

On the main street, nobody knew him. He was dragging a suitcase and Fanya R. walked behind him. They went down the slope, they passed by what had once been the threshing floor, saw new houses and handsome gardens, and an old DeSoto with a woman who looked like a scarecrow, wearing a wide-brimmed hat smoking a long thin cigar, and they came to Rebecca's house. He didn't recognize the house, but the sight of the aging Argentinean officer watering the garden, wearing a military cap, gave him a dull sense of belonging. Shaking with a sudden anger that gripped him, he grabbed Fanya R.'s hand and with his other hand, he pounded on the door. The door was hidden in a thicket of gigantic bougainvillea. The great-grandson of Ahbed opened the door, looked suspiciously at the Last Jew and the woman. The Last Jew said: We came to visit Mrs. Schneerson. The great-grandson of Ahbed said what he had been taught to say: She's not home and come back in a month and then you'll go again, and he tried to lock the door, but Ebenezer put a foot on the threshold and stopped the door. He said: You must be the grandson of Ahbed. The great-grandson of Ahbed didn't move a muscle, and said: I'm the great-grandson of Ahbed, and remove your foot, sir.

Tell the old lady her son has come back home, said Ebenezer.

Ahbed pushed Ebenezer, managed to lock the door, and disappeared. He put the suitcase down on the tiles at the entrance and waited.

A short while later, Ahbed opened the door a little and said: She said her son is dead, but since you're here already, come in. Fanya R. smiled. Ebenezer hugged her, and said: When we come to Israel, my mother will be excited. And Ebenezer tried to remember if it really was Rebecca, whose flyswatter he could hear now, curious. But he couldn't remember. When Ahbed asked them to come in to what was called the "salon," they walked like two frightened children. Ahbed locked the door behind them. Rebecca sat in an easy chair at a table with black domino tiles. Even Fanya R. could guess that Rebecca had just won a victory. She surveyed Ebenezer for a long time and her old beautiful eyes turned to Fanya R. She examined her impassively, and said: Ebenezer Schneerson, you were dead!

Her face was covered with a cloud of rumination and she looked as if she were trying to solve a riddle without help from anybody. She said: Now the Captain will have to move out of Boaz's house!

Whose?

Boaz's, she repeated. Ebenezer looked at her and tried to recall, but he couldn't. Fanya R. sat down on a chair, put her hands on the arms, one of which was carved with tiny features, and Ebenezer said: I'll live in Tel Aviv, near Samucl.

Who's Samucl? asked the old woman.

Samuel, said Ebenezer.

The old woman looked outside and saw the avenue of almond trees, and said: Where were you? He tried to think. Nothing concrete was clear to him. Where was I for so many years? He said: Samuel is my son, he came out of the camp and he'll come.

They told me you always wanted to go to America, added Ebenezer. Did you go? She smiled and wrung her hands. Ahbed entered the room and smiled. Ebenezer saw a carved bird on the windowsill. He looked at it and strong yearnings for the smell of sawdust filled him.

They were right, said the old woman.

But it's easier to find people here, said Ebenezer, Israel is smaller. And Rebecca said to Ahbed: Bring my son and that woman some cold juice and bring me wine. Ahbed looked at Ebenezer, blinked his eyes, tried to remember something, and went out.

He's the great-grandson of Ahbed, said the old woman. They always stay with me. When they attach Arabs to Israel, there's somebody to rely on. They're not Jews who disappear for fifty years and come to ask for Boaz's house for themselves.

Who's Boaz?

Your son. She said and smiled. And then she realized there was a danger lurking here whose nature she hadn't yet grasped. She looked at her son and thought about her father. A thousand years of life in distant places streamed from Ebenezer's face. She said: You left Ebenezer and you came back as some Diaspora Jew.

Fanya R. drank the juice Ahbed gave her. Rebecca started getting bored. For a moment she thought of Nehemiah as if he tried again to betray her and die for nothing. She said: Boaz is now my son, you were my son, maybe you still are my son, but you're old, Ebenezer, there were wars here and there's suddenly a state, there were locusts! Does your wife have sons?

She had daughters, said Ebenezer.

Rebecca didn't respond, she got up with the suddenness that was always typical of her, came to Ebenezer and kissed his cheeks. For a moment, she was soft, her fingers combed his hair, and then she hugged the back of Fanya R., who straightened up and leaned forward. Then they sat down and were silent. Ahbed brought black coffee and they drank and ate cookies and peanuts and tiny sandwiches filled with cheese that was sweet but sharp. The fragrance of basil stood in the air. After dark, they moved to the dining room and sat around the table. Ebenezer tried to tell in three sentences what he remembered. Rebecca fell asleep and Ahbed came and carried her to her room sitting in her chair. Fanya R. picked up a carved bird that contained a lot of force. Tears flowed from her eyes at the sight of the birds on the windowsills. Ebenezer said: Look at the beautiful birds the old woman has.

The next day, Mr. Klomin came. He told Ebenezer how awful the Holocaust was, and Ebenezer listened to him and tried to mutter something but couldn't. All he remembered were things he wasn't sure had happened to him. From Mr. Klomin's words, he understood who Mr. Klomin was.

These things I'm saying now, I also know from what I heard, how I came to Rebecca's house, how she kissed me, how I didn't know who Klomin was, how I didn't know who Boaz was.

When Mr. Klomin told about Boaz, vague things started to clear up in his brain. He stroked Fanya R. and inquired about Boaz, he was sure they were talking about Samuel. Klomin said: He hangs around the house of the Teacher Henkin who lost a son in the war. A handsome fellow. And Klomin took a photo out of the drawer and showed it to Ebenezer. Ebenezer smiled and said: That's Samuel. And Fanya R. said: That's an old picture of Joseph Rayna.

When his bags came from the port, Ebenezer went to Tel Aviv and bought the Giladi house. When Boaz came to see him, Ebenezer said: Samuel, and fainted. For three days Ebenezer wept in a closed room and thought. After he came out of the room he almost knew things he hadn't known before that he knew. Boaz, who was disappointed, didn't show his emotions. He was scared as never before in his life. Fanya R. told him about her daughters. Their skin, she said, was grafted onto the body of a German who was burned in a tank. But when Ebenezer tried to understand who Boaz was and how he wasn't Samuel, Boaz said: Never mind, it's not so important, he left the house, and when he got to the corner of Hayarkon Street, he entered a yard and banged his head against a wall for a long time.

Mr. Klomin, who envisioned the meeting between Boaz and his father, began to feel a certain closeness to his grandson, maybe because time wasn't working to his advantage now, as he put it, or because Dana became concrete before his eyes the moment Ebenezer called his son Samuel.

Once every two weeks, for years, Mr. Klomin and Captain Jose Menkin A. Goldenberg would meet in Tel Aviv to discuss their party affairs. Most of the people who had joined them over the years had died or were in old people's homes or in hospitals and had stopped being interested in the renewed Kingdom of Israel. A gigantic yoke of keeping the flame, as he defined it, fell on Klomin, and became heavier from year to year. The return of the last son gave him certain hopes that inconceivable things were happening. If Ebenezer came back, he said to the Captain as they walked in the street to their regular meeting place, all kinds of things can happen, he said and didn't elaborate. The two of them were up in years now. Whenever they'd walk in the street they'd discover a new city they hadn't known before, partly because they forgot. Suspicious-looking cars passed by and stopped at traffic signals that had just been planted on street corners. Mr. Klomin meditated aloud about the connection between the words grief and brief, dissect and connect, brave and wave, and then they went into the small old-fashioned café where they had once prepared the great revolt against the British Empire. They sat down in their regular places at the back window behind a gigantic bush that had turned gray over the years. Hidden from the eyes of passersby, they sat and whispered to one another. The Captain's uniform had faded long ago, a new replacement hadn't come. His once elegant hat looked shabby, even though he took such devoted care of it. He was already starting to forget for rather long periods why he ever had to go back to Egypt. As a sign of the passing years, he said to Mr. Klomin: I don't edit a French newspaper anymore, and Mr. Klomin, who had never believed the Captain had ever edited a newspaper in Cairo, thought to himself a bit, looked at the damp walls, the red plastic chairs, and said: Maybe you really didn't edit a newspaper for many years. The Captain's praise-wreathed past had faded with the years, bereft of that importance that had once been ascribed to it. And one of the two said, they didn't remember anymore which of them said it: Maybe we have to turn over a new leaf? And the Captain adjusted his folds that had grown flaccid, drank the thin coffee, and a shriveled old waitress, who remembered her youthful grace through them, said to her replacement waitress: Those were giant years, you felt electricity in the air, and what secrets they whispered there, and the new waitress came to them, bored, asked if they wanted anything, offered them the famous cheesecake and they laughed, in unison they laughed, and said: Us, cheesecake? Sometimes toast, not today, and then they gave in and ordered nut cake and said it was good, even though it had stood four days on the counter waiting for a defeated and hungry army, she pulled her apron, wiped a table that was already clean, looked bored toward another table covered with crumbs, and sat down to look at the street.

When the Captain, drinking coffee and chewing the hard nut cake, thought of what he had left of the past he had almost managed to live, he sank into depression, he thought of Rebecca, he thought of dark schemes he could no longer invent, and then a tear pearled in his left eye and he said to Mr. Klomin: But the memorial to Dante Alighieri I do have to erect.

It was because of the memorial, he said a few minutes later, that I came here fifty years ago, wasn't it. Mr. Klomin, who looked like a routed war hero who couldn't have been invented by the Captain even in his good days, pondered to himself: Boaz builds memorials, and here respected and unhesitating stands an ancient and firm fifty-year-old expectation. Not fair, he said sadly, really not fair . . .

Around them, people are selling and buying diamonds, exchanging earrings for foreign currency, and Menkin Jose Captain says: I've got a dim sense we won't succeed in establishing your kingdom, Klomin. And Klomin drinks the coffee, chews the unchewed cake, and says: The Prophets win again, Captain. He said that so sadly that tears filled the Captain's eyes. To the three hundred sixty letters he wrote to British commissioners, leaders of Israel, its ministers, noble American, French, and British leaders, chief rabbis, the Pope, the Dalai Lama, King Saud, the Prime Minister of Nigeria, the International Ladies' Garment Workers Union in New York and Left Poalei Zion in Brooklyn, no answer had come, except one, short and laconic, from

Ben-Gurion. Ben-Gurion wrote: I read your letter carefully, if we build our state with innocence, boldness, faith and wisdom, we shall be redeemed. Until we do we will not be redeemed. Respectfully, David Ben-Gurion.

Mediocrities are always celebrated here, said Klomin, great minds are stoned to death. The gigantic figure of the kings is corrupted by frustrated poets, the Bible is written testimony to the greatness of great dreamers despite its tendentious values . . . Everything's a lie, Jeroboam the Second was a great king whose figure was reduced by poets, and Jeremiah who called for betrayal and throwing up your hands gets a whole book. The Russian Revolution of nineteen five failed in Russia and succeeded here. Secular Hasids devoid of real greatness believe in the miracle drug of hackneyed rhymes. They started with a demonstration against Nehemiah Schneerson and now they're building a state of shopkeepers and an oppressed kingdom. We, Captain, we're the last ones who see what could have been. A great historical moment was missed, now maybe it's too late. I intend to write one last letter, Captain, added Mr. Klomin in a loud voice and the old waitress, who hadn't yet taken off her apron, recalled the stormy days of the great revolutions and wonderful arguments, I'll write a six-hundred-page letter: The last will and testament of one who thought up the state. I'll write what reptiles they are! How they turned possible redemption into a new ghetto, or in the words of the poet Tshernikhovsky, "The Lord God conquered Canaan in a tempest—and He will be imprisoned in straps of tefillin!" My letter will be testimony of memory and a memorial to Dana my daughter, guilt of Samaria against love of Zion!

But he'll erect my memorial, said the Captain, who had stopped listening to his friend's speech some time ago. I'll call the last letter the will and testament of the last Jews, said Klomin, my grandchildren will read the letter as we read Herzl's prophetic writings today. After they parted, the Captain stood with a South American firmness and the old waitress came to him, held out her hand, and said, I've served you for thirty years now and today I'm retiring, I just wanted to say what an honor it has been for me to serve you, she burst into tears and ran away. The Captain, who tried to wipe a tear from his eye, discovered to his surprise that his eye was dry. He walked along the street slowly, turned right, and ran right into a tree. His sight was failing now, but his honor didn't allow him to wear eyeglasses, and he walked to Boaz's house.

Climbing to the roof was hard for him, but he rested on every floor, wiped his sweat and the pathetic image of the waitress was still stuck to his eyelids. For thirty years she had served him and he hadn't noticed her. When Boaz opened the door, the Captain walked in and was caught in the last light fluttering on the roof and touching the leaves of the trees and plants and herbs that Noga planted in flowerpots and barrels. A few chairs and an old easy chair stood there. The Captain sat down in the easy chair, and said: You could have been my grandson but in the end I did succeed in being your godfather.

Godfatherhood is also an obligation on the part of the godson, said Boaz and smiled. Boaz surveyed the Captain with a certain affection, maybe a lot more than he allowed himself. There was some imagination in the Captain, even fictional, even not clear, that, instead of winning a position, honor in the big government of the world, he agreed to live with us here in this forsaken place. The splendid figure of the Captain now stood in the twilight and looked to him like the abandoned god of a treacherous kingdom.

After they spoke, Boaz said: But why the memorial, why now all of a sudden? Because I'm waning, Boaz, said the Captain in a gloomy despair and a betrayed sadness, Dante wrote the world and then tried to build another world, he's my bereaved son! I've got the money. You've got the knowledge. You build memorials for everybody. Build one for me.

Maybe, said Boaz.

No maybe, said the Captain. You owe me and you'll build. I'll pay.

Boaz asked: Is there a specific place that will suit the memorial?

The Kastel, said the Captain. From there Jerusalem was seen in ruins by Gottfried of Bouillon. There the poor Crusaders ripped their clothes in ten ninety-nine before they went up to conquer Jerusalem. From the Kastel, the city is seen in its wretchedness by pilgrims in all generations. From there Dante could have seen it if he had gone up to it. Do you know the mountain? he asked.

Once, said Boaz, I conquered it for you inadvertently.

There we'll erect the memorial, said the Captain, whose faith in it was only strengthened by the authority of the words.

Noga refused to come along. She told Hasha Masha: Henkin wants to go with Boaz and the Captain, they're going to find a place for the memorial to Dante. Hasha Masha said: They'll put that Italian on their committee, what do you have to do with Boaz Schneerson! But Henkin put on his hat and kissed Noga on the cheek, hugged Hasha and left the house. Boaz and Noga's roof was new to him. Walls enclosed the little grove Noga planted. A plane circled in the sky on its way to Lod Airport. Henkin stood in the center of the roof, looked at the rusting houses of old Tel Aviv, and said: I'm torturing myself, what do I have to do with this mountain? And Boaz looked at Henkin with the same ancient and piercing affection he saw in the eyes of Ebenezer when he thought he was Samuel, and said: That mountain was the most important place in Menahem's life, but I confused everything and you won't believe anymore, so what's the point of talking—

Boaz drove the car and Henkin and the Captain in his uniform observed the very familiar landscape. Not far from the place where Menahem is buried, Boaz turned right and climbed up the mountain. The air was fragrant and pure. A wind whistled in the treetops, the mountains at that hour were clear and free of mist and came close together.

On top of the mountain stood a ruined structure. Below new structures were seen and Jews from Iran, Bukhara, and Afghanistan dressed in colorful clothing were walking around among the structures. A woman in a purple *yashmak* called out: The mother of the sons calls the Lord! A gray-haired mustached man appeared, and said: The wicked of the wicked is before you my lady, and she said strangers came up above and he turned his eyes aside and saw a car and three people, one of them a general, he picked up the old rifle and the cartridge of bullets, shot one bullet into the air, and the colorful people stopped what they were doing and looked up, and the woman yelled: Kill, kill, but the man approached Boaz, Henkin, and the Captain aiming the rifle at them, and Boaz said: We're from the Prime Minister's office, searching for a suitable place for a tombstone for an outstanding Jewish commander named Dante Alighieri who overcame the wicked Romans. The man, whose rifle slipped down, recalled his distant youth in misty mountains in a distant land, and the other people approached and stood around him. One man said: Commander? We had a dervish who was the son of Queen Esther, and lived in the mountains. He was a great Jewish hero and the king of all the Persians. Did you hear of Ahasuerus? Esther was his wife. Then we came to the river. Remember what river would come to the Land of Israel? It was forty days across, forty days we rode in a truck just to get across to the other side. And then, the little girl born after the big rain died, and from there in airplanes, and you're a commander, you want a tombstone? Why not? Jews or non-Jews? And everybody laughed and startled the pure air with mouths full of white, crooked, and black teeth. As a sign of friendship, the man put the rifle down on the ground and started singing, and everybody hummed along with him. The singer reminded the Captain of the ancient melodies they'd sing in the Temple, which was taken to Babylon and from there came to Spain and was preserved in monasteries by conversos, who were then exiled to the east and came to Persia and India and Kurdistan and Afghanistan, and from those chants Dante Alighieri wove the Divine Comedy, whose melody was heard by Emanuel the Roman who knew the melodies he took in with his mother's milk and the hidden and mysterious notes were latent in him . . .

Then they stood above, and the people, except for that silver-haired mustached man, went to their houses and Boaz told about the decisive battle on the Kastel. Henkin stopped his ears. He didn't want to hear. And so Teacher Henkin, stubbornly but courageously, missed the only chance he was given in his life to hear about one battle in which his son fought wisely and heroically.

After Abdul Khadr el-Husseini was killed by mistake, said Boaz, and any one of us could have shot him, including Menahem, he said and looked at Henkin, all the Arabs fled and then came a reinforcement of commanders and we saw them enter the path, yelling, but they didn't hear and then it was too late and Simon Alfasi shouted: "Privates retreat, the commanders will cover the retreat," and thirty-three commanders were killed to defend Boaz and Menahem and Joseph. Afterward, the Arabs discovered the body of their leader and they fled . . . And that started the decisive turning point in the War of Independence . . . Menahem's one shot!

Or yours, shouted Henkin who heard the last words.

Or mine, said Boaz sadly.

Henkin started thinking about the next Independence Day: Nineteen years have passed and what am I doing? I'm helping erect a tombstone for Dante that will look toward Menahem's Jerusalem, while for my poets I left abandoned graves in the old cemetery of Tel Aviv. And out of pondering and an ancient sense of treachery, Henkin said: I see shadows on the horizon, Boaz, and Boaz said: What shadows, and the Captain looked and said: There will be a war, and Boaz thought: They're making fun, those old men, what war can you see, but he didn't say a thing and looked at the old Bukharan who started singing again.

In the evening, the Captain sat with Rebecca. Rebecca said: He's probably fed up with memory books and he wants to be a memorial to himself, but without my Psalms, he won't succeed. And the Captain said: But what will become of us, Rebecca? He thought about Ebenezer who had recently come back and painted his house, and Rebecca said: What will be? All my enemies are dead, all I've got left is you, Captain, Roots is waiting for me, you're suffering from eight diseases and you won't recover from any of them, what do you want from an old woman like me?

Tape / —

Boaz was one of the first to go. Then Noga was mobilized too. Hasha Masha asked, Why you all of a sudden? And Noga, who came to visit her, said: They'll find something for me, I'm not considered married and the lists got mixed up. People stuck pieces of tape on windowpanes, Rebecca sat in her armchair and contemplated her life and didn't find anything in it that wasn't compelled in advance. Planes flew low and shook the house. The great-grandson of Ahbed disappeared, but came back. At the airport, foreign residents were evacuated. The Captain said: They built an Auschwitz here with a philharmonic orchestra and now they sit and wait. Why don't they strike? He wore his uniform and asked to be mobilized, but nobody even paid attention to his lunacy. Dayan was appointed Minister of Defense. Eskhol delivered a speech. On television, hordes of Egyptian recruits were seen marching to throw the Jews into the sea. The nation of Israel, said the Captain, sees Chmielnitski and Hitler assaulting it, and I pity Nasser. He was the only one who pitied him at that time. Early in the morning, the red sheet was hoisted and without music, and in a thin still voice, the nation of Israel went to the great war against fat Frieda who lay under the dog, thought Ebenezer, the fist clenched for three weeks gaped open.

And five days later everything was almost calm.

Tape / —

She took off her clothes and put them on the cot. Outside reigned the impermeable desert dark. In the next bed he lay, she couldn't imagine how he looked. She played a game of imagining him from his breathing, from the smell of shoes and socks. She strained her eyes and saw shadows. Outside voices sawed. Her skin shuddered and she rolled herself up in damp army blankets smelling faintly of Lysol. She lay down, her eyes gazing at the ceiling of the tent. He said: Wonder what you look like in the light. She said: I also want to know what you look like. Every night you're here and not seen. In the morning you disappear before I open my eyes. By the time I come back at night, you're in bed.

My name's Boaz, he told her. I'm a grown-up child who survived the wars. Killing and not killed. On the Richter scale of my metaphysical biology, I'm a nine. Your wonderful youth can be smelled. All I know about you is that you've got a lover, that you have difficult dreams I can hear, you're somebody one can definitely fall in love with, if one forgets the inconceivable and unbearable problems of love. For years now I haven't managed to die in just wars, and in unjust wars I don't die either. Maybe justice has nothing to do with death in war? Now that the war is ending soon, I'm still here. During the day I shoot the routed enemy. You've got a female rustle among your clothes. When you undress in the dark, there are tears in my eyes.

She said: That's nice of you. My stupid officer pushes me around all day. He's got clean fingernails, smells like perfume. You sound like a person who flourishes in wars.

I make no demands on you. It's true, I love another man. But you come back with a smell of death and dark. Last night I smelled blood. You sound like a professional soldier. You bring weapons in your hands, you kill and sleep, sleep and kill. In that shelling you slept like a baby. I don't know why they put us in the same tent. My officer tried to start with me again today. I erupted. He has soft, warm hands. He talked to me about twilight in a distant city, said I remind him of that. It was cold and the sergeant on duty yelled: I'll put all of them under arrest, and all of them cleaned the mud and the mud kept coming in. As far as I'm concerned, you should go to jail for mud. I'll smoke a cigarette now. And you?

I'm trying to think if you're pretty. That drives me nuts. Do you have breasts? Big ones? Small ones? And your face, terrific, I'm not terrific either, few people like me. I don't believe in marriage. And I don't believe in love, either, but I'm starting to doubt my ability not to love. Why do people want so much to be loved? All the fools and dummies ultimately find somebody who loves them. And the worst bastards also have friends and women. You can see that from the funerals. The dumber the man the bigger his funeral.

Today I got out of the half-track. I went to search for a land mine. In the distance I saw people in the desert. Men in coats and suits and tunics and women in pants and head kerchiefs. They were straying, aimlessly, their eyes burning from the desert wind. Hundreds of men and women. One of them had a red scarf. I yelled at them to watch out. There are land mines, I said, and they didn't hear and weren't scared. They showed me pictures of their sons. Every one had a picture of his son, you know the high school graduation pictures they make with the faces of stranglers of old women? Those are their sweeties, and they were searching for their sweeties in the desert. Everybody asks if I know his son. Missing, they say. One woman told me: You surely know him. Surely, why should I know him, but I said: Maybe, maybe I knew him. She said, search for him for me. I've got to find him. "Surely," that's the compelling word, don't you think? You with your small or big breasts. After the woman with the red scarf disappeared I smoked a cigarette. Some of the sons in the pictures had scared faces. Do you think those with scared faces die more than those whose faces aren't scared? I'd like you to have my picture . . . with an erect cock. Like now. You'll take the picture with the erect cock, walk in the sands and ask if somebody knows me. Maybe some poor girl I once inserted a souvenir into. She'll say: The shmuck's buried not far from here. And you, will you weep?

And what do you do in civilian life?

Grave digger, prepare my financial future.

You're trying to be cynical.

Trying, that's right. Not living in the right man. A girl came to me, she's got long chestnut-colored hair and bright eyes. Not especially pretty, but belonging to somebody so temptingly. She said to me: I'm searching for a man. I asked if I could be the man. She looked at me contemptuously and I saw how she belonged to her somebody and I was jealous. And then she repeated: I'm searching for a man. I told her: What about his picture? She didn't have one. And she blushed because she didn't have a picture. She said: Listen, I'm searching for a man I love, and she didn't add anything more.

Will you also ask somebody about my cock, will you say then: I'm searching for a man I love?

Yes, she said, and she smoked a cigarette silently and her breath was fast, almost loud. You understand, he said, the girl put a semicolon after the man, because maybe he's dead. She didn't know his last name. She met him in a tent like this in Bir-Gafgafa in the dark. When there were still a lot more planes ripping the sky. She didn't know the declension: "I loved," everything was fresh and still in the present tense. Like the grammatical judgment of a language teacher. I turn over for a moment, the blanket stabs what's-his-name. Like this. She can't draw me the face of the lover. He had no geographical bearings or characteristics, normal or otherwise. No special signs. Only certain things, she said, swallowed those words. And then she said again with surprising speed: Things that can't be defined, she meant what happened to them together in the tent. Maybe she loved him because he died? How do I know? And if he died, maybe she'd love him forever. Isn't that safer?

She crushes the cigarette. Rustling is heard outside. Three half-tracks rumble up and brake. Music from the radio mixed with a roaring motor. The flash of pale blue light in the tent flap. A wind strikes the tarp. She sinks her head deep into the small hard pillow. I recall going out with my lover, she said.

He laughed.

And he's alive, she said.

Ah, but for how long?

A long time. Once he took me to the movies. That was soon after we met. He'd sit in cafés, go to matinees, waste time, sit next to me in the movies and even though he looked like a letch, he was afraid to stroke my back. I thought: Why doesn't he understand I've got breasts? Why doesn't he put a hand on my breasts, he thought I was a dangerous girl.

In the morning she sits at the teleprinter. Third shift. All the time she receives messages. Words appear—missing, missing, fell, fell, wounded. Names, numbers, identity tags. She drinks hot coffee from a cardboard cup and writes the dead. Suddenly she shrieks: Joseph Gimmeleon. Just yesterday he came into the teleprinter room and saw three girls and didn't know which one of us to desire more. So perplexed and lost he stood there. And I was the oldest. The officer with the soft sweaty hands didn't let him take us to the movies. He said: I'm from Haifa, and Talya made him a red paper flower. He stuck it in his shirt lapel and disappeared with Zelda. She phones the battalion. A field phone hums. A commander yells at Talya, come down from the line, she comes to a third in command who sleeps with her every third night. From the distance, from the war, a voice rising and falling like a roar answers her: What, what, Joseph, Joseph Gimmeleon, the body wasn't intact, they found a red paper flower. I'm coming tomorrow, and he hung up.

Bring you coffee, he asked.

Bring yourself, fool, she said.

I'm wiped out from the teleprinter, she said, but without naming names, and clean up your smell, don't want to smell death.

He stood in the tent flap. Took off his clothes. She strained her eyes but didn't see a thing. He said: Wait a minute. And then a car passed by in the distance and sprayed a little light. He stood there shaking and naked and she laughed.

He went to her and she said: You look like a skeleton. Want to touch you. Then if you want, you can. On a night like this I'm easily raped. Mainly by a living person, without a red paper flower, but don't try to be close or understanding, you'll just touch me and I you. In bed he hugged her and the shaking passed. Try to be romantic, she said, but without love. He said to her: I'll put a paper flower in you. She said: You're faking, you behave as if you know this body, think it's an instrument, be more careful, more calculating, you're sweet. And he said: No compliments, listen to the distant cannons, killing.

Then she stands up and he hugs her. Don't be a dead picture for me, she says. We fit in terms of height. Maybe we'll love each other again, she says, and they sway in an uncompromising prayer and things are forgotten. He steps on chewing gum and is disgusted. He also tosses her onto the bed, clings to her, that need to be loved by a real enemy who is you, and she puts her life on his erection and lies there, waiting, sweat pouring, that beauty of a mad lusty movement in a tent, you and I, two strangers. Listen, you can do with me what you want, but only in the dark and as an undesirable woman, as I am, don't relent, here I'm touching, touching with my feet the ceiling of the tent. Lick like that toward Mecca, yes press like that. Press . . . You think there's a God? I don't care. There are officers outside with national erections. You think there really are national goals. Here we can beget a Hebrew soldier for the ninth war, in this state a national mutation will take place and they'll beget children with rifles attached. You exaggerate, she said unemotionally. Everybody has a different name for what's happening here. Tomorrow you take the picture of that cock and walk in the sands and search for me. Ask horny soldiers if they knew me. Tell them you didn't know my first name or my last name. In that silence to penetrate to the throat and cut it. Generally, she says, I love first and only then do they come into me. Now it's vice versa. Who needs victory? Don't stop. I'm unable to love, he says, and she says: From death you came and to death you'll go, I'm lost between here and there.

And beyond them, far from there, people are killed. Bullets go astray at night. Airplanes go on final sallies. The teleprinter doesn't speak his name.

Then she smokes a cigarette. Silence. Pleasant odor of burned red war kerosene. If that smell is pleasant, it means I'm alive and well. The wind isn't blowing anymore, eh?

The wind isn't blowing, he said.

Talya had a boyfriend, she said.

You make friends fast. I've been here three and a half weeks and I've got only you. You've already got girlfriends, officers with wet hands, memories.

You should know me in civilian life. I silence the radio. But that's not important. My friend, Talya, had a boyfriend. Before the adjutant who slept with her. And I've also got an affair with you, even though I love somebody else.

Talya's boyfriend lives in America and sends her letters. She says that's convenient for her. She wants to know if she really loves him or not and the distance is a test. He'd come for every war. On the first plane he'd come. His unit loved him because he'd bring them presents—real jeans, lighters, American cigarettes. He once brought a mixer for one of them, she says.

Who?

Talya.

Oh. Give me a drag. He drags on the cigarette and puts it back in her lips. He looks at the dark, at the slit of pleasure of the juncture of her lips. A junction of pleasure of strength and softness. And she goes on: After the wars and the campaigns, Talya says, he goes back to America. He'd also bring whiskey. And for that war he came late. They had a pool about when he'd come and if. He came on the third day. From the airport he came straight here. His friends took blankets, a kitbag, and personal weapons for him. Even a little book of Psalms and the prayer of the warrior. He came straight to the desert with a James Bond case and a suit and tie, put on a uniform, and in two hours he went out in their half-track. Then he came back to Talya and she was in the clinic. They met by chance. They slept together one night. She says it was great. He forgot his James Bond case at her place and came back. The case was empty, she says. Why did he bring an empty case? Two days later, she went to his parents in Jerusalem. The father saw her and hugged her. The mother gave her a cup of tea. Talya sat in her filthy uniform and drank. They hung pictures of him all over the house. His father said: See how lucky we are, this time he didn't come. And the mother was glad the son didn't come, this time she had fears and dreams, but he didn't come so everything was fine. In America they're not fighting in the Sinai now.

I saw a father walking alone, he said. With a creased picture. He asks every soldier: Did you know him, did you know him? Me he didn't want to approach. He sat in the middle of the desert and dug, he searched for his son in a pit. Desperate. His son wasn't in the pit. All around were corpses of Egyptians. The wounded were brought from the Canal. He searched for his son in the pit, just because there was a pit there.

And there was one there who photographed a killed person, wore a *kippah,* and took twenty-eight pictures of the killed man from every angle until he ran out of film.

In the morning, the two of them came out of the tent. Not yet really morning, but they saw one another in the light. A pale desert light. Clear and pure. He started the jeep. She got in and sat next to him. Shadows of night and dew still mixed with sunrise. A gigantic convoy passed by them and they had to get off the road for a while and get out of the way. Sitting and looking, trucks with prisoners, soldiers with drooping heads, sleeping standing or sitting, two small buses full of singers, dancers, and mimes returning from the front, more prisoners with dead smiles spread over their faces, defective ammunition, spoils of crushed enemy tanks on carriages and command cars filled with wounded. One of the singers in the bus sang and the song was swallowed in the distant desert. The prisoners gazed with empty eyes. She flicked a cigarette. In the distance, civilians were seen, women with kerchiefs against the wind. Dogs running aimlessly, black and gray desert dogs, the light grows stronger, and a voice is heard: He comes only for wars, doesn't stay to live here, and now who will bury him? Then they drove on, a captured tank stood there, four foreign photographers wearing laced-up hats are posing the dead next to the tank. Moving the corpses and laying them in a nice position. While the photographers quarrel about where to put the last corpse of the rout, he spits and starts the motor. A soldier comes to them with a jerrican full of coffee. In the distance shots are heard. Three horses whinny and gallop toward the jeep, and she says: Like in the movies, while he takes out a transistor and puts it to his ear. The horses gallop and the shots cease. And then the horses disappear in the gigantic plain and shots echo once again.

People, old, young, women wrapped in kerchiefs, lie curled up in the desert. In their hands they hold photos. On their faces is the terror of the dream that may not be a dream anymore. He says to her: In an hour I'll take you back to the teleprinter! He wants her in the wet sand of the morning dew in the filtered and serene light, and when they stopped at a damaged car they saw a soldier connecting an electric razor to the battery and shaving. He stood naked in the morning chill and trembled. The soldier asked: Are you by any chance not dead people searching for their parents?

You're a son-of-a-bitch, he said to the soldier, we're going to make us our sons right here.

So who's the son-of-a-bitch here, said the soldier and went on shaving.

In the evening, after the teleprinter, he waited for her as if he hadn't seen her in a year. They went to the culture center. A month ago, Nasser said here that he'd throw the Jews into the sea. This doesn't look like a sea, said some sergeant major. But he wasn't laughing now. Airplanes tore the sky in sudden sallies. An arrogant atmosphere of numb tension prevailed. They sat facing a television set. They set up an antenna to receive broadcasts from Jerusalem that were just starting. Through the former Egyptian transmitter they can see the end of the war in the north. And H. Herzog talking about our forces. I'm drinking the wine of Latrun brought by the conquerors of Latrun, he thinks, and looks at H. Herzog talking about our forces, how terrific is H. Herzog, he's a General (Res.) and can talk; what and where to. He's also combed and talks with abysmal seriousness about wars. Wars aren't such a serious matter, H. Herzog. Our forces are a

youth with a paper flower who shaves naked at a destroyed car and then
dies. Or first dies and then shaves. Our forces is a man with a James Bond
case who comes to wars from America and they're still drinking his whiskey here. Our forces is also H. Herzog himself telling what our forces are,
what they do, did, will do.

When they went out they looked toward a dark point lighted for a moment by two spotlights. In the crisscross of the spotlights a half-track of the
Burial Society was seen. Instead of a cannon, a hut was set up there. In the
hut were our forces, their memory for a blessing. He said: See how they
pack the children whose parents are searching for them in the sands.
People dressed like crows with sidelocks and ritual fringes, and love thy
neighbor as thyself, they put the children in the hut on the half-track. In
their hands they hold prayer books they'd sometimes stick in their coat
pockets. Even the driver wears a *kippah,* but he doesn't wear a coat over the
prayer shawl. A young Hasid stood there, his face very pale, looked at the
crisscross of the lights and sang: This is what my heart desires, pity please
and do not overlook . . . He's also our forces, H. Herzog, he said.

When Boaz came to Rebecca's house, the old woman said, The Captain
died. Boaz didn't respond but went into the bathroom, waited until the
great-grandson of Ahbed brought him new clothes, filled the bathtub with
hot water, and sat for a long time and rubbed his body. Noga phoned and
he told her the Captain died.

Tape / —

Captain (Colonel) Jose Menkin A. Goldenberg died three days after the
war began. That was one of the rare days when Rebecca allowed the Captain to come when it wasn't Wednesday night. When he drank the eternal
tea the great-grandson of Ahbed poured for him, he saw Rebecca's legs
under the table. He said: I see through the dress, as if your clothes were
transparent, I don't see anything but bones and spots, he added pensively.
Outside, supersonic booms were heard, and Rebecca said: Watch out, Captain, you look like you are covered with clouds. The Captain said: When we
stood on the Kastel and talked about the memorial to Dante, I knew there
would be a war, I saw an army ready, but it wasn't ready, I saw things that
were to happen and that means I'm one foot in the future and the future
of a person over eighty years old isn't an alternative to death anymore. And

Rebecca said something and almost regretted the tone that didn't suit her, she said almost pleading: Don't die yet, I think I need you. He said: Interesting how beautiful you look without the clothes that disappeared from you, and she blushed and said: One by one they all go, don't let him take you, Menkin . . . not yet. Rebecca looked in his misty eyes and in her mind a memory surfaced of the river that pierced her, a sourish taste of blood rose from her insides to her lips and she said: When you see me naked after fifty years, Menkin, and I recall how I became pregnant from the river and begat Boaz, I start to be fond of you, Menkin . . .

In his attempt to smile, the Captain felt his bones dissolving, he stood up, kissed Rebecca's hand, and very slowly walked to his house. She watched him, but because her vision was blurred, she could see only an unclear mass walking on the path planted by Dana. The mass disappeared into the house and suddenly her throat felt dry. The Captain came to his room and felt the air running out of his lungs, his throat was choked, his body heavy. He lay in his bed, very slowly stretched his legs, even though it hurt, lit the table lamp, put his false teeth in a glass from which he sipped a little water, then he shook the glass to drizzle a little water on his hair, the glass was almost emptied, and he put his hat on his chest, his sword across his body, didn't take off his boots, but polished the medals he pinned on, and with his last strength, with a comb he held in a trembling hand, he combed the wet hair, and unable to see himself in a mirror he folded his hands, and when he saw the phosphorescent clock showing three a.m., he managed to pound the clock, stop time, and die.

Rebecca went into her room, locked the door, and for two days she didn't come out. When the great-grandson of Ahbed claimed that the corpse was rotting, she yelled at him not to come near her. Two days later, planes were heard passing over the house on their way north, and Rebecca went out of the room wearing a black dress and asked Ahbed to make her something to eat. She sat alone to eat and said: What great generals are starting to die now!

Nobody knew how to bury him. His splendid lying in bed evoked admiration and amazement mixed with an intoxicating atmosphere of victory. The rabbi waged a hard struggle not only with Rebecca but also with Mr. Klomin and a few other old men who began to show a suspicious fondness for the Captain. When Mr. Klomin went to the small church in

Jaffa, there wasn't a single person alive who remembered the Captain. In the beautiful house among swans and rare birds where the old man dressed in white sank into the ground, lived three old Arabs. The rabbi who left before in high dudgeon now returned from Roots in an almost philosophical mood, a sense of death stuck to him too, but he still firmly refused to bury the Captain in Roots. Rebecca argued with an implacable vehemence that her husband had founded Roots even though of course he wasn't to blame for the stupid name they gave the cemetery, and she had, she claimed, the right of veto. The phrase "right of veto" she had heard on the radio in interpretations of H. Herzog about the war Boaz was fighting now to make Nehemiah's desired and dubious future present, she said.

Nor in the Captain's papers did they find anything to indicate how to bury him. The valises and crates said: "To Boaz Schneerson." Rebecca and Mr. Klomin searched in those closets and cases with Boaz's name. Mr. Klomin, who wore white in honor of the resurrected kingdom of Israel—but also his joy for the kingdom and his worry about the disgrace that would be brought down on it by the leaders of Israel who surely didn't understand the greatness of the hour—didn't cover his pain at the death of his one friend. Among the objects they found a hundred and fifty poems, some written by the Captain and some ancient poems, handwritten, love poems to the throat and neck, the breasts and shoulders of a beautiful lady, addressed to Rebecca, even though they were never sent to her. She wondered how Joseph's poems had come into the Captain's hands, but then she said to herself with a logic characteristic of the Captain: He was an editor of a French newspaper in Cairo, so! In the suitcases were secret plans of various undergrounds, models of memorials to the poet Dante Alighieri, a plan, called "secret," for irrigating the Negev, a booklet in the Captain's handwriting titled "Indications of the Burial Place of Moses, Hagar, Jacob, and Alcibiades the Greek," and even Mr. Klomin didn't recognize the last name on the list or what he had to do with Moses, Hagar, and Jacob. There were descriptions of passes to the Land of Israel from the north, the east, and the south, including the Mitla and Gidi passes in the Sinai desert. Precise and old descriptions of the Santa Katerina rift in the Sinai which was now occupied, plans for war and crossing rivers, a war of armor against armor as a revolutionary tactic, which apparently had not yet been tried or had been tried before the invention of the tank. There were also books of the Jew-

ish religion and the Greek Orthodox religion, *Midrashim Eyn-Ya'akov* with
a dedication in an old-fashioned, curled hand to Yossel Goldenberg,
Argentinean books of war, "Books of the True Faith to the Children of the
Religion of Moses Who Saw the Truth," dried flowers, maps of lands neither Mr. Klomin nor the geography teacher—who was summoned—could
identify, maps of military campaigns with notes in a secret writing, copies
of Mr. Klomin's letters from a state whose name was torn from the enve-
lopes and its stamps destroyed. There were alphabetical lists of heads of
the underground and the Haganah in the thirties and forties, leaders of
Arab gangs, a list of the sexual perversions of high British officials, docu-
mentation of their acts, the copy of a secret correspondence between the
chief of the American air force and the British attaché about bombing or
not bombing the railroad tracks to Auschwitz, various notes, including an
announcement of the mufti of Jerusalem that "it's better for the English
not to support the Jewish foul deed and not to believe their lies about what
is happening in Europe as it were."

The American commander's rebuke of the pilot who mistakenly
dropped a bomb on the death camp of Auschwitz: "From now on, be careful not to waste bombs on areas close to attack targets like the A. G. Farben
factory, or any other industrial concentration." Rebecca and Mr. Klomin
also found Mr. Klomin's letters filed by the date they were sent, a journal of Boaz's life, faded brown pictures of anonymous handsome women
in splendid old fashioned garb in unidentified places, a little girl's curl,
and next to it an aging yellowed note: "Delicate Melissa." Names of the
Mameluke military commanders, dubious research on seaweed, on Swiss
democracy, history of the struggle for equal rights for women in the United
States, history of the tango, cooking recipes, Bible stories illustrated with
saccharine drawings, and an explicit request to be buried according to his
real religion (not identified), in the natural place (without any indication
of place), account books, checks and savings accounts in the name of
Rebecca and Boaz Schneerson and Mr. Klomin, in Egypt, Israel, Switzerland, Argentina, the United States, and Sweden.

They buried the Captain in two places. He was buried in the little
church in Jaffa and then his clothes were buried in Roots. The rabbi pretended not to see, and two tombstones were erected in his memory, one
in the churchyard and one in Roots. Despite the protests of the rabbi and

the director of the Burial Society, the schoolchildren, in white shirts, were forced to sing the national anthems of Israel, Argentina, Switzerland, the United States, and Egypt at the Captain's grave. Singing the last national anthem evoked strong protest even among Rebecca's supporters, but she insisted and it was hard to fight with her, especially since the young people were starting to come back from the war and most of the residents of the settlement were on their way to Jerusalem to see the miracle of the unified city. The consuls who were invited didn't come. Rebecca allowed the limited audience to see her shed a few tears at the grave. Mr. Klomin said: You missed the great kingdom of Israel that arose in spite of her foes, and Rebecca said: May you rest in peace, Captain, and when you come to your god, whoever he is, kiss his eyelids for all of us and be our advocate for our health and wealth.

On the way back from Roots, Rebecca walked faster than Mr. Klomin. She saw a castle in the clouds with a flag waving on it. In the castle, like a coil of silkworms, the Last Jew lay curled up. His eyes were shut and she felt a stab in her belly because when she sat on the deck of the ship and Ebenezer was inside her, she could sense the dream of Nehemiah Schneerson curled up in her, and then she saw Boaz come into the world and he was a copy of Joseph. She looked at the castle, the clouds moved, the mists scattered, and then she saw Ebenezer standing in the distance and looking at her. She called him to come home, and she said: The Captain is dead, Ebenezer, and he said: Before you looked at me as if you didn't see me. But she was too tired to answer him. They entered the house and when they sat in the room, Mr. Klomin started muttering vague words, his eyes were wet, crying now, he asked where was the queen who had once lived here whose sons had brought a disaster. He said: Dana will return from the Captain's house soon. Then he pulled out of his pocket a new map of "the liberated territories" that had been distributed two days before by the newspapers, and said: Greater Israel, the land of David, Solomon, and Alexander Yanai, and he started talking to the Captain and telling him the results of a poll of fifty-two members of the party who had died long ago, and then he bowed his head and banged on the table, Ebenezer started up and Mr. Klomin turned his face, smiled and said: In blood and fire Judah fell in blood and fire Judah . . . and he died. Rebecca said, Soon I'll be glad you came back, Ebenezer, see what a new plague of

death has spread here, and she thought of the plague of death that ran
rampant in the settlement years ago, and Ebenezer said: Samuel's forgetting machine is the watch set backward of the Last Jew! She looked at him
in amazement, shut Mr. Klomin's eyes, but Ebenezer, who was excited and
tried to understand what he had just said, wrote something in the little
journal he had started carrying in his pocket in recent months and wrote
in it things he thought, to know if he knew some things about himself. He
didn't understand what disease of forgetting could have afflicted Samuel,
and what was its connection to the watch set backward of the Last Jew—
which is me, and Samuel wasn't here at all. Rebecca who was already worrying about burying Mr. Klomin, forgot that Mr. Klomin never claimed to be
an American citizen, and so the strict rabbi, who replaced the local rabbi
who went to the desert to bury our forces of H. Herzog, didn't raise any
difficulties, even though he asked who guaranteed that Mr. Klomin was
indeed a Jew. Mr. Klomin was buried in Roots, next to the Captain, two
single strangers in the parking lot of Nchemiah's pioneer paradise, said
Rebecca, for whom phrases like "parking lot" or "right of veto" were new.
She told Ebenezer, I'm old now and what's in store for me, who else will
be taken from me, and then Boaz came back from the war and showered
and sat in the bathroom and talked with Noga on the phone and went to
the graves of the Captain and Mr. Klomin and let Rebecca read him five of
the hundred and fifty poems written by Joseph Rayna and the Captain for
Rebecca Schneerson and he fell asleep.

Tape / —

When he came to Tel Aviv the roof was locked. On the door hung a
note: Be back soon, wait for me. Noga climbed up carrying a bag of groceries. They kissed, it was oppressively hot and they stayed on the roof. Below,
horns honked as cars got stuck in the convoy. When they went into the
house and Noga set the table with the groceries she had just bought, he
noticed the pile of letters. There were invitations to memorials, construction bills, printed matter and pieces for proofreading; he kicked the pile
and yelled: Come on, let's blow this place. The windows were open and
from all of them came the song "Jerusalem of Gold." The song tells of how
Jerusalem was empty of people until the Jewish paratroopers conquered it.
Too bad we weren't defeated, said Boaz, I could have made you a beautiful

corpse. She didn't answer, looked around and thought of the Captain and Mr. Klomin, if only for them the war should have been won. Then they ate hummus at Shmil's restaurant and drank cold water from a whiskey bottle and looked at the vegetables heaped up in the nearby store and fish were brought in nets to the fish warehouse, and Boaz started the car, and said to Shmil: The hummus was great, Shmil, and they left. They parked the car, went into the hotel and spoke English. Boaz said: We're foreign journalists, and the woman smiled and said in Hebrew: Go up to room twenty-six. He sealed the windows, and said: The Captain shouldn't have died, Ebenezer is searching for Samuel, Talya's boyfriend died, I'm building tombstones, what a crappy victory!

Outside, maybe the sun set but they couldn't see. Downstairs in the lobby, colored paper strips were surely hung and the music was ear-piercing, but they didn't hear. They played child returning home to mother who's sleeping with the guard. Then they played boy whose father names him after his wife's lovers. Boaz said: I would curse your father if I knew which of his ninety-two women was your mother. And Noga said: You're killing Rebecca's saying, you should have said concubines. He said: It's an Arabic saying and I don't care. The lips burned. The air smelled of old urine, burning cars, and raw flaxseed oil. Noga thought: Is it truly possible to start all over from this moment? They crawled in imaginary battles and she played a girl who writes names on the teleprinter, stood before him only in a bra, he lay on the bed and she was ordered to be a vulture pouncing on a corpse. He didn't shut his eyes, lay without moving, tears flowed onto her cheeks but he didn't give up. When she hovered over him she looked artificial, transparent and airy, but when she landed she was heavy, and when he was filled with dread and yelled, she stopped and he signaled angrily: Go on! Go on! And the tears kept flowing, and Boaz said: Got to know how to celebrate victory before it turns into a bank account. She slapped his face and he played dead again, but his eyes were wide open. The ceiling was filthy and he said: You're a great vulture. Then, he squashed the vulture and kissed it and they lay there, and didn't move, like a couple of elderly lovers whose blood pressure would go up with every movement. They guessed the dark thickening outside and sensed the flow of the hours, the moments, minutes and seconds, and her insides were holding his power, and when a gloomy smile of triumph spread their lips, they fell asleep.

At dawn, Boaz woke up and was still inside her. When it hardened, she groaned in her sleep, but didn't wake up. Her lips were spread. After he got dressed he went down and bought coffee and rolls, butter and jam. And he came back. He opened the window, and when the light beams caressed her she woke up. She drank the coffee and ate two rolls with jam, sat up in bed, gathered the blanket and wrapped her legs in it, straightened her hair, and he said: I sat with the prime minister, and he told me to go see if the circles were really right. I went, but the foreign minister wasn't there anymore. Two young men were making emergency plans, but the Captain's plans were bolder. Then I bought pencils that said Made in China. Talya came and said the pencils belonged to her boyfriend and put them in the James Bond cube and went to screw the adjutant. She said: All the foreign ministers went to a parade. I was suspicious, but I didn't say a thing. I bought you coffee and rolls. Two armored troop carriers collided and I photographed their burned skeletons. Then I made them into a memorial to Dante, who invented the armored troop carrier. When children being taken to the Magen David clinic asked me what circles I was asking about, I fled. Then some man I didn't know and maybe looked like me came out of the camp with a barbed wire fence, maybe me, and one of the foreign soldiers standing there said: Now there'll be bread. A man I love and was a father to me said: Now I'm not alive anymore, we remained alive, but this life isn't ours.

Noga said: You dream nice, the coffee's nice, but you've got to go back.

He asked: Where, Noga? He was sad and silent: Where?

She didn't answer and looked at the window as if there really was something there she wanted to see.

Tape / —

Yes . . .

Yes, I also know when they left the hotel. How many tips? Not counted. Sees an article in a pamphlet "Kingdom of Israel," Number 34B. "Before his premature death (quote from the article), A. N. (Akiva Nimrod) Klomin managed to finish page six hundred of his big final letter. That was on June fourth, nineteen sixty-seven. Then Mr. Klomin heard the news, the weather forecast from the Golan to southern Sinai—one day before the war ended—he stood in his bed, sang Hatikvah to the window, and died. But there is also another version . . ."

Tape / —

The Hebrew poet Emanuel the Roman lived in Rome between 1270 and 1332. He knew Dante Alighieri, cured him of his illnesses, held conversations with him, sang him the songs of the Temple he knew from his mother's milk, and gave Dante the ancient meters from which Dante spun his rhymes. Maybe he also loved Beatrice. He was a learned man, a bon vivant, and a poet. Aside from philosophy, Bible interpretations, and sonnets in Italian, he wrote the *Notebooks of Emanuel* on the model of *The Wise One* by Rabbi Judah al-Harizi. A witty satire, splendid and restrained rhetoric, poems of lust and love, full of wisdom of life and wisdom of the world, his one poem begins . . .

Tape / —

My dear friend in cold and rainy Germany, here it is light and warm.

Thanks for your last letter.

I asked myself if I am really and truly open to you. Can there be friendship between us? To myself I thought: What is real friendship? Is it possible to understand our encounter at Ebenezer Schneerson's home as an attempt to capture a shadow, when two sides, opposite from one another, you and I, hunt echoes that cannot be captured? You wanted details and I generalize, but I am still horrified and amused by the thought that the Last Jew will be written, or is perhaps already written, by an aging teacher acting—as his wife puts it—his bereaved love and by Germanwriter, a man of the world, an artist who collects literary prizes, whom critics compare with Proust, Joyce, Thomas Mann, and Faulkner, but he's unable to write the story of Ebenezer, Rebecca, Boaz, and Samuel by himself and needs these tidbits, the limping investigations of Teacher Henkin . . . From the mendacity of the two of us, from our mutual helplessness, will a book come, or perhaps they will be notes for somebody else, for a better violinist than us who will write this book? Maybe a book should be written as books were written in the Middle Ages. First one version of Faust or Hamlet, and then

comes somebody else and writes another version, and on the
basis of that version, a play is written, or even a book, and then
comes somebody else and writes the new version and so on
until Goethe or Shakespeare . . . Jordana managed to weep at the
cemetery on the anniversary of Menahem's death. (Details!) She
encountered Boaz. They met in the Ministry of Defense because
of their common work. I don't know exactly how they met. I resented it, but I didn't say a word. Noga told me: "I love that sad
Yemenite woman, I love her lost betrayal of Menahem, her dependence on Boaz."

Yes, and the meeting with Jordana. We planned an outing for
the Committee of Bereaved Parents. On the phone, Jordana said:
We'll meet in a café, because it's hard for me to sit and discuss
these things in front of Hasha's mocking eyes. I'm no expert in
the new cafés, and I remembered Kassit Café, once a meeting
place for writers and artists, and I said: What about Kassit, and
she said, Fine. I walked there and thought that if I had sat in
Kassit after the war I would have met Boaz, who sat there then
and waited for me. Unlike me, Jordana took a taxi and so she
was late. After all the years when I hadn't set foot in the place,
the waiters looked as if they were still expecting those artists.
They waited on me nicely, immediately served me what I ordered, and smiled at me as if they were protesting the forsaken
youngsters with wild manes sitting there.

A young woman with open lips, shut eyes, sat there looking
as if she were rapt in mysterious thoughts. Artists yelled and
cursed one another, and when a person entered and wanted to
sit at an empty table, the waiter took it under advisement and
then allowed him to sit and I recalled Mr. Soslovitch and at the
same time also understood that he was dead, and at that very
moment, Jordana entered the café and looked extinguished.
Something in her face was depressed and bitter, she looked nervous, stood next to me distracted, I said Hello Jordana, I was so
glad to see her, and she said Hey Henkin and corrected it to
Hello Henkin, but the words were said distractedly, absentmindedly, she barely saw me, she sat down in a chair, muttered

something, excused herself and got up, went to the bar, next to where the owner of the place always slept with his enormous belly thrust forward and his legs stretched out in front of him and on his face a sweet glow of a giant teddy bear, asked permission to use the phone, dialed and sank into a long whispered conversation, I saw her weep a few times and then hang up decisively, amazed at the emptiness that filled her and very slowly she came to me, tried to smile through the screen of tears, said: You look great, Henkin, she sat down next to me, put her hands on the table, played a little with the salt shaker that had more grains of rice than salt, lowered her hands in astonishment, the salt shaker hit the pepper shaker with a bang that was maybe too loud for her. She groped in her purse, took out a cigarette and lighter, put the cigarette back in her purse, lit a cigarette that had been stuck in the corner of her mouth before, for a moment, she shut her eyes whose lids pearled with tears, opened them wide in a certain amazement, as if she didn't know exactly where she was and if she had already ended the long phone conversation, she inhaled deeply on the cigarette, and all I could see was a sadness spiraling up in a thin curling smoke, and I, maybe because of my sensitivity to her, maybe because of memories that surfaced in me, I looked at the man sitting at Soslovitch's table drinking beer and I tried to think about him, and Jordana played with the lighter and said: What a day, what a day, twice she said that, as if she weren't at all sure she had said what she said. The sorrow I saw in the meeting of her lips looked as if the smoke came to the soles of her feet and clouded my ability to talk with her about the outing we were about to plan. I said to her: The man eating gizzards and drinking beer is sitting at the special table. Maybe it was an attempt to distract, I really don't know anymore. Mr. Soslovitch, I said to her, sold locomotives. Ever since the establishment of the state he sells only one locomotive a year. A confirmed bachelor. Always dressed up, with a tie and a handsome hat.

Soslovitch loved artists and so he'd come here with the Cohen family. Mr. Cohen was then a bank manager or a financial advisor, I don't remember anymore, and Mrs. Cohen, a big, handsome woman (her father was one of the founders of Wadi Hanin and left her some land) had a house that served as a salon for artists and writers. I'm not well-versed in gossip, but Mrs. Cohen and Mr. Soslovitch fell in love with one another in nineteen twenty-nine, while Mr. Cohen used to travel a lot and seemed satisfied. He performed important missions for the new-born state, loved his wife's artists, and was a close friend of Mr. Soslovitch. Every Saturday afternoon they'd meet at Kassit, sit at the regular table, eat and drink. Sometimes they'd even hug each other emotionally, or would become pale and sing sad songs in Yiddish or Russian or Hebrew. Mr. Soslovitch would come alone every afternoon, sit at his regular table, and until he'd leave, nobody dared to sit at the table. Now a stranger is sitting there, and that's a sign that Mr. Soslovitch is dead. And so, out of thoughts of distant years I didn't even know I remembered, Jordana said, half pensively and half provocatively: What does that have to do with us?

What does that have to do with us? I asked.

Me? she said, blushed and repeated: What does that have to do, you burst into an open door and that doesn't suit you, Henkin. I said to her: I was trying to distract you from your gloom, and Jordana said to me: You're too old and wise to believe that if you tell a woman like me about a locomotive salesman who sold one locomotive a year, I'll forget what I'm weeping about. Did stories like that help you?

I was silent and drank coffee.

Then she ordered a beer and I saw the beer foam stick to the lips of the fragile madonna of death, and then she hissed between her lips: Son of a bitch, that Boaz Schneerson. She tried to smile, tears again pearled in her eyes, and she said: Let's drop the son of a bitch and talk about the outing. The son of a bitch said the stalactite cave is a delightful place, so I want some other place, Henkin, and now she almost yelled, since the girl who was meditating mysterious thoughts opened her eyes wide and looked at us in amazement and let her head drop on the table and fell asleep. I thought, Who sells us locomotives today? But that thought didn't help me, I couldn't really be concerned.

A few days ago, Harvjiaja brought me a story that was published in one of our journals. The story was written by a writer who fought in the war with Boaz and Menahem. In the story, Boaz appears, along with Noga, and Jordana, under the names of Aminadam, Mira, and Shulamith. I translate the story for you with the original names so as not to confuse you. The title of the story is "Vulture." The story annoyed me. Only after I read it did I understand what Jordana's rage meant. I wondered how the writer knew things I didn't know. But those are facts and from them we have to interweave "our" story. The writer's name is Nadav ben-Ami.

[A part is missing] . . . And Jordana left her office and went to the street. The light was dazzling, people who were scared of the heat weren't the shadows she had thought. She stood in line for the bus and since she didn't have anything to do with her hands, she straightened her hair and tried to squint her eyes because of the dazzling light. On the bus she stood crowded between people who were pungent with sweat and the driver yelled, but his voice was blended into the turmoil. When she squeezed her ticket, her hand was wet and the coins in her hand seemed to be swimming in water. The sights passed by in the blurred windows, and a woman sitting next to where Jordana was standing tried without much success to open the window wider. When she came to the stop, she got off slowly, which annoyed the driver who muttered something and even locked the door when the blast of the lock hit her spine. A sudden burst of wind from an air-conditioned shop made her shudder with pleasure. She turned to the street, which, now, at dusk, was empty. The night watchman in the big building, whose lower floors were built now, put a pita in his mouth filled with tomatoes and olives. The tomato dripped red juice and he wiped the blood of the tomato with a lace handkerchief. When he tried to smile at her he looked distorted because of the tomato and maybe also because the olive pit didn't come out in time, so he spat out the pit and the smile was crushed. But she had already crossed the street and didn't hear the curse. A car sped by and she jumped, the watchman couldn't help laughing, and the tomato dripped even more and she looked at the house, and didn't move. Just as the woman who lived alone in the house next door started hanging laundry on the clothesline, Jordana lit a cigarette and immediately let the cigarette drop to the ground and crushed it with her foot. The watchman looked at the cigarette and the tiny spark that still flickered in it. Jordana went upstairs, even though she didn't know where she got the strength to climb.

Noga sat on the roof and embroidered. Jordana looked at Noga and Noga raised her face and said: It's so hot! Jordana couldn't say a thing, she touched Noga's face, let her stroke her hand softly, and as they stood there obeying something remaining between them without words for a moment, they seemed to be hoarding an anger that had dissolved into their standing. Jordana drank water straight from the faucet and only then did she pour herself a glass of water from the jar she took out of the refrigerator and drank from the glass until she was amazed that there wasn't a drop left in it. Dead tired, she looked at the old grandfather clock without hands and allowed her clothes, with a light and unconscious help of her hands, to drop off her. When she stood in front of the grandfather clock, which she was apparently still looking at, but didn't see, air blew from the vaulted window and she saw the upper end of the wheel of the setting sun and a plane was seen cutting the air and descending on the way to the airport. The breeze lightened the heat a little and her sweat cooled. As in a daze, she moved to the shower. For a little while she stood unmoving under the stream of cold water. Then, without drying herself with the many towels hanging there, she put on a robe, and dripping water, stuck to the robe that was clasped to her, she went out to the twilight on the roof and looked at its serene riot, and Noga said: Sit

down, I'll make you coffee. And Jordana said: I'll make it myself, she sat and looked at Noga and saw again the woman
hanging laundry in the house next door. She got up, and without looking at Noga, she went to the kitchen, put on water,
waited until it boiled, poured Nescafé and some saccharine,
went outside holding the full coffee cup, and said: I dripped all
over your kitchen.

The wheel of the sun almost disappeared, leaving behind an
astounding wake. The shadows were starting to fill the roof and
penetrated between the flowerpots. Jordana, still dripping water, drank the coffee and started dancing. Noga came to her.
They stood so close they almost touched one another, Jordana
sipped the coffee she held behind Noga's back, the sun disappeared behind the department store, and Jordana said: What a
disgusting pink, and Noga looked at the old antenna and saw
a bird landing, cleaning its feathers, and soaring again. Noga
gently pinched a bush growing in a giant flowerpot, picked a
jasmine flower, brought it to her nose and smelled it as in a
long ceremony and then, gently, she moved it back and forth
in front of Jordana's nose. Jordana stood transfixed, her face
almost didn't move toward the flower, her nostrils expanded,
and then, with a quick movement, she tried to snatch the
flower from Noga's hands, and in a twinkling, Noga managed to
hide it behind her. When she moved and stamped on the floor,
the phonograph started playing. Jordana could move from the
spot, and so, even though she didn't pay any heed to it, she let
the half-full cup drop from her hand and shatter on the floor.
Only after the smash was heard did her hand start shaking
again. Noga didn't avert her face. Her back reconsidered, and
when Jordana came to her, she waited until she was clinging to
her and bent over, picked up a shard of the coffee cup whose
slivers were scattered around them and black coffee still
poured from the shard. The coffee was thick and a drop fell on
her shorts. Her leg was long and well-shaped, and Jordana went
down on all fours and cleaned the drop of coffee dripping from
the pants on Noga's well-shaped leg. Noga held out her hand,

and moved it very close to Jordana's long hair, got wet from the water still dripping from the hair and Jordana stopped shaking.

The woman in the house next door started playing her Italian singers, and Jordana said: They always sound as if in the last opera they die and only then do they live.

Get up, said Noga.

Jordana couldn't get up, but she couldn't say that. She was stooped, curled up in herself, before her the day broke and shadows deepened, the light was swallowed up rather than disappeared, a plane passed by and left a long darkening white trail behind, the roofs were swallowed up in the dark that was already heavy and its dimness was cracked by flashes of lights. The wind that had blown before stopped, and the air stood still again. They cleaned up the shards, swept the roof and washed it with water, and then Jordana tried to direct her body to the two pleasures competing with one another: the Italian from the house next door and the melancholy rising from Noga's phonograph, but Noga refused to be caught in her mood that may have been impossible, and the stumbling, that was right for her, maybe therefore something that accompanied her from the moment she left the office. When she fell she thought she wanted to burst out laughing, but she didn't know why she didn't laugh. Her head hit the floor that was just cleaned, and Noga said: Come, let's go in and eat something.

When they went in, Noga slammed the door and turned on a light. She put out a plate of cheese and rolls, butter, and a bottle of red wine. The phonograph went on playing, maybe because Jordana changed the record, even though the two of them weren't aware of that, the light from the vaulted window was red and vied with the light of the lamp, and the burst of air was stronger now. They ate in silence and then Jordana spread butter on a roll, put a triangle of cheese on it, chewed, looked at the zigzag snake of light bursting from the broken vault above the grandfather clock, and said: I went with him to Independence Park, Noga, there were homos there and a woman with a dog. We searched for shade, in the

distance I saw Henkin's roof, I ate lunch with him. Sad, Noga
. . . Boaz's father put up a new television antenna, and Boaz
didn't approve and didn't not approve. Near the demolished
wall of the Muslim cemetery, he told me he loved me. I said
to him: You don't love me, Boaz Schneerson, if you love, you
love Noga, and he said: Maybe I'm not using the right words.
I told him not to say anything, then he said, It's true, maybe
I am tied to Noga, but I need you. I told him, I love you Boaz,
say "love," don't say "tied," and he said, But Noga hates you,
and then I told him: So what, and I laughed, Noga's feeling is
stronger than your empty words.

Noga didn't say a thing and Jordana stood up, the roll in
her hand, finished a glass of wine, looked at Noga, and said:
How beautiful you are, Noga, you sit here, bring me into the
house, give me coffee, cheese, red wine, and Boaz, tell me
things so I'll understand him, what do all the ceremonies he
makes for people tell you, you do know how to obliterate and
you give him to me, some fine gift!

Maybe Boaz discovered my demon, only you know him,
nobody else does, when I loved Menahem Henkin Boaz came
and took that love too, even before he took me . . .

Noga started humming something that may have been
some echo to the music from the phonograph. She said: You
want to disgust me, to hurt me, but I'm protected, Jordana . . .
Got to say what happens on the roof on Lilienblum Street, on
that roof, not what happens in comparison with something
else. There are time differences—in Los Angeles it's now ten
hours earlier, but for me those are only words, now here and in
Los Angeles is the same time. I've got my own time; you're
there, Boaz is there, what happens to us, Menahem, you and
Menahem, me and Menahem, no love is that love, in that moment Boaz has to see himself in your eyes, or even "only" in
your eyes, that you will love him, that he will know how dreadful he is and of course wonderful, after the ten hours' difference he returned to me, and he was with me also ten hours or
ten years before, and always will be. This is home. This home

is not love or hatred and not what happens to you or to me or
to him, at the limestone wall of the Muslim cemetery.

When did I have more than ten hours? said Jordana.

When you loved Menahem, said Noga with sudden anger
that passed immediately.

Maybe, said Jordana, I once tried to feel what it is to be a
bereaved father or mother, Noga?

It's almost all I tried, said Noga.

Jordana opened the door, cast off the robe that had dried
long ago, stood in the pale light of the room, at the open door
where lights capered, and said: Once I came home from the
Committee of Parents, took off the marble look, I saw
Henkin's eyes in my mind, I thought: What is love for somebody who died twenty years ago? I sat in the big armchair I
had, with arms coated with disgusting black Chinese lacquer,
I shut my eyes and tried to banish the eyes of the fathers and
mother, I thought, I've got a son, I've got a son, I've got a son,
and I felt him inside me, I was pregnant, and he was there,
that son, I was happy, I didn't sleep, I just forgot I was some
existing Jordana, I was me, but in another place, maybe ten
hours' difference? Something like that, on second thought, I
hurt, I invented a child who dies, I gave birth to him, that hurts
but the pain was mine, I raised him in that ten hours' difference, and he was alive, he existed as you exist now in this
room. I didn't look at the clock, didn't know how much time
had passed, it was dark, I talked to him about grades at school
and then about flu and why you have to stay at home another
day and not go to school, and he went out and fell under a car,
I ran out of the house where I was apparently living, but he
was already crushed. After I returned from the cemetery, I
thought here, he's not with me anymore, he isn't even for himself. But for me that was something else, he wasn't anyplace
for anybody, not in Los Angeles, not here, not ten hours ahead
not ten hours behind, I sat in the armchair, I can't even de
scribe what I was feeling. I was choking, I tried to breathe, I
knew that if I woke up I'd be relieved, but I didn't want to, or

perhaps I couldn't. The knowledge that he isn't, totally isn't, no telephone would reach him, no letter would get to him, it was impossible . . . I gathered that emptiness from all the dead people I had filed, my nothingness was a dinosaur in me, swallowing every drop of air, I felt the emptiness penetrate again into my womb, but this time it was longing, like an ax, that cut the face, the feet, the cheeks, the roots of the eyes, his connection through me, cutting off from me, my eardrum was so taut that I could hear the heart beating, I started yelling, there was a wooden knife there, I brought it close, thrust it into my arm, blood flowed, I yelled, the neighbor rang the bell and then knocked on the door, I heard voices, I was in shock, the neighbor brought people, apparently I fainted, they broke down the door, I heard a siren, then I disappeared to it, I connected with it, there was one moment of bliss and pain and then I woke up in the hospital, they measured my blood pressure, tested my heart and blood, they bandaged me, my blood pressure was high, I said: My son died, my son died, and they were busy taking care of me and didn't pay attention. They gave me a shot of something and I fell asleep and came to only two days later and was loathsome in my own eyes, what a fuss I made for them, myself, I apologized to the neighbor . . . And then a week later I was eating lunch with the head of our department, we were eating in Olympia, suddenly I started yearning for the child, I looked at the people and they were eating moussaka and stuffed vegetables and shashlik and drinking beer and cold water and I was trying to eat and that yearning, like a flash that cuts the body and suddenly all the people became paper dolls and I saw them through walls and didn't sense them anymore, and I thought, that's how my people are, sitting in a meeting, in a car, suddenly that arrow that's stuck in them, like that, among people, among the living, next to shops, in a café, at the movies, suddenly you and the son, or the daughter, who aren't, and you feel and no word will express the feeling, and the tears have to roll in the belly, so they won't be seen, won't be misunderstood, and with whom to share this pain, and it's impossible, and another few times like that, I was sitting in the movies and suddenly I didn't have him there either, and on the seashore, among a crowd of people on Saturday, he wasn't, all the time crushed by a car, the expectation at night, I should have let months pass to get over the dead son I never had.

Jordana fell silent, she pinched her nipple lightly, found the stub of the mirror and looked at herself, Noga looked at Jordana in the mirror, saw the thin swarthy body and Jordana sucked in her belly and a spasm seemed to pass through it, she said: Right, I loved them, they were a yearning for something, Boaz is building an empire of dead people, I loathe that, and live with that, go to the Committee, smile, introduce parents to their sons, but inside I've got this son, once he was and remains forever, and Boaz, he's the only one besides you that I can talk to about that, tell him, today I met a dead person and then touch Boaz, know he's dead and he understands and somehow he also lives. What man would take a woman whose two men were killed and they say she kills her men, she's cursed. They say: Boaz loves the smell that comes from me, as from you, grows stronger from the death of others, mine, others, yours, vulture! He goes to war to be close to blood, meets you in a tent, you play Noga, he plays Boaz, and you can laugh at yourselves, me too, in his jeep, in his car, everyplace, with you, without you, shame, shameless, guilty, not guilty, I live without that official marble, without the curse, all of us in the cemetery, and it's allowed . . . And his grandmother who will live forever. Maybe Ebenezer . . . Once I went with Boaz to his grandmother, he told her: This is Jordana from the Ministry of Defense, as if I were the chief of staff. She smiled and told about the ants who would eat her someday. And Boaz, Boaz sat on her lap and she bounced her fist and stretched her fingers and said: Grandma baked a sweet cake, cut it in slices; gave it to Poopie, gave it to Moomi, gave it to Boaz, and then she sang some song in Yiddish, full of gloom and spiderwebs and he sat there, the one who meets dead people in my womb, who measures my veins to make them into threads to tie memorials, and listens to his grandmother talking to him as if he were five years old, and laughs . . . He sits in the lap of a woman who came to the Land of Israel before Ben-Gurion and Ben-Zvi, and hears about the bastards who destroyed everything for her and her husband who died on the shore at Jaffa, plays with her beautiful teeth, and she's like some ancient palace, a poster from Switzerland, elegant, and then he came to us two fools, and we're here Menahem's puss, with Henkin's words, stuck to our skin, in different planes of time, ten hours' difference, ten years, what's the difference, a Yemenite and a European, two beauties we, stretched to one another and he weaves us into his rage, hits, and we make him coffee. What, Noga, will be?

And the two of them stand there, Noga's legs touching Jordana's and Jordana lets Noga hug her, she has nothing to say, she holds Jordana and tears flow and you don't know which of them is shedding tears, or for whom they're shed, the phone rings and they answer the phone together and say he'll come back later and hang up and don't know where Noga starts and Jordana ends. The phonograph plays a Mozart concerto, the Italian opera on the next roof is over, the solitary woman there now has a television, rustling of a city, dark schemes, planes to Lod slice the dark sky filled with the roar of heat and then Boaz enters, glances at them, shuts his eyes, they're sunk in that hushed distance from one another like lovers, a feather touch, he washes his face, eats something he picked up from the table and then, when he starts combing his hair fear floods him, he wrenches Jordana away, pushes her to the torn upholstery, lies down next to Noga, looks into her crotch, averts his eyes to Jordana sitting cross-legged, and says: Look how charming she is, white, European, with her it's pressed and small like a seashell. He tries to laugh but doesn't make it. Now she started yearning and didn't yet want to know for whom. Again and again he strokes Noga's groin as she gnaws her fingernails, he tries to catch Jordana who slips away from him, and Jordana says: Let me love the two of you in the distance. She manages to climb onto the nightstand, cross her legs, disappear into the dark niche between the wall and the window with the opaque pane and he turns, caresses Noga, and Noga whispers: Not now. Offended, he hits her but she doesn't respond, goes on gnawing her fingernails, looking at Jordana sitting shrouded in shadows, and he says: Now! And Noga says: I don't feel like it, Boaz, not now, Jordana moves a little, her eyes measure the mattress at her feet, the closeness that had vanished before. He says: I want the two of you, I'm bursting from you, and then Noga said: Once you put a paper flower and were sensitive, now you're full of shadow, and Boaz yelled: Get down, Jordana, but Jordana didn't get down, not yet, and then the phone rang and he said: It's for you, Noga, who in the hell wants you? And Noga grabbed the receiver from his hand and whispered into it briefly, talked about some film they had to see and Boaz went to the kitchen and drank cold water and returned and yelled, Stop! Noga put her hand over the receiver and whispered: Stop, Boaz, and then he looked at Jordana and a slight smile started on her lips, and he said: What's going on here? A revolt of the streetwalkers? And Jordana laughed and then Noga whispered, Fine, see you, and replaced the receiver, went to the nightstand, bent over a little and started pulling Jordana's hands, which began, as in a dream, to stretch out to her with a pleasure Boaz couldn't bear, and Jordana shut her eyes and offered herself to anybody at all, she didn't care anymore, shuddering on the nightstand. Like a hedgehog, said Boaz, and went to the refrigerator and shrieked: Where's the beer, why don't they buy beer, and then he found a beer and drank it, put his head under the faucet and let the cold water stream and apparently also yelled because burbling noises came from the sink, and then Noga laughed and Boaz went to the other room and called out: Why isn't there any more beer? and Noga said: Because I didn't buy any, and he broke a chair, and Jordana said: Noga, he broke a chair, and Noga lifted her face and said: Jordana, Boaz Schneerson broke a chair, soon there won't be anything to

break in this house and then we'll all get married and get new
chairs from all the mothers and fathers, because there are
three of us and we've got a lot of fathers and a lot of mothers,
we've got Henkin and the whole Committee, and we'll get
chairs and clocks, and Boaz threw a chair leg that didn't hit
either of them, but could have, and said: You, you brought
Jordana here, not me, you invited her to live here, not me . . .
And Noga puts on the robe that Jordana took off, and says:
Me? I didn't bring anybody, Boaz, I opened the door and some
poor Jordana was standing there and I let her in, the ticket you
paid for, and Jordana approached Noga who seemed sunk in a
distant and maybe even malicious melancholy for a moment,
as if she borrowed it from another body, maybe from Los Angeles, ten hours behind, and Noga pushed Jordana away and in
a clear and quiet voice said: I'm my own rag, who am I? Do you
have any idea of the harmony you destroyed? Do you really
grasp who I am and why I am, and where I'm going and where
I came from, without any connection to you or Menahem
Henkin whom you killed or didn't kill. I myself became a memorial book for a fallen soldier who never was!

And then, again the empty silence of the south of the city
will swallow them. That dark will prevail, planes will go on
passing over the house on their way to the airport, Boaz is
softened with, without, Noga, Jordana, everything is again as
it was, but in the air there will be a sense that all that can't
happen and that it's not possible anymore, that we, said
Boaz, we take things too deeply, we can't do it simply, and
we can't do it not-simply, and at four in the morning they
woke up. If they had slept at all before.

Tape / —

Jordana went to the shower, stood and looked in the mirror and splashed cold water on her face, but she was still
blazing. When she went back to the room, Noga and Boaz
were sitting on the gigantic mattress. That pale light penetrating inside flickered and went out. Jordana said: I

dreamed of the dog we had in the village, his name was Haman, he was old, I dreamed he devoured you.

She looked toward the window, her face was molded in the flickering light, etched like the face of somebody else. She said: Poor old Haman was a Don Juan. In the days when he was a real dog, he'd make bitches pregnant like a fish. Now she was filled with an envy that flooded her and almost choked her. She looked at Noga and Boaz and they didn't see the tears: You'll always be with each other, she said, you'll have each other, that dog was a son of a bitch, like you! Then she said, he'd still run after the smells of bitches, but they didn't want him anymore. When he was fourteen or thirteen and a half, I don't remember exactly, which is like ninety years, Boaz, maybe a hundred, he started falling in love with cats. We had a cat named Incense, she was always pregnant or nursing six or seven kittens. Haman started wooing Incense, and then, the kittens. When Incense was in heat, he'd sniff her all day long.

You're weeping, said Noga.

Those tears have nothing to do with you, said Jordana, or with Boaz either, I'm thinking about Incense, I'm weeping for old Haman, who am I talking to? The window? The streetwalkers of teleprinters? I've had it. I'm jumping out the window, I left a cigarette downstairs and across the street is a night watchman as lewd as old Haman. By the way, in the end he died.

Who? asked Noga, and Jordana said: Poor Haman.

Boaz stood up and started getting dressed, he said: Come on, let's get out of here, and Jordana kissed him with a lust Noga couldn't bear.

The beat of footsteps in the empty night streets embarrassed them. It extinguished the rage every one of them felt for the walls, the sourness of the coming morning.

When they came to the old cemetery, they found a locked gate. The watchman was sleeping in the little cubbyhole at the entrance. Boaz folded the handkerchief, put it on his head and woke up the tired, angry watchman. Boaz told him: There are two women here who came last night from Hong Kong seeking the grave of their father who was murdered in 1938.

Come in the morning, said the watchman, shaking with rage.

In the morning they're on trial, said Boaz, they'll expel them from Israel, it has to do with the Ministry of Defense. I don't really understand you, said the watchman, maybe you speak Yiddish?

This is a matter of life and death, Boaz answered in Yiddish. He took out a hundred pounds and gave them to the watchman. Look, it's worth it to us and you can go to sleep. The watchman examined the money, sniffed it, and said: Come in, just don't wake anybody up.

Boaz loved the watchman's sense of humor kindled at the sight of the money. That's surely how he bribes dead people, he said, and Jordana giggled, but that was more than Noga did.

Be careful not to step, said Boaz. They walked on loose paths soaked with dew. Night on tombstones. Names of Tel Aviv streets. Heads of Zionism, heads of Tel Aviv, leaders of the *Yishuv*, history in a field of tombstones, said Boaz. A boy jumped from the third floor in nineteen twenty-nine. The women wanted to leave, Boaz didn't.

Then they sat on Manya Bialik's grave and hummed a song. Now they were drunk on something in the air, in the pale light that started appearing in the dark. Noga said: We're pathetic and melodramatic, and that's nice. Jordana felt disappointed and didn't know why. The magic engendered by the place was starting to fade. The graves were only stones on loose ground. It was four-thirty in the morning. The moon was setting. When they sang, Jordana said: I'm not singing, I'm not a European who sings in cemeteries, and I won't be buried here either.

You too, said Boaz.

I want a kiss, she said.

Take it from Noga, said Boaz.

Jordana touched the ground and said: Dew of death! And they started walking out, they trod on the tombstones as if they were fleeing from somebody. That amused Boaz, not Noga. They picked up flowers left by visitors in vases, whose water had already turned moldy. I need a little wine, said Boaz, and Noga said: He needs a little wine, Jordana. They came to the gate as dawn began to break. The light was pale and a reddish glow was lit in the sky and looked like a crazy spot, as if sentenced to destruction by itself and Jordana started weeping softly and nervously. Noga hugged her shoulder. They stood near the corner of Ben-Yehuda. Boaz told them to sit down and wait for him and he started running. He ran along Ben-Yehuda and Allenby, passed by a liquor store, broke the window, took out two bottles of wine, and kept on running. A terrifying ringing came from the store, Boaz ran in yards, passed by thistles and cats, a police car appeared through an opening of the buildings, cars were already starting to move, and he came home, started the jeep, went back, picked up his lovers who were sitting in an entrance to a building huddled together, opened the two bottles of wine, and they drank. After the wine warmed their bodies and the dust from the cemetery was shaken off, they drove along the street and yelled wildly at the locked balconies and came to Ebenezer's house. Ebenezer was Boaz's father. He left him when Boaz was a year old.

There was a woman there, too. She was his daughter and the mother of the daughters of the lover of his grandmother before she got married. The daughters died. They—

I've translated for you up to here, because strange as it is, I saw the end of this "story" with my own eyes. Boaz told me that when the author of this story came back from the war, all the neighbors went out to the balcony, tossed flowers at him, threw candy at him, and held a royal reception for him because he was wounded. Boaz said he stood there and looked and thought: That putz who didn't see half of the war I saw receives a national honor because they think he almost died, while if he had died he would have won more, while I, said Boaz, have to apologize.

What interests me is how the author knew those details, and maybe he didn't know, maybe I'm making it all up, maybe I'm mixing things? How do I really know all that happened? Maybe I'm inventing and you're thinking: Jewish knowledge, he knows what to call Boaz, Jordana, and Ebenezer. Maybe it's me. Everything is only an optical illusion. People come seeking the grave of Madame Bovary, is Madame Bovary really buried there, somebody told me that too, but when they tell me about me, about myself and I tell, what am I telling? What they said or what I know, but in that matter, I've got nothing to add, it's hard for me to meet somebody who was in Menahem's battalion, fought along with him, and never came to talk with me.

The yelling I heard clearly. It was five in the morning. Hasha Masha said: Henkin, don't open the window, and I didn't. I sat at our window with the old shutters you can see through, if only the opening, and I saw it all. Boaz behaved like a wild man. In his hand he brandished an empty wine bottle, Jordana and Noga sat in the jeep. I saw the two trying to sit off to the side, slightly bent over, so that if I were awake, I wouldn't see them, but they were also drunk apparently and Jordana wept nonstop and Noga looked vile and aristocratic in the light of dawn, and Ebenezer in his pajamas said: Who's there?

And Boaz said: Your son, Samuel!

Ebenezer went outside, and Boaz said: It's me, Samuel, and in his voice I heard reverence, maybe a certain cry for help, surely a supplication, some breaking of a savage. Yes, said Ebenezer, you're Boaz, the son of Rebecca Schneerson.

Boaz looked at his father. He yelled at Jordana and Noga: This is my father! He came to die in the Holy Land with a woman who is both his sister and maybe his daughter and the sister of his mother. Look at him, in his opinion, I betrayed the two people he loved, one Samuel and one Dana who's supposed to be my mother. Jordana, my mother Dana, was murdered by Yemenites.

Arabs, hissed Noga angrily.

Ebenezer went to them, he raised his eyes to my house, he did know I was watching, I knew he responded to my hidden figure, maybe he needed my help.

What do you want, Boaz? asked Ebenezer. Clearly he seemed to be wrapped in a dream. I'll tell you what I want, said Boaz, and approached his father. He pushed him toward the fence and for a moment I almost couldn't see him, but Ebenezer moved and then I saw his eyes. I'll tell you, I've got two women like Our Teacher Moses, one black and one white, the two of them belonged to the son of your friend there, and he pointed to the shutter where I was hiding, and now do for them what you did for Samuel, recite your fucking knowledge, you're in a nightclub, Ebenezer, you set clocks back, I'm Samuel, you're in a nightclub in Cologne! Ebenezer, who knew wood in its distress, on whose horrible death I grew up, in a nightclub, you're entertaining gentiles with your wonderful memory, turn on your crappy computer, why don't you start. I'm tired, Boaz, said Ebenezer, and his voice contained some submission. He haggled, but we knew he meant to do what Boaz ordered him to do, and I understood: That small chance that his son was Samuel . . . I wanted to get into bed, block my ears, but I sat fascinated. Ebenezer shut his eyes, looked obsequious like a Jew in your caricatures, and for a long time he recited the annals of the Mendelssohn family, as if anybody really cared to know who was the banker, who was the musician, and who was the philosopher. Hasha Masha put up water and blocked her ears with cotton and I sat and listened. The girls stood on the side, apparently already in despair at hiding from me, and Ebenezer recited. It was a cheap circus act, the setting was the seashore, lifeguards' surfboards on the way to the sea carried by tanned fellows, girls in blue on the way to school, the garbage truck on Yordei Sira Street, and he's telling about some woman he asked what she would do after the Liberation and she said: I'm going back home to my son who was a Hitler-jugend and she spoke proudly of her son . . . She went back home, she said, and waited

for her son, for her husband, and they didn't come. When she
discovered that her son had put her in the camp, and now neither
he nor her husband wanted to see her, she committed suicide in
a hotel, and then Boaz, a uniquely humiliating act, he went into
the house, brought out the hat of the Last Jew who stood humiliated, foaming at the mouth, stopped the woman delivering
milk who was trying to pretend not to hear and demanded
money from her, and she put half a pound into the hat and he
went to the two girls, Jordana and Noga, and demanded money
from them and they put it in the hat, and you could see they
were scared and did that as if they were possessed by a demon,
and Boaz took the hat and went back to Ebenezer and Ebenezer
said: Samuel, you always know how to surprise me, and I thought:
Well, at long last, I saw the Last Jew in a real performance, not
like when he recited and talked about you but just as in the
nightclub, and what a setting that was, a small street, a woman
delivering milk, construction workers on their way to work,
tanned girls and boys on their way to the seashore, the Hilton
on the left, and then surprisingly, without Boaz sensing anything, the Last Jew took the watch off Boaz's wrist. Jordana and
Noga didn't see, I did. Boaz wanted to go, his face was ashamed,
and the Last Jew said: What time is it, Boaz? And Boaz searched
for the watch and didn't understand where it was. And then the
Last Jew waved the watch in front of Boaz's face and laughed,
he laughed, really laughed, and said: There, there you wouldn't
have lasted a day, you're not Samuel, and he threw the watch at
him. And Boaz waited until his father went into the house, put
on the watch, and went down on his knees and chewed the wet
sand, even though the sun was a little warm now and his face
was black and he wept. Never did I see Boaz Schneerson weep.

Yours with friendship and the hope of seeing you again soon,

Obadiah Henkin

Tape / —

One warm morning, Rebecca Schneerson got up and looked at the window she had looked through but hadn't seen for forty-two years. She rec-

ognized handsome almond trees, a thick-trunked eucalyptus, a weeping oak, lemon trees, and expanses of flowers and greenery up to the edge of the horizon. In the distance, she saw the road that hadn't been in the window forty-two years ago. Rebecca put on a white dress, wrapped herself in a shawl, and went out. She walked erect and confident, even though it had been years since she strolled on these paths. When she came to the center of the settlement, children buying gum at the kiosk peeped at her. They said: Here's the witch come out of her hole. Yehiel, the shopkeeper, whose father remembered Rebecca, wanted to go outside to greet her, but a vague fear kept him from doing that. Now that Rebecca felt that there were no more enemies of life in the settlement, the children of the first ones, their grandchildren, and great grandchildren started loving her. Fears of her had been passed down as a legacy, but belief in their stories was even stronger than the worries, and there was talk in the settlement council of making amends for the ninetieth anniversary celebration. Among many candidates, thirty-one men and a woman were chosen as the founders of the settlement. Some of them did indeed found it, but Rebecca had long ago become the most senior and important founder of them all. She heard from a laborer who worked in her yard about the decision to fix the synagogue and call the main street, the Street of the First Ones, Nehemiah Schneerson Street and she told the reporter from *Our Settlement* who came to interview her (she even agreed to receive him), that the number of founders growing in inverse proportion to the realization of expectations worried her. Nehemiah died on the seashore in Jaffa, she said, and because of him, she had been living here for seventy-one years. There were ten families in the settlement at that time, then twenty, of the first four sons, only one was still alive, Ebenezer, who died and came back to life only because he went to the Holocaust. So, she added, Zionism has nothing to be proud of

Rebecca Schneerson went into Mr. Brin's small department store, and Mr. Brin, who had never seen Rebecca life-size, said: It's a great honor for me that you came to me. And she said: No honor, Mr. Brin, I didn't come to you but to the only store in the settlement where you can find a tape recorder. I assume that if there were two stores, the prices would be more reasonable. He tried not to pay attention to the complaint and bitterness in her voice and served her with an exaggerated devotion that disgusted her. Ever since the Captain and Mr. Klomin had died, and all her enemies

had been buried in Roots, she had lacked a certain adulation that Ahbed
and his friends couldn't grant her since they were too simple to recognize
her value.

Mr. Brin showed Rebecca Schneerson about sixteen different tape recorders, and since she didn't trust anybody, she chose the one Mr. Brin
claimed was not as good as the others, but she had to have it. She allowed
the disappointed Mr. Brin to wrap the tape recorder, picked up the package, and went home. She walked through the fields, saw the new houses,
the farms and trees and orchards and gardens, and the new school and the
community center and the old water tower, and she thought that in fact
this wasn't such a bad place, that there was nice air here and the view was
soft and beautiful and everything was painted now and not gnarled, people
built and improved, trees grew, flowers bloomed, yards multiplied and were
beautiful, the horizon stopped evoking gloomy expectations, the sky became softer and not exactly because of the cataracts in her eyes. She feared
those thoughts, as if some long way, maybe the longest she had made since
her forefathers' forefathers got her pregnant, a way that had gone on for
more than two hundred years, was coming to its end. She wasn't afraid of
the end, it wasn't death that scared her, what scared her was some more
absolute end, beyond death, an end that torments everybody and only its
contamination is felt, an end of what had been dreamed in her veins for
two hundred years—Secret Charity, the curse, the river that pierced,
Joseph and his poems of yearning, Nehemiah longing for Zion, could all
that simply vanish, only because there was never a solid basis for the dream
entrenched in some cosmic bitterness of a cruel God against those who
betray His command of destruction?

When she came back home, through a row of sprinklers that evoked an
amazement in her that she tried to chill, even though they'd water her
gardens and she didn't know, she tended to the tape recorder for a while
in her closed room, put the microphone to her mouth, and said aloud: One,
two, three, and when she turned on the machine, her voice was heard, and
even though she didn't recognize it at first, she immediately learned to use
it. She said: Recording number one, Rebecca Schneerson, to whom it may
concern and to whom it may not concern . . .

. . . Nehemiah was a handsome man. Boaz is my son. Ebenezer calls him
Samuel. Collectors of charity, who dreamed of Mr. Klomin's kingdom, in-

vented a state that is a little bit of a dream and a little bit of a ghetto and a little bit of a military camp and a little bit of flowers. My tears for eight years were for nothing. The Captain isn't here. Everybody died on me. Ebenezer was amazed that the Captain ordered flowers placed every week on Dana's grave. I wouldn't have done that. What do they know about the Captain? He was a swindler, cunning, naïve, and wise. How many wise Jews are there in this land? It's great wisdom to be a successful farmer, to build a good farm among Jews. Does the fact that I'm alive at least make me dead? I want to say something about Ebenezer. I married Nehemiah, not Joseph, and it's a lie to say I didn't love him. I wanted to save him in America and he didn't want to. Nehemiah taught me a lesson. He left me Ebenezer. Ebenezer went to search for the one he thought was his father, and in the end he married a woman who was both the daughter and the wife of his father. He comes to me and wants to know. What will I tell him? I think that even though Nehemiah was his father, Ebenezer is bound to Joseph and was born to bring Joseph back into the world through Boaz! Is it possible to love somebody, the son of somebody else, who grew in your belly, so that in the next generation your real son will come into the world? Ebenezer, the lost son. Whose son is he? The Last Jew, they call him. And I'll die after him. Lucky thing Boaz has no children. There will be a wilderness here with Ahbeds, as there was before we came here. But to tell Ebenezer I can't. I don't give birth because some man got me into bed. I brought two sons into the world. One was born by mistake from Dana in order to be my son again. Is he my grandson or my son? I lived the end of the story of Rebecca Secret Charity, but they don't believe in the satanic power of blood, in the awful flow of Satan. They believe in progress, they believe all awful things were an imagined curse with no foothold in the reality of progressive people who elect a hundred twenty fools to something they call a Knesset every four years, and they think they're successful and wise and clever because they learned to kill a few Arabs in tanks given them by gentiles, so that then it will be allowed, without any problems, to destroy them one by one . . . the river was at the end of my life or at the beginning and it's all the same, there was Joseph there, there was Nehemiah there, there were my father and mother. Ebenezer is the curse and he knows wood in its distress. Like an everlasting name he came back. He should be exhibited in a museum. . .

How much I wanted the love that would replace the dependence, the beauty, the yearning. Did I succeed in being promiscuous? Even that's a hard question. I remember once thinking I should let the Captain hug me, sometimes I did want to, but I thought, Is there somebody who can, with a few drops of water, put out the fire of hell burning in me? And life passed by. That's how it is. Life isn't what we live, but something that flows out of us. And I look around, Nehemiah and Dana died so that Boaz would be, Joseph isn't here, the Captain, I've got an avocado, flowers, fruit, chickens, a nightgown. What the hell don't I have? The flowers bloom, and I look around and ask what to tell Ebenezer, who wants an answer, and he's already past seventy, he wants to know, what will I tell him? That I'm ninety years old and can't say, so here, Ebenezer, with the only love I have left and that isn't aimed at anybody, not even myself, I swear, I'm telling you: *A fayg!* Up yours! Just up yours! It's not malice, be my son if you think so and want to be, not out of malice, you're quite lovable with all you've suffered with the woman you raised like a dried flower in one of Dana's old books, because I don't have anything else to say, not to you, not to the tape recorder, not to God, not to Satan, not to Rebecca Secret Charity, nothing. Up yours, that's what I've got to say, only that, up yours!

You're all that's left of Nehemiah. Of all the naïve founders, of that nation, of you, of me, up yours!

And then Rebecca turned off the tape recorder and started laughing and the laughter turned into weeping and she locked the door, put her head under the blanket, and wept as she had wept seventy years before, a whole day, nonstop, and then she got up, washed her face, sat at the table, and Ahbed said: What happened, Madame, were you weeping? Were you laughing? And she said: Bring something to eat, Ahbed, and he said: Were you laughing or weeping? And she said: *A fayg,* up yours, Ahbed, do you know what that is, up yours? So up yours to you, all your sons who will inherit the land Nehemiah sowed with Ebenezers who knew wood in its distress, into me they came, from me they didn't go.

Tape/—

Noga Levin knocked on the door fearfully. More than she was afraid to come, she was afraid of Henkin peeping at her from his house. She thought, What is he thinking, why is he looking? Fanya R. opened the door, invited her in without a word, and went to put on a robe. Noga was bundled up in a scarf, she hoped it made her look older. Last night she told Boaz: I'm going to Ebenezer, I want to look old and wise, and Boaz, who wanted to answer, suffered an attack of yawning she didn't cause and so he couldn't answer her. By the time he finished yawning her footsteps were heard on the stairs.

Ebenezer, who had slept in his clothes ever since the war, put a blue sailor's coat over the clothes he had slept in and went into the room. He said: What is the lovely flower in my house? She laughed because she didn't expect him to behave so gallantly.

Noga said: Sit, Ebenezer. He sat, watched the sun rise through the open bathroom window. I came to apologize for Boaz's behavior, said Noga, he didn't mean it, he had been drinking, he lives in tension, he's sorry for what was—

Ebenezer averted his face and didn't see the sunrise now. In the big living-room window you could see the fences of the port and the demolished buildings, and the abandoned shore. He said: Remind me of what you're talking about, some things I remember and some I don't. She sipped the coffee Fanya R. gave her and stirred while walking, which seemed to Noga like hovering, and after a few sips, when the tasty coffee was inside her, she repeated word for word what had happened at the house when Boaz and Jordana and she came from the cemetery. Ebenezer shut his eyes, stretched out his hands, and said: He meant what he did, and I was a fool!

You weren't, said Noga.

When I was a little girl, said Noga, as if she were talking to herself, I once came home from school and Mother met me on the stairs and told me to go up and wait in the house. I went up and the door was locked. I knocked on the door and Father didn't answer. I thought maybe he wasn't sleeping but listening to the news. I went up to the roof, from the laundry room, I slid on the water pipe straight to our kitchen porch. I loved to slide because it was also a little dangerous. I went into the kitchen and water was boiling on the stove. I turned off the stove, ate a few grapes from the refrigerator, and holding a bunch of them, I went into the living room. My father was lying in bed and the radio was off. His leg was stretched to the side as if he were about to put on house slippers and get up. I think he was smiling, but maybe it was a grimace, I said to him: Father, why didn't you open the door, but my father didn't answer. I went to my room, opened the schoolbag, sharpened a pencil, took out the books and notebooks and started doing my homework. And then I thought, Why didn't he answer me? He always answers me, but at the same moment I also thought there was something wrong with the eraser I had bought and I had to exchange it at Lichtenstein's. I picked up the grapes I had put on a plate where I would once mix sand from the Negev and went back to the other room. He was still lying there, the foot was on the way to the house slipper, he didn't move. Everything was in the middle—middle of a smile, middle of putting on a shoe, like a photo of somebody who is both running and standing still for eternity. I thought he looked like marble. I touched him, his hand dropped and stayed hanging in the air between the bed and the floor. I turned on the radio, after a few seconds, the music started, and then I looked at him and suddenly I understood. I didn't grasp how I understood, because I had never seen a dead person before. But that dead person was my father. I started yelling and stamping my feet until the neighbors came. In the ashtray was a cigarette and then I didn't have a father and I asked myself what exactly I didn't have, what I lacked, Mother would get hysterical and swallow pills and miss him terribly. Once I dreamed that my father came back and didn't want to see me, you can't imagine how that hurt . . .

Ebenezer got up and stood in the middle of the room. A beam of light penetrated inside and made the small squares of lacquer on the nightstand glisten, his eye was covered with a dark scrim, for a moment he looked both solemn and a scarecrow that birds aren't scared of anymore. Fanya R. gave him a glass of water. He said: I asked him to help me, I don't know who I am and what I am, how can I know who Boaz is or who you are or who Henkin is?

Henkin is writing a book about somebody who doesn't exist, maybe I don't exist, when they shot Bronya the Beautiful, Boaz came, or perhaps it was Samuel, and then somebody came and took him. And fifty years passed. Rebecca's here, and Dana. It's all words, Noga, he says and doesn't feel. Only Fanya R. All the rest is words. Germanwriter too.

Noga said: You scare me when you look at me and say those things, I can't understand.

I'm waiting for Samuel, said Ebenezer. All you say is only words, I've got to see Samuel, Boaz is Samuel, but he isn't either.

Noga got up and went to him. Fanya R. smiled. Noga didn't remember ever seeing a smile like that; as if what was hidden in her or shaped in her, some bitter memory, was disguised to itself and it was itself and at the same time its mask. Fanya R. said: I'm not a talkative woman. You're a beautiful woman, all that is a punishment from God! Boaz looks like Joseph, so how is he the son of Ebenezer? Ebenezer thinks his daughters died, because those are Joseph's daughters. Something for you and for our story. You know how awful it is at night here. Always yearnings and always those dreams he recites. I'm with him, so what, troubles Boaz needs, he's a Sabra, Israel, army buddies, a hero, what, why does he need all that with dead souls and dead bodies and yearnings for the dead, and my little girls who wait in Ebenezer's brain. He's got memories, he doesn't have Ebenezer, he's got Samuel, he doesn't have Boaz, my daughters left, Mengele, twins he loved. He did experiments, and then more, what do we know about Boaz, about Noga that's you or about a Yemenite woman who came here with pain and also apologizing, yesterday, says Boaz isn't to blame and now you come with a story like her, see how much I'm talking, but Ebenezer doesn't have all of you. He's dead, all Jews died, standing with a white flag, with Samuel, hitting gentiles who come, exile, exile, you don't know! Samuel is his son and how will you understand, you!

(Fragments of reels of recording for cataloguing: tapes [6/76 and tape 5/90] were ruined, these are fragments of them that remained—)

Women who look like Jordana and Noga are sitting in row twelve on the aisle in the movie house "Pa'ar" in Tel Aviv. A matinee and cracking sunflower seeds. A Lufthansa plane, a Boeing 747 flight 005 takes off from Cologne. Jordana is weeping and so she can't see the film that German-writer doesn't see on the plane because he's sleeping. Noga buys more sunflower seeds, comes back, and sits down next to Jordana.

Boaz took a Carmel Duke car and went to the desert to hunt vultures. He parked the car next to a wadi, took the rifle, and walked alone, in a good mood, whistled something, the gigantic desert, yellow and savage. The Carmel Duke car is made of fiberglass. When he came back with a dead vulture and searched for the car he saw a skeleton. Camels passed by there, saw the car, and ate it. They left only the chassis and the motor and the chrome. He walked a whole day until he came to Yotbata. From there he went home. For a week he laughed, even when he saw the vulture stuffed for a school in Jerusalem.

Boaz told Noga about the camels and didn't tell Jordana.

Jordana claims that Boaz doesn't love her because he didn't tell her about the camels. Noga tries to undermine her certainty.

Noga thinks: Jordana tastes like hot peppers and wormwood and cheese-cake.

Rebecca Schneerson dreamed she had wept for eight years. When she woke up she didn't know if she had dreamed she wept or wept and had really slept for eight years. She told Ahbed: I don't know what time is now. If now is now or not.

Ahbed asked Boaz what *a fayg*, up yours, means.

The Captain's grave moved at night. Bedouins camping there with the flocks they brought from the south trembled with fear. The son of old Avigdorov, who was considered one of the thirty-one founders and had once loved Rebecca, but didn't have the courage in his heart to tell her, toddled along for six kilometers in the heavy heat to tell Rebecca the Captain's grave moved. She said: Tea you won't get for that, but know that if he moves in the grave it means he's preparing for future wars. The Captain was lazy in his life, and even more so in his death.

Fanya R. was scared, went to the store, and bought two dolls. Then she hid them. The waiter who came to serve drinks at the party that was held someplace else and got the address wrong, buried the dolls in the yard for her, under a tree. She paid him in German marks hidden in a pillow. Ebenezer went to the place where there had once been a village named Marar and picked chrysanthemums. Then he tried to plant them in his garden.

Boaz sat in his house and very slowly burned his hand. He didn't feel a thing. Noga covered her face with a pillow and Jordana went into the street and read obituary announcements. She didn't know the dead people. In the morning she read in the paper that a man had died. She went to his funeral, stood there, asked herself what she was doing, but didn't have a satisfactory answer. Somebody asked her if she was a relative, and she said: Maybe. Then she went to the office. Boaz came with the seared hand bandaged for a memorial book for an artillery regiment. Jordana tried to pretend she didn't know him. They talked with an alienation that suited their mood. But her hand, her hand groped for him. She told him about Mr. Soslovitch, a locomotive salesman. Boaz said: If Henkin had come to Kassit when I sat there three days and waited for him, and Mr. Soslovitch ordered a beer for me and I didn't drink it, I wouldn't have had to write the poem. And I don't think Mrs. Cohen ever slept with Mr. Soslovitch. Then they talked about the fact that their love had to end and maybe was already ended. She wept. All she could say was, I love both of you, Boaz, I love you and I love Noga. He said: Maybe, and left.

Germanwriter finished writing the novella and went over the last proofs. Renate was sick. As mentioned above, they flew Lufthansa Flight 005 to New York.

In New York Sam Lipp said: You act Licinda, Licinda, but you're not Licinda. Nobody can be himself.

A conversation in Tel Aviv: You remember Samuel Lipker from the Sonderkommando? He's my son's commander in the reserves.

I thought he died, said the man.

No, he was on the ship with my brother. The name of the ship was *Salvation*. He hasn't been seen since. Now, she said, he's called Boaz.

Sam, asked Licinda, were you ever in Jerusalem?

Yes, said Sam.

I dreamed about a house, she said, and I know I got the dream from you, the house wasn't big and there was a bakery in it.

Sam said: That was my grandfather's house on Baron Hirsch Street in Tarnopol.

Rebecca Schneerson's cow barn, said the Minister of Agriculture in the official ceremony, yielded the greatest quantity of milk by three point forty-six percent of all the cow barns in Israel. I am honored to award the family representative the medal for increasing and encouraging production. The great-grandson of Ahbed climbs onto the stage and accepts the award on behalf of Rebecca Schneerson, and shakes the minister's hand. The minister's wife whispers to the minister. He looks like an Arab.

The great-grandson of Ahbed hears that and says: I don't look like an Arab, I *am* an Arab. And he adds in Arabic, *kata hirek*, and descends.

Boaz put his mouth to Noga's hand, caught her white hair, and in silence held her hair in his mouth for two hours and twenty minutes. Noga wept, but the tears she wept circumvented Boaz's head, and in an arc, like flying deer, the tears landed on his knee. When dawn broke, he turned his mouth away and said: Anybody who wasn't defending you, Noga, doesn't know what perfection there is in words.

Noga made him tomato soup.

Jordana called and said: I slept in my house and it was sad, but. And hung up.

Boaz thought of Samuel in the camp and didn't know why he thought of Samuel in the camp. He said: My father didn't forgive me for not being there and I didn't forgive either. And Noga said: Look who's coming, it's Kootie-and-a-Half, hello Kootie-and-a-Half, and Kootie-and-a-Half bent over, and said: Who's that beautiful Yemenite woman who's blocking her ears?

A hard land, said Rebecca Schneerson.

A hard land, said Fanya R. She didn't sleep at night. The letters from the newspaper get into my eyes, she said. What dreams there are that I left there and live here. Maybe we'll win the next war? And how alone is it together?

Tape / —

> New York, apologies for the delay.
>
> My dear friend,
>
> I meant to write to you on the plane, but I fell asleep. Renate is blessed with what can maybe be called psychosomatic wellness. Two weeks before I was informed of the trip, she was sick, but when they told me I had to fly to New York for the publication of the novella (*The Beautiful Life of Christina Herzog*), she recovered in a few hours. With my own eyes, I saw a red runny nose dry up. Your letter about Jordana and Noga, and the story you attached, evoked sad thoughts in me about my ability to understand the connections we're searching for: it was an instructive lesson.
>
> Two days before the flight, Renate dreamed she dropped into an ocean and then drove a black hearse. The lights went out and she couldn't see the road, she had to go on driving and started veering toward the steep slope, and when she woke up from the dream, she yelled: Friedrich, Friedrich, but since she hadn't called him in years, and I had meanwhile woken up, I brought her a cup of coffee in bed and she drank and then told me the dream and said that Friedrich had to be here. So she

went to the fortuneteller. For years now she hadn't been to her, but back when Friedrich died she had often visited astrologers and fortunetellers. You see, we also seek lost traces in quick-sand. Renate thought Friedrich was alive on another plane of time and his death was not absolute. Ever since, an essential change has taken place in her and she doesn't delude herself anymore, doesn't participate in séances to contact our son, has returned to the silent despair of those who submit. That dream before the trip brought her back to the fortuneteller named Ruth, like most of the women in the life of Adam Stein, whom we talked about, and whose old circus Friedrich used to go to, even though he himself no longer appeared in the circus and nothing remains of it except the name—"Adam's Circus." The fortuneteller looked at the cards, made Renate a hasty horo-scope, and after she talked with her about her nature and her past, things that need not be repeated here, she talked about the trip coming up in a day or two. There are encounters con-nected with the past in store for you, she said, and as for the flight, and you're flying soon, and Renate said: The flight's the day after tomorrow! The flight will be comfortable, she said and Renate said: But it's winter now and stormy, and the fortuneteller said, and I quote: "The flight will be smooth as butter."

When we were over the ocean, the head flight attendant came to us and said that the captain, who had seen me on tele-vision when I talked about my new book, invited me and my wife to the pilot's cabin. We went up to the cabin of the Boeing 747. The captain's name is Commandant Klein, and when we left Cologne after we took off, he said: Ladies and gentlemen, welcome to Lufthansa flight zero zero five from Cologne to New York, this is your captain, Commandant Klein speaking . . . And I thought about Adam Stein and I said Commander Klein caught me in the air, but Renate didn't pay attention and I shut up. Klein, a nice enough man, was excited by the modern in-struments he showed us, the up-to-date radar, the boards and the miraculous accessories, and the view from the pilot's cabin really was spectacular: you see the sky before you and you don't sense you're flying, you're up above, you're not aware at all of the plane behind you and beneath you, and below the ocean is spread out and you're alone before that stillness, a gigantic panorama of stillness and red and green lights go on and off and hum, we drank good coffee, we talked about politics and the fact that writers essentially lack understanding of problems that he as a captain and a practical man who "still remembers a thing or two," maybe understands no better, but surely different. We talked about economics, the Common Market, and then we parted with a warm handshake and a promise that when we flew over the state of Maine, we'd be invited back and could stay there until we landed in New York. That will be an unforgettable experience, promised the captain.

Later on, they showed some film and I fell asleep and didn't see it. Renate, who doesn't sleep much on airplanes, rented earphones and watched. I slept so soundly I didn't hear the head flight attendant come to invite us to the pilot's cabin. Renate decided not to wake me, and since she knew I wasn't as excited as she was by new technologies of pop-up toasters, automatic washing machines, transistors, and such instruments, and since she knew that the sight of the landing wouldn't be so important to me—and I could always imagine it and tell about it as if I had seen it, as she put it with a smile—she spared me the early rising and went up to the pilot's cabin without me. As she sat there drinking coffee Commandant Klein said we'd soon enter a strong storm. He showed her the radar screen, and she heard the voices on the radio, and as she told me later, she could see the storm right before her eyes. It was, she said, a gigantic black mass, like a threatening square at some distance in front of the prow of the plane. Renate said: But that can't be! The captain asked why not. (I'm quoting her because this letter is also addressed to Hasha Masha and I think Renate would want Hasha to know these things.) And Renate said, Because Ruth said the flight would be smooth as butter. The commandant laughed and pointed to the black storm at a reasonable distance from

the prow, but Renate insisted, it was important for her to believe. Later on she told me she thought she was red as a tomato,
and she said: No, it can't be, and when the pilot finished laugh
ing, Renate told me, she buried her face and looked at the floor
and thought of a beautiful Bible verse that Hasha translated for
her from Hebrew to German, even though it's also in our Bible,
but in Hasha's translation, the sting wasn't lost, she thought
about King David, of whom it was said that he was ruddy but
withal of a beautiful countenance. She liked the word "withal"
in that context. The wind velocity above Boston at the moment
is one hundred ninety knots, said Commandant Klein and he
wiped his nose, but the plane didn't dance. Renate asked: What
happened to your storm? and the captain said: Soon, the storm
simply moved left a little, and Renate looked ahead and did see
a storm and from above it looked like a gigantic black box moving left toward the ocean, and the captain said: Soon! But his
voice, she said, wasn't so confident, and it continued like that
until the landing in New York. The storm moved left, like a
snake, six minutes before the prow of the plane, and when we
landed in New York, Renate told me (I of course was sleeping),
the wind at Kennedy Airport was six knots, while only ten minutes before it was eighty knots. On the way, traces of the storm
were seen and as we were descending, cities and villages
wrapped in snow could be seen, and because it had already grown
dark the lights were seen sparkling after a decent washing, and
the commandant wasn't laughing anymore Renate had to give
all the members of the crew Ruth's address and phone number
and when she came back to me, she woke me up and said: We're
here, Ruth was right, and I woke up, looked outside and saw the
plane approaching the Lufthansa gate, and Renate told me the
story, brought me coffee in a plastic cup and I smiled. She didn't
tell me she gave them the address and phone number, because
she knew that would annoy me. She knew that my enemies, the
extreme rightists and leftists, would make mincemeat of me in
their newspapers. They'd write about the staunch rationalist who
went to a fortuneteller. For they wouldn't write that Renate went

to Ruth on her own, but would weave my name into the plot and would brew up a proper brew.

For two weeks I was quite busy. Along with my editor and a few other people from Harper & Row, I flew to six cities in a row, appeared on television and radio, held press conferences, was interviewed, lectured, and our young attaché, a handsome woman named Kristina, took Renate and me to a lot of cocktail parties, endless meetings; I even gave a lecture at the PEN Club in New York, I'm not complaining, in our day a writer has to play the clown, the portable philosopher, and I had to do that for myself and my publishers, my agent and Renate. I know that Schiller and Goethe didn't fly to public relations tours, but needless to say the times—and the people—have changed. After two crammed weeks I parted from the editor, the attaché, our consul, from some American writers, a few of whom I had met before, we took our bags, and instead of going to the airport, we went to a small hotel in Greenwich Village, slept quietly one night, and in the morning, I called Lionel.

Lionel was glad to meet me. I told him how much I liked the *Laments on the Death of the Jews*. He told me that he had high regard for me, after all, he said, I wrote the first article about you in *The New York Times*. And indeed, I remembered that he had written and was amazed that I hadn't thought about that, and after mutual compliments, I on the *Laments* and he on the novella, and after he expressed amazement that his *Laments* were now being published in all the countries of Europe except Germany, I said I was indeed astonished.

On our way to him, we bought white wine (made in Israel) and Renate bought a bouquet of flowers, and at a temperature of two below zero, in the cold wind blowing from the river, we came to Lionel's house. I must tell you that I was more excited than I had imagined.

Lily opened the door and was exactly what I had expected her to be, some undefined femininity, something between a lion and a summer flower. On her face the sadness of polished matter clean of sediments, was smiling serene, both deep and bright. At the age of forty, she looked rare, feminine, and an almost Mediterranean olive tone slipped among the northern tones as if they were bold storms on a marble surface. In her eyes is a dark touch and they look very bright, and yet the elusive gloom made them mysterious. She held out her hand and said in English: Welcome, she invited us inside and when we took off our coats and the warmth spread in our bodies, we offered the wine and the flowers and we saw Lionel. Lionel is tall, but not too tall, thin, his hair is silver and short and his face is lit by that light many Jewish intellectuals have, some mischievous flash in the dark eyes, wrapped in dark eyebrows, reflecting an alien, ancient melancholy, and when I looked at him I thought of the sentence of Spinoza (and Lionel's eyes reminded me of his), that God is celestial harmony and that His laws of morality are universal and hence are not an imitation of the laws of nature. Confronting Lionel's eyes, I thought that only Jews, that stubborn and wise tribe, could have created such a sublime and unnatural idea. Who if not the Jews had to know in their flesh how impossible that idea is, but the persistence in believing that there is a moral law that is not synonymous with the laws of nature, grants Hebrew tribalism the exciting, but no less annoying greatness. There was also some savagery etched on Lionel's face, something that strives for personal freedom, and I thought about the expression frozen fire, I thought to myself: Maybe that's how Joseph Rayna looked, or at least something from Joseph Rayna was looking at me and I couldn't take my eyes off Lionel, who was wearing a blue cashmere sweater and thin corduroy trousers and his hands are delicate, but not unmasculine. Lily persisted in speaking English with us, even when Lionel, Renate, and I were speaking German. I loved her for that, and in my heart, maybe I was also angry. The apartment is beautiful, the garden looked gray under the thin shroud of ice, I loved the furniture and the pictures on the walls. Later on, Renate told me that something in the blend (as she said) of the physical furniture, the pictures, the books and the atmosphere, reminded her of your apartment, although the apartments are so different. She talked about color and form that turn into an echo.

I thought about Cervantes's sentence that the pen is the tongue of the soul. Maybe the apartment is simply the thermometer of those who live in it. The conversation, of course, slid to the Last Jew. Never for a moment did I believe that Lily didn't know that Lionel and Sam are sons of the same father, but it was strange for me to think that Lionel didn't know that and that it was so important for those concerned that he not know. Later on, when I met Sam, I understood that he had to preserve lines of defense for himself and that he never trusted anybody—except Ebenezer and Lily—fully. After more than twenty years in the United States, he still felt foreign. As in his relations with Licinda, he always had to be on guard. Lily came from the same world of which Ebenezer is the last remnant. Deep in his heart, Sam Lipp believes that Ebenezer doesn't recite the Last Jew, but that he *is* the Last Jew, and everything seen in his eyes, and felt, is nothing but a delusion he's willing to live in, but whose logic he doesn't have to accept. That's strategic room for maneuver, a bit mendacious, a kind of pocket pogrom and anti-pogrom he keeps with him as a guarantee for his life. Thus Sam still sells his lampshade, hates what he can't forgive himself, takes revenge on himself for being prevented from taking revenge on the world that Ebenezer maintained was annihilated.

Sam's dreams are so strong that Lily started dreaming his dreams and sometimes she wakes up at night in a cold sweat (she told Renate this as she was drinking), gets up, goes to Sam and Licinda's room, and he's lying there, his eyes wide open, shaking, even Licinda started dreaming Sam's dreams.

I said I didn't know where Ebenezer was living today, but Lily glanced at me offended, since she knew very well that I knew, and then she said in German: Watch out, Sam does dangerous things, maybe what you don't know can sometimes be good.

Lionel told me he had found material in the public library that had been copied by a scholar from Brandeis University. It was a precise account of an evening in a nightclub in London where

Ebenezer performed many years ago. I came on that material, said Lionel, when I discovered that one of the laments I wrote was made into an opera and the composer, a German Jew named Weiss, found the libretto in the library. I found a few laments whose provenance I didn't know, they weren't exactly my laments, but one of them was very similar to my sixth lament, about the child who extracted gold teeth. You know the lament, he said confidently, and I did indeed remember it. The composition is called "Sources for the Burial of Moses, Story of the Golden Calf and Its Location," and the material Ebenezer recited was that composition—in addition to the other laments, including my lament and was composed from Ebenezer's words, by Yehuda Ber Avram ben Abraham and printed in Leipzig in 1984. And the year 1984 is still very far from us, said Lionel. I told him I knew about that composition and was quite amazed by it, and Lionel said that among the papers and manila files were annals of a Crusader (I immediately verified the story) and some meeting between SS Sturmbahnführer Kramer and Nehemiah Schneerson, husband of Rachel Schneerson, a meeting that was held, said Lionel, in nineteen nine. I was excited to hear these things and asked if he didn't mean Boaz, and he said: No, Nehemiah. Lionel asked if that was so important, since I looked quite excited and my face was surely beaming and I said Yes, yes. He told me: I've got a copy of this material and I'll bring it to you. We sat and drank the wine we had brought and Lily didn't talk anymore, but chain-smoked, with restrained pensiveness, and then Lionel came back and gave me a copy of the material, I glanced at it and then put it in my pocket.

In every person hides an image of a first love that may never have been. Lily was my first love, a love I didn't know. Dreams of my youth were embodied not only in the meditations of sin of Ukrainian guards, as Sam put it, but also in my own meditations. There was also a moment I still regret, a moment when I envied Lionel for robbing me of the right to love Lily and in my heart I expressed that explicitly: Our Lily! And I hated myself for that thought. Renate, who sensed something, stroked my hand and let me feel that she understood and forgave, but she wasn't willing for me to continue, and I stopped. That was a moment of wrath, like a demon that attacked, stayed in me and left immediately.

Lily, who maybe also felt it, laughed and looked at me as if to say: You're all alike! But there was also some sign of her own guilt in her smile; if you were forged of this matter, what was I forged of, she surely thought. But the moment passed. Lionel spoke excellent German, he told us about Sam's work, about his theater, and said that Sam had been working for two years on a new play based on the story of Joseph de la Rayna and that Licinda, Sam's girlfriend, was acting in that play. The premiere was tomorrow, and when he asked if we'd like to see the play, we agreed enthusiastically and arranged to meet the next day. Late at night, we went outside, Lily accompanied us, it was snowing, the wind was strong, and then the wind stopped, and Lily said: I know your books, and she linked arms with Renate, who was trembling a little from the sharp transition from warmth to cold. You're decent people, said Lily, but I'm really not at all sure it's good that you came, things aren't yet healed, got to watch out, everybody's conspiring against him, he fights me against Lionel, he's got a broken, corrupt laugh, he's always expecting the blow to land, that play . . . Sam Lipp isn't producing a play, he's creating the Fourth Reich. She glanced at me, smiled and didn't continue, changed the subject, and said: But it's better like this, you came, maybe it's important that we met, I have to defend Sam and Lionel, I normally don't speak German. In my childhood I sang "Spring, fields, how beautiful are the blue and copper mountains." I sang the "Niederlandisches Dankgebet, Wacht am Rhine." Yes, sometimes, between Sam's dreams, to protect him, she suddenly said in broken German, I have to dream or sing in German . . . and then she tore her arm out of Renate's and ran home.

We hailed a cab and went to the hotel. By ten in the morning, I was sitting in the public library, in a closed room, and poring over the material. Not until five in the afternoon, when I was so hungry I was dizzy, did I leave. I found very valuable material for our book, Obadiah, and I'll send you copies of all the material as soon as I can. The story about Kramer's meeting with Nehemiah Schneerson amazed me early in the morning, when I read part of the material Lionel gave me. Eating brings an appetite. Even if Kramer's journal, which I read in Ebenezer's house, was (as Renate says) my creation, and I don't accept that crazy version—the meeting between Nehemiah and Kramer absolutely cannot be the product of my imagination, no matter how fertile it is. In the report from London, Ebenezer tells about the meeting between his father and Kramer. (In his relation to the story, Kramer is not presented at all as a commander in whose camp he stayed. He tells a story of an encounter between a man—and only we, the readers, know was his father—and a German whom only we know was the commander of the camp where he stayed, in other words: he tells a story that is alien to him, unrelated, and that was enough to make me shudder.) Kramer, who was then a young man, went on a journey to the Land of Israel with an old German named Doctor Kahn, who never was a real physician. The two of them were residents of the village of Sharona, although Kramer was born in Willhelma, and only at the age of seven did he move to Sharona. The doctor, who had worked as a ship's physician for many years, collected butterflies, lived with an Arab lad, Hger, who was said to have been wounded once by mistake with his rifle, loved to swim, spawned children all over the east like some ancient god and spoke of turning Palestine into a German protectorate. On one of their journeys they came to a settlement in Judea, and that settlement was the settlement where Ebenezer was born (even though he doesn't mention that fact, and when he recited this story maybe he didn't know he was born there). They were caught in a storm, sought shelter, came to the house of Nehemiah and Rebecca Schneerson. Kramer (according to Ebenezer) describes Nehemiah as a handsome man for a Jew, hot-tempered like most Jews. And Rebecca (in his opinion) was the most beautiful woman he had ever seen even though she was a Jewess. Kramer told Nehemiah there would never be peace between the Jewish world and the Christian world, or the Muslim world. There won't be forgiveness, he said, until the so-called Jew of Jesus is taken out and the reality of the real Jews in the world is separated. Christianity, said Kramer, had a Greek, pagan tone, sublime and tragic in its essence. The idea of conscience and guilt feelings are the Jewish contribution that stuck to original Christianity. The Jews as a nation that rejects race—Gangbok—invented the ahistoricism of remorse. Pure chauvinism is foreign to Judaism, and there's nothing like pure chauvinism to cleanse and create, a solid element in the health of its nation. Would-be patriotic crusades have to be destroyed, he said, and then the Christian Jesus will be the natural god in the world where there are no witnesses to the Jewish betrayal of Him.

I won't weary you with the long speech Kramer delivered that night. We can be amazed only that he said those things in nineteen nine, if he really did say them. Kramer was drunk, drooling, and looked at the enormous expanses stretching to the Arab vines. He said: Today we no longer remember who was the first father of the eagle, evolution isn't only in nature, it also exists as a huge intellectual trap.

The argument was trenchant. Nehemiah's reasoning was, of course, ridiculous to the German. But despite all that, Kramer found Nehemiah charming. Maybe he saw him as a crucified one too miserable to worry about. He hated regretting pessimists and historical thinkers. For him, history was something that happens at this moment. He wanted to write to the German government, to describe the situation in the Holy Land, which monks and cunning spies were tempted to depict too romantically. He wanted to warn the government never to rely on the Jewish *Yishuv* that had German or Austrian subjects. He told Nehemiah: You've got a beautiful wife, and if I weren't a man of noble feelings, I would steal her from you. Afterward, Nehemiah went to visit him. The houses with handsome roofs, fields measured as with a ruler, the advanced agriculture, impressed Nehemiah. At night, he visited Dr. Kahn's room. He advised Nehemiah not to envy. He spoke with him about the splendid Jewish nation, which was beaten by all the great nations that lit up and went out, while it remained to tell that. He spoke with Nehemiah about the savage Germans, who sometimes had a stroke of wis-

dom, but lacked a tragic quality. They're even afraid of themselves, he said. The Jews have a rebellious, sober, and sad, maybe
ironic, surely tragic deafness, he added, ultimately they will de
feat the Kramer idea, just as your god overcame gods like Tamuz,
Apollo, Dagon and Ba'al. The field of defeat will always be the
hearts of men, he said sadly, and Kramer who heard the words
beyond the wall, scolded him and got in return the proud poetry
of an anthem and the finger held out to him as conciliation, and
then the doctor finished drinking a whole bottle of wine and
delivered confused speeches into the night.

Tape / —

In the evening, we went to the theater. The journalists had
raised great expectations for a long time, so there was a big and
curious audience. In the distance, I saw my publisher talking
with the charming attaché. They stared at me in amazement,
but were afraid to come ask me what I was doing there. Lily and
Renate went backstage and Lionel took me into the gigantic
auditorium, with a semicircular stage at the end. Actors were
already sitting on the stage, chatting among themselves. Somebody was weeping. They sat in a big camp with a barbed wire
fence. A gigantic clock hung over the stage. A group of musicians played music composed of jazz elements, Hasidic melodies, and what astounded me more: I could hear through the
first tune like a leitmotif—the fearsome and exciting anthem
of the Black Corps. It was a monstrous blend, and yet something pleasant was anchored in it. The musicians looked tired,
I remembered the sight of the small chorus in the Blue Lizards
Club in Copenhagen. Lily looked radiant. Her dress was light
purple, her hair was plaited into thin braids that crowned her
cascading hair. She smiled at me (now she returned with Renate
and sat next to Lionel), and said: I'm a disgusting woman and had
to challenge Sam. I'm scared of his Fourth Reich. Her beauty was
ingenuous and wicked, I tried to understand her desperate war.

Here I have to note something: In my youth, I tried to write
a description of the smell of a rose, and after many attempts, I
gave up. If I were able to describe the play, I would of course do

it, but when I returned home and tried to do that for you, for
me, I couldn't. I have six drafts of a description of the play, and
not one of them touches the terrifying and exciting, bold and
fascinating phenomenon we saw that night. Never did I see
theater like that. But when I say that, I say something about the
smell of a rose. Maybe the gist of the play can be summed up in
a few flashes and leave things there, so if you saw it someday
you'd understand what I meant.

What we saw was a combination of Ebenezer in a nightclub
and an attempt to convey with movement, music, acting, and
monologues the story of Joseph de la Rayna. The big clock was
set backward. We lived in two different times: a camp in the
last hours before the surrender and a person haunted by demons who goes to Safed in the late sixteenth century to bring
deliverance. The play was opened by Samuel Lipker, or more
precisely, an actor who played him, who explained a few things
about Ebenezer to the audience and announced that at the end
of the play, baskets would be passed around, and every spectator
would be entitled to contribute as much as he could for
Ebenezer's hungry dead daughters. The story of Joseph was
played in full: Joseph mortifies himself, leaves with his students
to bring deliverance, prophets warn him, snow on the mountains
of Safed, an intentional sin is greater than an unintentional good
deed, Joseph's wedding ceremony, also a Frank, the false messiah
with a Torah scroll and a whore on horseback. Destruction is
essential. Joseph burns down a synagogue. Rabbis mourn at the
throne, which is a stove in the middle of the camp, where soldiers
without hands clap their lips at other recruits going to die and
there sit Lilith and Ashmodai. They love the smell of divine incense. Joseph chews tallow. Smears himself with tallow. The students follow their teacher. Their tribulations, told by Ebenezer,
are sung by a chorus, danced by dancers, and then Ashmodai and
Lilith are caught. When the arrogant Joseph offers Lilith incense, a spark goes out of her mouth and burns the cords. Gigantic dogs assault the students. Joseph runs away. God yearns
for Lilith and Ashmodai. The synagogue burns down. A woman

translates for a lad the things said to him by a young woman who doesn't speak his language. Metaphysical pornography, Renate said to me. Joseph is flogged. All is lost. Salvation doesn't come. Ebenezer moves the clocks. A woman brings a dead baby into the world and actors sing numbers of death. Uniting with one another in human perversion. A bakery with a protesting woman put into an oven. Dogs metamorphosed into souls. Words incomprehensible at first and then blood-curdling. Silence, some epic of silence and movement, like animals who learned the annals of horror from the amoeba to SS Sturmbahnführer Kramer who sits and laughs, blinking at Ebenezer at the throne of God, in the middle of a camp with a human barbed wire fence. I'm trying and not succeeding. I know, but a seventh draft won't be hidden anymore. A dog's head on a tray. Ebenezer recites. Tells the history of the Jews from their end to their beginning. The Fourth Reich, says Lily, and tears flow on her cheeks, history of Joseph de la Rayna, Joseph Rayna, his sons and daughters, that horror, Henkin, descending to the dark depths to discover light, some catastrophe in the order of the universe. To save objects, the captain throws the ship into the sea and drowns. And during the play I felt I was in fact participating, acting in the play while sitting, the actors were acting me, I them, and we, one another, and between the silences movement and sorcery, as in some magic rite, sitting heavy, an awful silence broken only by the nervous laughter of the audience, a laughter at pictures from the present blended with the camp, Kramer, Ebenezer, Joseph de la Rayna living in Safed, then and now, as if all times were desecrated and the clock starts going forward and backward and the awful terrifying music and yet more beautiful, the increasing movement, a very thin freeze prevailing, so thin there are no words. Four hours passed and we didn't even go out during the intermission. The woman who gave birth to a dead son did that when some of the audience went to the bathroom. The actors eat and drink onstage. They themselves also constitute part of the set and they dance. Licinda is Lilith, and also the woman who lets some boy crush her breasts, as he reads the numbers of trains that went there in the voice of a stock market announcer reading stock prices and she's indifferent, her eyes extinguished, Joseph flies from Sidon to Greece and enters the dream of the Queen of Greece, who orders him killed. Deliverance doesn't come and won't come, there's only death which all of you, says Samuel, all of you are in and it is with you. The Fourth Reich, says Lily. Lionel hears parts of his *Laments*, Ebenezer recites with his eyes shut, the clocks are broken, words are lopped off, until it all ends in a thin silence. Only Ebenezer stands there and then falls. And then he laughs. He doesn't know who he is. Maybe he's dead. The actors start applauding the stunned audience and only then, Henkin, only then, does the audience wake up from a state I'd call hypnotic and come out of the role it has played: a spectator of its own execution, and applauds.

Never did I hear such applause . . .

We went outside. A cold wind was blowing. We bundled up. In the distance I saw the charming Kristina waving a flaccid good-bye to me and disappearing into a cab. My publisher came, shook my hand, and didn't say a thing, looked at me, for a moment he forgot why he had come to me, and he left. We went to Lionel's house. Later, somebody brought the reviews. We also heard the review on television. Sam closed himself in his room and didn't come out. I went to him. He was sad and quiet. A spark of anger flickered in his eyes. I don't like art, he said, I don't make art, what do they want from me, everything they saw was truth, somebody showed them, what's the big deal. But I couldn't pity him. He created a great work and he was suffering because of that. To create something great is to touch painful nerves, it's to try to create, to challenge, to change a world, and they come and say: Oh, it was awfully beautiful, I understood it.

One General Allenby, said Sam, wanted to scare the Sudanese and told them: I command you with a telegram, I sit here with weapons and supervise the wires. What does it mean to create? I translate dreams into theater. By the same token, I could have been a professional murderer or an undertaker, I've got no compassion, Melissa-Licinda is an open wound, I need her and Lily, that's all. I smiled at him and he looked at me, and then he confessed to me about the letter I had once sent him. Lily smiled the honeyed smile of a jungle queen in a Walt Disney movie, and Sam said: Did you see how my naked parents lay there! You must know, your wife could have been an excellent Jewish shawl, there's no future for that stupid past, trying to teach actors to act "it," not "about," what comes out? A review in the *Times*: Powder and milkshake. A crooner and a football player understand better. Who am I doing theater for and why? I don't have electricity in my hands and I don't have flames. I have to do theater. What does art do? Except that one man I knew built beautiful boxes to stay alive and then I too, because of him, and the life I have left isn't the life I wanted, you know how many came out of Auschwitz alive? Thirty thousand, another two days of war and not even one would have come out alive to tell.

Henkin my friend, a malicious thought came to me: The next time I'm asked about the heroes of my fiction, I'll tell whoever asks that he really should ask the characters about the author and not the author about the characters. I thought about that as a result of something that happened to me and that I'll tell you now. I'm not a person who acts impulsively. I stayed in New York to meet Sam, Lionel, and Lily. The meeting with Sam was disappointing to some extent. The night after the party, I invited him to a small bar, we sat and drank. He didn't talk about anything but his hatred for the play he had worked on for years. He didn't open up to me. I couldn't really make him talk, even when I gave him some information that should have interested him. When I tried to talk with him about Ebenezer, he shut up, then he said to me: For me Ebenezer is dead! And didn't go on.

When I told him about Boaz he was silent a long time and I saw three things at the same time. He envied Ebenezer, whose existence he didn't admit, he envied Boaz, and he felt a profound fear. He said: That's nonsense! I was the only son of the Last Jew. Licinda is the incarnation of Melissa. Melissa is the love of my stepfather's youth. He said that, since he knew very well that I know they're brothers. But he chose not to relate to that and I didn't press him. I'm afraid of those combinations, he said, those crossroads, of you and of me. The real world doesn't exist anymore and we're its last witnesses. Why embellish them? Melissa is dead so we'll act for her the death of the Jews as she sits at the throne of honor and sells lampshades for ten percent profit. If God were dead, said Sam, we wouldn't have to suffer so much, but He's not dead, He exists as long as Jewish suffering exists. And then I did the irrational act I alluded to earlier, I write you now, and my hand shakes. I did something like Ebenezer's request, when he told you to ask me for his two daughters, something like Renate's desperate attempt with the fortuneteller, I went to Connecticut.

I came to Washington Depot at noon and went to the official Ford dealer. Mr. Brooks was sitting behind a glass wall reading a newspaper. When I looked at him, he turned his chair around, took off his reading glasses, and tried to see me. I walked around the gigantic show room and a smiling woman came up to me, and said: Aren't you the German writer we saw on television? I read your last book, she said after I said yes. You want to buy a car? At that moment, Mr. Brooks came out of his office and approached us. An old man dressed meticulously, his hair white, his nose thick and some thread of taut harshness around his eyes, he introduced himself to me, and said that an honored guest like me—he had also seen me on television—warranted special attention, and I said: That's fine, your assistant was friendly and generous, and she smiled, maybe even blushed. I looked at him, I spoke, but I tried to think of my son. What arose in the back of my mind was an impossible blend of Boaz, Sam, Friedrich, and Menahem. He looked at me as he spoke and I'm not sure I heard what he said, I tried to understand his mourning, but his mourning was hidden under so many masks that I could almost see myself in his eyes. I was moved to pity for him, I can't explain why, never did I pity you, Henkin, or myself, or even Renate. I said: I came to meet you Mr. Brooks, and please forgive me, I wanted very much to see the house where Melissa grew up, but I can't explain why to you.

He made a gesture as if to stop me, and I stopped talking. He seemed to be trying to digest my words, to understand them. After a bit, he said: My brother's granddaughter, Priscilla, is a student at Smith College in Northampton, not far from here. A very distinguished college . . . When the Catholics came to Northampton, they built a splendid church there, next to the college dorms. Do you know what the scholars of Smith College did? They put the chemistry lab in a building next to the church. The windows of the chemistry lab face the windows of the church, and for fifty years, sir, the Catholics, now the majority of the population in the city, except for the members of the college, have had to suffer the stench . . .

I nodded as if I understood the parable, even though I didn't yet completely fathom what he was talking about, I felt the shining chrome of a new Pontiac and now, in his sterile church, between a Ford coupe, an elegant Mercury and a big white Lincoln, Mr. Brooks tried to smile. I saw the lines of his face refuse to illustrate a real smile. The layers of his face interwoven with thin red threads expressed some grievance, maybe anger, maybe even a threat, but under the threat I made out lines of serenity. He said: Melissa died years ago . . . I don't read books, sir, but I saw you on television and I read about you in *Time*. You look and sound like a rational and honorable man, you come from a country I admire for its practicality, its culture, its industry. Do you know how much I wanted to sell BMW and Mercedes? Listen, he said, and now at long last he managed to smile, I'd be glad to have you over to the house, let's go there, you'll have lunch at my house, but sir, Melissa no longer is, she's not in me, and now he almost raised his voice, she's not in the house, she's not in my wife, she's not finally and definitely, it's been many years since I stopped missing her, I've got two sons and one of them will surely take over my business, Priscilla can stay at her college, in the chemistry department and know she's still fighting an ancient war against Catholics, and with us, that's a rare, maybe desirable, case of a sequence of generations, sir . . . We're not like you, and it's too bad, he added sadly.

He took me to his office overlooking the showroom, ordered coffee for me, and went out. I munched a crunchy cookie, I drank the coffee, and I waited. He came back, we put on our coats, and went out into the harsh cold. We got into his white Lincoln Continental, the heat came on immediately, he started the motor and we glided to his house.

I won't weary you with the details of the meal. There were whispered conferences, the mounted hides are still there. We drank sherry, Melissa's mother is a charming, gentle old woman, much harsher than her husband. One of the sons asked me a lot of question about the two Germanys and I tried to answer him to the best of my understanding. The lemon mousse (after the ribs and roast potatoes) was excellent, and the more we talked, the more perplexed we became. Why am I here, they weren't the only ones who wondered, I also wondered myself and didn't know what to say . . .

I knew the moment of truth was approaching, I was worried, and so were they, and Mrs. Brooks, with that cleverness our wives call "feminine intuition," told me a young man came years before and then they found out that his name was Sam Lipp, and now everybody's talking about him. I told her: I'm doing research for a new book, maybe not so new, and I met a lot of people, including Sam Lipp. Mrs. Brooks showed signs of restrained excitement. For a moment she looked both desirable and shriveled, like some mounted hide of insatiable passion. She drank a lot of wine and her tongue became faster and maybe a little inarticulate. She talked about Sam Lipp, about the articles she read, that he isn't interviewed, that there aren't any photos of him, and nevertheless she said: I recognized him, I knew that was him. Maybe she recalled that dog, called her dog to come to her, it was a new dog, she patted his curly head with a sense of mastery, of revenge for Sam Lipp, some terrible sense for chilly melodrama. And then she got up, paced back and forth, and Mr. Brooks lit a giant cigar, smoked it slowly, and belched clouds of white smoke, and the maid brought a tray with coffee cups. Sam Lipp, she said, also went to the cemetery and we chased him. The dog betrayed us, we should have caught him, that famous stage director, what is he doing? I'm afraid to go to the play, Bud and Priscilla tell wonders and miracles about it. He patted the dog. The dog melted in his hands. I'm talking a lot. What hatred there was in him. Anger. What did I do? That anger of his. Melissa isn't his. He loved her, he said. Jesus!

I was silent and looked at the crease in my pants. Mr. Brooks was quiet and pensive and his look was caught in the smoke wisping up from the cigar. His face was impassive, and then suddenly, something in Mr. Brooks's dead face lit up. That flash I sensed in him before, something that would look inside, immune, creating stories about the chemistry department turned from an alloy of tiny red gills and miniature lizards into an almost savage audacity, and the shriveled silence turned into genuine rage. He said: There is in them that anger, the stubbornness, the cleverness, the nerve to get into the wrong places, where they're not wanted. There are reasons, natural reasons, aren't there? And you know, who knows better than you.

Yes, I said, and tried not to get upset, not to give it away.

No, that's not what was in him, she said. True, he's one of them, but no. Even then I thought, a trapped wolf, foreign, with a frightening, almost filthy beauty, some generosity in evil, some agitation in rottenness, his play, even then he tried to please . . . What did Melissa have to do with him?

And I knew she meant, What do I have to do with Melissa?

I told you, sir, said Mr. Brooks, somebody didn't build enough chemistry departments next to what could have been a cemetery! Those were strong words and I kept silent, Henkin! She shut up, and unlike her husband, she didn't trust me. The perplexity about my coming hadn't yet been explained. But he was swept up now in some old, gnawing enmity. He didn't know Melissa, she said, he tried to steal her! There was one who sneaked in, but we knew how to get rid of him, and now Mr. Brooks was incensed against the writer sitting there, and he barked: We're playing with words, what do you have to do with Melissa! What do you want after fifty years, what, what, what?

I said: I met Sam Lipp, and—

And what? Melissa wasn't his, she died before he was born! I'm investigating!

Investigating what?

I'm investigating the death of our children, I suddenly said, the death of Sam, who's disguised as living. The death of my son, the death of a boy named Menahem Henkin, the life of somebody who learned the history of the world by heart, Melissa is somehow interwoven in that story, I don't understand how, but I know and so I came here. Even before he met Licinda Hayden and called her Melissa, long before that, he was in love with Melissa and didn't even know her, just as I came from Cologne and find myself an unwelcome guest in your house, trying to know how you miss or don't miss Melissa. My son is dead. Sam Lipp, or as he was called before, Samuel Lipker, is also a fellow named Boaz Schneerson, and his events and the events of his father, I'm trying to write together with my friend who lives far away from here. He was in love with your daughter, knew her in another plane of time—an expression I learned from my spouse —and he's still searching for her, maybe in his disappointed love for Licinda Hayden who acted Lilith in his play . . .

I don't grasp what that has to do with it, said Mr. Brooks. He got up, his legs unsteady. He picked up the big glass ashtray standing there, and maybe he inadvertently dropped it and it shattered into thousands of slivers. At the sight of the smashed ashtray, he tried to smile, but his face managed only to grimace a little.

I do understand, Mrs. Brooks almost whispered. I remember looking at photos of Licinda Hayden, I saw her in *Time, Newsweek, The New York Times*. I remember looking at the photos and thinking, I know her, but I didn't connect it . . . now I do. Does Sam know about Melissa's closeness to Licinda?

I'm not sure, I groped for something opaque and astonishing that I heard in her voice now. Mr. Brooks said: I'm sorry about the ashtray. He called the maid to come clean up the slivers. We sat silent and pensive and waited until she finished. Mrs. Brooks got up and left the room a moment. Mr. Brooks said to me: She was a beautiful child, Melissa.

I know, I said.

She shouldn't have died, he said in a voice that cast off fifty years of thick walls, I should have listened to him and taken her to a hospital in New York, but I was too proud.

I'm fond of people who, at a certain moment, can say something contrary to the foundation of their whole life, and can feel human remorse, and I thought of my father who never could. I almost loved that man.

Suddenly there wasn't anything more to say. I looked out the window and saw the naked trees, the rebuked, aristocratic, frozen landscape wrapped in snow, an enormous sun startled me, as if your blinding light that exposes everything fell on me here of all places, a beam of light from another world, and I fell silent. And then Mrs. Brooks came back. In some way that seemed marvelous, but equally clumsy, Mrs. Brooks tried to connect Licinda with somebody who could have been Melissa. Maybe the fact that three strange men came during fifty years to love Melissa endowed her daughter—and even her yearnings for her had vanished with the years—with some importance, some metaphysical refinement. She was surely thinking of Lionel, of Sam, of me, she thought Licinda lived for us what Melissa could have lived eternally for her. I'm talking now of disappointment. I don't know, tangled threads unite us, and to whom am I telling these things! You? My self-mockery perplexes me and I almost suggested to them to establish an international committee of parents, without any distinction of sex, religion, race, or nationality, would Mrs. Brooks accept that idea? I was amazed at myself, not at her, she spoke about family, maybe a stub of memory of Licinda rose from there. Maybe she really did say that Licinda is a distant relative, and maybe I'm fantasizing and quoting things she didn't say, but there was one thing I'm sure she talked about—she talked about some rabbi named Kriegel who came to Providence, Rhode Island, in seventeen seventy-three, about her family graced with a Protestant minister named Stiles, who then lived in Providence and was an expert in Hebrew and wrote a book about that Kriegel. I thought: Where do I know the name Kriegel, and I recalled, contemplating that rabbi from Hebron who performed the marriage of Rebecca Secret Charity with her dead lover, Kriegel, who went from Hebron to America. Mrs. Brooks spoke of him with uncritical generosity, as if she missed him, and this is not the place to tell what she said, since that story has nothing to do with our issue, but at night, when I came back to New York and got into bed, I thought maybe I heard something that's important for us to know and I didn't yet grasp the end of its thread, and I also knew, a few seconds before I fell asleep, that maybe as I talk about Licinda, she herself is extraneous to the story, it doesn't concern her, but Lilith that she personified, or perhaps it's Lilith who personifies Licinda?

I went back to the public library and a fellow Lionel recommended helped me. He showed me some interesting research on Kriegel, relations with the Protestant minister Stiles, the sermon Stiles delivered in the synagogue on Shavuoth, how Kriegel came to America in seventeen seventy-three, wearing a turban, a handsome, radiant man. The connection, which I still don't understand, pleased me. Between Kriegel, Minister Stiles, Melissa and Licinda. Did Melissa grow up and become Licinda? Were the two of them distant relatives, was Captain Jose Menkin A. Goldenberg really—as I found out—the offspring of that Kriegel? Did he know he was his offspring? Could he have spawned his sons even after, beyond the generations that preceded him?

I sat with Lionel and Lily. It was late at night. Outside snow was falling. Sam and Licinda went out. Renate fell asleep. Then Lionel fell asleep too. Lily and I sat tired, our eyes almost shut, drunk, and sang children's songs. The next day, we flew home.

Dear Hasha,

I had a vision that lasted a whole day and I couldn't get rid of it. Menahem and Friedrich met in New York near Bloomingdale's. They went shopping. Friedrich bought leather suspenders and Menahem bought handkerchiefs and a belt. Menahem's hair was long and Friedrich's was shorter and the flap of a forehead could be seen on his head. Friedrich lied and said he had shot himself. Menahem said: You didn't shoot yourself, Friedrich, you shot somebody else and missed. They went to a Chinese restaurant. Neither of them knew how to use chopsticks. The old Chinese man laughed. They didn't know that was funny and ate with forks and knives. At the hotel, Melissa brought wine and they drank. Boaz came and jumped out the window. Menahem was impressed by the jump and Friedrich wasn't. They were drunk and sang. Friedrich was older than Menahem. They walked to the seashore. There was a cave there. Intense red colors were blended with sickly bluishness, a chaos of serenity they disappeared into dimness, as if out of weakness, wrapped in a thin halo of pinkishness, a kind of eternal sunset. Who said there's no life near death, they only said that there's no life after death! Everybody drowned there, alone. My husband claims I have a fever. I lie and write you. Maybe love is also preparing an alibi for the future, or the past. Menahem and Friedrich are consoled, they walked together on Fifth Avenue and laughed. Those were frozen tears of death. They flowed on him, on them, I felt an emptiness, maybe I yelled: Menahem, Menahem. I yearned for him.

Your love.

By the way: the director of your national theater held negotiations here with Sam Lipp to come to Israel to direct his play.

Love, Renate

Tape / —

Mr. Schneerson, do you really think ancient blood flows in us, don't you think you adopt a dangerous language? A kind of theatrical fascism, bereft of sharp positive critical thought—

I don't know what I think, my memory is me. I didn't ask others if they were fascists or progressives. Nor do I know where progressive people progress to. Thanks, Mr. Schneerson. No problem, when will Samuel come back?

Tape / —

And Rebecca Schneerson sat in her chair and felt in her bones how she was growing numb. When a giant bouquet of chrysanthemums came, sent by the grandchildren of the founders, she burst into a brief laugh. A note was stuck to the bouquet: May you live to a hundred and twenty. She looked at the floor and saw blurred spots. That cataract, she said, aside from that I'm healthy and could have had children, but there's nobody to do it for, she yelled at Ahbed: Put the flowers in a vase with a lot of water. See if the house is clean, and if they brought the jugs to the dairy, serve the mixture, and say if it's raining, Ahbed! He asked: Put out a finger? She said: Put! He stuck out a finger, got it wet a little, took a deep breath and said: It's not raining. Said the old woman: May Allah have pity, *Bidak Zuker*! He laughed and went off. The day began to leak to her through the cracks in the shutter, from the hayloft rose a sourish smell of wet straw. She said: There's a smell of flower piss here. In fact maybe she wasn't waiting for anybody, and so she drank black coffee Ahbed spiced with cardamom and basil. She lit a cigarette. At the age of ninety, she said to Horowitz's great-grandson, you start smoking cigarettes, it doesn't impair health or longevity anymore. Horowitz's great-grandson came with his classmates to congratulate her. The children wanted to see the birds. They were taught in school about the birds of the first son of the settlement who died in the Holocaust and came back to life. Ahbed explained to them: They come from the whole country, even from abroad, want to give a lot of money, but she doesn't sell. She keeps everything. Even the mosquito nets are kept. Maybe the anopheles will come back, she said. After they left, she shut her eyes and since she didn't have anything to do, she waited for evening.

In the evening, Boaz and Noga and Ebenezer and Fanya R. came and took her to the community center. The full community center was decorated. A plaque still hung on the wall: Ebenezer, who knew wood in its distress. The minister of education came. Rebecca Schneerson had reached her ninetieth birthday. They also came from the television and the radio. There aren't any wastelands now between the settlements, she said, buildings reach to Jaffa and China, and there's no place to weep. She wore a white dress and looked beautiful and svelte. When the committee chairman spoke, she shut her eyes. Everybody looked at her old indifferent beauty. Her long hair slid over her shoulders. Her skin was smooth and swarthy, her eyes flashed and she would have wanted a dead gleam to be muffled in them. They sang "How Beautiful Are the Nights in Canaan" and "Pity Please" and "Do Not Forsake Us" and "In the Fields of Bethlehem." She smoked a cigarette. The committee chairman said: In honor of her birthday, Rebecca Schneerson has started smoking. Then, they aimed the microphone at her mouth and she got up and pulled the microphone from its stand, as if she were a singer, and started talking with the microphone in her hand, and Boaz said to Noga: Look, Frank Sinatra!

Rebecca said: Now they want Rebecca Schneerson, not Dayan or Kojak. What's happening, maybe I'm an amusing woman. Years ago they were afraid of me. And I wept for eight years, there were problems, the dreamers died and Rebecca remained. Today they hear the Arabs returning to their houses at night from the yards and farms, and the last one to return at night is also the one who will remain here and that doesn't fit what Nehemiah dreamed, who like a Rudolph Valentino of Zionism, died on the shore of Jaffa.

The desert is a memorial to the God my forefathers knew in cellars . . . A poor Jew who died in the Holocaust tells Ebenezer a number of things that haven't yet been written and he follows the map and finds the Golden Calf. The God of Israel is hiding. The violence is as great as the evasion. In the riots of 'thirty-six, I sat with a rifle in my hand and waited, I didn't wash, three years I waited and they didn't dare come, but the Golden Calf was found for me by the counterfeit son A first Jew told a last Jew: It's a lost story. Chaos was in the beginning, chaos will be in the end.

And after the uproar died down, she sat and laughed. Boaz and Ebenezer went to the Captain's house. Rebecca sat and looked out the window. Her anger at the bushes Dana had planted hadn't yet faded. They're still here, she said angrily, but nobody heard.

When they entered the house, Boaz and Ebenezer looked at the Captain's shattered splendor, his medals, his faded uniforms, the ten tattered visored hats, the elegant carved sticks. You know, said Boaz to his father, when I was a child, Rebecca would give birth to me with groans. I'd sit on the chair and see her give birth to me over and over. You offended me, I'm seeking a connection and don't find it, a rather stupid situation. Aside from the gifts, the money, the phony maps and stupid war plans, he thought, what else did the Captain leave? Ahbed, sent by Rebecca, went up to the attic, brought down suitcases, and said: She said to open these suitcases.

The Captain's papers were there, along with Mr. Klomin's journals, and hidden in the side of the suitcase was a manila file. On the yellowing old-fashioned manila file was written in a fluent handwriting: "The Torments of the Life Filled with Modesty and Honor of Captain Jose Menkin A.

Goldenberg, as Recorded by Professor Alexander Blum in Nineteen Forty-Six, according to a Prediction in a Fascinating Performance of a Jew Named Ebenezer Called the Last Jew in a Nightclub in Paris Called The Gay Kiwi."

So you knew about him, said Boaz.

Maybe I also know about him, too, said Ebenezer. But he didn't know. He didn't know if he really knew. I didn't know and I don't know . . .

No.

. . . And the handsome poet then left the city and rode in the chariot of Countess Flendrik. Stunned that she almost succeeded in loving, the countess stayed in the city and became the dream girl of tired angels. There was total silence. Birds, stopped in their flight and shaped in books and pictures, were sold to tourists who burst out of holes in the rickety ceilings of seventeen kinds of sky hung there like every unexpected disaster. The woman called herself Milat. Milat's father was dead now in the honor he may have deserved, but his tombstone was defaced by rioters. She called herself Leila and Alima in turn, and with the fetus in her womb, she set out with the memory of the awful night stamped so deeply in her that she forgot it. The poet read her poems in high-flown Hebrew and listed for her the names of a hundred women who had gotten pregnant in his honor and she pitied him and let him touch her womb. With a rare deerskin valise she wandered and her belly swelled. Money she didn't lack. When she came to America she was adopted by Mr. Luria before his death. The only condition was that her son would be considered Luria's legitimate son. And so Avigdor was born, son of the lecherous poet with the eyes of a demon, adopted by Mr. Luria, who wanted only for her to tell him how bold and noble he was in his life and in his dying. After she buried Mr. Luria, she called herself Doña Gracia. She loved the stories of Hebrew maidens who served their God in secret. Spanish noble aristocrats loved them. Privately, they bore the tiara of their pride as it was later expressed. Even the boldest military commander Don Juan Garmiro, who granted Queen Isabella the greatest cities of the heathens, loved a maiden whose heart was torn between her love for him and her loyalty. When Doña Gracia decided to go to Lebanon to stay with the Countess, who was still searching in the mountains for the ancient gold of the Romans, she took her son and went. The Countess welcomed her gladly and anointed the boy Avigdor with goat milk and golden water, brought her by Arab traders from their long journeys in China

and India. Together they lived on an estate in the mountains, and in Aleppo
were Jews who wove wonderful rugs, and an old woman who lived in Sidon
knew the forgotten burial place of Jewish heroes who once ruled here. The
woman's name was Lilith. So in the fusty streets of Sidon they called her a
witch. Roman gold brought by desperate and forsaken Crusaders was found.
The Countess and Alima-Leila-Milat and Avigdor traveled to Italy and were
once again adopted by good people, who were able to grant them the final
and desired bliss. She slaughtered them and then wept, they slandered her
in the city. But backbiters aren't necessarily a valuable historical source.
Even though she was full of death and charm, there was some endless pro-
creation in her, a boundless youth. A pale man who kept wringing his hands
timorously saw her and called himself Goldenberg. When he died he was
buried with a politeness that suited him, because he claimed he was from
the mountains in northern Switzerland. The Countess came to warm her
body in a small hotel near Napaloya, and since they had already stayed in
Pelfonz and the sea was wide, they went to a small and distant island and
there Avigdor grew and became a sharp-witted lad, who could recite the
Divine Comedy in eight languages. He would invent himself in fictions, live
in them as somebody who needs a false biography, and then the Countess
got sick and disappeared, and Milat, Doña Gracia, went back to Lebanon,
married a balding Austrian consul filled with news and named Jospe, and
went from there with her Austrian husband in a coffin. She embellished the
coffin and put it in her cabin and played the mandolin for him, and thus they
came to a small Argentinean city where there were relatives who hadn't yet
come out of the cellars where the parents of their parents had put them, and
were called by Christian names. There she buried the consul, and the old
women who watched her and thought they were relatives began an extreme
forgetting that was much appreciated in those remote places. Then came a
bold American who wanted to move the Jews from Poland to the Land of
Israel in sealed trains, like the trains that would later take Jews to another
place. She learned to love his lined face. He adopted Avigdor, called him
other names, bought him a notebook so he could copy the poems in Hebrew
that were written for him by some father who may once have really begat
him. Together they swam in Buenos Aires, and because of the inventions the
American invented and were recorded in the name of her son, the lad was
given new citizenship and was called Jose after his mother Josefa Doña

Gracia, and when Avigdor-Joseph was twenty years old, he volunteered for the Russo-Japanese War, fought in the Japanese army, joined the routed Russian army, stirred his soldiers with speeches in fine French, which he acquired (along with the rest of his inventions) in Lebanon, with the Countess, and when he mistakenly killed a Japanese general who wanted to commit suicide out of boredom about a dubious victory and broke the heart of the attack regiment he led, he was awarded medals, which, in the market of Buenos Aires, were worth a title of nobility he had once been denied. So, he registered as Orthodox since that religion was less accepted, but was surely not understood as Judaism, and he could be sent on secret missions to the east, which he knew from his childhood. They told him: Why not Jose de Lupo, but he insisted and taught methods of warfare he'd invent himself, and with these methods the capital city was captured in the great revolution and so he was appointed commander first class.

All that may not have been and so maybe it was. Then Doña Gracia died and he buried her in a Greek Orthodox funeral ceremony, which he learned from ancient books he obtained in a long correspondence with the relatives of the Countess, who remembered him fondly from his youth, and thus he could get to the east and strike roots in the life of the colonial bureaucracy without evoking suspicion and that even enabled him to pretend, even when there was no need, to invent methods of attack and deception. Then there were wars that didn't have to be invented, and he learned not to fight in them admirably, and when he lived in Egypt, he came up with the idea that life is a corridor leading to a world in which his father and mother lived when there were still gods in the world, and only the great poetry of Dante Alighieri gave expression to the place where traces of things remained as they were before history was created which made everything monochrome, dark, and eager for destruction. And so he was enflamed by the great desire to erect memorials to Dante, which he established or didn't establish in various places in the world as tombstones people sometimes mistook and attributed them to somebody else. Giant tombstones where the names of those buried beneath them were sometimes fake. He felt superior in knowing that Dante Alighieri's tombstones conquered the world, and as reward for his happiness he would transport information from place to place, served so many masters that he had to peep in the small well-hidden bookler, written in code and based on key words from the Divine Comedy, to know who his real master was at the moment, and so he also started editing a newspaper nobody needed, and a little woman who was caught in the plot wrote the articles, received the payment of thirty-two subscribers with fictitious names and Jose, who was meanwhile also called Menkin and added the A to his name because of his love for mystery, initiated plans that certain governments paid enormous sums to acquire.

Tape / —

I don't remember anything, said Ebenezer. Why Menkin?

Maybe he was another father he didn't remember, said Boaz. They went back to Rebecca. The valise they brought was made of late doe/skin. Doña Gracia said: Boaz, who will expel the dust from your eyes, and she smiled. Outside schoolchildren sang songs in honor of Queen Rebecca, Noga chatted with Ahbed about the possibility of Jewish-Arab coexistence in the Land of Israel, and Ahbed said: Your husband buries Jews, and Rebecca said: Go to Dana's forest, and Ebenezer said: What forest, and she chuckled, and repeated: Go to the forest, and she added, It's my birthday and I want to talk with Noga, and after everybody left Rebecca said to Noga: Tell me about him.

And Noga suddenly pitied her.

She was holding a teacup with a silver handle, looked at the sugar cube on the saucer, sipped the strong tea, and said: What do I have to tell that you don't know, Rebecca? You came into a family that doesn't suit you, girl, said Rebecca, you lived with a dead lover. I know everything. Trying to be borne on wings and finding a butterfly in bed. Then a chrysalis. Then the children are shouting. I've got a son sitting there. I mean Ebenezer, a national wonder, knows by heart the annals of the Captain who came here to search for his father and found me. Ebenezer went to search for him, the father of your bridegroom—

He wasn't my bridegroom, said Noga, and the cup shook in her hand.

So he wasn't, but the father of somebody who was almost your bridegroom is investigating the annals of Ebenezer. Why do you have to get into all that? I'll die in another ten years, in nineteen eighty-four, I'll be a hundred years old.

Why all this bitterness?

Noga sipped the tea, put the cup down on the table, wrung her hands and crossed her legs sitting in the chair, and in the window, through the screen, flashed a sunbeam that turned the almond trees, the eucalyptus trees, and the prickly pear bushes into a hasty and wild blaze of chiaroscuro. She looked at Rebecca, and because of the dazzling light stuck in her eyes Rebecca vanished and was wrapped in a screen, as if she could no longer be touched. Outside the children sang Happy birthday Rebecca Schneerson and the Teacher All's Well conducted them. They were dressed in white and Noga stretched out a hand as if groping, lightly touched Rebecca's handsome cheeks, stood up, went to Rebecca and hugged her. Rebecca wanted to struggle with her, push her away, but stopped. She remained hugged by Noga, and a shudder went up her spine, when she turned her face to the window she no longer saw anything. The lenses of her eyeglasses were covered with mist and she couldn't, or wouldn't, wipe them. In total blindness, she could feel waves of love and refused them as she had done all her life, but now she didn't have even an iota of defiance or evil left. She said to Noga: I remember how a lion knelt before me, I didn't sing Hatikvah to him, I wasn't some Halperin! And Noga laughed, muttered something, put her lips to Rebecca's lips, kissed them lightly, and said: You're a beautiful woman, Rebecca, you're a brave warrior, but you won't break me.

Look, little girl, said Rebecca, and glanced in amazement at the other room where the quiet voices of Boaz, Ebenezer, and the great-grandson of Ahbed were heard, she smelled people and they walked around in her head, she used to say, and Ahbed came in for a moment, served Rebecca a glass of red wine, and Rebecca pushed Noga away from her, but stroked her face one more moment, as if she wanted to be sure that pure softness had indeed touched her. Ebenezer won't be alive in ten years, she said, and when he died in the Holocaust, I stood at his grave, from the second grave, he won't return. Somebody derides us, destroys us out of rage, doesn't hesitate, on the verge of a great degradation, and you come from a beautiful and sweet death of a boy who didn't burn in any fire. What have you got to do with us?

I want Boaz, said Noga, that's all, not all of you. I don't believe in circles with no exit—

And the Yemenite girl?

Noga looked at her and was silent. Then she lit a cigarette and asked

Rebecca if she wanted to smoke. Rebecca said: Yes, give me something
good. And Noga lit her an American cigarette, stuck it in the old woman's
mouth, and the old woman inhaled smoke into her lungs, and laughed:
Great like that . . .

Jordana doesn't matter, said Noga, they'll come and go, but Boaz will stay.
Maybe not?

He'll stay, said Noga.

I don't want him to, said the old woman.

I know, said Noga. Look, Rebecca, I know what you want from me.

What do I want, little girl?

I'm not a little girl anymore, and you sit here like a splendid and shattered palace and want Boaz to live in it with you, until the fire. Do we
bother you?

Who's we? asked Rebecca, and a cherished panic blew from Noga. Who's
we? Ebenezer and I.

Right, said the old woman and crushed the cigarette and now she was
alert and vigorous. She wanted to get up, but remained sitting, deeply
right, as that fool Horowitz used to say, deeply right I want you to move,
clear out, leave me Boaz, what is ten years in your life?

Noga smiled a thin smile that now popped up on her open lips, and the
concave line between the nose and the mouth sharpened became more
severe as the smile tried to invent a subsistence area. She looked at the
splendid old woman and said: That's not simple, Rebecca. We're not together because we want to be together.

No grandchildren, said Rebecca. That's forbidden! No great-grandchil-
dren, look at the great-grandson of Ahbed, he comes to stare at his grandfather's land, so there won't be forgiveness. I need him, said the old
woman. I didn't have anybody, the Captain died, Nehemiah died.

You've got Ebenezer, said Noga.

No I don't, said Rebecca. Then Rebecca contemplated and suddenly
saw herself in a ridiculous light she had never been in, and because she
didn't know how to behave in moments of weakness, she started shaking,
and because the weakness was strange to her, she also wanted to bark, but
the growls and the barks stayed inside her, deep inside her, and she looked
at Noga, and saw how beautiful the young woman was and for a moment, she
even thought: If I've lost Boaz, I've gained a wife, why should I ask, since

when do I ask, how do I know what I really want, how do people know what they want, why do I want to be dependent when I wasn't dependent on anybody, and she stretched out her hand and started stroking Noga's face, and asked her: Where are you from, who do you belong to, where did you come from before the death that brought you to Teacher Henkin?

Noga was alert to rapid changes. For some reason that pain touched her heart, the effort to win a position that was completely unnecessary. She loved Rebecca's face. That woman bows her head before death, doesn't want crumbs, but the whole, can kill Boaz to hold onto him. Her heart was stirred to pity, and Noga who knew only one love envied Rebecca, who could ask of her what people ask in old, unreliable stories. She almost said: Take him, but she knew that both Rebecca and she depended on Boaz more than he depended on them.

Late at night, everybody was tipsy. Even Rebecca tried to dance and fell into Boaz's open arms, and he hugged her as somebody who knew he had lost her that day to a girl his foster mother saw as a reflection of purity in the features of a murderer.

Tape / —

When Jordana disappeared, they phoned from the Ministry of Defense. Then Noga sat down, and Boaz, holding a narghila to plant a pinch of cannabis in it, put the mouth of the narghila he had brought from Mount Sinai to Noga's mouth, and Noga looked like an old Indian sunk in meditation, and Boaz went to drizzle water on the cannabis bush, which had meanwhile grown solitary in a brown flowerpot, where a fragrant jasmine bush had previously grown. The roof was crammed with flowerpots and smells, Noga brought spices she had cultivated and pruned and watered, and Boaz, who tried to check whether airplanes were continuing to fly low toward the airport, felt a pleasant giddiness, he landed next to Noga and stroked her back. Noga said, Jordana disappeared!

When? asked Boaz.

They haven't heard from her in months, and only now did they call, the bastards.

Boaz took off the cotton shirt, smelled his own odor, and tossed the shirt into the corner of the room. Then he stood up, his torso naked, and tried to let the thoughts run around in his brain. He said: If you hadn't given her Menahem, she wouldn't have run away!

Noga didn't answer, and pondered quietly. Her face was furrowed with new lines that would disappear later. Her eyes were sunk deep in their sockets. He saw her body harden and wanted to ask her to stop thinking about Jordana, but Noga thought of what he said and suddenly a distant pain condensed in her that tormented her again, and she said: Why when you want to pity do you attack?

He stood still and didn't know what to do with himself, Noga clasped the narghila, thrust her hands in it and tossed it to Boaz. He ducked and the narghila hit the pile of sheets Noga was about to put into the linen closet. Then she dropped her eyes, and said: Where did she disappear?

Boaz said: Why is that so important? Maybe she just couldn't take it anymore?

Noga got up and went to the kitchen, opened the refrigerator, looked at the row of eggs in their niches and picked up a carton of milk, opened it, tried to pour the milk into an empty space with no cup, changed her mind, put the milk in the refrigerator, and sat down in front of the old grandfather clock. The milk flowed on the countertop, and Boaz, who tried not to see Noga, pushed the pinch of cannabis into the narghila that wasn't broken. She searched for music, but on all the stations there was only talk. She turned off the radio and opened the chest, took out papers, and read aloud the numbers she had written at night after they returned from the unveiling of the memorial at the Dead Sea, when Boaz asked her to prepare the income tax report: the mileage doesn't fit the gas receipts, she said, and Boaz said: I can't calculate everything exactly. He saw Jordana's lost face among the memorial books, Obadiah Henkin strolling in the mountains and showing her where her beloved fought, tried to pity himself and Noga.

On the way to Henkin's house, they stopped at a café. Next to the wall, four men sat and talked. Around each one of them you could see the aura of foreignness. The old men yelled to one another in order to be scared less and to be present. Boaz could understand Jordana's not-being in the space between those men and themselves. He didn't know who they were, but they looked as if they were still expecting something that would never happen. And Boaz knew that wound, knew how to smell it in the distance, and Noga, who knew how much the pain costs afterward, asked Boaz to leave. He understood her fear and left. Henkin's house suddenly looked like a frontier. One window in Ebenezer's house was painted a new color. Why does he paint at night? he asked Noga, and Noga said: How do I know what your father does?

Obadiah Henkin sat at his table and looked at Boaz and at the door at the same time. Through the open door, Hasha could be seen carefully drawing Noga's wild hair off her forehead, and gave her a small round mirror. After they combed their hair and each looked in the little mirror, Hasha gave Noga a glass of cold lemonade, and Henkin said to Boaz: The story about Jordana has been worrying me a long time now. I didn't know what happened, the Shimonis said they saw her in Kiryat Haim. They went to the Galilee on their memorial day, on the way back they stopped for a cup of coffee, and in the distance they saw what Mrs. Shimoni described as a familiar back and then they made out her profile, but by the time Mrs. Shimoni stood up and found her coat hanging under three coats, she disappeared in the direction of what she described as a boulevard facing the highway. I really don't know what she's doing there . . .

Jordana's parents' family doctor knew some details he was willing to reveal. He told Noga: She went through a difficult experience. He didn't know where she lived or how to find her, but a doctor at the clinic in Kiryat Bialik called him about Jordana, and asked if she could take five-milligram Valiums and how to give it to her, and what were her reasons for needing Valium.

On the way to the suburbs of Haifa, cows were seen grazing near a field shaded by a row of thin-trunked cedars, and a heavy red horse was seen leaping with clumsy nobility. They bypassed Haifa and came to the suburbs in a heavy cloud of soot. The Carmel was buried in a giant bubble of sweetish stinking stickiness.

When they entered the small one-room apartment, Jordana looked docile, curled up in a giant armchair with torn upholstery, and remnants of foam rubber popped out of the worn back. In the small ugly mirror hanging next to the television that was on, she appeared sucking her thumb. Her eyes were fixed on the screen and on her face was a faded look. She raised her hand to beckon them in. On the screen was a teacher, the teacher was talking about decimals, it was a fifth-grade education program.

Boaz looked around, tried to take in the sight, maybe he even understood. He touched a leaf of a bunch of dead narcissi stuck in a blue vase, with no water. When he touched the leaf, dry white petals dropped off. The room had the musty odor of locked windows, orange peels, and skin lotion. Noga went to Jordana and hugged her from behind, and Jordana took Noga's hand, held it to her face, tears began flowing on her cheeks and she softened a bit, turned sideways toward the guests, stared stoned and stunned, tried to take her eyes off the screen, but when Boaz turned off the television the tears became clearer and hotter, and she turned the television back on in a panic, stared at the screen, as if she didn't see a thing, and Boaz turned it off again.

Jordana reached for the television, but fell down and Noga caught her. They picked her up and saw how thin she had become, sat her on a small sheet like a baby on a rough green bedspread. Jordana asked for water. Boaz went to the neglected kitchen, washed some glasses that were moldering in the sink, opened the refrigerator that held one egg, a rotten tomato, nuts, chocolate, and five jars of cold water that had been filled long ago and had turned yellow, took out some ice, put it in the glasses, poured tap water into them, and went back in the room. Jordana looked at him and for a moment, a smile ignited in her eyes. She drank two glasses of water in a row and asked for a cigarette. After she smoked a few minutes and smoke swirled around her face, she said: You remember that I once lost a child?

Noga looked at Jordana and didn't say a thing.

After that, I loved the two of you, and Menahem. Menahem I loved before. Then I couldn't. You shouldn't have found me, I don't belong to anybody Noga . . .

We love you, said Boaz, we were worried.

You don't love anybody, said Jordana, you're too distinguished to love. How's Obadiah?

He's worried about you, said Noga.

And about an hour later, seated on the sofa, her legs folded and her mouth gaping open, so blighted, beautiful against the background of the room laced with old wallpaper, Jordana said: Then I started watching television, they say I fell in love with it. I see all the programs in Israel, Jordan, and Lebanon, sometimes I get Cyprus. There's a guy here, Jacob, who set up an antenna for me with five directions. That's important.

Why is that important? asks Boaz.

'Cause I'm improving myself in a new direction, Boaz, at long last I'm building a past for myself that has a future.

Boaz got up and walked around the room, and Noga, who was sitting next to Jordana, hugged her. The infinite softness from Noga melted in Jordana a tremor that had begun to emerge when she took her eyes off the screen. You went out of your mind, Jordana, said Boaz, you've been imprisoned here day and night, sitting, what do you see, King Hussein, kissed wildly by officers of the armored corps? Cartoons? What are you wasting your life on!

This is my life, Boaz, and you have really no idea about somebody else's life. At night, when the light is over in the set, after the chapters of the Koran in Jordan, I see how the light pours into the screen, and then with four Valiums I fall asleep. And then Jordana yelled: I'm fed up, Boaz.

Then she whispered: The truth is I wanted to die, but I couldn't, death is too good for me, it belongs to those I love.

And Noga, Noga got up, maybe even darted up, and slapped Boaz's face. Her face bled pain, she started hitting the wall and Boaz in turn in a rage she didn't know was in her. Jordana tried to laugh, but her lips didn't move, she looked de trop and infantile and started sucking her thumb again. Boaz once again turned his face to the wall. An old calendar was hanging there, with a smiling swarthy girl holding a bunch of grapes.

When Boaz packed up her things, she didn't insist. He carefully wrapped the television, dragged the cartons to the big car, filled it so there was room for Noga and Jordana, and they left. He even paid the landlord. Jordana didn't look back, she just said: The new antenna you left here, too bad . . .

Boaz thought: What is it to sit in front of a television from three in the afternoon to twelve at night? But when he looked at her, she was dozing in Noga's arms. Noga, who had long ago wept at her outburst, but couldn't apologize, tried to signal something to him, but he didn't think of trying to understand. So deep was his contempt for Jordana. To himself he thought: She's leading me astray, that whore! When they got to the Henkin house, Hasha said: The undertaker's come, Obadiah.

Boaz left the two girls in the car. He removed an imaginary hat, turned to Hasha who was drinking tea at the table, and said: If you weren't the mother of my wife's husband, I would rape you. Hasha chuckled and said: You're scary, Mr. Schneerson, and she went on drinking her tea. After that,

Henkin went out and hugged Jordana, who trembled in his arms. When they brought her inside, Henkin was more solid than he had been in years, and said: Hasha Masha, she was found in Kiryat Motzkin, she's in shock and needs rest, for now she'll stay in Menahem's room. Hasha looked at her with eyes that were scared at first and then calm, and said arrogantly: Why not? I'll have grandchildren to raise and somebody's diapers to change. Suddenly she let her head drop onto the table, and her head banged on the table. Boaz managed to notice that when the album was shifted by the bang, squares crowned with dust frames appeared. He called home. The girl who worked there said: There were a few invitations, the newspaper reports of the ceremony at the Dead Sea were fantastic . . .

Boaz said: In all those years I never came into the room. He saw the closed yellow writing desk, the coat hanging on a hook, Menahem's cloth cap, the picture of Lana Turner, yellowed with age, the chair next to an old issue of the children's magazine. In the other room Hasha sits and measures him in the distance, she knows how to curb the sweep of hostility she reluctantly felt for him, and that thought brought a crooked smile to his lips. He yelled: If you loved me, Hasha, I might have been saved, and Hasha looked toward the room and saw Boaz putting down the television, seeking the connection to the antenna to bring the cord to Henkin's outlet, and she said: This house is dry, Jordana can live in your enemy's room, Boaz, in fact that's what you all deserve.

When Henkin went to Hasha, she let him hug her, stood still, and for a long time she stayed in his arms. Then she reached out her hand, touched Boaz, and suddenly flushed, came even closer, stroked him, pushed him away from her, touched his hand and moved her hand away, sat down and stood up again, and called out: Jordana, turn on your television. She calmed down, sat down, and for the first time in a long time she looked at the pictures on the walls. From one of them looked Menahem's face. She said: I didn't even succeed in hating properly. You're the most corrupt person I knew, but I know one thing, you once saved a child, once you really saved Menahem, why couldn't you save him when you really should have?

Henkin muttered something to himself and Hasha called to him: Don't mutter, Henkin, when you need to you know how not to be in the right place, give me grandchildren, Boaz, you hear me, give me a grandson, I want to be a woman, you hear? To be a good old woman. Jordana slammed the door and the announcer's voice was heard clearly. Maybe she was trying to imprison things, not to let them be heard, she had to give birth to her children from the giant set she loved, that filled half the wall of the room of somebody who was her lover and now strangers want to give birth to his grandson . . . In fact a son, she said, and then she didn't hear another thing.

When Boaz came two days later and Jordana looked at him, he saw a chilly darkened look in her eyes. He understood how total the blow was.

Three poets spoke, said Jordana, I watched them. One was fair-haired, with beautiful blue, somewhat scared eyes, full of black gold, he talked like the last man in the world, something both bombastic and blighted, measured and solemn, as if he stood on the frontier of ability, and so he had to find the most beautiful and elegant words to describe that frontier. The second poet was full of joy to be talking, and the third was a little suicidal, defeated, sad, spoke evil of himself, maybe it was a plea, I looked at him, I wanted him to be good, and after a few minutes, he started twisting, muttered something, moved a little, I think the microphone slipped away from him, and then he smiled, and after the smile he said a few things I wasn't listening to, but his eyes weren't so sad anymore, the gloom almost disappeared, I think I was good for him.

Boaz listened and didn't say a word. He had already heard about that from Noga. Noga spoke with the doctor. The doctor claimed that he refused to put her in the hospital because she wasn't really sick but was hiding from herself. The idea that she was able to cure people of their sorrow through television scared Boaz. He did what he had wanted to do for a long time— he went to the man Jordana had succeeded in smiling at on television and knocked on his door. The man gave Boaz a cup of coffee, complained that he hadn't been paid for the writing Boaz used in many memorial books and even published in three albums. Boaz didn't respond to the complaint and asked what had happened to him on the television program. The man was somewhat perplexed and said: I sat there, the two of them were talking and I didn't know what to say, I'm getting old, nothing happened, suddenly I felt as if strange eyes were looking at me, without understanding what I was doing, I moved, the microphone almost fell, I smiled, I wasn't there anymore, I spoke, what I said afterward was all right, somebody got me into a conversation, I spoke out of that somebody's mouth and I spoke to him at the same time. I felt enormous love pouring to me.

Jordana asked them to let her help people. Doctors at Tel Hashomer Hospital laughed at Boaz when he told them the story, but Doctor Lowenthal said it was worth a try. Doctor Lowenthal (whose son was killed in a plane crash at the Suez Canal) sat next to Jordana in the Henkin house as she looked at petals. There was a sad saxophone player. Jordana said he had been worrying her for some time. She concentrated on him, and after a minute or two, he started smiling. In the middle of the fucking program, he said afterward, I'm sitting and playing, feeling shitty, all of a sudden some woman says give me a kiss. And I smiled, it was weird with all the directors and cameramen around.

And one day, when they saw a soldier who had lost his eyesight skiing on Mount Hermon, Jordana looked at the screen, concentrated, and suddenly she shouted in terror, fell on the ground, bounced, and by the time Boaz bent over her and kissed her hard and hit her, she calmed down. After that she fainted.

They took Jordana to the hospital. She grew fat and lay in a locked room without a doorknob. She doesn't want to see television. Wants to marry Menahem. Boaz promised her there was a rabbi who married his grandmother's grandmother to a dead man and he'd bring her that rabbi, but it might take time because the rabbi died two hundred years ago.

So I'll wait for him, said Jordana. And Noga wept and then said: But she does help people, she gave them a smile, what does it matter if it's a disease? It's a disease that does good for others and for her. We should have left her in the suburbs, she was happier and Boaz had no answer. He thought about Herod. King Herod, he said, ordered a hundred Jewish grandchildren arrested and left in a pit until he died. On the day he died, he ordered, they were to be executed one by one. He said they were to do this so they wouldn't have a holiday when he died. And the queen of Norway, Sigrid, ordered all her vassal kings to come to a banquet in her palace, and when all the vassal kings came and ate and drank, she burned the house down on them, and said: That will teach them to lust for the queen of Norway.

Tape / —

Jordana lay, her eyes impassive, her body twitching, needing injections of tranquilizers every few hours. All she needs, said Boaz, is a television set to love. To know that they didn't teach me psychiatry ten years. For a month Jordana tossed and turned, stopped twitching and started reading the temperatures in various cities in the world in the newspapers. She repeated indifferently: If only I had a private room with a big television set, I'd be able to help people get rid of their sadness. When they came to visit her, she'd shut her eyes and list the temperatures in the cities of the world: Oslo—3 degrees, Amsterdam—6, Copenhagen—3, and then she'd grimace mysteriously, like a person who can see far beyond what's visible, and say: A barometric low is moving over Turkey and causing clouds there, and Boaz holds her hand and tells her how empty the house is without her, and when she heard that she burst into wild laughter, bounced, and sometimes they'd have to tie her to the bed.

Tape / —

Boaz begat Ebenezer, Ebenezer begat Joseph and Nehemiah. Joseph begat Shlomzion. Shlomzion begat Light of the Gentiles. Light of the Gentiles begat Joshua. Joshua begat Spear Father of the Mountain. Spear Father of the Mountain begat himself. And Spear Father of the Mountain begat Joseph who begat Rebecca who gave birth to Secret Charity who begat.

Tape / —

Dear sir,

You surely remember your visit to our house a few months ago. You came, as you said, to understand the house where Melissa was born. Ever since you came to our house Melissa has returned to live in the house. I'm old and close to the place where you wait for ghosts my father used to tell me about, and maybe the very idea that three men, years apart, came to seek my daughter who died fifty years ago, instilled in me a vague dread. Maybe that etched on life itself. Something happened to my wife and me. After fifty years, we're poring over old notebooks again. Reading Melissa's school essays, I sit at home, I practically don't go to the office anymore, my oldest son runs the sales center, and today I thought: Our governor, he's also a Jew, I hope he won't come searching for Melissa.

My wife read me a section from the diary of Timothy Edward, one of the first in her family to immigrate to America. In his diary he describes how he stood on the deck of the ship in the port of Amsterdam on his way to America. On the deck of a nearby ship stood a Jew and prayed. They started talking. The Jew was on his way to Jerusalem to prepare the "dust of the Land of Canaan." Timothy Edward was on his way to prepare the "dust of the Land of Canaan" in the new world. They talked all night. The grandson of that Jew was that Rabbi Kriegel who came from Hebron to our city two hundred years ago. We talked about him, remember?

And with that story that connects Licinda, Melissa and Sam, I came to Lionel's house. Those were embarrassing moments. Sam looked at me in amazement, and Lionel, Lionel is old but hasn't changed. The same aristocratic look, wounded and stubborn, the same perplexed imposing figure, the same force. At the sight of him, some anger that had been burning in me for many years vanished. All of us loved Melissa. That was the most ridiculous and sublime thing that had ever happened to me.

Two hundred and fifty years ago, two men became friends on the decks of two ships on their way to prepare the same kingdom in different places and now, on Melissa's grave, they meet again, I said, not without an overdramatic expression so foreign to my nature.

We talked all night. Sam began. He spoke a long time about Melissa's eternal beauty. And I, I was silent and drank whiskey.

I joined Sam on his trip to Northampton to see the students act parts of the play he had produced about a year ago. We flew in the Ford company plane. The idea that Ford was flying us there amused him quite a bit. Licinda didn't talk and we looked at the view below and tried to understand how our paths had crossed so many years after Melissa died. Below we saw snow-covered fields.

I told Sam what I told you about the Catholic church next to the chemistry lab. We were guests in the Gillette House. It was built about a hundred years ago with a contribution by Mr. Gillette, inventor of the razor blade. The girls of Gillette sang "Greensleeves" in thin, scary voices. Sam claimed that they

looked like Melissa. He also told them: You who will marry the
gods of industry, the leaders of this state, are acting in a drama
about burned curtains of the Ark of the Covenant! They
giggled nervously, and Sam said to Licinda: They're open to
indecent suggestions like Melissa, and she—to her credit—
didn't even answer. Sam, who drank a lot that night, lectured
to the students about what there no longer is in Northampton
(and I quote): Samrein or Samuelrcin. You're acting in a
drama about my naked mother! They turned their heads in
amazingly delicate embarrassment and one even wept silently.
He asked: Why should you act in a play about a diamond in a
rectum? You know that the man who lay there and thought he
was my father wasn't my father?

Joanna, the granddaughter of Priscilla and Bud, told me: I
feel as if I were chewing my mother's head, blood is flowing
between my legs and I'm laughing. And I, who never heard such
things, especially not from somebody in my family, stroked her
head with a gentleness which, if it had been in me years ago,
would have saved a beloved person from death. I walked with
Sam to the frozen lake. He went with a local rabbi to a meeting
of young Jews. When the rabbi started chatting and talking with
him about the meaning he found in his drama, he grabbed the
rabbi by the ear and bent it. The rabbi couldn't get away from
him and started twisting and shrieking, he bent over and yelled:
Why? Why? Why? And Sam lifted him up, cleaned the snow off
him, and said: I don't know why, sorry, but the rabbi was insulted and his ear burned and a few girls were gliding over the
ice in charming tights, and the view that was so Ukrainian in
Sam's eyes reminded me of my mother and my grandmother,
and I felt I was stumbling again, but I wasn't sorry. Then they
sang Jewish songs in a big house full of young people, and Sam
spoke, and Licinda said to me: I love that Jewish Jesse James,
and I told her I understood because Melissa loved him too.

Sam stood up surprisingly and informed them that he missed
the girls of Gillette. They aren't seeking a messiah in the plains
of Connecticut, he said, they simply belonged, he yelled. We

went to the theater. He said something had to be fixed in the sections that were performed for him, and the girls gave him a gift of a green cotton shirt that said "Smith College— a hundred years of superior girls." They played coins like those my mother played when she was a student here. It was late at night, and the sound was clear and terrifying. People came from the television station in Hartford to interview him, but he refused to be interviewed. Licinda bent her thumb hard until it broke, and Sam bandaged it and said: Tell her how much I love her. Licinda wept, but maybe she wept because of the pain. When we came back to New York, there was a storm and we landed in a cloud of snow. We went to their house and Sam told Lionel that the gentile girls stood naked in a church and sang his *Laments for the Death of the Jews* holding candles and were amazingly beautiful. Licinda went to the doctor and returned with a cast on her thumb. At night she lay with a thermometer in her mouth. Sam kept asking her what her temperature was, and she showed him her temperature with her fingers, but she didn't take the thermometer out of her mouth. They stole the destruction from me, said Sam, they made a play devoid of any risk or dread for the terrific girls of Gillette, that's how you get rich in America.

When he went to the Delmonico Hotel, I went with him. People were sitting around tables with bottles of wine and soda on them and turkeys and plates of pastry and vegetables and sweets. At the head table sat about ten dignitaries, and one of them said: Here's Sam Lipp, who has at long last deigned to honor us with his presence. And Sam, the focus of all eyes, stopped for a moment and asked in a loud voice: Where do I go? And the man said to him: To the table marked "Children of the Camp." I stayed at the end of the hall next to the journalists and in the distance I could understand how uneasy he was. Later he told me that when he sat there, he saw those people as they had been in April 'forty-five. With Ebenezer's eyes he saw them, and they were all dead, he added. When they applauded him, he stood up and applauded them. People at the head table talked, one after another. Behind them hung a sign: "Twenty-five Years of Liberation," and a gigantic picture of a concentration camp hung there. And then Sam got up went to the stage, whispered with one of the dignitaries, and the man smiled and there was a hush and Sam picked up the microphone, started walking back and forth, eyes fixed on the hundreds of people sitting around turkey and bottles of wine, and said: I was born in the wrong place, because they put me at the wrong table. I wasn't born in a camp but in my mother's house. Why are the tables arranged like that? Why not by professions: tooth extractors, gravediggers, experts in diamonds, in gold teeth?

The murmuring in the hall started right from the start. You're the only family I've got, he said, not paying attention to what was going on, except for Mr. Brooks, the father of my beloved Melissa, but she didn't wait for me either. What nerve is it to assemble every year like this? We should have devastated Europe and not be eating turkey, but we didn't. We should have destroyed America, who threw us to the dogs, but we're getting rich and living off her. We had Einstein and Oppenheimer and Teller, why didn't we ask them to devastate the Western world instead of Hiroshima? SS Kramer was more reliable. Until the last minute, he knew who the enemy was and what he had to do. Ebenezer knew too and as far as he's concerned, you're all dead.

He looked at them. After a few minutes, he started singing and they joined in, one by one, and sang a song called "Niederlandisches Dankgebet" as if he had hypnotized them. The head table sang too. They stood like slaughtered peacocks who had remained alive a few seconds, their eyes shut and sang innocently and devotedly, and the hall shook and the microphone whistled and screeched, and only the man sitting next to Sam looked pale and waved his hands, his name (I know because I saw him on television) was Eliahu Wiggs. He pushed Sam and slapped his face and the hubbub prevailed and Sam went on singing and everybody went on singing and then they assaulted the tables like a routed army and we left there.

You cannot understand, or you can understand better than anybody, how strange it is for a person like me to write these things. My background, my position, everything I was and did didn't prepare me for this week, but when you visited us, something snapped in me that may have been lying inside me for many years, that damn intimacy, almost despair, was born, something like closeness, to people who hundreds of years ago had cleared the forests of New England, burned in a foreign fire. As if I wanted to restore to Christianity what Sam Lipp, Lionel, and even you hold in your hand—some profound hatred, a shadow of a jealous and cruel God.

Before he ran away from the hall with Eliahu Wiggs's slap stuck to his face, he managed to take a few cookies. He stood at the cloakroom and with trembling hands he tried to put on the coat. He held the cookies in his mouth so his hands would be free. Eliahu Wiggs, furious, came out and yelled at him, but Sam couldn't answer him because his mouth was full of cookies. And suddenly I saw how two people could be hungrier than I ever knew. Eliahu wanted to slap Sam's face again, but the sight of the cookies was so attractive that he started weeping, quietly, and his hand that wanted to hit stuck to his body again, he turned his face right and left, and I thought: Those aren't the artificial tears Sam talked about before. With his skinny hand, he grabbed one cookie from Sam's mouth and started chomping it hungrily, and Sam held the cookies tight in his mouth and Eliahu wanted more and had to bring his thin, beautiful face close to Sam's mouth to snatch more, and suddenly it didn't matter what I or others saw, he put his face close and bit and Sam almost kissed him on the mouth and the two of them hugged or wrestled, and tears rolled on their cheeks and then Eliahu Wiggs pulled away, tears flowing on his cheeks, and disappeared into the hall.

We got into a taxi and Sam wanted to sleep for an hour, paid the driver in advance, apologized to him and me, and fell asleep. I sat and pondered what I was doing with him in a taxi, at night, in the cold, and the driver talked about the weather and about the near-accident of the Swissair flight at Kennedy Airport when he went there earlier, and then Sam woke up and asked the driver if he had aftershave and Sam got aftershave from the driver and sprayed a little on his face and told him to drive home.

I took Sam to my house. He and Licinda stayed with us for
three days. We looked at them yearningly. My wife hugged him,
drank too much, and said: If you want, you can marry Melissa,
and she passed out. We took her to the hospital and she's been
there for a month. I sit at her side and ask myself, What disaster did I bring down on her and on me? and I have no answer.

Yours,.

A. M. Brooks

Tape / —

Greta Garbo as Ninotchka goes into a restaurant. She says to the waiter:
Give me coffee without cream. A few minutes later, the waiter comes back
and says: We have no cream, Madame. Is it all right without milk?

In my reflection she is I, she's my memory, she's the fact that maybe it will
finally be revealed that I had no father. Not Nehemiah, not Joseph, an impure
spirit of holiness entered my mother in the river. The river is my father. Old
is my mother and cruel. Samuel is my son. Where are you, dear Samuel?

Tape / —

Dear Obadiah,
Some time ago, my phone rang at home and Sam Lipp, who
was on the line, informed me that he had come to town and was
living in a Lebensborn inn.
The name Lebensborn naturally made me shudder. When I
hung up, I said to myself: There can't be a hotel with that name
in our city. I took the phone book and scanned it and to my
amazement I found a hotel called Ludwigshaus-Lebensborn. I
assume the name doesn't mean much to you. But Samuel
wasn't so innocent. During the war, Lebensborn was a pretty
shady institution, yet was maintained by the heads of the party
and called "Institute for the Improvement of the Race." In fact,
it was a completely establishment whorehouse led by none
other than the Reichsführer in person. Aryan girls and officers
were brought there, mainly SS officers of impeccable race and
they could copulate and create a new generation of pure Aryans.
According to my father (to his credit he had total contempt for

the place), those were adulterous, purely bestial encounters, and human beings, said my father, could savor there the taste of protected, and even more important, legal promiscuity. In other words: Those were establishment, organized, numbered flirtations, and women whose husbands were on the front for a long time could come there anonymously (only the authorities knew who they were) and copulate with the best of the German men. According to my father, the institution was quite varied—and here you can hear the party member speaking—but at least here, unlike Paris, there weren't naked whores on skates with naked men running after them and falling and getting up and trying to catch them. There weren't impotent old men there peeping through the cracks. It was, my father added, an institution that was basically filthy, but clean in its operation, solid, even if full of adultery they called patriotic. I didn't ask him what he thought about that last word, maybe Friedrich did.

I told Sam I was coming immediately, and he said, and I could hear his smile on the phone: Don't rush, I've got something to do in the meantime. Maybe he was trying to hint to me that old patriots were still copulating there with heavenly girls. I put on my coat and went. He was waiting for me in what remained of a splendid lobby reminiscent of the old days. The building, like our famous cathedral, had never been blown up. He asked: Did you get a letter from Mr. Brooks, my first wife's father? I answered yes, and he said: That great man! We were sitting in his room. From the window Schiller Park could be seen, I used to play there as a child. We were sipping sherry from a bottle Sam had ordered earlier. The area was familiar to me from years gone by, and it had been a long time since I had set foot in that part of the city. Sam tried to explain something to me that was hard for me to understand, he said: Once I invented setting watches backward. Then I lived in reverse time and that's how the disease of forgetting was born, that lasted four years. My key was with Ebenezer and Ebenezer's key was with me. At Kennedy Airport I exchanged the ticket because I was afraid to fly to Israel, I wanted first to be in a place where

they invented the key to my reverse time, so I would come to
Israel and not somebody else.

The taste of the sherry, the sight of the park, a sweet
memory of my childhood, imbued in me an absurd sense that
everything became real only because it was said. If he had told
me the moon was a rectangle, I would have accepted it as fact,
so I could also see my mother sitting on a bench in Schiller
Park, reading a newspaper or a book. I heard the voices of the
old people who lived in the hotel and the voices came through
the walls, maybe they were singing. It was hard to hear what
song they were singing. Sam was a child whose mother called
him to come to her and gave him candy. And so we were able to
penetrate into areas of a place whose logic was different from
the logic we were used to. We didn't yet know where we were
and what the date was, and we talked, each one separately, but
together, about the other's childhood as if we had exchanged
identities. So we dialed together and somebody picked up the
phone and said Schwabe here, and I said: This is Sam Lipp, a
friend of Lily Schwabe, and the old man didn't even make a
sound of amazement or resentment and said Yes, and what can
I do for you, and I said to him: Lily, Lily your daughter, and he
said You must have the wrong number sir, these days people get
a lot of wrong numbers, and after a long time when I didn't let
him off the line he admitted he once had a daughter named
Lily, but not anymore. I'm an old man, he added, living on a
small pension, living in my own apartment, he didn't hang up,
maybe he tried not to be amazed, waited and I don't know exactly what he waited for, there was no longing or acceptance in
his voice, and when I hung up, Sam said: Maybe he really is the
man who knows who a disaster happened to.

Later on, Sam took me to a small club. I was born in this city
and I thought I knew it well, but the alleys we walked in were
strange to me. Sam knew that part of the city better than me.
I thought to myself: The old man sounds like an indifferent,
polite, and swinish murderer. Maybe he's a miserable person,
but I didn't say those things aloud. The ruins were restored and

Sam who knew the ruins before they were restored led me on
winding paths as if everything that had been built since then
hadn't been built yet.

I was surprised at the audacity of our architects who, when
they restored that part of the city, preserved completely what
had been and as they repaired and rebuilt, they even preserved
the hiding places, hidden ways, produced over many years, in
alleys where you could once evade creditors, police, or disgruntled women. Sam knew the way well, and I thought that if
those architects had to reconstruct a sinking ship, they'd do it by
preserving the sinking, even without preserving the ship. The
nightclub was dim and filthy. Women with dyed hair and puffed-
up hairdos sat on high stools with round, ugly backs. Ear-piercing
music blasted from a jukebox. In back, past the American
cigarette machine we saw a stage loaded with boards and rags,
a broken straw chair stood there and next to it, on its side, an
old spotlight. We drank beer, ate Greek olives. The owner was
a stocky man with a mustache, who addressed Sam: Your face is
familiar to me, sir, eyes like that I can't forget! Sam smiled
and said in a loud voice: Ladies and gentlemen, please set your
watches back four hours, the time is four-thirty in the afternoon, April fifteenth . . . And the bartender said with a joy
kindled in him. For God's sake, I remember him, the boy who
was . . . those eyes , , . and then one of the women sitting next
to me said in a loud voice: I'd screw with eyes like that and be
willing to die the way they die in Naples, and a woman sitting
next to her said: "After you see Naples." The first one said,
What does it matter before, after! And the bartender yelled.
Stop blabbing, and moved to the other side of the bar, hugged
Sam, and I sat there a stranger, while Sam, maybe really wasn't
a stranger . . . He climbed onto the stage and fixed the spotlight, plugged it in an outlet hidden behind boards and heaps of
paper, shut his eyes, and asked everybody to set their watches
back and they did, me too. One of the women started singing in
a soft, clear voice, her voice sounded as if it were composed of
glass slivers, Sam moved some old rugs, a mouse darted out to

the shrieks of some women, the spotlight was lit and illuminated the face of the woman singing and she sat down on the
broken chair, and the other women joined in and it wasn't like
a choir singing but flickers of sounds, like a vanished expanse of
audio mist. I waited for the bartender to smoke a Ritesma cigarette, pour light Rhine wine, and for gleaming aluminum insignia to be emblazoned on his shoulders, but everything was now
faded, part of that invented past now without real glory, I felt
how hollow everything is when it's out of place or time. Everything was divided into decimal fractions, which didn't add up to
any reliable equation. An old picture of a girl with stretched-out
legs, and a bird sitting on her belly, was discovered on a shabby
wall behind the lighted stage. Above the girl's head flew angels
of a saccharine nearly wiped-out color, the legs of the singing
woman spread by themselves, she wore high black boots and her
thighs looked gleaming and firm, and when she spread her legs
a rubber snake was discovered tied to her belt, and the snake
wound into her shaved crotch, and the moment the song was especially melancholy, almost whispered, Sam crushed her groin,
and the snake darted out at him and bit his hand and he stroked
the woman's crotch and she kept on singing. An innocent laugh
spread over her face, her eyes were wide open with a kind of intimacy, perhaps hope, she spat out the chewing gum hidden in
her mouth, shut her eyes and the bartender leaned over a little,
shriveled, his head turned to me, and Sam called out: Come
here, and I got up, looking stupid in my own eyes, but bereft of
willpower, I climbed onto the stage, I was Kramer, it took a
minute, my face changed, since the eyes looking at me saw him,
not me. I talked about the last defensive operation in the Alps,
about poor Eva who died in the bunker, how our holy soil was
defended. On my knees I sat, like a boy scolded in a classroom,
nobody was amazed, the bartender didn't move from his
scrunched position, the woman went on singing with yearning
eyes, I was defended by a bayoneted English soldier, Sam cited
the number of unemployed in Cologne, Leipzig, Hesse, and
Frankfurt in 'twenty-nine.

Sam's watch was set well, fat men smoked giant cigars and
drank whiskey and soda and sang a contemptible Hallelujah. We
prepared a putsch, Sam directed in silence, maybe we were too
drunk, earlier we had drunk seven glasses of beer, I wanted to
pee, but I didn't dare get up, the woman wept, it was in 'twenty-
eight that she wept, and the number of unemployed was worri-
some, inflation was rampant, the rubber snake dropped out.
Another girl, whose name I even remember, Johanna, sang
"Deutschland über Alles" and then a fat woman got up, rolled up
her dress and peed on the stage, wiped herself with a strip of old
newspaper and the pee flowed on the floor, and the woman on
the chair licked her lips, and Sam recited stock prices in June
'twenty-nine, the price of gas, the price of vegetables, the price
of newspapers, yearnings were born and I don't know whether
those were yearnings for what was or for what was after that,
faces were crying for help, I stood on my knees, somebody sang:
The shark has pearly teeth dear, and he shows them pearly white,
just a jackknife has old MacHeath dear, and he keeps it out of
sight, she yelled: He's a shark! And Sam said: Watch out for
sharks! To catch a shark you have to grab him by the tail, make
him lie on his back. He dies because his belly isn't connected to
the walls of his body, he's got a moving belly and he sheds it, said
Sam, and I muttered some of your words, Kramer, twenty-four
thousand teeth every ten years. And I, I can't move, I try to understand Sam and I know, know that deep inside me I do understand him, but I'm ashamed precisely because I do understand.
The bartender is now trying to return the clock to the present,
outside, somebody's knocking on the window, reality penetrates
inside with a wild daring and I want to get up and maybe I did,
the woman comes close to him and he kisses her and then slaps
Kramer and looks at him in amazement, smears his face with
powder he took out of some woman's purse and my head drops,
and the more I want to get up, the more I drop, and am covered
with powder, spew foam, and somebody thrusts a bottle of whiskey into my mouth, and I drink, and then, I stood, me, I who
once shot at low-flying planes, and I spoke about "paratroopers"

brought down by the bullets of our soldiers, the heroes, when the ghetto was burning, and how nice to see you landing dead from the roofs, from the burned houses, and I shot in retrospect, according to Sam's clock, reluctantly I aimed and shot into a propaganda film of the burning ghetto shot by my father and I was ridiculous in my own eyes, a chorus of fake women sang with artificial voices the anthem of the Black Corps of paratrooper shooters, Herr Reichsführer, the ghetto is no more says (inside me) SS Sturmbahnführer Stroop, and my father shoots pictures of his son shooting at the "paratroopers," and then the giant fire. And how beautiful it is to photograph the lapping fire, the houses collapsing, and they're still singing, and then Sam cuts his hand deeply with a knife he found on the counter, and I understand that Boaz left him the knife he took from Rebecca who took it from the knife-sharpener in Jaffa, it's all mixed up in my brain, maybe I'm dreaming, I and Jordana in the bath, hugged by a dream girl of death, the blood flowing on Sam's hand, I hit Sam and the spotlight, it's dark and the voices fall silent all at once.

The next day I woke up with a sharp headache between my eyes. The phone didn't stop ringing. The morning newspapers were hidden by Renate and our cleaning woman under the closets. Sam came to breakfast, jolly. The call from Mr. Schwabe was one of the only ones that felt strange and I said to Renate, Answer that call, and she picked up the phone and gave it right to me and I heard the strident, furious voice of the man even before I put it to my ear. He yelled and I held the phone away while, in my other hand, I held a cup of miracle juice Renate concocted to cure my nausea. He yelled: That man of yours, sir, came to my house, or perhaps you don't know, if I hadn't known you were an honorable man I would have honored you with a duel worthy of the name, and you wouldn't have been left with one ear to cure and even your nostrils would disappear along with what wraps them. I was smoking a pipe, suddenly there was a knock on the door, I opened it, and he stood, he stood there, you hear me? He stood there and smiled, pushed me into a chair and picked up the phone, you hear? And he dialed, I

heard distant voices in the receiver, I was scared, and he said
into the phone: Talk to Himmler, and he gave me the phone. I
heard shouts from the other end, what happened? What happened? She shouted there and I said: Schwabe here, and she
said: Who? And I said Schwabe of Badenstrasse and my pipe fell
down, it fell down, the pipe, and she said: You're Schwabe of
Badenstrasse, where's Sam, I said to her: I'm here and Sam is
standing next to me, you listening? And Sam pushed me and
yelled: Talk to her! And I'm an old man, what could I do, I said
Who is this? And she said Lily! What Lily, I said to her, what
joke is this, and she said, A really bad joke, maybe she wept, and
who is she, if she's Lily where was she all these years? And then
Greta came in, she takes care of me and I love her, she fixes
everything, sews, she said: What's happening? And she looked
at that man with a hatred I didn't find where to search for it
inside me, and Lily says What? What? Is this Schwabe and I
yelled: American filth, shit of American soldiers, you left a father in prison, took me years to crawl here, I found your stinking stockings in the empty house, and she laughed, she laughed
then too, and the old woman said: Enough, you'll get a stroke,
and the phone went dead and that Sam counts out marks for
the call, gives them to Greta and she took them, why shouldn't
she, but the heart is shaking with shame and even more, I'm
furious, eighty-one years old, what do they want, and from me,
and I hear Sam or what's-his name, laughing or yelling and Greta
isn't scared of him, no, she's not scared, her they measured for
a uniform of real Junkers, her they didn't take out of that music
and the pop and the long hair, and Sam told her, Tell how many
Reichsmarks you got, those Reichsmarks were brought to you by
Jews, and Greta sneered: The Reichsmarks are better from your
hand than from anybody else, and he told her the Jews were
coming back, and she said, There was no Lily, as if he had
asked, but she asked from inside me, And tonight, when she has
no teeth in her mouth, and that made the swinish clown laugh,
and then he took out a pack of lewd cards from Frankfurt, or
Japan, showed me, and said: You see, here's Lily with Jews! You

want to buy the pictures? And I, what can I do and even Greta was now yelling with shame, and I explain to him: I'm an old retired soldier, living on a small pension, what do you want from me, and I get mad: Lily? Where was Lily? And he said I came back home, Father, and kisses me, that filth, you hear?

I hear, I told him, and I drink another cup Renate gave me and my head is bursting. And he yells into the receiver, an old man with manly telephone power, I think for no good reason you were waiting for me, that Sam tells me, you sat in pajamas and waited, and I say: I wasn't waiting, I'm cheating death, I don't sleep at night because eighty-one-year-olds die at night, and he says, Waiting for death? Germans die standing up, sir, he told me, the filth, at three in the morning, nineteen seventy-three, and he tells me: Your daughter is a whore of Jews, and I yell: I don't have a daughter because I really don't, and he says a mothball of a woman and I remember every word, mothball of a woman, with a pedigreed womb, sing! He orders me and pushes Greta into the armchair where she was sitting and can't get into any deeper, and that friend of yours, tells me Take the cards, and hits me and kisses Greta on her toothless mouth and goes . . .

After Herr Schwabe hung up, Sam said with a calm that drove me crazy: Afterward I left his house and waited until the police car came. And then, after he said that, he fell asleep in his chair. I looked at him and suddenly my headache vanished. There's nothing like the sight of a lost person to cure a headache after such a night of drinking and humiliation. Renate took off his shoes and together we dragged him to the sofa, and the cleaning woman covered him and he slept for five straight hours. And then the evening papers came. When he woke up, we were busy reading. I wouldn't say those were especially thrilling moments. The papers made it clear that, at long last, my real face was revealed. The would-be rightist papers hinted at bitter things about my past and my dubious morals, and the so-called leftist papers explained without a shadow of a doubt that in the war I played much higher roles than had been thought. Of course, it was all formulated so that I can't sue anybody, and if I protested the injustice and the empty charge, I would look even more foolish.

They threatened me by phone, and friends who tried to encourage me said things like: I do understand you. Or: In your circumstances, it's easy to understand why, and so on . . . All of them hypocrites and flatterers. I decided to appear in a television interview and at least try to refute some of the charges against me. The producer of our television news is an old friend of mine. We were in school together, we once traveled together to Italy, Greece, and South America. He arranged that interview. It was an act of courage and resolution on his part.

In the television studio, I sat with Sam in the producer's office, the woman who prepared the report looked at Sam with wicked eyes and asked embarrassing questions. When she smiled she looked like a person who has started missing herself. Then I was interviewed and I returned home. I could have been interviewed in my house, but I wanted to be interviewed in the studio to impart much more credibility to my words, as if it wasn't only I who was talking, but the communications media. Sam drank hot chocolate and sat in front of the turned-off television. When the interview with me was broadcast, he turned on the television. We sat and didn't say a word, Renate smiled once and then averted her eyes and looked at Sam watching the program and her eyes suddenly became cold as steel.

And here are some news clippings for you.

. . . in his television appearance, he chose not to apologize. Nor did he try to cover up. He told candidly, and that candor has to be appreciated, how years ago he met a person who performed in nightclubs and was called the Last Jew, and about a fellow named Samuel Lipker who would lead him. He told how he investigated that person and now that Samuel—the American director Sam Lipp—came to our city, he swept him up into his world of horrors and made him act in his presence the commander who commanded both Sam Lipp and the one he called the Last Jew. Maybe what he said was candid, but equally unconvincing. Candor isn't necessarily a substitute for truth. Candor, like good intentions, is sometimes the road to hell. The poetic license our praised writer permits himself this time went beyond the boundary of good taste . . . On the contrary, the amazement about the past was even sharpened, his persistence in writing a book he can never write and doesn't write evokes a sense of intellectual impotence, ideological shallowness, and fear of critical readers, for if the book is so important to him, why did he write his other books? It is hard to accept as logical the fact of the clock set backward, the story about the fellow whose anger justifies disgraceful behavior in a nightclub and hectoring an old man, imprisoned in the past, who lives on a small pension, struck and pestered by a distinguished writer and a guest from America. Virgil (the moderator-A.S.) asked our writer why he had to go to a fortuneteller before his last trip to the United States, and didn't even get a satisfactory answer. Why does a writer try to pretend to be a beautiful person without delusions, when he secretly believes in superstitions of a clock set backward and secretly consults a fortuneteller . . . In his articles, he attacks the ignorance of what he calls worshippers of stars and signs. Our writer is caught here in naked hypocrisy! . . . Great amazement . . . As for the intellectual integrity of a writer whose past was restored without pangs of conscience, and along with streetwalkers, profiteers, and pimps, he presents a shameful play about the resurrection of the Reich, when in the same week, he writes a trenchant article against performing the Passion in Bayreuth, because as he puts it, it is a basic and profound insult to human moral values and to the Jewish nation.

. . . sometimes even hypocrisy has to be consistent, even if it concerns shutting one's eyes and tormented candor. Along with his friends, our writer is trying to condemn us, our society, to condemn us for what he himself calls in his articles "Teutonic arrogance, and the lost souls of the patriarchs." For many years he has demanded again and again that we stop making—as he puts it—"tours of exaltation and disgrace in the lost forests of ancient myths, and that along with the other nations of Europe we live the noble majesty of the civil world promised in the future, even if it is bereft of a real past" . . .

Or:

> . . . it is to be believed that he fell victim to a dangerous suggestion . . . A person doesn't set people back by an imaginary clock . . . His words were incredulous verbiage . . ."

Or:

> . . . I was convinced! Convinced that our author was an embezzler in his past, that those great moments of truth he experienced were wasted and he has to apologize for . . .

The studio was inundated with phone calls, Henkin. Hundreds of people called in. Most of them didn't scold me for denying my past or for falling victim to it. I was asked if my wife is indeed of Jewish origin, and when I tried to explain, I was flooded with insulting answers in a righteous and disgusting way. I was even asked why there are so many "last Jews" in Germany. When I told the questioner that only thirty thousand Jews live in Germany and most of them are old retirees, I was told that that was thirty thousand too many, I was accused of lying to the authorities of the Reich about my wife's origin, I was accused of being related to the fortuneteller and Sam Lipp. They called me a crazy leftist and a stinking rightist and an intellectual pig and a man of dubious honor . . . what wasn't said in those endless conversations. Even my son was conjured up. I was asked if my son was murdered, committed suicide, or died of natural causes, and why he had to be educated to hate his grandfather, and who taught the boy to challenge the grandfather, for after all he was only following orders. Friedrich, said one woman in a shrill and annoying voice, was a charming boy whose parents destroyed him, and he had to die to atone for their sins, but she didn't identify herself and I asked myself where were my three million readers where were the critics and journalists who wrote such nice things about me, and because of them and for fear of their criticism, I hadn't yet written *The Last Jew*, but they were in hiding, didn't express an opinion, were tranquil and silent. I asked myself where were my books, *The Lost Honor of Venus Daedelus? The English Lesson, The*

Awful Blow of the Soccer Goalie, where are my giant trumpet and the filmgoers, where is all that, but they weren't, they offended my son, they said: The apple doesn't fall far from the tree.

What I didn't know, of course, was that, after the interview with me, a television crew was sent to the club. They filmed the seedy ladies, the stage where they were acting that night, the bartender, and they got unpleasant comments from them. They also went to Lily's father's house and heard his version, and all that was presented to the viewers, as Sam, Renate, and I were waiting in front of the television set that Sam didn't turn on. That was a real bond against me, a bond only I was guilty of.

The next day, I complained to my agent, who apologized and said he had been at the sea. I told him: In the winter? In the ice? And he muttered something and I hung up. Then I hugged Sam and drank tea with lemon and the producer called. He said: I heard you're angry. Sam Lipp sent us to the club and to Herr Schwabe. He said it was your idea! Don't feel guilty and don't get mad at us . . . I told him: That's nice. I'm not guilty. You're not. My agent's not guilty. Only Sam Lipp is guilty. If so, how come I know that both you and I are guilty?

And then Renate said in a quiet voice that froze my blood. She said: I want Friedrich to be buried next to Menahem Henkin.

A few days later, Sam called from Marseille. He told me he was waiting for Lionel in Café Glacier. Lionel would come interrogate him about his crimes. Then he called from the hotel and said he was calling from Lebensborn. Hotels like that should be erased from phone books, he said. And I did complain at city hall and in the next phone book that name won't appear again. Sam said, I'm waiting for a ship.

Then he called me from the Rome airport. He reversed the charges. He said: The journey has ended, Café Glacier isn't what it used to be, sometimes you have to destroy. He asked forgiveness, he asked me to ask forgiveness from Lily's father, from Renate, from everybody. From what he said, it was clear but not explicit, that he was in trouble, but managed to flee. I was freed by a person named Leopold Bardossi, he said, I don't know Italian. I'm flying to Israel in an hour, he said, got to erect a memorial to the greatest Italian poet.

As I write this letter, Sam is surely in Israel. Renate and I will come in a week. Don't tell anybody about our coming. Please find us a room in a hotel near you. The Israeli cleaning woman we recently hired just told me that last night they called about Samuel. I don't know what it is, but I'm in a hurry to send the letter and I'll tell you in person about what's in store for us from this episode.

Yours as always . . .

Tape / —

The General Consulate of Israel, Trieste.

Consul: Adam Navon.

Dear Mr. Henkin,

I'm writing you in reference to Samuel Lipker. Among the papers we found in his room was a letter addressed to you and your name also appears in several of his papers.

Aside from you, he had the address of a German writer we have tried to locate, but his Israeli cleaning woman did not understand the issue, and then we learned that he had taken off for Israel and on the way had stopped in Italy, but it is not known where. I hope Samuel Lipker will get in touch with you. If he does, please get in touch with Mrs. Hannah Aharoni, secretary of our department in the Foreign Ministry in Jerusalem. My deputy, who will investigate the episode of Samuel Lipker's visit to the city, writes in his report:

Samuel Lipker was searching for a ship that was to sail for the Land of Israel on January first, nineteen hundred [sic!]. When he did not find that ship (it is now nineteen seventy-three [sic!]), he tried to burn down the only synagogue in the city. He provoked people, offended passersby, sold stolen goods at the port, and is wanted by the police. The press is going mad to take advantage of that man's behavior to gore Israel. The press says that Samuel was seen in the company of whores, a hashish dealer (the evidence here is confused), etc. . . .

It's not that these are important articles, although they do not indicate a great deal of affection. But on the other hand, when people are hit, gold watches are stolen from passersby who refuse to buy, people are flogged until they bleed, and anybody who tries to intervene—including a policeman who was badly beaten—is punished. . . . Apparently we must act, since we're the representatives of Israel here and even without all that our work is not easy. Please, therefore, if you hear something, let me know, and I will be grateful.

Yours, Adam Navon

Tape / —

Ebenezer and Fanya R. are walking along the seashore. Fanya is hopping, picking up snails and examining them. Ebenezer is trying to estimate the distance between himself and the turret of the mosque in Jaffa, and says: Jaffa is a rock. Jaffa of sundown. Jaffa of magic. Jaffa of abandoned smells. Let go of the snails, the sea wept them, nothing will influence me anymore. I dreamed a war will break out, I read the dream in a book that hasn't yet been written. That's what they say! The sea will be filled with blood. There's no iodine for blood of the sea.

In the distance a woman stands and yells at a child: Don't go in the water, Boaz. I told you not to. Listen, if you drown, don't you dare come back home.

Tape / —

Henkin reads Germanwriter's letter to Hasha. Germanwriter is going to Italy and from there he'll come. Henkin says: What will we do with Friedrich? And Hasha is silent. Henkin says: How, how, and Hasha says Shhh, Henkin. You're disturbing the rustle of the waves.

Tape / —

Boaz Schneerson: It's not just Noga. I live in a world I wasn't prepared for. And I'm half an orphan. Do you pity me? You're laughing! Jordana is woven of silken death, what are you woven of? They taught you to forget where you came from. At night, before sleep, an old nun read you sayings in Latin. You spat green blood. What exactly happened? Did you really find your dead father? Did you write a letter to the judge? The judge wrote to me. He wrote: In terms of morality, Noga Levin is right. So here you are, proof that you're right! The Last Jew, not our "last Jew," let him go into that sea, when he's thrown out. Let him throw up his hands, let him yell "I was right," and let him drown. What does it help to be always right? I'm not always right, but unlike you, I don't make Boazes miserable. Germanwriter is coming, Henkin's waiting for him. Your father never waited for another daughter, when he waited, he waited for you. The writer comes here to buy guided missiles produced by the military industry, rifles started with clothespins, Jewish genius, plastic tank turrets, dream-penetrating laser beams, water from the Jordan to alleviate material exhaustion—like planes that lost their fighting ability—sea sand to pulverize limbs, Jewish grenades to disperse student demonstrations, a philharmonic orchestra with stainless steel spires, the German leopards are supplied with soap made in Israel and in exchange they send us gas masks. What battle are the lords Herod and Mendelssohn preparing for us? The German command will buy Hebrew tents, go to Henkin, loathe him in my name . . .

And Sam Lipp—

Tape / —

Sam Lipp came to the old Ben-Gurion airport. When the plane extinguished its engines, the stewardess woke him up and said to him with a smile: I think we've arrived. He picked up his valise, brushed his hair, and got off. After a short bus trip, he came to customs. A policewoman hidden in a giant wooden basin stamped his passport; he walked slowly to the exit. Except for the valise in his hand, he hadn't brought anything with him. When he went outside, a hot wind blew and the light was still clear. In the distance he could almost love the ugliness surrounding everything like a wreath of thorns.

He got into a cab, stretched out, and said: The Hilton, Tel Aviv. He peeped out and through the windshield, the trees started becoming clear, the narrow road became more familiar, barbed wire fences posted in his mind between houses and boulevards faded away, he recalled that when he slept in the plane he dreamed he was walking on Baron Hirsch Street in Tarnopol carrying two challahs. Now, awake, he seemed to see the roads to Tarnopol. The driver was listening to music and smoking a cigarette.

Hebrew words on the radio became familiar. Syllables he didn't know before became a surer texture, for some reason he was afraid of history, the
structure of time, the molecules of relative time as opposed to absolute
time. He thought: Melissa is waiting for me at the corner.

At the entrance to the hotel, he paid the driver. The exorbitant price
didn't surprise him. When he came to the counter and said his name, the
clerk dialed and a few minutes later a tall beautiful girl appeared holding
a bouquet of flowers. She called a boy, put the one valise on a cart, and said
to Sam: Welcome to the Hilton! And she handed him the bouquet with a
ceremoniousness that seemed a little clumsy yet practiced. The beautiful
girl said she was the representative of the public relations department and
that the Hilton was proud to host him. She led him to a small room. He
apologized for the delay (she muttered to herself that they had expected
him a few days before), and after he signed the guest book studded with
the names of the world's great, beginning with the signature of Ben-Gurion
and then Frank Sinatra, he asked why it wasn't the other way around and
Frank Sinatra didn't come before Ben-Gurion, and she tried to smile, but
her teeth were too beautiful to waste on a meaningless smile, and they
went up together to the seventeenth floor and he was put into the big
suite. In one of the two rooms of the suite were bouquets of flowers sent
by the American cultural attaché, the national theater, and a telegram from
the Minister of Education and Culture on a silver salver.

A basket of apples, flowers, cheese, biscuits, cookies, and crackers stood
in the middle of the table. He picked up an apple and bit into it. The
beauty put some notes on a big nightstand, opened the closed drapes, and
he saw the lights of Tel Aviv. Sam said to the beauty: You're wasted in this
temple, and she smiled a professional and polished smile. Then a person
phoned and said he was the manager of the theater and was waiting for him
at the airport, and he had just heard he had come and he was sorry, but he
hadn't been home for five evenings when he had waited for Sam at the
airport. Sam apologized; fatigue was leaking out of him in drops of sweat,
and they arranged to meet the next day. The beauty checked the bathroom, Sam paid the boy who brought the valise and he wanted to pay her
too, but the two of them looked at one another, didn't say a word and he
said, Sorry, thrust the money into his pocket, and said: Thanks. She said:
If you want anything call me and everything will be taken care of immedi-

ately. He told her: Everything's confused, something's messed up there, and he pointed toward the seashore where Ebenezer and Fanya R. were strolling slowly. Everything became shadows, his body shook, and she waited, something of the pain that filled him infected her. He offered her a cigarette she lit herself because his hands were shaking too much to light it for her, and she smoked the long cigarette he had apparently bought on the plane before he fell asleep. The room smelled of flowers, aftershave, and apples, and he asked her to sit down and she sat down and dragged on the cigarette and he asked why she was so beautiful, and she said with a modest smile that she had been a beauty queen, and he said That's it, how is it to be a beauty queen? And she said, You see, you work in the Hilton, and he smiled, but something in him didn't smile, wanted to flee, but he was stuck to himself and since he couldn't do anything, his hands waved, his face was pale, and then the beauty recalled that he had to record his personal details and she took a form out of her jacket pocket, and he recorded the details and said I should have filled out the details in Lebensborn, too, and she asked what was Lebensborn, and he told her: A hotel to improve racially pure kingdoms, and he filled out the form, and she took it from his hands and glanced at it, and asked the meaning of the word *Gottgläubig* he had written next to the word nationality, and he muttered to himself more than to her: One who has a real German faith, and she said, You must be drunk, no? And he said, I drank all the way, did you ever host Heinrich Kramer here, and she said she didn't know, but she could find out, and he said: Never mind, never mind, and then she stood up hesitantly, waited, put out the cigarette in the ashtray, and apologized, it was clear from her face how sorry she was that the crushed cigarette dirtied the polished ashtray, but he smiled at her and she wiggled out, beautiful, and he lay down in bed, looked at the ceiling, time passed, he didn't know how much, an hour, two, five, he munched on the apples, ate cookies, and thought which side does a fish piss on. Then he went to the bathroom and saw toilet paper and thought: That's Jewish toilet paper, and he was proud. Then he wanted to laugh at his pride, but his face muscles were impermeable to his will and not far from him, a plane flew low over Ebenezer's house and landed at the little airport near the big chimney, which he didn't yet know was Reading Chimney, and he said: I've got to be objective, think objectively, formulate, maybe there's also objective faith, objective theater, objective pain and disgrace, and thus he fell asleep for a little while and awoke and called the public relations department and was told that the beauty had gone home and would come back later to a reception for the ambassador of Peru.

Time flowed somehow. He fell asleep, and when he woke up, he felt as if his body were crumbling, he turned on the radio and tried to watch it as if it were television, but the radio had no screen and he closed the curtain, lay down, sweated, and dreamed he was watering a tree and the tree refused to drink the water. Maybe he really did order the boy because he came in wheeling a cart with a pot of coffee and cookies, and what was clear was that he said: The ambassador of Peru is staying in the end suite, and then he told him: My name's Samuel Lipker, and the boy said, Fine, sir, and slammed the door behind him as if it were made of thin glass.

Then he apparently ordered more food because with his own eyes he saw him gorging himself in the mirror and a girl who wasn't young, but not yet a woman, picked up the dishes and went off, leaving him a toothpick and an intoxicating smell of orange piss. The radio was on and he now understood some of the words, and once again a cold sweat started creeping on his back. He decided to take a shower or perhaps he took a shower because he had nothing else to do. The water flowing felt nice on his body that was strange to him. In the shower he smoked a cigarette under the stream of water, and so he also started longing for Melissa and Licinda and the beauty queen. Apparently more time passed because when he picked up the phone he was already dressed and combed. They replied that the beauty had come, but wasn't in her office, and who wants to know. He locked them in the phone and locked his feet in his shoes and went out to the small balcony and looked at the sea. When he went out to the corridor, he saw a woman bent over the carpet plucking up grains of dust. The sight was depressing. He pressed the button for the elevator and waited. Downstairs he searched for the beauty. Then he thought maybe he should search for the ambassador of Peru, but he didn't feel like asking. He felt pressure in his chest and sensed an incomprehensible need to look in the various mirrors and identify himself. He broke into a locked room with a skill he hadn't used in a long time, and there was the beauty queen. She wore fabulous clothes, her soft thin hands gleamed in the light of the big chandelier and her bright eyes were more violet than green or blue. Her hair was fair but without a clear tone, as if it were made of cardboard. She was also laughing, apparently at the ambassador of Peru.

The ambassador was signing his name in the guest book after Sam Lipp's name, and he thought: She screws everybody, and went outside angrily. The sight of the charming beauty queen with the ambassador of Peru offended him. Outside he lit a cigarette.

Apparently he passed by the park because on the other side were rusted houses. He thought of a concept he didn't understand at all, he thought of a trigonometry of smell, something that reminded him of articles apparently written about his play. The city was full of one-way streets that became more and more familiar, burst out, and then disappeared. Even the boardwalk square was familiar to him, and he said: "Here's the square," as if he understood. An American girl with prominent nipples in her shirt passed by him and left a fragrant trail of white blood, he tried to see her from behind, but he didn't turn his face and so he lost her. He thought of the beauty kissing the bald head of the ambassador of Peru. Trees swayed in the wind and a precisely shaped cypress sharpened its crest to the sky. There were also stars, and he was glad about them. Beyond the window of a café, people sat and drank. He watched them and said to himself: Here's mother, here's mother, here's Aunt Leah, here's Lipkele. Here's Uncle Yom, here's Yashka, here's the Ukrainian. Maybe they sat naked in the café and policemen whipped them, but they smiled even though they had no teeth. He was terrified, but didn't do a thing about it. The manager of the café sat outside and read a score of "Making Whoopee." He thought, this is how they made a lady of jazz. And he thought about what Charlie Parker told him when he was hanging around New York searching for a celebration of authentic and well-woven social slime. The dead sat and acted his family for him. He wanted to break the window, and so he hurried on his way. Farther down was a boulevard, jazz and dead uncles, he thought, soda with straws, I'm walking in zigzags. Cafés full of sleepy young people, thinking thoughts. A girl wanted him to sign a petition against some occupation, he signed, in Hebrew, Samuel Lipker. He bought *Le Figaro* in a newspaper shop, because you could buy papers from all over the world there. It excited him that in a place of dead people you could buy newspapers in foreign languages and a little girl he had to notice could lick ice cream with a heartrending sweetness.

Apparently that night couldn't be reconstructed. An El Al plane reached its destination and Obadiah Henkin stood and waited for his guests. Boaz sat in Rebecca's house and heard how Nehemiah hated Joseph when he saw him in Rachel's face. Samuel Lipker saw a pair of legs in the opening of a house and next to the legs a small bottle of brandy. He stopped and looked at the legs and then at the owner of the legs. She smiled and licked her lips. Not far behind her appeared a shadow of a man wearing tight pants. Sam didn't say a thing and she became impatient. Finally he said to her: For ten dollars and the bottle too. She laughed and said: I'm not a whore for dollars, and that was the most beautiful thing he heard, a woman with a slightly charred face. On the mattress in the yard an open light appeared, blinking on and off, he tried to sleep with her, thought of the beauty queen in the hotel with the ambassador of Peru, but couldn't and he gave her another five dollars and heard yells not far away from there and stormy Greek music beyond the breakers of the sea. The mattress was filthy. The woman lifted her skirt, smiled, and held the bottle to her mouth and he drank from the bottle and forgot her and thought about the beauty and then lit her a cigarette. When the man in tight pants appeared, he ordered drinks for them all. The man saw the wad of dollars in Sam's hand, and yelled: There's a party and two other girls and three men immediately appeared.

The bar was dark with red lights burning in it. A fellow with an Uzi limped in. The fellow said to the bartender, who looked a little scared: That's an American sucker, what are you crying to me, and the soldier aimed the Uzi and laughed, and then they all laughed. Sam drank a lot and so did they. They told him to pay fifty dollars. He paid. Then he hugged them and started dancing. A buxom Greek woman tried to sing into a microphone, but an Arab tried to burn her dress. The scared bartender asked them not to cheat the American, but nobody paid attention to the bartender and took another thirty dollars from Sam. He also danced with the Greek woman. Then he said: That's like Paganini trying to compete with all of you in backgammon. They didn't really understand it and said: You want backgammon? And he said, Yes, and he let them cheat him at backgammon and he paid. And then he patted the fellow with the Uzi, crushed him, threw him at the lamp that went out immediately, aimed the other lamp at them, and also aimed the Uzi, cocked it and fired into the air. The police of the ten-twenty shift had gone now. He said quietly: Now stand up nice, and then he took all their wallets out of his pocket along with three watches and two chains with medallions and divided them, and they were too stunned to say a word, and he went to the counter, took out his dollars, counted, took more dollars out of the wallets and when his money was returned to him, he took five hundred pounds, and said to them: You wanted to fool me? Do you have any idea whom I've dealt with in my life? Do you have any idea who you're dealing with?

He sat down in a chair and burst out laughing. They looked at him. One of them wanted to get up and hit him, but one crushing blow was enough for him not to try again. Sam shot three more times into three foil cigarette packs pasted to the ceiling, returned the Uzi without a magazine to the limping soldier, and said: You don't understand anything, who's going to bring something to eat now, I'm paying!

And that was how the celebration began that ended later on the seashore when the Border Patrol, searching for terrorists, stopped them and he produced his documents (passport, certificate of honor from the Hilton, and a letter from the Minister of Education and Culture), and then they walked in the sand and sang. They said: What a real mafia this is, and he really took care of us, and the whore kept walking with him and went into the hotel with him, and in the distance he saw the beauty with three other women sitting and drinking coffee. He took the whore upstairs, took from his pocket a key he had previously taken out of the beauty's purse, opened the door of the suite of the ambassador of Peru, lay the whore on the bed, and she jumped up and down on the springy bed, and said: What a beautiful ceiling, and he said: You surely know rooms by the ceilings, and then he said: I'll be right back! And she wept at the sight of the wealth and beauty and the sea spread out in the window, and he went down, and the queen said with unrestrained malice: This isn't a hotel for such people! And he told her all that had happened, and he started laughing and there were tears in her queenly eyes, and he took her to his room and lay next to her, and said to her: Show me your gigantic artificial breasts, and she showed him, and then he entered her, and when he was inside her he called New York and said to Lionel: Listen, man, come here immediately, all of you, it's urgent, and he hung up.

Tape / —

Tonight (I'm talking into the tape recorder again), tonight something strange happened to me. I walked on the seashore with Fanya R. As usual, she picked up shells and threw them and I looked at the spires of the

churches of Jaffa. When we came to the marina, I fell asleep on my feet. I
don't know how that happened. My body stood still. You can say that a
person who just now turned seventy-two is liable to fall asleep on his feet,
but I'm not an expert in the lives of old people like me. From what I can
tell from what she said, Fanya R. tried to carry me, but I was too heavy.
Maybe because of the relation between the full moon and the low tide or
the high tide, I don't know exactly, but it wasn't possible to move me from
the spot, Fanya R. went to the Henkin home to call for help, but Henkin
wasn't at home and Hasha and Fanya R. called Boaz, but the phone was
apparently disconnected. They took a cab and went to Boaz (she told me),
went up to the roof and called him. I lay on the chilly sand and slept. And
then a rooster crowed. In my sleep I thought cocks were forgotten on the
seashore of Tel Aviv, but with my own ears I heard the crowing.

I opened my eyes. A bearded sculptor wearing eyeglasses was sitting on
the beach sculpting water. A policeman on a motorcycle passed by not far
away, but didn't notice me. The flash of a spotlight illuminated the beach
for a moment, and went out. When I turned my face, I saw the Hilton. The
rooms were lit up in a bold mosaic. Independence Park above me was dark,
but the moon lit up some trees and a sculpture that looked like a bird frozen in flight and a few pieces of limestone. I felt a need to die, to weep,
to eat hamburgers, and then I understood that the hundreds of hours I had
spoken, those dozens of tapes, had cast a high wall off me and I thought of
my life, was it nice, was it good? I didn't know what to think, that was the
first time in years I was almost liberated from all the people who had been
talking in me until then, and I'm talking now on one moment, I'm talking
not to myself, not to an anonymous audience, not in a nightclub, I'm talking to Germanwriter and to Henkin who will hear these things and will say,
Ah, Ebenezer stopped being a Last Jew, and if I stop being a Last Jew, will
they be able to write the book I wove for them from memories that weren't
mine, and suddenly I was alone with my life, with Mother, with the old
charred smell of the cowshed and the casuarinas and eucalyptus trees and
the fragrance of citrus blossoms, and an awful longing for wood, for the face
hidden in wood, burned in me, and I thought of Boaz, of a little boy I left
here so many years ago, of Samuel, the two of them I felt as if they were
struggling in me for a birthright, Esau and Jacob, in me, a hollow person
like me, who went to search for a father and found a disaster and now starts

returning from the disaster and bringing down more disasters. I longed for
Dana, but also for Fanya R. I thought about the German who came today,
about Hasha, about Henkin, about poor Jordana who went back to work at
the Ministry of Defense and still watches television every night, suddenly
I knew everything, but I didn't know anything, I didn't know other things
I once knew, I almost didn't know things told me by the dead people I had
amassed inside me and I kept myself from being myself, and that was how
I was saved from death maybe even more than the boxes I built for Kramer,
Weiss, and others, not everything was clear to me on the damp sand, I tried
to get up, but I couldn't, I knew Fanya R. wouldn't let me stay like that,
that she'd get help, and I waited, I wasn't afraid, I was tired, dead tired,
and hungry, and thirsty, and my body ached, but it ached me! And that was
my body that ached and I thought about Mother, about the awful life she
lived, about the curse that patched up her life like glue, I thought: I
couldn't be the son of Joseph because there's no wickedness in me, no
anger, no rage, no vengeance, no glorious words, there are no splendid
paper flowers in me, I'm not especially wise, I'm a simple man, like a
sponge, my wisdom is in my hands, I know wood in its distress as it says
on the wall in the community house in the settlement. I thought about
Boaz and knew that even though he's my son he's also the son of Joseph
and suddenly it wasn't strange anymore, I understood that there are things
I may never understand. I thought about Einstein's theory and I couldn't
recite it anymore, Kafka's stories, I didn't remember them, I remembered
Mother working from morning till night and Ahbed helping her, how I sat
in a corner, sucking a finger, hurting her bitterness, and how I wanted
somebody to love me, and there wasn't anybody to love me and a deaf girl
came and sat and looked at me, and then Dana and how Boaz was born and
the struggle between Mother and Dana over Boaz and I hated him then,
and Mr. Klomin and the Captain, and the children who plagued me because I wasn't like them, what a ridiculous thing I was, for a settlement of
people who had started entering gold frames, I had nothing, only the wood
and the passion to know who really was my father and how again and again
I imagined father Nehemiah, whom I envied because he might or might
not have been my real father, Nehemiah who died on the seashore of Jaffa,
so as not to betray his dream, and gloomy memories rose in me on the seashore, pure memories I hadn't remembered for thirty years, I, Ebenezer

Schneerson, an ashamed old man, who didn't hit me, who didn't strike or offend me in my life, and I, with a crooked back, in a hundred fifty night-clubs stand up and recite, so that Samuel Lipker can get rich, what a buffoon I was, but I loved Samuel, his boldness, my life was a contemptible collusion against myself, a pauper of shoe soles, who am I? Why am I? Something happens, a late awakening, second childhood, I know the limestone rocks now, the terror of barbed wire fences drops on me, Kramer turns into a distant picture, maybe I dreamed him too, but that's not important anymore and those yearnings . . . And I waited for Fanya R. I shook from the damp, I tried to sit up, but I didn't have the strength. But that wasn't important to me either, what was really important was after fifty years to be again somebody I once was, for good or for bad; what did they know about my thoughts, about my heavy and bitter meditations, when Mother and the Captain sat and talked and he would raise his voice and she, contemptuous but beautiful, and there was in her, beyond everything, some decency.

Tape / —

I'm Ebenezer Schneerson. I am suddenly me. I don't remember a thing except what happened to me, like many people, I'm just another person, love wood, lacquers, love the smell of sawdust, everything has dropped off me, I'm talking into a tape, maybe for the last time in my life, afterward I have and will have nothing to say, nothing to recite, I look around, the world's grown old. Only now do I understand that the trees Dana planted are no longer saplings, that our new house is old now and old-fashioned and nobody lives there. I see Ahbed and I don't know if he's the son or the grandson or the great-grandson, I try to shut my eyes, concentrate, nothing comes, I'm left with myself alone, a cockroach, like everybody, in the backyard of my life, with Fanya R., with a certain, unclear future, for a while, I have no more memories of others I'm only for myself.

Tape / —

The moment I came back to what I left years ago, today I know, was the moment when they met above, above me, in that room in the Hilton, and I didn't know. I saw many lights—I didn't see the one light he stood in, he looked outside and suddenly if he had yelled at me, from the balcony of the seventeenth floor I would have gone on reciting for him, and so the door was opened and slammed and I was finished, as I started, with some slow and uncertain dying toward nobeing . . .

Tape / —

Mr. Ofen, Opal Books Ltd.
Sir:

Everything you have read so far, what I said, what I wrote, what Henkin says and wrote, everything was said by the man we're investigating, whose life we have tried to restore and understand. The words were all his, even my words were his: these hundreds of pages! Will I be able to interweave the book? Will Henkin and I succeed? From now on, I begin a series of hypotheses, from now on I no longer know things right. I gave you the things in their language reinvented by Ebenezer, most of them true, always recited, from now on I'm left with myself alone, Ebenezer is no longer who he was, even though he's still alive, and I have nothing but questions, amazement, I want to fill up the space, to grant you some authenticity, not to stumble, I've been here two months now, you call, my agent calls, I've got at least to know where the paths are leading that were paved by Ebenezer and now I have to walk on them with Henkin.

My son Friedrich we buried on a warm day, when a western wind blew and handsome pines sheltered us. Friedrich is buried next to Menahem Henkin. As far as I'm concerned, that fact has a kind of brazenness. The ceremony was modest, but not unemotional. Between the rocks, on the plain where the olive groves of Samaria and the vincyard of the Judean Mountains meet, in the steep and rocky mountain pass, the Teutonic lad who was my son is buried. Like the Crusader Werner from the city of Greiz who ascended to a temple that wasn't his. On my son's tombstone, only his first name is carved: Friedrich. At the ceremony, I read a chapter from Psalms and the monologue from Macbeth: Out, out, brief candle! Life's but a walking shadow, a poor player that struts and frets his hour upon the stage and then is heard no more. It is a tale told by an idiot, full of sound and fury, signifying nothing. For a long time we stood still, evening descended, the trees rustled in the wind, and that was the first time I felt I was leaving Friedrich in a place that was truly real and not only yearnings and deceitful geography. In the back of my mind I saw an ancient father as the Crusader Werner from the city of Greiz, who was brought to Jaffa on a mule along with the corpse of Gottfried of Bouillon and afterward his brother Beaudoin became great and was king of Jerusalem. I thought to myself, You're not a king here but a guest on probation, and your roots will be in the air with the treetops in the ground and maybe you'll learn, after death, to long for what you never reach. In some place I then understood Rebecca Schneerson, the daughter of his great-granddaughter, the daughter and wife of Secret Charity, her zealotry, her hatred, her beauty. No person who is pierced by a river can live among living people. And Friedrich came home, even though this may not be the home he expected.

What I can say for sure—and the very word "sure" becomes strange and elusive in my eyes—is that Samuel Lipker started searching for traces of himself in a city he knew well and whose language and forgiveness he knew in his blood.

Ebenezer, who stopped being the Last Jew, looks miserable. Something very defined, that sharpens differences, was erased from him. He's no longer a man of mystery, but an old man who wants to atone for what he sees as his unimaginably exaggerated testimony. Boaz and he sat and talked. Boaz told him how he came to be what he calls "a vulture," when all he really wanted to do was nothing, just live, as people just die, and here are all the committees and the commemorations and the memorials and memorial books and Noga and Jordana. They talked about Boaz's childhood, about the Captain who converted him to Christianity or perhaps didn't convert him to Christianity, there's nobody now who knows what really happened. The two of them left the room, something that seemed to glow all night was dulled now, and when Boaz went to celebrate what he called "his new freedom," and we, Renate, Hasha, and I, sat and talked with Ebenezer and made him hot tea, Samuel Lipker went to the Ministry of Defense to find out if a person of that name was

killed in one of the wars. That seemed to be a rather logical
step, but later on, when I found out about it, and today I can't
say why, I thought maybe that was his last betrayal of logic.
Jordana, who had recently returned to work, saw him and said:
Boaz, what are you doing here? And I of course don't know if it
was Samuel who was offended at hearing the name Boaz, or
Boaz who was insulted when his father called him Samuel, but
the reaction was the same, anger, embarrassment, pain, maybe
even hope, so he smiled at her and took her to a small café, they
talked and she said: If I had a neat room, if they had gotten me
an established television, I could help people liberate them from
dread, I'd look at the screen and they would be purified. Samuel
Lipker grasped something we didn't, maybe that was a sponta-
neous response to the beauty of the swarthy queen of death,
maybe it was the old thirst for dark ceremonies. He said: Stop
playing the fool, maybe once you could cure people through a
television set because you were sick and sick people can work
miracles, but you're recovered now and you're dependent on
your sickness, you're acting the woman who can help, but you
know you can't anymore, that game is over. And when he hugged
her at the entrance to the small office building surrounded by a
garden heaped with papers and empty receipts, she felt, as she
told me later, that she was hugged by Boaz, who once knew how
to sleep with her, scold her, love her in his own way, but never
hugged her, didn't envelop her in that longing that was in
Samuel. She told him something strange, she said: That's exactly
how the dead would hug me. He told her: I hug you because
I'm a shadow of somebody and with me you can be free of your
dependence on death, and Jordana saw, or felt, life, real life, the
life people live before they die, starting to flow in her, to her,
from her, and she smiled, maybe she was happy at everything
there ever was, not because she loved somebody, but because
she didn't have to love anybody to accept herself as she was.

I have no idea what Sam did in the next three days. I was
busy with conversations with Henkin, I went to see the Museum
of the Holocaust and Heroism, so I don't know how it happened

or who really published the ad in the paper. Henkin thinks that Jordana, who still kept a key to Boaz's apartment, sneaked into the apartment, took an old picture of Boaz and printed the ad. Hasha, or perhaps it was Renate, is sure that Sam himself published the ad in the papers, while Henkin is sure it was Boaz. At any rate, the ad was published in the Friday papers, and it showed a photo of Boaz (or Samuel), with black tangled hair, burning eyes, and under the photo was the caption: Samuel Lipker, who came to Israel from Cyprus on May 14, 1948, is requested, for his own good, to come to room 1720 in the Hilton in Tel Aviv for his reward.

On that Friday, Noga and Renate went to Caesarea to search for antiquities. They returned happy and flushed from the wind, and Renate said to me: You walk in those soft sands and suddenly there's a coin that's been waiting for you for two thousand years. And then Henkin showed them the ad. Noga looked at the ad and said: That won't end well.

I went outside, it was a nice morning and an early autumn chill was blowing, I walked along Hayarkon Street, in the distance I thought I saw people I knew: Jordana, Hans Strombe, my childhood friend, the journalist Joachim Davis, Stephen Goyfer, the honorary consul of Colombia, and I thought: Why was the Captain devoted to the idea of the memorial to Dante Alighieri, what's the meaning of his story—the story of his life that was found among his belongings that may have been his life and may not—and I didn't rightly know, I thought maybe it was so simple it was impossible for me to see things correctly, particularly in light of the fact that this morning, there was in the paper a picture of one man who is two and I'm a father whose son is buried in two places and Henkin is father to a lad who was killed in two places, maybe precisely on that background I'm trying to see things that in a rearview mirror are perfectly normal. Maybe the Captain really loved Dante's great poetry with all his might, maybe he wanted to show that Dante's hell was human and pleasant compared with what the Captain envisioned for Ebenezer, and he came to the Land of Israel to try to prepare a spiritual awakening there that would combine the poet with the prophets, the memories, Jeremiah and Jesus, with whom he belonged in spirit, with those Pioneers who came to bring salvation, with the future victims of the idea of freedom of the vision of salvation, and Dante looked to him as Spinoza looked to the manager of the dairy on the settlement—as joining one thing with another, as a real model for the conjunction of poetry with its sources, not physical sources but heavenly ones in an Israeli version. In other words: A memorial to Dante isn't foreign to the landscape that produced great poets like Isaiah, Amos, or the author of the Psalms. Byron's Greece should have been the Captain's Land of Israel, and Goethe and Byron may have sought an excuse to build spiritual ropes to the real world in the wrong place. Here, in the place where God revealed Himself, who spoke from the mouths of Job and Amos, he should have lived the eternal life of a person who sang the lament of the possible world out of malicious and sublime love, out of dread of what was in store, dread that came from him and didn't penetrate heaven.

I climbed up to the Hilton and went to the public relations department. The stormy sea could be seen through the window. The beauty queen was filing her nails. She knew my name and suggested I sign the guest book, but I explained to her that I wasn't staying at the hotel, and she also agreed that it was better if I didn't sign. I asked her about Sam. She put her nail file in a drawer, locked it, scrunched her beautiful eyebrows, was silent a moment, and said: He's closed in the room, I can't talk to him, he's cruel.

I asked her if anybody had been searching for him, and she said: What do you mean, and anyway, I don't have detectives. I showed her the newspaper. She looked at the picture a long time and put her head down on the desk. I saw tears on the Hilton stationery. I stroked her head and told her how beautiful and wise she was and I left. The man in me added the word "wise" to stroke what I couldn't, or didn't dare, stroke. That was one of those easy moments when I discover how much grief a person has to have inside him to run away completely from the horny lad in every one of us. A flattery may bear fruit, but her tears were also tears I should have wept, not because she wasn't wise, but because I really don't know if she was wise or not, and I say "wise" to her because she's beautiful.

I found myself a table overlooking the bank of elevators and ordered coffee. Hours I sat. I ordered more coffee and ate cake. Women in bathing suits passed by. I was intent. And then I saw him come in. And when he groped in his pocket I knew he was holding the newspaper clipping. Hesitantly, he walked toward the bank of elevators and I saw him, even though he couldn't see me. The beauty queen passing behind him appeared in the mirror for a moment, so they couldn't even meet; the hotel detective I had spotted before lit a cigarette. Two laughing girls pass by, looking tanned and pure. Boaz stands intent, and then comes to an elevator, he steps inside, the elevator fills with people, the beauty queen is swallowed up in the opening behind the counters, a new light is lit above me. The waitress wants to be paid, because her shift has now ended. Very slowly the door of the elevator slams shut on Boaz's face, and here the story ends, from now on even my hypothesis won't have any basis in fact. What is Henkin doing? What's happening to the actors of the national theater who are waiting for Sam Lipp, and surely don't know that at this moment he's waiting in his apartment in the hotel for Joseph Rayna's last game of vengeance? And I sit—a person who once shot at low-flying planes, who saluted with upraised hand and yelled Heil—in the Hilton Hotel in Tel Aviv, in my mind's eye accompanying Boaz Schneerson, victim of a disaster brought by generations of seekers of deliverance and stubborn and angry people. And I feel that right here, at the moment of battle, the story I still have to write or recite like Ebenezer, is condensing, the story I have to reconstruct from the tapes, to fake myself in it, and I see the door of the elevator slam shut, and suddenly there is absolutely no certainty that what was said really was, that my son had to be buried far from home, that the elevator really is going up, and I see the red numbers jumping on the control board, trying to see the destruction, the haberdashers now locking their shops in the emptying streets, the climbers darting at crumbling and mourning chocolate houses, trying to get a foothold in this moment, I'm writing to you about it, something I started a long time ago, and to guess, to walk on the carpet, to come to the doorway, to wait with the creator of the Fourth Reich, and along with him to open the door, but I can no longer know what will happen now when those two men meet.

And on the seventeenth floor of the Hilton Hotel in Tel Aviv the elevator door opens and a person is seen getting off the elevator. He stands still. Waits until the door slams shut behind him. His face is tanned, a white hair flickers from his mane of hair, which doesn't seem to have thinned over the years. At the age of forty-five, he looks younger, but also older, than his age. He gropes in his pocket, lights a cigarette, walks on the carpet. His eyes are like the eyes of a hyena at night, thinks a cleaning woman passing by, carrying a bucket and a broom. He stops at a door. Beyond the door, as beyond the concrete wall that stood for years in Jerusalem and bisected the city, Asia, China, India, something distant, unknown, stretching out, beyond the door he stands, so he knocks.

The door opens and he can't see very well because of the glowing light from the open window. He doesn't say a thing, looks at somebody he may have to struggle with again. A locked yard with a tree and a hook and a bird, and distant music rises in his brain, he enters, and after the door is locked behind him, in the lobby a well-dressed, tall, heavyset man gets up, pays for his coffee, looks at the small light bulbs on the control board of the elevator, and leaves. Far away from there sits Rebecca Schneerson, facing a grove of almond trees, measuring herself in the windowpane, cleaned for her by the great-grandson of Ahbed and she wants in vain to touch the source of her prayers that could once make such a strong hatred throb in her that she gaped open a hole in the universe. Now she hurls empty looks and doesn't even hold the flyswatter anymore and she drinks wine as she sits for the men who couldn't make her forget the sweet smell of Joseph, who almost kindled in her her heavy and needless betrayal of love, and she thinks: Who am I waiting for, as if a pesky fly came and reported to her on the state of the farm, on crops that grew nicely, on a northwest wind, and she wants to know what's happening in a place where she doesn't know that anything is happening. She doesn't know that Boaz and Samuel are meeting now, she doesn't know that something that took place years ago, when two young men met and struggled, a struggle she really didn't pray for, is now reaching its conclusion. And Jordana, who dusted three thousand books waiting for her with pictures of eternal youths, returns to Henkin's house and teaches Noga and Renate how to clean the bluish rust off ancient coins, how the liquid forces the ancient letters and the ancient images to be exposed, and Renate looks at the countenance of Emperor Hadrian and sees how his face grows sad, how those features waited for her on the sands of Caesarea for two thousand years and nobody touched the countenance. A wind blew, rain fell, and after all those years coins emerged that were lost absentmindedly by some Roman soldier, who hasn't been among the living for ages, for Renate and Noga of all people, and now Jordana is cleaning them with a stinking liquid and the countenance of the Emperor Hadrian grows clear, and Noga, maybe, tries to listen to the voice of Boaz's ancient blood that has gushed up in her now too, and she thinks: Where did the blood disappear that poured here, on the sands, for thousands of years, the blood that went deep into the center of gravity of the earth, a place where Rebecca dug toward the sky, with the awful anger that pervaded her and is now starting to fade, as if after more than ninety years of life in a place where she didn't want to live, the anger is starting to be a needless, almost ridiculous embellishment, and you don't know who to be angry at anymore and you can't even be angry at yourself anymore, and so, Noga thought of her lovers, of Jordana who loved Menahem and Boaz, and now is maybe in love with Friedrich and will soon paste his pictures in the album and under each picture she'll write in her fluent handwriting: Place, date, general description, so she'll be able to look at his volume without opening it again, to guess the dim, grim force of time that doesn't turn hair gray anymore, and flows without moving, and Jordana goes to Menahem's room, turns on the television, wants to weep, tears seek her eyes and don't find them, and then she breaks the screen, but the ice cream man's ear-piercing music is heard outside and nobody hears the smashing blow, and Fanya R. yells: Stop it! We don't want ice cream! And the wrinkled man goes away routed, with his ice cream, and there aren't any children here anymore to sell ice cream to, says Hasha, and Jordana sits Henkin down and talks with him about renewing the activity of the Committee of Bereaved Parents and tells him that everybody is waiting for him and he has to do things, travel, search for new sites, the pain has to be extinguished, she knows, she gave birth to a dead son and she knows, she also broke the screen and Henkin sits and listens, looking at the beautiful Yemenite woman. What's happening there in the room, thinks Germanwriter standing up in the lobby of the Hilton, what's happening to them there that I can't guess, and Henkin thinks of what Jordana said, wants to answer her, maybe turn everything back, go back to the starting point, stand before his son a moment, and say to him: Menahem, you don't have to write poems, if you don't want to. Hasha Masha says you're a man of the sea. Henkin knew that no lad who came from Hasha Masha's womb would believe that Henkin who says those things really means them, and he can despise himself until he smiles at Jordana who strokes his hand and tries to lead him to battlefields where others fought for her and for him, and suddenly he says with a contempt that once was in Hasha but she doesn't have it now: Why don't you make love with something like a television, but she isn't offended now and moves to the agenda, he's going to tell me about the locomotive salesman, that sonofabitch, she said to herself, he thought that because of my love for Menahem he bought me for life, and I'm free to love whoever I want, she said and laughed, and Noga saw the laugh caught on her face like a wounded bird and she tried to get up, but her legs were heavy and she didn't get up, and Renate went to put on water.

Henkin thinks: That strange Yemenite woman, she endured everything and remained dry, from all the rain of death she

remained dry, and Rebecca sits in her room, Ahbed paces back
and forth, and she thinks: Something's happening, and then a
distant rage passes through her—not her own—one that went
astray and passed through her on the way to her sources, from
her toenails, which once stood at the river and let it pierce the
girl she was, to give up everything so she could be angry at herself, stumble on mastery, live a life that contradicted itself, so
that her life was a betrayal of her desires, to take vengeance on
herself, on the desires she didn't really have, and she said:
Somebody tells me up yours, somebody enters the room, does
to me what Nehemiah did when he committed suicide on the
shore of Jaffa, and when I was born the sun went out and a
rooster didn't die, deaf Joseph went to bring a new sexton to
the city, the rabbi of Lody who caused Napoleon's defeat at the
gates of Moscow, but the house of the Last Jew is still locked
despite the sudden shouts of that prompter Fanya R., the windows are slammed shut, the repainted shutters are closed, the
antenna sways in the wind, and in the hotel the tall beauty
queen sits down, in a purple dress and a white collar, next to
Germanwriter, who's about to leave, and says: So what will be?
Germanwriter, who thinks of avenging that moment when everything takes place, the moment when two men meet and you
don't know what happens to them, looks at the local beauty
queen who was international and came back to her scale, wringing her hands, and he notices that she's removed the red nail
polish and her fingernails are also pale, and he thinks: Did she
really kiss the Ambassador of Peru, did a whore from Hayarkon
Street really sleep in his bed on the seventeenth floor, as that
really was important to what happens to the writer deep in his
heart, where there were once stories that wanted to be written
as he used to tell Renate, and the beauty queen sits and starts
gnawing her nails, looking to the side, stealing a scared look at
the writer, and gnawing. He thinks: Let me have a hand, and he
says: Let me gnaw, and she says: Why not, and he gnaws one
fingernail and wants to laugh in the hotel lobby. He gnaws,
Germanwriter, the queen, a fingernail . . .

And he thinks about the hotel, about Henkin sitting in his house now, letting his thoughts roam free, pondering shelters, about Eva in the shelter when Goebbels comes and tells the Führer: The queen of Russia is dead, and Goebbels doesn't mean the queen of Russia, who managed to get routed at the last minute by King Friedrich for whom my son was named, he means Roosevelt, the miracle that may still happen . . .

The fact of the beauty queen's beauty, thinks Germanwriter, should have been an advance payment on the account of death. Some reply to life, to expectations, to dread, and isn't really a reply, not her face, not her bittersweet body, not even her measured grief about Sam, whom she spent a night with. It can be guessed how he asks Sam what happened in the room, and Sam tells him: He knocked on the door, we stood still, two mirrors looking at one another, he told me who he was, we talked about the struggle then, I tried to remember, I almost recalled, I told about the Fourth Reich. He was sad to hear about Ebenezer in the wretched nightclubs. We ordered vodka. We drank.

When he asked Boaz, Boaz will answer, Boaz will surely answer in similar language, will say: Somebody published an ad in the paper with my picture I came. The window was open, the planes that came a few minutes later to Father's house passed by the open window, their lights blinked on and off. We drank vodka. We talked about ourselves. I told about Rebecca, the Captain, the Captain's Dante Alighieri, I said, Maybe a monument has to be erected to Dante, to the fallen ones, to ourselves, to Henkin, to Menahem, to Friedrich, a gigantic monument where you can see the whole land and then die, and he smiled. We fought. We hit one another. He hit hard, but I wasn't weak either. We didn't know who hit whom, then one went out. I'm not sure who. And Sam will say, Right, and there was a beauty queen there. And Boaz will say: All of life, all that suddenly was, balled up for one moment and then silence.

A pianist wearing a toupee started playing old Hollywood songs. The queen got up and Germanwriter went outside and started walking in the street. And then he saw Boaz, and now it

was hard to know if that really was Boaz after the meeting in the
hotel, the one moment we all focused on, or perhaps it was
before, but it can't be denied that Boaz passed by in a jeep and
stopped and asked him to get in, and they took Noga who said:
What happened to you, were you wounded? And he said: I tried
to screw a lioness, and Noga said, Beware of us. And soon after,
they came to the settlement, the serene old houses in foliage
shrouded in shadows of nightfall, the great-grandson of Ahbed
opened the door and Rebecca was seen through the door as if
she were trying to classify walls, windows, and objects, not to
see the almond groves and the citrus groves, and on her face is
an old smile, no longer forced, as if the meeting that was or will
be between Samuel and Boaz extinguished in her the last ruse
she had brought with her to the Land of Israel on the first day
of the twentieth century, and he pondered whether, as
Goethe said, miracle is the beloved son of faith, what was seen
in Rebecca's eyes was the beginning of a fixed and constant
end, or a coefficient of the suicides on the verge of the last compromise a woman like her can make with what she had once decided her fate would be and it turned out otherwise, and then
she didn't allow things to take place, but reconstructed what
never happened. As if, with her own hands, she knocked down
her fate by bringing death and destruction on everything around
her, so she could realize in her body and mind what others
fought over, while she refused reality; some devotion to something sublime and yet hopeless at the same time. She hugged
Boaz, but suddenly her hands flowed off his body, maybe off the
bodies of Secret Charity and Joseph and Nehemiah and her son,
who is now maybe looking at the sea and the ripples of waves
on the shore at the yellowed boards and shells, counting the
memories he had lost, so he could at long last remember who he
really was and be Ebenezer who maybe doesn't really exist, and
start over to mutter and know wood in its distress. Rebecca's face
was weary, through the German she looked and saw the walls and
the objects she had classified before. On the walls, she said afterward, she counted nine million tears like the number of words

Ebenezer knew, tears she had wept for eight years so Nehemiah
would avenge her. That poor handsome man of mine, she said
softly, and nothing helped; the tears were waiting for her on the
walls along with the eyes that once, when she was a girl, she
packed in a suitcase with the names of dead people she took
down from the walls of the synagogue. The innocent smile of
Rachel Brin, who died of danger and didn't tell Lionel, now on
his way to the Land of Israel, who his father was, as if he didn't
know, as if he really didn't know Joseph and the Captain in his
blood, as if his *Laments* weren't based on the melody Rebecca
used to split the heavens with her anger, to protect Boaz who
would be saved in the war and so Menahem Henkin would die
instead of him. There's no pity, she said then, and she meant the
melody Emanuel the Roman taught Dante Alighieri and Joseph
taught his offspring, two hundred fifty-two offspring, and thousands of offspring throughout the globe, stumbling, routed, and
writing books, selling subscriptions, locomotives, irons, computers, building cities, teaching children, healers, maybe patients
and dying people, the whole kit and caboodle is this moment,
Germanwriter will think, maybe the whole thing is nothing but
one melody, some tune that came from the Temple through the
Spanish exiles to various corners of the universe, and that's how
those wretched and proud poor people could unite into one fabric, into a game of football with no winners but only losers. Like
me, he said, like Friedrich, Jordana's lover.

And Rebecca looked at the tears on the walls, the tears that
didn't want to return to her aged eyes, and she was silent and
maybe others said for her what she was supposed to say: The
end is inherent in the beginning, a pit makes a tree, a tree
makes a pit, so Ebenezer invented a book that hasn't yet been
written, but he knew it by heart, and by his estimate, she's a
hundred years old, and everything is filled with tears for something real. Battlefields of dead children, Henkin and rabbinical
responsa, holy walls, holy ground, graves, a holy wall, what does
all that have to do with my forefathers for whom God was to
gnash your teeth, rage, and glory they sought Him in vain. The

messiah will come someday when we don't need him anymore,
she said, big dreams bring small ends and Rebecca tried to hold
on, for the first time in her life, not to what others dreamed for
her, but to what she built with her own hands and didn't pay
any attention to—her farm, the fields, the citrus groves, the
Ahbeds, the fruit, the horses, the flowers in plastic awnings, the
vegetables, winter growths, the transparent air held in the cloths
of the fruit trees, the hens that don't stop laying, the prize
cows, she didn't seem sure that the farm she built as revenge
for Nehemiah's death existed, that everything that happened
did indeed happen to her and not to somebody else who was
pierced by a river, fell in love for a splendid and despicable
moment with a handsome poet under his wedding canopy,
killed a husband on the shore of Jaffa in a lion's cage as an en-
dearing reply to the ailments of the inspired soul of Michael
Halperin, her vision of the Hebrew army was never necessary,
while Klomin wove it into five thousand pages of letters of rec-
ommendation to high commissioners, ministers, famous people,
rulers, anybody . . . so Rebecca grew indignant and said: They
just go on inventing a past for themselves to console Nehemiah,
to understand poor Nathan whom I killed with a kiss when I
told him about the Arabs who gave me money, and she looked
at Noga and wanted Noga to give her Boaz until the day she
died and she wouldn't be with him, Noga who was already seen,
or perhaps would still see, Sam and would be confused and would
give birth to a son who would be both Sam's son and Boaz's son
and nobody would know, and more awful than anything—
Rebecca wouldn't know, and that would be the real up yours,
and Rebecca would ask and Noga would tell her: I'm not telling
you, Rebecca, and you'll die years later, a hundred years old she'll
be at her death and she won't know who is the father of the heir
of Secret Charity, and Ebenezer won't know because of not-
knowing, she'll say, and Noga will say: That's not right, Rebecca,
you knew and you didn't say. And I know too and don't say, and
that's the sweet revenge of the soft woman who was Noga who
one day, at the age of forty-five, when she'd become pregnant,

wouldn't agree to tell who was the father of the child, who would then go on being Joseph with green-yellow eyes and would live into the next millennium, when all of us won't be here and maybe he won't be either, if the destruction does come and the Messiah will come riding on an ass with broken legs, and will tarry, and won't come even after we don't need him, when everything will be or was, in the words of the chief of staff of the solar system, destroyed. And so, from Rebecca Schneerson's yearnings for a son, whom she delivered to herself at the trees and bushes planted by "that Dana," out of yearnings, the settlement could be seen in its splendor along with the rot eating it. Ninety years and the rot now comes to the roots of yearning, the spots of damp, falling walls, trees that came to fill the space of a furious light without corners, already rotten and falling in the rain, and Rebecca looks at them, or through them. What does a beautiful old woman with cataracts see? What can she see, thinks Germanwriter, maybe his architects could put her back together again, fill her interstices and the interstices of the settlement with a renewed antiquity, made of synthetic materials, and then the spider webs could be seen, and Rebecca said: Boaz, maybe we really didn't succeed in not loving. Was that a question or a challenge, thought the writer, and he didn't know, Noga tried to listen to the echo rising from the words, like a biblical old woman, some Jael the wife of Heber the Kenite, who killed her lover. Out of love and loyalty she killed! And I, who will I kill, said Rebecca as if she read her mind, who? Me? Who didn't I kill? My parents and my parents' parents I killed, so that Noga will give birth to a son and nobody will know who his father is and I will die without an heir, and the word "heir" came to her from television, when she'd watch the news and hear H. Herzog talk about our forces which was always Boaz in the desert, striking my enemy, sir, and what difference does it make who wins, she said, what's important is who loses, and I know how losers look, like Joseph's love poems, look at the settlement, they said there, and it's no longer known who said it, and they looked outside, the vineyard of Nathan's and Nehemiah's dreams. Rebecca

came to this place to plant shirt trees in America. Plain new
houses fill the interstices. Between Marar and the other Arab
village they built a passage then and it's now a settlement and
then it's "*the* settlement," and it swallows Nehemiah's old settlement, a settlement where we old women, who buried our buf-
foons in Roots, sit and knit ninety years, said Rebecca and sees
Yemenites, Iraqis, and Poles establishing a small town here and
in the river stuffed fish cruise in the Land of Canaan, near a
settlement where most of its founders submitted to the need to
dig a pit for the first ones next to the synagogue, close to the
community center named after Ebenezer who knew wood in its
distress, near the tombstone for Dante Alighieri that the Captain
didn't manage to erect, but maybe the whole settlement is a
tombstone for a poet, every poet, Joseph or Dante, what difference does it make, they all try to phrase a nonexistent and not
very important situation, some fictional space that happens because of people, because of the tears still waiting for her on the
walls, and in the distance sit the last old women of the settlement knitting sweaters for the grandchildren, who still come see
them in their fine cars, and the new houses straggle into one
another, lost, fearing the venom, from the dream they never
knew, children trying to learn it in the museum or the pit-of-the-
first-ones, the name of the Wondrous One is one of the founding
fathers and All's Well is old now and maybe dead, and Eve, a poor
old woman, lies in her bed and dreams of her chicks who went to
build her a state and came back graves, and one of them—Boaz—
sits in the Hilton and tries to be himself.

   And Germanwriter sits and eats sweet gefilte fish served him
by Ahbed and tells about songs he used to read to Friedrich and
Jordana shuts her eyes and ponders, who, who, who, he tells
about the songs and how Friedrich asked who sang those songs
and he said: We, I sang, my son, and then Friedrich refused to
read even one of my books, said Germanwriter, not even one
story, and I wrote for him and he didn't read, he went to his
grandfather and asked him: How could you? And he didn't read.
He fought me, read stories of younger authors, and in their war

against me maybe they were closer to Friedrich's grandfather
than I was and he didn't know, and he died, and we at least
tried to give an answer about something that no longer had any
meaning, but was the essence of our life, to know why we were
what we were, he didn't forgive, didn't read my books, said
Germanwriter, and Rebecca said: They're all like that, they die
and don't know, like those who live in Nehemiah's settlement
and read in the museum that Nehemiah built a model farm and
don't know who really built or why, anger built, not love of
kings, and what came out of all that? Ebenezer carved in wood
the face of Joseph, not his! And then they went from there, and
Boaz, if he was there, would say: This time not in a stolen car!
as if it really was important that he once stole a car, and he
adds: Maybe what I need to do is erect a big memorial, remember how we went to Kastel? And there Henkin could have met
Menahem if only he believed me, and on a high hill, fifteen
stories of a memorial, a revolving restaurant on top, conference
rooms, memorial rooms, and pictures of all those who fell in the
wars of Israel, thousands of standard-size pictures, and rooms
for those who will be, rooms of memory for those who died in
the Holocaust, for the ghetto fighters. Guides in uniforms will
explain the wars and the salvations according to the expressions
of those who fell, and a room will be devoted to Dante, maybe
a whole floor, to the poet who almost created a world from the
tunes of the Temple, and then they brought me an unwanted
salvation from the mouth of Rebecca, according to the Captain
who always brought good tidings, as if he came here because of
our wishes more than because of the illogical urgency to erect
a memorial to Dante here, and the memorial may not be
erected, because Boaz is trying to sink into the depression he
craves so much and wants to know who is the father of his child
and Noga won't tell and he doesn't know if, when he was with
Licinda as Sam, Sam wasn't with Noga as Boaz, or perhaps they
knew everything and kept quiet, or maybe those things didn't
happen and somebody is now writing the last words, his description of one indescribable moment, a moment when one

side of the coin met the other side. Somebody is now inventing
not only a past but a present in which those things take place,
and what happens is a prediction forward and backward, like
the history that's already disappearing from the world and only
historians are left without history, to describe something that is
no longer remembered, that disappeared with the houses of
Cologne where Germanwriter lived until he came to bury his son
next to Menahem Henkin who died instead of Boaz and didn't
want to be saved as Menahem wanted to live near the sea, with
Hasha Masha, and maybe with two orphan girls from Diskin or
even with Noga whose belly will swell and who knows who is the
father of her son, that wise woman, just as they won't know
things and we won't know who was the father of Ebenezer, even
though it's quite clear who his father was, if not the river, then
who, somebody who reads and listens to the tapes can know, but
Rebecca is silent and then silence prevails, and Germanwriter
thinks of his son and why he didn't read his books and hurts, now
of all times he hurts, just like Melissa, whose father wrote him
letters and tells, and calls Lionel, and Lionel goes to Connecticut, where he hadn't been since he was a boy in love and everything is different there, Mr. Brooks's awkward supplication
turned into "a lament on the death of little girls," his offices are
called "Melissa Inc.," and the sales center is called "Melissa Ford
Motors," and the main street is called "Melissa Street," and
there's a souvenir shop there called "The Shop of Poor Little
Melissa," and *The New York Times* published an article about the
city where masses of young people stream, and *Time* wrote about
it, and *Newsweek,* and they talk about Melissa whom Sam Lipp fell
in love with thirty years after she died, and a German writer came
to search for her fifty years after her death and miserable youths
stream here and stand at Melissa's grave holding signs, "We love
you, Melissa,"—and "There's life before death," and they go to
the shop and buy "Melissa souvenirs" and "Melissa dolls," and
some of them commit suicide there or try to commit suicide, and
they've set up a first aid station with a doctor and a psychologist
and a person who studies those cases for the University of Michi-

gan, and there's a game called "Game of Melissa Memory" and "Beautiful and Wretched Melissa Toothpaste," and a book with blank pages, with a picture of Melissa on the cover and everybody writes his sad thoughts there and sends them to a certain address and gets a raffle prize every month, and Hollywood is making a movie about Melissa and what happened to her after her death, and people pay high prices for cars, and from all over America they flock to buy Melissa cars. What a world, writes Mr. Brooks, and Lionel comes and everybody applauds him as if he were a hero, he wrings his hands, bends down, tries to flee, thinks about Licinda, asks her to come, but she doesn't, and Lily sits and is angry or laughs, who knows, and they go to Israel, to Sam, who is still locked in a room with Boaz or with himself, and they bring the smell of the great success of poor Melissa fifty years after her death and . . .

They visited Friedrich's grave. It was beautiful and delicate and a wind wisped in the treetops. Henkin seemed in tune with the landscape. Leads a group of parents to Nabi Samuel. And Germanwriter, who never broke his own pattern and didn't let himself fall like that, stands for one hour every day and reads his novellas and stories to his dead son, and the beloved Jordana brings people to see the writer who reads his works at the grave of a boy who didn't want to read his father's works, and Renate waits with patience and love, maybe a little contempt, which she inherited from Hasha Masha but she understands, like Hasha Masha she understands their need to love like that after death which they could fix, if they were able to fear life less, and he stands and reads his works and the wind is pleasant in Bab-el-Wad, where they died in the wars and read stories to dead sons who will be brought from far away by the Holocaust Fund of the needleworkers in Cologne to help their bereaved brothers in Israel.

Once in Cologne, Ebenezer said, Germanwriter recalls: If Moses hadn't grown up in an Egyptian house, would he have been able to think of rebellion? A Hebrew would have thought about uprising and not of a rebellion that is a revolution. Only

at a river with a king who's a god and whose divinity is geometric, tangential, and congruent with the laws of low tide and high
tide, the moon and the sun, only there, in harsh strips of ripples
of water, on the edge of the desert, could it have become clear
finally that a mighty mechanics of water regulation in an arid
desert is a kingdom, is the Lord, is God, the imprisonment of
revolts, and from that root of a river came prison and slavery and
uprisings and freedom. The river is geometrical freedom as well
as eternal slavery. In the desert the Egyptian turned into the
Jew. On Mount Sinai, they turn real and necessary tyranny into
the anarchy of an arid wasteland that burns in the blood. They
needed Moses and he, whose soul was embittered by revolt, of a
hard speech and of a hard language, an ancient desert aristocrat,
needed the grandsons of Jacob who were crazy for the wilderness,
filled with bitterness and depression, the spirit of rocky ground
of lost yearnings for a past they almost had.

And then he quoted the passage: Everything is foreseen and
permission is given. He said that was the whole Torah in a nut-
shell. So Samuel boarded the ship *Salvation* and went to the
Land of Israel, and at the same time he met Lionel and went to
America. It was some fateful decision before he was born. It was
known in circles of heaven that Samuel will die like that and
not otherwise, so he had to board the *Salvation*, fight the British, be sent to Cyprus, ascend to the Land of Israel, be the wolf
who learned to play seventeen different instruments. But permission was also given, and Sam is the permission given, so he
rebelled against his blood.

Thus pondered Germanwriter in the glow of nightfall. Henkin
and Hasha and Ebenezer and Fanya R. also sat in the room. All
of them were over seventy except Fanya R., and nobody could
know how old she was. There was a sense that everybody lived
in that moment when Boaz sits in Samuel Lipker's room and
something that can't be known is happening there, something
nobody can imagine, although the meeting is more imperative
than all the meetings discussed in the hundreds of Ebenezer's
tapes, in the letters Henkin wrote to Germanwriter and German-

writer to Henkin, what could have been more imperative than that meeting, decreed by fate in another thousand years when the last offspring of Boaz and Sam will sit in a spaceship, on the way to the stars of Andromeda, bound to the world along with the last human beings on their way to the cosmic explosion that will come after, or before, and then at that moment that was, and may arrive, it was decided that that meeting will be and everything that happened before, including Renate, "Rhapsody in Blue," the inflation of the 'twenties, the fate of foreign subjects in the Ottoman Empire, all that happened so that Sam and Boaz will be imprisoned together in a room. The moon was full, they sat in Henkin's room, there was a clear feeling that every single one of them destroyed his loved ones and in burying them entered the grave standing up, like Secret Charity, and resided there with the loved ones who died by their hand, or whose fate was decreed by another accidental assignment, who knows, and it was clear that they're united in a dark connection whose thread was in the hands of a Captain, and now it was impossible to ask him anything, that everything is vague and yet there was life and there were nice moments and there were days and there were wonderful nights and nobody succeeds in loving somebody who deserves his love, but in running away to something like love, to be saved from the vengeance of death, that maybe Rebecca was right when she married Nehemiah and not Joseph, for everybody whoever married Joseph Rayna paid a price that is then not forgiven, anybody who married love begat offspring who owed something that couldn't be reformed. And then you find love split on the shore of Jaffa and you pick up Nehemiah and don't restore him to life and abandon Ebenezer and Boaz is born and kills Dana and begets Sam and ends with a son Noga carries inside her and will be the object of the great destruction that people carried from one generation to another to avenge the empty heaven for their love for a peculiar nation that was forgotten in ashes.

And it was that evening, Noga sat pressed to the window, they were gloomy, Rebecca phoned and was worried about Boaz.

Henkin pondered and one of them, Sam or Boaz, slapped
Licinda's face, and Lily started speaking German, and Lionel
thought about a cookbook of medieval pilgrims like Shira Rabat-
Batim, and Licinda, angry, hurting from the slap, got up and recited one tape on the moment when Kramer is tied to German
soldier in a wheelbarrow, and Ebenezer sees Kramer and doesn't
yet understand how a German can be hungry and Kramer refuses
to eat or drink and Ebenezer envies him, hates him, is maybe liberated from him, at least he recites something to him, from
somebody's mouth, about identities and exchanging identities,
and Kramer waits, the hangman's rope will always find him ready
to die a patriotic death withheld from many, Boaz will think,
when Jordana looks at him with the chill hatred of a woman who
once loved, and there is no hatred chillier, quieter, more malicious than the hatred of a betrayed woman, and Licinda, whom
everybody lusts for, beautiful, lithe, and out of place, recites what
Sam crammed into her and they listen, eager to know what they
always knew, in love with her with an impossible love, getting her
pregnant artificially like some Joseph impregnating women who
was the father of them all, and Henkin says: Enough, enough, and
she stops and bursts into tears and then suddenly Jordana smiles.

And up above, in the suite overlooking the sea at whose shore
Rebecca Schneerson looked angrily seventy-three years earlier,
sit Boaz and his alter ego. After the wrestling, as they later told
Germanwriter, they drank vodka, what will they say to each
other? If there were an answer there would be no need for all
these tapes, but there isn't. Some moment requisitioned from
the space of time, from its own history, from the building where
the event didn't take place, and in Rebecca's house, with the
tape recorder next to her where she once recorded herself facing the rot of the old settlement, and all that's left of her is her
fictional past and fictional dreams of a polite Captain and a rabbinical prodigy, who went to a war to the bitter end against frustrated prophets and died on the shore of Jaffa, sits Ebenezer
and suddenly says: Marar is now a destroyed village, a sign that
I'm again listening to myself, and Fanya R. smiles at him sympa-

thetically, even though she's filled with envy for memories of
Dana on the road between Rebecca's house and Ebenezer's old
house, where the Captain lived and that was registered in the
name of Boaz Schneerson or in fact, although the old woman
didn't know, it was registered in the name of S.L.A. Ltd. because
of income tax regulations that weren't intended to tax the dead,
or were intended only for that, and Ebenezer says: There was a
time, he said, when I forgot Hebrew, Hebrew flew away and
wasn't, I spoke in so many voices that I forgot, and I'd recite
words in other languages spelled backward. When I had to open
a door I closed it. German or Polish I read from right to left, I
wanted to open a bottle and I put the cork in instead of taking
the cork out, and then Hasha Masha said: A big donation came
for the memorial, and Henkin went to the Ministry of Defense
and came back with weeping eyes and thought about what happened, or didn't happen, in the hotel on the seventeenth floor.
Germanwriter says: Right, it's ridiculous and cunning, but Brooks
senior sent a check to the government of Israel, and nobody is
willing to turn down money to create the memorial that Boaz
scoffs at and says won't be erected, but S.L.A. Ltd. will be the
initiator and Boaz will bury his head in his hands and say:
Enough, I'm not ready for that, and goes out, and Hasha sneers
in a whisper, "Melissa Gifts," "Melissa and All Her Suicides,"
which was created in the world by the poem of rage, a poem Boaz
wrote for my husband so he could love his son who loved the sea.

    And Lionel will sit at night and tell about his mother and
Rebecca will want to weep and won't be able to, and then that
moment will end as it began, with uncertainty, and one of them
will go out, Sam or Boaz, and a few days later, a siren will be
heard and Talya's friend from the adjutant's office won't come
this time because he didn't come back from the last war, and
they'll search for Boaz and Noga to give them orders, and Noga
will laugh with a belly full of a fetus and none of them knows
who the father is, revenge of a woman who found her father
dead in a room and loved a violent lad and stopped loving him
to live in Henkin's house and turn into a product of national

mourning until Boaz came and betrothed her to Jordana and
Sam and Licinda, in whose veins Melissa lived and this time
declared a revolt, and Rebecca pleaded, Give me Boaz, don't
bring a son into the world, who's the father of the son? And
Noga is silent, withdrawn, in love with her swollen belly, will
bring a son into the world and they won't know who the father is.
Joy filled her when they came to bring her a mobilization order
that was needless because the computer was wrong. She had long
ago passed the age and would no longer stay in a tent with Boaz
and play licentious streetwalker in light of the headlights of the
armored troop carrier in the desert, and Sam or Boaz, whoever
came out of the room and they don't know who, or perhaps they
do know and pretend they don't know, will go to the war that
started, and again they wait for Rebecca's expected disaster, but
she's silent, searching the sky to drill a hole in it, doesn't find it,
is offended to her last disgrace, and Boaz or Sam, in a uniform,
will go to the airport, three gigantic transport planes were parked
there, emergency doors gaping open, a unit of young soldiers sat
on what had once been a lawn. The sky is clear and no wind
blows. The roar of the motors is ear-piercing. Officers and non-
coms run back and forth, messengers come with flashes of orders,
whistles are heard on all sides. And he stands there, in a battle
uniform with sand stuck to it from a previous battle, washed but
not ironed. The insignia of rank aren't conspicuous. The green-
yellow eyes scare the recruits. He asks which of them was in the
last war, and there isn't one who had fought then. He explains to
them what they have to do: get into the planes and then
parachute into another field, and from there to the front. The sun
is beating down and he's sweating. He turns to a young soldier
who looks pensive and handsome, with curly hair, and calls out:
Soldier, get up! And the soldier gets up. Scared, you can see how
scared he is. Run to the canteen and bring paper and pencils. And
the soldier says: Yessir, and runs. The soldiers are sitting. Somebody starts humming, tomorrow when the army takes off its
uniforms . . . The soldier comes back. The planes are roaring. A

liaison officer comes and whispers something in his ear. First aid kits and stretchers are loaded onto the plane.

He orders the soldier who had returned and was standing at attention: Give every soldier a pencil and paper! They look at him in amazement, but nobody opens his mouth.

The soldier gives every one of the soldiers a pencil and paper.

They don't see that their commander is weeping, he's weeping with his eyes shut.

The sun beats down and the motors are ear-piercing.

May Jordana not love you, he says. And then he yells: This is an order, everybody has a pencil and paper. Everyone, every one of you now write a poem and give it to me with your first name, last name, serial number, and address.

He yells: That's an order! One soldier whispers: That commander was in all the wars, I'm not getting in trouble, and he starts writing. And the commander yells: You've got five minutes, so step on it!

And they write fast.

Forward! he yells.

He collects the poems, puts them in a manila file. Calls the sergeant. Sends him with the manila file. To put it in headquarters under the name of Schneerson until. The soldiers finish loading their gear and boarding the planes, once again a siren sounds. He follows them, swallowed up in the plane, and takes off.

And the moment up there doesn't end. They're still there, even though Boaz or Sam was swallowed up in the plane. And then everything ended and Noga gave birth to a son. Ebenezer died and was buried in Roots. Fanya R. will die after him. Lionel and Lily went back to America. Licinda will direct Sam's play at the national theater. Sam will stay or go, what do we know who's who. They came back. Three secretaries are trying to make order in the files of S.L.A. Ltd. Letters come from all over Israel, millions of dollars from the money of "Melissa Inc." And everything's desolate. Boaz sits and looks out the window. Sam is dusty inside him. As was said in the book Ebenezer quoted and that will be written in another few years, Rebecca will die on the seventh of Adar, the day of Moses' death, in nineteen eighty-four, a hundred years old she'll be at her death. After her burial Roots will be closed for lack of space. Next to Nehemiah her husband Rebecca will be buried. In the safe, along with the writings of the Captain, are the poems written by the soldiers, and Noga raises her son. He's got green-yellow eyes and he plays with the wooden birds once carved by a man named Ebenezer.

When the last of the Jews died, God held His breath a moment, and said: They're finished? And the director said: Yes. He said: There was something about them, what was it? And the director said: They loved You with all their heart. And He said: What a waste, and shut His eyes for another thousand years, that passed in retrospect, backward and forward. Marar is now in the lands of the town that was a settlement, the wine press is a museum like everything that never was, and Noga says to her son: Someday, if you write a poem, give it to me and I'll give it to your father. She didn't say who, and Boaz smiled and Licinda said: I know who the Captain was, he was the one poem of Joseph Rayna that took on flesh, stayed here and brought together the grandfather of the grandfather of my grandfather in the port of Amsterdam with the grandfather of the grandfather of your grandfather who was ascending to the Land of Israel.

And so, because of the baby whose father nobody knows, all these things had to happen, and in fact they didn't happen exactly like that, but it could have been the last of the Jews, it could also have been a dream and also rot and also a dying end, and anybody who tries to turn a dream into reality inherits disappointment, and Rebecca, who tried to turn anger into a dream, knew that better than the others, so she took vengeance on Nehemiah by letting his dream be a grandson whose father nobody knows and nobody knows when he'll be the Last Jew.